To Ray 12/17/09

Respublica

A Novel of Cicero's Roman Republic

Richard Braccia

Richard Braccia

authorHOUSE

AuthorHouse™
1663 Liberty Drive
Bloomington, IN 47403
www.authorhouse.com
Phone: 1-800-839-8640

© 2009 Richard Braccia. All rights reserved.

No part of this book may be reproduced, stored in a retrieval system, or transmitted by any means without the written permission of the author.

First published by AuthorHouse 11/30/2009

ISBN: 978-1-4490-4340-7 (sc)
ISBN: 978-1-4490-4341-4 (hc)

Library of Congress Control Number: 2009911472

Printed in the United States of America
Bloomington, Indiana

This book is printed on acid-free paper.

Dedication

For Catherine, my wife, and our daughter, Marian, and in memory of my parents, Michele and Anna, and my parents-in-law, Antonio and Maria.

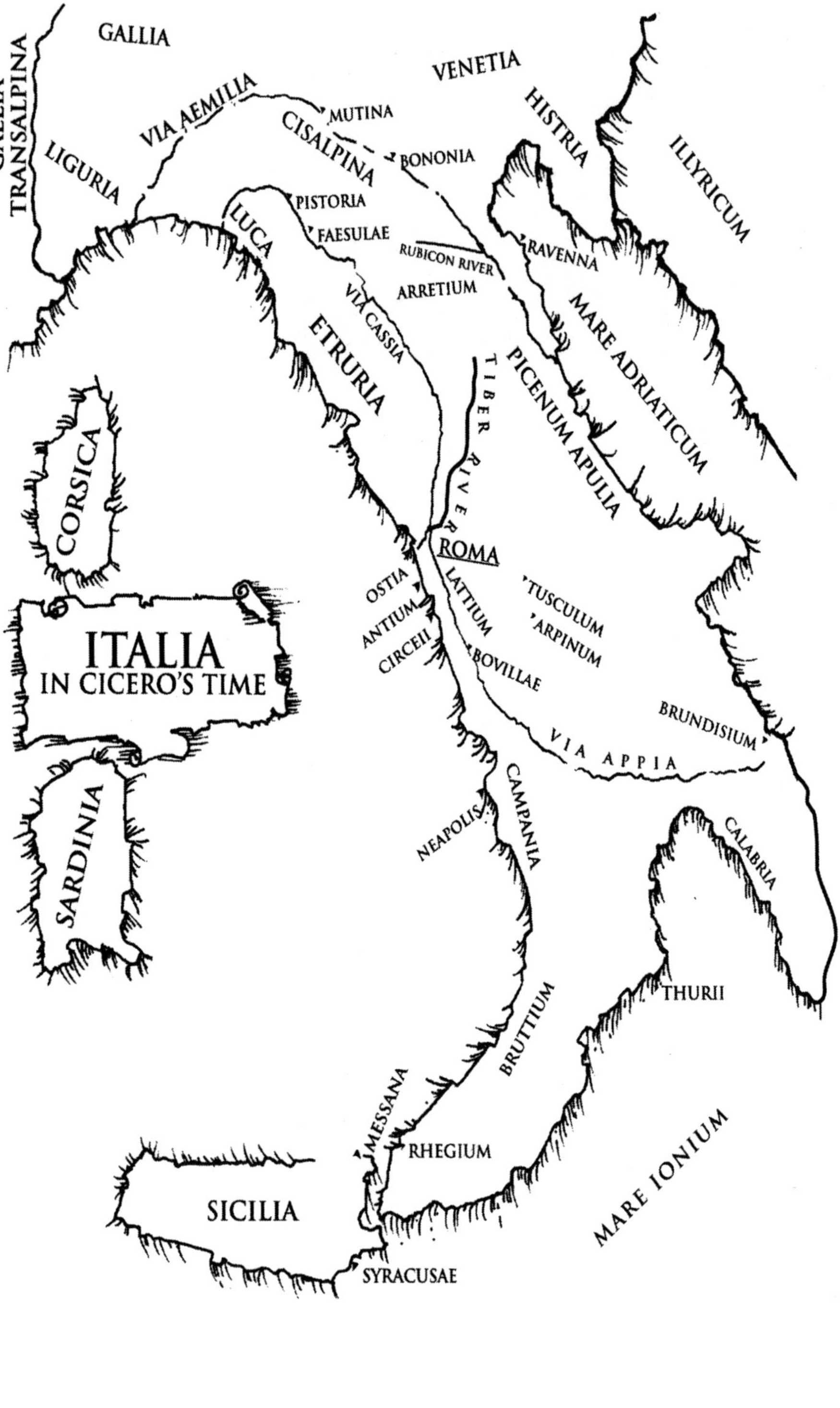
ITALIA
IN CICERO'S TIME
GALLIA
GALLIA TRANSALPINA
VENETIA
VIA AEMILIA
MUTINA
CISALPINA
BONONIA
HISTRIA
ILLYRICUM
LIGURIA
LUCA
PISTORIA
FAESULAE
RUBICON RIVER
RAVENNA
ARRETIUM
VIA CASSIA
ETRURIA
MARE ADRIATICUM
TIBER RIVER
PICENUM APULIA
CORSICA
ROMA
OSTIA
ANTIUM
CIRCEII
LATTIUM
TUSCULUM
ARPINUM
BOVILLAE
BRUNDISIUM
VIA APPIA
SARDINIA
CAMPANIA
NEAPOLIS
CALABRIA
THURII
BRUTTIUM
MESSANA
RHEGIUM
MARE IONIUM
SICILIA
SYRACUSAE

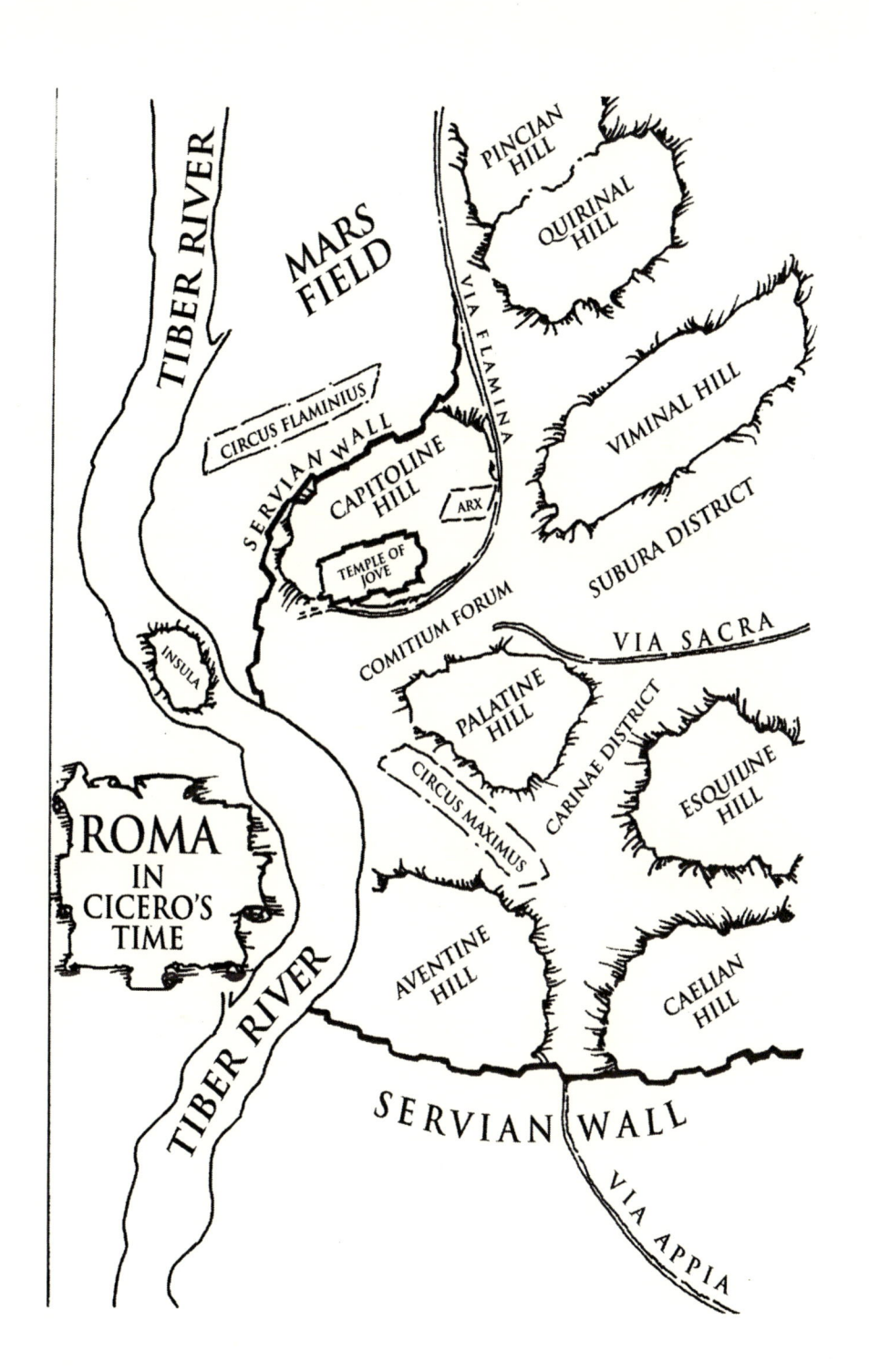

ROMA IN CICERO'S TIME

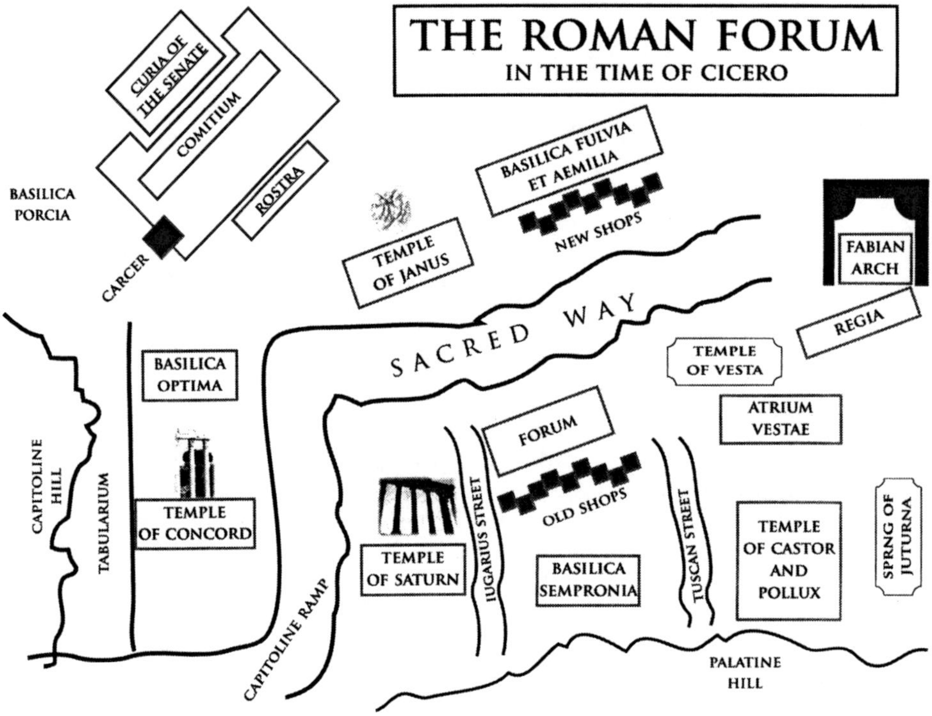
THE ROMAN FORUM
IN THE TIME OF CICERO
CURIA OF THE SENATE
COMITIUM
ROSTRA
BASILICA PORCIA
CARCER
TEMPLE OF JANUS
BASILICA FULVIA ET AEMILIA
NEW SHOPS
FABIAN ARCH
SACRED WAY
REGIA
TEMPLE OF VESTA
ATRIUM VESTAE
BASILICA OPTIMA
CAPITOLINE HILL
TABULARIUM
TEMPLE OF CONCORD
FORUM
OLD SHOPS
TEMPLE OF SATURN
IUGARIUS STREET
BASILICA SEMPRONIA
TUSCAN STREET
TEMPLE OF CASTOR AND POLLUX
SPRNG OF JUTURNA
CAPITOLINE RAMP
PALATINE HILL

SENATVS POPVLVSQVE ROMANUS
THE SENATE AND PEOPLE OF ROMA - IN CICERO'S RESPVBLICA

SENATVS

← CAN APPOINT A DICTATOR IN EMERGENCIES

AS PERMANENT DICTATOR, CAESAR EXERCISES POWER OVER THE SENATE AND ALL MAGISTRATES

→ IS COMPRISED OF FORMER AND CURRENT MAGISTRATES. IT IS RESPONSIBLE FOR ADVISING MAGISTRATES AND SANCTIONING PROPOSED LEGISLATION.

TWO CONSULS HAVE MUTUAL VETO POWER

ELECTS CONSULS, PRAETORS, AND EVERY 5 YEARS TWO CENSORS. LAW-MAKING

ELECTS CURULE AEDILES, QUAESTORS, LOWER OFFICERS AND SPECIAL COMMISIONERS. LAW-MAKING

ELECTS THE PLEBETIAN TRIBUNES AND THE PLEBEIAN AEDILES. LAW MAKING

TRIBUNES HAVE VETO POWER OVER MAGISTRATES AND FELLOW TRIBUNES

COMITIA CENTURIATA
ALL ADULT MALE CITIZENS ORGANIZED BY AGE AND WEALTH INTO 373 CENTURIES

CONCILIUM PLEBIS
RESTRICTED TO PLEBEIAN ADULT MALE CITIZENS

COMITIA TRIBUTA
ALL ADULT MALE CITIZENS ORGANIZED INTO 35 TRIBES OR ELECTORAL WARDS

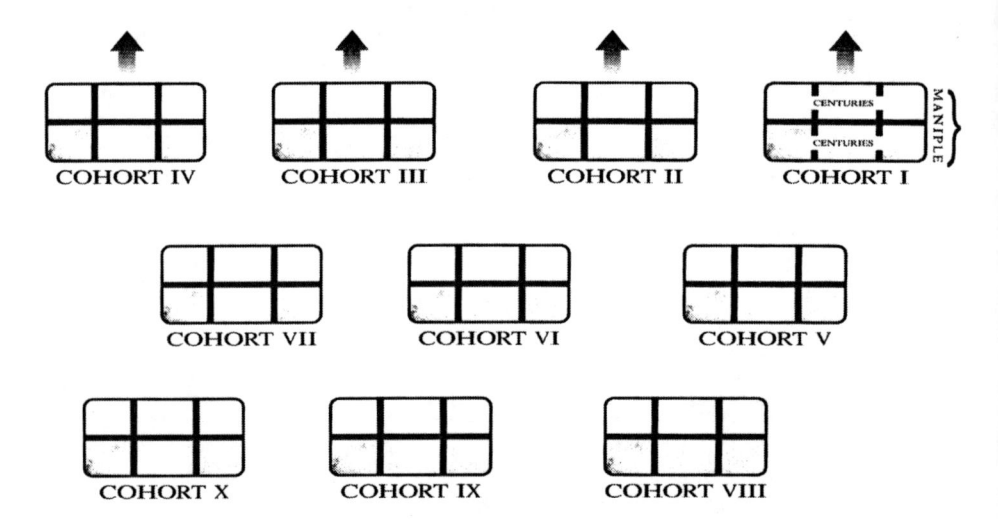

A ROMAN LEGION IN BATTLE ORDER IN THE TIME OF CICERO, CAESAR, AND POMPEIUS. THERE ARE THREE TO SIX THOUSAND MEN PER LEGION. EACH LEGION IS COMPRISED OF TEN COHORTS. THERE ARE THREE MANIPLES AND SIX CENTURIES PER COHORT.

EASTERN
IMPERIUM
OF CICERO'S TIME
SARMATIA
DACIA
PONTIC SEA
ILLYRICUM
ITALIA
THRACE
DYRRHACHIVM
MACEDONIA
CORCYRA
THESSALONICA
BITHYNIA PONTUS
ADRIATIC SEA
PHARSALVS
ATHENS
AEGEAN SEA
ASIA
IONIAN SEA
PATRIAE
CAPPADOCIA
GALATIA
CILICIA
TARSUS
ISSUS
RHODES
ANTIOCH
CRETE
CYPRUS
SYRIA
MARE NOSTRUM

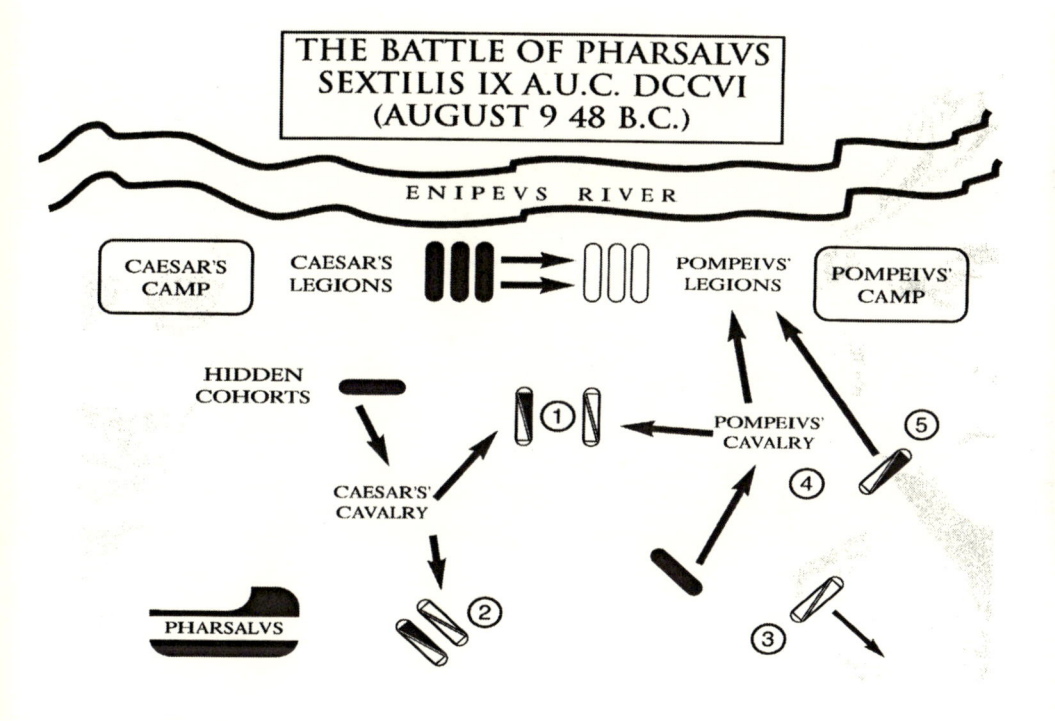

THE BATTLE OF PHARSALVS
SEXTILIS IX A.U.C. DCCVI
(AUGUST 9 48 B.C.)

ENIPEVS RIVER

CAESAR'S CAMP

CAESAR'S LEGIONS

POMPEIVS' LEGIONS

POMPEIVS' CAMP

HIDDEN COHORTS

CAESAR'S CAVALRY

POMPEIVS' CAVALRY

① ② ③ ④ ⑤

PHARSALVS

RIVER PO

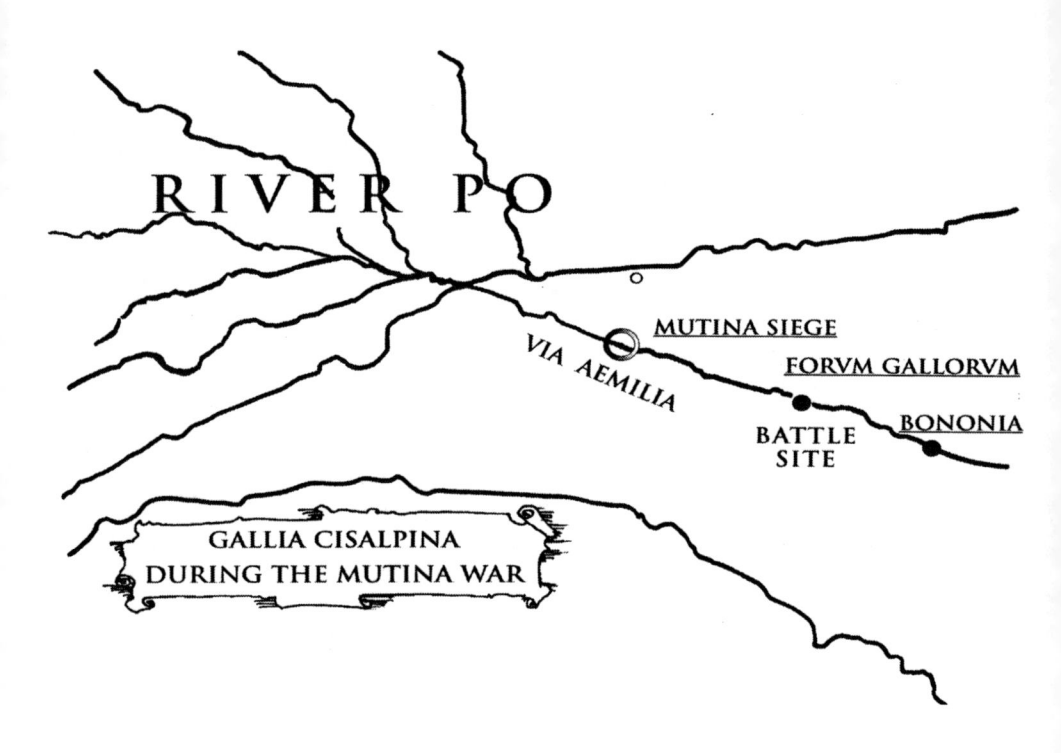

MUTINA SIEGE
FORVM GALLORVM
BONONIA
VIA AEMILIA
BATTLE SITE

GALLIA CISALPINA
DURING THE MUTINA WAR

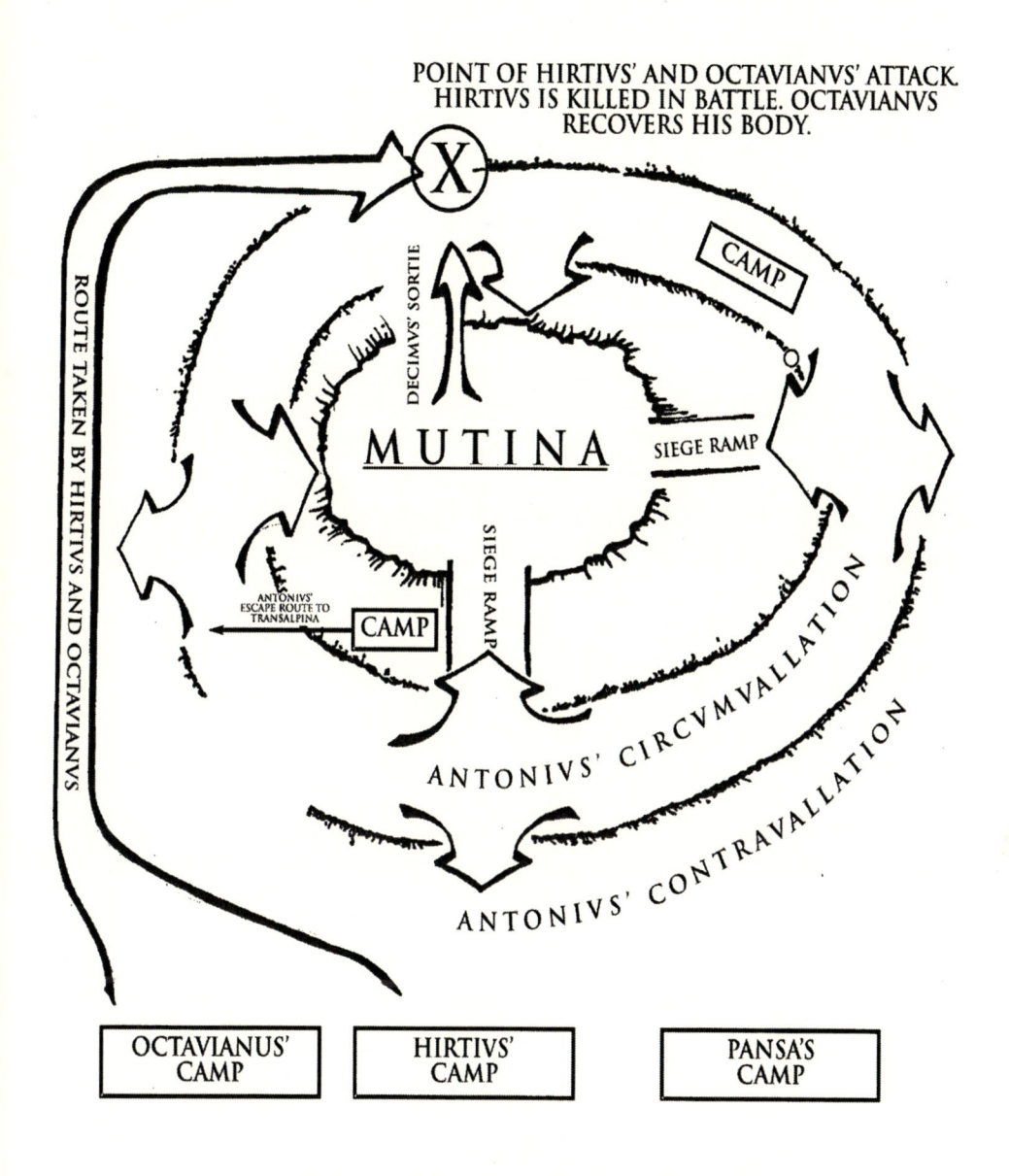

POINT OF HIRTIVS' AND OCTAVIANVS' ATTACK.
HIRTIVS IS KILLED IN BATTLE. OCTAVIANVS
RECOVERS HIS BODY.

Ⓧ

ROUTE TAKEN BY HIRTIVS AND OCTAVIANVS

CAMP

DECIMVS' SORTIE

MUTINA

SIEGE RAMP

ANTONIVS' ESCAPE ROUTE TO TRANSALPINA

CAMP

SIEGE RAMP

ANTONIVS' CIRCVMVALLATION

ANTONIVS' CONTRAVALLATION

| OCTAVIANUS' CAMP | HIRTIVS' CAMP | PANSA'S CAMP |

THE SIEGE AND BATTLE OF MUTINA –
NOVEMBER A.U.C. DCCX TO APRIL A.U.C. DCCXI
[44 B.C]   [43 B.C.]

Prologus (Prologue)

THE FACE IS SERIOUS, ALMOST sullen, yet possessing a handsomeness etched by travail and sorrow. His large, defined hands rest on the fine parchment scroll. Then, his right hand dips the reed pen into the ink jar and he writes across the top of the page:

RESPUBLICA
The Roman Republic of Marcus Tullius Cicero
Ab Urbe Condita DCCIX

On this last day of the year, the Great Man, Dictator for Life, Consul-Elect—yet again—Chief Pontiff, Prefect of Public Morality—a most dubious honor—the promiscuous cock-eagle, the laurel-crowned, bald-pated fornicator, Gaius Julius Caesar, celebrated, despite uncooperative weather, his most recent triumph. But this was not for victories over barbarous Gauls or treacherous Egyptians, or swarthy Numidians. Today's triumph was for his victory over our fellow Romans, over the sons of Pompeius Magnus.

I refused to walk in the procession of senators, his friends and parasites. So, I watched along with the multitudes, the foul, dirty "dregs of Romulus" as our Rex without a title, our Caesar rode in his triumphal chariot along the Sacred Road and through the Forum. Standing on the Rostra with your Uncle Quintus, Servius Sulpicius, and Atticus, I was close enough to his passing chariot to see a flash of anger cross Caesar's face when Tribune Pontius Aquila refused to stand respectfully for the triumphator.

The procession came to a sudden halt, as Master of Horse Marcus Lepidus rode up to the Dictator to convey some message. Calling for the crowd's silence, Caesar announced that Consul Fabius Maximus had expired. Indeed, rumors of the consul's death had been circulating even as the panoply of soldiers, senators, musicians, and Spanish captives paraded through the Forum. But that was not all. Caesar decreed that Gaius Rebilus would complete the expired consul's term, a mere fourteen hours! By Caesar's will, by his dictate, the remaining fourteen hours of a dead consul's term became the commission of a new appointee.

Gaius Rebilus stepped forward from the senators to accept the Dictator's appointment. As he took his place in line next to Consul Gaius Trebonius, the procession started off again amid the renewed cheering of the vulgar mob. Turning to my companions on the Rostra, I quipped, "I'll wager that no crimes will be committed during Rebilus' short term, for he is bound to be so vigilant in his fourteen hours that he'll not have time to eat, drink, sleep, or even relieve his bladder or bowels!"

They laughed at my witticism, but in reality there is nothing amusing about the state of the Republic when men are appointed to the highest offices by the nod and whim of a dictator as though they were porters working the grain barges down at Ostia. *O, what times are these!*

I had returned to Roma because I heard that Dolabella was back from Spain with the Great Man. So, I thought this would be a good time to nail my elusive ex-son-in-law and settle Tullia's dowry.

Tullia, my *Tulliola*. How I yet ache for her. The light has gone out of my life with her passing. I've been in darkness without her these last ten months.

Often times, parents who have lost children can at least console themselves. But Terentia and I, divorced almost two years now, have never even attempted to commiserate with each other. Instead, she badgers me – as she often did in our thirty years together. She insists that I make suitable testamentary arrangements for you. You would think she's burying her sorrow for Tullia's loss in financial plans for you, my son.

At least, your mother has a distraction, albeit a mundane one. I've written treatises on oratory, philosophy, politics, et cetera. But what good are these in a state that's not free? Though I bury myself in these intellectual pursuits, and encourage and subsidize your studies in Athens, the birthplace of democracy and learning, what fulfillment is there for me in these endeavors when there is no opportunity to speak freely in the courts, in the Senate, in the Forum? There is none—nor will there ever be as long as the Republic is enthralled to this dynast, this colossus!

I returned home in disgust and loathing over Caesar's arbitrary action, to find a short letter waiting for me. It was from Pompeia, the Magnus' daughter. She had to have written it with the very blackest bile. She wrote that I'd betrayed her great father; that I was an ingrate after all his services to me; that I was a sail-trimmer who set my course to the prevailing political winds, completely disregarding principles and patriotism. She almost accused me of complicity in her brother's death in Spain; and she praised her younger brother for continuing the struggle, unlike the accommodators and turncoats who've given in to the victorious tyrant. She puts me at their head.

I've pondered Pompeia's letter, trying to determine how much truth, if any, there may be in it. She is but the latest contributor to the ranks of my detractors. What is the truth of my life and my career—an odyssey of thwarted ambition and domestic failure? That I tried to serve the Republic, to save it, to preserve it?

Tomorrow is the Kalends of Januarius. Janus is the two-faced, two-headed god. He looks to the past and he looks forward to the future. Of the future, I can see only the further entrenchment of the Great Man's power and my own inglorious passing from this life. But the past—the past shows what I once was and what I could have been had my ambitions not been foiled and thwarted by Caesar. The story of his rise to power and prominence is the story of my own slow decline into virtual oblivion, a process that began in the year of my consulate, eighteen years ago. It was then that I achieved the pinnacle of my political career while Caesar, through intrigues and duplicity, conspiracies and alliances, launched his campaign to bring the Republic under his domination. He has used and abused, and he has exploited and discarded so many, including your father, in his meteoric ascent.

Marcus, my son, I write this testament for you so that you may understand the Republic that once was and how I endeavored to serve it. I have named it *Respublica,* borrowing the Latin words, *res publica*—the

People's thing, the common thing. This is the Roman designation for our commonwealth which has evolved over centuries into a melding of the Senate's authority and the People's power. However, under Caesar it has degenerated into an entity of his own personal domain. Though I cannot describe the private counsels of my rivals as I was never privy to them, I hope that, if the gods exist or if the Muses of the written word are not indifferent to the scribbling of an old man, then perhaps they or some other power or voice will provide you with insight into those circumstances and events that are beyond the scope of my account. Hopefully, a balanced history will emerge not only for you, my son, but for posterity, assuming, of course, that a future regime will allow it to be read. If so, then I hope that my failures and shortcomings as a statesman will be seen in the light of historical events. More importantly, Marcus, I hope that you will forgive my failings as a father. Please know that I have forgiven you the improprieties of youth, realizing full well that, as your father, I unknowingly set before you the opportunity for the most egregious of offenses.

In the summer of my consulate, with the elections only weeks away, I convened the Senate to receive extraordinary tidings—Gnaeus Pompeius Magnus, fresh from his Eastern victories, had landed at Brundisium. His return, after an absence of nearly five years, in the shadow of the imminent elections, would provide opportunities for ambitious, unscrupulous men to align and conspire, and it would require responsible men to be vigilant and courageous.

Liber I Consul
Caput I Cicero's Respublica

Seated on the curule chair, I patiently watched as the senators, some four hundred men, filed into the Curia Hostilia and took their seats on rows of wooden benches. They were an impressive sight in their white togas, like so many human sailing vessels gliding gracefully across the tiled floor as streams of sunlight from the high, narrow windows descended into the dark, brick interior of the Senate chamber.

As usual, the oligarchs entered together. This cluster of powerful men of consular rank steered the Senate in its deliberations and decrees. There was Quintus Lutatius Catulus, the First Senator, "Princeps Senatus," sleek, graceful veteran, well into his sixties. Next to him was Lucius Licinius Lucullus, in his late fifties, with a head seemingly helmet-molded from years spent on campaign. Both he and Marcius Rex, the same age, had commanded the Republic's legions in the Eastern wars. Lucullus' younger brother, Marcus, walked a few paces behind them. He had been consul ten years before, and as proconsul of Macedonia he had extended Roman hegemony over the neighboring kingdom of Thrace. Decimus Junius Brutus Albinus and Decimus Junius Silanus came after him, looking about the Curia with annoyance and irritation etched on their faces. Fat-faced, cleft-chinned Quintus Hortensius Hortalus, the brother-in-law of Catulus, looked at me from across the room and nodded. He had once been the chief advocate in the courts, before I displaced him.

These men had served the Republic at home and abroad, in peace and in war. They had been consuls and proconsuls. Catulus had even attained the office of censor, the crowning achievement of a distinguished career. Collectively, they represented the better part of a century's worth of valuable experience. Little wonder, then, that they should constitute the inner guiding council of the Senate, advising and counseling it just as the Senate advised and counseled the magistrates who steered the ship of state.

The oligarchs had admitted a junior member to their circle. This was Marcus Porcius Cato, great-grandson of the illustrious Cato the Elder. Cato the Younger, as he was commonly called, was about thirty-six years old at the time. He had fulfilled his obligatory military service before his election as quaestor, an office he had served with irreproachable probity. Tall and straight as a javelin, he was rigid and uncompromising in his personal and political affairs. Because of this, or in spite of it, he had many friends and several in-laws among the Senate, including Silanus, his brother-in-law. The veteran oligarchs were grooming him for great things.

The oligarchs were also the chief men of the optimates, the faction within the Senate that regarded itself as the best men of the Republic. They endeavored to maintain Senatorial ascendency over the opposing faction called the popularists, those senators who espoused the people's interests, usually for their own personal benefit.

On the opposite side of the chamber another group of senators caught my attention. The large, bald head of Marcus Licinius Crassus was unmistakable, and the plutocrat's paunch was quite discernable under his toga. Aged fifty-two, "Bald-Pate Money Bags" held at least half the Senate in his debt either for money or political favors. Like the oligarchs, he had been through all the offices of state, including the censorship which he had served not too amicably with Catulus.

At the time, Crassus was indisputably the richest man in Roma. He had made his fortune mostly from property confiscations during Dictator Sulla's reign of terror and partly from adroit speculations in public works contracts. His play for political power consisted of financing and sponsoring up-and-coming young men who would carry out his policies and programs.

My connection with the Crassus family extended back to the days of my young manhood when I had studied oratory under Crassus' celebrated relative known even to this day as Crassus the Orator. But Marcus Crassus, frequently called "Dives," the Wealthy One, and derisively as "Bald-Pate Money Bags," preferred collecting senators to collecting students. He may even have hoped to purchase me when I bought his splendid Palatine mansion just before entering on the consulate. He certainly held out for his price—three and a half million sesterces. As impolitic as it may have been to buy it from Crassus, the means by which I financed the deal were also questionable. Yet, over the years, I have grown deeply attached to this house, my primary Roman residence. Perhaps that is because it has become something of a prison for me, but one that shuts me out rather than locking me in.

My consular colleague, Gaius Antonius, seated himself next to Crassus. The scion of plebeian nobility, Gaius Antonius was porcine, ruddy, and broad. He had once been expelled from the Senate for insolvency. Through my efforts and with my support he had won election to the praetorate, in the same year that I achieved it, and so he had been re-admitted to that august body. In the first half of our joint-consulate, Antonius had been the front-man who proposed bills purportedly to benefit the people. In reality, the bills were bogus attempts at reform, and ultimately the only beneficiaries were to have been the men who actually contrived them—a typical popularist ploy. Bills for debt cancellation, land reform, franchise extensions, these I had successfully blocked from becoming law.

Crassus had succeeded in getting Antonius elected consul, but if "Bald-Pate's" schemes had proven totally successful, then Antonius' colleague would not have been myself, but instead Lucius Sergius Catilina. Sitting next to Crassus, he cast me a contemptuous glance and then followed it with a feigned, crooked smile.

Tall, lean, and rakishly handsome, Catilina was a declared candidate for next year's consulate, but this was not his first canvass for the Republic's highest magistracy. As a partisan of Sulla during the civil war, Catilina had participated in the proscriptions. Among his victims was his own brother-in-law and my kinsman, Marcus Gratidianus, who was also a relative of the popularist hero, Gaius Marius. Later, he had administered the province of Africa with such rapacity that he faced charges of malfeasance in office upon his return to Roma. These had kept him out of the consular race for one year, but upon his acquittal—achieved according to popular rumor through Crassus' influence—Catilina stood for the consulate again, this time in the same year as I. Having crossed factional lines from the optimates to the popularists, Catilina could easily be depicted as a self-serving turncoat, and I had succeeded in doing this time and again in my campaign speeches.

Catilina had the advantage of a long, patrician pedigree, while I was a "new man" without consular ancestors, an equite from Arpinum. Moreover, Catilina and Antonius had formed an electoral partnership, and their backer was Crassus with his virtually unlimited resources.

In those days, conditions throughout Italia were ripe for revolution. There was widespread discontent with the optimate status quo. Debt afflicted thousands of people, and its effects were exacerbated by the acute shortage of gold and silver coin which drove up interest rates to Olympian heights. There was a dangerous restlessness on the part of the urban mob, and veteran colonists settled in various parts of Italia were said to be bored, broke, and belligerent, anxiously awaiting fresh opportunities for war and plunder. The popularists expected, while the optimates feared, the triumphant return of Pompeius from the Asian war and his establishment of a dictatorship and with it new proscriptions, new confiscations, and new power alignments.

Catilina and Antonius exploited these conditions. While they were conspicuous in their promises of debt relief and other popularist reform measures, I denigrated these proposals, not because I opposed reform, but because the authors had their own political advancement at heart rather than the people's welfare. I also made the case that these proposals were inimical to the interests of the long-absent Pompeius. Moreover, I threw calumny upon the personal reputations of Catilina and Antonius, not at all a difficult task as their lives were checkered with tales of ribald debauchery and profligate bankruptcy.

Beyond vilifying the opposition—and there were many receptive ears for this propaganda—I cultivated staunch support from the business class, my own fellow equites, and from the senatorial class. They were reasonably disposed to look beyond my "new man" status and to see me as a trustworthy bulwark against any popularist agitation of the kind that Catilina and Antonius were likely to foment if they were elected.

Supported by these two powerful classes, and having cut the ground beneath Catilina, I was elected by a majority of the Centuriate Assembly's votes. However, my consular colleague was Gaius Antonius, who was returned in second place.

Now, a year later and with a new campaign season in progress amid the same prevailing fears and uncertainties, Catilina was yet again endeavoring to be elected consul. What was different was his electoral partner to his left.

This was Gaius Julius Caesar. An aura of triumph yet surrounded him from his Chief Pontifical election victory of only a few weeks before. His purple bordered toga, scarlet shoes, and the Jovian medallion suspended from a golden chain about his neck were the obvious insignia of his supreme pontifical rank.

Caesar had certain crucial advantages that had aided his progress through the course of offices. He was Roman-born of patrician parentage and he was descended of consular ancestors, though his father died having risen only as far as the praetorate. However, Caesar was connected with the popularists through marriage—his own and his aunt's. His first wife had been the daughter of Lucius Cornelius Cinna, the popularist leader who had succeeded Gaius Marius; and Marius had been married to Caesar's father's sister. In addition, Caesar's mother's kinsmen, the Aurelii Cottae, were definitely popularist in their politics.

Thus endowed, Caesar appealed to and easily won the support of the urban mob and the friendship of those senators who sought to use the populace for their own ends.

Caesar had once been on Crassus' payroll. Both his public and private debts were expedited by the old plutocrat. But things had changed for Caesar's finances after he had returned from his propraetorian governorship of Spain. The wealth he had accumulated from his victories over certain Lusitanian tribes made him nearly the financial equal of Crassus. Yet, Caesar continued his political association with Crassus even though money was apparently no longer a prime motive.

Caesar had scored a tremendous victory by winning election to the vacant office of Chief Pontiff. Though I had succeeded in thwarting his and his partners' other schemes, I could not prevent his pontifical election by a special convention of seventeen of the thirty-five citizens' tribes. Not even his rivals, older men, men who had been in the pontifical college longer than he, could outbid Caesar for the people's votes. Caesar's money and influence and fame extended too far and wide for him to be stopped.

He has occupied the Chief Pontificate during the last eighteen years, holding the power and wielding the prestige of Roma's most august religious office. Like a king of old, he has lived in the palatial Regia, the Chief Pontiff's official residence.

Caesar flashed a broad smile at me, one that made his brow furrow above his dark yet lively eyes, and his fair, wide face blushed. Whatever else may be said about him politically, he was an imposing presence, lean-limbed, fair-complexioned, dark-haired, possessing that special appeal known to the Greeks as *charisma*.

Crassus, Antonius, Catilina, and Caesar—the association of these four was no secret. They had been the prime backers of a far-reaching agrarian bill and a debt-relief measure which I had succeeded in talking down in the Senate in the early months of my term. But I knew their schemes were not yet at an end.

While the optimates, the so-called "best men" and the upholders of Senatorial power, privilege, and pre-eminence, and the popularists, men who used the urban masses and popular causes to advance their own careers, always sat on opposite sides of the Curia, there was yet a third faction. Often the votes of these neutrals had tipped the balance against optimate reactionary policies and popularist radicalism. It was to this group that I had always endeavored to affiliate myself, and I had cultivated the friendship of many of its members. Chief among them were Lucius Marcius Philippus, Publius Nigidius Figulus, Lucius Calpurnius Piso, Gaius Octavius Caepias, Marcus Terentius Varro, a kinsman of Terentia, and foremost among them, my dear, intimate friend, Servius Sulpicius Rufus.

With the exception of Varro, who had been serving as legate to Pompeius, all of the others, including your Uncle Quintus, were present and seated at their usual places.

After the auspices were taken and found to be favorable—for the caged chickens heartily ate their proffered seeds—I presented Pompeius' legates. Attired in civic rather than in military garb, Lucius Afranius and Metellus Nepos entered the semi-circular enclosure of the Curia and stood in the center of the floor.

Afranius, of medium stature, swarthy, and oily-looking, held several scrolls as he spoke. "Conscript Fathers, on behalf of my commander, Gnaeus Pompeius Magnus, we present the records of his acta, his decrees, and territorial arrangements in Roma's Eastern imperium. These we submit for your examination and ratification. My colleague, Metellus Nepos, brings you a written message from our noble commander, the Republic's great and loyal servant."

With this Afranius deferred to Nepos, a bronzed, granite-featured man. He unrolled a scroll, cleared his throat, and began to read Pompeius' message.

"Honorable Senators, Conscript Fathers, you and the People commissioned me to clear the seaways of Cilician pirates who for years had disrupted our maritime commerce. This, I have accomplished. You and the People commissioned me to terminate the long war against King Mithridates of Pontus, to stabilize our Eastern provinces, and to secure the frontier. This too I have accomplished."

Listening to Nepos, I could easily visualize Pompeius dictating the letter to a scribe in his command tent. It was almost like hearing the Magnus' voice instead of the legate's. I could not help but recall that the optimates had been adamantly opposed to both of these commands because they feared the conferring of such extraordinary power upon a single individual. It had taken tribunicial legislation pushed through the Tribal Assembly to grant these commands to Pompeius. In fact, my speech on behalf of Pompeius' command in the Eastern war had been my first political statement during my praetorate.

The senators' polite applause interrupted both Nepos' reading and my personal reverie. Then, he continued. "The old King died by his own hand. I interred his remains with all the honors befitting one of his rank and royalty. His ancestral kingdom is now the Roman province of Pontus. The details of my arrangements in our Eastern provinces, the client-kings and princes whom I have installed, the accounting of revenues and spoils, and the names of hostages are contained in the records which my legates convey on my behalf."

At this point, Afranius held up the scrolls as murmurings and chuckles and applause spread across the chamber. But Nepos, holding aloft Pompeius' dispatch with his bronzed, muscular arms, continued to read.

"Having discharged my duties to the Senate and the People, I have returned to my country. I will remain in Brundisium long enough to disband my legions as they disembark, but I will, as is my privilege, retain command of three praetorian cohorts. With these, I will retire to my estate at Alba Longa to await the Senate's ratification of my Eastern acta. I ask that the Senate assign land to my discharged veterans who have faithfully served their country and have vanquished Roma's enemies."

Nepos paused to catch his breath. He slyly looked about the chamber, taking in the senators' reactions. The optimates were plainly uneasy at the mention of land allotments, and the popularists, especially the Big Four, smirked vindictively.

Returning to the letter, Nepos read, "On behalf of my loyal legions and in recognition of our victories, I claim the right of a triumph upon the Senate's pleasure. In accordance with ancient tradition, I shall not set foot in Roma until these petitions have been considered and granted. As always, I am the Republic's loyal servant, Gnaeus Pompeius Magnus, Proconsul and Imperator."

The two legates handed their scrolls to an attendant and then sat down. Praetor Metellus Celer, the rotund elder brother of Nepos, rose from his seat. Recognizing him, I granted him leave to speak. "I propose that the Senate assure Gnaeus Pompeius of our good intentions toward his petitions," he announced.

Over loud murmurings, Antonius rose and seconded the proposals. But before I could submit them to a vote, Caesar rose and addressed the Senate. "Conscript Fathers, Gnaeus Pompeius truly deserves our thanks and good wishes for his victories and his pacification of the seas and the East. Surely, the Senate will allow him to triumph. But is the Senate prepared to grant his veterans land?" Then facing me, he announced, "This administration has denigrated all attempts at agrarian legislation that would have benefitted Pompeius' soldiers and thousands of the urban poor!"

Obviously, he was referring to me as the culprit behind the Senate's resistance to land reform. I shared with many in the Senate the view that such measures, while intrinsically good, can and have been used by unscrupulous men to advance their own interests rather than to benefit the needy. Then, as now, I believed in private philanthropy rather than in government action to ameliorate economic hardship. So, backed by the oligarchy, I had opposed agrarian reforms proposed earlier in the year by Antonius and by tribunes in Caesar's and Crassus' employ.

I studied Caesar as he spoke. His thin black hair was neatly dressed. He gave the appearance of being taller than he actually was. His dark eyes, especially when he glanced at me, had a penetrating force. There seemed to be a power in him that would have burst forth to envelope us.

Suddenly, Cato sprang to the Senate's defense. "The Senate will oppose *any* legislation that affects the state-leased lands in Campania," he declared in a stentorian voice that brooked no dissent. "These are not available for distribution. It was only right that any proposed bills affecting them should have been opposed by the consul and voted down by the Senate."

A round of applause acknowledged Cato's remarks. Over it, he continued. "Nor will the Senate countenance the forced eviction of citizens already settled on their own land."

The Campanian lands that Cato spoke of were a major source of revenue for the Republic, or more precisely, for the hundred or so noble families who had leased them for several generations. No one could dispute Cato's defense of these lands and the prohibition against government seizures and evictions. The problem was, there was hardly any other land available in all of Italia.

Cato had hardly finished speaking when Catilina stood and announced, "This administration has not only neglected the plight of the landless, it has also ignored the suffering of thousands of debtors all over Italia. The Eastern wars have drained gold and silver coin. Interest rates have been murderous. But now, thanks to Pompeius, the wars are over. The Senate must consider the people's welfare. The veterans and the poor need land! The homeless need shelter! The debtors need relief."

Every nerve in Catilina's gaunt face moved as he spoke. His sinewy neck strained with every agitated word. There was a dangerous, nervous desperation issuing from his tall, lean frame.

Though as presiding Consul I was prohibited from speaking in Senatorial debates, I nevertheless took to the floor before either Caesar or Catilina could resume their harangue. Deliberately, I aimed my words at Catilina. "Lucius Catilina, you speak of the hardships of the landless, the homeless, and the debtors. Are you sincerely concerned for their welfare? Or is it a mask you wear so that on their behalf you may threaten the peace and order of the Republic? We've heard your speeches to the Etrurian colonists who accompany you—a veritable legion of your own—as you make your canvass throughout the City. To them and to the City plebs you've made lofty promises, even to the extent of disrupting the elections if the voting appears to go against you. What have you to say to this, Lucius Catilina?"

Catilina did not back down from my challenge. Over the outraged din pervading the Curia, he shouted, "There are two bodies in the state: one is strong but without a head, while the other is old and weak with an infirm head." With these last words, he looked around at the Senate and then glared directly at me as he declared, "But I will provide the leadership so sorely needed by the People!"

Nothing could have been plainer. Here was a self-proclaimed popularist leader. Having made his declaration, Catilina haughtily walked across the floor and exited the chamber, leaving a stunned Senate staring after him.

Grimacing, Crassus and Caesar looked from Catilina to Antonius and then to me.

Three senators scurried after Catilina: Praetor Publius Cornelius Lentulus Sura, Gaius Cornelius Cethegus, a praetorian candidate, and young Publius Clodius Pulcher. The extent of their connection with Catilina was to become evident only later in the year.

I directed the Senate's attention to the Princeps Senatus, Catulus, who had slowly risen as soon as Catilina was out of sight.

"The consular and praetorian elections must be secured against any and all threat of disruption or violence," Catulus proposed in a raspy, haughty voice. "I move that the Senate postpone the elections so that guards may be stationed in Mars Field to protect the voters and all candidates."

Usually, when the First Senator spoke, his words were heeded. This occasion was no exception. Over the buzz and hum of approval, Lucius Lucullus rose and seconded Catulus' motion. I put it to the Senate's vote and it was passed with negligible opposition. Almost as an afterthought, the Senate also approved the proposed commendations for Pompeius after I reminded them that this had been their first item for consideration. Afranius and Nepos were dispatched to bring Pompeius the Senate's salutations.

Then, the meeting was adjourned and the Senators began to rise from their seats and file out of the Curia. Catulus beckoned to me. Turning aside from Quintus and Servius Sulpicius, I walked over to where the oligarchs were seated. Crassus, Caesar, and Antonius walked past me. "Bald-Pate" looked at me, smiled sardonically, and quipped, "Well played, Cicero, but the game is far from over."

IN THE TOMB-LIKE SILENCE OF the deserted Curia, the oligarchs took counsel about the Republic's business. Catulus commended me for my consulate, for serving the Republic's, and as far as they were concerned, the oligarchy's interests. "You've done well in checking Crassus and Caesar and their schemes. You know, when the annalists write of your term, they'll have to call it not the consulate of Cicero and Antonius, but the consulate of *Tullius and Cicero!*" The others chuckled at Catulus' witticism.

Yes, I had been their man last year to prevent Catilina and Antonius from attaining office together. Who would be their man *this* year to prevent a Caesar-Catilina pairing?

Cato asked, "How long will the elections need to be postponed?"

Catulus shrugged and shifted on his bench as he answered, "Until things quiet down."

"Whenever they're held, we'll need at least three thousand armed guards to cover Mars Field," Marcius Rex offered.

Lucius Lucullus added, "Protecting the elections and the electorate is not our only concern."

Catulus again shifted restlessly. He rose and stretched. "Yes, yes. It's imperative that we prevent a consulate of Caesar and Catilina. That would be an utter disaster for the Republic—for all of us." He looked around at the exclusive clique. "One or the other, if not *both*, must be kept out."

Both Quintus and Sulpicius had declared their consular candidacies. They would have been a formidable duo to run the government, but I doubted that either of them would have the oligarchy's backing. Why should they go with another Cicero, another "new man"? And Sulpicius was more envied than admired for his prodigious legal mind. No, it was all too obvious that they had already selected their candidate. I surmised that it had to be Marcus Calpurnius Bibulus. There could be no other reason for him to be sitting among the oligarchs during their privy session. Before long, my assumption would prove to be correct.

I watched him sitting next to Cato and I had to suppress my amusement at the uncanny similarities between them. Though Bibulus was older by about seven years, he and Cato possessed the same rigid, uncompromising demeanor, the same tough Stoicism. Strangely, the physical similarity between them was such that one who did not know better could have taken them for siblings.

"What's our policy on Pompeius?" Marcus Lucullus asked.

"For the time being, we'll watch and wait," was all that Catulus would offer.

"What game is he playing?" wondered Decimus Brutus. "With his legions at his back he could have *demanded* instead of petitioned."

"Pompeius' demands take the form of petitions," Catulus advised, "and remember: what he disbands today he could summon tomorrow. Imperators are never far from their legions."

The oligarchs nodded in acknowledgement of Catulus' accuracy. Then I spoke up. "Gentlemen, postponing the elections, though necessary, will allow Pompeius' veterans to come to Roma and to vote for whomsoever their commander endorses. We can't afford to ignore Pompeius for very long. Roman security in the East demands that his acta should be examined and ratified as quickly as possible. And land must be found for his veterans. The Senate must take this initiative before the popularists make it their business."

Hortensius took issue with me. "You spoke against every land bill, but now you want to give land to Pompeius' veterans. What a reversal!"

"You misjudge me, Hortensius. I'm against government hand-outs for the indolent, and I remain opposed to the enforced eviction of productive citizens from their farms. But discharged soldiers who've served their country are entitled to their farmsteads as a just reward for their service, providing, of course, that they're willing to work them responsibly and maintain them. Can the Republic afford to have thousands of discharged veterans swell the ranks of the unemployed? Or worse yet, have them become insurgents under unscrupulous demagogues?"

"Like Catilina?" Cato suggested.

"WHAT DO YOU SUPPOSE HE meant by that?"

That was Marcus Caelius Rufus' question upon hearing me relate my talk with the oligarchs. I remember him fondly, even affectionately. He was in his late twenties at the time and of equestrian pedigree from the town of Puteoli. His father had placed him under my tutelage to study oratory, rhetoric, law, and statecraft. He was an extremely handsome young man of dark features and lithe build. Always eager to listen, anxious to learn, he had sat in on many of our chats. It fascinated him to hear Servius Sulpicius' legalistic platitudes clash with Atticus' "in-with-everybody" and "money talks" sophistries. Having high regard for Quintus and me, he was respectfully deferential to us.

We were seated in the library of the Palatine house. Oil lamps illuminated the room as we refreshed ourselves on watered wine and fruit. We had moved into the house during Januarius, at the beginning of my consulate. Most of my books and documents were still back at the Carinae house, which Quintus and his family now occupied.

The Carinae district, so named because many of its houses were shaped like the *carinae* or keels of ships, had been the site of our first home when Father moved us to Roma from our ancestral home town of Arpinum, nestled in the Alban hills. Arpinum's residents had been enfranchised with Roman citizenship almost a century before my birth. However, Father had wanted his two sons to pursue political careers in Roma, the foremost city in Italia and the capital of an imperium surrounding the Internal Sea, what Romans liked to call *Mare Nostrum*, Our Sea. Unlike previous generations of Ciceri who had engaged in banking and commerce and local politics, Quintus and I were educated to run the course of honor and ascend the official ladder of political office in the Roman Republic.

Young Caelius reminded me of my early years in Roma, for his equestrian father wanted the same advancement for him. Regrettably, Father did not live to see me attain the consulate at age forty-two, the earliest legal age: a remarkable feat in and of itself, but especially for a "new man" without consular ancestry.

I responded to Caelius' question. "If Catilina tries any mischief at the election, he'll doubtless use the Etrurian veterans. They're practically inseparable from him."

Then Atticus asked, "Did they say anything about the Asian tax contract?"

I knew he would bring this up. I could only shake my head as Atticus muttered, "I'm not surprised." He leaned his broad, stout body back in his chair, reprovingly shook his bald head, and rolled his heavy-lidded pale eyes.

Atticus—Titus Pomponius Atticus—was a committed equite. At forty-eight years of age and a bachelor, he had no intention of embarking on a political career, or of marrying. His business was money, stocks, and provincial revenues. In short, his business *was business*. It had been this way for him ever since I had first met him in Athens during our philosophical and rhetorical studies. The mutual fondness between my friend and the Athenians was reflected in his assumed cognomen, *Atticus*. Several years later, after his adoption by a wealthy, but obnoxious uncle, his proper, full name became Quintus Caecilius Pomponianus. However, to us he was always Atticus.

In the wake of the Marian-Sullan civil war and the attendant proscriptions, Atticus could not imagine why two equite brothers would opt for politics over business. In our own defense, I would pedantically remind him that in Roma's ancient days, the equestrian class had consisted of those citizens wealthy enough to afford to maintain horses and thus constitute the first Roman cavalry. Later, the equites retained ceremonial public horses while they pursued commercial enterprises. Eventually, the honorary retention of public horses was discontinued if and when equites entered the Senate to pursue political careers. Feigning irritation, Atticus would tell me not to lecture him about equestrian origins, for, with or without horses, he would pursue business over politics without any misgivings.

Nonetheless, our dispositions and sensibilities were very similar. In time, the bonds between us became even stronger when Quintus married Atticus' sister. Unfortunately, the marriage has not endured as long as our friendship.

Our conversation took a different path with Sulpicius. "Yet, Pompeius wants to separate himself from his legions. That's loyalty to the Republic, or the shrewdest gamble I've ever seen him take."

We often teased him, calling him Sulpicius the *Ursus* because of his large, bear-like build and his thick crop of dark hair. His large, luminous, dark eyes were set off by a serious, benevolent face. In this year of my consulate, he had just turned forty-five. We had been friends for many years, ever since my early years as an advocate in the courts, even before my election as quaestor.

Servius Sulpicius was a widower. His lovely wife, Postumia, had died at about the time I was aedile. His son, the younger Servius, eschewed both business and politics, much to his father's dismay; instead, he engaged in literary and scholastic pursuits. Likewise, his daughter, Sulpicia, rejected even marriage and devoted her life, like her brother, to intellectual and philosophical endeavors. She was most certainly an anomaly, even in our age of the liberated Roman woman.

"It seems our Pompeius is in for a long wait before the Senate gets around to his agenda," Quintus suggested.

My brother, Quintus, my junior by little more than a year, was turning forty-two so that he would have attained the minimum age to seek the consulate. We were both often teased about our family name and referred to as "Chick-Pea the Elder" and "Chick-Pea the Younger." Our physical appearance was quite similar. We had the same medium stature and build, the same chestnut brown hair speckled with gray, the same light brown eyes, though his were lighter. While his facial features were more angular, more chiseled than mine, my nose and neck, especially the neck, were noticeably, even effeminately longer.

"Yes," Atticus agreed, "he'll wait and stew while all his work in the East will go to ruin. But he'll be in good company. The publicans have waited and stewed these last six months." Then to me he petulantly grieved, "Marcus, I can't believe you've not been able to get the Senate to budge on the Asian tax contract."

"Remember, my good friend," I began, "I've as much stock in the consortium as you have. I've given the Senate all the facts and figures about Asian crop failures and poor yields." Turning to my brother, I added, "Quintus, when you governed Asia you sent dispatch after dispatch warning them of the dire conditions."

My brother nodded in agreement. "The Senate's answer has been: 'What's that to us? The publicans took a gamble and overbid on the tax-farming contract. So now, poor yields or not, they'll have to collect and then pay up!' The Senate's not about to give them any kind of break. There it is—the Senate's unyielding position."

Atticus was not at all placated. He never was when the tax-farmers' Asian contract came up for discussion. "You know, of course, that Crassus' investment exceeds yours and mine together. And several of the leading bankers in the group have been turning to him for help. He doesn't lack friends or votes in the Senate, and it would benefit him mightily to earn the publicans' gratitude."

Hearing this, Servius laughed. He leaned forward and threw up his hands in a gesture of exasperation. "Those old men, those oligarchs and their minions, are a near-sighted lot. Their stubbornness in facing reality is ultimately harmful to the Republic, and Marcus, my dear friend, whom I love and respect, you're a party to it!"

"I?"

"Yes—because in trying to crash through the door and join their clique, you've turned your back on what's needed. Can you, can they, can *we* be so blind as to not realize it? *Land!* Not just for the veterans, but for that smelly lot—your 'dregs of Romulus'! That's what they need far more than cheap grain and free games. The *debtors!* Some relief must be extended to alleviate their hardships. There are precedents for such relief without provoking popular unrest or causing the equites to cough blood!"

Quintus and I looked at each other startled, and then I quipped to Servius, "Either of you could have used that as a campaign speech." Only Caelius laughed, while the others turned and looked at him sourly. I refrained from attempting any further witticism.

"Yes, Servius, you're right," I agreed. "But what's missing to bring about these changes? Is there a citizen-body out there that prefers labor and productivity over idleness and public welfare? The debtors are victims of their own financial mismanagement and profligacy. Should the government have to bail them out? The veterans? Of course, I agree that they should have farmsteads allotted to them. But if the Senate will not lead the way to constructive change, then popularist demagogues will fan the flames of unrest and strife. Ultimately, they'll have to be stopped because their idea of reform is to push aside the Senate and establish not a democracy as in old Athens, but a tyranny of the unbridled mob. That's how the politics of land reform have worked ever since the Gracchus brothers shook the Republic with their shameless agitations."

Caelius broke in, "That's how the division between the optimates and popularists first began. But will it ever end?"

Quintus looked at me and said, "I hope our sons will serve the Republic in a time of peace."

Servius opined, "It's a matter of leadership."

"That and more," I agreed. "The peace of our Republic is founded on the harmonious cooperation of the senatorial and equestrian classes. That is my ideal, and it is attainable."

"But so long as the Senate refuses to accommodate the publicans or their tax contracts," Atticus warned, "your precious 'concord of the orders' is in danger."

"And," Servius added, "as long as Gnaeus Pompeius and his reasonable petitions are ignored by the oligarchs, how can he serve as an actual 'rector' or 'moderator' of your ideal state? He'll either become the Senate's complacent pawn or he'll march on Roma as did Sulla and proclaim himself dictator; so much for your Republic, Marcus, and your 'concord of the orders'."

"But I remain confident," I assured them, "that Gnaeus Pompeius has great potential to be a modern-day Scipio Aemilianus, though Scipio's Roma was far different from ours."

Caelius asked, "If Scipio had his Laelius, his ally and counter-part in the Senate, then whom do you see as today's Laelius?"

Atticus, Quintus, and Servius looked with furrowed brows, raised eyebrows, and cunning grins from Caelius to me. Young Caelius was perceptive enough to realize that his question had been answered.

Before retiring for bed that night, I wrote a brief letter to Gnaeus Pompeius, pledging my continued friendship and support. The next morning, I entrusted the letter to one of my household staff and sent it off to Brundisium.

Caput II Omniscient Voice

PUBLIUS CLODIUS PULCHER WATCHES HIS four mentors. He is seated across a small table from Gaius Antonius. Both men drink watered wine and select morsels of delicacies from a silver tray. Lucius Sergius Catilina paces nervously, directing his attention to Marcus Licinius Crassus lying prone and naked upon a couch as a swarthy, nubile slave girl massages his broad, fleshy back and shoulders. Crassus' bald, oiled head shines under the room's oil lamps. Gaius Julius Caesar sits in a heated pool receiving the ministrations of another swarthy, nubile slave girl, probably the twin of the masseuse. This one now and again comes up for air from below the water. Clodius cannot see her face, but from Caesar's relaxed, serene expression, he surmises that the girl's submerged attentions have been satisfying.

Clodius smiles, hoping for an opportunity to sample the heated pool's delights. But he's distracted by Catilina's agitated voice.

"The veterans are here. Now's the time for us to seize power instead of waiting for the Senate to hold the election." Catilina looks at Crassus, annoyed at the man's seeming indifference.

Crassus opens his eyes and slightly raises his head from the pillow. "No, Lucius. I'm not disposed to imitating Sulla or Marius. It's not through soldiers' iron-shod boots that we'll take power. No—but through the Centuriata's votes."

"Can you really expect me to be so complacent?" Catilina responds. "I lost the election last year to the 'Chick-Pea'. Two years ago, I was disqualified from canvassing because some African provincials brought suit against me. Then my enemies tried to convict me of political murder..."

Crassus interrupts, "And I arranged favorable verdicts on both occasions."

"Yes, I've not forgotten that or your campaign help. That's exactly why I cannot afford to lose again!" Catilina's agitation increases as he takes big strides between Crassus' couch and the table where Antonius and Clodius sit.

"Come, come, Lucius, I've never pressed you for monetary returns." Crassus winks at the masseuse.

"Yes, I've not forgotten that either. But I've other creditors who do not have your forbearance. They want their money, and if I don't achieve the consulate I'm ruined." Catilina sees that Crassus is about to speak, and he turns emphatic. "Look, it's going to take one big push. Use the veterans to seize the Capitoline and the City walls and then arrest Cicero and the oligarchs...."

Now Crassus rises on his elbows. "And then you'll give Pompeius the ideal pretext to re-assemble his legions, march on Roma, declare himself dictator, and quite possibly, dispatch all of us. Is that what you want? Civil war? When we're so close to the goal? No, my impulsive friend, we don't tantalize Pompeius."

Catilina attempts to rejoin, "He and his legions could join with us in...."

"No!" Crassus snaps. We'll not invite Pompeius to march his legions on Roma. Put that out of your mind!"

By this time, Caesar has been sufficiently gratified in his bath and he rises out of the pool, dons a robe, and joins the discussion. "But we need his legions' votes."

"Yes, so true," Crassus agrees. "And we'll have their votes, however much it pains me to indulge Pompeius. Yes, yes, I know we need him, though he's always managed to steal what should have been mine. I cannot abide that man!"

Caesar knows well of Crassus' and Pompeius' mutual antipathy. During the civil war, it had been Crassus' victory at Roma's Colline Gate that had made Sulla the Republic's ruler. Yet, Sulla promoted Pompeius rather than Crassus with military commissions. Then, less than ten years later, when Crassus had crushed the slave rebellion led by Spartacus, it had been Pompeius who appropriated the victory by slaughtering a few thousand remnants. For this, the Senate had awarded Pompeius a triumph, but to Crassus the lesser honor of a mere ovation. And during their joint consulate, Crassus had had to conciliate Pompeius in order to forestall civil strife. No wonder Crassus cannot abide Pompeius!

"But in politics," Crassus says, "we often need those whom we loathe."

Then Antonius speaks. "Crassus, when I assume the proconsulate of Cisalpine Gaul, there'll be no shortage of manpower for us. I could recruit a dozen legions to balance and block Pompeius."

"Listen, Antonius," Caesar says, "don't get too comfortable about Gaul."

"And why shouldn't I, Caesar?"

"Because I want it for *my own* proconsular province!"

Catilina interjects, "That's *if* you win the consulate, Caesar."

Caesar chuckles and pours himself a cup of wine. "You know, Lucius, you're much too wound up about this election. Why don't you have a bath and a massage. It's an ideal way to take the stress out of canvassing."

"And exercise more restraint in the Senate," says Crassus, reclining again on the couch and beckoning the masseuse to continue. "There's no need to provide Cicero with darts and arrows to throw at you."

Caesar looks at Clodius as he takes a deep draught of wine. His face lights up with an idea. Turning to Crassus, he wonders aloud, "Do you think Publius Clodius might enjoy an excursion down to Brundisium?"

Looking up from his couch, Crassus, fully understanding Caesar's question, replies, "Well, why don't you ask him?"

Clodius knows immediately that, like it or not, he will be going to Brundisium to convey his mentors' greetings to Pompeius.

PRAECIA IS A JADED BEAUTY, though somewhat past her prime. Her auburn hair has been regularly treated to conceal the encroachments of age; her wide-set green eyes are outlined in kohl; her skin is like alabaster, and her chiseled features delineate a voluptuous mouth. She is renowned for her beauty, wit, and political sophistication. These traits she shares with her close friend and confidante, Sempronia Tuditani.

Sempronia, several years younger than Praecia, is the beautiful, hedonistic wife of the oligarch, Decimus Junius Brutus. Theirs was a marriage of early spring to late winter, politically motivated, but sufficiently passionate to produce a son, young Decimus Brutus. Golden-haired and hard-faced, Sempronia could match her friend in beauty, wit, intelligence, and political appreciation. But while Sempronia violated her patrician marriage vows with innumerable affairs, Praecia instead had eschewed marriage. She had been for years the mistress of Publius Cornelius Cethegus, a Senatorial boss and wire-puller among the "pediarii," the junior senators of quaestorian and aedilician rank. Praecia had been the channel though whom ambitious men sought to win over Publius Cethegus and Senatorial votes to advance their own schemes.

But Publius Cethegus has died, and Praecia has become the mistress of his younger brother, Gaius. Ruddy-faced, taut-limbed, and crowned with a mop of dark hair, Gaius is anxious to follow in his brother's footsteps. Partly for this reason, he has taken up with his deceased brother's mistress. For her part, Praecia sees advantages for herself, in spite of her own wealth, in pairing up with Gaius Cethegus. A candidate for the praetorate, Cethegus has also attached himself to Catilina, upon the example and recommendation of the urban praetor, Publius Cornelius Lentulus Sura.

Lentulus is a politician on the rebound. Several years earlier, he had been consul, but then, because of political improprieties, he had been among sixty-four senators expelled by the censors. His re-entry into the Senate has been accomplished by his election as urban praetor. In this, he has been aided by financial support from Marcus Crassus and by the influence of his own wife, Julia, the widow of Marcus Antonius Creticus and the sister-in-law of Consul Gaius Antonius. But Lentulus' ambitions are far from satisfied.

He has acquired a mistress in Sempronia, for a man of appetites must have an outlet beyond the confines of a politically motivated marriage. So it is at Praecia's house in the Caelian district that these four ambitious lovers meet for their trysts and their political talks – Praecia and Cethegus, and Sempronia and Lentulus.

In a well-furnished bed-chamber, Sempronia and Lentulus lie in each other's arms. Their love-making, as usual, has satisfied them both. Wistfully, teasingly, Sempronia asks, "Are you not at all afraid of bedding the wife of one of the oligarchs, especially since you've only recently been reinstated into the Senate?"

Lentulus stirs from his near slumber, opens his heavy-lidded brown eyes, and with a shake of his fleshy jowls, responds, "My only fear is not fulfilling my destiny."

"Yes, I know," the woman murmurs, for she has heard this many times before. But this time she pursues the point. "How are you so certain that you'll become *princeps*, Roma's leading citizen?"

Lentulus turns on his side so that he is directly facing her. "I'll tell you a secret, Sempronia, and I hope, though I don't believe, that you'll keep it in confidence. Not long after I'd been expelled from the Senate, I went to the Sibyl at Cumae. She told me that a third Cornelius – the first and the second having been Sulla and Cinna – will be prominent among his fellow Romans. I'll achieve this without Catilina and without Pompeius."

Sempronia is at first taken aback by her lover's assertion. Then she bursts into laughter. "But Lentulus, how do you know that you are *that* third Cornelius? Isn't Cethegus also a Cornelius? Could the Sibyl have meant Cornelius *Cethegus* instead of Cornelius *Lentulus*?"

Before Lentulus can respond, Sempronia again bursts into laughter. Then she recovers sufficiently to say, "I promise you, dear heart, your secret is safe with me. Yet, your association with Catilina is not a secret."

Lentulus smirks. "Today in Roma there are hardly any secrets – political or amorous." Saying this, he teasingly strokes Sempronia's exposed breast. She is aroused by his touch. Arching her back and stretching herself on the bed she purrs, "Not always, lover, for keeping confidences and secrets makes the game all the more exciting. Yes?"

It is no secret to Lentulus that his mistress loves and adores her son, Decimus, her one and only source of pleasure and pride in an otherwise loveless marriage to a man many years her senior. And Sempronia knows full well that of Lentulus' step-sons, his favorite is young Marcus Antonius. Only Julia, Marcus' mother, has prevented Lentulus from adopting the young man.

In an adjacent room, Praecia and Cethegus share a bed. Praecia reclines ever so seductively; her cream-colored arms, extending across the pillows, are draped by her auburn tresses. She listens as Cethegus describes his canvassing in the Senate, and he drops the names of scores of senators, familiar names like the Sulla brothers, Publius and Servius, Lucius Cassius, Marcus Caeparius. He says these have pledged themselves to vote for Catilina in the consular election and for himself in the praetorian election.

Praecia interrupts his frenzied litany. "Your brother would be proud of you. You want so much to be like him. Is it because you've inherited his mistress?"

Cethegus studies her large square face and calmly says, "Praecia and Publius Cethegus. Everyone knew of them, and anyone who wanted favors or commands sought them out. A rule of politics: useful alliances must be maintained. Publius knew this. That's why he commended you to me. But becoming my mistress? That was your doing." Placing his hand on her aroused nipple, he asks, "Has the younger brother serviced you at least as well as the elder?"

Praecia smiles and slides down enticingly. "Gaius… Gaius," she whispers as she pulls him onto herself and Cethegus buries his mouth inside her open lips.

AT THE REGIA, THE CHIEF Pontiff's official residence, four women sit in the atrium. It is near dusk and household servants have begun to light the bronze oil lamps. The walls are decorated with frescoes illustrating the gods and goddesses of the Roman pantheon. The tiled floor around the impluvium, a large water catch-basin located directly below the compluvium, the roof's aperture, is adorned with signs of the zodiac.

Aurelia, Caesar's tough, widowed mother is in her mid-sixties. She wears a plain white, long-sleeved stola and simple, unadorned sandals. Setting down her cup of watered wine, she asks, "So, Servilia, how are the children?"

The woman seated opposite her smiles broadly. "Oh, they're fine! Little Marcus Silanus grows more precocious each day, and the girls love to tease Marcus Brutus about his upcoming nuptials."

The women laugh, and Servilia winks at Julia, the sixteen-year old girl seated next to her grand-mother, Aurelia. Julia is betrothed to Servilia's son from her first marriage, young Marcus Junius Brutus.

"And how is Silanus?" Aurelia asks. "Feeling any better?"

"He's not had an attack of ague since this winter," Servilia responds about her current husband, Decimus Junius Silanus. "But I'm afraid he's still rather weak."

Aurelia nods thoughtfully. Her square-shaped face is sincere. It is surrounded by black and gray wavy hair. Her round, deeply-set brown eyes, her straight nose, and slightly protrusive mouth mark her as a woman not to be trifled with. She says to Servilia, "Don't allow him to exert himself," and then she smirks at the double entendre.

Servilia replies, "Oh no, of course not, at least not beyond attending the Senate's meetings." Even seated, she is tall and statuesque. She wears a blue palla draped over a short-sleeved mauve stola revealing her sensuous arms. Her hair is like golden wheat in summer, complementing her fair skin. Her hard, gray eyes are set within an oval face. A long, thin, slightly turned up nose extends over her bow-shaped mouth. She's a remarkably sensual woman in her early forties.

"And I hope that brother of yours, uh, excuse me your *half-brother*, doesn't agitate him." Aurelia reaches for her wine.

Servilia shrugs. "My husband has more forbearance for Cato than I ever could." In all truth, she cannot abide her obnoxious half-brother. She tries to steer the conversation in another direction. "And you, Pompeia? Aren't you thrilled to be the wife of the Pontifex Maximus, and very likely the wife of the next consul?"

Pompeia, age thirty-three, wears a haughty expression on her otherwise handsome face. Her auburn hair, more red than brown, complements the green, short-sleeved stola that accentuates her small but shapely figure. She manages an affable smile and says, "A woman could not desire a finer husband." But at the same time she thinks rather than says, *Nor could you, Servilia, hope to gain a more ascendant lover.*

Pompeia is not alone in holding unspoken thoughts. At the same time, Aurelia ponders, *O, Pompeia, why ever does my son keep you? You've never been any kind of mother to Julia. And you long ago ceased to be of any political use to him. You're a grand-daughter of Cornelius Sulla and* kin to Gnaeus Pompeius. *What of it? Sulla's long been dead and Gaius has made his own approaches to the Magnus. Yet, he holds onto you but consorts with that one, risking his own reputation and his entire career even in as permissive an age as this. Why? Why does he do these things?*

Aurelia looks at her grand-daughter. Julia is a beautiful girl-woman. How she resembles her mother, Caesar's first wife, Cornelia. The same black hair, brown eyes, and petite figure that Cornelia had had at the same tender age when Caesar had married her. Aurelia had loved her first daughter-in-law, now deceased for almost six years, as much as she dislikes her current daughter-in-law. It is no wonder that Aurelia is more like a surrogate mother than a grand-mother to Julia. The bonds between them are inseparable. So often, they even dress alike, as on this occasion. Julia wears a plain white stola along with her childhood bulla on a golden chain about her neck.

Suddenly, there are boisterous noises from the Sacred Way just outside the Regia. The women hear cries of "Caesar! Caesar! Caesar!" The women possess enough political sophistication to realize that the uproar must be from a crowd of electoral supporters. They stop talking and stare at each other in silence. Julia is aglow. "Tata!" She bolts for the vestibule just as her father enters it from the street. She hurls herself at him as though she has not seen him in days; in fact, she had last seen him in the early morning when he had left to attend the Senate meeting. Julia had expected him home earlier, for she had not anticipated her father's subsequent meeting with his partners. She is the apple of his eye.

Arm in arm, father and daughter enter the atrium. Aurelia exhales, "At last, my son, you arrive."

"We were beginning to think you had forgotten us," Pompeia puts in.

Caesar's only response is to raise an eyebrow at the two women. But his focus is on Servilia. He smiles cunningly and says, "Servilia! I thought I recognized your litter with its yellow and blue curtains matching your bearers' tunics."

Servilia smiles back with the same cunning expression. "I'm sorry. My litter has spoiled what I'd hoped would be a surprise."

Pompeia grits her teeth at this exchange. Aurelia must suppress a giggle at the sight of her daughter-in-law's discomfiture. The old dowager wonders, *What is it, Pompeia? That she and Caesar have been lovers, no doubt still are, or that she's still so beautiful, or that she's bold enough to flirt with him in your presence?*

Servilia rises from her chair. "Chief Pontiff, you've taken so long to return from the Senate, and it's grown late. I really must go."

"Please stay for supper," Pompeia invites with questionable sincerity.

"No thank you, Pompeia. I really must go. Good night, Aurelia. Good night, Pompeia." The women politely press their cheeks against one another, but Julia hugs Servilia and loudly kisses her cheeks. "Good night, my dear Julia. Any words for Marcus Brutus?"

"Well," the girl-woman hesitates, "does he still want to marry me?"

The women laugh, and Servilia promises, "I'll certainly ask him."

Caesar accompanies Servilia to the vestibule. Julia starts after them, but Aurelia calls her, "Julia!" With a cock of her head, the dowager signals for her to stay put. Pompeia cannot help but notice this, and she thinks, *Of course, Aurelia, allow your son and his mistress a moment of private leave-taking.*

In the vestibule, the janitor opens the bronze door and then faces out to the street. Servilia leans in close to Caesar. "Cato is going to run for tribune of the plebs."

Caesar is taken aback.

"Yes," Servilia continues, "he's their insurance, Gaius. If you win the consulate, with or without Bibulus, Cato will use his tribune's veto to check you."

"A good strategy," Caesar admits. "Thank you. But you didn't have to come in person to tell me this."

"Yes, I know." She turns her face up to his. Caesar pushes against her, takes her in his arms, and kisses her deeply on the mouth. Their respective tongues plunge and roll for prominence. Caesar's, as usual, wins. Catching her breath, Servilia exhales, "I must—must really go."

Caesar watches her go out the door and then enter her litter. As the bearers raise it upon their shoulders, Servilia smiles at him and her fingertips touch her lips to throw him an airy kiss. She is borne away as Caesar looks at the departing litter.

Servilia has been his lover, his mistress, his confidante since they were both widowed, she with a son, young Marcus Brutus, and Caesar with his beloved daughter, Julia. Thus far, neither can imagine life without the other, notwithstanding their current marriages to other spouses. However, unlike Caesar's, Servilia's second marriage has yielded children, three nubile daughters and a prepubescent son. She cherishes all of her children as truly as Caesar treasures his Julia.

When Caesar returns to the atrium, he finds only his mother. She says to him, "A word, my son, before we go into supper. Be careful. You're now Chief Pontiff and soon you may well be consul. Julia is engaged to Servilia's son. Don't let any – indiscretions – yes, indiscretions – mar your career, especially as long as *that one* is your wife." Aurelia gestures toward the dining room.

"What do you mean, Mater?"

"Gaius, I don't trust her not to give you back some of your own. You with Servilia, and *she* with – whomever! My son, don't invite scandal into your household."

"Mater, this very house is a fortress against scandal," Caesar offers not too seriously, "and the Chief Pontificate puts me above and beyond reproach."

But Aurelia shakes her head, clucks her tongue against her aging teeth and counters, "Not necessarily, Gaius, especially if you retain certain people in your circle."

"And they would be?"

"Catilina for one." Aurelia almost spits out the name. "His whole career is riddled with improprieties and scandals. He'll be a hindrance to you if you're both elected consuls."

Caesar only sighs and temporizes. "We'll see about that, Mater."

"And there's Pompeius. I can't figure him. He could have cowed the Senate into giving in to his demands by just parading his legions around Roma's walls. Instead, he disbands them to become a suppliant." Aurelia makes a sweeping gesture with the back of her bony, veined hand as if to clear the air of Pompeius Magnus.

"Remember, Mater," Caesar tries to reassure her, "his behavior of late is all very much according to his temperament. I know him, and I know what he wants, and how he'll go about getting it. And believe me, my assessment has been confirmed most intimately." Caesar looks at his mother slyly from below his raised eyebrows.

"Ah yes," Aurelia acknowledges. "During his absence fighting the pirates and Mithridates, you took frequent excursions down to Alba Longa. Yes, I remember. I trust the Imperator's wife was – *hospitable.*" Aurelia returns her son's sly, under-browed look.

"Mater, *hospitable* does not do justice to Mucia's generosity." Caesar smirks, holding his cocked head to one side.

"No doubt, no doubt, as generous, as hospitable as the lady who just left, or like Crassus' Tertulla, eh?" Aurelia shakes her head in feigned chagrin. "I dare say Pompeius would have done better to take her with him to the East. Mucia would have been in far less danger there instead of remaining with her children down at Alba Longa." She clucks her tongue. "It's too temptingly close to Roma – and to my ambitious son's amorous clutches."

The old dowager pauses, takes a few steps away from him, turns and then speaks again. "Again, Gaius, my son, be careful. For years, you've put the horns on Silanus and he's been too ill or too weak or too henpecked to do anything about it. You've put the horns as well on your biggest benefactor, but Crassus has been too wrapped up in himself to care about Tertulla's honor. But Pompeius –oh no! He won't wear the cuckold's horns and he won't be intimidated by your Chief Pontificate or your consulate. So, beware my son!"

Caesar approaches his mother. Taking her hands in his, he kisses their palms and their backs and then cradles them against his breast. "Mater," he says, beaming at her, "even the Olympians would take your counsel."

Looking up into her son's eyes, she replies tongue-in-cheek, "On occasion, my son, they probably have."

GAIUS MANLIUS IS A RETIRED centurion from the legions that had served the late dictator, Sulla. He lives in Etruria with some twenty thousand retired Sullan veterans. He is a friend and supporter of Lucius Sergius Catilina. Like so many other veterans, he is heavily in debt and in danger of losing his Etrurian farmstead. Seeking debt relief, Manlius has come to Roma to organize the Etrurian colonists as voters in Catilina's consular canvass. Wherever Catilina goes to solicit votes,

Manlius and a large contingent of veterans attend him as a legion-strength bodyguard and as a political machine.

Manlius is of medium height, of stocky and sturdy build, a tough, hard veteran in his mid-fifties. His iron-gray hair is close cropped to his formidable skull. He wears a military tunic secured by a metal-studded belt and hob-nailed soldier's caliga on his rough, calloused feet. His speech and manor are rough, blunt, and direct as befitting a man who has known the ways of the camp and of war all his life. "When are these accursed elections going to be held?" He demands to know of Catilina.

Manlius sits in the study of Catilina's Aventine house. Shelves and niches line the walls and here and there swords and other battle trophies are displayed. It is near dusk, and a bronze oil candelabra illuminates the room and delineates the battle scar traversing Manlius' olive-skinned visage from the left temple, down across the bridge of his nose to his right cheek.

Catilina shifts in his chair and with a shrug admits, "I don't know. It's up to the Senate."

"Lucius Catilina, each day they come down from the North – in scores, in hundreds, in thousands. They've come to vote for men who'll help them. They're camped out at Mars Field. But they won't stay forever. The longer they stay here, the easier it is for their creditors to seize their farms or take their children and wives into debt slavery."

Nervously, Catilina agrees, "Yes, I know, I know. I cannot help them if I'm not elected, and they must be willing to wait…."

"They won't wait forever. Will you, Catilina?"

"Listen to me, Manlius. I will be consul or I will seize the government by force!"

Manlius is taken aback by the hubris of Catilina's declaration, but his military bearing asserts itself.

"Do you understand?" Catilina asks, but Manlius hesitates to answer. Catilina leans forward in his chair. "Do you trust me?" Again, Manlius makes no answer.

Catilina rises and walks over to Manlius. "Manlius, you and I fought for Sulla because we believed that he alone could bring order to Roma by stamping out the popularist agitations of Marius, Glaucia, Saturninus, and Cinna and then restore the Senate's authority. But after Sulla, the Senate changed. It's dominated by men who've shut me out of the consulate, an office that's mine by my birthright. They would have me retreat into exile if I lose again. But I will not! Nor will I pass under the yoke of *my* creditors. I will take by force what is rightfully mine."

Catilina sees that his words have moved the veteran. He turns from Manlius and goes to the wall. A gilded silver eagle, its wings outstretched, its beaked face defiantly turned to the right, its talons grasping an acorn and lightning bolts, is perched atop a long oak pole leaning against the wall. Catilina takes the aquiline standard in both hands.

"Do you remember this?" he asks. "I took it from an aquilifer in Marius' army after I'd run him through. His comrades would have cut me to bits rather than lose their legionary eagle. But you came to my rescue, warded off their attack, and saved my life. I've never forgotten."

Manlius nods in recognition of the eagle and in the remembrance of the battle in which it had been acquired.

Catilina places his hand on the eagle's talons. "By this battle trophy, by this sacred eagle of the Great Marius, I swear on my honor as a Roman that I'll not abandon you or the veterans. Should I be defeated in the consular election, then we will march on Roma, and this eagle will be *our* standard!"

Manlius is impressed and finally convinced. He comes forward and places his hand on the eagle's talons right next to Catilina's. "On my honor as a Roman soldier, I'll not desert you, Lucius Catilina." Then the two men clasp arms in a gesture of Roman camaraderie and fidelity.

After Manlius departs, Catilina stares intently at the gilded image. The eagle conjures in him a reverie of sorrowful memories. "Gratidia, my beloved wife. Lucius, my son, our child. Did I abandon you to fight for the wrong cause? Had I stayed with you would you have perished by disease, by fire? Gratidia—where was you brother? Why did he not protect you? He betrayed us. But he paid with his life. Yes—I proscribed him. I executed him. I personally brought his head to Sulla, and seeing it, he no longer doubted my loyalty. I needed no reward, but still Gratidianus' property was given to me. Gratidia—forgive me. My son, forgive me."

"What are you doing, Lucius?" A harsh, besotted voice breaks his reverie. Catilina is startled. Turning away from the eagle, he says to the intruder, "Revisiting old memories."

Aurelia Orestilla, Catilina's wife, smirks and rolls her eyes. Unsteadily, she walks deeper into the study. Her scent of myrrh is accented by wine in which she has richly indulged. Her head, her fine patrician head copiously endowed with bronze-colored hair, is held high despite her tipsy condition. The crimson stola she wears has fallen off her left shoulder, and the skin and contour of her partially exposed breast is pink and supple. At age forty, she is still a beautiful woman, Catilina admits to himself while watching her approach.

The daughter and grand-daughter of patrician consulars, Orestilla had been widowed during the Marian-Sullan civil war when her husband, Flavius Fimbria was murdered by a popularist commander. She had been married long enough to conceive a daughter, born shortly after Fimbria's death. Despite her widowhood and fatherless child, she had been an attractive, desirable woman, especially as her fortune had not been seized by the Marians. Catilina had appreciated both her charms and her resources; she no doubt saw potential in him as a rising politician and a protector her herself and her daughter, even if she acknowledged the sorrow he bore at the loss of his first wife and son. They have been married for twelve years.

Orestilla says to him, "The election postponement is ruining our summer plans. Flavia and I had hoped to go down to Baiae to escape this stifling heat."

Off-handedly, Catilina replies, "You can go, Orestilla. But I must remain to continue canvassing. Perhaps I'll join you after the election."

"I appreciate that, Lucius. But you see, Flavia won't leave without you. And I dare not leave her."

Catilina is shaken by his wife's implication. He is not quick enough to find the right words because Orestilla, seeing his discomfiture, adds, "Don't bother to play the outraged husband, or should I say the outraged *stepfather*. I've seen how you look at her. And I have seen the way *she* looks back at you. You almost swallow her with every breath you take!"

Despite her impassioned words, Orestilla remains calm, the effect perhaps of the wine that has somewhat slurred her speech. She has more to say but....

"Mother!" The intrusive voice is Flavia's. She enters the room, surprising both mother and step-father. "You must be drunk or insane!"

"Drunk or insane, daughter, your mother knows of what she speaks," Orestilla spews back.

Flavia stands mid-way between them. At age eighteen, she has inherited her mother's well-endowed figure, though she is not quite as tall. Her hair is the same bronze color, but perhaps with a bit more of a copper aspect. Like Orestilla, Flavia is possessed of an alluring but rather long face with strong, sharply defined features. She looks from her mother to Catilina, hoping to find some indication of what next to say.

However, Catilina does not want to argue. "I've more important things to think about. I don't care if you stay here or go to Baiae together or separately. Either way, I'll not brook your wild accusations!" He brushes past Flavia and exits the room.

Orestilla calls after him, "While I'm here you'll never have *her*! You'll have better luck bedding one of the Vestals like 'what's-her-name'. You ought to try her again. Perhaps now she'll be more receptive!"

Outside the house, in the diminishing light, Catilina walks about the Aventine Hill. He sees shrines, temples, monuments, the houses of the well-to-do, and the multi-tiered insulae of the urban poor. Facing northeast, he sees the Great Circus flanked by the Palatine Hill with its splendid mansions and monuments bathed in the surreal light of the setting sun. On the opposite side of the Palatine, on the eastern fringe of the Forum, stands the Temple of Vesta, adjacent to the Vestal Mansion and the Chief Pontiff's Regia. From his vantage point, he cannot see these structures, but he knows that they are there. He wonders which of the Vestals could be tending Vesta's sacred flame. Could it be Fabia, she whom Orestilla's crude remark has touched upon? Could it be the Virgo Maxima herself, Licinia?

Catilina is well acquainted with both, as is Crassus. Both men and both Vestals are inextricably linked in an affair that long ago was judicially proven not to have happened. But Catilina remembers.

He had been denied Fabia. She was sacred, forbidden fruit. He has been denied Flavia, his step-daughter, equally forbidden fruit. Is the consulate yet another forbidden fruit that the Fates will deny him?

Remorse and guilt, lust and ambition, and fear of failure are the afflictions that wreak havoc upon the mind and soul of Lucius Sergius Catilina as he lives on the edge of bankruptcy.

NIGHT HAS DESCENDED UPON THE city of Roma. Within the circular, domed Temple of Vesta, the Vestal Fabia takes her turn holding vigil at the goddess' hearth fire – the fire which must never be extinguished lest disaster befall Roma. She kneels in supplication before Vesta's sublimely beautiful marble effigy mounted on a pedestal high above the hearth. Wearing the white woolen stola and palla, her hair set and braided with woolen ribbons beneath her veil, Fabia peers into the orange-red flame. She sees that that she would rather not see. With all her heart and soul, Fabia wishes to be free of the sight – the visage of Lucius Sergius Catilina.

THE APPIAN ROAD DESCENDS TO its southern terminus at the port of Brundisium. Five horsemen, Publius Clodius and his companions, have ridden for a week from Roma. They have made frequent stops along the way at inns and hostels for food and lodging. On the outskirts of Brundisium, on either side of the Appian highway, the tents of Pompeius Magnus' praetorian cohorts are laid out in strict Roman military grids. But there are no palisade or ramparts for the horsemen to negotiate, for the Pompeian soldiers are encamped on their own native Italian soil. Even before they are admitted by the sentries to the encampment, the horsemen spot the commander's splendid scarlet tent flanked by the cohorts' standards, gilded images affixed to wooden poles.

Publius Clodius rides ahead of them on a bay stallion. He and his companions wear tunics and short riding cloaks. Their equestrian skills allow them to sit their horses with minimal accoutrements. Clodius, in his early thirties and a junior senator, leads the others in age. They are in their mid to late twenties. Marcus Antonius, nephew of the consul, Gaius Antonius, rides a magnificent black. His friend and lover, Gaius Scribonius Curio, follows on a dappled gray. Decimus Junius Brutus, son of the oligarch, and the patrician rake, Publius Cornelius Dolabella, each riding sorrel mares complete the cavalcade. Clodius calls them his "wolf cubs." They are his friends and mates in debauchery and intrigue. But before their drinking and whoring, Clodius' mission must be accomplished.

Publius Clodius is admitted to Pompeius Magnus' presence while the "cubs" wait outside the commander's tent. The Magnus sits at a campaign desk strewn with scrolls and various paraphernalia. He wears a brown leather military coat adorned with the Roman eagle, its wings outstretched across the coat's chest. There are minimal furnishings in the tent: a few campaign folding chairs, a pair of bronze candelabra, and the commander's vexillum, his personal standard, surmounted by a gilded eagle on a solid wooden pole. Off to the side, the Magnus' armor and crested helmet are set upon a cross-shaped rack. Clodius has time to take all this in, for he sits, quite impatiently, across the desk from Pompeius, and waits, and waits for the Magnus to finish reading a wax tablet. Clodius cannot know that it contains a letter from Consul Marcus Cicero. But he assumes it must be important enough to justify the commander's rudeness in having a visitor wait upon him. Pompeius' furrowed brow and squinted eyes show a perturbed concentration on the letter.

At last, the wax tablet is put aside with a smirk and a rough gesture. Pompeius now looks up directly at his visitor. His tone is officious and yet familiar. "Publius Clodius Pulcher, you have my complete attention. What news do you have for me?"

"Imperator, the Senate has deemed it necessary to postpone the consular election." Clodius cannot help but notice the lack of surprise on the Magnus' face. He begins to suspect that others, perhaps the author of the very letter that Pompeius has been reading, have so informed him. "Your friends have sent me to relay to you their hope that your discharged legionaries will take advantage of the postponement; that they will come to Roma and vote for those candidates – your friends – most likely to support your interests. Your friends desire to meet with you, at your convenience, to make further plans."

Pompeius listens attentively. Each mention of *friends* brings to his mind's eye bald-pated Crassus, nervy, sinewy Catilina, bull-faced Antonius, and sleek, intriguing Caesar. His association with these men extends back many years, and even during his absence in the East, there had been no lack of correspondence between them. *They want to make further plans,* Pompeius repeats to himself. Is that with or without an electoral victory?

Pompeius hears Clodius say, "Your friends are confident that you will encourage your legionaries' civic duty."

The Magnus nods his acknowledgement. "You may tell *my friends* that as my men march and camp and fight when and where they are ordered, so too do they vote as they are ordered, especially if their interests and mine are concerned."

Clodius presumes to encroach upon the Magnus' humor. "Your friends will be most gratified to hear this. They surely realize all too well that their interests and your legionaries' interests and your interests are virtually inseparable."

Pompeius resents this presumption. He glares coldly at Clodius and says, "You see, Publius Clodius, disobedience has no place in my legions. Which reminds me – I should thank you for your help in procuring my Eastern command."

Clodius is caught off guard.

"You see, had it not been for your mutiny against your brother-in-law, Lucullus would have completed the war, and I would not now be awaiting a well-earned triumph. Tell me, have you led any mutinies since then?"

Pompeius references a notorious episode in Clodius' military service in the East some five years before. Political influence and family connections had then protected him, and after a brief stint under another brother-in-law, Marcius Rex, he was elected quaestor and thereby entered the Senate. Nevertheless, Clodius is irritated at this reminder, and Pompeius' irony does not escape him. He gives back measure for measure to the Magnus.

"No, Imperator, I have not." After a brief pause, Clodius hurls his own missile. "But I'm curious to know—have you killed any Roman citizens lately?"

Pompeius hardens like stone. He has his own episodes of infamy, for as a young commander under Sulla, he had cold-bloodedly executed popularist leaders, most conspicuously—after promising him clemency—Marcus Junius Brutus. For such treachery, Pompeius had come to be called by optimates and popularists alike the *young butcher*. The reminder of his butchery casts a pall over the Magnus.

Like any wise strategist, Pompeius chooses his battles with the utmost circumspection. He will not take on Publius Clodius now, especially since the young man's older brother, Appius, is a strong, aspiring presence in the Senate. No, it is best to allow this Pulcher to leave unmolested. Pompeius thereby calls for his guards to escort Clodius and his traveling companions out of the camp.

In the privacy of his command tent, Pompeius calms himself by reviewing Cicero's letter. The consul assures him of the Senate's goodwill and of his own continued support. Cicero will do all within the power of his office to achieve the Senate's ratification of the Magnus' Eastern acta and to arrange for him the honor of a triumph, an honor mandated by his spectacular achievements in the East. But Cicero warns that the question of land grants for the discharged veterans will prove more difficult to achieve as there are, as Pompeius must fully realize, vested interests opposed to land re-distribution initiatives. Cicero urges Pompeius to be patient.

Pompeius sets down the letter and feels that his umbrage at Pulcher has subsided. Yes, he will be patient. He will see to the veterans' discharge. He will pledge and he will promise and he will secure all that they deserve from him and from the Republic. But he will also endeavor to achieve for himself all that he, Pompeius Magnus, deserves.

"POMPEY THE GREAT! POMPEY THE Great! Pompey the Great!" Clodius exclaims with a feigned expression of climactic release as he masturbates a phallic-shaped dry sausage. He and his companions erupt into drunken, raucous laughter.

They have come to a dockside tavern in Brundisium's harbor, hardly an appropriate venue for noble Roman manhood. Yet, despite the greasy, cramped, cooking-fired, smoke-filled, rustically furnished room, peopled with sordid riff raff—or perhaps because of this squalor— Clodius and his "wolf cubs" are very comfortable. The wine is cheap, in price and in quality; the food is edible though far removed from Epicurean tastes, and the young men need a place to stay the night before heading back to Roma.

Pounding away at the dry sausage with ejaculatory glee, Clodius proclaims, "Pompey the Great—that conceited, vain-glorious prig!"

Over the renewed laughter, Marcus Antonius shouts, "And with good reason!"

"What?" Clodius responds. "You think Sulla gave him the title 'Magnus' because his rod is *this* big?" They laugh, Curio spewing a mouthful of rancid wine over their table.

Curio, curly-haired, small and spare in build, recovers sufficiently to say, "If so, then his wife should have been content to wait patiently for his return. But gossips have it that Mucia's not been fallow all these years."

The cubs all pronounce a resounding *"Ahhh!"* Then Decimus Brutus, the masculine image of his vivacious mother, Sempronia, ventures to ask, "Antonius, is it true that your kinsman is among her lovers?"

"Who?" Antonius is not certain that he even heard the question correctly. He leans his bullish head toward Decimus so that the meager oil lamp light shines off his handsome, young bull's face.

"Why, Caesar, of course!"

"Oh… well… just because he's my mother's distant cousin—I don't think of him as kin." Antonius holds up the empty wine beaker and beckons to the serving wench to bring a new filled one.

Clodius wipes the sweat from his brow with the back of his hand. "Kin or not, yes—Caesar's kept Mucia quite diverted in her husband's absence."

"That is," Curio puts in, "whenever his wife and Servilia can spare him."

Clodius takes feigned umbrage at this remark. "About as often as you can spare Antonius, eh Curio?" Clodius sniggers at Curio's deadpan face. It is no secret among them that Antonius and Curio have shared many an intimacy. Antonius confirms it only by an impish grin as he pours himself a fresh cup of wine from the new beaker. Clodius catches the eye exchanges between Antonius and the buxom serving wench. He adds, "Or perhaps as often as Antonius can spare *you*, Curio. You know, Mucia is my brother-in-law's half-sister."

The cubs by now are too inebriated to follow Clodius' relationship pathway. But Dolabella—handsome as a marmoreal Greek god—asks, "Which one?"

"Metellus Celer, the urban praetor."

"Yes, yes, now I remember. Between the half-siblings and the adoptions Roma is one big stewpot of family connections. Even Marcus Cato and the indomitable Servilia are half-siblings." Dolabella looks from one cub's face to another, searching for approbation.

"That connection, as well as her own 'knock down' beauty, makes her quite a prize," Antonius admits.

Dolabella wonders aloud, "Was Caesar having her *before* or *after* her husband's death?"

Antonius searches the inn's ceiling timbers before he answers guardedly, "Probably *before*, but…" here he lowers his voice to a slurred whisper, "don't speculate in her son's presence."

The five drunken men snigger at this, for they all know the crude, lurid gossip holding that Servilia's son, young Marcus Junius Brutus, is Caesar's and Servilia's love child.

"Young Brutus prefers the late Marcus Brutus to Gaius Caesar as his father." Saying this, Antonius winks lecherously at the passing buxom serving wench. "Having lost my own father, I can empathize with Brutus who lost his when he was just a boy. It was during the civil war…."

"No!" Decimus Brutus interrupts. "It was after Sulla's death when the popularists tried to overthrow his government."

"Yes, you're right," Antonius is quick to acknowledge, "and of course you'd remember better than I because Brutus is your kinsman. Anyway, Brutus senior surrendered to Pompeius after being promised honorable captivity—whatever that meant." He takes a slow, thoughtful draught of wine. "Pompeius had him executed quicker than a wounded gladiator."

"Hail Pompey the Great!" exclaims Clodius, still manipulating the sausage. "And with one stroke he earned the unyielding hatred of young Brutus, his uncle, Marcus Cato, and the young, widowed Servilia."

"Widowed," Antonius puts in, "but not for long. She arranged a new marriage for herself."

As if on cue, Curio completes his lover's thought, "To Decimus Junius Silanus. Odd, isn't it, that Brutus and his step-father should have the same *gens*." He pauses for comments, but there are none. "At any rate, he fathered on Servilia three daughters – three Junias – and a son, little Marcus who's about four by now. Unless—could any of them be *Caesar's?*" The drunken cubs laugh into their cups.

Clodius then slurs, "Servilia's a beauty alright, and quite a dish for Caesar, as mistresses go."

Antonius qualifies his friend's remark. "She's more than just a mistress. She's a friend, an advisor, and, most conveniently, soon to be his daughter's mother-in-law. Family—always the family for us Romans."

Antonius' irony brings out further laughter, laughter that flows as easily as the truth among drunken friends.

"But she's too haughty for me," Clodius opines. "Now his wife, Caesar's Pompeia, there's a stack of pulchritude—no pun intended. Beauty, brains, desirable, and, I hope, accessible. Wouldn't mind diverting her, in *or* out of the Regia. Is she related to *Duxie?*" Again, he makes masturbatory gestures with the sausage. He is pleased with his clever diminutive version of the Latin Dux—Commander.

There are shoulder shrugs all around the table, except for Antonius. "She might be, but only remotely. She's actually Dictator Sulla's granddaughter. If ever there was a political marriage, that's Caesar and Pompeia."

Clodius pipes in, "A well-descended spouse, a prominently connected mistress, and dalliances with the Magnus' wife—Caesar has more than ample furrows to plow." Drunk almost to the point of oblivion, the cubs nevertheless burst into promiscuous laughter.

His speech slurred by the cheap wine, Antonius manages to say, "His ambitions exceed patrician furrows."

Dolabella, his speech equally slurred, announces, "They're saying he's a sure bet to win the consulate."

"But Catilina's another story. He might even be a handicap for Caesar." This is from Curio.

Antonius, turning serious, as serious as his stupor will permit, says, "Caesar has the Roman mob sewn up within his toga folds as surely as *Bald-Pate* Crassus has the equites cinched into his money bags. But Pompeius has the legions and the fame and the glory—the pacifier of the seas, conqueror of the East, he's...."

"A prig!" Clodius explodes. "A conceited, vain-glorious prig!" He works the sausage for emphasis. "Shall I tell you all what real power is?

It's the *mob*! He who controls the mob rules the streets and the guts of Roma."

"Is that your goal, Publius?" Dolabella asks.

Clodius smirks and takes a long draught of wine. "My present goal is to help Caesar and Catilina win the consulate."

"And should they lose?" Curio asks. "Or, what if one or the other loses? What then?"

"Expedience!" Clodius coughs up. "As a matter of expedience, I'll support whoever can best advance my interests."

Antonius laughs sardonically. "In other words, you'll desert whoever is no longer useful to you?"

"My dear Antonius, such is the art and practice of politics." Clodius raises his eyebrows and nods at Antonius.

The buxom serving wench comes around to the table again and asks if she can provide anything else for the men. She is not pretty, but her question is sufficiently inviting. Her eyes lock with Antonius'.

Rising from the table, Antonius slurs, "Excuse me, companions, but I mustn't let this opportunity pass. That's also the art and practice of politics." He staggers off with the girl.

Clodius laughs and calls after him, "Go to it, Marcus. It's about time you gave *Curio* a rest!" Decimus Brutus and Dolabella laugh as Curio, barely able to hold up his head, looks sheepishly after Antonius. Clodius pours himself and his companions another round of wine. "You know what I like most about Marcus Antonius? He doesn't put on airs—well, at least not in our company. He's plebeian nobility, like Curio, *not* patrician like the rest of us, but plebeian. That his uncle is consul and his step-father is praetor—doesn't swell him at all."

Dolabella says, "But Gaius Antonius and Lentulus Sura are not political prizes. Not too many years ago they were both expelled from the Senate, and...."

"...his father led a desultory campaign against Cretan pirates," Curio interjects, "and died shortly after with the Senate's honorary title of 'Creticus'. Marcus doesn't like to talk about him."

"So perhaps our Antonius has practical reasons for modesty," opines Dolabella. "There hasn't been an admirable Antonius since his grandfather, the renowned orator."

Looking at Antonius' vacant space at the table, Curio offers, "You know, I think Marcus has more affection for his step-father than he ever had for his own father. Lentulus has taken him under his wing."

"His step-father—yes," Dolabella agrees, "but he certainly must care for his uncle."

Clodius chortles through his wine. "Yes, no doubt, especially since his uncle is also his *father-in-law*!" He faces Curio. "Curio, you're to be admired and commended. It's a special man who can distract Antonius from his cousin-wife, but apparently *not* from a willing tavern wench." He spews his wine-soaked words into Curio's distraught face.

The combined effects of the cheap wine and Clodius' sardonic words and foul breath overpower Curio. His head plops down on the crude wooden table. Clodius laughs, coughs, and retches onto the littered floor. Decimus Brutus and Dolabella see the tavern's walls spin around them.

Clodius and his wolf-cubs have visited drunken oblivion before. They have always recovered. They will recover yet again—in time.

Caput III Cicero's Respublica

OVER THE NEXT SEVERAL WEEKS, the consular canvassing continued without incident. The candidates, Caesar, Catilina, Bibulus, Servius Sulpicius, your Uncle Quintus, and the lately declared candidates, Pompeius' legates, Lucius Afranius and Aulus Gabinius, were plainly visible in their fuller's chalk-coated togas—our traditional Roman "toga candida," the garment worn by officially declared candidates. The Senate and the senior magistrates, myself in particular, were most vigilant for any suspicious incidents as we continued to collect a security force to safeguard the elections. However, by mid-Quinctilis—by which time the elections were ordinarily held—there had been no decision as to when the postponed elections would actually take place.

There were preparations of a different kind in our household, for your sister, my "Tulliola," was to be married. She had been betrothed from the age of thirteen to Gnaeus Calpurnius Piso. The marriage contract had been smoothly negotiated, and I had provided Tullia with a generous dowry to bring to her husband. That had been three years earlier. Now, at the age of sixteen, my daughter was to marry a man twice her age. But the age disparity was not terribly unusual for marriages of the time.

I liked young Piso. He came from a patrician family and he was a kinsman of that Lucius Calpurnius Piso who was one of my friends among the neutral senators. In fact, as young Piso's father was deceased, Lucius Piso sponsored the young man as a surrogate parent. It was expected that young Piso would run for the quaestorate in a couple of years and, if elected, he would gain admission into the Senate.

Even now, eighteen years later, I can picture them, my Tullia – my heart, my soul – and her bridegroom, standing before the altar of our household spirits. The atrium was festooned with garlands of flowers, laurel, and roses, and rows of chairs, benches, and stools had been provided for our guests. Terentia and I sat in front, closest to the altar. Was she thinking, was she remembering as I was our own wedding day seventeen years before? Our marriage, like Tullia's, had been parentally arranged. This daughter of an equite, your mother, brought me a bountiful dowry.

By custom, Tullia's hair, chestnut brown like my own, had been arranged in seven locks by her mother using a spear-shaped comb. She wore the flame-colored veil of a virgin bride. Next to her, Piso was tall, thin, and fair, once could say even delicate. He wore a plain white toga, and his head was adorned, as was Tullia's, with a crown of myrtle leaves.

Tullia resembled me more than she did her mother. Yet, her appearance on this nuptial day brought to mind Terentia's lovely face on our own wedding. As a bride, Terentia had been tall, stately, and reserved. Now, she was still a handsome, well preserved woman of thirty-three. Her dark, brown hair had few traces of gray, at least few enough for vanity to tolerate, though she did not consider herself vain. Her soft, brown eyes, which could flash with an imperious temper, were mounted on finely chiseled cheeks bestride a strong mouth, straight nose, and shapely chin. Her figure, though somewhat matronly from having borne two children, was yet firm, supple, and even attractive beneath her white stola and palla.

Terentia was very much the modern Roman businesswoman, carefully monitoring her investments and accounts and her woodlands in the environs of Roma while collecting rents from her apartment buildings in the City. Yes, a modern Roman woman whose business acumen and independence meshed with the ancient virtues of frugality, piety, and domesticity.

Our marriage had settled into a mutually complacent arrangement, our last occasion of spontaneous passion having occurred when you, my son, were conceived. At the time of Tullia's wedding, you were almost two years old and you had not yet been weaned off your wet nurse. You were an adorable infant, the fourth Marcus Tullius Cicero in a line that went back to my grandfather in Arpinum, our home town in the Alban hills southeast of Roma. During the wedding ritual you kept straining to break free from your nurse's arms and run off to play with your cousin, young Quintus.

Older than you by a year, Quintus junior had already been spoiled into a fiendish brat by his mother, your Aunt Pomponia, a short, doughty, ill-tempered but innocuous shrew who hardly ever seemed to run out of ways to frustrate and exasperate your Uncle Quintus. Turning to them in the row behind us, I could discern that Quintus and Pomponia must have had another of their chronic tiffs. I noticed Atticus sitting with them, wearing an ironic expression that seemed to say "I'm so glad I'm a bachelor, and I'm content to remain so!" His phlegmatic, tranquil temperament was in stark contrast to his sister's frequent hysteria.

Contentment. How elusive it could be both for those married and those unmarried. Sitting to Terentia's left in the front row was her half-sister, Fabia. A priestess of Vesta since the age of thirteen, she glowed with a serene expression of contentment. She wore the white palla, stola, and veil of the Vestal Virgins, those guardians and tenders of Mother Vesta's sacred, eternal flame. At age twenty-eight, Fabia was still as beautiful as she had been when Terentia and I were first betrothed. A sculptor would have had to combine Vesta, Juno, and Minerva with Roma just to approximate her sublime beauty. No wonder she had had so many suitors before her parents enrolled her as a novice in the Vestal College. Among her suitors had been Lucius Catilina.

Though I placed no credence in any of the gods and goddesses of the Roma pantheon, I respected their servants and gave public acknowledgement to the deities.

Fabia was Terentia's confidante, just as Atticus, Quintus, and Servius were mine. Though there was a slight physical resemblance between them, with Fabia clearly the more comely of the two, their personalities and temperaments were vastly different. Fabia had never, to my knowledge, shown the ill-temper, the imperiousness, the officiousness that so characterized Terentia. These traits in Terentia impelled her time and again to interfere in my political and business affairs. Yet, she would never have tolerated my interference in her accounts and affairs. Whether she conducted them herself or turned them over to her Greek freedman, Philotimus, I was not privy to them until her endeavors were completed. About Philotimus, it is difficult to imagine a retainer who inspired more distrust and loathing than he. Fortunately, I had little to do with him.

In preparing the guest list, I had had to cross Terentia. She wanted to exclude the Claudia Pulchra sisters, even though two of them were married to oligarchs and the youngest was married to the urban praetor, Metellus Celer. Terentia believed the gossip alleging the sisters' promiscuity and their incestuous relations with their youngest brother, Publius. It would have been impolitic as well as impolite not to invite them, especially as Lucullus, Marcius Rex, and Metellus Celer had helped me to attain the consulate and had supported me during my term in office. So, over Terentia's objections, I insisted on their being invited, and they and their spouses attended. They occupied the front chairs to our left.

Most conspicuous among them was Celer's wife, Clodia Pulchra Metella. Like her youngest brother, Publius, she pretentiously spelled and pronounced her name plebeian-style with an "o" instead of its correct patrician rendering with an "au." From across the room, those dark eyes of hers, those languid, ebony pools, fetching, mystifying, brought to mind an earlier time in my life. Before Quintus and I were matched with Pomponia and Terentia, our family and the Pulchers had become very close. They were of old, patrician stock, but unfortunately they were not too well off financially. A marriage alliance of the elder Claudia daughters with Quintus and me had been discussed, at least tentatively. There would have been advantages for both families—patrician connections for us and equestrian money for them. But somehow, our families grew apart. Perhaps Claudian aristocratic snobbery asserted itself over our rural equestrian pedigree; perhaps Father caught wind of some unsavory goings-on among the Pulcher siblings.

At any rate, both Quintus and I ended up with equestrian brides. Like so many things in life, these were mixed blessings. Of course, Terentia was well aware of our past connection with the Pulchra sisters, but she had a particular antipathy toward Clodia. I had gleaned bits and pieces of her conversations with Fabia, and from them I inferred that Terentia suspected Clodia of having amorous or at least erotic designs on me. Since we had moved into the Palatine house, we were situated only a short distance from Metellus Celer's house. Perhaps this proximity fueled Terentia's misgivings.

Most recently, gossip mongers had been churning out tales of Clodia's latest fascination, a young poet from Verona who was her husband's protégé. It was commonly joked about Metellus Celer that his wide girth kept him from seeing in his own house that which all of Roma claimed to be going on. Amazing what the Roman public could know and what an occasion, a wedding for example, could bring into one's house.

Our Chief Pontiff, Caesar, stood at the altar waiting for the Rex Sacrorum, Lucius Claudius, to pronounce the omens favorable—a final, tiresome time; they had been declared propitious the evening before as well as at dawn. No unsightly marks or blemishes had been detected in the entrails of the sacrificial sheep.

I looked from Caesar to the guests seated behind us and on our right. There was vivacious Servilia sitting between her husband, Silanus and her half-brother, Cato. Servilia's striking beauty was fair, as fair as Clodia Pulchra's was dark. She could have been taken for a Gallic or Germanic beauty clothed not in the furs or hides of the northern barbarians but in the palla and stola of a Roman matron.

Slanderous gossip had it that Servilia and Caesar had been lovers when both were between spouses. Moreover, rumors speculated that they were yet intimate with each other, that a special bond connected them in the person of Servilia's son, Marcus Brutus, named for her first husband but allegedly fathered by Caesar.

Servilia's body language toward Cato betokened a feline antipathy, but she leaned across him to clasp hands with and smile warmly at Cato's wife, actually his second wife, young, fecund Marcia. Daughter of Lucius Marcius Philippus, prominent among the Senatorial neutrals, Marcia was much admired for her forbearance with the unyielding uprightness of Cato. Jokesters lampooned Catulus and Hortensius for supposedly coveting the young woman. Fortunately, I was denied the sight of them appraising Marcia's charms as they were both indisposed and therefore unable to attend the wedding.

At least old Decimus Brutus was present, twitching impatiently as his quite younger wife, Sempronia, looked askance at him. Somehow, she did not quite fit with him. She had given him a son, now almost old enough to start his public career, but there was something of the libertine about her, something trying to hide beneath a façade of matronly reserve.

So much for the oligarchs. Courtesy as well as politics required that Marcus Crassus be invited. After all, he had once owned our house. He was with his wife, Tertulla, the widow of his deceased elder brother, and by the saucy accounts of gossip-mongers, Caesar's intimate friend. They sat together with Caesar's mother, the formidable matriarch, Aurelia, and with his wife, Pompeia, the late Sulla's grand-daughter. She was apparently Caesar's gesture of reconciliation with the optimates, but they still distrusted his popularist leanings.

Seated between mother-in-law and daughter-in-law, almost as a buffer, was Caesar's lovely daughter, Julia, the offspring of his first wife, Cornelia, the daughter of the deceased popularist leader, Cinna. Julia was about a year older than Tullia and engaged to Servilia's son, Brutus. The two young women were quite friendly, a relationship stemming from but not prejudiced by their fathers' political encounters. Even Terentia was quite fond of Julia. She was amused by the times she had overheard Tullia and Julia discuss their imminent weddings and in particular the mysteries of the nuptial night.

My consular colleague, Antonius had sent word that he could not attend due to a flare up of his gout.

Besides Metellus Celer, the other praetors of the year were present with their wives. There were Gaius Pomptimus, Lucius Flaccus, and Lentulus Sura, whose wife, Julia, was the widowed sister-in-law of Antonius.

The leading men of the neutrals were in attendance sitting behind the oligarchs. Gaius Octavius was with his wife, Atia, Caesar's niece, large with child, while widowed Servius Sulpicius and Lucius Philippus were unescorted. As Lucius Piso was like a father to my son-in-law, Terentia arranged for him and his daughter, Calpurnia, to sit in front with us.

A conspicuous absentee among the guests was Lucius Catilina. As a gesture of political amity and in respect of his consular candidacy, I would have invited him. But Terentia was adamant in her refusal to allow it. As I had prevailed in the matter of the Pulchra sisters, she won out in excluding Catilina. It had to be this way, not just for Terentia, but more importantly for Fabia.

The old house in the Carinae would not have comfortably accommodated so large a gathering as this. Fortunately, the Palatine atrium was spacious and sufficiently commodious not only for the ceremony itself but also for the dining couches needed for the nuptial feast.

At last, Rex Sacrorum Lucius Claudius pronounced the omens favorable, and the Chief Pontiff beckoned to the bridal couple. Tullia removed her childhood locket, the traditional bulla, and placed it upon the altar. The Chief Pontiff poured a libation of wine, and placed two spelt cakes upon it. Then, he broke another in half, giving each half to the bride and groom. Joining their right hands, they spoke the ancient vows.

"Where you are, Gaius, I am Gaia."

"Where you are Gaia, I am Gaius."

Tullia and Piso, now wife and husband, ate of the spelt cakes and drank honeyed wine from the nuptial cup. Family and guests applauded and exclaimed, "Feliciter! Feliciter! Feliciter!" The newlyweds sealed their holy covenant with a kiss.

We took our places on the dining couches and partook of what Atticus called, "an Epicure's delight." Accompanied by the music of lutes and auloi and by poetic recitations celebrating love and matrimony, we feasted and communed well into the evening. The conversation was animated and cordial, highlighted by many warm wishes for Tullia and Piso.

After several hours, we formed the nuptial procession to escort the newlyweds to their new home. Accompanied by a score of torch bearers and my lictors, we walked down the Palatine and made our way through narrow, winding streets to the Esquiline district where Piso had a modest house. To the cheers of the wedding guests, many of whom were undeniably besotted, and the ribaldries of some vulgar passers-by, Piso lifted Tullia over the threshold of his house, imitating an ancient tradition to forestall the bad omen of a bride tripping upon entering her new home for the first time.

We left them to begin their new life together. As we made our way back to the Palatine, many of our guests took their leave to return to their homes. While bidding farewell to someone, I glimpsed a group of hooded men walking past us. Fabia, walking beside me, was startled upon recognizing the man who walked in front of them. She leaned over to me, whispering with fear in her voice, "Catilina."

I looked back after them, but they had vanished into the dark street.

THE CONSULAR AND PRAETORIAN ELECTIONS were finally held early in October. This was an unprecedented delay of four months. The Centuriate Assembly convened in the grassy expanse of Mars Field under the shadow of the Janiculum Hill. From atop its summit, the praetor Metellus Celer hoisted the traditional red flag signaling the voters to take their places in their designated centuries.

The Senate had succeeded in hiring close to a thousand guards to protect the voters and prevent any disruption. They had come from Reate, tough, reliable mercenaries, fully armed. Gladiator schools in Roma, Pompeii, and Capua had provided troops of burly, brutish swordsmen. Even freedmen, both Italian and foreign, and retainers and slaves of both senators and equites had been conscripted for security duty. These were what the Senate had to hire in the absence of a regular police or vigilance force. But the Republic should not have been faulted for this, for traditionally, the lictors and attendants of the magistrates had served to keep the City rabble in cheek. Now, we were in different times, and Catilina had been too loud and menacing in his threats.

By lot, I secured the presidency of the elections. From my vantage point on the electoral podium I surveyed the thousands of citizens clustering into their centuriate enclosures set off by wooden posts and heavy ropes. They were a mish-mash of Roman manhood. The equites were easily recognizable, their white togas off-set by twin purple stripes on their tunics. Their gold finger rings and crescent shaped shoe buckles glistened in the autumnal sun. The senators in their white togas and tunics with broad purple stripes included in their number current office holders, whose togas were bordered in purple, and declared candidates whose togas had been rendered a stark brightness from having been smeared with fuller's chalk.

How many of these candidates in their *togae candidi*, their *pure* candidate togas, could really be called *pure*? Certainly I could vouch for

Quintus and Sulpicus. But there had been rumors of rampant bribery by Caesar, Catilina, Bibulus, and a handful of other candidates despite the severe anti-bribery legislation I had sponsored earlier in my term.

Catilina's arrival at the polls was greeted by cheers from the vulgar, brown and gray-clad masses, the urban trades-men and City parasites who lived off the state's dole of cheap grain, wine, oil and public games, the ones who so eagerly sold their votes to the highest bidding candidates.

The mob's acclamation of Catilina rivaled that given to Caesar. At least his attendants were somber, dignified servants attached to the pontifical and augural colleges, while Catilina was escorted by droves of ex-soldiers, veterans of the late optimate dictator, Sulla. He had settled them on Etrurian farmsteads twenty years before. They were a rough, tough-looking lot despite their rather advanced ages. They appeared to be in their fifties and early sixties. It was from such as these that I, that we of the Senate, had reason to expect some interference, some disruption of the elections.

Sulla's were not the only veterans here, for the soldiery of Pompeius were also conspicuous in their leather doublets marked front and back with the word "Magnus." While many of them escorted Pompeius' legates, Lucius Afranius and Aulus Gabinius, still larger numbers shouted Caesar's name. Was this Pompeius' idea, a pairing of Caesar with one or the other of the Magnus' legates? Though he had written thanking me for my support and again pledging his loyalty to the Senate, the Imperator had not confided in me his preferred candidates.

Armed guards had been posted on both the outer and inner perimeters of the centuriate enclosures. There was also a detachment of horsemen stationed on the Janiculum slopes. Even on the electoral podium, besides my twelve lictors bearing the bound rods and axes, symbolic of consular imperium, there was an equal number of armed guards whose duty was to safeguard the ballot urns.

All of these precautions, and the day's oppressive heat—most unusual for October—made for a highly charged atmosphere. If there was to be violence, I reckoned it better to occur here in Mars Field, some two miles from Roma's northwestern limits, rather than in the City itself. It was most fortuitous that our customs and traditions banned the centuriata, by its nature a military assembly of the citizens, from convening within the City limits. Hence, its meeting place was usually Mars Field.

I had added my own touch of dramatic stagecraft by wearing a coat of mail. Glistening in the sun, it was visible beneath the folds of my toga, and I wanted it to be so. Catilina and his cohorts were put on notice that as consul I was prepared for any trouble they might provoke. My consular colleague, Gaius Antonius, was unnerved at the sight of it. His porcine face dripped with the sweat of apprehension.

Upon my signal, the trumpeters sounded the fanfares of attention. Then, the augurs, including Rex Sacrorum Lucius Claudius, took the auspices. The omens were good—the entrails of the sacrificial sheep were healthy and without blemish, and the sky was clear of thunder, ominous clouds, and the flights of ill-omened birds. The elections could then proceed. By lot, the favored century of the first class of citizens was selected to cast its votes. One by one, the members of this selected century came forward from their enclosure. They walked up the wooden ramp to the electoral podium, each man depositing his small clay ballots in the consular and praetorian urns. It took roughly half an hour for these hundred voters to cast their ballots and then half as long for the ballots to be tallied by the attendants.

The choices of the first voting century were always regarded as auspicious, denoting the gods' preferences. If I believed in them, I would have to say that on this occasion they were perverse, for Julius Caesar and Marcus Bibulus held sway over the other candidates. The balloting continued with the remaining centuries of the first class and the tallying of the votes. By the time the second class's votes were counted, it was clear that the Republic's new consuls were to be Caesar and Bibulus.

This election exemplified a basic truth of Roman electoral proceeding. The inherent preponderance of age, seniority, rank, and wealth in the eighteen centuries of equites and in those of the first and second classes had provided the numerical majority needed to translate the oligarchy's designs into actuality. While I commiserated with Servius Sulpicius and Quintus for their defeat, I was relieved that Bibulus had been elected to check Caesar and to exclude Catilina. For the second consecutive year, Catilina had been defeated in his attempt to win the consulate.

The subsequent balloting of the third, fourth, and fifth class centuries was virtually a needless formality. One hundred twenty-three of the total one hundred ninety-three centuries had decided the contest well in advance of the less affluent, though more numerous citizens and the urban rabble whose votes counted for nothing. Block voting as opposed to individual one-man-one-vote mathematics characterized all Roman citizen assemblies. Perhaps future societies would look back on us scornfully, but this was how the Roman Republic attended to the business of electing its magistrates.

With the lowering of the red flag atop the Janiculum, the assembly was adjourned and the citizens began their return to Roma. I caught sight of Catilina as he walked by the podium. His face was flushed and taut. From among the Etrurian veterans who accompanied him there was loud murmuring like the ugly clenched-teeth growling of vicious dogs. He looked up at me. His glance was full of venom.

The elected praetors were solid, optimate men. Several days later, the citizens convened in their Tribal Assembly in the Comitium, the large oval pavement flanked by the Curia and the Forum. They voted for next year's aediles and quaestors without difficulty or incident. A short time after that, the plebeians voted in their Concilium for the new tribunes. Three of the ten men elected were Marcus Cato and two popularists, Titus Labienus, a Pompeian legate, and Publius Vatinius, known to have Caesarian connections.

I speculated that the oligarchs intended Cato's tribunate to deter any radical popularist initiatives that Caesar's and Pompeius' tribunes might venture.

So, all of the elections had come off without disruption or violence. The security measures had not been in vain. The veterans, both Sulla's and Pompeius', began their exodus from Roma. But neither I nor the oligarchs were lulled into any false sense of security.

Caesar would be consul as of the Kalends of Januarius. He would have to be watched. So would Crassus, though he was not an elected magistrate. I reckoned that by now Pompeius had completed the discharge of his legions. The latest news concerning him was that he had arrived at his Alban estate and was taking his ease in the bosom of his family. But no one knew precisely what was on his mind. I remembered speaking with him in years past and he had been impossible to figure. His words were laconic and cryptic.

And Catilina? Though defeated in his second consular bid, I could not help but feel that more would be heard and seen of him soon. A strong sense of foreboding filled me when the Senate decreed the discharge of all security forces that had been assembled for the elections. My forebodings would be well justified.

Omniscient Narrative

A GREAT THRONG ACCOMPANIES CAESAR from Mars Field to the Regia in the Forum. These are Caesar's voters, city trades-men, equites, soldiers, veterans as well as those not yet discharged, and all manner of City rabble. There are cries of "Caesar!" "Victor!" "Consul!" Along the way, the non-voters, women, children, and slaves are carried up in the grand procession. Arriving at the Regia, Caesar waves triumphantly and smiles broadly at the enthusiastic crowd, and Crassus stands beside him on the portico. He repeats this gesture several times until he thinks it wise to bid them farewell. Then with the utmost grace, he retreats into the pontifical mansion with Crassus following closely behind.

Once in the grand vestibule, he says to Crassus, almost off-handedly, "Where's Catilina?"

Crassus shrugs. "You expected him to be here? No, my dear Gaius, I'm certain he's at home licking his wounds as would be expected of a two-time loser."

Caesar stops short. "You're very cruel. Such sentiments you no doubt would have had for me had I lost."

With a laugh more like a grunt, Crassus replies, "But you won, Gaius, and Catilina lost. These are two immutable facts. Now I've no time for commiseration with him, because we've much to plan."

"Yes, of course," Caesar agrees, "and so much of our planning must include Pompeius." Caesar notices the chagrined cloud that passes over Crassus' face. "By now, he's probably at Alba Longa."

"What makes you think so?"

"Mucia wrote me. She was expecting him by this time," Caesar reads much into Crassus' smirk.

"So considerate of her to tell you well in advance of her husband's homecoming." Crassus' cheek swells where his tongue is pressing.

They cross the threshold into the spacious, brightly illumined atrium where Caesar's women have gathered.

"My son, my son!" exclaims Aurelia as she clasps her arms about his broad, togated shoulders. "I did not think it possible that I could be as happy or as relieved as I was when you won the Chief Pontificate. But, you know, I'm even happier!" Mother and son hold each other and stare into each other's tearful eyes. "Gaius Julius Caesar—Consul! Your father, your father—the fates did not allow him to ascend to such prominence, but you, my son...."

"Tata! Tata!" The voice of the girl-woman interrupts their tender moment. "My Tata is Consul of Roma!" Julia storms into her father's arms, almost displacing Aurelia, but the old dowager holds her place.

"Is there room for Caesar's wife?" The hard, icy, and yet almost pleading voice is Pompeia's. Caesar looks from her to his daughter's beaming face. Without any exchange of words, Julia understands and grants her father's wish. The space in Caesar's arm that she relinquishes is then filled by his wife.

"Congratulations, my *husband*," Pompeia says with unmistakable emphasis on the last word. She gives an almost defiant look at Aurelia and then kisses Caesar hard on the mouth.

Utterly amused at the domestic politics being played out in his presence, Crassus purses his lips so as not to smirk. But he cannot avoid winking at Caesar.

Despite the chronic mother-in-law and daughter-in-law friction, the Caesar family has much to celebrate. The Regia resounds with happiness. But such is not the case in Lucius Catilina's house in the Aventine district.

Catilina reclines on a dining couch, a half-filled goblet of wine in his hand, and he stares past the geometric mosaics adorning the dining room wall. Since returning from Mars Field, he has been drinking heavily. Orestilla has noticed that he adds only miniscule amounts of water to the potent Samian wine. She also notices that he has hardly touched his food. Reclining opposite to her husband, she looks from him to her daughter whose face wears anguish and pity over Catilina's mood.

"Some food might help, Lucius," Orestilla proposes. "If this is not to your liking, we could...."

"No, leave it!" Catilina's voice is brusque. "You imagine that I'm concerned about food?" He takes a long gulp of wine.

Flavia knows as well as her mother what engages Catilina's thoughts. Unlike her mother, she is bold enough to mention it. "Father, take my dowry and use it. It doesn't matter. Use it for your own purposes."

At this, Catilina turns from his concentration on the wall and squarely faces his step-daughter. "Good, generous, beautiful Flavia," the words spill out haphazardly, "your dowry and even *all* of your mother's estate would not be adequate for what you call my *purposes*." Then, turning to his wife, he asks, "Why Orestilla, why aren't you having some wine? Why should today be different from any other day? Because of the election? Because again I've drunk the bitter dregs of defeat? No—drink, my sweetness! No need to abstain on my account." He pushes his goblet toward Orestilla with such force that it falls over, the wine splattering on her stola's breast.

Rather than recoil, Orestilla leans toward him. "Let's go from here, Lucius. From this house. From Roma. From Italia. How far must we go to evade your creditors? To Greece? To the East? To the barbaric Parthians?"

Catilina laughs drunkenly. His heavy eyes are bloodshot, his hair disheveled. Turning to Flavia, he nearly spews the words, "Your mother's a very practical woman. Shake your creditors—easy—run—exile—banishment. No!" He pounds his fist on the table causing plates and cups to jump. "I'm neither drunk enough nor cowardly enough to run. Caesar has his consulate. Crassus has his man elected. What further need have they of me? I'll show them. I'm not finished yet. I've hardly begun."

Much to the two women's surprise, his drunken stupor abates somewhat for him to say, "I'm grateful to you, my dear Flavia. And yes, to you, my darling Orestilla. You would offer all you have – and we would be ruined. No… thank you… no. I know men, men like me—desperate men—men who won't run or be enslaved. No, my two lovelies, great things are about to happen. You'll see!"

Flavia and Orestilla look from Catilina to each other. In place of the younger woman's former pity and anguish for her step-father there is now alarm. And upon Catilina's wife, the beautiful, jaded Orestilla, an expression of anticipatory dread floats over her face, and fear descends upon her neck and into her breast, causing her heart to pound furiously beneath her wine-stained stola.

WITHIN DAYS AFTER THE CONSULAR election, Catilina assembles twelve men in the cellar of Marcus Porcius Laeca's house on the street of the Scythe-makers in the valley between the Palatine and Caelian hills. Catilina has known these men intimately for many years. All but three of them are senators. Lucius Statilius, Publius Capito, and Gaius Cornelius are the only equites in the group. Whether senators or equites, these are desperate men, men whose ambitions have been frustrated and thwarted, men whose personal fortunes have been squandered profligately. Catilina has recruited these desperate men, knowing that they are likely to venture anything to relieve their misfortunes, acquire wealth, and fulfill their ambitions.

The praetor Lentulus Sura stands next to Gaius Cethegus. A former consular expelled from the Senate, Lentulus' election to a second praetorate had facilitated his re-admission. Cethegus, ambitious to be the Senate's fixer and deal-maker, smarts from his recent defeat in the praetorian election.

The praetorate had been held three years before by Lucius Cassius Longinus, but thus far the consulate has been closed to him as his campaign debts continue to rise. Publius Autronius Paetus and Publius Cornelius Sulla, only two years before, had been elected consuls. But then charges of electoral bribery had banned them from office, and they were subsequently expelled from the Senate by censorial review.

Marcus Porcius Laeca, their host, is a senator of aedilician rank. His campaign for office and the expenses of mounting spectacular entertainments for the Roman mob have caused him to incur onerous debts.

The remaining senators are of quaestorian rank: Marcus Caeparius, Lucius Statilius, and Publius Clodius Pulcher.

The men stand around a large oblong table with Catilina at its head. Their togas are covered with dark, hooded cloaks. The room is purposely poorly lit for their meeting is most secret. There is barely sufficient air to allow for several candles to illuminate their faces, faces that show Catilina his friends' intensity and commitment.

Catilina's eyes move from face to face as he speaks. "Are we not Romans? Or are we but aliens? Are we not free men, citizens of the Republic? Or are we but slaves or exiles?" He waits for the words to penetrate. Then, with clenched teeth he continues. "We *are* men, *Roman* citizens! We will *not* be relegated to the status of aliens, exiles, or slaves. We and any and all who choose to follow us can take and hold what has been denied us by the oligarchs—offices, commands, wealth. Have you the courage for this?" He pauses again long enough to extract a dagger from his toga folds. "Have you the courage for this?" he asks again.

Catilina cuts across the palm of his right hand without the slightest grimace. He shows them the dark crimson line of blood emerging from the cut. A third time he says to them, "Have you the courage for this?"

Not a murmur of dissent follows. "Good! Then each of you take the dagger and do as I have done. Anyone who will not, leave now for you cannot be trusted to hear my plans."

Catilina passes the dagger to his left, to Lentulus Sura. He does not hesitate to slash his right palm and pass the dagger to Publius Sulla. In but a few moments, the dagger has made its progress around the table. Each man performs the gruesome ritual, ending with Publius Clodius at Catilina's right. Catilina sheathes the bloody dagger. Then he walks about the table, clasping each man's bloodied hand, their blood mingling together in a secret enterprise.

Arriving at the table's head, Catilina is satisfied of the men's fidelity. "We may well have to spill more blood to accomplish our purposes, but whoever among you might betray us, know this—your blood is irrevocably damned."

The men listen intently as Catilina lays out his plan for taking over the Roman Republic. Publius Clodius wonders if these men realize, as he certainly does, that the hand-cutting and blood mingling ritual is converting them into Catilina's conspirators.

ALBA LONGA IS AN IDYLLIC paradise crouched amid the Apennine foothills southeast of Roma. It is watered by several small Tiber tributaries that render it a verdant landscape of forests and meadows. Here, Pompeius' renowned estate is situated. There is more than ample ground for his praetorian cohorts, nearly a thousand legionaries, to have pitched their tents. They are an impressive sight to the party of travelers that proceeds down the Appian Road. Two litters are born by sixteen burly slaves, and two mounted men are accompanied by a score of footmen and attendants. Consul-elect Julius Caesar and Marcus Crassus have come with their litter-borne wives to call upon the Magnus.

It is both a political and a social visit. Pompeius and Mucia set before their guests a stunning table of roast pheasant and squab, asparagus and artichokes, Campanian wines and Sicilian cheeses, and Picentine figs and Apulian grapes. The dinner conversation revolves around the recently held elections in Roma and family concerns.

Crassus and Tertulla hold forth proudly about their sons, Publius and Marcus, both of whom will soon begin their military service. Mucia is equally indulgent in praising her adolescent children, young Gnaeus, Sextus, and Pompeia. Caesar speaks in superlatives of his daughter, Julia, but in mentioning her imminent wedding he is circumspect in not mentioning his prospective son-in-law. It would defeat the purpose of their meeting with Pompeius to mention by name the son of the man whom Pompeius had had executed.

The talk of their children discomforts and irritates Pompeia, for she and Caesar have no children of their own despite having been regularly intimate during their several years of marriage. Though unspoken, she resents Caesar's dotage upon Julia, whom she regards, along with the dowager, Aurelia, as a rival for Caesar's affection and attention. Even here at Pompeius' table, she must contend with Tertulla, who strives with unabashed assertiveness to monopolize Caesar's attention.

During the dinner, Pompeius eyes Mucia suspiciously, noticing that she avoids eye contact with Caesar. Yet, Caesar endeavors to engage her in conversation whenever Pompeia and Tertulla allow him an opening.

Eventually, the women excuse themselves for the purpose of touring Mucia's garden, and the men are left alone to fulfill the main purpose of their meeting. The political talk that ensues lays the groundwork for the Caesar-Pompeius-Crassus triumvirate. Land is to be secured for Pompeius' veterans. His Eastern acta are to be ratified. Crassus' fostering of the publicans' Asian tax contract will be legislated. Finally,

Caesar is to be posted with an extensive Gallic proconsular command. The means to achieve these ends? The Senate first, as is required by law and tradition. But if it should prove obstructive, then the triumvirs agree that the Senate will be overridden and recourse will be made to the People's assemblies, the Tribal and the Plebeian Concilium. They have two strong, able tribunes in Titus Labienus and Publius Vatinius. They expect all manner of hindrances from Caesar's consular colleague, Marcus Bibulus, and from Marcus Cato, the oligarchs' hand-picked tribune.

"Have you figured on Catilina?" asks Pompeius after taking a draught of wine.

"Catilina? What are we to figure about him?" Crassus is annoyed even at the mention of his erstwhile protégé.

Pompeius purses his lips thoughtfully. "He must be part of the equation."

"Why?" This is from Caesar, both alarmed and curious.

Pompeius exhales deeply and passes his sharply tipped tongue over his lips. "He came to see me down at Brundisium, he and six others."

"When was this?" There's alarm now in Crassus too.

"At about the middle of Quinctilis, when the elections are customarily held. Publius Sulla was with him. So was Autronius Paetus. The others—I don't know them. They were probably Senate juniors."

"He came to welcome you home?" There is no conviction in Crassus' query.

"That, yes, but more besides. He proposed that I march my legions on Roma...."

"Heinous bastard!" Crassus erupts.

"...to coincide with his using Sulla's veterans from Etruria to put the City under lock-down. He said he and I would take the consulate and then we'd make a deal with the two of you."

"By Jove's great cock!" again Crassus erupts.

Caesar is amused by his friend's blasphemy. "Would it be ingenuous to ask what response you gave him?'

Pompeius drinks again, clears his throat, and tilts his head toward Caesar. "I thanked him for his offer, very generous of him." After an uncomfortably long pause, he continues, "Then I told him that I would await the outcome of the consular election." Another uncomfortable pause follows. "I've not heard from or seen him since then." Another drink is taken and the Magnus strokes the flesh beneath his prominent chin. His two guests, his friends, his fellow-triumvirs, mull over what they have learned.

The silence is broken by Caesar. "There can be no equation with Catilina disrupting our plans with sedition and violence. Agreed?"

Crassus and Pompeius nod their heads, their lips turned downward in assertive acquiescence.

"We must dissociate ourselves from him, but we must be careful not to antagonize him. Above all, we must not implicate ourselves in his plot." Caesar taps his upper lip thoughtfully.

Again, Caesar's partners nod. Pompeius asks, "So?"

"Cicero?" Crassus infers rightly.

"We'll let Cicero dispose of Catilina for us." Caesar reaches for a goblet of wine on the table. "He'll rid the state of a nuisance, perhaps even a great danger. He'll earn the gratitude of all good, loyal citizens. And perhaps, in gratitude for this opportunity we're affording him, he'll cooperate with us."

"No doubt, Pompeius," Crassus says, "you just might be called on for some soldiering against seditious citizens."

Pompeius raises his cup. "Gentlemen, to our triumvirate—may it serve us and Roma!" The triumvirs join their cups together.

While the triumvirs make their plans, Mucia and her guests stroll through the verdant paradise of the garden. The autumnal profusion of shrubs is in rich display. They sniff and fondle and flatter each plant, but their conversation has become icy, flat, and superficial. Ironically, they constitute a non-political triumvirate. Each woman, though perhaps unbeknown to the others, has been intimate with Caesar. What experiences they could share if they were but willing to divulge them. Mucia is beautiful, stately, a reserved patrician lady. Tertulla, the eldest of the trio and the most matronly looking of them, is still a handsome specimen, tall, broad of girth, yet voluptuous as a ripe melon. Pompeia, the youngest, is the most desirable of the three, even if Mucia's stateliness and Tertulla's voluptuousness surpass her own charms. Pompeia suffers what the other two have not known—neglect. Pompeia knows full well that she is Caesar's political trophy wife, and this realization stings her eyes, tightens her throat, and beats against her breast.

Mucia's mind replays a conversation she had had with Pompeius when he had first arrived at Alba Longa. Leaving his senior centurions and military tribunes to disband the remaining legions that were to arrive at Brundisium, Pompeius had hastened to see his wife and children. They had had a happy reunion after a separation of several years. The children had grown physically and had matured emotionally in his absence. The boys were almost old enough to don the *toga virilis* of Roman manhood, and Pompeia, age fourteen, had blossomed into a lovely flower of young womanhood, strongly resembling her mother.

Consumed with pride in his children Pompeius had commended Mucia for rearing them so admirably in his absence. With an edge in her voice, Mucia had replied, "Of course, my husband, they are *my* children too, you know."

Pompeius' mood had suddenly changed. "Mucia, some rather disturbing reports came to me when I was in Greece. Amidst all the preparations for embarking for Italia I...."

"What kind of *reports,* my husband?"

Annoyed at having been interrupted and by Mucia's repetition of *husband*, Pompeius had shot back as though he were addressing one of his soldiers. "Reports about you, Mucia, or more precisely your, how shall I put this delicately, your social activities."

"Social activities?"

"Activities unseemly for the spouse of a Roman proconsul and imperator, and for the mother of his children."

There had been a pause with Pompeius scrutinizing his wife while she collected her thoughts and considered the best response.

Mucia had then asked, "What is your intention, my husband?"

"Stop playing your servile game, Mucia!" Pompeius had exploded. Then, after calming somewhat, "What do you have to say, Mucia?"

"To gossip, slander, or innuendo I make *no* acknowledgement. But to my husband and the father of my children, I ask again, what is your intention? Tell me and I will do your bidding."

Glaring coldly at her, Pompeius could not help but be impressed with how Mucia stood up to him. "You will know my intentions, Mucia, all in good time."

The recollection of the scene plays out in Mucia's mind. She has yet to know his intentions.

AT THE TEMPLE OF VESTA in the deepest part of the night, the Vestal Fabia kneels in holy attendance upon the goddess' sacred flame. This night she is not alone. The Virgo Maxima, the Chief Vestal Licinia, kneels by her side.

"What do you see, Fabia?"

"A mist surrounds a bridge. There's a man standing amid a group of men. They're trying to cross it. At the opposite end there's another man, standing alone." Fabia describes the visions appearing to her in the midst of the sacred fire.

Licinia asks, "Who are they?"

Straining to see within the flames, Fabia hesitantly says, "The man with the others is Lucius Catilina. He's holding a sword as though he's about to strike someone."

"Who's the other man?"

"I can't make... no, wait... it's my brother-in-law—the consul Cicero. Now there are lictors with fasces on their shoulders standing on either side of him. Licinia! The men with Catilina have vanished. They've left him. No wait—now they're at the other end of the bridge. They're standing behind Cicero. Now there's nothing but fire." Tears and sweat beads cover Fabia's face.

At the same deep hour of the night, Publius Clodius Pulcher meets with Crassus and Caesar at the former's Palatine house. Caesar and Crassus have recently returned from Alba Longa. What awaits them is further news of Catilina's conspiracy. The nature of what Clodius has come to tell them demands that they meet in the seclusion of Crassus' study.

"At least he required only a cut palm rather than a scarred cheek," Crassus opines sardonically. "That would have disfigured your *pretty* face, Pulcher." He throws in the pun for good measure.

Caesar ignores the sardonic pun. "It is not entirely of your own volition that you've come to us, is it Publius?"

"No," Clodius freely admits. "Catilina specifically told me to relay to both of you together this message: He would have your support in his enterprise; either *that* or your departure from Roma because he cannot guarantee your safety. He offers you this warning out of respect for your previous association."

"Bah!" Crassus snorts. "He's mad! Totally mad!"

Clodius says, "I suggested that he speak with you, with both of you, but he was adamant. He has no wish or need to meet with you. His course is set. Either you join him or you leave the City or you forfeit...."

"What about Gaius Antonius?" Caesar interrupts.

"You may have to negotiate for your lives with him," Clodius warns. "Catilina plans for Consul Antonius and Praetor Lentulus Sura to eliminate—that is to say—to kill Cicero, the praetors, and the oligarchs and all other non-supporters—such as yourselves."

Crassus asks, "Why wasn't Antonius at the meeting?"

"I don't know. Perhaps he was afraid to cut his own hand." Clodius smirks with satisfaction at his own sarcasm.

"Contemptible madness!" Crassus exclaims. "He's going to destroy all that we've worked for—even if he doesn't succeed in killing us. Gaius, we've got to get rid of him—now!"

As though ignoring Crassus' entreaty, Caesar says to Clodius, "Publius, tell him that he may rely on us."

"What? Are you mad too?" Crassus erupts.

Caesar evades the question. "Publius, how's your sister?"

Puzzled at the apparent non sequitur, Clodius asks, "Which?"

"The one who, like you, affects plebeian status, the praetor's wife, Clodia Metella."

"She's well—I suppose."

"And your love life?"

Further puzzled and piqued by Caesar's innuendo, Clodius replies, "And just what do you mean by *that*?"

"No, no, don't be alarmed," Caesar assures him. "Your partner, Publius, how is she?"

Recovering, Clodius admits, "Oh—Fulvia? I'll be seeing her tonight, as soon as we're finished here."

"Excellent!" Caesar now turns to Crassus.

"Yes, of course. Excellent!" Crassus now begins to see where Caesar is headed.

Turning back to Clodius, Caesar asks, "Publius, if you're going to be a go-between for Catilina and us, have you the stomach for more sinister work?"

"More sinister than Catilina's plot?"

"Yes, decidedly—because, you see, Publius, if you fail, you may well forfeit your own life. But if you succeed, you will have rendered a most patriotic service."

Clodius hesitates, his eyes darting suspiciously from Caesar to Crassus and then back to Caesar.

Caesar sighs. "Well, think about it, Publius, and please convey our respects to your sister *and* to Fulvia. Go now. You mustn't keep her waiting."

After Publius departs, Crassus and Caesar stare at each other for a long moment. Crassus breaks the silence with a series of names. "Clodia. Fulvia. Clodius. Cicero?"

Caesar nods, "Yes."

"Brillant!"

Caput IV Cicero's Respublica

I REMEMBER THE NIGHT THAT Clodia Pulchra paid us a late visit, a visit that aroused deep-seated stirrings in me as well as Terentia's suspicions. It was past midnight on the Ides of October, a few days after all the elections had been completed, and I was about to retire for the night. Clodia had been accompanied to our home by a large, burly slave and a diminutive maid-servant. When I met her in the atrium, she had them withdraw to the vestibule. There was a twinge of suspicion in my tone as I greeted her, for I could not imagine what she could possibly want at such a late hour. To have refused to see her would have been most impolitic because, after all, she was Praetor Metellus Celer's wife. He had been a valuable ally during my term, and for that matter so had Clodia's older brothers, Appius and Gaius.

When Clodia returned my greeting, she removed her veil, revealing the thick, long, raven-colored hair framing her oval face and falling back upon her neck. The ebony of her eyes set in liquid white pools shone in the oil-lamp light. Her scent was of jasmine and roses.

"Consul," she began so formally, "I'm sure you'll excuse this late intrusion after I've told you the reason for it." Her voice was a throaty, sultry whisper. Straight-forward and precise, formal yet without ceremony, she resumed before I could reply. "You life is in danger. Before the month is over, there will be a rising against the government." Her sensuous mouth and full lips seemed to have a life of their own. She paused, her ebony eyes holding on me. I felt shaken by them as much as by what she had said. I could not speak, but she must have sensed the question forming in my mind. "Catilina—Lucius Sergius

Catilina is conspiring to seize the government and murder you, and the praetors, including my husband, but *not* Lentulus Sura—he's one of the conspirators—as well as many senators. He has many desperate friends."

"And how do you know all this?" I finally asked.

Clodia smiled, pleased and contented with herself. "An intimate source."

"I need to speak with this *source*. Immediately!"

Again, she smiled a reassuring smile. "It can be arranged."

Almost as an afterthought, I inquired of her, "Does Metellus know?"

"No, not yet."

So, she had bypassed her own husband, the urban praetor, to divulge this alarming news to me. As if to dispel any doubt from my mind, Clodia whispered, "It's all true, Consul. As senior consul, you should have been told of this before anyone else."

I asked her to wait for me in the atrium while I withdrew to my bedroom to fetch my toga and cloak.

"Whatever does *she* want at this time of night?'

I wheeled about and saw Terentia. "Well," she demanded again, "what does she want?"

I sighed, impatient, fatigued. "She told me something that deserves to be investigated. If there's anything to it, I'll tell you later. Now, I'll need Tiro."

"But *what* did she tell you?" Terentia persisted. She was more often than not persistent and insistent. "Marcus, what did Clodia Metella need to tell you that you cannot confide in me?"

"Terentia! I don't have the time now! I cannot—I *will not* discuss it now. But know this: If what she says is true, it's serious. More than serious, it's dangerous."

"But dangerous to *whom*?"

"Great Jupiter's balls! Terentia—do you never stop?"

Terentia muttered something about Hades as she marched out of the room. She passed my faithful secretary, ever so efficient, Tiro, who moved to one side to allow her to pass.

"Tiro!" I called. "It's good you're still awake." He had been taking dictation from me when Clodia's arrival was announced. "Listen carefully. Go to my brother's house. If necessary, wake him. Tell him to come here immediately. It's important that we talk."

"Yes, Dominus."

"Then go to Atticus and to Servius Sulpicius. Give them both the same message. Take some company with you—four or five of the household staff. Report to me when you return, or when I've returned. Don't be long. Now go!"

Even as I spoke, it occurred to me that I would need some protection as I had no idea where Clodia was taking me. So I called after Tiro, "Wait! Before you go, wake Alexio. Tell him to arm himself and to meet me in the atrium. Very well, that's it. Now make haste, good Tiro."

The young Greek bowed and said, "I understand, Dominus," before departing.

For dictation and courier service and personal attendance, Tiro was and remains unparalleled. But in the event that I was to need a personal bodyguard, then big, brawny Alexio the Illyrian, our household steward, was the man to take along. For added security, I placed a dagger in the cincture of my tunic. Then, grabbing my toga and cloak, I proceeded out to the atrium to rejoin Clodia.

Marcus Caelius, my pupil and protégé, accosted me in the corridor. "What's happened?"

"No time now to explain, Marcus." I pushed past him and then stopped, turned to him, and added, "Why don't you come along. It might prove educational for you. But bring a weapon. A dagger should suffice." He followed after me.

Clodia stood waiting for me. As I approached her, I looked at her small, lithe figure, the full bosom pushing against the draping folds of her saffron-colored stola and blue palla. The coloring of her face, neck, and arms was an amalgam of rose and olive and cream. She replaced the veil over her head, but I could still see the raven tresses framing her face. Almost off-handedly, I announced, "This is my pupil, Marcus Caelius Rufus." He bowed ever so politely, and she in turn smiled studiously at him.

Alexio appeared in the atrium from another doorway. "Dominus," the steward began without the least trace of somnolence, "Tiro tells me you wished to see me."

"Yes, yes, good Alexio. First—here, help me with these," I said motioning to the toga and the cloak in my arms. As he helped me on with them, draping the toga over my left shoulder and then around my right side and fastening the cloak to my shoulders, I explained, "We're making a little trip tonight, Alexio, although I don't actually know where we're going." Saying this, I looked at Clodia.

"To the Subura. My litter will carry both of us comfortably," she teasingly offered.

An elegantly draped litter attended by eight sturdy bearers and four torch-bearing slaves was waiting for us. Clodia and I sat in it while her maid-servant walked beside it. Caelius walked on the opposite side next to Alexio. Clodia's slave walked ahead as the litter swayed along the dark, narrow streets.

Then, as now, the Subura was an unsavory district of plebeian riff-raff. The distance to be traversed was not far, and in the misty darkness there was hardly anyone stirring about to obstruct our route. Clodia's slave knew exactly where he was to take us. Except for telling me that we were going to see an acquaintance of hers, Clodia said very little. She stared at me, and in the torchlight I could see a mysterious smile play upon her lips as her black eyes glowed excitedly. Clodia and the swaying litter were a stimulating combination.

The litter stopped before a small, stone house, one of many such dwellings clustered together. The bearers set it down, and we alighted from it. The torchbearers lit our way to a door. Clodia knocked upon it three times, paused and then knocked another three times. The door opened and Clodia and I stepped in, leaving the others to wait outside.

Clodia introduced me to her acquaintance. This was Fulvia, granddaughter of the formidable plebeian leader of a by-gone era, Gaius Sempronius Gracchus. She was a small, lithe woman with flame-colored hair secured by a jeweled hairpin, and complexion the red-brown color of Arretine pottery. I estimated her age to be about twenty-four, the same as Clodia's. She was not wearing a palla, and the contours of her full, round bosom clinging to her cyan stola could easily be seen. Her scent was of spikenard and myrrh, and her eyes were an exotic amber color.

Fulvia was deferential to us, offering refreshment which I declined. I looked from her to Clodia anticipating an explanation. Clodia said, "Consul, my brother, Publius, is Fulvia's lover."

"He'll arrive within the hour," Fulvia huskily offered.

"Fulvia has told me that my brother's been boasting of great wealth that he's expecting to acquire very soon," Clodia said.

"Wealth through murder and revolution," Fulvia added, "and he's said that Catilina is the agent of all this. He's told me much during our times together, wild, lunatic stuff. So, I contacted Clodia and told her."

I nodded and said off-handedly, "Two patriotic women."

"But we're also concerned about our own survival," Clodia reproved. "I won't have my brother sacrifice himself in a plot that's doomed to fail."

"And it *will* fail, Consul," Fulvia assured me, "because you will expose and destroy it; and we, we three will help you. You can prevail upon Publius to betray Catilina."

"Is he willing to be an informer?" I asked. "Which of you would know better?"

The two women looked at each other and then turned to me. "Wait for him and ask him yourself, Consul," Clodia suggested.

I assured them, "I will."

We arranged for Clodia's attendants to hide with the litter and the bearers in an alley behind the house. Fulvia conducted Clodia and me to a room, actually more like a closet, adjoining her own bedchamber. We waited patiently, silently for Clodius' arrival. The door was only slightly ajar, affording minimal air. Fortunately, we did not have long to wait.

We heard some stirring, some talking from Fulvia's room. Clodia nodded at me upon hearing her brother's voice. It was a rather deep, albeit nasal voice, and he sounded rather winded. He laughed the way a stallion would whinny. Then there was silence. I listened more intently, and I noticed Clodia looking at me, and smiling. Then I noticed the strange aspect of her nose, small, pointed like a sparrow's beak.

Sounds from the other room became more distinct. Heavy breathing, sucking sounds, sounds of quick, wet kissing, moaning cries, creaking wood. Clodia was looking at me all the while, her lips parting, her ivory teeth gleaming at me. A sweet, exotic fragrance emanated from her neck and bosom. I felt enclosed, trapped, put upon, as though Clodia were enveloping me. And I took pleasure in my own entrapment.

But when the room fell silent, Clodia looked away from me. She motioned toward the door and whispered, "Now." We pushed open the door and walked in upon the two spent lovers sprawled upon the disheveled bed, reeking of perfume, sweat, and semen. There was no surprise or embarrassment in Fulvia's response. She merely drew the coverlet upon herself. But Clodius was visibly alarmed. His eyes, as dark as his sister's, appeared to be popping from their sockets. His mouth was open and his lips quivered as if he were trying to speak. Frantically, he looked from Clodia to me and back again several times before his sister spoke.

"Dear brother, show some modesty before Consul Cicero," Clodia reproved him.

Fulvia giggled and extended the coverlet to him so that he could shelter his deflated rod. He was thin, but quite sinewy and muscular, a fit man in his early thirties. His skin coloring was identical to Clodia's olive, rose and cream complexion, and his hair was the same raven-black as his sister's.

"Publius dear," Fulvia began, "your sister and I have asked Marcus Cicero to have a talk with you."

"About your friends and about your future," Clodia broke in.

Now, Clodius was recovering from his initial shock. He sat on the edge of the bed, poured himself a cup of something from a ewer on an adjacent table, drank long and deeply. He looked at the two women and then at me before admitting, "Consul, as you see, I've nothing to hide from you."

"Nor do I want you to hide anything from me, Publius Clodius," I replied as I carefully approached him. "I know of your association with Lucius Catilina. I know he's plotting subversion against the Republic. But I do not know the specifics."

"So, Consul," he snorted back, "you want me to be your informer? Is that it?"

"I expect you to be a loyal citizen and to help me stamp out the seditious designs of disaffected men."

Clodius smirked and nodded an approval that was more mocking than genuine.

From Clodia came an entreaty. "Publius, don't be a fool. Here's a chance to redeem yourself. Don't cast it aside." At the same time, Fulvia's hand passed over his naked back as if to encourage him further. I was close enough to see their faces quite clearly in the dim oil light of the room. I noticed how Fulvia's nose was rather large for her face and slightly bent to one side. Actually, in purely physical terms, she was quite attractive. And Publius Clodius possessed a handsomeness that was delicate, almost feminine. No wonder that in later years we all referred to him as Clodius *Pretty-boy* and thereby made a pun upon his surname, Pulcher.

"What remuneration might I expect?" he asked of me.

Now we were getting somewhere. I told him, "Work with me and I'll promise you immunity from prosecution. I'll support your canvass for future offices, providing of course, that you don't espouse any radical, popularist programs. And, most important of all, I'll give you money for your patriotism."

He smiled at my irony, but I continued. "In return, I want names, dates, places, anything and everything pertaining to Catilina. Agreed?"

Clodius nodded. "Agreed." Clodia and Fulvia exchanged furtive glances of satisfaction. "As a gesture of good faith," Clodius offered, "I'll tell you Catilina has compiled a list of enemies, senators and equites, who are to be killed. Consul, your name heads the list."

WITHIN HOURS AFTER HEARING CLODIUS Pulcher's disclosures, I met with Quintus, Atticus, Servius Sulpicius, and Marcus Caelius. Quintus was shaking his head in dismay. "I still think it's a trap," he was saying, "and Clodius was too eager to talk to you. He could be playing a double game, telling you what Catilina *wants* you to know!"

"But even so," Servius countered, "there's something in this that must be probed."

Atticus asked, "Can you move against Catilina?"

"No—not yet," I replied. "I've testimony from one man about a plot to overthrow the government, murder me and scores of senators and equites, set fire to selected districts of the City, and all of this is to coincide with an uprising of the Etrurian veterans on the twenty-seventh. If I go to the Senate with this—and remember, I dare not reveal my source without sacrificing him to assassination by his confederates—all I'll achieve is public hysteria...."

"That would be enough to stop them!" Quintus interrupted.

"*Delay* them, brother, but not stop them. No—I need harder proof and from sources that I can safely reveal."

"Yes, you're right," Servius quickly agreed. "What about this Gaius Manlius?"

"Clodius says he was a high-ranking centurion under Sulla. He's organized some ten thousand veterans into a strike source. They're to march on Roma when Catilina gives the word."

"Well, you know Etruria's beautiful at this time of year," Servius said lightly. "Unless you need me here, I'll go up there and have a look. You say Clodius said Faesulae and Arretium are the muster areas? I'll have a look and then get back to you as soon as I can."

We all looked at Servius and then at each other. He spoke again more emphatically. "I'll go."

"Very well then," I agreed, "but don't take any undue risks."

"You may be in greater danger *here*. Guard yourself well, Marcus." Servius smiled reassuringly at me.

"How many women are involved in the plot?" This was Caelius' first entry into our conference.

"For certain two," I replied, echoing what Clodius had told me. "Decimus Brutus' wife, Sempronia. She's also Lentulus Sura's mistress. And Praecia—she's nestled up with Gaius Cethegus, one of the losers in the praetorian canvass."

"What about Catilina's wife?" Atticus inquired.

"I don't doubt that Orestilla knows what her husband is up to, but Clodius did not mention her as an accomplice." I thought of something and then added, "I don't think Sura's wife is involved even if her brother-in-law, Gaius Antonius, is in it."

"What about these two *daughters of Venus*?" Servius asked.

"I don't know. I can't be sure. Of course, I'm not prepared to trust them."

"I should hope not!" Atticus interjected. "Though Clodia's of pure patrician lineage, the other one is steeped in plebeian radicalism."

"Fulvia's mother, Sempronia, is Gaius Gracchus' daughter. She's very old by now," Quintus speculated. "But her father, Fulvius Bambalio, died some time ago."

"Yes, true enough, and Sempronia's lawyers found a loophole in the Voconian law so that her unmarried daughter could inherit a considerable legacy." I nodded reflectively, remembering what I had seen earlier in the night at Fulvia's house. "Wealthy she may be, but she lives in the Subura, the most plebeian of all Roman neighborhoods."

Then I remembered something unrelated to the feminine angle, something that turned our discussion in a different direction. "Clodius said that Catilina had been in contact with Pompeius. But if I know him well enough, he'd have nothing to do with this madness. Still, I'll write to him and try to gauge his disposition. I've had no word from him in several weeks."

Atticus beamed with a suggestion and gesticulated with his large hands. "I could arrange a meeting for you with Afranius and Metellus Nepos. They've told me they're going down to Alba Longa to see the Imperator."

I saw merit in his idea, but I amended it slightly. "I'll prepare a letter for Pompeius and then, Atticus, you can have them deliver it to their commander." Atticus agreed and then mentioned that he would contact Pompeius' legates as soon as my letter was ready.

"I'll go with them," offered Quintus. "But brother, you should look closer to home. Two of your fellow magistrates are wrapped up with Catilina."

I nodded in agreement. "Lentulus Sura is too desperate to be bought off. But Antonius is more tractable. I think I might have a way to neutralize him."

"What about Caesar and Crassus?" Servius asked. "Didn't Clodius say that Catilina would *deal with them*?" When I had acknowledged this, Servius wondered aloud, "Whatever does that mean?"

"We'll see," I replied. "Clodius will report to me directly or through his sister. It's convenient that she's my neighbor."

"Are you going to tell the oligarchs about any of this?" Atticus raised a good question.

I hesitated before answering and even when I spoke there was indecision in my voice. "I'll tell them what I've discovered so far, of course without mentioning Clodius by name. Doubtless, they'll want to know my plans."

"I still don't like it," Quintus insisted. "It's all so neat and tidy—Clodia, then Fulvia, then Clodius. It's as though someone were putting them up to it."

"Then the deeper we dig, the sooner we'll learn the complete truth of this whole business," I hopefully suggested.

"So, Marcus, what are you prepared to tell them of your plans?" Atticus asked.

"That I will stop Catilina and keep Pompeius loyal to the Republic."

I WAS IN A FRENZY of activity over the next several days. First, I wrote a letter to Gnaeus Pompeius and sent it off with Afranius, Metellus Nepos, and Quintus. I informed him that the Senate had not yet considered his petitions, but I reminded him of my constancy in his service. I also reminded him that he was held in the highest regard as the Republic's loyal commander and the great vanquisher of Roma's enemies. He was trusted to be aloof to any entreaties by disloyal citizens for his aid and cooperation in their subversive enterprises. Finally, I expressed the Senate's reliance upon his loyalty to and patriotism on behalf of the Republic.

Having sent this off, I met with Gaius Antonius about two nights after Clodia Pulchra had first come to see me. He looked like a tired old bull metamorphosing into a boar. Though only a few years older than I, he looked many years my senior.

His was a checkered political career. Expelled from the Senate, he had been re-admitted with my help when we were elected praetors. As an associate of Crassus, he had attained the consulate. Now, he was a confederate of Catilina along with his brother-in-law, Lentulus Sura. Besides this conspiratorial connection, they shared a special fondness for young Marcus Antonius, Sura's step-son and Antonius' nephew and son-in-law.

To drive a wedge between them and to pry Antonius away from Catilina, I played upon my colleague's acquisitive interests. "Antonius, I know of your association with Catilina," I told him without ceremony or equivocation. "I know of his heinous designs against the Republic.

When I move against him, all who are with him will fall with him. But I offer you an opportunity to extricate yourself from the catastrophe awaiting him. At the same time, I offer you an opportunity to enrich yourself."

I could see from his furrowed brow and anxious expression that I had hit a nerve, and so I pushed my advantage without giving him a chance for denial. "In the proconsular lots, you were assigned Cisalpine Gaul, while I was assigned Macedonia. But there are far greater prospects of enrichment available in Macedonia. Wouldn't you think so? Besides, Macedonia is farther removed from Roman scrutiny, no?"

Antonius smiled crookedly, nodded, and almost coughed his reply. "Marcus Cicero, are you trying to buy me?"

"I'm buying your neutrality, Antonius. Withdraw from Catilina's group and I'll give you Macedonia with all of its lucrative advantages." I knew I had him! Arching my eyebrows and inclining my head toward him, I drove a final personal condition into the bargain. "Naturally, it's only fair that I expect some share of the provincial proceeds. Well, what do you say to this?"

Antonius rose from the table where we had been sitting. He slowly walked around it to a small wooden box on an adjacent table. When he opened the box, I saw the waxen death mask of his deceased wife. "Truly, this is a good likeness," he spoke absently. "How my Antonia resembles her mother." Then he turned and faced me. "Antonia is all I have."

Contrary to common belief, men who would make revolution are not always without spouses, children, loved ones. But having these, their actions are all the more desperate.

"Gaius Antonius, if you put yourself outside the law, even this house of yours is forfeited to the Republic. For your daughter's sake and your own safety, take my offer. You'll be guaranteed security and wealth."

He touched his wife's death mask and solemnly intoned, "I will do as you propose."

NEXT, I REQUESTED A MEETING with the oligarchs. We met at Catulus' house in the Palatine district. Cato arrived late, reeking of wine.

They listened with rapt concentration as I told them that I had discovered Catilina's conspiracy to overthrow the government and kill some of the Republic's leading citizens, including myself.

"There are a dozen men, senators and equites, working with Catilina here in Roma. There are also two women involved." I avoided looking at Decimus Brutus, as his wife, Sempronia, was an accomplice. "Perhaps there are others as well, but they've not been revealed to me."

"You know them by name?" Marcius Rex asked.

"Yes—I have names." I quickly ran off the names of Catilina's conspirators, all but my informer, Clodius, and the women. "Also involved are those veterans settled by Sulla in Etruria during his dictatorship. Their leader is an ex-centurion, Gaius Manlius. They're to march on Roma in conjunction with a rising in the City."

"And these risings are to happen when?" inquired Lucullus.

"My source"—I said this almost ironically for Publius Clodius was Lucius Lucullus' brother-in-law—"has said on or about October twenty-seventh."

A collective sigh was released as their heads wagged and their faces darkened with outrage and umbrage. Yet, they were not totally convinced.

Catulus observed, "That's less than two weeks away!"

"Arrest them! Arrest them all!" tipsy Cato blustered.

"We cannot at this time," I offered, "because we don't have tangible proof of their designs." Purposely, I spoke of *we,* rather than *I* because I wanted them to share the responsibility with me.

Cato again blustered, "Then get it! Who is your informer? Have him—have her testify against them!"

"Marcus Cato," Hortensius intervened, "you know, of course, that the informer, whoever he or she may be, must remain anonymous. If, uh, rather, *when* the conspirators are caught in the attempted execution of their plot, then the informer could testify against them. Is this not your intention, Consul?" Hortensius turned to me with this last statement. He was smooth and so perceptive.

"I can move against them *before* they act, but I need hard evidence to substantiate even my informer's testimony. Without it, in the Senate's eyes I'm inventing the entire business. They'll ignore my warnings, and Catilina will have a free hand."

"Why doesn't he just go off into exile?" Marcius Rex asked almost as a non-sequitur.

"Catilina and his confederates are too desperate, too stubborn to do anything that sensible. They want to reverse their ill fortune and they can do this only by revolution, by overthrowing the existing order. And Catilina wants what he believes was denied him—the consulate. He intends to have it even if it means betraying his country."

"What then do you want from us, Marcus Cicero?" Lucullus asked.

"Your cooperation and your readiness to support me. We'll need the military, especially if there's a rising in Etruria. The only soldiers in all Italia are Pompeius' praetorian cohorts. You should not hesitate to use him, before Catilina tries to win him over."

"Pompeius!" snapped Marcius Rex.

"Perfect excuse for him to proclaim dictatorship," Lucullus interjected. "Pompeius indeed!"

"This is no time for dredging up old resentments and petty jealousies," I reprimanded them. "Think of the Republic. It's threatened by a gang of dangerous, subversive men. Lucullus—can you not stifle your umbrage at losing the Eastern command to Pompeius? Marcius Rex—can you not stifle *your* umbrage at losing the naval command to Pompeius? Can you both not put aside your petty resentments for the safety and welfare of the Republic?"

They did not reply. Instead, they glared at me with simmering, noble rage. The tension in the room was broken only when Cato hiccupped.

"Pompeius alone may prove inadequate," Catulus mused.

"Should there be need of other commanders," I replied, "then assign Gaius Antonius and the urban praetor, Metellus Celer, to raise levies from among the colonists in Picenum and other regions. My brother could be assigned as legate to Antonius."

Hortensius cast me a suspicious glance upon hearing me mention Quintus. Slyly he remarked, "Consul, it's as though you want your brother to spy on your own colleague."

I nodded and replied cryptically, "I have my reasons for suspicion."

The oligarchs looked at one another, smirked at inebriated Cato, and then turned to me. As if by collective agreement, Catulus, the Princeps Senatus, First Senator, spoke the meeting's final words. "If Catilina is truly plotting subversion against the Republic, the Senate has at its disposal the *Ultimate Decree*. If necessary, we will issue it. We will expect you, Marcus Cicero, if so empowered, to use it to the fullest possible extent so that the Republic may be preserved. That is all for now. Thank you, Consul, for your report. Of course, you will keep us informed."

I returned home, confident and satisfied that I had the oligarchs' support. My ego, however, was somewhat bruised by Catulus' dismissal as though I were a student whose lesson had been concluded. Also, his mention of the ultimate decree weighed heavily upon my thoughts.

Senatus Consultum Ultimum—the Senate's Ultimate Decree empowered the consuls and all other magistrates to take extra-constitutional measures to save the Republic from destruction. It had been invoked twice before—to put down the agitation of Gaius Gracchus and his followers, a generation before my birth, and then to authorize Consul Gaius Marius to quash the popularist revolt led by Saturninus and Glaucia, a political rupture occurring when I was but a child. Now, Catilina might necessitate this extraordinary measure. It was an onerous responsibility for a consul to shoulder. Though I hoped it would prove unnecessary, its utility strengthened my resolve.

DURING THESE DAYS, AS I arranged meetings and waited for news from Servius in Etruria and from Quintus at Alba Longa, I could not withstand Terentia's entreaties to be made privy to my preoccupation. So I told her all that had been disclosed to me first by Clodia, then by Fulvia, and finally by Clodius. When she persisted in her questioning, I told her of my meetings with Antonius and with the oligarchs. She wanted to know about the conspirators: of Gaius Cethegus—a would-be power broker, a junior senator ambitious to be a dispenser of political favors, but now reduced by debt to sedition; of Publius Sulla, nephew of the late dictator, who took a strange fork in the road in choosing to follow Catilina. His uncle's shade in the Underworld may have been convulsing at Sulla's involvement in sedition against Roma and against the Senatorial order that the Dictator had espoused. And Sempronia.

How strikingly, vivaciously beautiful she had been at Tullia's wedding. But as Lentulus Sura's mistress she was not only his bed partner but his confederate in treason too.

"Lentulus Sura," Terentia mused, "wasn't he expelled from the Senate so many years ago?" After I acknowledged that this was true, she added, "How could Julia have married such a creature?"

"Well, Terentia, consider her situation. She was widowed. Her husband, Marcus Antonius, had just died after achieving some minor victories against the Cretan pirates during his consulate…."

"Oh yes, I remember now," Terentia interrupted, "and the Senate gave him the title 'Creticus'."

"Yes, that's true. At any rate, he left three orphaned sons, and I suppose Julia wanted the boys to have at least a step-father."

Terentia made clucking noises like a frustrated hen. "But Marcus Antonius was a distinguished man, even if his operations against the pirates were inconclusive. That Julia would have accepted as a second husband one as dissolute and reckless as Lentulus Sura is beyond my understanding. And then he betrays her with Decimus Brutus' wife. What a sinkhole of immorality and profligacy these patricians had made of Roman society! Oh, Fabia! Fabia, Fabia."

When I asked her why she mentioned her half-sister's name, she dismissed my question as unimportant. Instead she urged me to move aggressively against Catilina and his conspirators. Yes, of course! Now I understood. Terentia wanted revenge against Catilina for the scandal of ten years past when he and Fabia were accused of sexual misconduct. Though both had been acquitted, the scandal hung like an ugly cloud about the Vestal Fabia, compromising her in the public's mind.

"Terentia, as consul I will protect the Republic from all harm and I will bring to justice all who threaten it with sedition." She was satisfied with this.

Having opened up my counsels to Terentia, I felt intimately drawn to her. We kissed and embraced each other like newly found, unhindered lovers. For the first time in many months, we shared a conjugal bed and with it the release of an abundance of pent-up passion. It was in these all too rare, tender times, that I realized how much I loved Terentia.

SIX DAYS HAD PASSED SINCE Clodia had come to me. Neither Quintus nor Servius had returned to Roma. Within the City, there was no insurgency from Catilina or his conspirators. The waiting for something to happen, for some news, for some outbreak, afflicted me physically and emotionally. And then I received a message from Fabia. She asked to see me urgently at the Vestal Residence. Strange, I thought, that she would not come to me, for she regularly visited Terentia. Yet, there was something ominous that I gleaned between the lines of her note. I told the messenger that I would meet Fabia shortly.

The Vestal Residence was and remains part of a complex of structures flanking the Sacred Road not far from where it enters the Forum. The circular, domed Temple of Vesta is directly adjacent to the Vestal Residence. Directly behind them are the Public House and the Regia, the Chief Pontiff's mansion and office.

My lictors successfully and officiously cleared our way through the streets packed with pedestrian, animal, and vehicular traffic. By this time, I was conditioned to ignore the crude cat-calls of "Chick-Pea" from foul plebeians and slaves. But the stench of garlic, sweat, and human and animal dung that assailed my nostrils was intolerable. I turned to Alexio and bade him have the lictors push more aggressively through the openings that they had made for us.

After almost an hour of start-stop-and-go progress, we arrived at the Vestal Residence, a large, rectangular stone edifice. An attendant—female, of course—admitted me to the atrium. Although all Romans of genteel stock received their visitors in the atrium of their homes, here in the Vestal Atrium this formality was strictly observed. It would have been cause for gossip at the least or outright scandal had a male visitor been conducted to any other part of the residence.

I had been here several times before, and I was always fascinated by the statues of former Chief Vestals that adorned the atrium's perimeter. Their faces and figures possessed a quiet, tranquil, almost blissful beauty that soothed the discomfort of the journey and helped to settle my jarred nerves. They filled me with anticipation for the sight of my lovely sister-in-law. But my anticipation was dashed when, instead of Fabia, Caesar crossed the marble floor to greet me.

"Welcome, Consul," he began. "I wanted an opportunity to speak with you secretly. This seemed the most likely place." He waved his hand about the room. "As Chief Pontiff, even the Vestals have to accommodate me." He must have noticed the distrustful look I gave him, for he quickly added, "I asked Fabia to ask you to come here. You see, Marcus, what I have to say to you must be said in the most secretive circumstances. Your coming to the Regia or my coming to your home would have aroused suspicion, and I dare not put it in writing."

I resented his power over Fabia, a power that could compel her to send me a bogus note. "Very well then," I said suspiciously and with unconcealed irritation. "You have my attention."

Caesar moved in closer to me and spoke in hushed, urgent tones. "Lucius Catilina has invited me to join him in a plot to overthrow the government. Among others, he plans to execute you, Crassus, and Marcus Bibulus. He says he and I will share the consulate; he's going to seize and re-distribute the wealth of the victims, and then assign proconsular offices among his supporters. He says there are to be two marches on Roma—one from the north, the Etrurian colonists, and one from the south, Pompeius' cohorts. Pompeius is to share power with us. Catilina assumes that I'm with him."

"I see." Affecting as much surprise as I could manage, I pulled back from him as though this news were a shocking revelation. "In telling me this, Gaius Caesar, you hope to play a double game, don't you? Should Catilina win, you'll profess your loyalty to him and reap the rewards of murder and revolution. But, if I destroy him, you can always say that you came to me and …."

"That's not quite how it is," Caesar interrupted. "First, I know that you'll destroy him. I know it because I'll help you. Second, in return for my help, I want your support in my consulate."

At this I was genuinely shocked, and I smiled at his success in catching me off guard.

Slowly, he moved away from me and toward a corner of the room where there was a four-piece statuary group. There was a marble image of the goddess, Roma, seated like a haughty matron on a cathedra chair. Behind her on marble pedestals were bronze, life-like renderings of the Roman divine triad: Jupiter, grasping scepter and thunderbolt in his hands; his wife and queen of the gods, Juno, tall, broad of breast, a face of daunting power; and helmeted Minerva, goddess of wisdom and good counsel.

"Impressive, aren't they?" Caesar considered them. "Not really as grand as the Capitoline images, but the arrangement conveys the same essential truth: Our Roman cosmos is governed by the divine triumvirate—Jupiter, Juno, Minerva. Our Republic ought to be administered by a triumvirate of mortal men." After saying this, all the while studying my reaction, he began moving back toward me. "Cicero, the time has come for change, the kind of change that you've opposed. But in my consulate a new order will come to Roma. You and your men of property are a vital part of this new order, as integral to it as Pompeius' military and Crassus' publicans."

Yet a second thunderbolt! That Caesar was in league with Crassus was an established fact. But now, was I to infer that Pompeius was in tow with them as well? Here was Caesar enticing me to join them. I thought of Quintus. Why had I not heard from him?

"Without that order," he continued, "there's the mob, restless, and fractious, ready to do violence in the streets at any demagogue's bidding; there are the veterans, like those in Etruria, easily led astray by the wildest promises; over all these sits a selfish, complacent Senate."

"But you've exploited the mob!" I protested.

"No—I've tried to contain them, to occupy them, to reduce the numbers of the indolent and the indigent by putting them on their own farmsteads. But you and the Senate would leave them as they are so that a Catilina could inflame them. And there will always be a Catilina to shake the Republic and upset the Roman world unless my—*our* new order is realized."

I saw no purpose in prolonging this dialogue. "Gaius Caesar, thank you for your warning *and* your offer. I hope for the Republic's sake that I can continue to rely on your loyalty to Roma. But I tell you frankly, I never trusted you and I cannot begin to trust you now, even though you're turning on an old partner in order to embrace a new partner."

Caesar smirked. "Marcus, I sincerely hope you will change your mind and join us, for your sake, and for the Republic's benefit. Farewell."

With that, he turned and was gone through a side exit. The silent, stone faces of the Vestal statues and the divine triad with seated Roma seemed to be staring at me with vacant eyes.

When I returned home, I found Quintus and Atticus waiting for me. Quintus had good news. He said that Pompeius was ready and willing to serve the Republic in whatever capacity the Senate was to commission him. Pompeius did admit to being approached by both Catilina himself and by his agents, but he and his soldiers, both those with him and those discharged, were for the Republic. As relieved as I was to hear this, I was still uneasy at Caesar's intimation of collusion with Crassus and Pompeius.

Quintus went on to say that he had accepted Pompeius' hospitality and had rested at Alba Longa for a few days before returning to Roma. I was annoyed that he had not returned sooner, given the impending crisis, but my annoyance passed when he told me that he had noticed some friction between Pompeius and his wife, Mucia. Also, Metellus Nepos and Afranius, while garrulous and amiable during the trip to Alba, became sullen and reserved in Pompeius' presence. I attributed their change in behavior to deference toward their commander, but Atticus reminded us that Metellus Nepos was Mucia's half-brother and as such he may have been disturbed at any domestic discord.

"I'll tell you this as well," Atticus continued, "the money-men are smelling civil war. Money has practically disappeared despite the millions that Pompeius is said to have brought back from the East. Something's bound to break soon."

In dismay I could only agree with him. "If only there were some word from Servius, some proof, something I could take to the Senate. They'll take no pre-emptive measures against Catilina without hard evidence, and they'd only regard me as a hysterical fanatic. Even if I brought charges against him in the Court of Public Violence, he could bribe the jury into acquitting him or he'd slip off into exile and continue his plotting from afar."

Quintus and Atticus shrugged. "So then," Atticus mused, "here we are on the brink of revolution, but we have to wait for it to happen before we can stop it."

How it pained me to admit that he was right. Time was running out, but I continued to hope for an opportunity.

The little sleep that I had during those tense days was afflicted with disturbing images. In one dream that I remember after all these years—and I had it on the night following my meeting with Caesar at the Vestals' Residence—I saw before me the seated effigy of the goddess, Roma. On the wall behind her, five blood-stained togas were hanging on pegs. Off to one side, there was a statue of Vesta whose marmoreal features resembled Fabia's. A figure approached from behind Roma. I could not at first identify it, except that it was a man clothed in the military garb of a commander, a proconsul. He came upon the seated statue and began to fondle her breasts and to kiss the nape of her neck. Suddenly, the statue came to life, swooning in ecstatic, orgasmic delight at his touch. The statue of Roma had changed before my sight to Aurelia, the old dowager mother, and he that caressed and fondled her was her own son—Caesar.

Repelled by this scene, I turned from it to face the image of Vesta. But it was surrounded by swirling mists of vapor and, like the image of Roma, it began to come to life. The veils and stola and palla dropped from her body, and Vesta-Fabia became Clodia Pulchra, smiling at me and extending her naked, supple arms to me as beads of water glistened on her breasts and belly.

I had this dream several times, and each time I awoke from it in terror. The deepest conjuring of mind and soul manifested Caesar's ambition to possess Roma, to have his way with her just as Oedipus, albeit unknowingly, had possessed his mother after taking his father's life and throne. What about my *own* ambitions? How was my service to the Republic, to my adopted commonwealth, revealed in the images of these women? That I earnestly revered the one while the other enticed and repelled me at the same time betokened more than just my own political ambition. What else then? No wonder the dream filled me with terror!

"Dominus, there is a caller in the atrium."

I recognized Tiro's voice in the dark.

"It's Marcus Licinius Crassus, Dominus. He must speak with you at once. He has urgent business to put before you." Tiro was emphatic even as he lit an oil lamp. "The noble Crassus says that lives are at stake."

Rising frantically from my bed, I threw a robe over my sleeping gown and followed Tiro into the atrium. Crassus stood there, wrapped in a traveler's hooded cloak and looking like a peripatetic scholar. He greeted me cordially and apologized for the late call as he pulled a small roll of parchment from his toga sinus.

"This was brought to my home not more than an hour ago," Crassus said placing the scroll in my hand. "My porter could not identify the bearer. Whoever he was, he left these as well." From his cloak, he pulled out an additional six scrolls, the same size as the first, and bound together.

Unrolling the parchment and holding it an angle so as to cast sufficient light upon it from the standing oil lamp, I found it contained a short, ominous message.

"To Marcus Licinius Crassus, you are marked for death by Lucius Catilina and his faction. Flee Roma and escape the general massacre."

There was no signature. Upon inspecting the other scrolls, I found that each was tagged and addressed to a different senator. Though I did not open them I presumed that they contained the identical warning. Even Crassus concurred in this assumption, or he would not have brought them to me. The script was not his. I was certain of that. But it could have been written at his dictation. The whole business could have been a ruse. Yet, he could easily know what Catilina was up to, and he was giving me the shafts to hurl against him. It was a gamble, but I decided to take it.

I convened the Senate for the next morning for an emergency session. Despite the short notice of the summons, the Curia Hostilia was full. Even Catilina was there, bold and defiant as ever.

"Conscript Fathers, I have discovered an insidious plot to overthrow the Republic and murder the magistrates and many men among the senatorial and equestrian orders." Finally, I was able to announce what I had known for the last week. The faces of the oligarchs were filled with satisfaction. *"It's about time!"* they seemed to be thinking.

"Only several hours ago, irrefutable proof was brought to me by Marcus Licinius Crassus." I held up the scroll Crassus had brought to me. Amid the Senate's muttering and buzzing, I had the scroll conveyed to Crassus and I asked him to read it aloud. When he did so, the mention of Catilina's name in connection with a general massacre struck horror into the senators' faces.

Seizing on the moment, I brought out the other scrolls. Reading the names of the addresses tagged to the scrolls, I had these senators read aloud their respective letters. My gamble paid off handsomely. Starting with the praetor, Metellus Celer, followed by Marcus Bibulus, consul-elect, and then by Metellus Scipio, Lentulus Spinther, Lucius Domitius Ahenobarbus, and ending with Marcus Claudius Marcellus, the identical ominous warning was heard. The same mention of Catilina and his faction and of a general massacre in each of the six letters caused all eyes to focus on Catilina.

Throughout the readings, Catilina had sat impassively on his bench. Now, over the hubbub of the Senate's outraged clamor, he stood up and, without invitation or leave, he addressed them.

"Senators, it is not enough that you've twice kept me from attaining the consular office that is my birthright as a patrician of the Roman state. Now, this *calumny* is laid upon me! I'm branded as a rebel and traitor to my country. This comes from a non-Roman, a foreigner, a *new man* who presides where I ought to be. If you believe him, if you accept the evidence of anonymous notes that the consul probably contrived to have written, then you are doing his bidding as slaves, *not* senators! For myself, to convince you of my innocence, I will put myself into the custody of any of you willing to have me or any senator whom the consul will appoint as my custodian." Catilina looked about the chamber, showing no sign of intimidation or discomfiture.

There was dead silence in the Curia as Catilina surveyed the senators. His face tightened when Gaius Antonius looked away. Publius Clodius was running his fingers around his mouth and chin, and Lentulus Sura was visibly shaken.

"Well then," Catilina announced at last, "if no one will have me, then I place myself in the custody of Marcus Porcius Laeca. Let him be responsible for keeping me under house arrest. Will you accept this responsibility, Marcus Laeca?"

Like a polished actor responding to a cue, Laeca stood and made a great show of accepting Catilina into his custody. I smirked at the sham, but I was not yet ready to denounce Laeca as one of Catilina's conspirators.

From Marcius Rex came a proposal for the declaration of a *tumult*, a state of emergency. The proposal was seconded by Lentulus Spinther, one of the recipients of a warning letter. The proposal was then carried by a hefty senatorial majority. Bodyguards were decreed for me, for Antonius, and for all the praetors. (At this point, I did not mention Praetor Lentulus Sura as one of the conspirators.) In addition to the men of Reate, who had been retained since the consular and praetorian elections, young equites and junior senators were to comprise these armed escorts.

All was going well. I wanted desperately to introduce the problem of the Etrurian colonists, but without proof of their militant plans my work against Catilina would have been vitiated. Clodius would have confirmed it, but I would then have had to expose him as my informer and that would have been the end of his service to me. Just when I felt the floor slipping out from under me, I saw Tiro waving frantically at me from the Curia's foyer. I beckoned to him to enter and he did so, but with much reluctance, for slaves, women, and non-senators are generally not admitted to the Senate's deliberations. He whispered into my ear the most divinely sent news. By the time he had finished telling me, behold, Servius Sulpicius was entering the Curia.

He had just arrived at my home and Tiro had conducted him to the Senate. Attired in riding clothes, he looked fatigued and winded. Yet, there was a glow of excitement emanating from his face. The senators looked at him, leaning their heads together to speculate about his sudden appearance. From the nod of approval he gave me, I surmised that he wanted to address the Senate. So I called for silence and bade them give him their attention.

Taking a deep breath, Servius began cautiously as though the Republic's fate hinged on what he was about to say. "Conscript Fathers, I have just come from Etruria where I spent the last several days witnessing a muster of veterans. Their numbers are equal to at least two full legions. They are armed and ready to march on Roma from their encampment near Faesulae. Their leader is a centurion from the days of Sulla, one Gaius Manlius. I learned they are in league with men here in the City, men who are plotting to overthrow the Republic from within!"

The Senate erupted with cries of "Treason! Sedition!" Servius sat down, winded but satisfied that he had accomplished his mission. Then I took the initiative. "Senators, Conscript Fathers, you have heard additional proof of the seditious designs of disloyal citizens. *Citizens?* By their plotting they render themselves *enemies* of the Republic. Conscript Fathers, what is your will?"

Over the hubbub, old Catulus rose and motioned for silence. "Consul," he intoned so solemnly, "there can be no delay. Faced with murder and insurrection from within the sacred precincts of the city and an armed uprising from Etruria, the Senate's decree of a tumult must give way to more severe measures. I propose that the Senate issue the Ultimate Decree—that the consuls be endowed with emergency powers to see to it that the Republic suffers no harm!"

Thunderous applause greeted Catulus' motion. His brother-in-law, Hortensius rose above it to second the motion. I put it to a vote, and by overwhelming voices the Senate's Ultimate Decree was passed. Then, empowered with virtually dictatorial authority, I maneuvered for position against Catilina's conspirators. "Senators, I propose the following measures for the Republic's security. First, that armed guards be assigned to the Senate, the Forum, the Capitoline, and to all City gates. Second, that Gnaeus Pompeius Magnus be commissioned to lead his praetorian cohorts to Etruria to contain the rebels. Third, that Consul Gaius Antonius be commissioned to raise troops from among the loyal colonists in Etruria. In this commission, the Consul should be assisted by Quaestor Publius Sestius, by the Military Tribune, Gnaeus Plancius, and as legate, Senator Quintus Tullius Cicero. Fourth and finally, that Praetor Metellus Celer be commissioned to recruit soldiers from our veteran colonists in Picenum."

The oligarchs must have prepared their friends and cronies well, or perhaps the danger was clearly perceived to be imminent. There was no objection to any of my proposals. But as the Senate by acclamation approved them, I saw Catilina and Porcius Laeca sneak out the door. The others of their faction kept their seats for any number of reasons.

Julius Caesar was then on his feet. At first, I thought he too was going to leave, but instead he cocked his head back and eyed me. "As the Senate has secured measures for the Republic's safety, let it not forget its responsibility to protect the rights of all citizens." He announced this in a resolute, pontifical voice as though Jove himself were speaking through him. "In the past, even within the living memory of many here, the Senate has used the Ultimate Decree to commit political murder! Let the Senate not repeat the injustices of the past, lest it bring divine retribution upon our country."

He resumed his seat as the stunned Senate tried to recover its composure from the alarming events of this session.

I was satisfied with the turn of events. My gamble, based on Crassus' letters, Clodius' disclosures, and Servius' timely arrival, had paid off. The Senate's decree and my proposals had Catilina and his conspirators at bay. Now, I hoped that our courier would reach Pompeius speedily so that he could take the field against the Etrurian rebels.

So much had happened in so brief an interval since Clodia Pulchra had come to me on the Ides of October. By the twenty-first, a mere six days later, the Senate had empowered me in its Ultimate Decree to defend the state. I was prepared to do just that.

Omniscient Narrative

Lucius Catilina and Marcus Laeca exit the Curia with hurried, stealthy steps. When they reach the portico, they stop and Catilina looks back contemptuously. He can yet hear Cicero's voice.

"Caesar. Crassus. They betrayed us." Catilina grits his teeth, snarling out the words.

"What about the letters?" urges Laeca.

"Cicero's own slaves could have written them for Crassus, or Crassus or Caesar could have had them written. It matters not. They're in league with Cicero to destroy me." Catilina puts his hand against one of the six fluted Ionic columns supporting the Curia's unadorned pediment.

"We are discovered!" Laeca faces him impetuously. "Now what do we...?"

"Get a messenger off to Manlius! Tell him to be ready to march on the City. He'll get the word soon. And get the word out to the others. We'll meet tonight and plan the disposal of Caesar and Crassus."

With this said, Catilina descends the broad, flat steps connecting the Curia's portico to the Forum's pavement. Laeca watches him pass between the stairway's supporting platforms, each broad and high enough to hold a huge tripod chafing dish. Each night coal and wood are burned in them to illuminate the Forum. Laeca wonders who has illuminated Catilina's conspiracy.

An hour later, by which time the Senate has concluded its business, the steps are crowded with the senators descending in pairs, trios, and clusters discussing the Consul's revelations. Praetor Lentulus Sura, Gaius Cethegus and Marcus Caeparius weave their way through them. They cross the steps diagonally and ascend the Rostra where three of their faction, the equites Gabinius Capito, Gaius Cornelius, and Publius Statilius are waiting. They have heard of this emergency session of the Senate where Consul Cicero was to divulge critical news concerning the Republic's safety. As non-senators, they are banned from even waiting in the Curia's foyer.

Statilius carelessly beckons to the three senators, and for this he is reprimanded by Lentulus Sura. Capito is flushed with anticipation. "What has happened?"

Cornelius is quick to add, "We saw Catilina and Laeca come out, but they ignored us and went their separate ways. Is something amiss?"

Lentulus Sura is direct and concise in his reply. "*Amiss*?!" It seems we have an informer or two or more in our midst. Cicero has had the Senate declare the Last Decree and Catilina has put himself in custody under Marcus Laeca." With this last piece, a crooked smile plays across Sura's mouth. "He'll get word to us about the next meeting."

Cethegus proposes another angle. "We have to get word to Orestilla—unless Catilina has already sent a messenger."

Sura grimaces. "Perhaps, and then again, perhaps not. Let the women take care of that."

A SENATOR, GAIUS OCTAVIUS CAEPIAS, arrives at the Curia and is surprised to see the Senators descending the steps. *Have they adjourned already?* He is winded and happily excited. His friends, Marcius Philippus and Nigidius Figulus, hail him from the portico. They walk down to meet him as Octavius hurries up the steps, weaving this way and that to avoid colliding with the senators. However undignified such haste may be, for him it is entirely justified.

"You're late, good friend!" Marcius Philippus tells him. "Come along. We'll tell you what's transpired."

"But not before I tell you the blessed news!" Octavius pauses to catch his breath. "Atia has been delivered of a boy. I have a son!"

His friends congratulate him, patting him heartily on the shoulder. Figulus is inspired to pronounce, "The ruler of the world has been born!"

Near dusk, two litters are borne to the house of Lucius Catilina in the Aventine district. When the bearers set them down, Praecia and Sempronia emerge and walk to the door. Once admitted by the janitor, they pass to the atrium. They wait a moment or two before Catilina's wife, Aurelia Orestilla appears. She is not surprised to see them.

"Sempronia, Praecia, welcome. Welcome to you both," Orestilla is cordial to the women, but there is an edge in her voice and in her bearing.

"Orestilla, we've come here to tell…." Sempronia begins but Catilina's wife cuts her off.

"That my husband has placed himself in what we Romans call *custodia libera*. Yes, you needn't have bothered to make the trip. Catilina's messenger arrived almost an hour ago."

"We're sorry, Orestilla," Praecia offers, "sorry that Catilina cannot be with you now. But at least from Laeca's place they can continue what they've thus far set into motion."

Orestilla shakes her head and waves a dismissive hand at her visitors. "He'd have done better to take me and my daughter into exile with him. I would gladly have gone. So too would Flavia. Instead, he's committed himself to making war on the state. He can't possibly win. His chief allies have deserted him, and Pompeius is a cagey reptile, and there is at least one traitor in the cabal."

Sempronia heatedly counters her, "Your husband is a brave man. He won't desert his friends by running off into exile. Nor will he pass under the Senate's yoke. His men will find the informer and they'll silence him."

"And the two of you," Orestilla says disdainfully, "what do you hope to gain from their sedition?"

"Freedom from my creditors, and a chance to unload an aged, bore of a husband." Sempronia nods her head emphatically.

"And I want the power and influence that I once enjoyed among ambitious senators," Praecia admits candidly.

"And I want my husband," Orestilla sighs.

Caput V Cicero's Respublica

FOR SEVERAL DAYS FOLLOWING THE Senate's declaration of the Ultimate Decree, all was comparatively quiet in Roma. Armed patrols of volunteers maintained their surveillance, and Catilina was deterred from attempting any commotion. Each day, Cato summoned him to appear before the Court of Public Violence. But Catilina did not appear. He confined himself to Laeca's house, a most convenient place of self-arrest where he could hatch new intrigues.

My bodyguard accompanied me everywhere—a troop of eighteen young equites armed with swords, daggers, and cudgels, attired in leather, bronze-studded coats, and spoiling for a fight. The leaders of this armed escort were my son-in-law, Piso, my pupil and protégé, Marcus Caelius, and a junior senator, Titus Milo, who was eager for advancement under my influence.

Much to Servius Sulpicius' chagrin, Publius Clodius also served as a bodyguard. In this capacity, he could easily and inconspicuously relate the latest news of Catilina's intrigues while also performing an act of public patriotism. But Servius, like Quintus, did not trust him. In his mind, Clodius could very well have been commissioned by Catilina to assassinate me, and serving in my bodyguard would have afforded him a perfect opportunity to strike—*if* that had been his purpose.

Actually, the only noteworthy news from Clodius was that Catilina had added Caesar and Crassus to the conspirators' death list. Catilina was convinced, and with good reason, that these two had betrayed him. However, Catilina's agents had been unsuccessful in striking down his erstwhile partners. Both the Chief Pontiff and the Plutocrat had taken extensive security measures of their own. They had hired their own cohorts of thugs as bodyguards. The Regia and Crassus' Palatine house were ringed with armed guards. Caesar and Crassus were taking no chances. Though they may have had their own informer, they certainly would have inferred Catilina's vindictive designs even without one. At any rate, I had my suspicions that Caesar or Crassus or both could have been playing both sides.

The news from our military commanders was encouraging. From Picenum, Praetor Metellus Celer reported enthusiastic veteran and junior levies. Such reports were echoed by Gaius Antonius and confirmed by Quintus from lower Etruria. However, farther north, near Faesulae, the news was more troubling. On October twenty-seven as foretold, the veterans declared their open revolt against the Republic.

Omniscient narrative

On the southern slopes of Faesulae thousands of canvass military tents are pitched. A ditch surrounds them, topped by an earthen wall and wooden palisades of sharpened stakes. This has been easy work for the veterans of Sulla's legions. They have not forgotten how to pitch and fortify an encampment, no matter that one of Etruria's most thriving towns lies above it. The brown-grey walls of Faesulae rise above the military quadrants of the retired legionaries' camp. But it is more than a camp. It is their base of operations, the site from which their revolt against the Roman Republic has been launched. From here, when the word has been given, they will march south to Roma and secure their demands.

As many as the ramparts can hold have occupied them. Many more, in centuries, maniples, and cohorts have formed up on the slopes outside their camp. Their commander, Centurion Gaius Manlius, dressed in the battle uniform of leather coat overlaid with a harness of metal scales, stands at their head. He faces a contemptibly smaller force at whose head stands Imperator Gnaeus Pompeius Magnus. The Magnus wears his most splendid armor, the leather and bronze cuirass molded to his torso's musculature. Like Manlius, he wears no helmet because he wants the rebels to recognize him, to remember him from their service under Sulla.

Pompeius surveys the alignment before him. He says to his legate, Marcus Petreius standing only a few paces to the rear, "I number them at about ten thousand, including those on the ramparts."

"That's about right," the battle hardened legate admits.

Behind Pompeius and his legate are the Magnus' three praetorian cohorts numbering some one thousand legionaries, the commander's personal troops. They are armed and arrayed for battle, shields and javelins in hand, helmeted, and grim faced. But Pompeius is gambling that there will be no fight.

The warm October sun bears down on them, and the only sounds to be heard are of birds flying overhead and the neighing of Pompeius' horse held by an aide.

At last, it is Pompeius who breaks the silence. "Veterans and citizens, your assembly under arms here is illegal and treasonous. I order you to disperse, dismantle your camp, and return to your homes."

But the veterans do not budge. Gaius Manlius responds, "Imperator Pompeius Magnus, many of these men do not have homes or farms to return to because they've been stripped of them by greedy, merciless publicans. Many of them face enslavement for debt—enslavement not only of themselves but of their wives and children as well. We want nothing more but assurances of debt relief from the government. We'll commit no belligerent acts unless we are first assailed by you or by other forces that Roma might send."

"Gaius Manlius, I remember you. You were a fine soldier, perhaps Sulla's best centurion. I recognize many of the men standing behind you. All of you know that the Republic will not brook rebellion and sedition. If you refuse to disperse and strike your camp, then you will be dealt with as enemies of the state. Additional government forces are coming and I can easily and quickly re-muster my legions. What say you, Centurion?"

Gaius Manlius cocks his head back and flairs his nostrils defiantly. "We will hold our ground! But when the time comes, unless the Senate promises us debt relief, we'll march on Roma, and we'll push aside anyone foolish enough to stand in our way!"

Thunderous cheers erupt from the veterans' ranks. Manlius is pleased. He turns to his men, signals to lower-ranking centurions and decurions to lead them back into camp, and then he turns back to face Pompeius. The Imperator realizes full well that the confrontation will now degenerate into stalemate. He does not know for certain if additional disgruntled veterans will swell the rebels' ranks. But he is certain that Consul Antonius and Quintus Cicero will be bringing the levies from lower Etruria. Watching the rebels withdraw into their camp, he conceives a strategy for the Picene levies being recruited by Praetor Metellus Celer.

Cicero's Respublica

Upon receiving these reports from Pompeius and his fellow commanders, the Senate voted commendations for them.

At about the same time, the Kalends of November, an auspicious dedication took place. A magnificent statue of Jupiter, Best and Greatest of the gods, was to be unveiled in the Jovian Temple on the Capitoline. A procession of pontiffs, augurs, Vestals, equites and senators moved up the Capitoline Ramp and congregated at the podium before the Temple. I was among them, and so was Caesar, sublimely regal in his Chief Pontifical toga, its purple-bordered hem draped ceremoniously over his head and the Jovian medal and chain hanging about his neck. I saw old Catulus regarding him with potent envy, for the Princeps Senatus still coveted Caesar's high office.

Actually, there was more reason for Catulus' umbrage. This dedication of Jove's statue marked the completion of the Capitoline Temple's restoration after the ravages it had endured during the Marian-Sullan civil war of an earlier generation. Two years before, when Catulus had been Censor with Crassus, he had failed to fulfill his pledge to repair and restore the edifice to its former magnificence. Now, still smarting from his defeat in the recent Pontifical Contest, Catulus resented Caesar's triumph in completing the Jovian restoration.

Five white bulls, bedecked with ritual garlands, were sacrificed in honor of Jupiter as Rex Sacrorum, Lucius Claudius officiated. When struck with fatal blows by the sacrificial attendants, they fell upon the stone altar with mournful thuds. Though I did not realize it at the time, I can now reflect on and appreciate the prophetic irony inherent for me in their sacrificial deaths. Their blood flowed down upon the altar's walls, and then onto the pavement as the fire of their holocaust reached up to the Temple's pediment.

Then, Caesar conducted us inside through the long cella to the high, draped colossus. Upon his signal, the newly restored marble and bronze effigy was revealed. Jove's head was a solid mass of wavy, shoulder-length hair. His full beard encompassed broad, high cheek bones, and thick-set lips were poised as though he were about to speak. A gown draped over one shoulder and half of his muscular chest. His massive arms held the scepter of dominion and the thunderbolt of divine retribution. He was seated on a throne, actually more like a cathedra chair. His feet were sandaled and his shins were bound in caliga shoes.

This Capitoline Jove was easily three times the size of the effigy in the Vestal Residence. Similar to its Vestal counter-part, this one was flanked by statues, of similar size and detail, of Juno and Minerva. The Queen of the Gods and the Goddess of Wisdom had not, however, had to be restored as they had not suffered any of the ravages visited upon Jove or his temple during the civil war.

While this day of dedication belonged to Jupiter, my attention was drawn to Minerva. From my deepest heart, from my most profound thoughts, agnostic though I was, I appealed to Wisdom for guidance in the crisis that now beset our Republic. My reverie was interrupted when our Chief Pontiff looked up at the cold marmoreal visage of our Roman pantheon's chief god and solemnly intoned, "May Jupiter, Best and Greatest of the Gods, protect the Republic and the Roman People."

Though I never espoused any belief in the state gods, I found the ceremony politically useful over the next month.

"HE TOLD US HE'S GOING to leave Roma, make a show of going into exile at Massilia. But it's all pretense. He's really going to Faesulae to take command of the veterans." Clodius Pulcher said all of this in one breath. He was such a fast talker, and if I leaned too close I was invariably sprayed with his saliva.

It was the first week of November, and he had come to me late at night disguised as a slave wearing a *birrus* that covered him from head to ankles. I could not help but marvel at this young rake's inventiveness.

"But Catilina wants Lentulus and Cethegus to handle things here while he's up north," he quickly added.

I was not at all surprised. Who else but these two?

"Catilina's no fool. He knows that one of us is the informer. When we met tonight at Laeca's I'd take an oath that he deliberately looked at me when he said, 'May the traitor be impaled and gutted.' We all looked at each other after he said it."

"Is that it?" I asked.

"No. He told us to wait until he'd brought the veterans to the Milvian Bridge before we start setting the fires and beginning our attacks. Then he asked for two volunteers to undertake a special mission to the Consul."

"What???"

Clodius seemed amused by my startled reaction. "Yes—he wanted two of us to visit you...."

"When?"

"Tonight, or tomorrow. He wasn't very clear about it, and he didn't say for what purpose." Clodius looked at me mischievously from under his brow. "Anyway, Lucius Vargunteius and Gaius Cornelius volunteered. So then, he dismissed the rest of us and spoke privately with them. By the way, Gaius Cornelius is an equite. Interesting, no?"

I remembered Clodius telling me upon our first meeting that Catilina had put my name at the head of his death list. Naturally, I assumed that Catilina was sending two of his confederates to assassinate me.

After sending Clodius off with instructions to keep me informed, I then told Tiro and Alexio to anticipate certain *visitors* over night. I posted my lictors and bodyguards to cover all entrances to the house as I suspected that Vargunteius and Cornelius might employ slaves or other hired riffraff to break into the house to kill me and others as well.

Terentia got wind of these security precautions. "So," she fumed, "expecting an assassination and I'm the last to know!" She kept you, my son, and your nurse with her in her own bedchamber. I posted one of my bodyguards at her door. To some unknown god, I was grateful that Tullia was married and safely out of harm's way at her husband's house.

Arming ourselves with daggers, Servius and I stayed in the library. We waited in armed vigilance as the night slowly, tediously passed into the pre-dawn twilight. Our vigil ended when my porter came in to tell me two men were in the vestibule requesting an audience with me. He identified them as the senator Lucius Vargunteius and the equite, Gaius Cornelius.

What audacity! I thought. Not by stealth had my would-be assassins come, but instead they were calling like early morning petitioners. So, I told the porter to have the vestibule guards escort them to the atrium.

He departed. But not a moment later he was back with Marcus Caelius. They were both agitated and almost stumbling over each other. "They've gone, Dominus!" the porter exclaimed.

"They were looking about suspiciously," Caelius put in. "They must have suspected a trap. Without a word, they turned, picked up their togas, and bolted out the door."

"Damn them!" I hissed.

"Shall we go after them?" Servius asked, almost dashing toward the door.

I pulled on his arm. "No. Let them go." I sighed, shaking my head with much irritation. "We've blundered ever so stupidly. Our own security scared them off."

"At least you're alive to tell about it!" Servius rebuked me with a hint of sarcasm. "Would they have run off without trying to slit your throat if there were *no guards*?"

"I'd wanted to catch them in the act and then present them as evidence to the Senate." Then it occurred to me that we had an opportunity, as Servius and Caelius looked at me with confused anticipation. I told the porter to find Tiro and bring him to me. As he departed to execute his task, I said to Servius and Caelius, "The Senate will hear about this strange, hurried visit of Vargunteius and Cornelius."

Caelius was still confused. His handsome, refined face bore signs of fatigue and strain, but at my request, he went off to join the other guards in the vestibule. Then Tiro entered and I said to him, "Good Tiro, send out criers to summon the Senate." He turned to go, but as an afterthought, I called to him, "No, wait! We'll meet at Jupiter Stator's Temple instead of the Curia. Alright, that's all. Now go!"

About three hours later, the Senate convened in the designated place. The Temple of Jupiter Stator, Roma's first marble temple, had been built two hundred years ago to commemorate our legions' heroic stand against Roma's Samnite foes. Jupiter, the *Stayer* of defeat was,

I thought, an ideal setting in which to tell the Senate of the near attempt on my life the previous night. In size, it was perhaps a third of the Curia, but its high walls were furnished with wooden benches to accommodate meetings of the Senate.

Tight security was strongly in evidence. I had stationed armed guards along the high stretch of the Sacred Road leading up the Palatine Hill to the temple's entrance as well as within its vestibule. Both the place itself and its assigned sentries made for a highly charged atmosphere as the senators entered and seated themselves.

After the traditional preliminaries, I rose from the presiding consular chair and proceeded to explain how I had foiled an attempt on my life. I even mentioned Vargunteius and Cornelius by name. The Senate did not appear to be roused by this announcement, perhaps because it was another in a line of accusations against the scheming, plotting Catilina. But then, I saw him casually enter the chamber and take a seat as the senators began murmuring and whispering. His very appearance here was an unbearable affront. Changing my tactics, I tore at Catilina directly.

"How long will you try our patience, Catilina?" I began. "You dare show yourself before the Senate when all your designs are fully known. You plot to massacre the Republic's leading men, to lead rebel veterans against our City; and you sent two conspirators to kill me in my own home!"

Catilina shouted back, "Can you produce them or even their weapons? Are you so certain their purpose was to kill you?"

I ignored his remarks and pressed on with my attack. "Time is running out for you, Lucius Catilina. For your insidious plots against the Republic, you deserve nothing less than death, for such would our ancestors have demanded for one so heinous. But until all of the Conscript Fathers are convinced of your guilt, you will live and you will be closely watched."

It was inappropriate and inauspicious to speak the words *dead* or *death* in the Senate. I did so deliberately for Catilina's conspiracy did not deserve oratorical delicacy. As I spoke, Catilina's head sagged deeper and deeper upon his chest. Before long, I could see only the top of his head, his black and gray hair surrounded by the folds of his toga and tunic upon his shoulders. The senators sitting near him rose from their seats and moved away from him as though to escape contamination. Before I was half-way through my tirade, Catilina was isolated on one side of the chamber. I noticed how Caesar and Crassus watched him, both fear and pity showing on their faces.

"Catilina, leave Roma! Your confederates will follow you, brandishing their arms for all to see. Your self-consignment into custody was a sham! I know that Marcus Laeca is one of your conspirators, and you have continued to meet with them at his house. That's where you plotted my death!"

"If the Senate decrees that I should leave Roma," he interrupted raising his head and glaring at me, "then I will! Put it to a vote!"

"Catilina, the Senate's silence affirms their desire that you should leave Roma," I retorted. "Leave now! But leave not as a martyr so as to make me appear as your persecutor. Go as the subversive parricide you truly are. Go to Etruria, join your partner, Manlius and his rebels at Faesulae. I know that this is what you have actually planned to do. The sooner you leave and put yourself at the head of the rebels, the sooner you will convince all citizens of your danger to the Republic."

I paused and looked from Catilina to the bronze effigy of the god before concluding. "May Jupiter Stator and all the gods protect the Republic and punish its enemies!"

An eerie silence filled the chamber as Catilina slowly rose to speak. "Conscript Fathers, all of you know my noble lineage. What would one so rich in patrician forebears hope to gain by subversion against the state? Can the Senate accept these unsubstantiated charges from this *new man,* this *foreigner,* a political upstart claiming to be the guardian of the Republic?" He paused long enough to scan the senators' faces. In particular, his gaze fell upon Caesar and Crassus. "When I saw the consulate, my birthright, denied me and given instead to the unworthy, I took up the cause of the debtors, the landless, the indigent. And for this, the Consul accuses me of sedition! He would lead all of you in hounding me with firebrands as though I were a hunted wolf. I could consume all of you and your fires with blood and total ruination!"

Now, the Senate erupted with cries of "Assassin! Traitor! Villain! Parricide!" But over the din, Catilina shouted, "So be it! As of this day, I retire into exile at Massilia." He paused long enough for his eyes to locate the Princeps Senatus, Catulus. "Quintus Lutatius Catulus, I commend my wife and child to your keeping."

With that, Catilina stormed out of the chamber as the senators continued to shout accusations and deprecations upon him. The oligarchs and Crassus and Caesar sat impassively, but Lentulus Sura and Cethegus rose from their places and followed after him.

By nightfall, we learned that Catilina had in fact left Roma.

Omniscient Narrative

Lucius Catilina rides at the head of seven horsemen along the Cassian Road. Having departed from Roma with Cicero's harangue and the Senate's denunciations ringing in his ears, he has stopped off briefly at Arretium. There, he seeks out six men, intimate friends, debt-ridden rakes, men who have nothing to lose as their lives have already been squandered in profligacy and prodigality. Catilina has been in contact with them, and they are acquainted with his desperate enterprise. It requires little coaxing to persuade them to leave their meaningless existence at Arretium and proceed with him further north to the rebel camp at Faesulae. Catilina holds out to them the prospect of plunder and sudden wealth.

This expectation sustains them the whole way up to their destination. The Cassian Road cuts through Pompeius' praetorian cohorts' encampment. The Magnus has anticipated Catilina's arrival, and he orders his soldiers to allow the party of horsemen to pass unmolested. Outside his command tent, Pompeius watches sullenly as Catilina rides by. Catilina looks back cautiously at Pompeius, one hand gripping his horse's reins while the other grasps his sword hilt.

Pompeius is unnerved at the sight of a silver eagle standard borne by a slave riding behind Catilina. He is further unnerved when the horsemen pass by. Each man has strapped to his back the fasces, the rods and axes of a Roman consul.

"What madness is this?" Pompeius says through clenched teeth.

His legate, Marcus Petreius, is equally stunned: a rebel against Roma assuming the insignia of a consul and having a slave carry a legionary eagle. "Imperator, we must stop them!"

"No. No, let them go. Assemble the men to see this," Pompeius orders.

The rebels recognize Catilina from their camp's ramparts. Thunderous cheers greet him as he and his men enter the camp. Gaius Manlius salutes him and then, at Catilina's order, he assembles the veterans. Catilina mounts the rampart where he can be clearly seen both by Manlius' men and by Pompeius' legionaries. The Greek slave, Demetrios, holds Marius' silver eagle just behind Catilina. Manlius remembers it and the pledge that he and Catilina had made on it.

Catilina's six unofficial lictors flank him on the rampart. They hold the fasces upon their left shoulders. Publius Furius, Titus Annius, and Gaius Flaminius, Sullan colonists at Arretium, are thrilled by the military panoply presented by the rebel formation and Pompeius' cohorts. Marcus Tongilius, Lucius Publicius, and Quintus Minucius look at their friend, their partner in debauchery, and marvel at the gamble he has taken.

Catilina holds up his arms and the rebels' cheering ceases. He speaks for both his own followers and for Pompeius' benefit. "Soldiers of Roma, I, Lucius Sergius Catilina, have taken the title and fasces of a Roman consul. This office has been denied me several times, but I assume it now so that I may lead you to seek justice and reparation from a government that has wronged you." Then, directly to Pompeius' legionaries, he offers, "Any of you under the command of Pompeius Magnus are welcome to join us."

Pompeius Magnus, standing at the head of the cohorts' formation, has been listening intently. He calls out in his most stentorian military voice, "Lucius Sergius Catilina, you are a traitor to your country, and all who follow you are traitors," and then to his own men, "and any who would even consider such villainy are also traitors." Turning back to the rebel rampart, he continues, "All who have joined you, Lucius Catilina, are free to return to their homes. But you and Centurion Gaius Manlius must surrender and return with me to Roma. You want justice, Catilina, and I promise you shall have it."

From the rebel camp to Pompeius' formation there is complete silence, like the silence before battle. Catilina motions to two veterans standing on the rampart. "Give the Imperator our answer!" At the very same instant, Legate Petreius orders a squad of soldiers forward to protect Pompeius with their shields. Years of combat have honed the legate's perceptions. Suddenly two javelins are hurled from the ramparts. They pierce the ground only inches away from Pompeius' feet.

Cicero's Respublica

A few days later, having received the latest dispatch from Gnaeus Pompeius, I went to the Forum and addressed the assembled citizens from the Rostra. I told them that Catilina's departure had not been into exile, but instead to the rebel camp at Faesulae. For this, all loyal citizens should have been grateful because now Catilina was openly the Republic's enemy. He had taken the title and fasces of a Roman consul, in flagrant violation of the constitution.

I announced that the Senate, upon receiving Pompeius' dispatch, had declared Catilina, Manilius, and their followers to be public enemies. I urged all of Catilina's confederates and parasites to leave Roma and join their leader in open defiance of the Republic so that all would know them for the traitors they were.

There was scattered heckling and cat-calling from some of the coarser elements in the crowd, probably Catilina's supporters or general trouble-making riffraff. I never had much regard for people in the mass, and by that time, the general citizenry, the very lowest common denominator, through indolence, the dole, and unemployment, had degenerated into such a disreputable state that I privately called them *the dregs of Romulus* and *Romulus' feces*.

Continuing my address, I characterized Catilina's followers as consisting of six groups. Patrician and plebeian nobility, riddled with debt and hoping for revolution to liberate themselves from their creditors, were his main strength. Then there were the politically ambitious but financially insolvent who aimed to secure by revolution the offices that they coveted but could not obtain by legal canvassing. The bankrupt veterans of Sulla's regime made up the third group, and these hoped for new opportunities for havoc and plunder. Next, there were debt-ridden political and social derelicts from all over Italia, and these were not much better off than assassins, parricides, outlaws, renegade shepherds and fugitive slaves. And at the very bottom of the heap of seditionists were Catilina's intimates, perverted libertines and rakes.

Again, I urged those conspirators still remaining in the City to flee to Catilina's camp, for they would surely be discovered and destroyed if they lingered among loyal citizens. Finally, I called on the citizens to guard their homes and their Republic against traitors, and I called upon Jupiter and all the gods to safeguard Roma.

When I went home, I was accompanied by a great throng of senators, led by the oligarchs, and equites, among whom were Atticus and the prominent bankers, Publius Considius, Gaius Oppius, and Lucius Balbus. To have had the joint support of these two orders of propertied citizens was the fulfillment of my long cherished goal for the Republic: a concord of the orders, senators and equites combined to forestall civil commotion and maintain the status quo. Maintaining this *concordia ordinum* would be crucial in bringing about Catilina's ultimate destruction and in preventing any subsequent popularist agitation against the harmony and tranquility of the Republic.

CATILINA HAD BEEN GONE FOR a week. Stalemate prevailed up in Etruria, as Pompeius reported. The levying of troops continued under Antonius and Metellus Celer. Loyal veterans from lower Etruria had augmented Pompeius' forces to about seven thousand men. I hoped that they would not have to be used in violence against their countrymen.

One of Pompeius' dispatches reported that slaves from Arretium and Faesulae, numbering upwards of five hundred men, had tried to enlist in Catilina's rebel army. Catilina made a great show of rejecting them. Standing atop his camp's ramparts, he told the fugitives that his struggle was for the rights of Roman citizens, *not* for the emancipation of slaves. Catilina ordered them to return to their masters without delay before their escape would be noticed and they would then be subjected to severe chastisement.

The runaway slaves did as they were bidden. I was relieved to realize that Catilina's attempted revolution was not as all-encompassing as it might have been. However, Clodius informed me that Lentulus Sura was angry that Catilina had not exploited the opportunity of employing slaves to augment the rebel forces.

If Roma were a living, breathing entity, then in those days she lived and breathed ever so anxiously. Each day brought with it the fear of turmoil, of arson, of vile assassination. That the conspirators attempted no violence was due more than anything else to dissension between

Lentulus Sura and Gaius Cethegus, or so Publius Clodius led me to believe.

Omniscient Narrative

At Praecia's house in the Caelian district, an impromptu meeting of Catilina's chief men takes place late at night in early November. A starlit sky and a full moon cast light through the skylight of Praecia's atrium. A few small oil lamps burn and provide additional illumination. Lentulus Sura and Caius Cethegus, conspirators in a desperate enterprise, want as little light as possible to fall upon them, lest their plans should be seen and conveyed beyond the atrium's four walls. Praecia and Sempronia, vain to their very cores, accept the dim oil light and the natural moonlight and starlight as flattering to their painted faces and figure-fitting garments.

Praecia has dismissed her slaves and household servants for the night. She and her guests have been well furnished with a tray of wine, water, and assorted fruits and sweetmeats. But the delicacies have not been touched. Though they speak in hushed tones, they do not disguise their agitated edginess.

"We'll wait," Lentulus says most emphatically. "When Catilina has brought the veterans to the Milvian Bridge, we'll put the word out to ignite the fires in the Carinae, the Forum, and the cattle market, and the Palatine, and then...."

"Why must we wait?" Cethegus cuts in.

"Because Catilina so ordered."

Cethegus gesticulates nervously. "He's been up in Etruria for a week. *What* is *he* waiting for? The whole City is getting tighter each day."

Lentulus agrees. "But he'll get word to us when...."

"How? With Pompeius blocking him? With more government troops going up to Faesulae almost every day?" Cethegus leans forward in his chair so that he is almost nose to nose with Lentulus. "But if we commence our operations here—*now!*—some of Pompeius' troops may have to be sent to Roma. That'll take pressure off Catilina so that he can break through and link up with us."

Lentulus shakes his head and is poised to respond, but Praecia's mouth and tongue are faster. "Is it totally impossible for messengers to travel between Faesulae and Roma?"

Sempronia answers. "Probably not—not if they're clever and if they can negotiate around the Cassian Road."

"All the more reason for us to wait for Catilina." Lentulus pulls away from Cethegus to face Sempronia, seated to his left. "Those veterans of Sulla know the back-roads and sheepfolds of Etruria. They'll have no trouble going around Pompeius. So, we'll wait!"

Cethegus is still not convinced. "We're wasting time. Government troops and Cicero's security are increasing, getting tighter, more expansive, just like a fisherman's dragnet."

"Cethegus," Praecia pulls on her lover's arm, "could you send a messenger to Catilina, someone who can detour the Cassian Road?"

"I suppose so, but why? For what purpose?"

"Let him know how bad things are for us here. Tell him to move on Roma soon or we might be finished."

"No, Praecia!" Lentulus counters. "I say we wait until Catilina sends word that he's on the march."

Cethegus again puts himself nose-to-nose with Lentulus. "Praecia's right. Remember, Cicero has an informer in our group. He *knows* who we are, and he's been urging us to leave Roma and go to Catilina. What's in Cicero's mind, eh? How long before he sends his guards and lictors to drag us out of our beds and arrest us? Once that's done, *who* will give the orders for our freedmen and slaves to set the fires and kill Cicero and the oligarchs and magistrates, eh?"

"Lentulus, we cannot wait indefinitely for Catilina to make up his mind." This is from Sempronia, looking directly into his eyes. Then turning to the other, she says, "Cethegus, we cannot be rash and impetuous and act on our own without Catilina and the Etrurians."

Lentulus throws up his hands in an exasperated gesture. Sempronia considers the dilemma for a moment. She voices her idea. "Send a messenger to Catilina by an indirect route. Tell him that we must act in concert by a certain date—I don't know, say the Ides of November. Give him a specific date by which to move, or else all is lost."

Cethegus erupts. "*Time*! Time again! A messenger—by an indirect route would need *time* to get to Catilina and yet more time to return!"

Lentulus now exercises his rank. "I'm praetor and the only magistrate among us. It's *my* decision to make and...."

Cethegus cuts him off, "Tortoises move faster than you decide. We cannot...."

"And you, Cethegus, are more frantic than Aesop's hare!" Sempronia is sufficiently in tune with Greek fables to connect Lentulus with the slow, lethargic tortoise suggested by Cethegus and the rash, impetuous hare personified by Praecia's lover. "The two of you must compromise, but don't discount Catilina from your calculations."

"We need an equalizer," Praecia suggests.

"What do you mean?" Cethegus is puzzled.

"Something to bridge the gap between us in the City, and Catilina and the veterans at Faesulae; something to give us long-range striking power." Praecia purses her lips and looks over at Sempronia.

"Like mounted troops?" Lentulus speculates.

"I think that's exactly what Praecia means," Sempronia observes presciently. "I didn't know we had an Amazon among us."

The two women exchange sly, lupine smiles, and Lentulus and Cethegus regard each other with smoldering resentment.

Cicero's Respublica

IRONICALLY, AS CLODIUS REPORTED DISAGREEMENT between the conspiracy's leaders, I had to contend with dissension within the government. One day, not long after Catilina's departure, Catulus and Cato approached me like a pair of greedy procurers.

"Consul, you actually know who's in Catilina's group?" Catulus asked.

I told him I did, and then he caustically hurled his next question.

"Then why haven't you arrested them? You've been given the Ultimate Decree. You've driven out Catilina. Yet, you won't move against the traitors here in Roma!"

"Just so!" Cato affirmatively put in.

I met their challenge head-on. "You saw how I dared Catilina to come out openly against the Republic? Well then, I'll tease, cajole, and harangue them into making some blunder in which they'll be trapped and caught. Arrest them now and all we can do is charge them with conspiracy against the state."

Cato blustered, "Isn't that sufficient grounds for their arrest?"

Turning to him, I asked, "Could you even bring Catilina to court? Just as he ignored your summons, so will the others. We're dealing here with men—and women—who have nothing to lose. In time, they'll make their move and I'll be ready for them?"

"But Consul," Cato objected, "the year is almost over. You'll be out of office in a few weeks. Then...."

"Then I trust your protégé, Marcus Bibulus, will deal with them as decisively as I would. And let's hope that Gaius Caesar doesn't hamper him."

Catulus chuckled at this. "Perhaps we might help each other. If we accuse Catilina's chief supporters, would you back us?"

I affected confusion, but I knew exactly whom Catulus meant.

"You see," he continued, "we have *our own* informer, at least that's what we're calling him. He'll accuse 'Money-Bags' and 'Cock-Eagle' of aiding and abetting Catilina. We all know they've supported him in the past. All that's needed is for you to press the charges before the Senate. The Republic will be relieved to be rid of them. Without them, perhaps Catilina's other conspirators will be discouraged and they'll leave too. Consul, you've started the play by driving out Catilina. Now, let's finish it by driving out the others."

I considered Catulus' personal animosity to Crassus and Caesar, an animosity shared by Cato. Despite the old oligarch's exalted status in the Senate, I refused to allow him and his young Stoical fire-brand to steer me off my original course.

"Gentlemen," I began after a moment's hesitation, "these two men have brought me evidence against Catilina. Whatever their connection with him may have been, it no longer exists. Catulus, I will not betray them to vindicate your defeat by Caesar in the pontifical election, or to help you settle old scores with Crassus. Nor will I help you, Cato, to vent your spite upon Caesar because of..."—I chose my words carefully—"certain innuendoes." I dared not mention the rumors that Caesar was the lover of Servilia, Cato's half-sister. But I inferred that he understood correctly.

They were both taken aback by my blunt speech. Catulus muttered, "The Chief Pontificate should have been *mine*! You know *that*! All Roma knows it!"

I nodded. "But it doesn't matter now. He bought more votes than you."

"You mean *Crassus* bought them!"

"The same thing," I sighed.

Cato broke in, "Between the two of them, the whole Republic is up for sale. 'Money-Bags' puts out the sesterces and 'Cock-Eagle' puts up his rod!"

Such vulgarity was typical of Cato, though he was also known as a prude. I replied in kind, but without being very specific. "Marcus Cato, if you want to chastise Caesar for his peccadilloes, then you can accuse him of immorality in the civil court. But don't throw Catilina at him to soothe your fraternal sensibilities."

Cato fumed, but he did not reply. Catulus jerked back his head as a signal. They turned to go, but over his shoulder, Catulus gave me a stern warning. "I hope you'll show more courage and enterprise in the days ahead."

A few days later, one Lucius Vettius, a senator of quaestorian rank, a slight, insignificant man, accused both Crassus and Caesar of conspiring with Catilina to overthrow the government. In so charging them, Vettius had to incriminate himself as a former member of Catilina's gang. But Clodius had never mentioned him to me. He may very well have been a conspirator and perhaps there were others as well, yet unnamed.

I noticed how the oligarchs, especially Catulus, smirked triumphantly at Vettius. He was their pawn, their *informer*. I was prepared to speak on behalf of Crassus and Caesar, for I could not afford to alienate them, even though they formerly had been Catilina's associates. But before I could speak, Crassus had indignantly risen to deny and denounce the accusation. He spoke briefly but passionately, calling Vettius the tool of envious, petty men who were too cowardly to accuse him directly. "I have far too much invested in the Republic to plot its destruction," he announced before walking out of the Curia. After that day, he did not attend Senate meetings for the short balance of the year.

Caesar's response was equally impassioned but far more theatrical. Addressing the Senate, he claimed that the dignity of the Chief Pontificate was assailed by the base, groundless charges. He said that I could be called on to confirm his assistance in exposing Catilina's conspiracy. Finally, he approached Vettius directly, rebuked him for showing disrespect to the Chief Pontiff and consult-elect, and then he seized the little man by his coarse hair and dragged him, screaming in protest, from the Curia. Over Vettius' protests, Caesar declared that one so base as to accuse the Chief Pontiff of the Republic did not deserve to sit among the Conscript Fathers of the Senate.

Many of the senators—Caesar's friends, no doubt—laughed at this comical display. Others—in particular the oligarchs—sat in frozen horror at Caesar's bold affront to the Senate's dignity.

Upon my motion, the Senate dismissed Vettius' charges as groundless. No doubt, far too many senators were under obligation to Crassus, both financially and politically. That was that, though I was certain that I had not endeared myself to the oligarchs.

In retrospect, it would have been far better for the Republic had I been less protective of Crassus and Caesar.

As Servius Sulpicius and I were leaving the Curia, a senator, Quintus Fabius Maximus Sanga, asked to speak privately with me. He said he had urgent information.

Fabius was the son of Quintus Fabius Maximus Allobrogicus, surnamed honorifically because of his conquest of the Transalpine Gauls nearly sixty years before my consulate. Fabius was the principal patron of the Allobroges, a position he had inherited from his famous father. He took this quite seriously, for he knew that in their eyes he *was* Roma. He could make the difference between the tribe's peaceful submission to the Republic's policies or their recalcitrance and rebellion.

I believe Fabius was about ten years my senior, but he had never ascended higher than the rank of aedile. He bore a striking resemblance to contemporary busts of his illustrious father. As he was known for his honesty and loyalty, I had no reason to doubt him when he told me that he had urgent news for my attention.

"Consul, you may not be aware that three Allobrogian envoys have lately arrived in the City," he said. "They are waiting to be received by the Senate."

I admitted that I had heard of their arrival. Fabius took a deep breath, looked about the Curia's foyer to make sure we were not being seen or overheard, and continued in an intense, but mincing whisper. "They sought me out to tell me that... certain men have approached them... with a view to enlisting their tribe's help in a particular enterprise."

"These *certain* men?" I inquired.

Fabius answered as though checking his recollection. "Publius Umbrennus, a Gallic freedman to Lentulus Sura; also, Gaius Cethegus, Marcus Caeparius, Gaius Capito, and Publius Statilius."

Recognizing these men as Catilina's conspirators, I inferred the enterprise for which they had suborned the Gauls.

"The Allobroges have many grievances," Fabius continued, "especially against the last few governors. These men know of their discontent. They offered help if the Allobroges will foment rebellion in the province and provide horsemen for Lentulus, Cethegus and for...."

"Catilina?"

Fabius was taken aback by my anticipation, but he nodded in agreement.

"What else?" I asked.

"The envoys say they want peace with Roma," Fabius insisted. "They're willing to expose traitors in return for concessions from the Senate. They say they've been fleeced by both equites and governors, and they've nothing but contempt for them. But if the Senate gives them relief and justice, they'll guarantee their tribe's loyalty."

This was an opportunity that could not be ignored.

"Fabius Sanga, you are a true patriot of the Republic." I said this while grasping his arm in political fellowship. "Tell the Gauls I'll intercede on their behalf with the Senate. But you *must* bring them to me. If they'll cooperate, we can set a trap for these traitors, catch and expose them. If they do this, the Republic will be forever grateful to them."

Fabius nodded intently. "I assured them of as much, Consul."

Several hours later, well past dusk, Fabius brought the three envoys to my house. They were gray-beards wearing Gallic britches and brightly colored cloaks. After Fabius' introductions, we spoke in Greek, for many of the Transalpine tribes had adopted this tongue from the Greek colonists at Massilia and Narbo on the coast.

Ambrax, apparently the senior of the group, confirmed all that Fabius had already told me. In addition, he told me that Lentulus Sura had confided in them his belief in an old oracular prophecy. According to it, three Cornelii were to have had the mastery of Roma. Lucius Cornelius Sulla, the Dictator had been the first. Then his rival, Lucius Cornelius Cinna, had attained control of the state. Lentulus reckoned that as he was of the Cornelian gens, he would be the prophecy's third master.

I knew that Lentulus Sura put much stock in prophecies, portents, and such. He probably assumed that the Gauls did also, for he was apparently playing on their superstitions.

Then, Bracco admitted that Lentulus and his conspirators were preparing to set fires in different City wards on December seventeenth—the feast of the Saturnalia. During the confusion of the fires, the conspirators, their hirelings and slaves, were going to kill the chief men of Roma. Bracco explained that the conspirators had chosen the Saturnalia for their attacks because they expected the City's defenses to be relaxed owing to the festivities.

There were inherently dangerous aspects about this holiday owing to the tradition of masters trading places with their slaves. Add to this the horrific element of organized incendiarism and methodical murders, and the result could be complete anarchy and chaos. These ruminations took hold of my mind when the third envoy spoke.

Celtillus mentioned that the conspirators wanted the Allobroges to supply a force of horsemen for Catilina's army in Etruria and another for use in Roma itself. In return, the conspirators promised that they would secure Senatorial recognition of the Allobroges as the chief tribe of the Transalpina, friends and allies instead of *subjects* of Roma.

I could not help but admire the terrific brilliance with which the conspirators had hatched the plot. Instead of one day of token freedom on the Saturnalia, the conspirators were probably offering their slaves much more if they did the vile work of arson and murder. They understood all too malevolently the demoralizing effects of widespread incendiarism and violence on a populace living mostly in wooden and stone dwellings and routinely lacking anything approaching a city fire and police force. But most frightening of all was their attempt to make common cause with Roma's traditional foes—the Gauls. And there was I—negotiating with them.

Resolutely, Ambrax declared, "Consul, we've shown good faith in confiding these things to our patron and in coming here. We expect you Romans, you men of the she-wolf, to show good faith to the Allobroges."

I gave them my pledge that their people's grievances would be heard and redressed by the Senate. But first, the evil, insidious plot against the Republic would have to be destroyed—with their further assistance. They agreed to cooperate fully.

So, I instructed them to obtain signed letters from Lentulus and the others on the pretext that their people's chiefs would want written proof of the Romans' fidelity before sending horsemen and committing the tribe to war.

The envoys eyed one another and tacitly agreed. Then Ambrax mentioned that the conspirators were to have Publius Umbrennus conduct them to Catilina's camp at Faesulae. I asked when they were to depart, and Celtillus answered, "In about a week... on December second, well after sunset." He said the conspirators preferred that they leave at night so as to attract less attention.

"By what route?" I asked them, though logic and geography provided a ready answer.

Fabius answered for them. "By the Cassian Road... northward across the Milvian Bridge."

I had inferred correctly. "Good. Now when they've given you their letters, tell Fabius, and then we'll speak again. Remember—a signed and sealed letter from each of them—from Lentulus, from Cethegus, from Capito, Caeparius, and Statilius. Don't delay! Time is running out!"

Before the Gauls departed, Ambrax remembered a name that he had heard the conspirators mention: Publius Clodius.

"What about him?" I asked."Was he with the others when you spoke with them?"

"No," Bracco replied. "They seem not to like him. They spoke ill of him. But they want to send him with us to their leader's camp."

I told them not to be concerned about him. Then, the Gauls and Fabius took their leave.

Two days passed before they returned. In the interim, I confided all this to Servius, Atticus, and Caelius. Then, I brought two praetors, Lucius Flaccus and Gaius Pomptinus, into our circle of confidences. With Fabius and the Gauls, we took counsel and set a trap for the conspirators. I hoped the envoys would be true to their word.

I HAD GIVEN UP ON Publius Clodius because, though he continued to serve in my bodyguard, he had not passed on to me any significant news of Catilina or the conspirators. Then, very much to my surprise, he came to me after dusk on December second, the feast of the *Bona Dea*, the Good Goddess. Terentia had already left for the Regia where she, as a consul's wife, was to preside over the exclusively female rites. Tullia and Pompeia were to be there along with the invited women folk of senators and magistrates.

Clodius wore the slave's disguise, an ankle-length hooded *birrus*. Strangely though, his eyelids were heavily darkened with kohl like an actor about to perform a woman's role on stage. However, I didn't think of it at the time because I was so preoccupied about the Gauls and their imminent departure from Roma. So, I assumed that Clodius' eye make-up was nothing more than another eccentric Pulcher affectation.

He told me he was making his final report. Lentulus and Cethegus were sending him to Catilina's camp with certain Allobrogian envoys. He was surprised and I think a bit disappointed to hear that I already knew about the envoys and their contact with the conspirators.

"Go with them," I urged. "Find out what's going on within Catilina's camp,"

He laughed sarcastically. "I won't live to report *that*! They're sending me up there to be killed! Don't you see, Consul? They're on to me!"

"But *how*?" I demanded.

"Too many missed opportunities when I might've assassinated you—that's *how*! If I wasn't trying to kill you, they surmised that I was informing on them." He laughed that high-pitched, nasal horse whinny of a laugh. "Either Lentulus' freedman or the Gauls themselves or their attendants will kill me once we're outside the City; or perhaps they'll let Catilina do it once we've arrived at the camp. Now do you understand?"

I was not prepared to tell him of my plans. Yet, I tried to persuade him that he need not fear to go with the Gauls.

"Are you *mad*? Or do you take me for a simpleton? I'm not going anywhere with the Gauls, not for Lentulus, Catilina, or *you*! I'm going underground, into hiding until it's safe for me to come out!"

I offered him the protection of my house, but he refused. When I offered him more money, he roared a contemptuous laugh. "*More money??*! You've given me *nothing*—not as much as a copper *ass*!" Then, after composing himself, he looked directly into my face, smiled, and said, "Good fortune to you, Cicero. I'm off to make my own. Farewell!"

With that he was gone. But before long, Publius Clodius Pulcher would be back to wreak turmoil and havoc upon my life.

Our plans had been well laid. I had no doubt of the loyalty and reliability of Flaccus and Pomptinus. They were to lead a party of armed men in an ambush on the Gallic envoys as they and Umbrennus were crossing the Milvian Bridge. I was less certain about the Gauls. It was agreed that for appearance's sake, they would offer token resistance. I hoped they would not double-cross us, fight their way across the bridge, and run like the Furies to their own land.

Waiting for news of the ambuscade, I paced in the library like a caged animal, now and then looking over volumes of Plato and Aristotle. But the comfort I sought from them eluded me. I had a sense of foreboding, of some imminent disaster that was to befall me. Perhaps Publius Clodius Pulcher's visit had irritated me more than I realized.

Despite the guards stationed in and around the house, I felt very much alone. Terentia was attending the Good Goddess mysteries at the Regia. You, my son, were asleep in your nursery, your nurse sitting near you. For some reason or other, Atticus and Servius delayed in coming. I was becoming annoyed at their tardiness when Tiro appeared at the door and announced that Clodia Pulchra Metella had arrived.

Omniscient Narrative

The purple-blue star-lit December sky is clear and cloudless. Evening has brought a short respite from the winter rains. A crescent moon overlooks the arched stone and wooden Milvian Bridge spanning the Tiber River just beyond the Janiculum Hill and Mars Field.

A party of horsemen approaches the southern side of the bridge. Some of them carry pine torches to light their way. All of them are hooded to keep out the winter chill. In the van rides Publius Umbrennus, the Gallic freedman of Praetor Lentulus Sura. Behind him ride the Allobrogian envoys, Ambrax, Bracco, and Celtillus and their attendants—all together a party of about a dozen men.

They enter upon the bridge, their horses' hooves clattering upon its wooden planks and cobblestones. When they are at mid-span, torches appear at the farther end. Alarmed, Umbrennus halts the cavalcade. A stern commanding voice rings out. "Stop where you are, Gauls! I am Praetor Lucius Valerius Flaccus. I arrest all of you in the name of the Senate and People of Roma!"

Umbrennus turns his horse about and rushes for the southern side of the bridge. Praetor Flaccus, his lictors and armed guards quickly move onto the bridge. At the same instant, from the near side, Praetor Titus Pomptinus and his lictors and guards lunge out of hiding and storm onto the bridge. Realizing they are trapped, Umbrennus and two of the attendants draw their swords and attempt to fight their way out. Praetor Pomptinus calls out to them, "Dismount and surrender! You cannot escape!"

The envoys offer no resistance. They and most of their attendants dismount and stand by their horses, holding their reins with one hand and holding the other aloft in a gesture of submission. The praetors' guards overpower and disarm Umbrennus and the two resisting attendants. Troops of horsemen from each end converge on the center of the Milvian Bridge. Horses are brought forward for the praetors. The lictors assist them in mounting.

"Ready?" Flaccus barks. "Alright, now let's take them to Consul Cicero."

The mounted government troops, the praetors, their lictors and guards escort the Gallic party back into the City. Umbrennus and the two resisters have been bound and gagged to preclude any escape attempt. Likewise, the envoys and their attendants are made to walk alongside their horses. It may take them longer to reach the consul's house this way, but the praetors are taking no chances of losing any of their quarry. Praetor Pomptinus sends two guards ahead to bring notice to Consul Cicero of their success.

Cicero's <u>Respublica</u>

"What does she want?" I snapped at him. But Tiro was spared answering my question when *Juno of the Black Eyes* came into the room as though she were in her own house. *What presumption!* I thought. Tiro bowed gracefully to her and to me after I dismissed him.

"You are welcome to my home, Clodia." I tried to be gracious to her, but in all truth her arrival surprised and intrigued and discomforted me all at the same time.

She removed her veil, letting her raven-black hair shine in the oil lamplight. Her eyes—those ebony pools of inviting yet strangely sinister light—sparkled as she smiled and cooed a captivating reply. "I trust you are not terribly occupied, Consul."

"I'm at your service, Clodia," I assured her.

"*Are* you? That's good of you, and generous of you, too." She moved closer to me, increasing my discomfiture. "I want you to know that I'm annoyed at what I hope was only an oversight on your wife's part."

"*Oversight?*" I repeated, trying to recoil.

"Yes. You see neither I nor my sisters were invited to participate in tonight's Good Goddess mysteries."

"I'm sorry," I told her, "but I know nothing about it. Quite frankly, I've more important things on my mind."

Clodia kept moving in on me like a lupa stalking her prey, all the while leering at me with a predatory lasciviousness.

"Have you any idea what the women do at the Regia?" she teased. "In so many ways they celebrate their subjection to men and their bonds of womanhood—subjection and bonds." She paused and slid her tongue across her teeth. "You know, we could have our own rites here. Does that appeal to you, Marcus Cicero?"

She pushed herself up against me so that I could feel her firm bosom against my togated chest. She aroused me, and yet she repelled me. The thought of taking her then and there raced through my mind. Why not? She was offering herself like a bowl of ripe fruit, a cup of honeyed wine. Take her! Betray Terentia? No! Betray Metellus Celer? Would it matter to him? How many lovers had they both kept from each other?

Was not the young poet of her household her latest conquest? So then, Marcus, take her and have done with it. She wants me! You want her! Take her—on the table—clear your books and scrolls and tablets or take her into a side room. But do it now!

And Clodia's face and Clodia's body and Clodia's aura—were all so alluring and inviting.

Omniscient Narrative

At the same time that the praetors apprehend the Gauls on the Milvian Bridge, the Good Goddess rites are in progress at the Regia.

The Regia is surrounded by Caesar's hired guards. It is illuminated from without by torches and from within by numerous olive oil lamps. The litters of the attending women have been parked off the Sacred Way and are watched by their bearers. They sit and squat and stand about several charcoal fires, warming themselves against the chill night air.

Within the Regia, every statue of a male deity has been draped or removed and closeted; for the rites of the Good Goddess, known to the Romans as the Bona Dea, celebrated every December second, either in the Regia or in the house of the presiding consul, are strictly closed to males of all stations of Roman society.

The Bona Dea may well be the equivalent of the Greeks' Agathe Theos, and she is related to Hygieia, the goddess of Health, and to Damia. Usually, the Romans' proper name for her is Fauna. There is a shrine to her situated on the *saxum*, the sacred precipice on the Aventine Hill where it is believed that the City's founder, Romulus, had first taken the auspices.

On this night, the Regia is alive with the cackling, giggling, and energy of several score of Roman women, old, young, middle-aged, mothers, grand-mothers, daughters, sisters, wives of Roma's senators and equites.

A group of musicians—female, of course—is admitted through the main portal, escorted through the vestibule, and into the expansive atrium. They are young women, dressed in matching outfits of red, long-sleeved, ankle-length stolas girded at the waist with leather bands, and gold-trimmed sandals. Each carries an instrument—a lyre, a sistrum, an aulos, cymbals, and one curious-looking musician carries a small hand drum.

Very likely these musicians have performed at many a Bona Dea night. They are not at all fazed by the goings-on; except for the curly blonde one with the drum. This one conspicuously stares about at the vine and laurel and flower bedecked atrium and is taken with the statue of the goddess, undraped for this one special occasion each year.

The Bona Dea stands upright in bronzed glory on a pedestal of marble. She is life sized. Her abundant hair descends to her waist. She is broad of hips and broad of shoulders. Her breasts are large, appetizing spheres which she cups upward in her hands. Her legs are like the trunks of fig trees joining together in a pubic triangle, rich, vibrant, fecund like Egypt's Nile Delta. The goddess' eyes stare blankly straight ahead on either side of a large, pendulous nose above full, voluptuous lips.

Facing the Bona Dea from the opposite end of the atrium is the Roman phallic god, Priapus. Like Fauna, he has also been brought out of storage for these annual rites. His humongous, erect organ has gained the rapt attention of so many of the women this night. They have touched it for good luck and fertility, laughed at its exaggerated dimensions, and solemnly prayed to it.

The curly blonde musician has showed a most peculiar fascination with both deities. And she has been noticed by a maid-servant named Abra. Abra has been ladling out wine from a large terra cotta jar. However, the tipsy and giddy women who shamelessly partake of it call it "milk" and its container they call the "honey pot." Abra beckons to another maid-servant to relieve her at the "honey pot" so that she may follow the blonde.

The blonde has been looking in on various rooms adjoining the atrium. In one, she sees a nubile girl held over a matron's lap and a pair of bare-breasted women lash her back with strips of animal hide. The matron intones, "May Fauna grant you health and fertility, my child!" In another, a circle of women, their hands locked together, swirl ecstatically as intoxicating incense is burned in each corner of the room. In yet another room, Terentia, Consul Cicero's wife, presides over what appears to be a group prayer session as she leads the women in a methodical litany of petitions for blessings and favors from the Bona Dea.

All the while, Abra has been watching the blonde and suppressing the urge to laugh aloud. Blondie almost seems taken by the sight of Pompeia, the Chief Pontiff's wife. She's an attractive specimen of womanhood. Pompeia and her mother-in-law, Aurelia, the Chief Pontiff's mother, stand on either side of Terentia.

Abra starts to approach the musician on the pretext that she has become separated from her colleagues. She stops, however, and bows politely as the Chief Vestal Licinia and several other Vestals cross her path. Abra counts them as they pass. They number five, and she knows that one Vestal must be on duty at the hearth fire. The Vestals enter the room where Pompeia, Aurelia, and Terentia are now about to offer a sacrifice at a shrine.

Blondie also watches them, clutching the drum ever so tightly. Suddenly, a hand with sharp nails grabs Blondie's arm. "What happened to your girls?" Abra asks. "Don't you want to play your little drum? I'll help you find them. And if we can't, why, we could always play together, no? Come, come sweetheart—come with me!"

Blondie is alarmed. This encounter should not have happened. Abra begins to pull on the musician's arm. Instinctively, Blondie pulls away. "No... no, I don't think so!"

Abra is dashed by the voice. There is a deep though nasal quality about it that does not jibe with the rest of the musician's appearance. She reaches out for Blondie and notices this time the muscular feel of the arm.

"Curse you, bitch! Stay away from me!"

The voice is distinctively masculine!

Abra cries out, "A man! A man! Profanation! Sacrilege! A man! A man!"

There is pandemonium. Women and girls are screaming in the atrium and from the adjoining rooms. Blondie is beset by the women as he tries to run for the exit. They pull at him, scratch him, slap and punch him. He sees Pompeia, Aurelia, and Terentia enter the atrium. He recognizes the Vestal Fabia, the Consul's sister-in-law, just as a powerful hand pulls the blonde wig from his head.

"Clodius! Clodius Pulcher!" The nearest women shriek. "Profaner! Sacrilege! Sacrilege!"

The intruder has been knocked to the tiled floor, the women kicking him with well-aimed sandaled feet. He sees the Consul's wife and the

Chief Pontiff's mother and wife looking at him and by their expressions he knows that they have recognized him.

He rises frantically and enraged hands pull the red stola from his body revealing, unmistakably, a man. Luckily, the path to the vestibule is unobstructed. He bolts through it like an athletic champion. The female janitor at the front door offers no resistance as she is too shocked by the sight of a naked man running head long. The intruder disappears into the Sacred Way. The litter bearers and Caesar's guards imagine that the naked, bleeding man running off into the darkness must be a demonic apparition.

In the atrium, screams have given way to tears—tears of anger and outrage, and for some, of amusement and laughter. Aurelia, as Chief Pontiff Caesar's mother, seizes the initiative ahead of her daughter-in-law. "Women of Roma, the rites of the Bona Dea have been profaned by the presence of a man! All traces of his presence here must be obliterated, and then the rites and sacrifices must be repeated!"

Murmurs of assent as well as dissent float across the room. "And I promise you, women of Roma, that this profanation will be brought to the attention of the Chief Pontiff and to the Senate!" Aurelia sees approval in the expressions of Licinia, Fabia, and Terentia; but there is resentment in Pompeia's eyes.

Cicero's Republica

"Dominus!" Tiro called from the corridor. "The praetors Flaccus and Pomptinus have sent word. Their mission is accomplished."

I extricated myself from Clodia and headed for the atrium. But her taunting, teasing, tempting face remained fixed in my mind.

Atticus and Servius arrived just as I was hearing the report of the praetors' messengers. The planned ambush had indeed succeeded. We had not long to wait before Flaccus and Pomptinus arrived with their quarry. The Gallic envoys appeared satisfied with their efforts. Ambrax handed me a satchel. Upon opening it, I found it contained letters from the conspirators. The Gauls had kept their word. My fears about their loyalty had been unfounded.

Praetor Flaccus gave me a brief report. His and Pomptinus' men had closed in on the Gauls from both sides of the Milvian Bridge. Contrary to what we had expected, the Gauls did not put up even a sham fight but surrendered promptly. Concluding, Flaccus said, "Consul, We've brought you a bonus." He pushed forward Umbrennus and two others who were bound and gagged. At my command, their gags were removed.

I said to Umbrennus, "You are freedman to Lentulus Sura." Reluctantly, he nodded. Then, I realized what Flaccus had meant by *bonus*. Standing next to the Gallic freedman were the senators, Gaius Capito and Marcus Caeparius, dressed in Gallic britches and cloaks.

"These two were trying to pass as torchbearers," Pomptinus explained. "They tried to make a run for it but we caught them."

I looked at both men, pronounced their names, and shook my head in dismay. But neither man spoke. Suddenly, Umbrennus cried out, "Consul, grant me leniency and I'll give testimony!"

"Treacherous Gallic dog!" Caeparius sneered.

"Keep these men bound and under guard," I instructed the praetors. Then turning to Tiro, I ordered, "Send out messengers. The Senate is to meet at the Temple of Concord just after dawn." Servius and the praetors were surprised at my choice of a meeting place. I chose it because it was closer to the Forum than was the Curia, and the word *concord* played into my statecraft endeavor to bind together the Republic's propertied citizens against subversives.

To the Gauls I said, "Come to the Senate. Your testimony and these"—I indicated the satchel of letters—"will complete this business."

"We will come to the Senate," Ambrax replied after he and his colleagues nodded at each other in agreement.

"I hope the Senate will remember what we have done for Roma," Bracco announced.

Again I assured them that the Allobroges would be treated fairly by the Senate.

"This one has boasted of his weapons." Celtillus indicated Caeparius with his baton of authority. Caeparius was clearly shaken by the revelation, but he made no attempt to deny it. I dispatched Marcus Caelius and two of my lictors to Caeparius' house to search for this stash of weapons. The Senate's Ultimate Decree empowered the consuls to undertake such searches and seizures.

Then, I instructed Flaccus and Pomptinus to send some of their lictors and guards to bring Lentulus Sura, Gaius Cethegus, and Publius Statilius to the Senate. They were not to be arrested, but escorted under conspicuous guard. The praetors immediately discharged their orders, my lictors went off to Caeparius' house, and Tiro was off to summon the Senate.

Suddenly, I remembered that I had left Clodia back in the library. But when I returned there, she was gone. Perhaps she had used the rear door to leave. I was grateful for her discretion, and then I noticed she had written something on a wax tablet on the table: *Don't make the same mistake twice.* Using a stylus, I rubbed out the message and wished I could have rubbed her presence out of my mind.

When the Senate convened, I told them of the conspirators' Allobrogian connection. Umbrennus' testimony confirmed this, but Capito and Caeparius protested their innocence. Lentulus, Cethegus, and Statilius rebuked me for having had them hauled to the Senate under guard as though they were criminals. Then I presented the letters to each of the conspirators. Reluctantly and shamefully, each one acknowledged his signature and seal.

I had commissioned two senators, both friends of mine, Marcius Philippus, Cato's father-in-law, and Publius Figulus, a Pythagorean sage, to record verbatim the proceedings of the Senate. At my direction, they read aloud the conspirators' letters to the Allobrogian tribal chiefs. Murmurings and mutterings of shock and outrage floated across the temple's lofty, marble interior as the senators heard how Roman citizens, senators and equites all, had conspired with the Gauls—Roma's traditional enemies—to bring fire, ruin, and murder upon the City.

Each of the Allobrogian envoys testified in Greek. Fortunately, as most Roman senators of the time were bilingual, they had no difficulty understanding the envoys' Gallic-accented speech. When they had finished, Capito and Caeparius retracted their earlier statements of innocence. Desperately, Lentulus and the others tried to controvert the evidence. Again, I called on the envoys to bear witness. Seeing that denial was futile, the praetor broke down and acknowledged his guilt. His accomplices followed suit.

In fulfillment of my promise to the envoys, I spoke on their behalf, praising their loyalty to the Republic and urging the Senate to hear their grievances and redress them. The Senate voted a commendation for the Gauls and decreed a thanksgiving to the gods in honor of my services in uncovering and thwarting the conspiracy.

Following this, Marcius Rex made two proposals. First, that Lentulus Sura, having acknowledged his guilt in a seditious plot against the Republic, should relinquish the office of praetor. Without dissent, the motion was seconded and then approved. Lentulus was too shaken and confounded to do more than nod in acquiescence.

Marcius Rex then proposed that the conspirators be remanded to the custody of several senators. As if to test their loyalty to the Republic, Caesar and Crassus—though Crassus was absent from the Senate—were respectively appointed custodians for Lentulus and Cethegus. Capito was assigned to Marcus Bibulus; Statilius to Marcius Philippus; and Caeparius to Publius Spinther. At this time, the Senate was not prepared to consider their ultimate disposition.

No sooner had this second proposal been seconded and approved when the two lictors that I had sent to Caeparius' house appeared at the entrance to the temple. I beckoned to them to enter. They did so, and trailing behind them came a score of Senatorial attendants. Each carried an armful of assorted weapons—swords, daggers, clubs, spears, and javelins.

The elder of the two lictors reported to me directly. Then, I announced before the entire Senate that these weapons had been confiscated from Caeparius' house—weapons that were to be used to slaughter Roman citizens. "Unless, Conscript Fathers," I suggested facetiously, "you are prepared to believe that it is merely Caeparius' *hobby* to collect an entire arsenal of armaments!"

The cache of weapons was the final piece of corroborative evidence.

After nearly three hours of testimony, inquiry, and deliberation, the Senate adjourned. I proceeded to the Rostra, a hundred paces from the temple's steps, and addressed the citizens on these most recent developments.

The Roman people, especially those coarse elements, those *dregs of Romulus*, could always be counted on to be fickle and noisy and irreverent. Nonetheless, I appealed to whatever patriotism I hoped that they might possess. I equated myself to Pompeius as the defender of the Roman people here in the City just as he had defended Roma's imperium over the seas, extending it over foreign lands.

Appealing to their superstitions, I told them that the recent restoration of Jupiter's Capitoline statue was a sign of the gods' favor. Truly, had not the gods prompted the Allobroges to betray the conspirators and to remain loyal to Roma? Therefore, I urged them to celebrate the decreed thanksgiving to the gods who had chosen to deliver Roma from the strife and bloodshed and civil dissensions that had afflicted the Republic during the previous two decades.

The danger was almost past. I urged the citizens to continue in their vigilance and in their trust in the gods. For my part, I would persevere in the remaining weeks of my consulate and in my subsequent public life to be worthy of their gratitude.

That day, the sun was shining brightly on Roma, and on me. The winter rains of political turmoil were at least briefly dissipated.

Caput VI Cicero's Respublica

FATIGUE HAD BEGUN TO SET in by the time I returned home. The tension-filled, sleepless night, like so many I had had during the entire crisis, began to take its toll on me. My head was splitting with pain and my bowels were knotted with anxiety. I asked my physician, Metrodorus, to prepare a draught to relieve my symptoms. After taking it, I lay down in my room for a few moments' ease. But this proved to be short-lived, for Terentia insisted on speaking with me about a strange occurrence from the previous night.

"Fabia, Aurelia, and Licinia, and I were offering a sacrifice at Fauna's altar," she explained. "There were about seventy women with us, but many more were out in the atrium; perhaps about another fifty in the adjoining rooms, having their own observances."

Listening to her, I visualized the whole scene, though I had never been to the Regia during a Good Goddess celebration. That would have been unthinkable as well as illegal. Fauna, the Roman goddess of procreation, was identified with the Good Goddess. Her statue in the Regia's atrium was generally kept veiled or closeted until it was time for the women to celebrate her rites. I pictured the atrium festooned with vines and holly and pine branches and illuminated by numerous burning oil lamps with perfume pervading the entire room. The sounds of sistrum, lyre, cymbals, and drums probably were to be heard from hired musicians. My imaginings were not unfounded, for in other years, when Terentia's role had been less pivotal, she had told me how the Regia had been decked out for the rites. Likewise, when she mentioned women *in adjoining rooms, having their own observances,* my mind conjured up scenes based on the idle, careless talk of our female household slaves who had attended upon Terentia in years past. Images of matrons and their daughters and daughters-in-law ministering to the Good Goddess; of matrons symbolically flagellating young, nubile girls held across their mothers' laps so as to render them fecund; of tipsy women ladling out wine from a large stone urn—their *honey pot*—and cackling, giggling, and teasing each other inanely; of young married women gathered about an image of Priapus, the phallic god, and laughing hysterically, gesticulating lewdly, exchanging ribald tales of copulation.

"Suddenly, a great, prodigious flame shot up from our offering. We heard screaming from the atrium, and we held our breath in terror. Someone was shouting from behind us: 'A man! A man! Sacrilege! Profanation! Sacrilege!' We turned around and rushed to the atrium. There was a figure on the floor, and the women were clawing at it, kicking it, cursing at it. Pieces of clothing were torn from the body of a man. His curly wig fell to the floor as he leapt up and ran like a frightened beast. We assailed him all the way to the street with our curses, pummeling and kicking him. We watched him disappear, bruised and naked, into the night. Then we returned to the atrium. The rites were pronounced violated, profaned by a man's intrusion. They would have to be repeated. Aurelia said she'd report it to her son. I had to tell you."

"And so you have," I said to her, pulling a warm compress from my aching forehead. "And now, Terentia...."

"Marcus!" she interrupted. "We saw him. We know him. There's no mistake! It was Pulcher—Publius Clodius Pulcher!"

"What???" I gasped, pulling myself up from the bed. "What would he have been doing there?"

"I don't know, other than crashing for curiosity's sake." But then Terentia reflected before adding, "Though Aurelia has an idea...."

"Terentia, are you absolutely certain it was Publius Clodius?"

"Marcus," she said ever so emphatically, "as certain as I know you are the father of our children!"

What a lunatic act he had committed, I thought. And why? Then, like a bolt of lightning it hit me, and my aching head throbbed with the realization. Clodius was trying to hide in the Regia. This is what he had meant by going "underground." His darkly painted eyelids were an anticipation of his female musician's costume—his passage into the Regia, into hiding, into sanctuary. But something had gone wrong. Somehow he had been recognized. Perhaps he had been betrayed. Terentia had said that Aurelia had an idea. Did the old dowager know who had arranged this bizarre business with Clodius? With every idea my head ached and throbbed. *Caesar.* Caesar was behind this. It was bizarre, comical, and brilliant.

"As Chief Pontiff, Caesar must conduct an investigation into this affair," Terentia was saying. "This sacrilege strikes at the very core of Roma's soul. It must be expiated. The Senate must see that...."

"Yes, yes, Terentia," I broke in, "all in good time, but just now the Senate has far more important business to consider."

She was aghast that I didn't share her resentment over the Good Goddess. But before she could complain, I told her all about the arrest of the conspirators, referring to them as the *Catilinian Five*. However, I did not tell her about Clodia Pulchra's visit.

"What's to be done with them?" she asked. "What are your plans?"

In all truth, I could not answer her, for I did not know at that moment how very dangerous the conspirators could prove to be under house arrest.

Omniscient narrative

Julia Antonia and her three strapping sons come to the Regia by mid-morning on December third. They have no difficulty being admitted, for she is the Chief Pontiff's kinswoman. However, she has come not specifically for Caesar, but for Caesar's charge, her husband, Lentulus Sura.

She is a handsome, middle-aged, rather stout, olive-hued woman. She wears the attire of mourning, a black palla draped over her gray stola, and her sons wear the same colors, although only her eldest, Marcus, wears the toga of manhood. The other two, Gaius and Lucius, are still too young to have put aside the purple-bordered toga of youth. Their mourning attire is for Lentulus Sura, caught in the act of sedition against the Roman Republic, and remanded to Caesar's custody. Julia is distraught and fearful and angry.

"Cousin, I implore you," she entreats the Chief Pontiff, "please help him."

Caesar assures her, "I'll do all I can for him. You know I will, Julia."

"Could you not allow him... allow him to slip away to...."

"You dishonor yourself and me by such a question." Caesar shakes his head. "Your husband could have left Roma long ago. He could have joined Catilina or gone anywhere else. But he stayed, and plotted and was arrested."

"My sons revere him as a father, most especially Marcus. He cannot...." Julia bursts into sobs. Young Marcus attempts to comfort his mother.

At that moment, two household servants accompany Lentulus Sura into the Regia's atrium.

"O, Publius! Publius!" Julia sees him and dashes into his extended arms. "What's going to happen now?"

Lentulus embraces Julia and kisses her cheeks and mouth and forehead.

She repeats, "What's going to happen now?"

Lentulus looks at her blankly and then turns to Caesar as though he has the answer.

Caesar beckons to Julia's sons. "Come with me, fellows. Give your parents some privacy."

After they have left the atrium, Lentulus draws his wife closer to him. He looks to ascertain that they are alone. "Julia, listen to me now. Get word to Sempronia Brutus. Tell her to send a messenger to Catilina. He must march on Roma—now! I was wrong to wait. He must...."

"Sempronia Tuditani? The wife of Decimus Brutus?" Julia is perplexed. "Is *she* in this too? Or, should I ask, are *you* with *her*?" Julia begins to back away from him. "You would pull me into your treason by using me to contact your mistress? O, Lentulus! You've betrayed your country! You've betrayed your people! And you've betrayed me! No! No! No! Marcus! Gaius! Lucius! Come! We're leaving!"

"Julia—wait!" Lentulus implores, but to no avail.

The three youths enter the atrium, stunned to see their mother even more distraught than before.

"Bid farewell to your father," she commands them. "Farewell, Cousin, and thank you," she tells Caesar.

Julia heads for the vestibule as her sons dutifully shake hands with their step-father. They nod politely to Caesar before following after their mother. Lentulus stands, shaken and forlorn, a pathetic, forsaken man.

"Caesar… would you…?"

"You know I cannot," Caesar replies. Nodding toward the departed company, he adds, "You needn't fear for them. I promise you."

With that Caesar signals his two servants to escort Lentulus back to his room. But Caesar is not for long alone with his thoughts. Aurelia enters the atrium. "Gaius, I must speak with you on an urgent matter."

"Yes, Mother, what is it?" He breaks his reveries and tries not to show the annoyance boiling up within himself.

"This house and the sacred rites of the Good Goddess were violated last night by a male intruder!" Aurelia advances upon her son to drive home the point. "This sacrilege necessitated the cleansing of the house and the repetition of the rites."

"Well then, thank you, Mother. Thanks to your fastidiousness the rites were truly validated."

"*Validated?*" Aurelia snorts in outrage. "There are at least three women besides myself who identified the profaner. It was Publius Clodius—dressed up like a female musician! The rites, my son, require far more than validation; the offense needs to be expiated, and the offender must be punished."

Caesar attempts to extricate himself from his mother's demands. "It's going to have to wait, Mother. You know that the Senate has a criminal conspiracy to quash."

"And you, Gaius, as Chief Pontiff and consul-elect, must surely know that offenses against the gods are no less heinous than offenses against the state. If you doubt me, your own mother, then ask Terentia Cicero! Ask Virgo Maxima Licinia! Ask the Vestal Fabia!"

At that instant, Pompeia enters the atrium because her mother-in-law's shrill voice has attracted her attention.

Aurelia sees her. "Ask your *wife* what Publius Clodius was doing *here*! Did he sneak in here last night at *her* invitation? Did they have an engagement? Why don't you ask her?!!"

Pompeia flushes with rage. She clenches her hands into white-knuckled fists that she raises across her breast. "You malicious old hag! How dare you!"

Caesar attempts to intervene. "Mother, you are implying a most dishonorable insult upon my wife, and upon me. It is not your affair to meddle in my marriage. Please...."

"Listen to me, my son...."

"*I* won't listen to base calumny!" Pompeia shouts. "I've done with it!" She stamps out of the atrium and heads for her own bedchamber.

"My son, if you fail to pursue this matter because you want to spare *her* any embarrassment, then I say to your face that you shame the gods! As Chief Pontiff, you *must* bring this profanation to the Senate's attention—*now*! And rather than protect *her* reputation, you should strive with all possible discretion to secure the Bona Dea's rites from exposure and further violation!"

Caesar breathes deeply. His jaws are tightly set lest he issue any disrespectful words. When he is sufficiently composed, he says, "I need no one, not even *you*, Mother, to tell me my duties—as Chief Pontiff, as consul-elect, or as a husband. It is time, I think, for you to realize this. Now, if you will please excuse me, Mother."

Aurelia watches her son walk down an adjacent corridor, where he will keep his own counsels.

At Crassus' house, Gaius Cethegus is ever restless. He has been comfortably accommodated as Crassus' custodial charge. His energies, however, are directed at Catilina's revolt against the Republic.

Cethegus has written a short note on a small scroll, for Crassus has been generous with his library. Now, Cethegus needs a courier to deliver the note to Praecia so that she can then send its message to Catilina's rebel camp in Faesulae. He relies on his masculine charms as he targets Crassus' wife, Tertulla.

Cethegus plies her with flattery—her beauty, her ancestry—of which he is so embarrassingly ignorant—her handsome, virtuous sons, Publius and Marcus, and on, and on, and tirelessly on. Inevitably,

Tertulla asks him, "What is it, Gaius Cethegus? Do you want me to help you escape? Aren't you comfortable here? Have not my husband and I treated you with all due hospitality?"

Discovered, Cethegus laughs like an apprehended, mischievous child. "No, Lady Tertulla," he sheepishly admits. "You and the esteemed Crassus have been paragons of hospitality. As for escape, well, far be it from me to compromise you in so rash an undertaking."

"Well then?" Tertulla's eyebrows arch in an affected puzzlement.

Cethegus now turns intensely serious. "*This*, Lady Tertulla," he says holding up the scroll. "If you could send this short missive, a token of my eternal love for a woman whom I probably will not have occasion to see again, it would give me great comfort."

"Oh? And who might she be?"

Cethegus whispers the name, *Praecia*. "Please, if you would do this for me, Fortuna will surely smile upon you." He places the scroll into Tertulla's open hand. She looks at it, smiles tenderly, and then looks up at Cethegus' anxious face.

"Darling, would you care to read it?"

Cethegus assumes that the question is addressed to him. He is about to answer her, when he hears full, round words coming from behind him.

"No, my love. Why don't you read it first." Crassus enters the library and walks around Cethegus to stand beside Tertulla. Cethegus is too mortified to move or to speak. Beads of sweat form on his brow and temples.

Crassus takes the scroll from his wife's outstretched hand. He fingers it as though it were a toy. "If you wanted to see your mistress, Cethegus, you should have asked, and I would have arranged it. You needn't have tried to flatter my wife into sending your *love* note. Or, is it a *love* note? Hmm?" Crassus breaks open the seal and unrolls the parchment. He reads aloud: 'Dearest Praecia, I am under guard in the house of Marcus Licinius Crassus. You must get word to Catilina. He must march with all speed on the City or all is lost. Yours, Gaius Cethegus.'

Crassus looks up from the note. He studies Cethegus for a long moment, savoring his charge's utterly defenseless position. He hands the note to Tertulla and she peruses it quickly. "Well, Marcus," she says, "it is a *love* note, of sorts." Tertulla looks at Cethegus and purses her lips to suppress a laugh.

"Gaius Cethegus, I'm surprised at you!" Crassus shakes his head reprovingly. He takes the note from Tertulla, holds it up, and says, "This is yet another piece of incriminating evidence against you. How sad."

Cicero's Respublica

My uncertainty about the conspirators was accentuated when Consul-elect Marcus Bibulus visited me with his mentor, Marcus Cato. Servius Sulpicius had arrived about an hour earlier, and then Marcius Philippus and Publius Spinther arrived only moments after Bibulus and Cato. They were severely agitated. By mid-day, the five of them had my head spinning.

"Consul," Bibulus began, "I must tell you that Gaius Capito tried to bribe my steward into delivering this message." He handed me a little scroll. It was addressed to Sempronia Brutus, and in it, Capito urged her to notify the other conspirators to leave Roma and get word to Catilina to march on the City at once. Even as I read it, Bibulus spoke on. "Luckily, my steward brought it to me. But we can't be sure about the other four, especially Lentulus and Cethegus. They might already have sent out messages with Caesar's and Crassus' connivance."

Philippus and Spinther complained in the same vein about their respective charges—Statilius and Caeparius. Then, even more emphatically, Bibulus added. "The conspirators cannot be kept under house arrest indefinitely, especially where two of the Senate's custodians were, perhaps *still are,* Catilina's accomplices. The Senate must judge them and decide their fate."

The onerous responsibility of directing the Senate's disposition of the Catilinian Five sent waves of nausea through my bowels, and painful pangs assailed my head.

Then Cato interjected, "Under house arrest, they could continue to plot and conspire, though they're apart. And there's even the possibility that they could be rescued by their confederates. By the gods! This whole house arrest is almost as much of a sham as Catilina's self-consignment!"

The ever jurisprudential mind of Servius Sulpicius offered an appropriate rebuttal. "Our laws and traditions do not provide for long-term imprisonment. We all know this. Roma has always allowed both suspects and the condemned to go into exile."

"*Exile!*" Cato exploded. "Just what they would want—so they could go straight to Catilina! If the government gives them that privilege, we will look weak and indecisive, and the Republic's enemies will take renewed courage from our irresolution. But deal decisively with them and we strike a death blow at the heart of Catilina's rebellion."

"So you would dispense with the laws to save the Republic?" Servius challenged.

Cato shot back lividly, "To save the Republic the Senate has issued the Ultimate Decree!" Turning to me he asked almost menacingly, "Consul, will you shrink from the power that the Senate has entrusted in you? Or will you use it with vigor to destroy Catilina and his minions and save the Republic?"

"Be careful, Marcus," Servius warned me. "Though you have extraordinary power from the Last Decree, if you wield it arbitrarily you may find yourself its victim. Bring these five before the Senate and they may vote to condemn them, but *you* will bear the onus of their condemnation. So, I urge you—don't allow the Senate to judge them. The Senate has no power, even with the Last Decree, to function as a court of law. The law is best served if you keep the conspirators under arrest, increase the guards on them, but try them in the proper courts once Catilina's been captured or destroyed."

This was well-reasoned in complete compliance with Roman law and custom. Yet, Cato's argument, based on the need for quick, decisive action, was equally sound, especially when Bibulus added a final observation. "Don't be deluded, Consul," he advised, "that Caesar will cooperate with me in bringing them to trial. You know he'll scour the laws for some trap, some minutiae to get them off. Your term expires in less than a month. Don't hold their judgment for the New Year. Act now, Consul, before it's too late!"

I pursed my lips, sighed deeply, and then said to them, "Gentlemen, the Senate will meet tomorrow morning at the Temple of Concord." That day was to be the Nones of December—December fifth. I could not realize then that that year's December Nones would prove to be the most crucial of my entire life.

Yet, in anticipation of it, I struggled through another sleepless night. Anxiety and uncertainty weighed heavily upon me. I must have lain awake in my mental anguish for some four hours when Terentia came into my bedchamber. She slid into bed with me, touched me and tried to comfort me. But I was too tense and preoccupied to respond to her caresses. Sensing my discomfort, she sat up and tried to comfort me in a different way.

"Marcus, I didn't tell you everything about the other night," she whispered. "There's more that you ought to know. Fabia and I were praying and offering sacrifice to the Good Goddess for you, Marcus, for your success in suppressing Catilina's plot. It was then that the great flame shot up from the altar. Later, Fabia told me that this was a sign, an affirmation of the goddess' approval of your actions. Fabia would surely know this."

She must have seen the incredulity registered on my face, even in the dim oil-lamp light of the room. "Marcus, put aside your disbelief long enough to hear me. For your sake, I'll break a promise I made to my sister many years ago. I'll tell you what she had me promise never to reveal to anyone."

I attempted to protest. "You needn't break your word, Terentia, not for my sake. It would be unfair to Fabia."

Terentia was oblivious. "Fabia is blessed, or perhaps she's *cursed* with the divine sight." Again, seeing my disbelief, she became emphatic. "Yes, it's true; she has seen visions of events before they've happened. During her years of service to Mother Vesta, while tending the sacred fire, she's had visions. She saw the birth of our children. She saw your election to the consulate and she told me the year it would happen. And she saw Catilina's defeat and his plot against the government. She confided these visions to me and swore me to secrecy. Now, seeing you distraught with fear and misgivings, I've foresworn myself to encourage you, to strengthen your resolve. Yet, you continue to doubt. On the night of the Good Goddess rites, did your ambush not succeed? Did the Gauls not remain steadfast? The following morning, did the conspirators not confess their treason? The gods are with you, Marcus. Fear *not* to do what's necessary!"

Terentia seized my shoulders as if to add to the earnestness of her words. I did not doubt her sincerity in all that she had told me. The idea that lovely, pious, almost ethereal Fabia was psychic intrigued me, for though I do not believe in the gods, I still have much credence in signs, portents, and dreams. But how could I *act* on them? How could Fabia's visions or Terentia's inspiration be the basis for official policy? The answers to these questions did *not* come with the dawn.

THE TEMPLE OF CONCORD WAS under heavy guard that morning of the Nones of December. Built and dedicated more than half a century earlier to commemorate the Senate's suppression of the Gracchan revolt, the *Concordia* had been lampooned by pundits at the time who quipped that it should have been named the Temple of *Discordia*; political factionalism and strife remained rampant since that time. I hoped there would be no discord today as the Senate assembled to deliberate the fate of the Catilinian Five.

Most of the senators in attendance belonged to the optimate, aristocratic faction. There were but a few of the popularist group and of these Caesar was the most prominent. My entourage of equites—led by Caelius, Piso, and Milo—escorted Servius and me into the temple's rectangular cella. The senators were seating themselves on wooden benches against the high marble walls. I was hoping that the concord we had attained at our previous meeting two days earlier would again prevail. Yet, there was a heavy, sullen air about this day's meeting; or perhaps I was still troubled by the previous day's discussion with Bibulus, Cato, and Servius, and by Terentia's nocturnal revelations.

The preliminary sacrifice and the taking of the omens were performed expeditiously. Then I addressed the Senate in order to present the day's business. "Conscript Fathers, we meet here today in this hallowed place dedicated to Concord to decide the fate of five men who, by their own admission and by the preponderance of irrefutable evidence, have conspired to make war on the Republic. They have been in the custody of five trustworthy citizens. Yet, they have continued their intrigues by attempting to communicate and correspond with Catilina and his rebel army at Faesulae.

"When you issued the Ultimate Decree, Fathers of the Senate, you charged me to see to it that the Republic suffers no harm. I have used it like a sword in its scabbard—cautiously, judiciously, prudently. But these five men, Lentulus Sura, Gaius Cethegus, Publius Statilius, Marcus Caeparius, and Gaius Capito, pose a continued danger to all citizens despite their arrest and confinement. As Consul, I have recourse to you, Conscript Fathers. *You* must decide their ultimate fate. I submit their case to the judgment of the Senate."

Having laid the issue before them, I then began to poll the senators for their opinions, beginning with the consuls-elect. Gaius Caesar, though returned first in the election, deferred to his colleague. So, Marcus Bibulus spoke first and briefly. He proposed that the conspirators suffer the extreme, Ultimate Penalty, and the confiscation of their property.

I assumed, of course, as I was certain many others did, that Bibulus was using polite language to advocate the death penalty, for words such as *death* and *execution* were anathema in the Senate.

Then Caesar took his turn. Even now, nearly twenty years later, I can still see him standing before us, a tall, lean, dark cock-eagle reproving us as if we were school children who had forgotten our lessons. "Conscript Fathers, take care that you do not destroy our laws and traditions in your zeal to save the Republic." Caesar's opening statement echoed Servius' words from the previous day. He paused to survey the chamber imperiously and then continued. "The Ultimate Penalty, by law and tradition, cannot be imposed on citizens without their right to appeal to the People assembled in the Centuriate Assembly. Again, by law and by tradition, should the People deny their appeal, the condemned have always had the right to go into exile. Yet, the Senate has given the Consul the Ultimate Decree, and he in turn has made you the arbiter of their fate. Will you, Fathers of the Republic, condemn the conspirators to the extinction of their lives as Bibulus has proposed and thereby violate the rights of citizens and in so doing violate our laws and traditions?"

I remember wondering, *What is he up to? What trick is this?* The oligarchs eyed each other nervously as low murmurs passed through the temple. Caesar continued, "Yet there is a way to protect the Republic and avoid the travesty of violating these citizens' rights." He paused again to augment the senators' anticipatory suspense. "Let the conspirators be imprisoned in different custodial cities throughout Italia—imprisoned for the rest of their lives. Let the Senate ban any attempt to consider their release, and let their properties be forfeited to the state."

Now, the murmuring grew louder. What Caesar proposed was nothing less than innovational in Roman jurisprudence. Life imprisonment was totally contrary to our customs and practices. Even citizens condemned to death had the option of voluntary exile as Caesar had mentioned. But clearly he and all of us knew that such an option would not and could not be offered to the Catilinian Five, for surely they would flee to the rebels' camp. Caesar was looking at me as if he were reading my thoughts.

"Execute these men," he continued, "and you extinguish all their sensibilities, all their pain, and all their sufferings. But life imprisonment will afford them time to reflect on their treason against the Republic. Imprison their bodies so that their minds and spirits will be imprisoned in the perpetual knowledge of their treason and disgrace. And they will know that their families will suffer privation through the confiscation of their properties."

Caesar's argument was soundly reasoned, but I could not help believing that there was an ulterior motive to his radical proposal. Was he trying to afford Catilina's men a chance to escape, a chance at life? In any event, the senators of consular rank supported Bibulus' proposal. But when the praetors-elect and the praetorian-ranked senators were polled, there was an impasse until Servius Sulpicius proposed an alternative to the Caesar and Bibulus options.

"Imprison the conspirators," he offered, "confine them in the Carcer and keep them there until Catilina is either captured or destroyed. Then, bring them to trial on charges of treason."

Essentially, this was the same proposal that Servius had voiced the day before, except for his mention of the Carcer, the official state prison. This was unusual in that only foreign enemies awaiting execution were kept there. To imprison Roman citizens in the Carcer was unprecedented. Still, his proposal avoided the extremity of Bibulus' execution measure and the innovation of Caesar's life imprisonment proposal. It was not without merit, but under the circumstances it would have aided the conspirators and Catilina.

I pointed this out when, seeing the Senate divided and confused by the conflicting proposals, I took to the floor and addressed them.

Summarizing the proposals of Bibulus, Caesar, and Sulpicius, I emphasized what I was certain had been Bibulus' original intention, namely that the conspirators should be executed. "As Consul," I proclaimed, "I am ready to carry out the Senate's decree and to bear the responsibility. Therefore, think first of the Republic's security rather than of my own personal safety. The welfare of the people is the supreme law."

Then, the consular, Decimus Silanus rose to speak. In an embarrassing about-face, he announced ever so apologetically that when he had spoken in favor of Bibulus' Extreme Penalty, he had understood it to mean perpetual exile and *not* execution. "After all," he sheepishly announced, "that is the only conceivable Ultimate Penalty for Roman citizens."

A wave of dismayed sighs and moans swept across the temple, and I saw Cato shaking his head and rolling his eyes over his brother-in-law's sophistries. In the midst of the Senate's continued confusion and before the aedilician and quaestorian-ranked senators could be polled, Cato requested leave to speak. I consented, and then the young firebrand proceeded to attack Caesar's proposal in the most virulent language. "Conscript Fathers, our exalted Chief Pontiff would have us believe that life imprisonment for the conspirators is far more severe than extinguishing their lives. He would have us believe that we must not violate the laws and traditions of the Republic by executing these men without granting them an appeal to the People and without allowing them the choice of exile rather than the termination of their lives.

"But our Chief Pontiff ignores reality in his devotion to legalities and traditions. These men, in their evil designs against their country, have forfeited their citizenship. They have rendered themselves enemies of the Republic and traitors to the Roman People. Hence, they have *no right* to appeal to the People for clemency. Nor should they expect punishment for their crimes *less* than would be visited upon rebellious, seditious aliens."

I saw many senators nodding in approval of Cato's impassioned speech, and there was definite murmuring of approbation when he paused long enough to notice an attendant handing Caesar a small scroll. Then he resumed his oration with even more passion than before. "In proposing life imprisonment for these traitors, the Chief Pontiff is merely protecting his associates, or should I say *former* associates? What guarantee is there that they would not be rescued from their confinement? Indeed, how do we know that some demagogic tribune might not agitate for their future release? The same man who speaks so eloquently about upholding our laws and traditions proposes that which is totally foreign to Roman law and practice. There is *no precedent* in Roman jurisprudence for life imprisonment! He would have us trust the Italian cities that may well harbor others of Catilina's subversives! Look, Conscript Fathers! Even *now* he sits before us and reads a note from one of them! May we not know if Lentulus Sura has written him? Or perhaps Cethegus has some urgent plea? Perhaps, *any* of the others have petitioned him?"

Cato crossed the floor and came to stand next to Caesar. Facing me, he announced, "Consul, I demand that the contents of this note received by the Chief Pontiff only moments ago be divulged to the entire Senate!"

Caesar smiled sardonically and nodded, "As you wish." Rising from his seat, he walked over to Publius Figulus who, with Marcius Philippus, had been recording the deliberations. Caesar handed him the note, whereupon Figulus, appearing somewhat confused, looked at me for direction. I shrugged and bade him read the note. In a strong but monotonous voice, he read aloud: *"My dearest Gaius, my thoughts, as always, are with you. Be on guard. Yours eternally."* He added, "There's no signature, but only the letter *S*."

Suddenly, there was an eruption of laughter from all parts of the temple. Silanus squirmed and shifted uneasily in his seat, for he doubtlessly inferred, as we all did, the identity of *S* to be none other than his wife, Servilia. Flushed with rage and embarrassment, Cato scurried over to Figulus and seized the note from his hands. Amid continuing guffaws of laughter, he flung the little scroll at Caesar like a child who no longer wanted to play. "Take it, *drunkard!*" he bellowed before returning to the center of the floor.

I could not help but chuckle at Cato's projecting a personal foible upon Caesar who, despite whatever else may be said against him, was not then or now reputed to be an excessive imbiber. Of course, it would have been quite impolitic of Cato to reproach him for being his half-sister's lover.

The comic interlude distracted Cato so much than when he resumed his speech, he was only able to reiterate his earlier points. He accused Caesar of wanting to spare the conspirators from execution because of his former association with Catilina. He said Caesar's life imprisonment proposal was a sham and a ruse to facilitate their eventual rescue or release. In this, he reflected exactly my own unstated views. By the time he had finished, he was still scarlet with rage and embarrassment at having been made the butt of Caesar's joke.

Seizing the momentum that Cato had initiated, I rose and asked the Senate to make a division—in effect, to vote. But out of three proposals advanced, I selected Bibulus' measure and stipulated that the Extreme Penalty should be understood by all to mean execution and the forfeiture of the conspirators' property to the state.

I rejected Caesar's proposal because of its inherent flaws which Cato had articulated, and I could not accept the temporizing nature of Servius' proposal because it flew in the face of the urgently dangerous situation impinging on the Republic. In retrospect, I realize now more than I did then that Servius was offering a compromise situation which, if accepted by the Senate, would have spared me tremendous personal and political liability.

Like soldiers on a drill field, a definite majority of senators, the oligarchs and optimates and many neutrals, rose from their seats, crossed the floor, and stood next to Bibulus. A few, including, much to my dismay, Servius Sulpicius, remained seated. Caesar was most prominent among the dissenters.

Before I could announce the obvious outcome of the vote, he had risen to obstruct the proceedings. "Consul, and Conscript Fathers," he declared, "think well on what you are about to decree. You have constituted yourselves as a court of law when you have no real authority to do so. Not even the Ultimate Decree gives you that authority. You have condemned to execution five *citizens—not aliens*—but Roman citizens, and you have denied their right of appeal to the People. For this violation you will incur the People's wrath and the gods' disfavor! And you would magnify the outrage of political murder by seizing the properties of the condemned. It is one thing to imprison them and confiscate their holdings; but to execute them, to *murder* them *and* inflict impoverishment upon their families is nothing less than a shameless travesty that pollutes our deepest virtues. Therefore, I move that at least this portion of the Senate's decree be stricken. I will not...."

Outcries of "Yield! Yield! Desist! Withdraw!" poured onto Caesar's words from the majority clustered about Bibulus. Cato rushed over to him and bellowed, "Will you dare obstruct the Senate's decree to save *your* conspirators?"

Caesar glared at him malevolently but did not reply. Instead, he made for the exit, all the while hounded by Cato and a score of senators who baited and reviled him. Titus Milo and the bodyguard attempted to block the door just as several senators, including Servius, rushed over to Caesar to shield him with their togas from any violence that Cato and his friends might inflict.

Looking back at that moment, I realize that it was in my power to destroy Caesar, if not by direct volition, then at least by my passivity. Obviously, had I chosen to do so, we would not today live under his regal shadow. But I could not brook the idea of violence committed in the Senate against the Chief Pontiff, whose very person was sacrosanct and inviolable, even if it was Caesar. So, I signaled Milo to allow Caesar and his group to pass unmolested.

Then, without further dissent or obstruction, the Senate confirmed its decree of execution for the Catilinian Five.

At sunset on the Nones of December, they were escorted under guard from their custodial charges to the Carcer, the official but hardly adequate detention center. But they were not to be detained there, as their stay would be strictly transient. Then as now, the Carcer was an ugly eyesore of a stone edifice situated about three hundred paces from the Temple of Concord where the conspirators' fate had been debated and decreed. Armed guards kept at bay a considerable crowd that had gathered to watch the grim proceedings. They and the entire Forum were bathed in an eerie, blood-red light from the setting sun's rays.

Out of respect for Lentulus Sura's former praetorian office, I personally accompanied him by the hand to the Carcer's entrance, while the others, Cethegus, Statilius, Caeparius and Capito, were accompanied by my lictors and guards. They seemed resigned to their fate, for they made no protest, even when their togas were removed and they were bound hand and foot.

I announced each of their names and then pronounced the Senate's decree for their execution. Several crude catcalls shot out from the crowd. I heard my name bandied about—a few *Chick-Peas* here and there. This did not unnerve me as much as the sight of the conspirators' togas hanging from iron hooks on the Carcer's front wall. A twinge of remembrance brought to mind the dream that had disturbed my sleep earlier in the crisis. Chills of foreboding descended from the nape of my neck to the base of my spine. I braced myself to ward off fear and nausea.

One by one, the conspirators were lowered into the foul, dark, dank subterranean chamber of the Carcer. Ironically, the chamber was called the *Tullianum*. There, they were quickly seized and methodically strangled by official executioners.

The whole process took only a few moments. When informed by the prefect of executioners that the business was completed, I turned to the assembled senators, equites, and citizens and solemnly announced, "They have lived."

My own words meshed with the cries of "Savior!" and "Father of the Country!' and "Defender of the Republic!" as senators and equites accompanied me home in a splendid torchlight procession. Among the equites were Atticus, Lucius Balbus, Gaius Oppius, and Publius Considius. Unfortunately, Servius Sulpicius was not among the senators, and his absence, his lack of support, distressed me in what was otherwise the climactic apogee of my triumph over Catilina and his seditionists. So I thought at the time.

The conspirators' bodies were disposed of efficiently and most unceremoniously, burned in Mars Field and their ashes scattered to the winds. However, I arranged for Lentulus Sura's ashes to be sent to his widow since he had been praetor. Heralds were sent to various districts of the City to announce the news of the executions. Two couriers were sent to Etruria to convey the same tidings to Pompeius. I trusted him to exploit the news to his advantage and to the Republic's benefit.

Omniscient Narrative

CRIERS AND HERALDS, ACCOMPANIED BY torch-bearers and trumpeters, make their rounds through each of Roma's districts. Several shrill trumpet blasts precede the same dire tidings: Traitors to Roma and the Roman People—by the Senate's decree and under the auspices of Consul Marcus Tullius Cicero—have been executed in the Tullianum chamber of the Carcer. The names of the executed Catilinian Five conspirators are announced with exacting enunciation.

The Caelian district, where Praecia lives, is one of the first areas removed from the Forum to get the news. Her maidservants, trembling with fear and sorrow, report what they have heard in the streets and crossroads. Though they may not have known of the conspiracy, they certainly knew of their mistress' intimacies with Cethegus and her friendship with Sempronia and Lentulus Sura.

Praecia is not incredulous, though she is pierced and shaken. How often had Cethegus told her that death was in the offing if they were discovered and taken? This is why he had pushed for immediate action in the City in advance of Catilina's march. So now it is done. Her lover, her protector, her partner is dead; he and his confederates have been executed. What of the others? Could they still be in the City? If they are, would they dare venture anything now? What of Sempronia? Has *she* heard the news of Lentulus' death? What is going to happen to them—to herself and to Sempronia? The Consul's reach and the Senate's decree will surely catch them in the government's net. Sempronia at least has her husband, the old oligarch, Decimus Brutus, to intercede for her, if he would be so disposed. *But Praecia, who will be your intercessor? Who will venture to protect you now? Flee, Praecia! Get across the river. Go north, perhaps to Faesulae and Catilina's camp. For what purpose? No, it's over, Praecia. Face the truth. You hold reality in your hands. That is the only escape.*

Praecia dismisses her servants. To the household steward she speaks of important documents stored in a chest in the atrium. The contents are to be distributed in the morning. Surely, that is when they will discover her. She retires to her bedroom and bolts the door behind her.

Praecia examines herself in the bronze mirror. She is yet beautiful in her mortal twilight. Yes, it is worth cheating whatever else the Fates may have in store for her. Her fingers nimbly remove the leather belt about her waist and her bosom heaves with apprehension. She lets her palla fall from her shoulders. The flesh revealed is yet firm. The anticipation surges through her, arousing her, stiffening the pink-brown nipples. Stepping away from the mirror, she mounts a bed-stool so that she can reach up and secure one end of her belt around a ceiling beam. She pulls on the belt. It is securely taut. Now, the belt's opposite end caresses her long, slender neck. It is knotted several times, its tightness ushering her to the portals of oblivion. Both ends now tight, taut, twisted, she lunges off the stool. The air is squeezed out of her; her neck snaps, and her body jerks and then for several minutes it swings to and fro before coming to rest in deadly inertia.

Early the next morning, the bolted door is broken down by Praetor Flaccus' lictors. Sent by the Consul to arrest Praecia, Flaccus is nonplussed to see that he, and the Consul, and the Republic have been cheated by a dead, but beautiful, and utterly resourceful woman. He orders her body to be cut down from its improvised gibbet. In addition to reporting Praecia's suicide, Praetor Flaccus will also report that she had provided posthumously for her slaves' manumission.

WITHIN A MILE OF THE Capena Gate, a sprawling necropolis lies enshrouded in an early December mist. A sad, funeral procession slowly approaches from Roma along the Appian Road. Its destination is the large, multi-tiered tufa stone columbarium belonging to the Cornelius Lentulus clan. At its head walks Julia Antonia, the widow of the ex-praetor Lentulus Sura. It is early morning on December six, the day after Lentulus and his confederates have been strangled in the Carcer, their remains cremated in Mars Field. As a former praetor, Lentulus rates a special privilege denied the others. Their ashes have been scattered carelessly, but his have been preserved in an alabaster jar and given to his widow.

Julia holds the jar of ashes to her breast, draped in black stola and palla. Her eldest son, Marcus Antonius, walks beside her, holding her arm, supporting his aggrieved mother. His younger brothers, Gaius and Lucius, walk directly behind. Like their mother, the brothers are attired in mourning black as are their household attendants.

As the procession draws near, cemetery attendants push open the large bronze doors of the columbarium, the repository of scores of vases holding the ashes of the Cornelii Lentuli who have lived and then passed on to eternity. Julia enters the dim, somber interior honey-combed with scores of arched niches. An empty niche draws her attention. She walks toward it and when she is close enough she sees the copper name plate indicating her husband's place.

Julia raises the urn to her lips and kisses it solemnly. Then she places it in its reserved niche. Turning away and covering her mouth she makes for the door. There is a veiled figure just outside the entrance. Julia strains to recognize it, but it is not until she steps over the stone threshold that she realizes it is Sempronia Brutus. There is no mistaking the haughty beauty of that face even under the thin veil.

As though Julia needed assurance, or perhaps to offer her own commiseration, Sempronia lifts the veil from her face. Her eyes are swollen with grief. Tears run down her cheeks as she opens her mouth to speak. But it is Julia's voice that is heard. *"Lupa! You* dare to come *here!"* Julia follows this reproach with a discharge of spit into Sempronia's face. She is paralyzed with shame and dread as Julia, her sons, and household attendants move past her and begin their return trek to Roma.

They have been some time on the Appian Road before Sempronia slides down along the doorpost, a crumpled mass of black and gray wool sobbing onto the back of her hands.

Cicero's Respublica

Early in the morning of December six, I hosted a meeting of the oligarchs. We had just settled down in the library when Tiro announced that Praetor Flaccus had arrived and was waiting for me in the atrium. I told him to bring the Praetor to our meeting. Old Catulus, who looked and sounded more dyspeptic than ever, seemed to take umbrage at the interruption. The Lucullus brothers looked at each other as though tossing between them an unspoken question: *What now?* Decimus Brutus was stretching his neck and grimacing at some invisible pest. Cato was running his fingers along the edge of the inlaid table. Marcius Rex and Hortensius were examining some of my volumes of philosophy and jurisprudence.

When Praetor Flaccus entered, he seemed reluctant to speak in the oligarchs' presence. In response to my encouragement, he proceeded to tell us of the suicide of Cethegus' mistress. The oligarchs appeared not to be surprised by this news. Their cynicism and inherent masculine superiority could not afford them any display of emotion. But I was moved by such an act of desperation, suicide being generally associated with males rather than with females. More importantly, I had hoped that Praecia might have been willing to divulge further details about Catilina's conspiracy. Her suicide obviously had precluded that possibility.

I looked at Decimus Brutus and thought about his wife. Sempronia had been a conspirator and Lentulus Sura's mistress. It had been my intention to arrest her after Praecia had been taken into custody. Now, the woman's suicide shook my resolve. As much as I hated temporizing and differentiating among expedients, I decided to implement certain exceptions.

"Gentlemen, seven conspirators are yet at large: Autronius Paetus, Publius Sulla, Lucius Vargunteius, Lucius Cassius, Gaius Cornelius, and Porcius Laeca. I've attempted to arrest them, but my officers tell me that they've apparently fled the City. They may have joined Catilina or they may have gone elsewhere. We simply don't know."

I rose from my chair and circled the table, all the while carefully considering my next statement. "Will the Senate condemn these in absentia and confiscate their properties?"

Hortensius' legalistic mind was spinning on my every word. "In accordance with the Senate's Ultimate Decree, yes, yes, Consul, they could certainly be condemned in absentia. But—did we not hear you say that *seven* conspirators are at large?"

"That is so," I acknowledged.

"Well then, who is the *seventh*?"

I turned from Hortensius, braced myself, and looked at Decimus Brutus. "It gives me severe distress to tell you, Decimus Brutus, that...."

"That my Sempronia was a conspirator?" Decimus Brutus stretched his neck forward to thrust the question in my face. "That she was Lentulus Sura's mistress?" Decimus Brutus held up his hand as if to forestall any further word from me. "Consul, spare me your solicitude. I've known since... since before yesterday." He looked at me as though he were reading my thoughts. "You want to know *how* I know, Consul. Well, I'll tell you!"

He looked at his fellow oligarchs before continuing. "You know, this whole business started with a round of letters. Well, I've had one too. No, I don't have it with me." He sneered and looked at me disdainfully. "It was Julia Antonia. It seems that an unfaithful husband brought out a betrayed woman's patriotism."

The oligarchs considered him with all the sympathy that they had been unwilling or unable to show for Praecia.

"Consul," Decimus Brutus said to me, "I'll turn her over to you." With that, he began to rise.

"No, wait," I offered. I swallowed deeply and considered every face in the room. "Decimus Brutus, we will relegate your wife's disposition to you."

The old man was stunned speechless. The oligarchs eyed each other in disbelief. "Are you with me on this, gentlemen?" I asked of them.

A moment of silence was broken only when Catulus spoke in that ever raspy voice. "You accept this responsibility, Decimus Brutus?"

A barely audible *yes* escaped from the old man's mouth.

Cato then interjected, "Why this exception, Consul?"

I tried to ignore him. "Gentlemen, there's one thing more. I ask that the Senate's confiscation decree be waived for Lentulus Sura's widow and for Aurelia Orestilla."

"*What?!?!*" Cato exploded. "What madness is this, Consul? I don't know about the rest of you, but I see a touch of *Caesar* here!"

"Will *you* shut up, Cato !" I turned on him abruptly. "There's no need for another Nones of December debate!"

Lucius Lucullus asked, "But Consul, why this reversal, with Catilina's rebels still in the field?"

"One woman has taken her own life," I replied. "I already have the execution of five men on my conscience—however necessary it was. I allowed for Sempronia to be adjudged by her husband. I don't want either Julia Antonia or Aurelia Orestilla to take their own lives because they've been deprived of a roof over their heads. Just these two exceptions, gentlemen; can we not afford at least this degree of compassion?"

In the end, and despite Cato's stubborn resistance, the oligarchs agreed to my proposed exceptions. Remembering that Catulus had been charged by Catilina to safeguard Aurelia Orestilla and her daughter, I inferred correctly the old oligarch's reason for supporting my proposal.

I realized equally well that Caesar would have appreciated my efforts on behalf of his kinswoman, Julia Antonia.

However, compassion for the conspirators' womenfolk did not preclude my speculative inclinations. Subsequently, when the conspirators' properties were seized and then sold at public auction, I endeavored to purchase several units using Atticus, Milo, Terentia, and her freedman, Philotimus, as proxies. Looking back, it may have been an impolitic move on my part, but I profited handsomely, and I justified my gains as dividends for saving the Republic from seditious and disaffected men.

Curiously, as the oligarchs were leaving, Catulus took me aside and whispered, "Consul, this affair of the Bona Dea intrusion has to be considered. After all, you've shown remarkable compassion today in your solicitude for the Catilinian women. Truly, are not the women of Roma entitled to the same consideration. They were scandalized by the intruder—whoever he was. They—and the Good Goddess—deserve justice. Do you agree, Consul?"

I had not heard such a well reasoned argument about the affair since Terentia had first told me about it. When she had, I had the Catilinian Five on my mind. Now, Catilina's rebels and the at-large conspirators were most prominent in my concerns. Nevertheless, I agreed with him in principle, and he seemed to be placated, at least for the moment.

Omniscient Narrative

With Catulus in the lead, the oligarchs walk from Cicero's house to the south side of the Palatine Hill. The residents of the area are energetically engaged in their morning activities. Slaves scurry to and fro. Children cavort in the streets. Litters of fashionable ladies negotiate the human traffic. The grand mansions of prominent citizens attest to the Palatine's concentration of power and wealth.

No one in the party breaks off to go to his own house because they know that Catulus has something to say to them, something that could not have been divulged to Cicero. Catulus halts with the Great Circus fully in view below the Palatine's south side. "Cicero will be out of office in a few weeks," he says while surveying the grand, empty stadium. "Caesar will be Consul with Bibulus. We can trust our man to veto any dangerous bills from Caesar. But now, with Catilina and his army up in Etruria, the thought of his escaping, joining forces with Caesar, is altogether unsettling. And Pompeius—his loyalty is as the tides."

Catulus turns to his colleagues. "The Circus has its inherent dangers for the charioteers, and so it is in the political arena. A wrecked chariot in the path of a charging team is a terrible obstacle. We may have an opportunity to throw an obstacle in Caesar's path—to block him, to compromise him."

Lucius Lucullus infers, "The Bona Dea scandal being the obstacle?"

Catulus renders a smug, contented smile.

ALONG THE CASSIAN ROAD FROM Roma ride two horsemen. Couriers from the Senate, they have been en-route to Faesulae for two days since they were dispatched late on the Nones of December. Twice they have changed horses. They have spent one night at an inn at Clusium. On the morning of the seventh they come in sight of the tents of the Republic's forces before the walls of Faesulae.

Brought to Pompeius Magnus, they render the Senate's greetings and deliver Consul Cicero's message. The Magnus shares the news with his legates and with Consul Gaius Antonius and Senator Quintus Cicero, both of whom have recently arrived with their levies from Lower Etruria. He goes out of his command tent to his waiting horse. He mounts and, accompanied by several mounted soldiers, including his standard bearer, he rides up to the ramparts of Catilina's rebel camp.

"Lucius Sergius Catilina!" Six times Pompeius calls out at intervals. The rebels cluster on the front rampart; they realize something is amiss. Their numbers have grown in the several weeks since they declared their revolt against the Republic, but so have the government's forces. Yet, there have been no clashes, no sorties, no advances and no retreats on either side.

Catilina appears on the ramparts and recognizes Pompeius below. "Gnaeus Pompeius, has the Senate agreed to our demands?"

Ignoring the question, Pompeius replies, "Lucius Sergius Catilina, news has been brought to me. On the Nones of December, the Senate decreed the execution of five of your conspirators. Lentulus Sura, Gaius Cethegus, Publius Statilius, Marcus Caeparius, and Gaius Cornelius *live no more*. The terms remain the same: you and Gaius Manlius are to surrender at once. All who follow you are free to return to their homes or be adjudged traitors to the Republic if they remain with you. That is all. I will await your answer, Lucius Catilina."

Pompeius and his soldiers wheel about and gallop back to their camp. On the ramparts, Centurion Gaius Manlius speculates, "Could it be true?"

Catilina is lost in his own thoughts, but he rouses himself sufficiently to say, "I can't afford to gamble that it's *not* true. I've had no word from Roma since those five were arrested." Then resuming his commander's demeanor, he orders, "Assemble the men. They can follow me, or they can leave. That's the choice of free men."

"Follow you *where?*" the centurion asks.

Catilina looks directly into Manlius' eyes. "To Gaul."

THE NIGHT PASSES SLOWLY. BOTH the rebel camp and the Pompeian camp are well lit and securely guarded. But there are sounds of movement, of horses' hooves and marching feet, from the rebels and from the direction of Faesulae. Pompeius keeps vigil without any trace of alarm. It is obvious to him and to his legate, Petreius, that Catilina is breaking camp and fleeing north. Consul Antonius and Legate Cicero are disturbed at Pompeius' complacency at the rebels' escape.

"Imperator, shall we not advance?" Quintus offers.

"No, Cicero. We'll not venture anything in the dark. We'll reconnoiter at first light."

Antonius is impatiently alarmed. "You *want* them to escape?"

"I want them out in the open, on the move, and the only place for them to go is north." Pompeius smirks and his face is a mask of irony.

At the first rays of dawn, Pompeius and his aides and officers ride unopposed into the rebel camp. The tents are still standing. Embers of old fires yet burn weakly. Here and there, groups of veterans sit or stand in a mood of resignation and submission. Pompeius reckons their number at about two thousand. He halts his horse next to a grizzled veteran of about sixty years. "Good morning, Father. So you had second thoughts about Catilina, eh?" Pompeius regards the old soldier with filial respect. "You know where he's headed?"

The old soldier's toothless mouth moves. "Cisalpina," he says. "Damn cold this time of year. Enough snow to bury a man... maybe all of them."

"And how many of *them* are there, Father?"

The old soldier shrugs. "Six, maybe seven thousand. But they won't last. Many of them, old like me, sick, weak. They won't make it to Gaul. Winter march through the mountains—*nah*. That's why we stayed."

"You're right, Father!" Pompeius chortles. "Petreius, give these men food and send them off to wherever they wish to go, but *not* north. And break up this camp."

"Yes, Imperator." Petreius wheels his horse about to execute his orders.

Pompeius calls after him. "Breakfast for all units. Then strike camp and we march."

Petreius extends his arm in a salute to his commander and then rides off.

Consul Antonius leans over his horse's neck and pats the beast. "Catilina will have a good headstart."

"True," Pompeius agrees. "But he won't get far. In fact, he won't get farther than Pistoria."

The Consul and Quintus Cicero exchange quizzical glances. "Imperator, might you take us into your confidence?" Quintus dares to ask.

Pompeius looks up at the cold, hard December sky and its menacing clouds. "While you gentlemen were collecting levies, I arranged for Metellus Celer to march with his Picene recruits to the Cisalpina and occupy the Apennine passes ascending to Pistoria. His five thousand men are in position even now."

Antonius and Quintus marvel at Pompeius' strategy. "Congratulations, Imperator!" Antonius offers.

"That's somewhat premature, Consul. It's not over yet." Pompeius calculates. The forces under him and Antonius number about eight thousand veterans and recruits. He hopes that desertions will deplete Catilina's army and that the weather will not play havoc upon his own pursuing forces. More than this, he hopes that a pitched battle can be avoided so that Roman and Italian countrymen will not spill each others' blood.

While Catilina retreats toward the Cisalpina, his remaining six conspirators hide in Roma's port city, Ostia. They have fled hither since their five confederates had been executed. Here they hope to take ship and leave both Roma and Italia, but their ultimate destination is a source of dissension among them.

"Take the next ship for Sicilia," Lucius Vargunteius urges.

"Go beyond Sicilia," Porcius Laeca adds, "to Africa Province, pass through Numidia, and then on to Mauretania."

"But why Mauretania?" Autronius Paetus asks. "Its rulers have split the kingdom between them. If Bogudes doesn't sell us out, then surely his brother Bocchus will!"

Porcius Laeca reminds them of a small detail that Catilina had once mentioned to them. "Publius Sittius, an equite from Nuceria, has been operating in Mauretania for years. He has a considerable mercenary army, Romans, Italians, Iberians, and Africans. He bounces back and forth between the two kings. If Catilina escapes, I'll wager he'll go to Mauretania; and even if he doesn't make it, there are plenty of opportunities there for us—expatriates, just like Sittius."

"Too risky!" Publius Sulla opines. "I've no reason to trust this Sittius any more than I trust the Mauretanians."

Sulla looks out at the harbor where grain barges from Sicilia and Egypt are docked and waiting to be unloaded. "My illustrious uncle the Dictator had clients and retainers in Epirus and Greece. My name should yet carry some respect and induce their support."

"*Epirus?*" Lucius Cassius is intrigued. "Yes, I suppose—better Epirus than Mauretania."

"I'm with you, Sulla," says Autronius Paetus. "To Epirus!"

Porcius Laeca insists upon Mauretania, and he wins over Gaius Cornelius and Lucius Vargunteius.

"Then that's it," Gaius Cornelius remarks. "At least we'll have an easier time getting a ship for our destination. How are the three of you going to make it to Epirus?"

"We could all take the same ship down to Rhegium," Sulla suggests. "There we'll split up. You three to Sicilia, and we'll ship across the Ionian."

"You've a long voyage!" Vargunteius smirks. "Can you afford it? If we traveled together to the same ultimate destination we could share our resources—limited as they are."

"Listen to me, all of you!" Sulla declares. "I want no part of Mauretania, or Publius Sittius and his mercenaries, and I'm through with Catilina! I'm going to Epirus and then to Greece even if I have to row the damned ship as a galley slave!"

"May your uncle's good fortune accompany you, Sulla." Porcius Laeca is resigned to their separate paths. "I hope some of that good fortune will visit Catilina, and protect Praecia and Sempronia."

The conspirators fled Roma in such haste that they have no intelligence of Praecia's suicide or of the fate that awaits Sempronia.

DECIMUS BRUTUS SUMMONS HIS NAMESAKE son. Father and son meet in the elder's study. The elder Decimus has spent several hours in seclusion meditating upon his rights as a Roman husband and considering his prerogatives as a senator of consular rank. What he has decided to do is in line with Roma's *mos maiorum*, the ways of the ancestors. Never mind the past generation or two that have seen remarkable advances in Roman female emancipation, at least among the patrician and plebeian nobility, in economic and social spheres.

"What I am about to do, my son, I do *not* out of cruelty, but out of justice," Decimus tells his son. "Do you understand?"

Young Decimus Brutus would rather be out carousing with his fellow-cubs, the young men whose wont is to drink and to whore about with Publius Clodius Pulcher. But Clodius has virtually vanished. He has not been heard of or seen since before the Bona Dea profanation. Decimus fondly remembers the excursion they had taken down to Brundisium. Theirs had been a festive progress to and from the port city.

"Yes, Father," the young man replies. "But I don't know who or what this refers to."

Decimus Brutus reaches for a birch rod hanging on the wall. "You'll see. Come with me."

With a huff, Decimus Brutus walks out of the study and into the corridor. The son follows his father toward his mother's suite of rooms. A pair of sturdy slaves stands guard at the open door. Father and son enter and find Sempronia pacing to and fro across the marble in-laid floor.

"What's the meaning of this?" Sempronia demands. "You've kept me under guard in my own rooms for the last three hours! How dare you, Decimus! My son—what has he told you?"

"Mother – I, I...."

"Never mind, son," the father interrupts. "All you need do is listen and watch." Decimus Brutus turns to one of the slaves, "Fetch two of her women, the biggest—that would be the Ligurians." The slave goes off to do as he is bidden.

Decimus fingers the birch rod menacingly as he speaks. "Your mother has consorted with traitors to the Republic. She has been the mistress of one of them, at least one that I know of. She has betrayed and dishonored me, and you, my son, and she has betrayed Roma."

Sempronia's face turns to a mask of terror. Her eyes well with tears as she comes to realize that the birch rod in her husband's hand is not a mere prop. Yet, she holds up her head and sets her face in utter defiance.

"Sempronia, five of your confederates have been executed, and one, your special friend, Praecia, has taken her own life. I can't be sure if it was bravery or cowardice that impelled her to hang herself. No matter. Your punishment has been put into my hands. Be grateful, wife, that there will be no public scrutiny, I'll see to that. Instead, as your husband, I invoke the ancestral rights of corporal authority. And after you have been chastised you will be confined to your own rooms—forever. You'll have no further opportunity to go about and intrigue and whore with anyone."

At that moment, the slave returns with two large, big-boned slave women. They see the terror in their mistress' eyes. They feel the tension in the room. But they say nothing and do nothing but bow to their master.

"Your mistress needs you," Decimus sneers. "Hold her securely against the pillar, her back facing me. Now!"

The two women do as they are ordered. Sempronia's defiance begins to slacken. "No, Decimus—please no!" Her face and bosom are pressed against the cold, marble pillar as the two slave women tightly crisscross her arms on the pillar's reverse side. She is unable to move.

Decimus Brutus advances upon his wife. He rips the back of her stola revealing the sensuous, broad shoulders. Another tear and Sempronia's waist and buttocks are exposed in all their curvaceous beauty. The stola drops to the floor encircling Sempronia's ankles. Her legs, the legs that had parted and enveloped Lentulus Sura, begin to shake. But Sempronia is unable to pull away from the pillar. Her protests and pleas are unheeded.

Decimus Brutus steps back several feet from Sempronia and the pillar. He catches sight of his son turning away. "No, Decimus. You must look. You must learn the fate of unfaithful wives!"

"Gods, Decimus! Send him away!" Sempronia implores. Then she shrieks in pain as Decimus applies the birch rod methodically upon her shoulders, buttocks, and legs. Welts and blood emerge upon the supple flesh. Decimus grows winded with each stroke and sweat pours down his face. Decimus the Younger watches in horror. He would run from the room were it not for the two slaves blocking the doorway. His mother's humiliation, his mother's torn, bloodied flesh sicken him. He cannot help but double over and retch.

When he looks up again, it appears that his mother has fainted. Yet, she is held in place by the slave women. Decimus Brutus plies the rod. *Thirty-three...Thirty-five...Thirty-nine.* Decimus Brutus stops, wipes his brow, and then throws the bloodied rod to the floor.

"See to your mistress!" He snaps at them. Upon seeing his son's discharge on the floor, he bellows again, "And clean up this room!"

Sempronia is gingerly carried to her bed and laid prone upon it. She begins to regain consciousness as the women cleanse her wounds and daub them with olive oil. Her sobs are punctuated with curses for her husband. The two slave women also weep and beg their mistress' pardon.

In the corridor, young Decimus tells his father that he will never forget what he has witnessed.

The College of Pontiffs, at the request of Quintus Lutatius Catulus, convenes at the Regia. The Pontifex Maximus Gaius Julius Caesar presides. They meet in the conclave chamber at a long oaken table. At their head sits the Chief Pontiff. To his immediate right sits the Rex Sacrorum, Lucius Claudius, followed by Marcus Licinius Crassus and Marcus Valerius Messala. To Caesar's immediate left sits Catulus, and then Marcus Licinius Lucullus, and Decimus Junius Silanus.

Theirs is more of a political rather than a religious fraternity. The pontiffs have all been co-opted into the college, but Caesar has been elected by a special election of seventeen of the thirty-five tribes. There are men like Catulus, with far more seniority than Caesar, who regard his election as a political perversion. Both optimates and popularists are represented on the college. With the exception of Catulus and Silanus, they are sound and robust in health. Silanus is afflicted with his chronic ague, while Catulus is strangely lethargic, pale, with a most irritating, raspy voice.

Nevertheless, Catulus commences the business of their meeting. "Pontifex Maximus, thank you for consenting to meet with us today." His tone is unctuous and fawning.

"I'm always at your disposal, gentlemen." Caesar is equally unctuous and fulsome.

"I... that is, *we* wanted to know what steps you anticipate taking in regard to the Bona Dea sacrilege committed last week." Catulus hopes that he has cornered Caesar.

Caesar replies thoughtfully, "I see."

Catulus prods on. "Surely, you realize that an offense to the gods, committed at a time when the Republic struggles to suppress rebellion and sedition, requires, indeed *demands*, investigation and propitiation."

"I'm informed that the attending ladies have repeated the rites. That should serve as sufficient propitiation. Is that not so, Lucius Claudius?" Caesar turns to the Rex Sacrorum for confirmation.

The elderly pontiff nods agreeably. "The Virgo Maxima has so informed me."

"But there remains the matter of investigation, no?" Catulus' irritation begins to rise. Turning also to Lucius Claudius, he adds,

"Surely, our Rex Sacrorum must have heard the rumors—I say, *rumors*—that the profaner was his own kinsman, Publius Clodius Pulcher."

"We should investigate—*rumors?*" Caesar coyly asks.

"No, *Chief Pontiff!*" Catulus pronounces the title with unmistakable sarcasm. "It is the profanation that needs to be investigated, the culprit found and punished if the gods are truly to be propitiated. *That* and nothing less is required—*Chief Pontiff.*"

Caesar looks directly into Catulus' face and sees the old man turning scarlet as his chiseled jaw is firmly set. He says, "It was my understanding that under the Senate's Ultimate Decree all matters not pertaining to the political crisis must be deferred."

Marcus Lucullus offers his opinion. "Deferred—but *not* indefinitely. With all respect, Chief Pontiff, you have made no attempt to broach this matter in the Senate. If you will not, then others may well do so."

"Perhaps any of you?" Marcus Crassus queries. He notices Decimus Junius Silanus glaring hatefully at Caesar, but the cuckold keeps his peace. It is all too apparent that Catulus is their mouthpiece.

"It is our right, I dare say our *responsibility* as pontiffs to do so," Catulus declares, as he turns and considers Caesar venomously, "especially if *you* will *not* do so."

Marcus Valerius Messalla offers an acute observation. "Concerning Publius Clodius—he's not attended any Senate meetings since before the Bona Dea, and he's not been in Cicero's bodyguard as he used to be."

"What are you suggesting, Marcus Messalla?" Crassus asks.

Messalla replies, "Just a hunch—that somehow the profanation is not just a matter of religious sacrilege. There's more to it. Perhaps there's a political element."

"It would not surprise me if it's all somehow tied up with Catilina's plot!" Catulus declares accusingly. "That is all the more reason for an investigation, Chief Pontiff."

Caesar has by now had enough. He rises from his chair. "Thank you, gentlemen. I will consider carefully what has been said here. Good day."

The pontiffs rise, bow respectfully, and then depart—all but Crassus. He whispers to Caesar, "You'd better have a talk with *Pretty-Boy*. It's best to prepare him. Give him time to think about his options."

Deep in thought, Caesar nods in agreement.

Cicero's <u>Respublica</u>

I convened the Senate—again in the Temple of Concord—after receiving Pompeius Magnus' dispatch from Faesulae. He had announced under the ramparts of Catilina's camp that the Senate had executed the Catilinian Five on the Nones of December. He had urged the rebels to disperse after first surrendering Catilina and Manlius into his custody. But neither Catilina nor Manlius had come out. Pompeius had waited and watched, bracing for a possible sortie from the rebel camp, but this had not occurred.

Instead, what he had expected and hoped for *did* happen. The rebels, reduced now by desertions to six or seven thousand men, abandoned their camp by night and marched northward. Their obvious destination, Pompeius reported, was the Cisalpina, and ultimately unconquered Gaul of the far north. His plan was to pursue and trap them between his cohorts, now reinforced by Consul Antonius' levies, and Metellus Celer's forces. Having anticipated Catilina's attempted dash for Gaul, Pompeius had planned for the Praetor to occupy the northern Apennine passes near Pistoria. The Imperator promised that before the year was out, he would have Catilina and Manlius—either in bonds or their heads on pikes.

The Senate voted commendations for the Republic's commanders with fervent hopes that the rebellion would truly be quashed in the remaining two weeks of the year—if not sooner.

Then, the Senate's attention was diverted to another issue. Beginning with Catulus, and then continuing with the Lucullus brothers and other senators who were pontiffs, augurs, and custodians of the oracular Sibylline Books, there were speeches and calls for the investigation of the Bona Dea sacrilege committed on December second. Obviously, their wives, daughters, sisters, mothers and mothers-in-law must have insisted on this. Yet, each senator resolutely and passionately maintained that the profanation was an endangerment of the Republic's moral rectitude in the gods' eyes. Their statements echoed Terentia's reasoning.

And as Terentia had insisted on the intruder's identity, each of the senators named Publius Clodius Pulcher as the known or at least *suspected* profaner. To everyone's surprise, Lucius Lucullus, Clodius' own brother-in-law, made a motion for the postponement of all public business in the new consular year until the alleged intruder was tried on the charge of *incestum*, or ritual sacrilege. Just as surprisingly, Marcius Rex, also Clodius' brother-in-law, seconded the motion.

How sublimely crafty they were! In putting this sacrilege matter at the head of all public business, the oligarchs sought to delay and obstruct whatever reform agenda Caesar would have initiated once his consulate began. What made the proposal especially detrimental was the fact that no one knew of Clodius' whereabouts. As long as he remained absent and in hiding, his sacrilege trial could not commence, and Caesar's consular program could be deferred indefinitely.

Yes, it could be argued that the oligarchs were harming the Republic's orderly political affairs for the narrow, selfish purpose of thwarting a popularist consul-elect. But they could counter this with their devotion to and observance of the state religion. After all, the Lucullus brothers and Marcius Rex were members of religious collegia, as were other oligarchs. Even Caesar, as Chief Pontiff, had to concur, at least publicly, with their motion. Had he quibbled with it, he would have appeared to be religiously insensitive to the scandalous profanation. Yet, as consul-elect, he had to have realized that by supporting the measure, he would be frustrating his own political agenda. What a *confounding* dilemma it had to have been for him!

Caesar voted with the majority to approve the proposal, as I did also. I was certain, though, that he had some stratagem by which he would surmount this barrier. Time would tell.

AFTER THE SENATE ADJOURNED, CATULUS and I visited Catilina's wife, Aurelia Orestilla. As Catulus was her guardian, as per Catilina's public pronouncement, I asked him to accompany me because I felt duty-bound to tell her of her husband's flight.

She and her daughter, a most attractive young woman named Flavia, received us with a frigid haughtiness. I was not surprised. Briefly, I told her the latest news concerning Catilina.

"So, Consul," she said with icy bitterness, "you've not only driven him from Roma, but from Italia as well. But it won't be over for him or for you until either his head or *yours* is nailed to the Rostra! Now get out of my house!"

So much for any hint of gratitude I might have expected from her. Catulus assured me that she had been equally abrupt with him on previous visits.

As I made my way back home, I found myself sorely missing Servius Sulpicius. The vote on the Nones of December had driven a wedge into our friendship. I noted his absence in the Senate, as I noted Crassus' absence as well. In my deepest heart, I hoped that this Catilina rebellion would be destroyed soon so that all disruption, personal and political, would be ended.

As Catilina and Pompeius played their *cat-and-mouse* game in the north, the Senate was torn over the Bona Dea affair. There were various proposals for the constitution of a special court to try the case, all of which brought forth much discord and controversy, especially between optimate and popularist senators. Several times the Senate adjourned without any consensus.

It was not until the last day of the year that the Senate's argumentative factions reached a compromise. The court for the sacrilege trial was to be presided over by a reliable optimate, the praetor-elect, Marcus Valerius Messalla. The jury was to consist of fifty-six men to be empanelled from the senatorial, equestrian, and plebeian classes, with the defense counsel having special latitude in their selection. The prescribed penalty, upon conviction, was to be perpetual exile and confiscation of property—the gods' curse for ritual sacrilege. All that was lacking was the alleged profaner.

We were also lacking word from Pompeius about Catlina's capture or destruction. He had promised to deliver the living body of the traitor or his head by the end of the year. It would have given me tremendous satisfaction on my last official day to have announced in the Senate and from the Rostra that he who had plotted to overthrow the Republic no longer lived or that he had been apprehended. But this honor did not fall to me.

Having written an official report of my consulate, I went to the Tabularium to deposit it in the official state archives. I had written at length of my endeavors against popularist schemes, but I did not directly mention Caesar or Crassus. However, I made up for this omission by playing up Catilina's conspiracy and its suppression. Here again, though I mentioned all of the conspirators by name, according to Publius Clodius' disclosures, I did not name him as my informant. I thought it best to avoid implicating him in the conspiracy. In this way, no citizen would have had reason to charge and prosecute him for complicity. Moreover, I had originally promised him legal immunity, and I intended to keep my word. Besides, he presently had the profanation/sacrilege charge hanging over him like Damocles' sword.

From the Tabularium, I proceeded to the Rostra. As was the custom and right of every outgoing magistrate, I was prepared to address the populace and summarize and defend my consulate. But no sooner had I ascended the Rostra when I beheld the bronzed, scowling visage of Tribune Titus Labienus protruding from the crowd. He had begun his term back on December tenth. With a voice reeking of accusatory menace, he called out to me, "Consul, as you have caused Roman citizens to suffer death without trial and appeal to the People, you are unworthy to address the citizens!"

Jeers and catcalls erupted from two hundred men around the tribune. I tried to speak but their jeering persisted. Again, Labienus bellowed his objection. "Consul, as Tribune of the Roman People, I *forbid* you to speak to the citizens whose rights and sovereignty you have violated! Stand down, Marcus Cicero!"

As if on cue the mob took up the chant – "Stand down, Marcus Cicero! Stand down, Marcus Cicero! Away with you! Away with you!"

It was impossible to continue. Yet, before descending from the Rostra, I shouted over the din, "By my efforts, the Republic was saved from arson, murder, and sedition. I trust the Roman people will remember this!" My lictors pushed a path through the pressing crowd as I walked down the Rostra steps and across the Forum.

The incident put me in a foul mood for the rest of the day. Though convinced of my own probity and certain of the support of the Senate and the equites—the greatest beneficiaries of Catilina's suppression—I had a profound, loathsome fear of the mob and of what it could become under reckless, demagogic tribunes.

The triumph I had achieved in destroying the Catilinian conspiracy would prove to be short-lived. Caesar would exploit my success in order to debilitate me; and my relations with the Pulchers, as well as certain indiscretions, would be my undoing.

Liber II Exsul (Exile)

Caput VII Cicero's Respublica

THE NEW YEAR BEGAN WITH the formal inauguration of Gaius Caesar and Marcus Bibulus on the Capitoline mount. The new consuls swore to preserve, protect, and defend the Republic of the Senate and People of Roma. Contrary to common expectations, there were no radical pronouncements from Caesar and therefore no reactionary, confrontational utterances from Bibulus. But Pompeius' issues – land grants for his veterans and the ratification of his Eastern acta – had yet to be considered. Similarly, the tax farmers' Asian contract was still a bone of contention between senators and equites, one that threatened to disrupt the concord of the orders that I had labored to establish.

There was still no sight or even word of Clodius, and so the sacrilege trial was still pending. All other business was contingent upon expediting the Good Goddess affair. However, within a fortnight after the consular inaugurations, momentous news came from Pompeius.

Omniscient Narrative

CATILINA'S REBEL ARMY ARDUOUSLY TRUDGES through the Apennine Mountains. The buffeting winter winds, intermittent snow, supply scarcities, and disillusionment induce scores and then hundreds of deserters to fall out and straggle by the wayside. Catilina pushes on – his destination is the Cisalpina Gallic province, and from there to unconquered Gaul, known to the Romans as Gallia Comata, Long-Haired Gaul. Should that prove infeasible, he will then take the maritime route along the Transalpine coast, stop at the allied Greek city of Massilia for succor, continue along the Iberian coast and eventually cross the Pillars of Hercules into the kingdom of Mauretania. There, he is bound to be received by his friend, the Italian freebooter, Publius Sittius. These are Catilina's thoughts as he spurs his horse forward against the north wind.

Periodically, he mounts a cliff or promontory and looks south and sees the long, extended line of Pompeius' pursuing cohorts. Each time he looks, the pursuers seem to close the gap between themselves and the rebels. But he is confident that he can escape them.

His confidence, though, is shaken when his scouts report that the mountain passes ascending to Pistoria are occupied by troops. They identify the vexillum of Praetor Metellus Celer. Catilina realizes that he is trapped. There is no time for indecision or vacillation.

He orders his tired, cold, hungry men to turn south. They will fight the army that he assumes must be equally tired from the arduous ascent through the mountains. Besides, he reckons on an easier fight as one of the commanders is his erstwhile associate, Consul Gaius Antonius. Then again, there is also Pompeius to consider. He has no doubt that the Magnus will fight. Still, Catilina resolves to take on the closer enemy.

He forms his battle line in a narrow valley strewn with newly fallen snow. Gaius Manlius commands the right wing; a former Decurion, one Vir Faesulanus, takes the left, and Catilina plants himself in the center. The silver eagle of Marius is held aloft directly behind his right shoulder. Catilina addresses the men, tries to buck up their flagging spirits, assuring them that while the enemy may win, it will be a costly victory. Dismounting, Catilina smacks his horse's rump, sending it careening across the field. Those of his men who have horses follow his example – they will all share the same danger from afoot.

The Pompeian troops spot the rebels' battle formation. The Magnus immediately orders the bucinators to sound battle orders. Addressing the soldiers, he tells them that he will not waste time attempting to negotiate with rebels against the state. All of his soldiers' exertions will be consummated in this battle.

But not for Gaius Antonius. He complains of an attack of gout, exacerbated by the winter, mountain march. He will not participate in the battle. Pompeius sees through the ploy – Antonius is obviously unnerved at the prospect of fighting his former confederate. As the malingering proconsul heads to the rear, Pompeius makes his command dispositions. Quintus Cicero will command the right wing in Antonius' stead; the legate Marcus Petreius is to take the left wing. Pompeius will command the center, and his reserve line will be jointly commanded by Quaestor Sestius and Military Tribune Plancius.

Despite his unwillingness to negotiate, Pompeius calls out across the snowy expanse to Catilina. If Catilina and Manlius will surrender, Roman bloodshed will be averted. In response, the rebels shout back defiantly: "Death before surrender!"

Pompeius orders his lines to advance and the ensuing battle is a merciless fight. Catilina and the entire center, the men clad in worn metal-studded leather coats, bronze helmets, and knee-length *braccae*, surge toward the Pompeians, cutting down all in their way. The rebels' swords, daggers, and cudgels steep themselves in the blood of the Republic's soldiers. Though clearly outnumbered, the rebels cut and slash and thrust forward in their valiant fight without once turning about. For this reason, they fail to see, until it is too late, that Pompeius' flanks have extended themselves.

In the confines of the narrow valley, the Pompeian flanks circle and envelop the rebel wings, attacking them, and slaughtering Manlius, Faesulanus, and their men. The iron-helmeted and ring-mail armored soldiers of the Pompeian flanks link up and begin to press in on the rear of Catilina's veterans.

Advancing to within several paces of Pompeius – conspicuously mounted on his charger – Catilina is surrounded and dispatched by a score of swords. The Marian silver eagle falls by his side, pressing into the bloodied snow.

When the victors inspect the rebel dead, they see that none have wounds on their backs. None made any attempt to flee. The rebels have perished to the last man. The snow-laden battlefield is strewn with the human wreckage of war; corpses, severed limbs, swords, shields, and javelins litter the crimson drenched, snow-bound earth.

Manlius' body is barely recognizable from the wounds it has sustained. It is carried before Pompeius. Coming upon Catilina's corpse and verifying its identity, Pompeius orders its head, and that of

Manlius, to be lopped off and sent to Roma along with the tidings of victory.

Pompeius oversees the gathering up of the dead, both rebels and government troops, and their cremation with all due military honors, the beating of drums and the plaintive blaring of bucina and cornu. The Magnus acquires a battle trophy – Marius' silver eagle. His cohorts and the veterans levied by Antonius and Quintus Cicero acclaim him, *"Ave Imperator! Ave Imperator! Ave Imperator!"*

Cicero's Respublica

Consul Caesar presided over the Senate and sullenly read Pompeius' dispatch: Catilina and his rebels had been defeated and destroyed in a pitched battle near Pistoria. The victorious Imperator sent the severed heads of Catilina and Manlius on pikes, as he had once promised he would. Caesar arranged for them to be exhibited on tripods in the Curia's foyer so that the Senate could indeed verify them.

Overjoyed at the news, the optimates proclaimed a thanksgiving to the gods for the destruction of the Republic's enemies. As would be expected, the popularists sat impassively, taking the news with the same sullen demeanor with which Caesar had presented it. From the tribunes' bench in the foyer, there were outcries from Tribune Labienus and Tribune Vatinius against what they called the unlawful execution of Roman citizens. But they made no attempt to veto the Senate's proceedings.

The Lucullus brothers moved for certain provincial dispositions. Proconsul Metellus Celer was to govern Cisalpine Gaul in my stead as Pistoria was only a short remove from the province. Gaius Antonius was to proceed to the governorship of Macedonia as per the agreement that I had made with him. Quaestor Publius Sestius and Military Tribune Gnaeus Plancius were to accompany and serve under him in administering the province. Pompeius was commissioned to remain in Etruria to pacify and police the region until the Senate deemed it rid of all rebel activity or – though the Senate did not publicly admit this – until such time as they were willing to allow him to return to Roma. Finally, the praetors Pomptinus and Flaccus, who had served me so loyally, were appointed to the respective governorships of Transalpine Gaul and Asia.

In all of the Senate's proceedings that day, no mention was made of my consulate or of my services in exposing and suppressing the Catilinian conspiracy. This omission and the tribunes' agitation against the "unlawful" – as they called it – execution of Roman citizens annoyed me. My only contribution to the meeting was to propose that Catilina's remains – that is to say, his head – should be given over to his widow and daughter. Otherwise, it, and Manlius', would have been thrown from the Tarpeian Rock of the Capitoline Mount – a symbolic gesture accorded to traitors.

I was happy that the Senate approved my proposal. A small gesture, perhaps, and in the same vein as my motions for Sura's widow and for Aurelia Orestilla to be allowed to retain their properties. Yet, I hoped that this might offset the news that had the business community astir: I had exploited the Catilinian Five and the conspirators who had escaped. Acquiring their confiscated properties through proxies at public auction, I in turn sold them and profited so lucratively that I was able to make a substantial payment to Crassus on the Palatine mansion. Also, I purchased two additional villas, one at Pompeii and the other at Antium.

Though I was far from impervious to rumor and gossip, it had seemed expeditious to override my political conscience in acquiring these properties, especially from such controversial sources. This was only fair compensation for my services to the Republic. But I was also looking to another quarter for additional revenue. If Antonius were true to our bargain, and if his quaestor, Sestius could be relied upon to be thoroughly circumspect, then my share of the provincial proceeds from Macedonia would enable me to expedite what was yet owed to Crassus for the Palatine house.

Now, seventeen years later, this house, splendid though it is, has become a virtual prison for me whenever I am in Roma, and my rural estates are like places of exile when I am away from the City. This imprisonment, this enforced exclusion is Caesar's work. It is the measure of his triumph over the Republic and the depth of my own submission.

Caesar – how polite, how accommodating he was on that day when, as presiding Consul, he presented Pompeius' dispatch. But just when I thought that we were about to adjourn, he shocked us all by presenting Publius Clodius Pulcher.

Like a shade returning from the Underworld, he came before the Senate looking ever so dignified in his senatorial toga and purple-striped tunic. In his attire and on his face there was no trace of a comic actor or disguised impersonator. His manner was reserved and cautious. "Senators, I stand in the shadow of suspicion of having offended the gods, at least one god in particular," he announced in that distinctive, nasal voice. "In your punctilious observance of propriety due the gods, you have enjoined all public business until I am judged and my alleged offense expiated. This is a black mark against my name. I will not have it said that Publius Clodius Pulcher obstructed the public business of the Senate and People of Roma. You have decreed that I must be tried, and so at your command, I shall. And in my trial and in my acquittal the offense against the Bona Dea will be expiated."

A round of applause, mostly from the popularists, greeted his announcement. The optimates, particularly the oligarchs, looked wary. Presiding over the Senate and having introduced Clodius as though he had been hiding in his toga folds, Caesar's demeanor and his solicitous ministrations toward him spoke volumes. Something was afoot here. The whole business, however dignified and decorous on the outside, smelled of collusion; and what a comedy there was to behold once the trial began!

The comedy's first act was Clodia Pulchra visiting me the next morning along with the usual cadre of petitioners. But unlike the others, she was splendidly beautiful and fetching. Her raven tresses were impeccably dressed; her ivory-colored stola accentuated her physical contours and the saffron palla cascaded recklessly about her sensuous shoulders. I took her aside to a room adjoining the atrium, oblivious to the other callers' mumbled speculations.

"Marcus Cicero, I want you to defend my brother." Clodia's ebony eyes fixed on me. "He risked his life informing on Catilina's gang. You would not have been able to destroy them without him. You *know* it! Now he needs your help. You won't deny him. And you'll be most *sweetly* rewarded."

"Is it specifically *my* help that he needs? I'm certain that he has quite formidable help already." I smiled with as much charm as I could muster.

"You owe him *your* help!" Clodia's eyes flashed. "What does it matter who else is helping him?"

"Clodia, the whole business reeks. For your brother's sake, and for yours, and yes, for *mine* as well, I'd just as soon stay out of it."

She looked at me intently, breathing out spite through her flaring nostrils. "Then make sure that you do just *that*! Thank you for your time, Marcus Cicero."

Clodia departed with an air of haughtiness, looking back at me once over her shoulder. A slight smile played upon her voluptuous lips.

Omniscient Narrative

"Pompeia, I've considered our situation most carefully." Caesar says this to his wife who stands before him straight and unyielding. "It's to no purpose for you to give testimony, to be questioned, to be...."

"Are you sending me away? Is that it?"

Caesar rises from his chair, walks around the table where various scrolls and tablets are laid out. He reaches for a particular scroll and hands it to Pompeia. "It is necessary that we terminate our marriage. I've provided generously for you – your dowry is returned to you forthwith. A house in the Carinae is at your disposable. A new husband is ready for you too, if you'll have him – Tribune Titus Labienus. He's a widower."

Pompeia sneers, "Most generous. But you must want something from me."

"Only that you leave Roma *now* – before the trial begins."

"Why? What are you afraid of?"

"I fear nothing – except *not* fulfilling my destiny. I'll not have this trial interfere with it."

Pompeia turns and makes for the door of the Regia's library. She stops and turns back to her husband. "You must know, despite whatever Aurelia may have told you, I had nothing to do with Pulcher or whoever it was that profaned the rites."

"Yes, Pompeia, I know."

"You *know*?" She asks incredulously. "And yet you would resort to *this*?" She holds up the scroll containing Caesar's bill of divorce. "Why? Is it a whim? Or your mother's venomous inspiration?"

Caesar swallows hard; he is annoyed at the barb directed at his mother. "Because, Pompeia, you must be above suspicion in *this* as in all things." He pauses and looks plaintively at the woman who has been his wife. "Farewell, Pompeia, and good fortune to you."

Cicero's Respublica

Ordinarily, trials were conducted in the open air of the Forum. However, this one was held in the Aemilian Basilica lest the inclement winter rains interfere with the proceedings. Clodius' advocate was young Gaius Scribonius Curio, much to the annoyance of his optimate father who did not hold the Pulchers in high regard. The effeminate rake packed the jury with the dregs and riffraff of the City rabble, while the prosecutor, Hortensius, succeeded in maintaining a modest proportion of respectable citizens from the senatorial and equestrian classes.

Hortensius had asked me to assist him in the prosecution, but I decided to remain aloof because of Clodius' services to me against Catilina. Naturally, I did not extend this confidence to Hortensius; nor did I tell him that I suspected collusion between Clodius and Caesar. A short time later, Terentia was to misunderstand my motives.

Terentia, Fabia, and the Chief Vestal Licinia were the first, second, and third in a veritable procession of witnesses to identify Clodius as the female-disguised intruder. But Curio impugned their testimony. "Are we to believe," he mockingly wondered, "that Clodius' beauty makes him a likely female impersonator? And in the pandemonium of screaming, outraged ladies, you could identify Publius Clodius? Why would he commit such a ludicrous prank?"

Of all the witnesses, only Aurelia, Caesar's old dowager mother, had an answer to Curio's question. She said with a malevolent accusatory tone, "He was looking to have an affair with my son's wife!" The spectators guffawed and howled with laughter, and some of the cruder elements called out: *What Pulcher, tired of your sisters? Did you bring Fulvia to make it a threesome?"* The raucous laughter did not subside until Praetor Messalla, the presiding judge, called for order.

The prosecutor called on Caesar concerning Aurelia's allegation, but he had no knowledge of any connection between Clodius and Pompeia. "Why then," Hortensius asked, "did you divorce your wife?"

Caesar replied cryptically, "Caesar's wife must be above suspicion."

Hortensius had no rejoinder for this. Instead, he looked up at the judge's tribunal and threw up his hands in utter frustration. Not only had Caesar divorced his wife, for whatever motives, but he apparently had spirited her out of Roma; neither defense nor prosecution could summon her to testify.

Several days into the trial, Publius Clodius testified on his own behalf. When both defense and prosecution counsels inquired of his whereabouts on the occasion of the Good Goddess rites, he insisted that he was at Interamna, about sixty miles distant from Roma, inspecting some family properties.

So *this* was to be his alibi! Not only was he *not* the profaner, but he *wasn't* even in Roma! His alibi not only stalemated the trial, but it also provoked an acrimonious argument between Terentia and me.

WE WERE TALKING ABOUT THE trial over dinner when Terentia asked me, "When did you last see Publius Clodius?"

I hesitated before answering, "On the day that the Catilinian Five were arrested."

"Wasn't that December second?"

"Why…yes," I cautiously replied.

"The very same day as the Good Goddess?"

"Just so."

"Then you knew Publius Clodius could not have been at Interamna if you spoke with him only hours before the rites."

I looked at her anxiously, uncertain about what she would next hurl at me.

"Marcus, you've kept out of the trial. Is it only because Clodius had been your informer?"

"And what other reason could there be?" I was trying to make light of it.

"Oh?" she exclaimed. "You know so very well! Clodius was not your first or only informer. *Clodia Pulcher* too had your ears and eyes and perhaps *more*!"

"Terentia," I protested, "your insinuation is absurd."

"Absurd?" she repeated, rising from the dining couch. "You chose not to assist in the prosecution. You sat there and heard him lie and you made no move to disprove his alibi! And you're holding back *only* because he was your informer? That's *cow dung* straight from the cattle market! Isn't it because Pulchra *Black-Eyes* has bewitched you? I *know* she was here on the night of the rites. I know she came to see you then as well as before the trial began."

"Look, Terentia," I countered, "I've no doubt that Clodius *is* the intruder, but only because he was trying to hide from Catilina's men who were out to kill him."

"And Clodia?"

"Damn her! She has nothing to do with this or me or anything!" As so often happened in these confrontations with Terentia, I was losing my patience.

"*Prove it!*" she demanded.

"What?"

"Go to Hortensius," she demanded again. "Offer to give testimony. Tell them all that you saw and spoke with Clodius on the Good Goddess day. I've seen how *Black-Eyes* looked at you each day at the trial. I've seen *you* look back at her. So then, Marcus, prove to me that there's nothing between the two of you. Go destroy her brother's alibi. *This* alone will satisfy me; this and *nothing* else!"

There was no reasoning with her. When the trial resumed, I testified for the prosecution. I publicly admitted to speaking with Publius Clodius only hours – no more than three hours – before the rites. However, I did not divulge the reason for my communication with him.

As I spoke, I noticed Clodia Pulchra staring at me, smiling that mysteriously enticing smile. I was getting caught up in that smile when Hortensius proclaimed, "Roma to Interamna – all in a matter of three hours! Even upon Mercury's winged heels that's an improbable feat!"

There was scattered laughter at Hortensius' wry comment. Now I saw Clodia Pulchra shaking her head as her brother glared at me with an expression of hateful vindictiveness such as I had often seen from Catilina. Fulvia was sitting next to her lover; her visage was like red-brown stone which hurled evil and wrathful spite at me. At another quarter, I saw Terentia beaming with sublime satisfaction.

The court was adjourned so that the jury could deliberate and vote. During the next two days, there were rampant rumors of jury tampering and bribery. Hushed speculation mentioned Crassus as the source of the bribes. On the third day, Praetor Messalla announced the jury's tally: thirty-one for acquittal and twenty-five for conviction. Hortensius threw up his arms in dismay and disgust. Turning to the cackling jurors, he upbraided them, "You should have requested a bodyguard to protect your ill-gotten gains!"

We began to leave the basilica. In the press, Publius Clodius came up to me and through a malevolent grin he hissed, "You'll pay for this, Marcus Cicero!" He had moved a few steps away when his sister was before me. Smiling balefully and shaking her head reprovingly, she whispered with equal malevolence, "You've made another serious mistake."

In the light of subsequent events, her words proved to be prophetic.

With his acquittal bought and secured, Clodius was spared the penalty of perpetual banishment. Now, he was free to pursue his political career with the backing of his new friends – Caesar and Crassus.

While the rumors and speculations of Crassus' bribery continued to grow, neither the Senate nor the pontifical college pressed for an investigation. It seemed that everyone wanted to dispose of the whole business. But for me, Clodius' acquittal, or more specifically my role in almost precluding it, was to impact injuriously upon me. In placating Terentia's groundless suspicions – perhaps they were *not* entirely groundless – I had had to antagonize the Pulcher siblings.

However, the Pulchers had their own share of troubles. Not long after the trial, Lucius Lucullus divorced his wife, the eldest Claudia, on grounds of immorality and adultery. In doing so, he severed the political ties between his Licinius clan and the Claudii Pulchri. Almost at the same time, the oligarch, Marcius Rex, suddenly died of unknown causes at the age of sixty. Wild rumors held that his wife, the second Pulcher sister, had contrived at his death.

At the beginning of Februarius, Decimus Silanus succumbed to his chronic malaria – an affliction visited upon so many by the adjacent Pontine marshes. They have yet to be drained and cleaned out.

The greatest blow to the oligarchy befell them when Catulus, the Princeps Senatus, died of a stroke. Caustic wits said his death had been the result of shock over Clodius' acquittal. But the religiously attuned, like Fabia and my Pythagorean friend, Figulus, said that the gods were about to wreak calamity upon Roma because of the compounded sacrilege of judicial bribery.

But if the deaths of three of its members weakened the oligarchy, then at least they afforded the survivors the opportunity to delay further Caesar's consular agenda. Three deaths became, at Consul Bibulus' motion, three consecutive periods of mourning. Public funerals, processions through the Forum and out to Mars Field, eulogies for Marcius Rex, Silanus, and Catulus consumed several weeks. Caesar was again frustrated. The optimates held forth.

Omniscient Narrative

There are numerous caves in the vicinity of the Appian necropolis. Social derelicts have made their homes in many of them. They feed off the vermin that haunt the extensive graveyard. Many live by beggary of the well-to-do who come out on memorial days to decorate the gravesites of their loved ones. But one inhabitant of this morbid world is not of the sub-class of social derelicts; nor does she live off the vermin or off the charity of the privileged.

Maga Venefica hails from Etruria. The name she has taken for herself describes what she is and what she does. She is an old, decrepit hag whose torso is twisted grotesquely and whose face is so pocked and scarred that she conceals it with a coarse veil. The walls of her cavern hold skulls of humans and beasts. A score of candles of varying sizes illuminates the dark recesses of the dank, fetid cave. She has had many visitors, particularly females. Today, two women seek her intermediation, for Maga Venefica is a practitioner of the art of divination through necromancy.

The two women who have come to her are mother and daughter – the widow and step-daughter of Lucius Sergius Catilina. Aurelia Orestilla bears a cylindrical leather chest. The two women are dressed in the darkest, most somber trappings of mourning. They sit at the flat-topped stone that serves as the crone's table or bed or altar.

Orestilla states their business. "Maga Venefica, we would know of Lucius Sergius Catilina – my husband and my daughter's step-father. He was driven from his country, hounded, and killed by his countrymen. *This* is *all* they have allowed me of him." Orestilla pushes the chest forward, pulls back its leather flaps, and reaches in with both hands without the least tremor or hesitation. Then she extracts the severed head of Catilina.

The visage is a mask of aggressive contempt, gashed and bruised, its open eyes staring off into infinity; its hair matted with blood and sweat. Congealed blood encircles the neck where a swift, sharp sword had severed the head from the torso. From such human relics, Maga Venefica is reputed to summon knowledge and truth.

"Tell me, tell me all that led to *this*, and all that will come from it," Orestilla pleads. "I'll pay whatever you ask."

The crone leans toward the grisly relic, sniffing at it and passing her hands around it and then cocking her head. The words escaping her mouth are in an alien tongue, probably ancient Etruscan, Orestilla and Flavia surmise. After several minutes in which these gestures are repeated, she speaks in a heavily accented Latin. "Four men who were with him betrayed him. One is dark and marked with beauty. One has the face of a pig. One is of vast wealth but without hair. And one is head of state and the chief bridge to the gods."

Orestilla matches the descriptions to Clodius, dark-haired, dark-featured, almost femininely beautiful; to Gaius Antonius, whose porcine features complement his demeanor; to Crassus, the rich, bald-pated political schemer, and to Caesar, Consul and Chief Pontiff, the Romans' head *pons* or bridge to their deities. These four have been Catilina's partners. Yet, Antonius had taken soldiers against Catilina; and Crassus dropped Catilina immediately after the last consular election; and Caesar, to whom Catilina had personally appealed, had deserted him. When Catilina had suspected an informer in his group, Orestilla now remembers, it could have been none other than Clodius, he who had attempted to escape assassination by profaning the Bona Dea ceremonies.

"Two men have destroyed him: the one by his tongue and voice, the other by his command and sword. Both shall meet the same fate as this one." Maga indicates Catilina's head. "The one in his own country and by his own countrymen; the other by aliens in an alien land; and of those who betrayed him—all but one will meet death by violence."

Orestilla knows that Cicero's incessant oratory in the Senate had forced her husband to flee Roma; and Pompeius had coordinated the military maneuvering that ultimately destroyed him and his rebels.

Gurgling, retching noises emerge from Maga's throat. She spits bile and blood at her bare feet. "This is what they say of him who was your husband and *her* step-father. He will be defamed and scandalized. But the time will come—ages, ages from now— when he will be renowned as one who would have brought your Roma to a new life. They will write of him and talk of him and they will try to know him; but clouds and mists will surround him so that he will never truly be known apart from the evil that will enclose him as you enclose him in that box. You have a grave for him, yes? You have a marker for him, yes? Then *bury* him! He would not have you keep him like this."

Distraught, Orestilla turns to Flavia. "Give her the purse—*all* of it. Let's get out of here."

CLODIUS PULCHER TAKES A DEEP draught of wine, Falernian vintage, Caesar's favorite. Hospitality is never lacking in the Regia, especially when political discussions are in progress. Saved from the shadow of condemnation, Clodius is grateful to Marcus Crassus who provided the money, to his sister, Clodia, and to his lover, Fulvia, whose agents distributed the bribes to the jurors, and to Caesar who remained steadfast and loyal, even to the point of divorcing his wife. But with each cup of wine that Clodius replenishes, he is reminded of how the outcome of the trial could have been very different.

"Cicero! That provincial ingrate! Traitor!" A profusion of denunciations falls out of Clodius' inebriated mouth. "You know I didn't get a damned *ass* from him despite his promises to reward me. And then he testifies against me!"

"The Pulchers are not in high esteem just now," Crassus observes. "Rumor and innuendo often have more weight than proven truth."

"And just what does *that* mean?" Clodius slurs his words.

"It means that your sisters' reputations are working against your family. Lucullus divorces your oldest sister, charging infidelity, and the second one is whispered about as her husband's conductor to the Underworld." Crassus does not mince his words.

"Well, Crassus, perhaps that's why Marcius Rex did not include me in his will, despite all the assurances he'd given me." Clodius laughs spitefully.

"In any case, Publius," says Caesar, "you *must* behave. There's to be no tweaking of Lucullus' nose or any instigation against any of the oligarchs or the optimates. We can't afford to give them any pretext to obstruct us any longer."

Clodius becomes very serious. "Gaius Caesar, you must believe that I had no designs on Pompeia when I…."

Caesar waves off the disclaimer. "You would have infiltrated so easily if my mother's maidservant had been less perceptive."

"Or if you could have disguised your voice to match your musician's costume," Crassus drolly puts in.

Clodius erupts in his high-pitched, nasal laugh, the same laugh with which he climaxes with Fulvia later in the evening at her Subura home. Equally satisfied, Fulvia giggles at her lover's release. His rapture is contagious; his tight, sinewy body envelopes her bosom and waist as her legs hold him.

"Publius dear, I've thought of an excellent way to celebrate your acquittal," Fulvia whispers to her lover. Her amber eyes lock his gaze above her as her fingertips trace circles upon his shoulder blades.

"But Fulvia, we've celebrated it many times just as we've done now. Of course, if it's another round you want, well if you'll…."

"No, no, no, dear heart. Not yet. I was thinking of something else, namely, your career. You haven't forgotten it, have you?"

Clodius considers her question before responding. "Why should I have forgotten it?" He removes himself from atop her and then reclines next to her. "I'd have no chance of a career had I not been acquitted."

"Well then, what's next? Aedile? Or are you going to pass that over, wait till your age permits and then run for praetor?"

"What are you getting at, Fulvia?" Clodius is perplexed by her questioning.

"Only this, dear heart – you know and I know that a political career is an expensive enterprise, particularly if the necessary funds are – well, *limited*. And the Pulchers' resources in recent years have been quite restricted, no?" Fulvia has turned on her side to face him as she manipulates his nipple.

"So?"

"Publius, you'll go far, especially with the backing of …."

"I'll go far even *without* them!" Clodius declares.

"Of course you will, Publius, and I want to be with you as you rise." Fulvia smiles at him tenderly, though she is in earnest. "The Roman electorate likes their magistrates married. It lends them… an advantageous *respectability*." She pauses and waits, her fingertip doing its work on his aroused nipple. "Marry me, Publius Clodius, and my dowry will go far in funding your rise through the course of offices. You need it, and want it, as much as I want a career politician as my partner."

Clodius turns to her and kisses her deeply upon the mouth. Fulvia pulls away from him, restraining him with her hands on his chest. "Perhaps you need to ask your *sister*?" They both laugh. "And how is Clodia anyway? I've not seen her since the end of the trial."

"She's busy," Clodius says with a mischievous grin. "She's jilted her poet from Verona. Nice fellow too. He's truly devastated. I know. I've read his letters. And Clodia's taken up with a new flame: Cicero's friend and pupil – young man by the name of Marcus Caelius Rufus. We became friendly serving on Cicero's bodyguard. I introduced him to Clodia and, by Juno's teats, the erotic sparks flew between them!"

The same erotic sparks draw young Marcus Caelius Rufus into an ever deepening abyss of wanton lust and manipulation. He is well over his head and he knows it too, as truly as he knows that he has never before known such gratification. That Clodia Pulchra is married, that her husband is a propraetor governing a Gallic province, only accentuates his pleasure with her. She is a surreal vision bearing down, grinding down upon him to their mutual climactic exhaustion. He cannot know as he fondles her firm, full, sweated breasts that for her, for this raven-haired, black-eyed beauty, he is her spiteful strike against Cicero. For as she rides Caelius with the abandon of an equestrian Amazon, so too would she have dealt with Cicero, the young man's mentor and teacher. Through half-closed eyes, she almost imagines Cicero rather than Caelius writhing beneath her supple loins.

The February night is clear, cool, and starlit. A litter with blue and gold livery is borne through the streets of the Subura by eight hefty slaves. Two slaves bearing torches light the way through winding streets no wider than alleys. The litter is set down before a modest brick and stone house. A veiled woman clad in gray and black stola and palla alights from it. Two maidservants accompany her to the door. Before she can knock upon it, it is opened and then closed behind her after she enters the dimly lit vestibule.

Gaius Julius Caesar takes her into his arms and kisses her ravenously on the mouth as his and Servilia's body coalesce into a throbbing mass of wool. Several moments pass before they disengage and then walk deeper into the abandoned house, through the atrium and into a small bedroom.

"While waiting for you, dearest," Caesar relates, "I was reminiscing about this house. I was born here, grew up here. My daughter was born here, and my Cornelia died here. When I moved to the Regia last year, I left so much of myself here."

Servilia says, "I too have left much of myself here," but she's thinking that the Subura house, Caesar's ancestral home, has been far more comfortable and convenient for their trysts than the insula flat that he used to rent from Crassus.

Caesar stokes the blazing coals in a brazier on the floor, the room's only source of heat on this winter night. Servilia is thoughtful. She says, "Wasn't it at this time of year that Cornelia passed? The same time as your aunt, no?"

"Yes, within a few days of each other."

"You loved her deeply, didn't you?"

"Cornelia? Oh, yes," Caesar admits. "That was part of Pompeia's problem with me, my abiding love for my first wife."

Servilia removes a shroud from a couch and sits on its edge. "Did she resist the divorce?"

"Why would she? She knew she'd lost her usefulness for me."

"You made sure she'd know it, cold, calculating bastard that you are," Servilia smirks.

Caesar is taken aback. "Are we going to argue, Servilia. If so, then I'd rather save my argumentative energy for Bibulus and the Senate."

Servilia removes her veil and palla, draping them over the couch's head board. Her wheat-gold hair frames her oval face and descends upon her neck and shoulders. "Shall we talk about Decimus rather than argue?"

"If you like." Caesar walks toward her.

"When he died, I felt no remorse or guilt at having betrayed him. He knew all along, but he never reproached me. In the end, he wanted to speak, but he could hardly breathe. I don't think he could even see me. I had the children come in to kiss him good-bye. The sight of them, each one kissing him and saying 'Farewell, Tata' tore into my heart. I'd have wept had not Marcus Brutus, young stalwart Marcus, held me in his strong arms; such arms as his father had when he held me as a young bride. When at last his labored breathing stopped, his mouth gaping open, I reproached myself for feeling no remorse, no guilt. It was, I…."

Caesar interrupts, "If you felt guilt or remorse, then you would not be here now."

Servilia looks at him dismissively. "I'm in mourning."

"Yes, I know." Caesar sits beside her on the couch, takes her in his arms and kisses her passionately on the mouth. Tears descend on Servilia's cheeks, but they do not deter him from slipping the stola of mourning gray from her shoulders. Servilia then unfastens the *strophium*, the linen band supporting her voluptuous breasts. Caesar has peeled off his cumbersome toga. With Servilia's help he pulls his tunic over his head revealing broad shoulders and a hairless, muscular chest. He is upon her, his chest pressing down upon her bosom. Servilia's hands and knees push his loincloth down along his thighs. She is enraptured when he enters her, riding, thrusting, caressing her, his mouth buried in the pleasure of her breasts.

Their climax is achieved with concurrent moans of ecstatic release. Their passion spent, they lie in each other's arms as the brazier's embers glow red and hot. Servilia is first to speak. "It's been years since we were both free at the same time. Should we care about what is seemly in the public's eyes? Should we begin to care *now?*"

"I'm Consul now," Caesar replies. "We must both care about appearances. When the optimates run out of stratagems to thwart me, I must have staunch allies to protect whatever I achieve in my term. If not, everything I will have done will be taken apart by Bibulus and the Lucullus brothers, and, most especially *your* Cato.

"Oh, please!" Servilia protests. "He's *not my* Cato, even if he is my half-brother. But your allies – Crassus and Pompeius – aren't they enough for you?"

"We'll see. Pompeius is soon to celebrate his triumph. I already know he's not pleased that his issues are still not even considered; and will he and Crassus be willing to put aside their mutual antipathy? So you see, my sweet pomegranate, how important are allies and appearances."

Servilia leans closely toward him, her breast nuzzling against his chest. "Have you considered the possibility, especially for appearance's sake, of an alliance between us?"

Caesar is surprised. "The alliance of our children's engagement is more than just for appearance's sake."

"No, no, Gaius. Not them; a closer alliance between *us*!" Servilia teasingly smiles at him. "Have you ever thought that I might be more useful to you as your *wife* than as your mistress?"

Caesar stares thoughtfully into Servilia's eyes

Cicero's Respublica

Seven months after his return to Italia, Pompeius at last celebrated his triumph over the Cilician pirates and King Mithridates of Pontus. For several days, the Field of Mars had been occupied by his soldiers, his hostages, animals and vehicles of all sorts as preparations were made for his victory parade. A break in the winter rains proved to be auspicious, a bright, cloudless day enveloping the City.

Pompeius' procession through the Forum was the most spectacular panoply that I had ever seen up to that time, and it certainly was far superior to any in which I had had occasion to participate. There were exhibits of the prows of captured Cilician ships, and there were hundreds of wagons loaded with the rich booty of scores of Eastern cities. Hostages from more than twenty Asian nations preceded the triumphator. The most important captives, the wives and younger children of King Mithridates, were remanded to the Senate's custody, as was young Prince Tigranes of Armenia, whose namesake royal father had been Mithridates' ally. However, the old king himself was missing from among the hostages. Roma's implacable enemy for a quarter-century had died by his own hand rather than be taken alive to be exhibited in a Roman spectacle. There was instead an effigy of the dead king, whose appearance caused the masses to cry out their opprobrium in thunderous tones that nearly drowned out the blaring martial music of drums, tuba, cornu, bucina, and sistrums.

The Consuls, Caesar and Bibulus, and their lictors, led the senators at the procession's van. I walked among them, flanked by Quintus, who had recently returned from Etruria, and Servius Sulpicius and Marcus Varro. Unusual though it was, Varro had chosen to walk with the senators rather than ride on horseback with Pompeius' other legates.

Resplendently clad in triumphal purple and burnished armor, his face painted vermillion and his head crowned with the victor's laurel, Pompeius rode in a magnificent *quadriga* drawn by four gallant black stallions. His handsome adolescent children, Gnaeus, Sextus, and Pompeia, stood beside him as he drove his chariot. An old slave stood behind him in the chariot, as custom required, whispering into the triumphator's ear, "Remember, thou art mortal!" so as to discourage delusions of divinity amidst all the triumphant acclaim. If he were embarrassed by the raucous adulation of the mob, the triumphator's vermillion paint concealed his blushing face. White-clad grooms held the horses' bridles lest they be frightened by the press of the cheering multitudes lining the Sacred Way. Pompeius' lictors and other attendants kept the mob at bay. Following his chariot were additional ox-drawn carts carrying even more spoils from his victories. These were followed by Pompeius' legionaries, formed up in maniples and cohorts, their helmets, body armor, and shields burnished to an intense luster. Their legionary eagles and other military ensigns were held proudly aloft by standard bearers with wolf and bearskins set upon their heads and tied about their shoulders.

At the time, I thought that Pompeius had attained the apogee of his career—the quintessential militarist basking in the glory of the highest tribute accorded victorious commanders. The people were wild in their acclamation as his chariot was guided up the Capitoline ramp to Jove's temple. There, Pompeius would offer sacrifice to Jupiter for his conquests.

Standing with the senators and our attendants on the Capitoline summit, I could not help but notice several ironies in all of this adulation. First, despite the fact that Pompeius' most recent victory had been over Catilina's rebels, not a word was spoken of it, nor was there so much as a miniscule cipher alluding to it on any of the victory placards. Perhaps Pompeius did not want his triumph to touch on any event of civil discord.

Secondly, Mucia, Pompeius' wife and the mother of his children, was not present. I wondered if this accounted for Metellus Nepos' grave bearing during the whole parade as he rode with the legates. Marcus Varro whispered to me that all was not well between Pompeius and his spouse, and this was impacting upon Nepos, who was very fond of Mucia, his half-sister. I knew not if Nepos had conveyed these tidings to his brother, Metellus Celer, up in the Cisalpina.

Thirdly, Pompeius triumph was celebrated against a backdrop of frustration with the Senate. Ever since the Good Goddess trial had concluded, and in the aftermath of successive periods of mourning to honor the deceased oligarchs, Caesar had attempted to gain the Senate's sanction for an agrarian bill providing land allotments for Pompeius' veterans. But the optimates had resorted to the same tried and true measures of obstructive filibustering to prevent a vote. Without the Senate's affirmative sanction, Caesar was thus enjoined from bringing the bill to the Tribal Assembly where it would most probably have been passed.

Caesar's attempts to propose ratification of Pompeius' Eastern acta and to remit some portion of the publicans' Asian tax bid also had met with the same staunch opposition. Under Lucius Lucullus, the de facto successor to Catulus as Princeps Senatus, the oligarchs were resolved to prevent Caesar's bills from finding a path to the people's Tribal Assembly. Consul Bibulus and Tribune Cato were equally adept at thwarting Caesar in the Senate.

Matching this political stalemate was my own disillusionment with the concord of the senatorial and equestrian orders that I had effected during my consulate. So long as the optimates remained opposed to accommodating the tax farmers and to expediting Pompeius' Eastern acta, the Republic would founder in the throes of dissension between these two propertied classes.

Pompeius had to have been aware of all this. No one wondered at his obvious umbrage when, upon alighting from his chariot at the Capitoline and hearing the old slave intone yet again, 'Remember thou art mortal,' the triumphator cast the senators a darkly, sinister glare and replied, 'Yes, only a man, triumphant, yet frustrated!"

After this, he proceeded into the temple, accompanied by his children and attendants, to offer sacrifice to Jupiter for his victories and to deposit his triumphal laurel crown at the base of the deity's statue.

MY FRIENDSHIP WITH POMPEIUS WENT back to the time of my youthful and *only* military service. It was during the Social War when Roma was trying to suppress the rebellion of the Italian allies. I had just turned seventeen and I was serving in the legions commanded by Pompeius' father, the Consul Gnaeus Pompeius Strabo. The younger Pompeius was my age, but unlike me, he loved being a soldier. Though I never cared much for the military life, and I was not a very good soldier, I developed a deep friendship with him. Despite his innate aptitude for soldiering, he was a refined young man whose scholastic sensibilities complemented my own.

During the Marian-Sullan civil war, Pompeius had raised three legions among his family's clients and retainers in Picenum for service under Dictator Sulla. He served with admirable rigor and fidelity. For his victories against the popularist armies in Sicilia, Africa, and Spain, he had been awarded the title *Magnus*, the Great, by the grateful dictator, but not, I fear, without some grudging irony. Nevertheless, Pompeius thenceforth styled himself as Gnaeus Pompeius Magnus.

Seven years before my consulate, Pompeius and Crassus had suppressed a wide-scale slave uprising that had infected most of Italia. Both men were ambitious to attain the consulate, but both were ineligible: Pompeius because he had not served in any of the lower magistracies; and Crassus because insufficient time had elapsed since the termination of his praetorate. Notwithstanding these caveats, the two ineligible candidates made common cause. Backed by their legions, they cowed a reluctant Senate, faced with the threat of armed force, into waiving their respective disqualifications and allowing them to canvass to their ultimate electoral victory.

However, long-standing jealousies and petty rivalries led to much friction between the consuls during the early part of their term. Their enmity could very easily have erupted into civil war had not a Senatorial delegation persuaded them, for the sake of the Republic's tranquility, to put aside their differences and become reconciled.

Much to their surprise and dismay, the Senate found that the reconciled consuls worked quite amicably in eradicating the last vestiges of the late Sulla's constitutional settlement. The consuls sponsored legislation restoring the full powers of the tribunate, which Sulla had severely curtailed, and they lifted Sulla's ban on election to higher office for those who had served as tribunes. In addition, they reorganized the composition of the juries, eliminating the Senatorial monopoly and providing for the empanelment of equites.

It was during the consulate of Pompeius and Crassus that I successfully prosecuted Gaius Verres, the extortionate governor of Sicilia, and thereby displaced Hortensius as leader of the Roman bar. The reformation of the juries was implemented as a result of Verres' conviction.

The tribunate that Pompeius had helped to restore served him in good stead over the next several years. He received his extraordinary command against the Cilician pirates by means of a law proposed by a tribune, Aulus Gabinius, who subsequently became a Pompeian legate and one of his main supporters in the Senate. A year later, another tribune proposed his appointment to the command against Mithridates. My support of the latter measure steered it over the Senate's concerted opposition and through its passage by the Tribal Assembly, but *not* without irritating the optimates.

They saw Pompeius as a renegade from the optimate faction because of his consular actions; but the equites and the urban masses idolized him as their new champion. A very conspicuous supporter of Pompeius' consular reforms and of the extraordinary commands proposed for him was Caesar. As Crassus' protégé and the urban mob's favorite politician, he saw gains to be made by supporting the ascendant Pompeius.

Eventually, Crassus came to fear and distrust his former colleague so much that, over the years, speculation had it that his schemes and the popularist measures that he had supported during my consulate were designed to build up his own political counter-weight to Pompeius.

Gnaeus Pompeius had been through two wives prior to Mucia. As he had changed marriage partners, so too had he changed his political affiliations. This indeed was a major part of his frustration with the Senate, and of theirs with him. The Senate in general and the oligarchy in particular feared him. They believed he was ambitious for supreme power over the state, the same supremacy currently held by Caesar. Their fear and resentment of him showed in their refusal even to consider his Eastern arrangements and land grants for his veterans. It was so easy to see Lucius Lucullus' hand conducting this opposition, for Pompeius' victories over Mithridates and his pacification of the entire East could have been garnered by Lucullus had he not been recalled from his command, due to equestrian and popularist pressure, and then superseded by Pompeius.

I believed I knew Pompeius well enough to understand that his ambition was to be of service to the Republic. Of course he wanted and did attain fame, prestige, and power, but *not* inordinate power. He wanted only to be pre-eminent in the affairs of state, especially where military commissions were concerned. Harkening back to the Republic's major statesmen of the generation before my birth, I envisioned Pompeius as a contemporary counter-part of Scipio Aemilianus, and I saw myself as the modern counter-part of Scipio's friend and ally, Gaius Laelius. So confident was I in Pompeius' integrity and circumspection that when I theorized about a *rector* or *gubernator* for the state in my political treatise, *On the Republic*, I had in mind none other than Gnaeus Pompeius Magnus.

Only a few days after his triumph, I invited Pompeius to dine with us. He graciously accepted, but he came without Mucia, and his dinner conversation avoided mentioning her at all, despite Terentia's inquiries. She must have become irritated at this because after dinner, she excused herself and departed from the dining room, claiming to have to look in on you, *little Marcus*. So, Pompeius and I were left alone to exchange confidences.

He had not changed much in the five years since he had received his special commands. He seemed strong and physically fit. His ruddy complexion contrasted with the stark whiteness of his toga. The head was still broad, perhaps even puffed up from his recent successes. The hair was still thick, brown, but touched with more gray, though not as much as my own despite our being the same age. His high cheekbones and firm brow complemented his full, straight nose. Pompeius always prided himself on resembling contemporary portrait busts of Alexander the Great. In fact, he was often referred to as *the Roman Alexander* in acknowledgement of his Eastern conquests, his victories upon the seas, and his military services of ten and twenty years before.

"You've done very well for yourself, Marcus," he observed as he looked about the room, admiring the decorative murals. "Yes, yes, a very fine house."

I detected a slight tinge of envy in his full, baritone voice. Why should he have been envious of me or my house? He had a grand townhouse in the Palatine district, a massive estate at Alba Longa, a mansion at Tibur, and various properties throughout Italia.

"We're very comfortable here," I replied.

"So I suppose Quintus and his family are still at their old place."

"At least for now," I shrugged. "They'd been looking to relocate after he returned from Asia, but they didn't find anything that suited them."

My allusion to Quintus' propraetorian governorship of Asia some three years earlier gave Pompeius an opportunity to redirect the conversation.

"Yes, he was an able administrator. Pity there's such bad stuff out there: crop failures; revenue shortfalls; pity." Pompeius pursed his lips thoughtfully.

"Yes," I acknowledged. "The tax contractors have already felt the squeeze."

Pompeius reached for a cup of wine from the table, took a deep draught, and nodded. "Of course, Asia is but one problem. Move further east and you'll find client-kings in Galatia, Cappadocia, and a score of other countries who sit uneasily on their thrones because they don't know if the Senate has or will confirm them. Move north and you'll find uncertainty over the borders between Pontus and Bithynia. Go south and there's the same uncertainty between Cilicia and Syria and Judaea. All this uncertainty can undo my labors in the East."

I realized all too well the accuracy of his descriptions.

"Not at all a pretty picture," he continued, "especially if you take account of the Parthians. Instability in our Eastern provinces is a perfect invitation for them to invade and annex territories."

"Yes, yes, I know and...." I began but he interrupted.

"And the Senate in all the months since I returned has done nothing but review, or at least *claim* to have examined my arrangements, while the entire East could well disintegrate. *Gods!* What stupidity!"

All I could do was shrug and admit that he was right.

"Their delay and temporizing is a deliberate, calculated insult to me. But what's more, they've used my veterans to pile further insult upon me. These men have fought and bled in wars against Roma's enemies. They're entitled to their bonuses and land. The bonuses I've already paid them out of my own resources, but land allotments must be assigned by the Senate. The longer they delay, the more I lose face with the men who've counted on me to provide for them."

"Gnaeus, you know I've urged the Senate to expedite all of your needs, but it seems they're committed to their own agenda."

Then Pompeius vehemently turned on me. "Truly! You too had your own agenda when you were Consul. You struck down every reform proposal put forth by the tribunes, even the agrarian bill which would have set up the means to distribute land to my veterans!"

"Gnaeus, the men who proposed these measures were not your friends. They were only posing as such." My counter-argument was not convincing.

"So then, Marcus, you presume to know who are and who *not* my friends? Who are *your* friends? The ones for whom you executed Roman citizens without trial?"

I was shocked not only by what he had said, but also by the accusatory tone in which he said it. Such presumption from a man who had not hesitated to execute Sulla's enemies during the civil war was trying my patience. I replied firmly and steadily, "My actions were for the salvation of the Republic, and I've earned the eternal gratitude of all responsible citizens. I would remind you, Gnaeus, that you had a significant part in crushing that subversion."

"You needn't remind me of my services, Marcus. Remind the *Senate*, and especially the oligarchs, that it was my men who destroyed

Catilina's rebels in battle while you and they executed Roman citizens without so much as a hearing."

Again he accused me!

"They've had me at their service for years. Clean out enemies all over the imperium. Clear the seaways! Vanquish Mithridates! Subdue Catilina! They gave me extraordinary power, but when I used it to fix and settle boundaries and set up kings loyal to Roma, they start to hem and haw and quibble!" Pompeius' ruddy complexion was flushed with anger.

"You don't suppose you've given them reason to equivocate?" I offered.

"Have I?" He looked at me quizzically with an ironic twist of his head. "I could have marched on Roma and demanded my own terms!"

"Yes," I replied, "I remember at least once when you almost did as much."

"Not this time! Instead, I disbanded my legions and played the *suitor*; and this is how they reward me!" He paused momentarily to rise from the dining couch. "If your speeches cannot help me, Marcus, then I'd best look elsewhere for the support I need to achieve my ends."

Having said this, he summoned his attendants, bade me a perfunctory good night, and took his leave. I sat alone for some time in the dining room thinking of what Pompeius and I had discussed. I recalled how Caesar had once implied a connection with the Magnus and Crassus. Pompeius' words played in my head: *"I'd best look elsewhere for the support I need to achieve my ends."*

Pompeius' concern for his veterans caused me to remember that there had once been a time when military service in the Republic's legions was based upon land ownership. A man served in the wars against Roma's enemies because he had a stake—a farmstead, a plot of land, however small—to defend. But those days were gone, a consequence of Roma's rise to imperial prominence. The emergence of the *latifundia*, extensive, landed estates worked by slaves, caused the Roman and Italian yeoman class to shrink into near oblivion; masses of poor, derelict citizens swelled the urban mob. At the time of my birth, poverty among the citizens had become so widespread, and Roma's military needs were so pressing that Consul Gaius Marius resorted to recruiting the indigent and the landless into the legions. Unprecedented though it was, the practice became the norm over the next two generations. The legionaries soon became unquestionably loyal to their commanders—instead of to the Republic—and staunchly dependent upon them for promotions, bounties, and rewards, and most especially for land grants upon their discharge from service.

This woeful pattern of recruitment from among the pauperized citizenry, their long-term service in the legions, and the discharged veterans' need for land grants has been the bane of the Republic and remains so even to the present day. Hence, Pompeius was perturbed at the prospect of losing face with his disbanded legions; and the Senate was at a loss as to how and where to settle some twenty thousand of his discharged veterans.

It was late, and I felt very much alone.

THE WINTER RAINS DISSIPATED WITH an early spring in that year of Caesar's and Bibulus' consulate. It was early Martius, less than a fortnight after Pompeius' triumph. Quintus, Servius, and I were on our way to the Curia for a Senate meeting that Caesar had convened. How amazed we were to see the Comitium occupied by the Tribal Asembly! Each of the thirty-five tribes had taken its place in the wide, expansive, paved oval of the Comitium. City rabble and rural folk in their coarse, brown and gray and drab homespun garb, equites in their white togas and narrow-striped tunics, and a great multitude of veteran soldiers easily recognizable by their leather doublets, comprised a virtual sea of Roman manhood stretching from the Rostra to the Curia's steps. They stood facing the Curia and sent up chants like the subdued rumbling of an underground beast. *"Land! Land! Land! Caesar! Caesar! Caesar!"*

There were no senators among the Tribal Assembly, at least none that I could notice as we pushed our way through the throng to the Curia. No doubt they were assembled in the Curia, and this is what made us so uneasy, that the Senate should have been convened at the same time that the People's Assembly was gathered in the Comitium. This unprecedented occurrence did not bode well.

We entered the Curia in time to hear Consul Bibulus berating Caesar for having convened the Assembly and the Senate at the same time. "What is the meaning of this?" he was demanding to know.

"This is nothing less than subversion of the constitution and it will not be allowed. I myself will disperse them if you will not!" Bibulus was starting for the door, but Caesar halted him when he addressed the Senate.

"Conscript Fathers, there are those among you who have repeatedly obstructed any discussion on the urgently needed agrarian bill." Caesar's gaze fell upon Tribune Cato, who sat on the tribunes' bench in the Curia's foyer. Then, as he continued, he faced the oligarchs, the Lucullus brothers, Hortensius, and Decimus Brutus. "The Senate has had an opportunity to lead in the cause of reform. But it has shirked its responsibilities to the people. I give you one final opportunity to take the initiative. Will you not desist in your obstruction?"

Suddenly, Cato was on his feet bellowing into the chamber, "Veto! Veto!" The oligarchs and their numerous optimate followers applauded the tribune's interposition as they had dozens of times before. But this time Caesar was not to be deterred. Summoning his lictors and indicating Cato, he ordered, "Arrest the tribune!"

Four lictors walked over to Cato as the Senate sat in paralyzed shock. They laid hold of him, violating the sacrosanctity of the tribune's person. They pulled him from his bench while he resisted. Pandemonium broke forth from both optimates and popularists, and Bibulus shouted above the din, "In the name of the Senate and People of Roma, I demand the release of Tribune Marcus Cato!"

Caesar looked about the chamber. There seemed to be a silent exchange between him and Pompeius and Crassus. Perhaps he reasoned that his purposes would be better served without turning Cato into a martyr. He called after his lictors, "Release him!" The lictors did as they were bidden, and disheveled, distraught Cato resumed his tribune's bench.

"If the Senate will not lead, then it must *follow* the people." Having said this, Caesar walked out to the portico and began to descend the steps into the Comitium. His twelve lictors elbowed a path through the assembled press as he made his way to the Rostra. The people turned from the Curia to face the Rostra as Caesar mounted it and then began to read the agrarian bill. Cato, Bibulus, and a score of optimate senators and their attendants were following closely behind, and with Quintus and Servius, I followed upon them.

Though I could not hear what Caesar was saying, I knew the basic provisions of his land bill from having heard it promulgated in the Senate on numerous occasions. A commission of twenty men, steered by an inner council of five, was to be empowered to buy all remaining public land in Italia and re-distribute it to indigent citizens and to retired veterans. Both the commission and the inner council were to have full access to the Republic's Treasury funds stored in the Temple of Saturn. The spoils reaped by Pompeius in the Eastern war augmented these funds at least a hundred fold. There had even been speculation that the Campanian lands, though excluded by the bill's provisions, might be included by subsequent amendments sponsored by Caesar's employed tribunes.

The bill was nowhere near as comprehensive as the measure that I had spoken against during my consulate, and it prohibited forced evictions. I had been inclined to support the bill in the interests of Pompeius' veterans and for the sake of reducing the glut of the idle, boisterous City rabble.

But Caesar was resorting to demagoguery to have his way. Trampling upon the constitution by summoning the Assembly with the Senate yet in session, he went further still by overriding the Senate. Bypassing their required sanction of the bill, he was presenting it directly to the people for a vote. This was nothing less than revolutionary, as revolutionary as what the Gracchus brothers had initiated nearly a century earlier. As they had provoked reaction, so too did Caesar.

Cato bounded up the Rostra, vetoed Caesar's reading of the bill, and then wrested it from his hands. A scuffle ensued between Cato and Caesar's attendants. Consul Bibulus got into it with his men. Seemingly from out of nowhere, someone dumped a bucket of dung on Bibulus' head, while some other rowdies attacked his lictors, seized their fasces, and broke them apart, scattering fragmented rods over the Comitium's pavement.

Most of the jostling on Caesar's behalf was done by Pompeius' veterans who apparently had been placed strategically in the Comitium. With the Cato-Bibulus obstructionists held at bay, Caesar introduced Pompeius and Crassus on the Rostra. Cheers shot up from the crowd for both of them, but more so for Pompeius. Calling the Assembly to order, Caesar asked Pompeius his opinion of the agrarian bill.

"I will support it!" the Magnus confidently announced.

"What of the opposition?" Caesar asked as if on cue.

"For all their swords of opposition," Pompeius proclaimed, "I'll raise up swords *and* shields to defend the law!"

Tumultuous cheers greeted the Magnus' pronouncement. In turn, Crassus then voiced his support for the bill and the Assembly cheered its approval.

There they stood, the three dynasts – Caesar flanked by Pompeius and Crassus. What he had intimated to me during my consulate, Caesar now publicly revealed to be an accomplished reality—a coalition, a triumvirate of the Consul's popularist mob, the Magnus' soldiery, and Crassus' equites.

Caesar proceeded with the reading of the bill without further interruption. Afterwards, he announced, "Now, let the citizens vote to accept or reject the Julian agrarian bill."

"Hold!" An anguished cry pierced the air. It was Bibulus, besmeared with dung and blood, whose hysterical voice cried out from the Comitium pavement and silenced all. "By ancient law, no public business can be transacted if the Heavens are being watched. Beware, Gaius Caesar! Beware citizens! I'll be watching the Heavens for any and all inauspicious signs. While I do this, you are enjoined from voting on this and all other measures. If you proceed, you do so in violation of the consular auspices, and *all* your measures are null and void! Think well on what you do, Gaius Caesar!"

With that, Bibulus, Cato, and their attendants withdrew amid crude catcalls and jostling from the rabble. Undaunted, Caesar conducted the vote. To no one's surprise, the Assembly passed the agrarian bill by an overwhelming voice vote. But this was not the end of Caesar's trampling upon the constitution. The Senate was required to take an oath of support for the law. Reluctantly, I did so, along with Cato, the Luculli, Hortensius, and the optimates. We consented not out of fear of Caesar's reprisals, but rather out of spite, for we believed that Bibulus' continued observation of the skies would ultimately invalidate Caesar's law and our oath.

As Bibulus watched for inauspicious signs from the security of his home, Caesar ignored this archaic ritual and steered his legislative agenda through the Tribal Assembly. On behalf of Caesar, Tribune Labienus secured for the tax-farmers a one-third remission of their

Asian contract. Atticus and other financiers speculated that Caesar even reaped handsome dividends for himself and his partners. Also, Pompeius' Eastern acta were at last ratified; again Tribune Labienus functioned as Caesar's executor.

Caesar rewarded his triumviral partners by arranging for them to sit on the quinqueviral board of the land commission. The other members were Caesar's elderly kinsman, Lucius Aurelius Cotta, and Pompeius' legates, Lucius Afranius and Marcus Varro.

To augment the board's authority and to expand on the land bill's scope, Tribune Publius Vatinius secured passage of a second agrarian bill. This one realized the optimates' worst fears. Large tracts of public land in Campania, theretofore leased only to the Senate's preferred tenants, were now to be accessible for the board's purchase and redistribution. Pompeius' discharged veterans, some twenty thousand men, were the designated beneficiaries.

Caesar made no attempt to conceal his initiatives and policies. In fact, he took pains to make sure that they were manifested to all, especially to the literate citizens. His cooperative tribunes pushed through the Tribal Assembly a bill requiring the daily publication of the Senate's deliberations and all activities of the citizens' assemblies. Designated the *Acta Diurna,* these bulletins would inform the general public about their government's policy formulation as well as pinpoint those individuals, like Cato, who stood in the way of measures beneficial to the people.

So it was that Caesar, frustrated and exasperated by Senatorial delays and obstruction, took matters into his own hands. Like the tyrants of ancient Greece, he plied the populace but to the detriment of the polity, and achieved his own and his partners' ends. But as his term continued, there would be further outrages.

Omniscient Narrative

Gnaeus Pompeius Magnus has assembled his family in the atrium of his Palatine mansion. He sits upon a cathedra chair as if he were about to receive reports from his legionary tribunes. But he is not attired in military garb. Instead, he wears the toga and tunic of a senator. He is immaculately groomed as are his children, Gnaeus, now almost seventeen and soon to don the manly toga; Sextus, at age sixteen, is not far behind his brother; and Pompeia, almost fifteen.

The children stand to Pompeius' left. They are ill at ease, for they sense that something is amiss between their parents. Their mother, Mucia, standing to Pompeius' right, looks at them reassuringly. Of the three children, Pompeia most closely resembles her mother—the same stately, reserved, patrician bearing. Mother and daughter have the same rich, brown hair, the same alabaster skin, hazel eyes, a long nose and full lips extending over a wide mouth. Sextus is an amalgam of both parents, while Gnaeus is virtually identical to his father.

Pompeius nods his head in a curt acknowledgement of his wife's presence. He holds in his right hand a scroll and regards it as though it were a commander's bronze baton. "Children, I have called you here to inform you that as of today your mother is no longer my wife." Pompeius holds up the scroll, and the children and Mucia infer that it is a bill of divorce.

Mucia and the boys show no emotion, but Pompeia's lips begin to quiver and tears begin to well in her eyes. Pompeius' voice is hard and pragmatic. "Your mother, during my absence, as I was fulfilling the Republic's orders, either forgot or did not care to behave like the wife of Gnaeus Pompeius Magnus. Therefore, I am terminating my marriage with her."

The two boys swallow hard. Pompeia looks to her mother and sobs openly. They hear their father say, "I care not should you wish to visit your mother after today." Then Pompeius speaks to Mucia. "Your dowry is forthwith returned to you. Please notify me of any discrepancies in the tally." Then to the children he orders, "Gnaeus, Sextus, Pompeia—kiss your mother and bid her farewell."

The children obey their father, for they have been taught and conditioned to obey unquestioningly. The boys bear up quite stoically as they kiss Mucia's cheeks and embrace her. But Pompeia weeps profusely, and Mucia's maternal comfort does little to alleviate the young woman's emotional pain.

Mucia accepts the divorce with an icy composure, neither admitting nor denying Pompeius' accusations. She harbors many secrets and confidences. When they will be most useful, when they will do the most good or have the greatest effect, she may well divulge them. But for now, she leaves behind the man who had been her husband, and the life she had shared with him.

Gaius Julius Caesar, Consul of the Roman Republic and Chief Pontiff, receives two politically prominent visitors. Leaders of the ever narrowing faction of Senatorial neutrals, Lucius Calpurnius Piso and Lucius Marcius Philippus are both flattered and intimidated by the Consul's request for a meeting. But they will not allow themselves to be remiss. They come together to the Regia at the appointed time. Expeditiously they are shown in to the Chief Pontiff's office where they are comfortably seated on the visitors' side of a large oak table. Caesar, all smiles and exuding bounteous charisma, sits opposite them.

Preliminaries are exchanged quickly, refreshments are presented, and then Caesar turns to political affairs. "It is my understanding, Lucius Piso, that you are a cousin, albeit a distant one, to Gaius Cornelius Cethegus, who unfortunately was executed for conspiracy against the Republic."

"That is so, Chief Pontiff." Piso is uncertain whether to address him in his consular office or according to his pontifical status. Piso's head is square-shaped. His dark eyes are dominated by thick, bushy eyebrows that run in a straight course across his brow. His face is lean and long and his cheeks are sinking, hollow depressions.

"Also," Caesar continues, "you voted against the execution of the conspirators. Is that not so?"

Piso fidgets in response to the question. "I voted out of moral conviction, Chief Pontiff, not out of family loyalty."

"Certainly, of course, of course. I don't mean to impugn your vote. But tell me, Lucius Piso, do you have strong opinions about the executions on the Nones of December?"

Hesitating at first, Piso breathes in deeply before replying, "The executions were unjust. All Romans are entitled to trial and appeal before the citizens in the Centuriate Assembly." Piso wonders if he should continue. Has he said enough, or perhaps too much?

"I see. Thank you, Lucius Piso. I'm told—I've *discovered,* as Marcus Cicero used to say— that you are going to run for consul in this year's election."

"*Discovered!*" Piso declares, picking up on Caesar's joke upon Cicero.

"Well then, I offer you all my support, and that's considerable. My friends, my allies, money, favors."

"Most generous, Consul," Piso turns the address from pontifical to political. "And in return?"

Without missing a beat, Caesar delivers the *quid pro quo*. "You will support and maintain my policies during your consulate. Agreed?"

Piso nods his head thoughtfully. He wonders what Caesar could possibly want of Philippus who does not plan to seek the consulate, at least not this year. He gives the inevitable reply. "Agreed."

Caesar smiles before delivering his next missile. "Your daughter – Calpurnia – is she presently betrothed?"

"There are some suitors." Piso knows exactly where the conversation is going.

"A marriage between the Calpurnii and the Julii would be mutually beneficial, don't you think?" Caesar holds out his hand, extending it across the table.

Piso does not hesitate to take the proffered hand. "Done!"

"And done!" Caesar now maneuvers to his other guest.

Philippus, dour-faced and bald, has followed the conversation like a predator stalking its prey. He is prepared. "Yes," he responds to Caesar's question, "I too voted against the executions on moral grounds." Yes, he responds again, he has strong convictions against the summary execution of Roman citizens, notwithstanding that his son-in-law, the optimate fire-eater, Marcus Cato, had so persuasively argued for the conspirators' execution. And yes again, he will support and maintain Caesar's policies, even though he objects to the rough-shod manner in which the agrarian bill was carried.

Caesar is pleased with the man's candor. Somewhat off-handedly— but not enough to fool wise Philippus—Caesar mentions that his niece, Atia, will likely become a widow before long. Her husband, Gaius Octavius Caepias, is very ill and bedridden. Philippus, also widowed, ought to consider marrying again. Atia is a good woman, attractive, intelligent, and desirable. Moreover, her young children will need a surrogate father.

Philippus agrees to be available and ready. He and Caesar clasp hands to seal the bargain. Caesar has triumphed.

How long does it take for a man to die? A man of some sixty years of age, of generally sound, robust health—how long might it take for a regimen of poison slowly, but regularly mixed in his food, in his wine, to take effect?

Sempronia ponders these questions each day since she began her desperate, methodical program to rid herself of Decimus Junius Brutus, the husband who so cruelly, so archaically disciplined her for betraying him, for consorting with the Catilinain conspirators. He is the very same who keeps her confined like a hostage in her own rooms. She is not allowed visitors unless they are supervised by Decimus' own slaves rather than household servants. However, she is permitted her own women without restriction, and her beloved son, young Decimus Brutus, has ready access to Sempronia as frequently and for as long as he may desire.

A generous gesture, a trustworthy allowance from the old oligarch, and Sempronia exploits it. Maternal solicitude, ever genuine, turns and gives way into matronly solicitation for aid; and finally, and most recklessly, she wields her considerable feminine wiles. Decimus is manipulated, cajoled, and ultimately seduced and suborned to his mother's will. She plays upon her son's horror of his mother's physical abuse. The husband had constrained her to submit to the ordeal, and the father had ordered Decimus to watch.

And watched he had, no matter how much he had been repelled and sickened by the sight of the punishment inflicted upon his mother. Sempronia has regularly reminded him of this. She has planted seeds in her son's heart and mind; these bring forth a harvest of hatred for his father. He will do anything to save his mother and avenge her shame and humiliation upon his father. And Sempronia has been virtually boundless in her promises. She has sealed them with deep, penetrating kisses into Decimus' mouth, her bosom, more wantonly than motherly, pressing against his firm, young body.

He will do anything for her.

Intriguing with Sempronia's trusted women, he arranges meetings with the most disreputable apothecaries whose shops extend from the Forum and infiltrate the Subura. Samples of mandrake and belladonna are measured out, bought, secretly conveyed to the Brutus household's kitchen and blended into the Master's food in such small amounts that his palate will not detect the foreign substances; but in time, their deadly effect will secure Sempronia's liberation and vindication; and young Decimus Junius Brutus, already fettered in incestuous intrigue, will mark his incipient manhood with parricide.

SERVILIA'S LITTER IS SET DOWN on the curb just outside Caesar's old house in the Subura. She is early for their appointment, but she does not have to wait for him. Caesar is always expecting her well in advance. It is as though he still lives here rather than at the Regia.

There are passionate kisses and hungry embraces between the lovers in the vestibule. They move on to the usual bedchamber. But before either of them has a chance to disrobe, Caesar draws Servilia down next to him on the bed. She sees that he is pre-occupied, for his brow is furrowed and his dark eyes have a troubled aspect about them.

"Servilia, there's no easy way for me to tell you this. I'm sorry, but the engagement between our children must be broken off, for political reasons."

Servilia is stunned. *"Broken off?"* she manages to say. "And for *what* political reasons?"

"I must make of Pompeius a firmer ally."

"Pompeius?" The woman's face is flushed from rage. "Pompeius and Julia? Of all people, why *Pompeius?*

"Because I need him."

"He murdered my husband, my son's father. He betrayed him; promised him amnesty and then killed him. He's a *murderer!* What does Julia say about this? Would she accept a *murderer* for a husband?"

Caesar is resolute. "It doesn't matter. She'll do what is needed. Servilia, you must understand that it has to be this way. This is no reflection on you or your son."

"What about *me?* Or should I say *us?*"

Caesar shakes his head and smiles resignedly. "We can continue on the same path—status *quo.*"

Servilia's irritation doubles her rage. "We're both free. Why should we not marry?"

"We're not truly free. We have been suspected and rumored about for years."

"So what?" Servilia explodes. "Why are you now bothered by rumors and suspicions?"

"Because, my love, Caesar's wife must be above suspicion."

Servilia's patience breaks. She lunges at her lover, her palm striking him hard on the face. "You're *not* talking to *Pompeia* now, and this isn't the Bona Dea all over again! Whom have you singled out as your new wife? Who's to be your new *trophy*? Well? Are you taking Pompeius' daughter to wife? Or would that offend the public's sensibilities? Whom are you going to marry, eh?"

Caesar attempts to pacify her. "It's a matter of allies and alliances. That's why Pompeius is marrying Julia."

Servilia shoots back, "Julia already has a *father*. She doesn't need another."

Ignoring her sarcasm, Caesar admits, "I'm counting on Lucius Piso winning one of the consulates for next year, and so...."

"*Of course!* So it's to be Calpurnia Piso!" Servilia bolts up from the bed. Caesar tries to caress her back, but she violently pulls away from him. "Thank you. I've learned today the full measure of your love. *'Caesar's wife must be above suspicion.'* But Caesar's mistress can be the subject of rumor and jokes and innuendo. That's it, isn't it?"

Caesar rises from the bed and faces her. "When my term expires, I'll be going up to the Gauls. I'll be away for some time, and I won't be allowed to return to Roma without losing my imperium. But perhaps...."

"Keep your imperium! Keep your provinces! Keep your allies! Go pounce on hordes of Gallic tarts! *We* are *through!* Farewell, Gaius Julius Caesar."

Servilia haughtily walks out of the bedchamber. She struggles to compose herself as she finds her way down the corridor, across the atrium and to the vestibule.

Caesar looks after her, realizing that he's had the first defeat of his consulate. *Was it inevitable?* He wonders. Knowing the animosity that Servilia has for Pompeius, could he realistically have hoped to retain her with Pompeius replacing Marcus Brutus as Julia's husband? More than this, he misjudged the depth of her love. But in Caesar's mind, the scales of political calculation take precedence over the yearnings of romantic passion.

Caput VIII Cicero's Respublica

CAESAR'S LEGISLATION ON BEHALF OF his partners kept pace with a network of matrimonial alliances. Pompeius divorced Mucia, alleging her infidelity during his absence in the East, or so common gossip had it. Some of it even connected her with Caesar. But the divorce may have been politically motivated so that Caesar and Pompeius could solidify their political union with a personal bond. In a highly publicized wedding, Pompeius, within days of his divorce, married Caesar's daughter, Julia.

At the time, she was about a year or so older than my Tullia. She was a lovely nineteen year old girl married off to a man some thirty years her senior. It was not known then nor is it known now if she had any misgivings about it, but their marriage proved to be successful, at least in most publicly observed respects. Julia's youth and vitality brought warmth and joy to smug, aloof Pompeius, and he was utterly devoted to her. Even his adolescent children got on surprisingly well with her, though they maintained close ties with their mother, Mucia.

For her part, Mucia contracted an enviable marriage for herself. No doubt with the intervention of Pompeius, she married the Magnus' legate, Marcus Aemilius Scaurus. Scaurus' pedigree was most illustrious; his namesake father had been Princeps Senatus for many years, right down to the eve of the Sullan era. Young Scaurus had become Sulla's step-son when his widowed mother married the notorious dictator. During Pompeius' Judaean campaign, Scaurus had been second in command. On his own initiative, he had led an expedition into the territory of the Nabatean Arabs.

Even Caesar's ex-wife, Pompeia, entered into a new marriage with triumviral connections. Her new husband was the stalwart, scowling-faced tribune, Titus Labienus. I surmised that Caesar and Pompeius had negotiated the nuptials.

For himself, Caesar took as his wife, Calpurnia Piso, the comely young daughter of Lucius Calpurnius Piso, kinsman of my son-in-law, Gnaeus Piso. The elder Piso was being spoken of as a likely candidate in the forthcoming consular election, while my son-in-law told us that he would seek election as quaestor.

The optimates lampooned the triumvirs, holding that Caesar, having divorced his *Pompeia*, could now espouse his *Pompeius*. The women who socialized with Terentia speculated that Julia's marriage to Pompeius had sorely irritated Servilia. Her son, Marcus Brutus, and Caesar's Julia had been betrothed since before puberty, and Servilia hated Pompeius for executing her first husband, the elder Marcus Brutus, during the post-Sullan disturbances.

To placate her annoyance, Caesar was said to have given her a rare, precious pearl. Nevertheless, this did not prevent Servilia from marrying her son to the daughter of Appius Claudius Pulcher. This Pulcher was none too fond of Caesar or his partners.

Another marital connection between Servilia's family and the optimates was effected when her elder, estranged sister became Lucius Lucullus' new wife; an ironic union inasmuch as this Servilia was hardly a model of virtue to replace the divorced, allegedly adulterous Claudia Pulchra. It was rumored that the only vice she *lacked* was incest with her brother, Servilius Caepio, who had died several years before; or with her Stoical half-brother, Cato. There was avid speculation that the marriage would not last long. However, probably because of Cato's and Lucullus' mutual admiration, it lasted long enough for Servilia to bear her husband a namesake son.

Marcus Cato, the diehard optimate tribune, quipped that the Republic was being turned into a marriage bureau. However, this witticism ironically turned on him, for before the year was out, his widowed father-in-law, Marcius Philippus, became second husband to Atia, Caesar's niece, shortly after her husband, Gaius Octavius, had died. Caesar proved to be remarkably adept in the game of matrimonial politics.

In the midst of these political marriages, another pairing was effected, though not one of politics or matrimony. Marcus Caelius, the young equite from Puteoli, my protégé as well as a former member of my bodyguard, came under the predatory sway of the *Black-Eyed Palatine Medusa*—Clodia Pulchra. He had started consorting with Publius Clodius and soon became part of the jaded smart set of Pulcher, young Gaius Curio, Marcus Antonius, young Decimus Brutus, and a rake named Quintus Fufius Calenus.

Caelius was no fool—or so I thought. He knew what he was getting into, and he was oblivious to public opinion. He saw Clodia as an erotic extension of or supplement to the education in law and statecraft that I had provided him. Her beauty, her wealth, her directness appealed to him and whetted his appetite. She must have made it clear that she wanted him, and having her would not have been a difficult endeavor as her absent husband, Metellus Celer, was governing Cisalpine Gaul.

But if Caelius or Clodia expected Celer's provincial tenure to extend into a second year, they were mistaken, especially when Caesar's ambitions came into play. Fresh on the heels of his agrarian legislation, he was encouraged to challenge the Senate on the issue of the consuls' proconsular duties.

In their attempt to curtail Caesar's ambitions and, by extension Bibulus' as well, the optimates had decreed that the supervision of Italian cattle trails and forests would comprise the consuls' proconsular duties. This, instead of provinces and legions in Roma's imperium, where ambitious men could cultivate wealth and power and clients, this undistinguished posting was to be the Senate's clipping of the *Cock-Eagle's* wings.

Caesar would have none of it. Through his loyal tribune, Publius Vatinius, and the fully 'cooperative Tribal Assembly, Caesar was appointed to the proconsular governorship of Cisalpine and Transalpine Gaul and Illyricum for the unprecedented term of five years. Thus, Caesar's imperium would extend in an arc from the Adriatic Sea through the Alps and to the Pyrenees range.

Tribune Vatinius met with little opposition, aside from Consul Bibulus' continued sky-gazing from the security of his own house, and of course, the unmitigated but futile obstruction of Tribune Cato. At every Senate meeting, marked by the absence of most of the optimates, and every assembly of the citizens, where the popularists and equites and Pompeian legionaries prevailed, Cato's was the lone, dissenting voice trying in vain to block Caesar. His vetoes were ignored, and time and again, he was bodily removed either by Caesar's lictors or by Tribune Vatinius' ruffians.

In fact, the one-sided administration of the year was in many quarters derisively spoken of as the consulate of *Julius and Caesar*. I found this curious because the late Catulus had once referred to my own year of office as the consulate of *Tullius and Cicero*, especially after I had blocked and then neutralized my colleague, Gaius Antonius.

There had been revolutionary precedents of tribunes infringing on the Senate's prerogatives of appointing proconsular magistrates, but not since the days of Marius. Caesar trod the path of revolution heavily. He wanted and needed a powerful and prolonged proconsular command, one that would allow him to build up a formidable military base and to shield him from prosecution for his consular illegalities. Thus, with the obvious agreement of his triumviral partners and through Tribune Vatinius' manipulation of the Assembly, he had secured his proconsular objectives.

I wondered if Caesar truly appreciated what he was about to shoulder. The Transalpine tribes were restless. In particular, the Allobroges were never accorded the considerations that had been promised them. It was one thing for me as Consul to have promised concessions, but quite another for the Senate to act. They did not, and so the Allobroges were inciting rebellion among the other tribes. Propraetor Pomptinus was hard-pressed to contain them.

Omniscient Narrative

THE TRIUMVIRS MEET IN THE Regia. They are seated around the great oak table in Caesar's study. They take stock of their gains and advances thus far.

The agrarian commission is working with admirable energy and efficiency. It is well-funded, especially because of Pompeius' bounteous endowments from his Eastern campaigns to the state treasury; and it is well-staffed by the triumvirs themselves as well as by their friends and some neutral senators. Pompeius is anxious to go down to Campania and begin his commission duties. His discharged veterans will be grateful to receive their allotments seemingly from their commander's hands.

Crassus happily acknowledges the grateful relief of the tax-farmers for the remission of their Asian contract. He reminds his triumviral partners that the equites' gratitude has added significantly to their individual coffers. They have ample reason to be gratified; and Pompeius is certain that the confirmation of his Eastern acta will promote stability for many years hence.

"Before we proceed with further self-congratulations," Caesar announces with a sardonic smile, "there are two other issues that we need to address. Crassus and Pompeius look to Caesar with anticipation. Their recent successes are put aside as they listen attentively.

"Envoys from King Ptolemy Auletes have arrived in Roma to request on behalf of their sovereign a new treaty of alliance." Caesar reaches for a small, flat loaf of bread from a bronze plate on the table. "I don't need to remind you of the crucial importance of Egyptian grain reaching Roman bellies. Given that, the *Flute-Player* king ought to be recognized and allowed to retain his throne—of course, for the right price."

Crassus grimaces at this. "Roman bellies would be best fed if we finally annexed Egypt. Ptolemy's predecessor bequeathed his kingdom to Roma. When I was Censor, I came very close to acting on it."

"Yes, I remember," says Caesar. "But this *will*, if it exists at all, has never been found. We cannot annex without it. Besides, I don't think we should unnecessarily antagonize the Senate further by bringing up annexation at this time."

Pompeius adds yet another angle. "Marcus Crassus, we all know how you'd covet the honor of heading a Senatorial commission to annex the Nile Kingdom." Pompeius has hit a nerve, judging from the dark pallor that descends over Crassus' face. "Annexation of Egypt would serve to destabilize our alliance. So, I agree with Caesar—no annexation of Egypt, at least not now. Although, part of Ptolemy's fee for his continued crown ought to be the surrender of his bankrupt brother's island kingdom of Cyprus."

"*Cyprus?*" Caesar is bemused, and he notices that Crassus appears to be as well.

"During my campaign against the pirates, many of them had made Cyprus into a formidable stronghold, probably with Cypriot Ptolemy's collusion. It's only fair that he should be stripped of his island kingdom. Besides, control of Cyprus would augment Roman naval power in the Eastern waters." Pompeius convinces his partners, and so they agree to retain Ptolemy on the Egyptian throne for a price yet to be determined, but one that will include Roman acquisition of Cyprus.

Next, Caesar brings up a Gallic issue. "A German king, one Ariovistus, has invaded Gaul upon the request of various Transalpine tribes, particularly the Allobroges. It seems, the German doesn't want to return home. I'll have to deal with him when I take up my proconsulate. But for now, Ariovistus should be placated so that he won't commit any further aggression, especially against the Transalpine and Cisalpine provinces."

Crassus asks, "What's your idea of *placating* the barbarian?"

"I was thinking, perhaps some honorific title, say—*Friend and Ally of the Roman People.*"

Caesar's partners chortle in admiration of his irony and statecraft.

"If he believes that he's our friend, he'll be less likely to be aggressive." Caesar convinces his partners. "One thing more: Let the Senate issue decrees concerning Ptolemy and Ariovistus. I don't want Labienus or Vatinius playing through the Assembly—unless the Senate should again prove intractable."

"Why?" Pompeius asks.

"A diplomatic gesture from Caesar calculated to restore some measure of dignity to the Senate in matters of foreign policy." The Consul has spoken.

Cicero's Respublica

CAESAR AT LEAST SUPERFICIALLY ALLOWED the Senate a nominal role in foreign policy. The optimates had ceased attending the Senate, but the popularists and neutrals responded to his summons. It was these men who granted his request for a resolution declaring a German king, Ariovistus, to be Friend and Ally of the Roman People. This Ariovistus had intervened in a war between rival Gallic tribes, but he was loath to lead his people back to their German homelands across the Rhine, so appealing were the prospects of land and plunder in Gaul. Hence, Caesar wisely thought to flatter the barbarians into a pro-Roman complacency, at least until he would have to deal with them as proconsul.

Caesar's machinations secured another senatorial resolution. This one gave official recognition to the rule of Ptolemy Auletes of Egypt. He was the latest in the Greco-Macedonian dynasty that ruled Egypt for nearly three hundred years. The Senate's resolution on his behalf removed the likelihood of Roman annexation of Egypt—at least provisionally.

From the days of Sulla's dictatorship there had been rumors of a will from an earlier ruler, another Ptolemy, which bequeathed the Nile kingdom to Roma. Whether or not this will actually existed was a matter of mere speculation, for it had never been found. But ambitious expansionists were so often ready to use it as a pretext for annexation. When Crassus had been Censor, he and Caesar had endeavored to appropriate Egypt in order to advance their own powers, but the scheme had been blocked by Catulus and the oligarchs; they feared the prospects of Nile Valley wealth in the wrong hands.

Now, much of that wealth was rumored to be flowing into the triumvirs' greedy fists. It was said that the price for Auletes' recognition was six thousand talents, a sum equivalent to Egypt's total annual revenue. At least, the King sat securely on his throne, and the triumvirs had a reliable ally in the ruler of one of the world's wealthiest kingdoms.

In early April, the Senate's attention was again directed northward to the Cisalpina by reports of Metellus Celer's death, the result of a freak accident: He had fallen from his horse and broken his neck. Upon Marcus Varro's motion, the Senate proclaimed a period of mourning for the deceased propraetor. At the same time, Pompeius moved that Caesar should assume the vacant governorship even before the end of his consulate. The Senate's approval gave Caesar the unprecedented simultaneous imperium of both Consul and Proconsul. He could now begin to recruit soldiers and to gather resources.

Strangely, I was not bothered as much by this innovation as I was saddened by Celer's death. He had been a good friend and a reliable ally during my consulate. Considering this and to observe all civilities, Terentia and I called on Clodia Pulchra to express our condolences. Terentia was loath to go, but on this rare occasion I prevailed on her to put aside her enmity to the Pulchers and to accompany me. Actually, in view of Terentia's suspicions against Clodia, I was surprised that she did not *insist* on coming with me.

As befitting Roman custom, Clodia's house bore the somber trappings and flora of mourning. She and her sisters, like a triad of Gorgons, wore austere, somber blacks and grays, but they were far from grief-stricken. She was polite and warmly receptive of all the sympathetic callers, among whom were Pompeius and Crassus. I was certain that Caesar too would have visited had not his pontifical status, by tradition and custom, precluded his presence at a household visited by death.

Marcus Caelius hung closely by Clodia, ready to comfort his mistress in her transition to young widowhood. What a *sham* it all was! Could she have read this thought on my face? Her face with its constant, enigmatic smile and those luminous black eyes seemed to say to me: *I've taken Caelius because you wouldn't have me.* My rejection had earned her spite.

The Pulcher brothers were there with their spouses. When I saw Publius and Fulvia, I thought, *Well, Clodius, you've gained a wife, but at the expense of a mistress!* I overheard their conversation with young Gaius Curio and Marcus Antonius. It was typically Clodian, vulgar and insipid. Its most memorable line was Clodius' remark that *"Gallic horses are a strong breed. Celer's horse survived the fall and is ready to be ridden by the next governor."*

My only extensive conversation was with Metellus Nepos. I could see that he was very saddened by his brother's death. They had been quite close, both socially and politically. I could also see that he was bothered by Clodius' tasteless remarks. "It's one thing to be cousins with him," he whispered to me as he shook his head in dismay, "but how could my brother have tolerated having *him* for a brother-in-law as well? It's no wonder that he wants to be a *plebeian*. He shows the crudest plebeian breeding even among his own kin, and I freely admit it even though we Caecilian Metellans are of plebeian stock, but at least plebeian nobility."

"What's *that*?" I asked in alarm. "You say he *wants* to be a *plebeian*? Is this more than just spelling and pronouncing his name plebeian style?"

"Yes, though it's not widely known yet," Nepos replied. "He's been petitioning Caesar to transfer him to the plebeians. They can have him as far as I'm concerned. But Caesar's not responded as yet. He's more interested in getting Pompeius appointed to Celer's vacancy in the augural college."

Clodius—a *plebeian*? What gain was there for him in this social demotion? There was but one door open to plebeians, and always closed to patricians—the office of Tribune of the Plebs. Now my head began to throb and a cold, sweaty foreboding enveloped me. Clodius as tribune would be a demagogic menace to the Republic and a deadly scourge for me; and if Caesar sanctioned his transfer to plebeian status, then Clodius could be the triumvirs' weapon against the Senate's tampering with their arrangements.

I CONFIDED MY FEARS TO Quintus, Atticus, and Servius the next evening over a late supper. They did not find them unfounded, but they also encouraged me in the hope that if indeed Clodius were to be the triumvirs' tool, then they could foil his actions against me. "That would depend," Quintus said, "on how cooperative you're prepared to be." Though I had testified against Clodius to destroy his alibi at the profanation trial, I had neither said nor done anything to interfere with Caesar's legislation.

"But dissent is beginning," Atticus observed. "Here, look at this." He pulled from the folds of his toga a small book and handed it to me.

"*Trikaranos,*" I read the title aloud. "Marcus Terentius Varro," I read the author's name and then looked up to see Atticus smiling cunningly at me.

"*The Three-Headed.* Varro's take on the *Big Three*," he explained as I perused the book's contents. "It's just been published. Yes, my copyists handled it. It's strong stuff: the three-headed beast of Caesar-Pompeius-Crassus devouring Roma into oblivion."

"But *Varro* wrote that?" Servius asked incredulously. "He's one of their men. He's on their land commission—one of the inner circle!"

I passed the book to Quintus. "This is not dissent. It's Varro's exercise in letters and propaganda. Very likely they've commissioned him to write it so as to dissuade any optimate resistance to their rule."

"Nonetheless," Servius said to Atticus, "weren't you taking a chance in publishing it?"

"Businessmen thrive on taking chances," Atticus replied, "and if Marcus is wrong about Varro's motives, then perhaps someone will write a rebuttal. If so, my house might also publish it. But for your sake, Marcus, I hope you won't attempt it. You need to remain as inconspicuous as possible."

"It makes no difference who speaks up or who doesn't," Servius commented. "All of Caesar's laws were carried by force in violation of Bibulus' watching the auspices. Therefore, they're technically invalid, and Caesar is liable for impeachment. No wonder he wants to fortify himself with a long, powerful Proconsulate so that he'll put off a likely prosecution by any of the oligarchs."

Quintus passed the book to Servius and added, "And he'll need favorable consuls to protect his laws against the Senate's tampering while he's in Gaul. So, he's backing his father-in-law while Pompeius supports his men, Aulus Gabinius and Metellus Nepos."

"And reliable tribunes would further his interests," I grimaced saying this. "Clodius could be as serviceable to him as Vatinius and Labienus have been this year."

"But again, Brother, he needn't be *your* enemy if you're careful. Circumspection counts."

CAREFUL. CIRCUMSPECTION. THAT IS WHAT Quintus said. But it is virtually impossible to be cautious or prudent enough with a tyrant's politics, especially if one believes in the existence or even the possibility of a free state.

The Senate was called into session by Caesar only days after the news of Metellus Celer's death. I attended because I had been informed that we were to discuss public funeral arrangements for the deceased propraetor. There were scores of senators, alighting from their litters at the Curia's steps, while others were walking across the broad pavement of the Comitium. In the latter group, Gnaeus Pompeius was walking with Caesar and Tribune Labienus. Caesar's lictors preceded him across the Comitium.

Suddenly, a slight man dashed between the files of lictors and, brandishing a dagger, he lunged at Pompeius. Parrying with the folds of his togated arm, Pompeius deflected the dagger blow while Labienus seized the assailant by the neck. Instantly, Caesar's lictors turned about and closed in to subdue the attacker. Caesar ordered them to take him to the Rostra. Ascertaining that Pompeius was not hurt, Caesar then walked to the Rostra where six lictors ringed the fellow, pinning him to the deck.

A crowd of spectators had formed around the Rostra. Senators, equites, and urban rabble were all anxious to know what was amiss. Caesar ordered the man to stand, but the lictors kept him under restraint. I could see by his white toga and broad purple stripe on his tunic that he was a senator. But more than that, I recognized him.

"Who are you?" Caesar demanded.

The man hoarsely, breathlessly replied, "Lucius Vettius." This was the very same man who had accused Caesar and Crassus of complicity with Catilina, the man whom Caesar had then dragged from the Senate.

"Who are you?" Caesar again demanded. "Say your name so that all may hear it!"

"Lucius Vettius!"

"Why have you attacked Pompeius Magnus?"

"To free Roma!" cried Vettius. "To deliver Roma from its tyrants… all *three* of them!"

Caesar looked out over the shocked spectators. They were still and as silent as statues. "At whose bidding?"

Vettius replied defiantly, "Those who love the Republic and who would see…."

"Who *are* they?" Caesar bellowed with every sinew in his neck straining. "*Name* them!"

After a long moment's hesitation, Vettius pronounced the names of Lucius Lucullus, Quintus Hortensius, Decimus Brutus, and—*Marcus Cicero.*

The shock that pierced me at that instant was as penetrating as an assassin's dagger. This was a completely bizarre fabrication. If the oligarchs had plotted to assassinate any or all of the triumvirs they had *not* included me in their counsels.

I was hearing Caesar offer clemency to Vettius if he would name his accomplices. He again hesitated before speaking: "Gaius Curio the

Younger and Marcus Junius Brutus." Caesar was visibly unnerved at the mention of Servilia's son. Motioning to the lictors, he ordered them, "Take this man to the Carcer. Place guards to watch over him." Lucius Vettius was practically dragged away as indecorously as Caesar had dragged him by the hair across the Curia floor less than a year earlier.

When Caesar presided over the Senate, he made no reference to the Vettius incident. Instead, as I had been informed beforehand, he proposed a public funeral for Metellus Celer as soon as his body was delivered from the Cisalpina. Without dissent, the senators approved his proposal.

I sat through the brief session with intense discomfort and loathing because of this bogus assassination attempt on Pompeius. Trying to tie his partner more closely to himself, Caesar used the very same man whom the oligarchs had previously used. Paid informers like Vettius would accuse anyone so long as the price was right. But why was he throwing *my* name into this black business?

Caesar convened the Senate the very next day, and he had Vettius brought under guard before them. Vettius repeated the same testimony that he had made the day before on the Rostra. But he omitted Marcus Brutus' name. I leaned over to Quintus and Servius and whispered, "A night has passed since Vettius' first disclosure. Time enough for Brutus' mother to make a *nocturnal intercession*." They smirked mischievously at my witticism.

Caesar ordered Vettius to be detained yet again in the Carcer. He announced that the Senate would convene again the next morning to investigate further into the Vettius affair. But in fact there was no further investigation into this mystery; for on the morrow, Tribune Labienus announced that the prisoner was found dead in his cell, his head smashed against the stone wall.

So, it seemed that Vettius had served his purpose, whatever it had been, and now he was expendable. My outrage was unbounded and not to be restrained. I made an impromptu speech on this occasion that surely overcompensated for my months of silence.

I disparaged Caesar's entire consulate: his disregard for the constitution; his bypassing of the Senate to get his laws passed by the Assembly; his neglect of the consular auspices. I even went so far as to suggest that the Vettius affair was Caesar's creation and that Vettius' death was not apparent suicide but instead murder in which Caesar himself was implicated.

The Consul and his triumvirs made no attempt to reply; nor did they stir in their seats. All the senators present sat in a deafening silence. But I could not bear to remain longer. I started for the exit when suddenly I heard a nasal voice call after me. "Marcus Cicero!"

I stopped and turned about to see Publius Clodius standing. Strangely, I had not noticed him in attendance.

"Marcus Cicero," he called yet again, "I hear you've bought *another* house."

Quite a non-sequitur, but I inferred that he was alluding to the villas that I had recently purchased with the proceeds from the sale of the Catilinian Five properties. So, Clodius wanted to spar verbally with me and he had chosen the weapon of public gossip and rumor. I could have turned and continued on my way. Instead, I decided to do battle.

I replied with sarcasm equaling his own, "It's *not* the same as buying a *jury!*" The senators burst into laughter. The allegedly bribed acquittal at Clodius' profanation trial was also still being turned by gossip-mongers.

Undaunted, Clodius shot back, "They did not credit you even upon your *oath*."

"Twenty-five credited me, Clodius, but thirty-one wanted their *money* up front!" The Senate laughed again and many applauded my rejoinder.

Then Clodius looked about the Curia, raised his arms as though in supplication, and called out, "How long must we allow him to lord over us like a *king?*"

"Don't confuse me with your *brother-in-law!* Your *Rex* left you no inheritance; and I doubt you'll have one from Metellus." Over the Senate's continued laughter, I hurled my last barb. "Clodius, you'll have nothing but what the jury spared you for—*death*—ruin and death!"

His only response was to sit down, silenced and defeated. I surveyed the Curia and saw Caesar looking from Clodius to Pompeius and then to Crassus. I had said all that I wanted, and so I took my leave amid the senators' applause for my verbal victory.

METELLUS CELER'S FUNERAL WAS A very dignified and somber affair. His corpse was borne in a procession of official dignitaries from his Palatine house through the Forum to the Rostra. Hired mourners kept up a wailing lament accompanied by the shrill, piercing blare of pipes. Metellus Nepos eulogized his deceased brother as a devoted son of the Republic. Then the procession resumed its progress skirting the Capitoline Hill, proceeding northwest to Mars Field where Metellus Celer's remains were set on a pyre and torched.

I studied Clodia Pulchra through the flames that enveloped her husband's corpse. Veiled in black, she returned my gaze, and we held each other in view for several moments. The flames snapped and licked at their prey, consuming it. Soon, clouds of billowing smoke were ascending to the heavens. Clodia's veiled visage seen through the raging fire seemed to betoken some imminent disaster, some impending tragedy.

Publius Clodius was standing by his widowed sister's side. We regarded each other warily. Next to him was Fulvia, proud and contemptuous; and Marcus Caelius, standing by Clodia's other side, was so entwined in his mistress' snares that he was oblivious to my presence. Then Clodia parted her veil so that I could clearly see her face. Her eyes welled with tears, and she looked at me ever so pitifully.

EARLY IN MAIUS, ANOTHER EQUALLY somber ceremony took place in the Forum. On the portico of the Temple of Castor and Pollux, with Caesar presiding as Chief Pontiff, and Gnaeus Pompeius witnessing as newly designated Augur, Publius Clodius was officially adopted into the plebeian family of Marcus Antonius. Antonius, my consular colleague's nephew, was a few years younger than his adopted son, but that was not a hindrance. He must have been well compensated.

Thirty lictors, representing the original thirty *curiae* or wards into which the Roman citizenry had once been divided, ringed the portico between the grand marble statues of the divine twins, Castor and Pollux, and their matching, rearing horses. A considerable crowd stood on the Forum pavement below watching the proceedings.

Castor remains unique among Roma's temples in that its portico is approachable only from the side staircases. There is no front approach, only a high, almost defensive wall. Aside from Capitoline Jove's site high atop its namesake mount, Castor is the most fortress-like temple in the Forum. This setting for Clodius' formal plebeian adoption turned out to be well chosen in view of his subsequent actions.

At the conclusion of the ceremony, Clodius stood at the very edge of the portico and announced his candidacy for the tribunate. Beginning his campaign then and there, he promised to defend his adopted plebeians against all abuse by public officials.

The election campaign season soon began in earnest. Caesar, to no one's surprise, endorsed his father-in-law, Lucius Piso, while Pompeius' legates, Aulus Gabinius and Metellus Nepos maintained a bogus competition with each other. The optimates, still heeding Consul Bibulus' obstructive sky-gazing, did not vigorously campaign against the triumvirate's candidates. However, a notable optimate candidate in the praetorian race was Cato's brother-in-law, Lucius Domitius Ahenobarbus. In the tribunicial contest, several optimates and neutral candidates competed against Clodius.

The elections were held on time and without incident. The triumvirs' men, Piso and Gabinius, captured the consulate, and Lucius Domitius was returned at the head of the praetorian polls. In the tribunicial race, Publius Clodius was elected as first tribune, and an ominous sense of foreboding again fell upon me. Atop Castor's portico, he announced his official policy: to distribute *free* rather than subsidized grain to the unemployed citizens and the poor; and to bring to justice any magistrate who had caused Roman citizens to suffer death without trial and appeal to the Roman People.

Foreboding gave way to a ponderous sense of doom befalling me as I realized Clodius' revenge. I confided my fears to Terentia and she wept at my peril. So did Tullia when I told her. My son-in-law, Piso, recently elected quaestor, told me that he would support me against any and all adversaries.

I sought out Pompeius to gauge his disposition. He told me not to worry because Clodius was to be kept on a tight rein, and he guaranteed that he would protect me against all harm. Then he told me he would be in Campania for the summer tending to the settlement of his veterans and discharging his duties on Caesar's agrarian commission. The prospect of his absence vitiated against his protective assurances.

Soon after meeting with Pompeius, I was visited by Caesar. He was very cordial despite my scathing speech against him in the Senate. In fact, he was extraordinarily solicitous, so much so that he offered me a legateship on his provincial staff in order to shield me from any Clodian mischief once the tribunicial term began. It was a most tempting offer, and Caesar was quite sincerely extending it. Of course, I realized that his ulterior motive was to get me out of Roma so that I would not attack his legislation while he was in the provinces. He could not be sure of my silence if I remained. This is where Clodius would affect me. If I were not cooperative, then he would use his tribunate to hound me for executing the Catilinian Five; in this way, he would avenge himself upon me for testifying against him.

In the end, I declined Caesar's offer because I did not want to compromise myself by accepting his aid. Also, I fortified myself by recalling Pompeius' assurances of his support. What is more, I expected and *hoped* that at least the in-coming consul, Piso, the kinsman of my own son-in-law, would extend me the protection of his high office. Grasping for every conceivable hope for aid, I was certain that the optimates, especially the oligarchs, and the equites would not forsake me.

IN THE EARLY AUTUMN, CAESAR was addressing the Senate. This time, a fair number of optimates was present. Despite their opposition, he was saying, he had succeeded in attaining all his goals for the good of the Republic. He warned that if opposed in the future, he would mount upon their heads like a cock upon hens. Just then, some unknown, unseen voice cried out, "*That's* a difficult position for a *woman* to assume!"

A slowly rising swell of laughter spread through the Curia. Caesar himself even laughed. He was used to being lampooned as the "husband of every woman and the wife of every man." That he was reviled as a woman was an allusion to the old scandal of his young manhood, when he was reputed to have been the subordinate partner in an affair with King Nicomedes of Bithynia.

But Caesar was not in the least fazed, and he had an appropriate reply. "Semiramis of the Amazons *could* do so! She—and *they*—mounted very well, despite their *sex!*"

Yes, Caesar had veritably mounted upon the optimate opposition; he had violated the Republic and its laws and traditions; he had satiated himself with power—or *had* he? That remained to be seen. But surely he had taken steps to stifle any potential opposition. I was part of that opposition that he meant to silence, and I was to feel the full fury of the tyrant's power.

Caput IX Cicero's Respublica

PUBLIUS CLODIUS PULCHER BEGAN HIS tribunate early in December. Since his electoral campaign, he had grown a beard, Claudian black hair adorning his jaws, chin, and upper lip. He had recruited a cohort of City riffraff augmented by a troop of hired gladiators. With these, Clodius set about fortifying Castor's temple. His operae dismantled the temple's side steps and set up barricades in their place. A wooden ramp and scaffold were installed to afford access to the temple's front steps and portico. Clodius posted guards all along Castor's perimeter. No one dared oppose him.

Tribune Clodius then officially promulgated his legislative program. He promised free grain, wine, and olive oil for the urban unemployed—*free*, not cheap, state-subsidized as had been the case since the time of the Gracchi. He proposed the restoration of the workingmen's collegia, banned several years earlier for their notoriety in street violence.

To prevent obstructions of a religious and therefore technical nature, Clodius proposed a bill enjoining all magistrates, especially consuls and tribunes, from invoking the ancient Aelian and Fufian laws. These measures, having been used by Consul Bibulus, could have nullified all popular assemblies while the heavenly signs were being observed for ill omens. Clodius was taking no chances. Like Caesar and the ex-tribunes, Labienus and Vatinius, Tribune Clodius even delved into foreign policy. He proposed Roman annexation of the island of Cyprus from a debilitated relative of Egypt's ruler, Ptolemy Auletes.

The annexation was entrusted to Marcus Cato, whom Clodius extolled as the only trustworthy Roman to undertake the mission. In addition, Cato was empowered with the special assignment of mediating civil strife between rival political factions in the Greek city-state of Byzantium on the Bosporus, and of facilitating the return of its exiled citizens. His specific title was to be propraetorian quaestor, giving him the imperium of a provincial governor and entitling him to appoint two legates.

This commission could well occupy Cato for the better part of two to three years. He confided in me his reluctance to go, especially because he knew all too well that he was being honorably removed from Roma so as to prevent his interference in the triumvirs' plans. Yet, it was beneath him to refuse a commission from the Tribal Assembly or the Plebeian Concilium.

Tribune Clodius' final and most ominous proposal was the banishment of any Roman magistrate who had ever caused citizens to suffer death without trial and appeal to the People. The further realization of my own vulnerability shook me to the core. The Tribune had fashioned the shafts that the Assembly in time would hurl at me.

Caesar had withdrawn just outside the City walls to Mars Field. There he was recruiting a legion from the City rabble for service in his provinces. There was no shortage of volunteers. I wished he could have taken the whole deplorable lot with him, but there were still hundreds and even thousands that paraded about the Forum and the Comitium with Clodius. And Consul Bibulus, even in the remaining weeks of a completely ineffective consulate, responded in the same way as he had throughout Caesar's tenure. He still watched the Heavens for inauspicious signs.

Directly responsible for the recruitment of the Caesarian legion was the junior senator, Gaius Claudius Pulcher, the middle of the three Pulcher brothers. So ironic was it that this family should be thus politically divided. The eldest brother, Appius, was a staunch optimate hoping to take a *lacuna* in the oligarchy's diminishing ranks. Yet, Gaius had volunteered for military service on Caesar's proconsular staff, while Tribune Publius was to be the triumvirs' weapon to keep the Senate in check. Notwithstanding his optimate allegiance, Appius had married off a daughter to Marcus Brutus, the son of Caesar's reputed mistress, and another to young Gnaeus Pompeius. How the two young men summoned up the wherewithal to tolerate their family tie was a mystery, for Brutus' father had been killed by Pompeius' father. What a warped situation, almost as warped as my own.

I hoped against reality that my circumstances would improve with the New Year when the new consuls took office. But my hopes were dashed. Consul Gabinius, fat and oily-haired, his forehead scarred with curling iron burns, was cold and aloof to my entreaties for help. Consul Piso, upon whom I had relied because he was my son-in-law's kinsman, was all posturing gravity, twitching, bushy eyebrows, and sinking, hollow cheeks when he haughtily pronounced that he could do nothing against a tribune in arms.

Not long after the consuls took office, Clodius' legislative proposals became law. Now, his shafts were ready to be hurled. I began to wear a sordid toga, the gray garment of mourning, and I let my beard grow and kept my hair disheveled. Thousands of equites, sharing my forebodings, attired themselves in mourning as well and, braving Clodius' mob, escorted me through the Forum to show their support. But Consul Gabinius ordered us to disperse and to dispense with our mourning attire as it was, in his words, "unnecessary and inappropriate."

"Given that, Consul," I replied, "is it any wonder that we are in mourning? Is it not fitting that we mourn for the Republic when it is ruled by a venal coalition? When a tribune makes himself an armed demagogue? When he and his gang seize and fortify a temple of the gods? When the Consuls of the Roman People offer nothing but acquiescence and complacency? *All* good citizens ought to be in mourning for their *country*." However, my words had no visible effect upon him.

I called upon Pompeius, but his porter told me that the Magnus was out. Later, Tiro told me that he had seen Pompeius slip out the back door while I was waiting in the vestibule. Obviously, he was too embarrassed at his own ineffectiveness to face me.

Utterly disheartened and betrayed by the man upon whose constancy I had so deeply relied, I went to the oligarchs. It was now early Februarius, and the harsh winter rains made my plight all the more painful. The oligarchs offered little to alleviate my crisis. Cato invited me to go with him to Cyprus. Yes, he assured my stunned incredulity, he had formally accepted the People's commission to undertake the island's annexation.

"As they want me out of Roma, so too, they want *you* out of the way, and for the same reason!" Cato declared. "So come with us to Cyprus and then to Byzantium. There's safety and honor in it." Cato explained that he had already arranged for his nephew, Marcus Brutus, to serve as his legate. I would have had the other legateship.

But I declined, reluctantly. What was the difference between accepting Cato's offer and accepting Caesar's protection? Both offered an expeditious foray into official service. Yet, I held both options to be ignominious retreats.

The Lucullus brothers urged me to stay and fight against any prosecution Clodius might initiate. Hortensius, on the other hand, betrayed a virulent antipathy and envy by urging me to spare the Republic so much civil strife and to retire into exile. With flagrant sarcasm, he even suggested that my exile could be spent helping Proconsul Marcus Bibulus supervise cattle trails and forests in Latium, Picenum, Umbria, and Samnium. Perhaps, he reasoned, with the termination of Clodius' tribunate, and Bibulus' cattle and forest duties, it might then be safe for me to return. Hortensius wisely desisted from his discourse when I glowered angrily at him. However, much of his cynicism may have resulted from his wife's fatal illness, a fact that I discovered only later.

Go with Cato on the Republic's business *or* go with Caesar on his proconsular staff; stay and fight, though it might provoke civil strife, or go into voluntary exile. These were the opinions voiced, but one voice was silent, incapable of speaking, seized in moribund paralysis; Decimus Brutus was said to be dying.

Omniscient Narrative

THE OLIGARCH DECIMUS BRUTUS LIES motionless on his bed, a paralyzed shell unable to speak, to move, to respond. He sees through glazed eyes his wife and his son who stand by his bedside.

Sempronia, with malicious tones, tells him, "Decimus, would you have believed me if I had told you that I would have my revenge? I swore I would with every stroke of the rod right up until I passed out. All during my recovery I cursed you. You thought to lock me away, to make a prisoner of me in my own quarters, didn't you? But you didn't consider the loyalty of my own women, nor did you think of our son."

Decimus stands slightly behind her. Taking his right hand in hers, she places it upon her breast and leans back upon him as he instinctively fondles it. "You tortured me but you caused your son to hate you for it, and I made his hatred grow. Together we've brought you to near oblivion with every morsel and every sip that passed your lips."

The moribund Decimus is transfixed by his wife's confession. His eyes widen in alarm.

"Decimus, Decimus, your ways, the old ways are dying with you. Wives will no longer be their husbands' chattel." Sempronia grows more enraptured by her son's touch. Decimus is shocked by the sight of his son toying with Sempronia, but as he cannot move or speak he is helpless in his outrage.

Sempronia continues her spiteful harangue. "Yes, I loved Lentulus Sura. I was with him many times. We had each other in every imaginable way. He was everything. You are *nothing*. And Decimus, I want you to know"—here she takes her son's other hand and presses it to her other breast—"yes, *our* son, I've had him too. We've had each other while you kept me locked up."

Decimus the Younger shakes with impassioned arousal at his mother's display of their intimacies. His jaws are firmly set as he passes his hands over Sempronia's breasts, kneading them over her soft stola and hardening her nipples. She leans back against her son's chest, her hands clutching her son's thighs over his tunic. Her spiteful words are interspersed with enraptured moans. Her head is set under Decimus' chin and through half-closed eyes she sees the dim light of life leave her husband's face. His ultimate breath wheezes forth from his open mouth at the same instant that Sempronia emits a decisive, ecstatic moan.

She recovers from her frenzy and leans forward to peer more closely at her husband's lifeless body. "Yes, he's gone." Turning to Decimus she whispers again, "He's gone. Thank you, my son."

Decimus looks at his father's corpse, considering it for a moment. Then he turns back to his mother. "You have your freedom, Mother. Now, let me seek my *own!*"

"What do you mean?" Sempronia asks in alarm.

"This business stays between us, mother, *all* of it... Father and *us*. But it's finished. You understand? I'm leaving immediately. You can see to his funeral on your own."

"But where are you going?" Sempronia frantically clutches at the sleeve of his toga.

"To Caesar's camp out at Mars Field. I'm going up to Gaul with him, if he'll have me. I need to get out of *here!* Away from *this!* Away from *you! I can't bear even to look at you! You* disgust *me!*"

"*Decimus!*" Sempronia calls after him as he runs from the room. But she knows her son. She has not lost him for good; he is her accomplice in incest and murder, a high price for her freedom and her revenge, and an abyss of shame and guilt for him.

Proconsul Caesar's encampment at Mars Field is a neat, rectangular aggregation of canvass tents and broad quadrilateral lanes. Though located only a few miles beyond Roma's northwest walls, the camp could easily be situated in some hostile land. Caesar's recruits, men from the City rabble, most of whom are veterans of past military service or the sons and grand-sons of such veterans, have constructed an earthen rampart encircling the camp, surmounted by wooden palisades. Secure against possible attacks from the Senate and its retainers, the camp is also Caesar's exercise in military discipline and regimentation.

Gaius Claudius Pulcher is the camp prefect. He is meticulous and exacting, and Caesar trusts him implicitly. He and the Pulchers have had a long history. Political rivalry between Caesar and the eldest brother, Appius, whose ties are strongly optimate, has been incessant. Caesar has been political mentor for both Gaius, and most recently, Publius Clodius, and he has been an intermittent bed-fellow of the three Pulcher sisters, with a special partiality for Clodia, the youngest.

However, Gaius Pulcher is only one of several young Roman nobles who have volunteered for service on Caesar's staff. The former tribunes, Titus Labienus and Publius Vatinius, having served the triumvirs so effectively during Caesar's consulate, are rewarded with legateships. For Labienus the tie with Caesar is also social, for he has married the Proconsul's divorced wife, Pompeia.

Caesar's triumviral partner, Marcus Crassus, swells with paternal pride in presenting his sons, Publius and Marcus, slated for equestrian prefectures under Caesar. Marcus Antonius and his most intimate friend, Gaius Curio, have also secured staff positions—Antonius through his family connection to Caesar, and Curio in spite of his optimate father's objections.

Twelve lictors bearing the rods and axes of Caesar's imperium stand at attention near the entrance of the scarlet command tent. One of them breaks ranks to escort a new arrival, young Decimus Junius Brutus, to Caesar's presence.

Attired in military breastplate, scarlet cloak, and knee-high greaves, Caesar is busy at a large camp table. Wax tablets, parchment scrolls, styluses, maps, and assorted paraphernalia are neatly arranged before him as he methodically peruses one item, sets it down, and then moves on to another. His secretaries are hard-pressed to keep up with his quick, precise movements.

With all respectful deference, Decimus introduces himself, adding that his father, the oligarch well known to Caesar, has just died. To honor his father's memory, Decimus wishes to serve on Caesar's staff in any capacity that the Proconsul may see fit to assign him. Caesar is suspicious of the young man's seeming indifference to his father's passing, especially as Brutus does not care to observe a period of mourning.

"Proconsul, it is my understanding that you will soon depart for Gaul. If you will accept me, I am ready to leave with you, even now," Decimus declares. "I will honor my father more in service to Roma than in attending funeral rites that are best left in my mother's care."

"Your mother would not benefit by having you for a few days?" Caesar cannot begin to appreciate the irony of his words.

Decimus replies with a sardonic edge to his voice, "Sempronia has had as much comfort from me as I'm capable of giving."

Caesar is still undecided until Marcus Antonius vouches for him, as does Gaius Curio. Decimus is well known to both young men as a member of Publius Clodius' "wolf cubs."

"Well then, Decimus Junius Brutus, from this day you are appointed to Proconsul Caesar's staff. I trust that you, that *all* of you, will make the most of this opportunity."

As the new appointee is welcomed with handshakes and backslaps, Pompeius and Julia arrive. She is totally aglow with love for and contentment in her much older husband. It does not seem to faze her that Pompeius is even older than her father. Caesar kisses her cheeks and embraces her.

Pompeius' attendant carries a sheathed pole which arouses Caesar's curiosity. The Magnus removes its covering to reveal the silver eagle of Gaius Marius. "I took this from the battlefield of Pistoria where Catilina and his rebels were vanquished. *Here!* It's yours now, and it's only fitting that it should be." Pompeius points to the standard's shaft where the words, *Gaius Marius, Consul et Imperator* have been carved. "It brought him many victories in his glory days." Beneath his arched brows, he adds, "I'm glad it did nothing for *Catilina*. May it bring *you* good fortune and victories."

Caesar takes the standard in both hands and looks up at the eagle's outstretched wings. "Victories for *us!* Thanks, Gnaeus." He hands the trophy to an aide. "Excuse us, gentlemen." Caesar dismisses his staff. The young men file out leaving the triumvirs and Julia. Rather than ask her to leave, Caesar proceeds with triumviral business, oblivious to his daughter's presence. "Lucius Claudius understands that he is to function as Suffect Pontifex Maximus in my absence?"

"Yes," Crassus replies. "As Rex Sacrorum he should take precedence over the whole pontifical college."

"But hope that he enjoys good health for many years," Pompeius interjects, "because if and when he dies there will be a hard fight among the optimates for his office."

"These Pulchers are a healthy lot," Caesar quips. Then he asks about the latest news from the City.

Comprehending his full meaning, Crassus responds, "They're both still in Roma, but Cato's making preparations to depart. He's appointed his nephew and his protégé, young Marcus Favonius, as legates."

Caesar asks, "What about the oligarchs?"

Pompeius answers, "The Luculli are keeping low and quiet, though Hortensius is complaining a lot about Bibulus having a dishonorable proconsular posting over Italian cattle trails and forests."

"And the consuls?"

"They're both aloof to Cicero as though he were from *terra incognita*," Crassus answers.

Pompeius adds, "And your tribune is straining at the leash like a hunger-crazed hound at the scent of meat."

"*That* menacing, eh?"

"Rest assured," Crassus says, "With Clodius on the loose and a pair of *do-nothing* consuls, the optimates won't try anything."

"How very disappointing for Cicero. After all his efforts on their behalf, they can't or won't so much as lift a finger in his defense." Caesar clucks his tongue against his teeth and shakes his head in wonderment.

"Tata," Julia speaks for the first time. "Is it so important that Cicero be put out of the way? Is he *so* dangerous to you, to *all* of you?"

Caesar indulges the political naivete of his daughter. "Julia, he has the potential to be more dangerous than all the oligarchs and optimates combined."

Cicero's Respublica

I WAS BETRAYED BY THE very men whom I had striven to defend. Now they wanted only to spare themselves hardship even though they had foisted onto me the onus of executing the Catilinian Five. The lot of them filled me with disgust and loathing.

Early in March, the winter rains abated somewhat. Clodius' operae were feasted and entertained by games and theatricals in the Circus Maximus. Each day his numbers swelled. From atop Castor's fortified portico, he harangued the dregs with denunciations of my consulate, most especially the Catilinian executions. I tried to stay as inconspicuous as possible, and as calm as my jagged nerves and torn spirit would allow. Though my family and friends constantly offered their support and encouragement, they could not pull me from the abyss into which I was sinking each day. Returning home one day after another fruitless attempt to see Pompeius, I found Terentia waiting for me with a letter from Caesar. He was still outside the walls, ostensibly making final preparations to depart for his provinces. But I knew better. He was waiting for a resolution of my crisis. Cato had already left for Cyprus, taking with him Marcus Brutus and a junior senator, Marcus Favonius, a friend and protégé, as well as a handful of lictors and various support staff. So Caesar tarried out in Mars Field to see what I would do. His anticipation was all too clear in his letter, for again he offered me a legateship on his staff. He made it so tempting that it would have been almost impossible to refuse. Terentia urged me to take it. She reasoned that I would be under Caesar's protection and the family would be spared any assault from Clodius.

But the prospect of military service among the wild Gauls did not sit well with me. Moreover, I thought it a dishonorable accommodation to put myself under obligation to Caesar. I knew the triumvirs wanted me out of Roma, out of *their* way.

So, I began to consider going into an honorable exile, one without Caesar's or Cato's protection. Doing so, I would keep Clodius at bay and at the same time I would stand up for my consular actions without provoking civil discord.

When Terentia failed to deflect me from these considerations, she demanded to accompany me into exile. But I had to argue this down as well. Terentia's occasional flare ups of pains in the joints were becoming more chronic, and they would preclude her making a long journey with me and remaining away for some indefinite time.

I thought at first that I might retire to one of my rural villas, Tusculum or Asturas, or perhaps even down to our homestead at Arpinum. However, when I discussed my intention with Quintus, Atticus, and Servius, they advised against it. For my own welfare, they urged me to avoid staying at any place where I might be readily found. Atticus recommended Brundisium. He said I could stay with a mutual friend and client, an equite named Gaius Maenius. Yes, Atticus was thinking ahead, anticipating what I thought, what I feared, what I dared not say aloud. Brundisium by the sea was the departure port for the East. Might it actually prove necessary?

Even now, so many years later, it pains me to recall that tragic time in my life. There was a tearful, pathetic farewell to Terentia, to Tullia, to you, my son, to Fabia, to Pomponia and your cousin, Quintus. My son-in-law, Piso, told me he would resign his quaestorian posting to Bithynia and remain in Roma to support me. Good Piso, loyal, faithful Piso; if his consular kinsman had a fraction of such devotion I would not have had to go into exile.

Accompanied by Quintus, Atticus, and Servius, and with the closest of my household staff, Tiro, Alexio, and my physician, Metrodorus, I went to Capitoline Jove's temple at dawn on the twenty-first of Martius. A cold, heavy silence, a silence as of death, hung over the temple's magnificent cella. Shivering in the dawn's cold, I went to the statue of Minerva, Roman goddess of Wisdom. I drew from the folds of my toga a small figurine of the goddess and placed it on Minerva's pedestal. How ironic that I, a confirmed agnostic, should make this gesture, this offering. Why? Was it for the wisdom to follow the right course? Or, was I looking for the spirit to strengthen me, to sustain me, and to protect my loved ones in my absence?

The sun had not fully risen by the time we arrived at the Capena Gate, the portal to the Appian Road. Struggling against the cold that penetrated me despite the two cloaks I wore over my toga, I bade farewell to Quintus and my friends. Atticus had arranged for a horse-drawn coach to transport me and my attendants to Brundisium. We had a few satchels of clothing, some food for the journey, a little money, and much foreboding about the future. The pines and cypresses along the Appian Road, like silent, verdant sentinels, guarded our journey and obscured the scant rays of the vernal sun as they swayed in a gentle breeze.

ON THE VERY DAY THAT I departed, Clodius had the Plebeian Concilium, or at least that portion of it dominated by the City riffraff, formally banish me from Roma for a distance of four hundred miles in every direction. His law also confiscated my Palatine house and all the movables within it. By mid-day, Clodius' mob ascended the hill and attacked the house, pillaging and ransacking it, and then destroying it brick by brick, stone by stone. Using his kinsman, Lucius Claudius, the Rex Sacrorum, Clodius declared the leveled site consecrated to Libertas, thereby technically precluding any attempt to rebuild upon it.

Fortunately, Terentia, having been alerted by her freedman, Philotimus, took you, my son, and the entire household staff to Vesta's temple for refuge before the dregs arrived. But Clodius learned of her whereabouts. So, after destroying the house, the mob descended upon the temple. Chanting obscenities, they surrounded the edifice and Clodius demanded that Terentia come out to them. Fabia could not prevail upon her to remain inside where the mob would dare not enter.

Terentia was always a strong woman, and her strength did not fail her now. She went out to them, and her calm, aloof presence silenced their howls and catcalls. Clodius demanded that she accompany him to the

Treasury at the Temple of Saturn to give an accounting of my properties. Terentia agreed. With serene composure, she walked through the midst of the mob with Fabia walking ahead of her and Philotimus trailing a few steps behind. She went to Saturn's with Clodius showing her all due deference, and made the necessary deposition. Afterwards, he and his attendants escorted her back to Vesta's. Clearly, the presence of a Vestal Virgin among them induced the rowdy mob to some degree of civility. Though rough, brutish and profane, the Roman rabble is simultaneously consumed by a superstitious awe of these servants of Vesta.

The news of these occurrences was conveyed to me in letters from Atticus, Quintus, Servius, and Terentia which I received several days after my arrival at Brundisium. In his letter, Quintus added that Caesar left for his provinces immediately after the Concilium had passed the banishment law. It may well have been his departure that prompted Clodius to incite the mob's destructive fury. Combined with Caesar's absence, Pompeius' aloofness and the Consuls' indifference served to fortify Clodius' militancy. Within a week after my formal banishment, the mob poured out of Roma to plunder my suburban estate at Tusculum and my seaside house down at Antium.

The news sickened me: my loved ones chased out of house and home; our properties seized, plundered, and destroyed. I had been certain that my removal from Roma would have satisfied the triumvirs, but I was grossly mistaken. They indulged Clodius in the fullest vengeance he could have taken upon me, short of killing me. Grief and dismay overwhelmed me and dissipated my reason. Pain and instability assailed my head and bowels. Were it not for Metrodorus' medicines and ministrations, and Gaius Maenius' hospitality, I would surely have died.

About Gaius Maenius, he was one of a small circle whose generous, unfailing solicitude for me during that dark time stands firm in my memory after all these years. He was a stocky, portly man in his mid-fifties, olive-complexioned, his few remaining hairs combed forward over his broad, bald head. In association with Atticus, he operated a thriving export/import emporium in Brundisium. His hospitality was boundless.

After a few days of recovering my senses and strength, I resolved to leave Brundisium, as it was within the four hundred mile interdicted area, and to cross to Dyrrachium on Macedonia's coast.

It was early Aprilis, and at that season of the year the winds were in our favor. A small vessel carried us across the Adriatic's sullen, gray waters in a day. But I was profoundly depressed. A ponderous sense of betrayal weighed upon me like a stone that would have pulled me into the depths of the sea. Tiro, Alexio, and Metrodorus watched me intently, perhaps suspecting that I might throw myself over the ship's side and end my misery in the watery abyss.

The white limestone cliffs of Dyrrachium came into view. Our vessel was secured at the dock, one small inconspicuous ship among hundreds in the port. Hiring porters to help us with the few belongings we had taken with us, we made our way through the teaming dock street to the nearest Roman administrative center. All along our route we heard *koine*, common Greek, spoken by cargo masters, stevedores, and sailors as well as some Latin from customs officials. Though I still wore the sordid attire of mourning and my face bore four months of beard, the officials recognized me as a Roman. They directed me to the office of the Proconsul Gaius Antonius.

Still the porcine beast with whom I had been consul, Antonius was wearing military garb. Sitting across his desk from me, he regarded me suspiciously. Of course, my appearance was like that of a suppliant, which indeed I was. I explained that I was in exile because of Tribune Clodius' enmity and his vindictive legislation. I asked my former colleague for refuge. Antonius listened to my plight, all the while fidgeting impatiently with his sword hilt and his signet ring.

Finally, he spoke. "Marcus Cicero, I cannot guarantee your safety here as there are many exiles in these parts, especially Catilina's followers." He shook his head reprovingly. "In a few days, I'll leave for the north to start a new campaign against the Thracians. They need to be pushed back beyond the border. You can come with me, but again, I can't guarantee your safety."

He was cold and detached. In fact, I think he was pleased at my predicament. As an afterthought, he added, "That matter we agreed on has been taken care of by Sestius here. He'll tell you about it." Saying this, he indicated Publius Sestius, the quaestor, who sat by his right and slightly behind him.

Sestius was also attired in military breast-plate, tunic, leather kilt, boots and cloak. His hard, lined face showed concern for me and annoyance at Antonius' indifference. He nodded at me and then addressed his commander. "Proconsul, I've completed two years of service. With your permission, I request leave to resign my office and return to Roma so that I might work on behalf of Marcus Cicero's recall."

Antonius was surprised by this announcement. Showing a laxity so uncharacteristic of Roman governors, he answered, "I suppose you'd go even if I refused leave. Well, what difference? No doubt we'll all be in for a prosecution when we return to Roma. Marcus Cicero, by this time next year we may *all* be in exile with you." He laughed cynically.

Then Gnaeus Plancius, military tribune, stood up by Antonius' left. His burnished armor complemented his tanned, chiseled face. "Proconsul, before we start on the campaign, let me accompany Marcus Cicero to Thessalonica. He should be safe there. As soon as he's properly housed, I'll join you at the border." He turned to me after speaking. I could see on his face the same genuine concern that Sestius had shown.

"Very well then," Antonius agreed with an impatient sigh. "Good fortune to you, Marcus Cicero." With that, our interview came to an end. But Sestius took me aside privately. He told me that my share of the province's revenue had been deposited at the Artemisian treasury vaults at Ephesus. It was safe and waiting for me. Though Antonius took no pains for my safety, at least he had upheld his part of our bargain. Nevertheless, the losses I had sustained since being exiled probably counted for more than whatever might be in my account at Ephesus.

I thanked Plancius and Sestius for their solicitude and assured them that I would never forget them. Pride stifled my tears. Sestius gave me a ledger of the deposited funds. Then I bade him farewell as he was to take ship for Brundisium, while Plancius was to escort me to Thessalonica.

We traveled by horseback along the Egnatian Road, the well preserved highway cutting through the mountains and plains of Macedonia.

After three days, we arrived at Thessalonica, the provincial capital. It was an ancient Greek town whose masses of stone edifices straddled the Egnatian Road and overlooked the azure Aegean Sea.

As he had promised, Plancius arranged for our billeting in the vacated quarters of one of Antonius' legates. He stayed with us a few days and then returned to his duties under Antonius, but not before I thanked him again and assured him of my undying gratitude.

Our quarters were comfortable, though somewhat austere; we settled in, the days passing into weeks and months. Exile afforded me much time to reflect on my young life, especially my childhood at Arpinum and our family homestead there. I remembered the afternoons I spent reading below the great, ancient oak tree, the oak of Marius, beside the gently flowing Liris River. I would stare up into its mass of green leaves, the sunlight streaming through them, and it was like looking into the face of Eternity.

What was my life all about? I was an outcast, condemned to disgraceful exile, my life in shambles, my family driven out of house and home. I wrote to Terentia and regretted all the pain I had caused her. I wanted nothing but to see her once more, to see Tullia and little Marcus a final time, and then die in Terentia's arms. I could barely raise my head above the abysmal depression in which I was mired.

As I wrote, I contemplated a dagger and considered making an end of my life, my worthless, purposeless existence. However, some force that I could neither recognize nor understand stayed my hand. I remembered the statuette of Minerva that I had left at Capitoline Jove's temple. I wondered if the Roman *prudentia* and *sapientia* had merged with the Greek *sophias* to stunt my own agnosticism, to stay my hand against a self-inflicted death. I yet waited.

Omniscient Narrative

Tullia travels by coach out to Tibur, a community east of Roma. Spring is evident in the blossoming trees and shrubbery that flank the road. However, the young woman cannot appreciate nature's beauty because she is preoccupied about her father's plight. Outlawed and exiled from Roma, Marcus Tullius Cicero now resides in Thessalonica, provincial capital of Macedonia. Tullia has come to petition for her father's recall and restoration, but upon arriving at Pompeius' mansion, she learns that the Magnus is not at home. It is just as well, she reasons, for her business is really with Julia, his wife and Proconsul Caesar's daughter.

Julia is most hospitable to her young visitor. She warmly greets Tullia in the spacious atrium. Refreshments are served as the two young women sit near the impluvium. Sunlight descends through the skylight in the roof. "My husband is in Campania," she explains. "He's working on the land commission. Whenever he's away, he prefers that I stay here at Tibur. It's really a beautiful house. If you'd like, I'll show it to you."

"Julia, my father had a beautiful house in Roma, as well as villas at Tusculum and Antium." Tullia's voice is traced with sadness.

Julia is discomforted by Tullia's remark. "I'm sorry you came all this way not to find my husband. Perhaps...."

"It matters not because I really came to see you, Julia."

In their dress, in their coloring, in their bearing, the two young women could almost be sisters. In a sense, they *are* because their respective fathers are leading statesmen of the Republic.

"What would you have of me, Tullia?"

Tullia swallows hard so as to hold back her tears. She has never begged for anything in her life. Perhaps Julia has never been petitioned for anything. She looks squarely into Julia's eyes. "I ask, I implore you to intercede on my father's behalf. You are the daughter and the wife of two of the chief men of state. Speak to your husband. Write your father. Please ask them to allow my father to return to his country and to be restored to all that was taken from him. I beg of you, Julia. *Please!*" Suddenly, Tullia leaves her chair and is kneeling before Julia.

"No, Tullia... don't! This is unseemly and...." Julia stops at the sight of Tullia sobbing into her own hands. She leans forward to embrace and comfort the suppliant. "Neither my father nor my husband appreciate my interference in their politics, but never mind that." Julia takes Tullia by the hands. She reaches into her stola's sleeve and extracts a handkerchief. With it she dabs the tears from Tullia's cheeks. "I promise you, Tullia, I'll do whatever I can to persuade them. I give you my word, as Caesar's daughter and Pompeius' wife." Julia smiles benignly at Tullia.

The exile's daughter composes herself and smiles back appreciatively. "Then I am content. Thank you, Julia."

As a gesture of good faith, Julia confides in Tullia certain annoyances that Pompeius has lately endured. These specifically relate to the demagogic tribune who is principally responsible for Cicero's banishment. Tullia listens attentively, engrossed by each word, recording each event in her mind so that they can be transcribed in a letter.

TERENTIA SITS ACROSS THE ORNATE obsidian-covered table from Servilia. A platter of sweat-meats and a beaker of watered-wine rest undisturbed upon the table within easy reach of the two mature women. Though Servilia has offered refreshment, Terentia has politely declined.

"This is not altogether a social call," Terentia admits in a most business-like tone.

"You've hardly had to call on me before today, Terentia. Please don't think that I don't appreciate your visit. Truly I'm honored that the wife of a former consul should call on me." Servilia smiles reassuringly at her guest.

"A *former consul*... yes," Terentia agrees, "and now he's an *exile*."

"And he is doubtless the reason for your visit. Why do you imagine that *I* can be of help either to you or your exiled husband?"

Terentia knows she must proceed cautiously. The golden-haired beauty sitting across from her already knows the answer to the question. If Servilia is going to be coy, then Terentia must be diplomatic in her supplication. "Yes, Servilia, I need your help now. You are held in such high regard because of your family, and because... because...."

"Because I was Caesar's lover? I've no qualms about admitting it to you since you're reluctant to say it. But I must emphasize that I *was*, and not just because he's in Gaul for the next five years." Servilia begins to feel a resurgent longing for the man who had been her paramour. "But I'm sure you don't care to know the particulars of our, what shall we call it, our *falling out?*"

Without missing a beat, Terentia responds directly, "No, because that's *none* of my affair. But I'm certain you still carry some influence with him, at least enough to merit a letter from you on my husband's behalf."

"You give me much credit, Terentia. In fact, you flatter me." Servilia pauses to consider her petitioner. Terentia is a handsome woman of strong features and stalwart bearing. Clearly, she is not a woman who could be easily dominated, if at all, by her husband. Servilia smiles in admiration of Marcus Tullius Cicero's devoted wife.

"Before my son went off to Cyprus with his uncle, he told me that Cicero was invited to go with them. Yet, he refused. Why?" Servilia is curious as to whether her own inferences are correct.

"For the same reason," Terentia proudly replies, "that he did not accept a position on Caesar's staff. My husband was loath to accept any offer that would have compromised his integrity."

"So he preferred banishment instead?" Servilia wonders aloud. "What you call integrity others might call *foolishness*. Of course, I can empathize with him if he refused Cato for personal reasons. You see, Terentia, I've never been able to abide my half-brother." She shakes her head in dismay.

"My husband did not believe that the Furies would be unleashed against him, against us, if he went into voluntary exile." Terentia looks squarely into Servilia's eyes. "Clodius Pulcher and his mob made my husband an outlaw. They destroyed our home, and the profaner himself had our land declared sacred to...."

"Yes," Servilia interrupts, "I know. From my balcony I saw what they did." She shakes her head again. "This City rabble can be a voracious beast, especially under a creature like Pulcher." She sighs deeply, purses her lips, and then offers, "Very well then, Terentia. I'll write to Caesar on Cicero's behalf. But, there are two things for you to consider. First, you must realize that as long as Pulcher rules the Roman streets nothing can be implemented for your husband, and that monster's tribunate is only half-over. Second, you should have a talk with someone who presently has Caesar's attention… namely, his wife, Calpurnia."

CALPURNIA, DAUGHTER OF CONSUL LUCIUS Piso and wife of Proconsul Julius Caesar, is a pretty young woman in her mid-twenties. She resembles her consular father in her square face, but unlike her father, her cheeks are high and full and her eyebrows are neatly trimmed. Her dark-brown hair is handsomely dressed in a chignon at the back of her head. Bright vivacity sparkles in her hazel eyes as she listens to her visitor's petition in the Regia's atrium.

Terentia has followed Servilia's advice in seeking Calpurnia's help. But Servilia had apparently been oblivious to the Cicero family's relationship with the Pisos. Terentia's son-in-law is a kinsman to both the Consul and his daughter. This connection, coupled with Consul Piso's refusal to help Cicero, have caused some degree of embarrassment for Calpurnia.

"I've been married to Caesar for about a year," says Calpurnia. "I don't know him as well as others." She blushes at this oblique reference to Servilia, a reference quickly caught by Terentia. "Our marriage is purely a matter of political alliance. Certainly you know this, Terentia."

"I know," Terentia admits, "and your father's aloofness and detachment are based upon that alliance. Families and politics in Roma are interchangeable. Your cousin, Gnaeus, my daughter's husband, is committed to helping my husband. He even gave up his elected office so that he could work for Cicero's recall. Could not your father at least… but no, no, I suppose that would be beyond any expectations."

"Look, Terentia," Calpurnia's voice betrays exasperation, "they don't allow me to meddle in their affairs. I don't know what to offer. What… what would you expect of me?"

"You would not need to ask that, Calpurnia, if it were your father or your husband who had been outlawed and driven from his family and from his country."

SEVERAL DAYS LATER, THE REGIA is visited by two Vestals, Fabia and the Virgo Maxima, Licinia. Ordinarily, when Vestals go to the Chief Pontiff's residence it is to see him about religious matters such as rites, festivals, or the needs of their college. But in Caesar's absence, such concerns would be addressed by the Rex Sacrorum.

Lucius Claudius is held in high regard, especially as the duties of Chief Pontiff devolve upon him. But the Vestals' business is not with the Rex Sacrorum. Instead, they request an interview with Aurelia Caesar, mother to the Chief Pontiff.

The old dowager receives them in her private apartments. She knows that her daughter-in-law has been visited by Terentia. So, she does not even feign surprise when the Vestals humbly ask her help on behalf of the exiled Marcus Cicero.

At first, Aurelia is somewhat indignant, not about Fabia or Licinia, but about Cicero. "He could have gone with my son to Gaul! Why didn't he, eh? Too proud, was he, to accept help from the Caesars? Or was he convinced of his own invulnerability? Well, he learned otherwise... and his family had to suffer because of him!"

The Vestals look at the old dowager through supplicant eyes. Their patience is not strained, nor do they forsake their pious bearing. In particular, Fabia strives to keep her emotions in check. She has seen her half sister, Terentia, now resident in the Atrium Vestae, weep bitter tears each day for her banished husband. She has watched her pray to the goddess Vesta for Cicero's speedy recall and his safe return to Roma. She will not antagonize the old dowager by attempting to defend Cicero's decisions or actions.

Finally, Aurelia's reverential respect for the Vestals asserts itself. Putting aside her umbrage at Cicero, she tells the Vestals that she will write to her son and plead on their behalf for Cicero.

The Vestals are profoundly grateful. Before they depart, Aurelia shares a piece of family history with them. When Caesar was a hunted fugitive of the Dictator Sulla, she and the Vestals had pleaded for the young man's pardon and return. She will remind Caesar of this when she writes him. She is certain that he will remember it.

ATTICUS, PRE-EMINENT EQUITE, WHOSE FINANCIAL and political contacts are nothing if not all-inclusive, comes calling upon Roma's most esteemed, yet most despised plutocrat, Marcus Licinius Crassus. Investments, interest and rent rates, and provincial tax yields are the issues most frequently turned over by the two leading money men; but, not today.

As they stroll in the blooming spring garden of Crassus' Palatine house, their conversation turns on the exiled Cicero. "He was foolish not to have gone with Caesar," Crassus declares, "damnably foolish! But he was even more foolish in another way." The bald-pated plutocrat pauses in both his speech and gait, turns to face Atticus head on before revealing, "He should have come to *me*!"

Seeing the surprise registered on Atticus' face, he goes on to say, "We go back a long way, Cicero and I... well, alright perhaps not directly. When he was a young man he studied oratory and rhetoric under my illustrious cousin, the one they still call 'Crassus the Orator.' When my sons were youngsters they studied the same stuff under Cicero. Why do you think I gave him such a good deal on that house... uh, that is, the house that *was*."

"He would not agree that it was a good deal," Atticus throws in with an eyewink. "He's always said you were a tough haggler."

"Bah! If *he* were selling it *he* would have held out for double... *no triple* what I settled for!" Crassus shakes his head, his lips turned downward. "What's it worth now to him? To me? A non-existent house on a big plot of Palatine Hill dedicated, sanctified to Libertas? What's it worth?"

Atticus retorts "Marcus Crassus, I didn't come here to speculate on City real estate."

Crassus' face flushes with annoyance. "That house, for which Cicero still owes me more than a million sesterces, could still be standing intact if he had come to me!"

"It's no secret that Tribune Clodius is your creature... yours, Caesar's and Pompeius'."

"And therefore I could have prevented the pillaging and destruction of that house, for which I am still owed a considerable sum, if only Cicero had had the common sense or the plain good manners to seek me out. He could have gone with Caesar or gone into his exile and I would have put my protective web over his house and all his properties, and his wife and son would never have been driven out." Crassus pauses again. "Your Cicero's a hard man to figure."

Now Atticus sees an opening and he exploits it. "What if Cicero were to be recalled and his properties restored?"

"But only with the full agreement of Caesar and Pompeius!" Crassus emphasizes.

"That's a given. But if he's recalled and his properties restored, then you want full payment of the balance?"

"How perspicacious you are, Titus Atticus! No wonder you're such an astute financier. But let's be absolutely clear about it. The Palatine site has been sanctified. It's most unlikely that that house will be restored to him. My position is this: Restored or not, I'm owed one million sesterces for the razed house. I'll support Cicero's recall *if,* and only *if,* he'll honor his obligations. Clear?"

Atticus thinks for a moment before replying. "You know as well as I that Cicero is honorable. As far as the sanctification of his land is concerned, well, the gods can always be accommodated, because Caesar *is* Chief Pontiff."

IN THE BROAD EXPANSE OF terrain between the Latin and the Appian Roads, gangs of surveyors, their attendants, free laborers, and slaves are measuring and plotting prospective farmsteads for Pompeius' discharged veterans. The vernal sun floods the Campanian plains with light and warmth.

Pompeius Magnus and his retinue, attired in riding tunics, short cloaks, and boots, are riding along the older highway, the Appian. They are nearing the municipality of Pompeii, and the inherent irony of their location does not escape the triumvir and land commissioner. Mount Vesuvius' conic summit can be seen to the north, its billowing smoke being the only darkening aspect of an otherwise sun-drenched day.

The Magnus is flanked by Quintus Cicero and Servius Sulpicius. He is politely and respectfully attentive to their pleas and entreaties on behalf of the man to whom Pompeius owes so much in the way of political patronage. Pompeius infers from their petitions on behalf of exiled Marcus Cicero that his own aloofness, his own omissions, have impelled the former consul, the man roundly praised as Savior and as Father of the Country, into ignominious banishment.

As they ride on and talk, Quintus and Servius become even bolder. They remind Pompeius that his victory over the Catilinian rebels was in many respects a consequence of Cicero's crushing of the conspiracy in Roma. If Cicero's empowerment by the Senate's Ultimate Decree enabled him to execute the conspirators summarily, then the same measure authorized Pompeius to do battle with Roman citizens and former soldiers of the Republic. If Cicero's exile is valid, then every magistrate who took up arms to crush the sedition ought to share in his disgrace.

From the mouth of Servius, such statements are tempered by his acknowledgement that he voted against the conspirators' execution.

"Yet," Servius insists, "the Senate's majority decreed their execution and, as presiding Consul, Cicero dutifully carried out their decree."

Pompeius reins in his horse and the entire cavalcade halts. "I'm well acquainted, Servius Sulpicius, with your jurisprudential expertise; but at this moment, I don't need you to lecture me. Instead, let me remind you both of a political reality. An assembly of the Roman People passed a law of banishment and property confiscation against Marcus Cicero."

Quintus is quick to point out, "An assembly of Roman citizens convened by a tribune in arms, a tribune seeking personal vengeance upon a former magistrate. Pompeius Magnus… is Tribune Publius Clodius Pulcher truly your *friend*? Is he truly serving your interests when he releases foreign hostages that you brought back to Roma from *your* victories? When he drains the Treasury of spoils that *you* deposited so that *his* City rabble can have free grain? How many of your veterans will get land if the commissioners run out of money, if they can't buy Campanian land because Tribune Clodius has plundered Saturn's Treasury? Again, is Clodius truly your friend? Your *pawn*, yes! But your *friend?*"

Pompeius is nonplussed at Quintus' boldness. Even Servius looks at both men with trepidation. After a moment's pause, the Magnus asks, "You should consider, Quintus Cicero, just what you are willing to offer for your brother's recall. And remember this: I'll take no action without consulting my colleagues."

FULVIA'S LARGE HANDS PAT HER abundantly round belly. "Baby sleeps now," she says to her sister-in-law, Clodia Pulchra, "otherwise he'd be kicking like an angry goat." She and Clodia are lounging in the garden of Fulvia's Aventine house.

"You're so sure it's a boy?" Clodia takes a sip of wine after the remark.

"Well, I hope it is… for Publius' sake… another Publius Clodius Pulcher in the making."

"Is the world ready for another?" Clodia quips and both women laugh. "But Fulvia, did you run out of cork or wax or both to leave your vagina open to receive my brother's seed?"

"No, Clodia, nor did I tire of anal intercourse; and I was not slow to withdraw before he spilled. All these tricks I know as well as you.

No, Clodia, I wanted this child." She again pats her belly. "I want him or *her* to be born in this house where my grand-father once lived; this house from which he set forth on what turned out to be his last day."

Clodia says, "It's a pity that your mother could not have lived to see this house again *and* her first grandchild."

Only a few months before, Sempronia, daughter of Gaius Sempronius Gracchus, the renowned, martyred hero of the plebs, and Fulvia's mother, had passed away in her sleep at the ripe Roman age of sixty-five. Fulvia has channeled her sorrow at her mother's death into joyful anticipation of her baby's birth; and she has striven to recapture the past. The Aventine district has traditionally been associated with popularist politicians ever since the time of the Gracchi. Fulvia and her demagogic tribune husband have spared no bother or expense to purchase the house that had once belonged to Gaius Sempronius Gracchus. Yet, they still retain Fulvia's house in the Subura.

"Do you see much of your neighbor, Aurelia Orestilla?" Clodia asks facing in the direction of Catilina's house.

"No. She and her daughter keep well to themselves. But when they venture out, they're always together. Do you think what they say could be true?"

"What? Catilina and Flavia? Why not? The step-father and step-daughter copulated while Orestilla was preoccupied." Clodia launches a manifesto. "Men are such shameless users! Ever since the Sabine women were raped by Romulus and the first Romans. They take and use us to advance their own political schemes while shutting us out of the whole process, especially marital alliances."

Fulvia braces herself, for she has heard before what Clodia is now about to say again.

"In my youth, I'd had to obey my father's wishes and comply with his arrangements that I marry Metellus Celer in order to reinforce our family's alliance with the Metelli. So too did my sisters have to obey, otherwise there'd have been no firm union between us and Licinii Luculli and the Marcii Reges."

Clodia pauses because she is reluctant to mention the name of her brother's victim. She looks down at the serpentine mosaics on the atrium floor before speaking again. "Yes, I loved Cicero in my youth. I wanted him, but I could not have him. Nor could my sisters;

instead, the three of us were forced into loveless marriages where, by contract, we had to submit to conjugal embraces and then look for love in numerous affairs. Even Cicero had to obey his family's wishes and marry for money instead of for love. Yes, we married, but we kept our independence. We knew all the stratagems to prevent conception, and we used them. But, you know, sometimes I think about the kind of mother I might have been. Had I loved Metellus, I'd have been a good mother to our children. I've been fond of Appius' and Gaius' children, and I'll love *yours*."

"As you should, Clodia, because my child has the blood of the Gracchi, the Fulvii, and the Clodii Pulchri." Fulvia beams with maternal pride.

"You love Publius, don't you? Do you love him as his wife differently from the way you loved him as his mistress?"

"As his mistress," Fulvia replies, "I was not espoused to anyone." She looks squarely at her sister-in-law.

"Yes, I broke my marriage vows as a protest against the men who lord over us and use us as pawns. They say that old Decimus Brutus brutalized his wife because she'd supposedly been involved with Catilina. The old bugger died and, from what Sempronia has confided in me, she was vindicated upon him."

"Clodia! Really?"

"So she said! Remember that men are shameless users and they deserve whatever vengeance is meted out to them! For example, Cato married Marcia after divorcing Atilia, who had given him two children. He claimed she was unfaithful. Who knows? But just before going out to Cyprus, he divorced *Marcia* just so Hortensius, recently widowed, might have a young, healthy *breeding cow* to give him more children."

"That's bizarre!" Fulvia snorts.

"But entirely true! And when, or if, Cato returns from his mission, Hortenius will probably divorce Marcia so that she'll remarry Cato. How they *use* and *abuse* us! What about *their* infidelities? Have you considered, Fulvia, why men keep *mistresses*? Is it because of a lack of love from their wives? Is it dissatisfaction? Disillusionment? I've learned that they seek much more than illicit love or mere carnal pleasure. Yes, they seek a repository of confidences, of hidden truths and fears, of ambitions both petty and grand. So it has been with every lover

I've had. Some day, I hope to discover Cicero's secrets, his fears and ambitions, though we may well wonder if he is worth the bother."

"What of Marcus Caelius?" Fulvia asks slyly. "What confidences has he reposed in you?"

Clodia's face darkens and her mood becomes sullen. "I've had him totally ensnared, wrapped up in the folds of my palla. I've worked my charms on him." Clodia teasingly cups her breasts over her scarlet stola. "He's been mine, entirely mine. But lately, he's been quiet, locked in his own thoughts. Something's festering in him."

"Memories of his *mentor?*" Fulvia suggests. "*Ohh!* He's waking up! Look how he stretches!" Fulvia holds the sides of her distended belly.

Clodia smiles broadly at the undulating movements across Fulvia's dome of a belly; they are plainly visible underneath her yellow stola. "Will you deliver here in Roma?"

"Oh no, he'll be due by mid-summer. You know how impossibly hot our Roman summers are. No, I'll go down to Antium, if I'm able to. Why don't you come with me... you *and* Caelius. Publius' tribune duties demand that he remain here. *Ohh!!!* Feel *this!*" Fulvia places her sister-in-law's hand upon the site of the baby's kick. "Perhaps he doesn't want to be born anywhere other than in *Roma!*"

Touching Fulvia's belly, Clodia replies, "Then it *must* be a boy, for only *males* dare to make demands even *before* coming out of the womb!"

Publius Sestius, recently arrived in Roma from his quaestorian duties in Macedonia, goes to the Esquiline public baths. It is not only the comfort of steam room, massage, hot, tepid, and cold baths that he seeks; he also wants the latest political news of the City, particularly any details concerning the exiled Marcus Tullius Cicero. Having disrobed, he wraps a towel about his loins and walks into the marble-veneered steam room.

The vapor is so thick and pervasive that Sestius cannot at first recognize any of the occupants. But a voice calls out to him, "Sestius! Publius Sestius! *Here!* Join us!" A towel-hooded, sweating man materializes before him. It is Milo, Titus Annius Milo, a junior senator and one of the leaders of Cicero's bodyguard during the Catilina crisis. "Come, sit with us!"

Milo is a muscular, solidly built man possessing a physique that veteran gladiators would envy and strive to attain. His face is square, seemingly carved from granite, and his chin is reminiscent of a legionary's shield in its stalwart protuberance. The sharp, blue eyes below the furrowed brow are like beacons in the steam-filled chamber.

Milo conducts Sestius to a place on the walled tiers. Amid the steam, Sestius recognizes another familiar face. Gnaeus Calpurnius Piso, Cicero's son-in-law, a veteran of his father-in-law's bodyguard, raises his sweated face and smiles. "Welcome back, Publius Sestius. You've arrived none too soon."

"Only yesterday," Sestius says. "It's good to be back."

"Don't speak on that, Publius, until you know what you've come back to you." Piso's tone is cynical and bitter, belying his benign face and delicate, slender physique. "Tribune Clodius and his gang still control the Forum and the Comitium. His vetoes prevent the Senate from even considering any motion for Cicero's recall. The consuls venture nothing. Pompeius and Crassus scurry back and forth from Roma to Campania giving out parcels of land to the veterans. They've refused to meet with me, though Quintus, Sulpicius, and Atticus have pleaded with them for Cicero. The oligarchs are just as indifferent. I've spoken with senators of junior rank. At least they've been willing to listen, but their only response is to shrug their shoulders."

"Don't include *me* in that!" Milo objects. "They know, as you know so well, that there's nothing that can be done unless we first defeat Clodius with his own tactics."

"What are you saying?" Sestius asks as the steam takes effect, drenching him with sweat.

"I've told him"—Milo directs his thumb at Piso—"scores of times. Organize gangs to drive back Clodius' men, re-take control of the Forum and the Comitium by force of arms, even if we have to bring in troops of gladiators. That's not a difficult task for me, I assure you! That's the only way to defeat him and enable the Assembly to convene."

Milo turns fully toward Sestius. "Look, I've already decided to run for tribune for next year. What about running with me, Publius?"

"I was thinking about it all during the trip back," Sestius admits with a cagey grin. I think we'd make a considerable duo as tribunes."

"We'll have to be," Milo agrees, "because I wouldn't put it past Clodius to seek re-election to the tribunate.'

"What?" Piso exclaims. It's illegal!"

Milo laughs a boisterous guffaw. "Will you listen to him! Illegal! My balls!" He grabs his own crotch. "Clodius and illegalities are meant for each other! Besides, re-election to the tribunate is not strictly illegal. It's merely not, not…."

"Customary and traditional," Sestius completes Milo's statement. "There are precedents. Long ago, Tiberius Gracchus sought a second tribunate."

"And was killed trying to get it!" Milo declares.

"But his brother, Gaius succeeded in getting a second term," Sestius continues.

Milo interrupts yet again, "And after failing to win a third term he too was destroyed!"

"So this is how Roma discards its demagogic tribunes?" Piso muses. "Violence must be met with violence. Roman against Roman… even in the City streets?"

"Fight fire with fire and iron with iron!" Milo asserts. "That is—if you want your father-in-law recalled."

Piso thinks, shaking his head in dismay. He looks up at Milo's sweaty, granitic face. "Every day I watch Tullia weep for her father. I don't know any more what to say to her. It seems that…."

Sestius interrupts Piso by putting his hand on the young man's slender arm. He lifts his chin toward a towel draped figure sitting on the tier only a few feet away from them. They cannot be certain how long this person has been present or how much of their conversation may have been overheard.

Milo cautiously rises and approaches the stranger. When he is close enough, he lays his iron-clad grip on the figure's shoulders and turns it around, coming face to face with Marcus Caelius Rufus. *"Ha!"* tough Milo exclaims. "Look who we have here!" Milo turns back to Piso and Sestius.

Caelius brusquely breaks free of Milo's grasp. He realizes all too well that the interlocutors suspect him of eavesdropping, and, as Clodia Pulchra's lover, he will most likely pass on what he has heard. Ultimately, Tribune Clodius would be informed.

"Have we disturbed your rest, Caelius?" Piso asks sardonically. "Your mistress must exhaust you beyond endurance so that you could not even show your face to your old friends."

"Don't hold it against him, Piso," Milo offers, patting Caelius on the shoulder. "Perhaps he has much to sweat out."

"I'll leave so that you three can go on with your planning," Caelius mumbles as he starts for the exit.

"You needn't leave," says Milo. "Join us. Come back to us!"

Caelius stops and turns to face Milo.

"Remember how we guarded Cicero when he was consul? Now, can we not work together to return him to Roma?" Milo's piercing blue eyes hold Caelius fixed to the tiled floor.

Piso joins in, this time without sarcasm. "He was like a father to you, Caelius. Would you abandon your own father to take up with his enemies?"

Caelius protests, "I did not vote for any of Clodius' laws. How could I? I'm not a plebeian. I'm not even a senator because I've yet to start my career."

"When you do, Cicero will be a better sponsor for you than Clodius, or any of his kin, and that includes the *Lupa* that you've been pouncing on." Milo's hard face betrays no sign of sympathy for Caelius' predicament.

Piso says, "I gave up my elected office so I could stay in Roma and help Cicero. Sestius here gave up his office in Macedonia, came back so he could run for tribune with Milo and work for Cicero's recall. You think you're excused from helping him just because you're too young to canvass? Caelius, you have a moral obligation to pitch in and help us!"

The tears from Caelius' eyes merge with the sweat beads on his reddened face.

Cicero Respublica

In Roma, the wheels of change were beginning to turn. Pompeius was regretting that he had betrayed me. This, Tullia related in a letter she sent me after speaking with Julia and asking her to intercede on my behalf. But there were political reasons for Pompeius' change of heart. He was angered at Clodius' release of Prince Tigranes from official custody. Clodius had apparently been receptive to proffered bribes from the Armenians for the crown prince's release. Clodius had also despoiled Pompeius' Eastern treasury deposits to fund the mob's free food. In neither instance had Clodius consulted Pompeius. Atticus, Servius, and Quintus wrote me about this as well.

Terentia wrote me about her meeting with Servilia. So wise was it of her to plead my cause with Caesar's mistress instead of first calling upon his wife. But neither Servilia nor Calpurnia was able to give any substantive assurances. However, Terentia also wrote of Fabia's meeting with Caesar's mother, Aurelia. Like her son, the old dowager held all the Vestals in high esteem. Terentia was certain that there would be some movement from the mother-son-Vestals nexus.

With the approach of the consular elections, Metellus Nepos, Pompeius' man, and the optimate, Publius Lentulus Spinther, announced their intention to work for my recall. Among the tribunicial candidates, Titus Milo and Publius Sestius were also verbose on my behalf. In describing these political developments, Servius mentioned that he and Quintus were also entering the consular race. In effect, they were all canvassing for my recall.

Atticus wrote that he had gone to Crassus to gauge his disposition. Old "Bald-Pate" said he would concur with his colleagues on the question of my recall; but he wanted assurances that he would be paid the balance owed him for the Palatine house, a house that had been destroyed, leveled, and its site consecrated to Libertas.

In my panic over an imminent prosecution, I had not considered Crassus as a crucial policy maker among the triumvirs. I had been too preoccupied with Caesar's intentions, Pompeius' unreliability, and Clodius' enmity. Would it have made any difference to the tragedy that befell me if I had gone to Crassus for aid? I still owed him more than a million sesterces for the house. Though he had helped me expose Catilina's conspiracy, my indebtedness to him might have ruled out his assistance. After all, I was certain that he and Caesar had sacrificed Catilina to exposure and destruction. But Clodius was their new creature, and he was not yet expendable. Then again, Crassus might have been willing to offer protection if for no other reason than to protect one of his debtors. Yet, as he had not proffered aid, I had been above asking it of him.

During the first weeks at Thessalonica, I endured many a night of fitful, tormented sleep. Chaotic images swept through my dreams. I experienced no relief until after the encouraging news from Roma began to arrive. This and the sleeping potions that Metrodorus prepared calmed and soothed me into a tranquil somnolence.

My dreams lost their anarchic fury and became mosaics laden with real people and familiar places, albeit often in utterly surreal settings. In one, I recognized my fellow Arpinate, Gaius Marius. He was arrayed in the garb of a triumphator, and he directed me to seek refuge in a nearby temple that he indicated. I saw a plain, unadorned Roman temple with Etruscan columns. Then I found myself standing within its colonnaded interior. I was alone and it was silent and dark. But gradually, it became illumined by a great light whose source I could not discern.

I had this dream several times. It was a far more comforting vision than an earlier one. Terentia, Fabia, and Tullia were walking along a colonnaded corridor toward an effigy of the Roman-she wolf, whose pendulous teats were like inverted fleshy cones. At the lupa's pedestal lay Clodia Pulchra and Fulvia, their naked bodies entwined in an orgasmic embrace. Suddenly, an effusion of blood from the she-wolf's breasts gushed upon Clodia and Fulvia and splattered the white garments of Terentia, Fabia and Tullia.

I also dreamt of my brother riding across a broad river and coming toward me. Mysteriously, he disappeared into the river; but just as suddenly he reappeared. Local seers told me that it was the gods' true assurance of my eventual recall.

But the affairs of men are not the same as the realm of dreams. I waited and hoped.

Caput X Cicero's Respublica

THE EARLY SUMMER OF EXILE at Thessalonica was a hopeful time. My spirits were lifted by the anticipation of good news concerning the consular elections at Roma. I fought off the temptation to consider the possibility of further setbacks. The fair weather strengthened my confidence and hope. The azure waters of the Aegean Sea reflected the brilliant sunshine and brought cool breezes throughout the town. A day did not pass without thoughts of home, of Terentia and the children, of Quintus and his family, of Servius and Atticus. But one day, as I looked out upon the sea, I thought of my mother.

My memories of her were few and vague, for she died when Quintus and I were quite young, in fact before we moved to Roma. Her name was Helvia, and she was of equestrian lineage. I remember Father speaking fondly of her diligent attention to every detail of life at the Arpinum homestead. She had to be attentive, for Father was always preoccupied with his books and accounts, and his health was not especially robust.

Helvia was extremely thrifty, though her frugality was a trait that I unfortunately never developed. I remember when she would preserve wine she would seal both the filled and the empty jars so as to prevent pilfering household slaves from draining a jar and then claiming that it had been already empty.

Recalling the *sealed jars* of Helvia was like an affirmation of my life. As a public figure, I was always open to scrutiny, and impolitic words and actions could be my undoing. This had indeed been the excuse, if not the reason, for my banishment. But I also tried to keep a few *sealed jars* away from public scrutiny, even though my proxy purchases became the subject of much speculative rumor and gossip. I was determined to keep the Macedonian revenues in the *sealed jars* of my account at Ephesus.

Sestius' records showed that an amount equivalent to one and a half million sesterces had been set aside for me. This was a hefty sum, enough to pay off the arrears to Crassus and still have a tidy amount remaining, though not enough, I feared, to cover my other losses. For Antonius to have been able to reserve this sum for me, he must have done a rapacious job of fleecing the provincials so as to stuff his own coffers. No wonder then, that he expected to be prosecuted upon his return to Roma.

In addition, Antonius was liable for other malfeasances. Before returning to duty, Plancius had told me that the wars against the Thracians were actually provoked by Antonius on the pretext of the tribes' incursions across the province's border. So, there was the possibility that the triumvirs' men in the Senate or the optimates might charge him with waging illegal wars.

At the same time, Caesar was fighting Helvetians and Germans in Gallic territory beyond the Cisalpine and Transalpine frontiers. I wondered what the Senate would have to say about that. Would it matter? Would it deter Caesar from becoming a conqueror? After all, they could not prevent his rise as a popularist champion; nor could they block his consular program, though they certainly attempted most arduously to do so. Were it not for his trampling upon the constitution, I could almost admire his indefatigable energy and spirit, even though he had used them to victimize me.

From the transgressions of Antonius and Caesar, it was a short passage of memory to the triumvirate and to the self-serving oligarchs. What they all had in common was an established name. A name is an essential element in Roman politics. Men like Caesar, Pompeius, Crassus, Antonius, Catulus, and the Luculli inherit theirs with fame and distinction attached. Others, like my countrymen, Marius, and I, must labor to make our names known. In my case, the family name—derived from an ancestor whose face must have had a prominent *cicer* or chick-pea feature—was almost a liability. Acquaintances had advised me to drop *Cicero* or change my name before embarking upon a public career. But I had refused. Instead, I said that I would make my name as great and as memorable as the founders of Roma.

In retrospect, what a vain pronouncement that had been! My name was now that of an exile. Marcus Tullius Cicero—banished from the state that he had striven to defend against subversives who would have destroyed it. Such thoughts, such realities, like ugly foreboding clouds, warred upon my optimism and enveloped me in dismay as I gazed upon the azure sea.

An early casualty of the war within my spirit between optimism and dismay was my physical, virile energy. Had I so desired, I could have partaken of the city's available practitioners in erotica; but I thought it below me as a senator of consular rank. More than this, I completely lacked sexual desire, even sexual thoughts during my entire exile. However, I longed for Terentia, to be with her so that I might be comforted by her, as an infant desires the comforting embrace of its mother and the warmth and security provided by her bosom.

Following the regimen of my physician, Metrodorus, I took various remedies by mouth and by direct application upon my dormant organ. Unfortunately, these proved to be ineffective. It pained me to contemplate the loss of my virility as a consequence of the loss of my citizenship. I hoped that my eventual recall and the restitution of my properties, my presence once again among family and friends, would restore my life-force.

As Minerva had been my recourse for wisdom when I had set out upon the road to banishment, I began to consider the Greek god, Asclepius, and his Roman equivalent, Aesculapius, as restorative media for my virility.

Omniscient Narrative

Tribune Publius Clodius Pulcher has convened the Concilium Plebis in the Comitium. His armed operae ring the assembly area, standing on the steps and pedestals of temples, basilicas, and monuments. It will soon be time to elect the magistrates for the ensuing year, but the Tribune's concern on this early summer day is with the current year's Consuls.

Both Gabinius and Piso have been steadfast in their non-interference in his tribunate, so much so, that the state has been run by Tribune

Clodius, his operae, and his ever-ready Plebeian Concilium. He has ingratiated himself with them so deeply, so thoroughly, that the City plebeians need only hear his proposals once and then by acclamation they render them into law—demagoguery at its most flagrant.

Now, Clodius proposes lucrative proconsular postings for the Consuls: Syria for Gabinius and Macedonia for Piso. There is no dissent; no mention is made that by tradition it is the Senate's prerogative to assign proconsular duties; that is of the past. Most expeditiously, the Concilium Plebis confers Gabinius and Piso with their provinces, and Clodius is reassured of his continuing clout with his adoptive plebeians.

After the Concilium is adjourned, Clodius returns to his Aventine home, the house that had once belonged to his wife's grand-father, Gaius Gracchus, in whose radical footsteps Pulcher appears determined to follow.

The old house has been the birth site for Clodius' daughter, recently born of Fulvia. She had been certain to be delivered of a boy, but both parents dote on the infant girl, named Claudia, in accordance with the father's *gens*. The infant suckles at her mother's breast, for much to Clodius' surprise, Fulvia wanted no wet-nurse for her baby.

Clodius paces across the atrium floor, telling her of his most recent handling of the plebeian assembly. He is pleased, he is satisfied, and yet bothered. He has received no assurances from Caesar of a second tribunate. "Without a second term," he complains, "how can I keep the mob in *their* pockets? How can I block the Senate and the tribunes that are likely to get elected? If Milo and Sestius and others like them get elected, they'll start the wheels turning for Cicero's recall. Besides that, they may even try to bring me up on charges of public violence."

Shifting the infant to the other breast, Fulvia reminds her husband that the triumvirs have engineered the outcome of the Assembly's vote. It was doubtlessly their will that Pompeius' man and Caesar's father-in-law should be well placed for their proconsulates. "Besides, a second tribunate, or even seeking it, could prove to be unlucky," she says smiling down at the suckling infant. "At least it was for my great-uncle, Tiberius Gracchus. He ran afoul of the Senate merely by canvassing for a second consecutive term; and my grand-father, Gaius Gracchus, who served two terms, was driven to take his own life after he failed to win a third term."

"Since we've moved into this house, Fulvia, I've heard about nothing but the *Gracchi*," Clodius protests. "You'd probably bring them back from the dead if you could."

Fulvia's face turns stern. "They yet live in memory—mine as well as the memory of those Romans whom they died to help!" She looks down and coos at the infant at her breast. Looking up again at Clodius, she says, "Publius, perhaps they have you in mind for other offices, aedile, or even praetor, and in time, the *consulate!* So don't stew over this. Don't waste any energy that could be applied elsewhere. You have it in you to be greater than the Gracchi, and Tribune or not, you'll still control the Forum and the streets, as long as you have your *collegia*."

Clodius is mollified by the logic in Fulvia's words. He leans over Fulvia, kissing her neck and shoulders, and then he kisses his daughter on her tiny forehead. But he seems troubled again. "Caesar's busy with his Gallic campaigns. Here, Pompeius is angry because I released the royal hostages. He'll not support me. *Balls to him!* The Lucullus brothers and the remaining oligarchs are shunning the Claudians. Appius is too cautious, and Gaius is still up in Gaul." A brief pause and reflection follow, and then he adds, "There's only one other strong man in Roma whom I must cultivate."

Fulvia follows his thoughts perfectly. "Marcus Crassus—and you may rest assured that *he* knows it too."

The suckling infant has fallen asleep at her mother's breast. Pleased with herself as both mother and counselor, Fulvia covers her bosom with her stola and smiles reassuringly at her husband.

Cicero's Respublica

By mid-summer, the news from Roma was that, after delays and disruptions by Clodius' thugs, the magisterial elections were at last held. Lentulus Spinther and Metellus Nepos won the consulate. There were also many pro-Cicero men elected among the praetors, aediles, and quaestors. However, one glaring exception among the praetors was Appius Pulcher, the elder of Clodius' brothers. Though I had never been at enmity with him, he was firmly aligned with his brother's political stance against me.

Among the elected tribunes were Titus Milo and Publius Sestius, outspokenly favorable to my recall; but these were offset by the hostile tribunes, Quintus Calenus, Publius Bassus, and Sextus Serranus, and others who were at least believed to be neutral. Though my hopes were lifted by the positive electoral results, I realized all too well that supportive magistrates were insufficient to bring about my recall unless the triumvirs agreed.

When summer gave way to the autumn rains, I received a letter from Quintus. He wrote of an interview he had had with Pompeius. The triumvir said he would support my recall only if Caesar was so disposed to it. Quintus further wrote that the tribunes-elect, Milo and Sestius, had also been present at the meeting, and Pompeius had given them assurances of his *conditional* support for my recall.

The new tribunes would take office early in December, and Clodius would be out. But the consuls and other magistrates could not initiate measures on my behalf before their terms began in Januarius.

A week after Quintus' letter, I received one from Servius. He related that an attempt to discuss my recall in the Senate had been vetoed by Clodius. Servius feared that the expiration of Clodius' tribunate within the next several weeks would not preclude his further interference in the Senate's deliberations.

Another letter from Quintus told me of his meeting with Caesar at the Proconsul's winter quarters in Ravenna. Having completed two successful campaigns in a single year, Caesar had billeted his legions in winter camps well beyond the Cisalpine and Transalpine frontiers. Accompanied by Milo and Sestius, Quintus had petitioned Caesar for my recall, even offering himself as a personal guarantee.

Caesar was agreeable to it, but only on certain conditions. A resolution of the Senate and its confirmation by the Centuriate Assembly were to be required. Also, and most crucial of all, I was required to support the triumvirs' agenda, or at least to abstain from all political activities not in line with their plans.

So again their price was my accommodation. Would I be willing to pay it this time? I could not help but perceive that there was something else that Quintus omitted from his letter, something between the lines that I could not quite put my finger on.

WITH THE YEAR'S END AND Thessalonica enshrouded in a gray, foreboding winter, I looked back at the nine months of my exile. I remembered how I had wanted to end my life. What force had stayed my hand and given me the will to live? My agnosticism was undermined as I considered the Stoics' belief in a Divine Intelligence, a Divine Mind ruling the Cosmos. Was it this deity or force that fortified me with the will to live? I likened this recognition to an earlier mystical experience, the one that I had had when, as a student at Athens, I was initiated into the Elysian Mysteries. I had emerged from the ritual convinced of life's continuity, of the soul's existence and its transcendence beyond this world's parameters.

No matter what lay ahead in the New Year, I was resolved to face it. While Roman honor and dignity would have condoned suicide over the disgrace of banishment, I opted for life, entrusting myself to the spirit that had guided me during the last nine months.

THE NEW YEAR BROUGHT A change in the provincial administration. Gaius Antonius was out, and Lucius Piso was in as the new proconsul. As he had predicted, Antonius was prosecuted on charges of provincial malfeasance upon his return to Roma. Convicted, he went into exile on the island of Malta. Though Antonius had taken few pains for my safety or comfort during my exile, I hoped that *his* would be tolerable.

However, when Piso was Consul, he had refused to help me against Clodius' mob. So I was not especially anxious to see him. But how was I to avoid him if he came to the provincial seat of Thessalonica? If I returned to Dyrrachium, I was certain to encounter him on the connecting Egnatian Road, and I did not feel safe at any other city in the whole province.

In the end, I remained in Thessalonica. By mid-Januarius, much to my surprise and discomfort, Piso arrived with his lictors, staff, and legates. Among them was the former praetor, Lucius Valerius Flaccus, who had been of invaluable help in the Catilinian suppression. Having been informed of my residence in the city, Piso sent Flaccus to seek me out. When he found me, I could not refuse to meet with him. It was through his intervention that a meeting was arranged with Proconsul Piso.

As always, he was all twitching eyebrows and hollow cheeks, but, despite his military uniform, his gravity was diminished. His aloofness and detachment were gone too. Perhaps this was because we were now far from Roma and away from Clodius. He inquired about my health and comfort, noting that I had grown leaner in exile. Indeed, with my unshorn hair and nearly a year's growth of beard, I probably looked more like an itinerant Greek philosopher than a Roman senator.

"Many senators are anxious for your recall," he informed me. "There are those who've said that you should simply be invited to return rather than be officially recalled." He paused and considered me with what appeared to be genuine sympathy. "As long as you... need to be here... I'll pass on to you whatever news comes from Roma."

I thanked him for his solicitude as I struggled to suppress my resentment of his earlier refusal to help me.

"You know we were compelled by that *creature*," he said apologetically. "Gabinius and I were little more than chorus members in a Greek tragedy."

"Except it was *my* tragedy," I answered bitterly. Then, restraining myself from further rancor, I acknowledged the truth of his remarks. "Yes, it was Pulcher having his revenge on me and doing Caesar's bidding. Yes, you and Gabinius recited your verses so very well." I have never been a forgiving man. Yet, I felt sorry for Piso. He was trying to make amends, perhaps out of genuine contrition or because he was my son-in-law's kinsman.

Unlike Antonius, Piso remained in Thessalonica. He did not resume his predecessor's campaigns against the Thracians, but he sent his legates and military tribunes, including Gnaeus Plancius, to the legions stationed on the northern border. He extended many dinner invitations which I at first declined. But I relented by early Februarius, as my anger diminished, and thereafter we became frequent dining partners.

I HAD HAD NO NEWS from Roma in over two months. I attributed this to the contrary winds prevailing in winter. But by early Martius, I received a letter from Quintus; it contained the most tragic news sent to me in all the months of my exile. So tragic were these tidings that Quintus had delayed in writing them down and sending off his letter.

At the beginning of the year, Consul Lentulus Spinther had tried to raise the question of my recall in the Senate. With each attempt, the tribunes Bassus and Calenus had alternated in vetoing the Consul's proposals. This happened all through Januarius, and Pompeius and Crassus merely sat at their places and watched in silence. Then Tribunes Milo and Sestius tried another tactic. Convening the Tribal Assembly, they attempted to invite public discussion of my recall. At the very least, they expected the hostile tribunes to interpose their veto. Instead, they encountered Clodius and his gang of gladiators and armed riffraff. His tribunate had expired, but *not* his tyranny over the Forum. He and his operae still occupied Castor's temple, converted into a veritable fortress. From there, they converged on the Assembly, swinging their swords and cudgels at all who stood in their way. The Forum ran with blood that day, its pavement littered with the wounded and the dead. Even the sacrosanct Tribunes Milo and Sestius were among the wounded.

Quintus, Servius, and Piso had been standing on the Rostra with the Tribunes when the attack began. Clodius' men called out my brother's name upon recognizing him. They pulled him off the Rostra, punching and pummeling him, tearing the toga from his body, dragging him to the Forum pavement, a bloody, bruised wreck they left for dead. Others who were struck down were piled upon him, nearly suffocating him.

The survivors, both the wounded and the unscathed, dispersed, and then Clodius' gang retreated back to their fortress-temple. After nightfall, my brother found the strength to extricate himself from the mound of corpses. Clutching his way cautiously in the dark, he managed to get home where Pomponia and young Quintus, believing him dead, were already grieving for him.

Pomponia nursed her husband to a thorough recovery over the next several weeks. But Quintus could not shed his sense of guilt at having survived the assault; for Piso, my son-in-law Piso, had been one of its casualties. My poor Tullia, my poor "Tulliola" was widowed and not even nineteen years old. What beastly fate was *this?* What had become of law? Of decency? Of order? The Republic had become the domain of *demagogues* and *mobs*! It was not enough that I had been driven into exile. My brother had been beaten almost to death, and Piso was *murdered.*

Quintus closed his letter by regretfully observing that the recall initiative had become stalemated. Why was Pompeius silent in the midst of this anarchy?

The elder Piso and I grew closer through our mutual sorrow. If I had ever doubted the depth and sincerity of his love for his young kinsman, I could no longer do so after seeing the outpouring of grief for him. Moreover, Piso's expressions of sympathy for my widowed Tullia were no less genuine.

About three weeks later, a letter from Servius told of Milo's attempt to prosecute Clodius for public violence. But the gangster refused to appear in court. Instead, accompanied by his gladiators and riffraff, he went about the Forum and announced his candidacy for aedile in the next election.

Added to my grief at Piso's death and Tullia's bereavement was a renewed, deeper depression at the turn of events in Roma. Depression gave rise to desperation and cynicism. Writing to Quintus and Servius, I recommended that they advise Milo and Sestius to "fight fire with fire." Clodius was at war with the Republic and with all semblance of orderly government. "In time of war," I wrote, "laws are silent." Clodius could not be stopped unless the government used the same tactics. So I urged them to recruit gangs, arm them, and seize the Forum and the Comitium. Use against him the same weapons that he had used, but use them with even greater force and ferocity. This was the only way to contain the anarchy into which the Republic had fallen; only then could the Senate and the People's Assembly legislate for my recall.

My new depression was reflected in the gray-slate color of the Aegean Sea in winter. The optimism I had felt when notified of the election results was dashed by the chaotic conditions prevailing in Roma.

Ironically, my advice was already under discussion among Quintus, Servius, Milo, and Sestius before I sent the letter. Atticus and a consortium of equites provided the funds to purchase troops of gladiators from the schools at Capua, Nola, Pompeii, and Neapolis. To these were added bands of armed, young equites and even some elements of the City plebeians whom Clodius had failed to win over. Thus fortified and equipped, Milo and Sestius occupied the Forum and the Comitium.

From his vantage point atop Castor's portico, Clodius saw this and ordered his gang to attack. The fighting was fierce, but indecisive. A second and a third day the two gangs clashed in the Forum amid the edifices of the gods and the basilicas of the law. By the fourth day, Milo's and Sestius' men had gained the upper hand.

These events had happened during Martius and Aprilis. I learned of them through letters from Quintus, Servius, and Atticus which I received early in Maius. By that time, as I subsequently learned, the shift in the powers had become so evident that the Senate could meet without fear. Tribunes Bassus and Calenus absented themselves from the Senate. Many senators, both optimates and neutrals, made speeches on behalf of my recall.

By early June, even Pompeius found his voice. He proposed a series of decrees in my honor: a Senatorial commendation for all communities and individuals who had rendered me assistance during my exile; an invitation to all Roman citizens residing in every colony and municipality throughout Italia to come to Roma to vote for my recall; and finally a Senatorial decree, to be ratified by the Centuriate Assembly, formally nullifying my banishment and recalling me from exile.

The Senate approved each of the decrees by a vote of four hundred sixteen to Publius Clodius Pulcher's sole dissenting vote. Clodius' brothers were absent from the Senate on the day of the vote: Appius because of his praetorian duties, and Gaius, having been discharged by Caesar, was canvassing for next year's praetorate. Just as well, for I could not imagine them approving any measures favorable to me.

The date set for the Centuriata's recall vote was the fourth of Sextilis, the day before my Tullia's nineteenth birthday. I received word of these preparations by mid-Quinctilis. Atticus' business contacts were predicting a massive turn-out from the equites all over Italia and from the farming communities, despite the fact that the farmers would be very busy harvesting their summer crops. The roads were bound to be clogged with thousands of travelers en route to Roma.

I too would be on the move. Anticipating a favorable outcome, I made preparations to leave Thessalonica and head back to Dyrrachium so that I could more quickly cross to Italia. My confidence in a successful vote was not at all unfounded, for the Centuriata, the same Assembly that voted for consuls and praetors, was dominated by elder, propertied citizens, rather than the plebeians who held sway in the Concilium Plebis. Moreover, I calculated that the eighteen centuries of equites would certainly tip the balance in my favor.

I bade farewell to Piso and thanked him for his hospitality. He wished me good fortune, especially with the recall vote; he also allowed me to use one of his couriers to convey a letter to Dyrrachium for transit to Roma. In this way, I sent word to Terentia and Tullia of my intention to cross to Brundisium on the fourth. Assuming favorable winds, I expected to arrive there on the following day—my "Tulliola's" birthday. I took it as a good omen that the vote was to be taken the day before her birthday; I missed her so much that I felt I had to be on Italian soil on that day, even if I did not see her.

Our journey to Dyrrachium was swift, safe, and uneventful. Passing through the same pastures, mountains, and villages that we had seen eighteen months earlier was a poignant reminder of how my fortunes had been reversed. Once in Dyrrachium, we rented quarters and waited for about three weeks until it was time to make the crossing.

WHEN THE TIME CAME TO cross over, we had no trouble securing passage on a Greek vessel, and our crossing to Italia was without incident or mishap. The sight of the Italian coast filled me with joy. As we sailed closer to the port, I beheld a veiled figure almost like a spectral apparition in the morning mist. Torches and lanterns on the quay revealed ships of various sizes anchored by the dock; porters and stevedores were busy at their tasks of loading and unloading cargoes. Straining to make out the veiled figure, I at last recognized my beloved child, my Tullia. My heart leapt into my throat as I called out to her. "Tullia! Tullia!" Frantically, I waved my arms high above my head.

Recognizing me, Tullia called back, *"Tata! Tata!"* The few moments it took for the vessel to be anchored and secured at the dock seemed like an eternity. I bolted down the gang plank to the quay, embraced and kissed my Tullia. We were both drowning in our own tears.

Tullia's face was visibly marked by the sorrows of the last year and a half. All the fear, pain, anxiety that I had borne in exile was reflected before me as though Tullia were a mirror to my very soul. She was only nineteen on this day of our reunion. But her face and bearing were that of a woman almost twice her age. We stared into each other's tearful eyes for a long moment, taking in the reality that we were at last together.

"I left Roma as soon as we got your letter," she said between sobs. "I wanted to be here for you when you arrived. We *all* wanted to be here, but Mother thought it best to stay for the vote. She said she'd send word to us as soon as she heard. Oh, Tata, I can't believe you're really here! I've missed you so!"

I held her closely and comforted her. "I'm here with you. We'll all be together again soon." I realized that I had misspoken because young Piso could not possibly be with us, except in spirit. Looking around the dock, I asked her, "Who came with you?"

"Mother had Philotimus escort us." She indicated two slave women from Piso's household who were standing a few paces behind her, and from my own household, Lucia, a doughty Latin who had been Tullia's nurse. The three of them bowed respectfully to me, and I acknowledged them.

"But where's Philotimus?" I asked as I looked about the quay for Terentia's cunning Greek freedman.

"He's back at Gaius Maenius' house. Atticus told us to stay with him. He's been so kind, so gracious. He can't wait to see you."

"That's fine. But Phiolotimus should have been here with you. The port of Brundisium is no place for unescorted women. Come on! Let's get out of here. I've never understood why this is the foulest port in all of Italia. On the other side of the sea, Dyrrachium is a scented garden compared to *this!*"

Tullia giggled meekly at my barb against Brundisium. Tiro, Alexio, and Metrodorus each paid their respects to her. After hiring some porters to help us with us our baggage, we proceeded to Gaius Maenius' house. The old equite welcomed me with open arms and extended to us the full hospitality of his household. Grateful as I was for this and his earlier solicitude, the remembrance of the days before I had crossed to Macedonia, those sad, uncertain days, vitiated against the joy of my return.

That evening, after supper, the town's chief officials and leading citizens came to Maenius' house to welcome me back to Italia and to wish me a safe and expeditious return to Roma. Over the next several days, as we awaited news from Roma, citizens of all classes and tongues saluted me and expressed similar sentiments.

Nearly a week after our landing at Brundisium, Terentia's couriers sought us out and gave us the splendid news—the Centuriate Assembly had overwhelmingly approved my recall! Immediately, we made preparations to set out for Roma. The city officials gave us a laudatory send-off comprised of sacrifices to the gods and speeches honoring my services to the Republic.

Hiring a coach, we proceeded up the Appian Road intending to reach Roma in about a week. But news of our imminent approach preceded us into every farmstead, village, and town. Communities turned out to cheer us, entertain us, and feast us. We could not refuse their hospitality, though I longed to be back in Roma, to see Terentia and you, my son, and Quintus and all the others. The triumphant receptions given us each day by the communities along the ancient highway delayed our arrival at Roma until the Nones of September, one month after I had landed at Brundisium.

Drawing nearer to Roma, we saw many of the roadside's monuments festooned with holiday garlands. Arching over them, the once lugubrious pines and cypresses now seemed aglow as the late summer's sunlight streamed through their bushy crowns sending shafts of light upon our path.

We halted briefly just outside the Capena Gate. Several hundred citizens lined the roadway and cheered upon recognizing me. I waved at them, but then I alighted from the halted coach. I wanted to see young Piso's monument. Tullia pointed it out to me, a short, cylindrical, fluted stone among scores lining the roadside. Its inscription read: *Gnaeus Calpurnius Piso*. Good Piso sacrificed his life for me. Tullia wept, and I held her closely to me.

"Enjoy this triumph, Marcus Cicero, for it will be short-lived."

Tullia and I wheeled about and saw two women standing a few paces away. They were dressed in mourning stolas and pallas of black and gray. The elder of the two spoke again. "You drove my husband out of his country, away from his family and countrymen. So, you have learned what that is like. You have your daughter at your side as you return." She faced the young woman standing next to her. "This is *my* daughter—whose step-father you drove into exile."

I could not recognize them. They were somehow familiar, but I could not place them. The elder woman's voice and her words jarred my memory at the same instant that she spoke again.

"I am Aurelia Orestilla, the widow of Lucius Sergius Catilina, and this is my daughter, his step-daughter, Flavia. I say yet again, Marcus Tullius Cicero, enjoy this triumph, for it will be short-lived."

I wanted to reply, but I was at a complete loss as to what to say. The encounter disturbed me, overshadowing my return with a note of tragedy. Tullia and I remained fixed in our places. I felt her quivering beside me.

"You will see us again," Aurelia Orestilla said, and then she and her daughter walked off. We were both relieved at their departure.

I turned back for one more glance at Piso's grave marker. Suddenly, the very same mystical feeling that I had had in exile, when I had refrained from using the dagger on myself, the sense of life's continuity despite death, surged through my being.

Resuming our progress, we passed through the Capena Gate and into the City. It was decked out and adorned in a holiday spirit. Crowds of equites, senators and plebeians, men, women, and children escorted us through the streets in a triumphant parade to the Forum. There, the temples' columns and the Rostra were adorned with laurel and oak boughs. But I also saw blood-stained pavements—the evidence of bloody battles between Milo's and Clodius' gangs.

In returning so triumphantly, I had changed my sordid toga of mourning for the white, Roman senator's toga. But I still had the beard and untrimmed hair, the legacies of my banishment. Amid the cheers and acclamations of the citizens, I mounted the Rostra. In every direction, there were thousands of people—senators in their white togas and purple-striped tunics, equites in their double-striped tunics, and the gray and brown-clad plebeians. Now and again, Clodius' riffraff catcalled and heckled, but Milo's and Sestius' gladiators kept them at bay. What an occasion for a speech!

"If it is through my ancestors that I have a country, then it is through the Senate's constancy, the Roman People's goodwill, and the benefactions of the immortal gods that I and my services to the Republic are vindicated, and I am now safely restored to it with peace, honor, and dignity." And so, I began, however extemporaneously, my first official address upon returning from banishment. I chose my words with care, imparting thanks and acknowledgements to those men who had helped secure my recall, while reining in the acrimony that I would have wanted to hurl at my enemies.

Both Consuls were on one side of the Rostra, lean, ruddy Lentulus Spinther and bronze, granitic Metellus Nepos. Turning to them, I announced, "Consul Lentulus Spinther, your labors on my behalf were unceasing. Consul Metellus Nepos, you put patriotism above family connections to serve my cause. To you both, I offer my deepest thanks." I delicately alluded to Metellus Nepos' family tie to the Pulchers, as his deceased brother, Celer, had been Clodia's husband.

On the opposite side of the Rostra, I saw Pompeius and a few steps behind him, Quintus and Servius. "Of Gnaeus Pompeius Magnus, whose services to the Republic are innumerable, I acknowledge before the Senate and the Roman People, his renewed and restored loyalty. Without him, I know I would not have the privilege of addressing my countrymen.

"Of my brother's loyalty, there were never bounds or conditions. Even at the risk of his own life, he persevered against armed opposition to bring about my recall. No less in perseverance and loyalty was my dear friend, Servius Sulpicius Rufus."

Though I did not see Atticus on the Rostra or standing among the equites, I extended thanks to their order for their unfailing support even before I had gone into exile. "To that class of citizens into whose ranks my birth and ancestry place me, I acknowledge your support, your loyalty, your solidarity in my service."

Then, I changed tack. "The enmity of one tribune, backed by self-serving men, drove me into banishment. But the goodwill and loyalty of two tribunes, Titus Milo and Publius Sestius, backed by the men of law and order, brought me home to country and family."

At the mention of family, I looked lovingly at Tullia standing a short remove from Quintus and Servius. She was beaming at me, and yet there was a sad aura about her. "To do so," I continued, "they had to meet force with force, swords with swords, violence with violence. For those who opposed my recall attacked peaceful, lawful assemblies of the Roman people; they struck down citizens who tried to help me, like my own brother; and they killed others, like my daughter's husband, young

Piso. Only when they repulsed the foes of orderly government could Milo and Sestius enable the people to sanction my recall, confirming the Senate's decrees."

The heckling and cat-calling of Clodius' hooligans became more pronounced during my allusions to them, though I dared not mention my enemy by name lest I provoke a riot. "Those forces of anarchy and lawlessness were abetted by consuls who turned deaf ears and hard hearts to my plight. Gabinius and Piso, not by commission, but by their apathy, their indifference, their volition, became my foes. And though I would not call Caesar my enemy, I know that he was silent when others called him this." This was my only reference to the man who had been the will behind my banishment. It would not have been politic to say more on that occasion.

I thanked the citizens for their attention and then I stepped down from the Rostra. I made directly for the Forum's eastern end, to the Vestal Mansion where I was certain Terentia was waiting for me as she had not been on the Rostra. The press of the crowds accompanying me slowed my progress. Senators, equites, and plebeians extended themselves to clasp hands with me, to congratulate me, to touch the hem of my toga as though it were a sacred talisman. When at last I arrived at the Vestal residence, I found Terentia and Fabia standing on the steps with other Vestals amid a score of attendants.

I walked up the steps, and Terentia extended her hands to me. Taking them in my own, I smothered them with kisses. Then, I kissed her mouth, embraced her, and held her for a long moment. Eighteen months away from Terentia! I did not realize until I held her how much I had missed her.

The crowds were cheering and applauding our reunion. I could feel her shaking in my arms. Was it joy at seeing me again, or was she embarrassed at our public emotional display? We pulled back from each other, looking into each other's faces. Terentia's eyes were red and swollen with tears. Lines and shadows had visited her face since I had left. Her hands and arms were stiff, evidence of the ravages of her joint pains.

Neither of us spoke as we looked at each other, at least not with our voices. But our eyes and our tears spoke volumes. Terentia touched my face, caressing the full beard that had been only stubble when I had gone into exile.

Fabia ushered us inside while the crowds yet cheered and applauded. Tullia, Quintus, and Servius followed. Once inside the atrium with its statues of former Vestals, I saw you, my little boy, my son, Marcus. How you had grown! You were almost five now. I called to you, "Marcus! It's Tata!" But you clung to your nurse's skirt in fear at the sight of this long-haired bearded stranger.

Terentia picked you up and brought you to me. "This is your father, Marcus," she said to you almost reprovingly. "Of course you *do* remember him. Go on! Kiss your father. Hug him!"

Obediently, you came into my arms, your red tunic getting tangled between your legs. I held you ever so closely as yet another flood of tears gushed forth. You pulled at my beard and passed the back of your hand across your cheeks where my beard had tickled and scratched you.

Little Marcus and Tullia, Terentia, Fabia, Quintus and Servius—I was home—home at last! But, strangely, Atticus and Pomponia were not with us.

At dusk, Quintus and Servius escorted me to Capitoline Jove's temple. On the way, they told me that Atticus had had to leave Roma for business concerns in Picenum. He was expected back before the end of the month. Atticus' presence would have made my home-coming complete. About Pomponia and little Quintus, my brother would only say, most evasively, that they were both indisposed.

As we made our way up the Capitoline steps, I remembered the day of my departure into exile eighteen months earlier. What fears and uncertainties held me captive that day and for most of the next eighteen months.

Upon entering the Temple, we went directly to Minerva's statue. Her cold, marmoreal visage stared down at us from vacant eyes below the rim of her raised helmet. Her armor and shield glinted in the torch-lit cella. The sacred owl on her shoulder was barely visible in the shadow of the goddess' helmed head. By her sandaled feet at the statue's pedestal, where I had left it eighteen months earlier, was my statuette of the goddess. I felt profound, yet unspoken gratitude to some unknown but perhaps not unknowable deity.

WE WENT BACK TO THE old house in the Carinae district. Pompeia was happy at my return, but her greeting and disposition was noticeably guarded and reserved. I attributed this to some row that she and Quintus must have had. Their son, young Quintus, ran into my arms upon seeing me. I do not know how he did not knock me over. For a child just two years older than you, my son, he was solid and strong.

Quintus and Pompeia had changed the old family house very little over the years. Being there again brought back so many memories of my childhood and young manhood. But these memories dissipated as Quintus and Servius told me of what had transpired in the month intervening between the recall vote and my actual return to Roma. I listened attentively as Metrodorus painstakingly cut and shaved the beard off my face and then trimmed my hair.

"Only days after your recall," Servius was saying, "the Assembly voted for the new consuls, Marcius Philippus and Gnaeus Marcellinus."

A good sign, I thought. Marcellinus was an optimate and Philippus was a neutral, though he had married Caesar's widowed niece. But I had to ask, "Why were the elections delayed?"

"The Senate wanted as large a turnout as possible," Quintus replied, "so they thought it best to hold your recall vote ahead of the magisterial elections."

"I'd have thought that Clodius might've tried to exploit that delay."

"Possibly," agreed Quintus, "but Milo and Sestius proved to be more than effective checks."

Metrodorus tilted my head so as to better catch the oil-lamp light. Necessity impelled me to keep my mouth shut as he was scraping around my lips.

"The praetors and other officials have been chosen as well," my brother added, "but not the aediles. Milo has blocked every attempt at their election because *Pretty-Boy* Pulcher's hot for it."

"Clodius has played havoc with the grain reserves by giving them away to the mob," Servius observed, "and the great influx of citizens to vote for your recall has put a further drain on the City granaries."

"And just as Roma starts to feel hunger pangs, Ptolemy *Flute-Player* gets kicked off his throne by the Alexandrian mob and his unscrupulous eldest daughter," Quintus put in. "So he comes to town and asks the

Senate to put him back on or there might not be sufficient Egyptian grain to feed Roman bellies."

"So then, Marcus," Servius concluded, "there you have it!"

As Metrodorus was now applying the blade to my right cheek, I was able to ask, "What has the Senate decided to do?"

"About *Flute-Player*? There's been no decision yet," Quintus replied. "But they know what the King expects. He paid Caesar and Pompeius well for his kingdom. Right now, he's staying at Pompeius' Alban estate, waiting for the Senate's answer."

"What about bread?" I asked.

This time Servius answered. "They're saying that the new quaestors will have to appropriate the funds to buy grain from wherever surpluses can be found. Crassus has even suggested that the shortage is a hoax created by Pompeius. Lately, they've been at odds with each other." Then, he paused and looked at me intently and asked, "Marcus, what are your plans?"

I had Metrodorus pause long enough in his barbering for me to reply, "To get back my land and my house; and to curry Pompeius' favor."

When Metrodorus had completed his task, he handed me a small bronze mirror. Looking at the reflection in it, I saw a man whose face was etched with lines of sorrow and bitterness, a man whose hardened face looked older than his forty-nine years. His hair, though now neatly trimmed, had far more gray than it had eighteen months earlier.

AT THE NEXT MEETING OF the Senate, Consul Metellus Nepos invited me to speak. I used the occasion to express again my gratitude for the Senate's loyalty. I reiterated many of the same points I had made earlier in my extemporaneous address in the Forum. But I did not wax at length on them. Instead, I segued into the grain crisis, insisting that the emergency required swift, decisive action. "There is but one man with the skill, the administrative ability, and the boundless energy to undertake the task of saving the state from calamity."

I paused and focused on Pompeius. The expression he wore said it all. The calm, almost smug reserve told me that he was expecting what I said next.

"Conscript Fathers, I propose the appointment of Gnaeus Pompeius Magnus to the task of grain curator for the Republic. He should be entrusted with imperium over all grain-producing provinces and tributary states and communities for no less than five years. He should be entrusted with all necessary funds, ships, and legates. The Senate must not fail to do its duty: Commission Gnaeus Pompeius Magnus!"

Thunderous applause greeted my proposal. Gnaeus Pompeius looked squarely at me, his eyebrows arched, and a peculiar smile played upon his lips. Crassus, however, made no attempt to conceal his contemptuous scowl.

There was hardly any debate after Marcus Varro seconded the proposal. He reminded the senators of Pompeius' diligent efficiency in carrying out an earlier extraordinary command, the one that led to his eradication of piracy on Roman seas. But the Lucullus brothers and Hortensius were joined by Marcus Bibulus—recently returned from his proconsular cattle and forest duties—in arguing against the conferment of such power on any individual as inherently dangerous.

Inevitably, in short order, the Senate voted in favor of my proposal over negligible opposition that included Clodius, *both* his brothers—for Gaius had returned to Roma to be elected praetor for the ensuing year—and their faction.

Accepting the commission, Pompeius appointed Quintus and me as his first legates. He announced his intention to procure grain for the citizens with all deliberate speed. Privately, he thanked me for honoring him with the commission. I told him it was the least I could do in view of his services on my behalf. However, when he told me that he would continue to work for my interests, I knew better than to accept his assurance at face value.

Next, the Senate took up the issue of Ptolemy Auletes' restoration. I supported the motion for Lentulus Spinther to undertake the task as soon as he began his proconsulate of Cilicia. In the wake of my recall vote, the Senate had exerted its traditional prerogative of assigning proconsular provinces. Thus Spinther had received Cilicia, while his colleague Nepos had been assigned to Nearer Spain.

There was a considerable divergence of opinion on the restoration issue. While Crassus' friends and debtors spoke for his appointment, others favored Pompeius for the task, insisting that a grateful Auletes would furnish his benefactor, Roma's newly appointed grain curator, with abundant food. However, Pompeius gave no inkling of any interest in the job, and those who knew him well enough knew that this did *not* necessarily mean that he did *not* want it.

It was speculated that Pompeius was hoping for the appointment of his friend and former legate, Aulus Gabinius. As Proconsul of Syria, Gabinius was the closest to Egypt and this would have made his commission preferable to the other candidates. In the end, the Senate gave the nod to Lentulus Spinther, and so the Egyptian question appeared to be settled. It probably did not sit well with Auletes that he would have to wait four months before Spinther could initiate the restoration. He departed from Pompeius' Alban villa and went to Tarsus in Cilicia to await Spinther's arrival.

Omniscient Narrative

On the Capitoline Mount, between the majestic Temple of Jupiter, Best and Greatest of the gods, and the Temple of Juno Moneta, the Republic's official mint, a wall of kiln-baked bricks has been constructed. Measuring sixteen by nine feet, it faces the Forum and the Comitium in the valley below, and it is situated directly above the roof of the Tabularium, the official state archives edifice, whose multiple arched stone tiers are built into the Capitoline's southern face.

The wall is part of Publius Clodius Pulcher's monument to his own tribunate. Its construction had occupied the summer months of his wild tribunate, while his gang of ruffians and hooligans had turned the Forum and the Comitium into their own private campground. Now, though his tribunate has ended, the gangster oversees the placement of four bronze tablets upon which his tribunicial legislation has been inscribed in deeply-carved Latin letters. A team of masons and metalsmiths labors to mount, bolt, and secure the tablets to the brick wall, while a coterie of Clodius' men stands guard around them. The late September sun is graciously generous in its light and warmth upon their tasks.

Clodius, attired in a white toga and purple-striped tunic, and his companions watch the installation. Though it is overdue, it pleases the erstwhile tribune; it gratifies his wife, Fulvia, who is again with child, and it amuses their guest, Marcus Antonius, Clodius' friend and adoptive plebeian father.

"Well, Publius, it's the *Twelve Tables*—minus eight!" Antonius quips flippantly.

"If I'd had a second tribunate," Clodius returns, "there'd have been an additional eight plaques—at least."

The workmen hammer the bolts into the corners of the second plaque. Clodius' smile calls attention to it. "That one's special for me. It's the one that outlawed the *Chick-Pea*."

"Your *Chick-Pea* is back, and I've heard he's making noise for Pompeius' benefit." Antonius' flippancy is increasing, and he notices that Clodius' irritation is also on the rise. "Are you going to do anything about it, or will he be making louder noises?"

With an icy tone, Clodius replies, "You should ask those questions of Caesar when you return to Gaul."

Fulvia senses her husband's annoyance and she attempts to redirect the conversation. "Marcus, how long will you be staying in Roma?" Her impregnated belly is conspicuous beneath her green stola and buff-colored palla.

"Only long enough to visit Antonia and my mother and brothers. Then, I'm off to Syria." Antonius' flippancy now takes on a swaggering cockiness.

"*Syria?*" Clodius is taken aback.

"Why Syria?" Fulvia asks with a teasing lilt to her husky voice. "Have you had a falling out with Caesar?"

"Far from it. I've been transferred to Proconsul Gabinuus. Caesar wants me to command his horse. I've even brought a contingent of Gallic horse with me. They're camped out at Mars Field."

Clodius is puzzled. "Gallic cavalry for service in Syria? What's going on?"

"It's what's going to happen about the Egyptian King." Antonius is quite pleased with himself.

Clodius smirks. "Lentulus Spinther's got that job. *Chick-Pea* moved it and the Senate decreed it."

Antonius assumes the officious air of one who knows what others cannot even begin to fathom. "I promise you, Publius, if Caesar wants the King restored by Gabinius, then that's who'll do it!"

Clodius is uncomfortable being corrected about Caesar's intentions. "Whoever does it, the sooner Ptolemy is restored, the better it'll be for Roma's hungry mob."

"Is Curio going with you?" Fulvia asks. She sees by Antonius' reaction that she has hit a nerve. She also sees that Clodius has noticed it. She wonders, *Is Antonius trying to put behind him his intimacies with Gaius Scribonius Curio?*

"No!" Antonius snorts. He's staying on with Caesar."

"Well, perhaps both of you could benefit from a brief respite." Fulvia's tongue presses against her inner cheek.

Ignoring the barb, Antonius says, "I'll stop at Malta on the way and visit my uncle."

"Oh yes, poor Uncle Gaius Antonius. What might it take to recall him from exile?" Fulvia muses.

Clodius has been thinking of something that will surely unnerve his cocky friend. While Fulvia has but left the door ajar to Antonius' sensibilities, he will push it wide open. Turning his attention from the third plaque's installation, he says to his friend, "You ought to take your wife with you down to Malta."

"Of course, Antonia's coming with me. She wants to see her father. She misses him very much."

"That's fine, Marcus. Then she ought to stay with him. She'd be safer in Malta than here in Roma."

A quizzical mask comes over Antonius' Taurus-like face. "Why? What are you talking about?"

Fulvia giggles and shakes her head. "Publius… *must* you?"

"I wouldn't be a true friend otherwise. Look, Marcus, don't be alarmed. Well, actually, you should be, because it seems that our mutual friend, Publius Dolabella, has been prancing around your Antonia like a stallion in heat since you've been in Gaul. He might grow bolder when you're as far away as Syria. *Beware!* Take her with you to Malta and then leave her there with her father."

Antonius flushes with anger so that his face matches the scarlet of his leather-bound tunic. *"Dolabella?!?! I'll squeeze the seeds out of him like a pomegranate!"* His muscular hands are clenched into aggressive fists.

"His marriage to the heiress really hasn't settled him down,' Clodius says so facetiously.

"Nor has fatherhood," Fulvia adds, tongue-in-cheek.

Their tandem taunts are not without foundation. While Antonia herself may be above reproach, Dolabella's rakish reputation renders any woman fair game for his plying charms

The workmen have mounted and bolted the fourth and final plaque. They stand back and to one side so that Clodius can view the completed monument. "Well done! Well done! Very well done! I've been immortalized in brick and bronze." Turning to Fulvia, he says, "And when you, my *Fulvy-plum*, give me a son to carry on my line that will immortalize me in flesh and blood."

The workmen begin to gather up their tools. Their apprentices and slaves clean up the debris from the completed task. Rough woolen cloths are used to buff the newly-mounted plaques. Clodius is pleased. He has a completed monument to feed his vanity. He has a second child on the way, hopefully a son. He enjoys the personal satisfaction of having discomforted his boastful, cocky friend and adoptive plebeian father. He is supremely popular with Roma's life-blood—the urban mob. He is yet a power-house of demagogic energy.

Indeed, Clodius is well pleased with himself.

Cicero's Respublica

I embarked upon my own agenda when I petitioned the Pontifical College for the restitution of my confiscated property on the Palatine. In my address, I reviewed Clodius Pulcher's enmity to me since the Good Goddess scandal. His tribunate, I told them, was a weapon sharpened and unsheathed to be used against me because I had destroyed his alibi. But I argued that Clodius' banishment law against me was invalid, as indeed was his entire tribunate. This was so because his adoption into plebeian status had occurred in violation of the consular auspices.

Here, I was treading on dangerous ground, for the Pontiffs knew all too well that Caesar had engineered Clodius' adoption in flagrant disregard of Bibulus' religious sky-watching. But I dared not mention Caesar directly.

Now these Pontiffs included the optimates Marcus Lucullus, Marcus Messalla, Consul Lentulus Spinther, the triumvir Marcus Crassus, and two new members, Marcus Aemilius Lepidus and Quintus Metellus Scipio, who had been co-opted to replace the deceased colleagues Catulus and Silanus. These were the men to whom I appealed for the restitution of my land and my house.

A notable absentee was the Rex Sacrorum, Lucius Claudius, who was the surrogate Pontifex Maximus during Caesar's proconsulate in Gaul. As he was related to Publius Clodius, I had anticipated opposition from him. So, as Lucullus was senior Pontiff, it fell to him to preside over our meeting in an audience chamber of the Regia.

When I had concluded my appeal, Lucullus conducted a brief deliberation with his colleagues before announcing their decision. "Marcus Tullius Cicero," he intoned, "we will recommend to the Senate that the confiscation of your property and its consecration be overturned. We will further recommend that the Senate appropriate the necessary funds for your home's reconstruction and for the repair of your damaged properties. Finally, we will recommend that the Senate decree the removal of the tablet containing the law of your banishment."

I was elated at their decision. So too were Terentia, Quintus, and Servius. I suspected, however, that the Pontiffs' decision had been pre-approved by Caesar. Quite expeditiously, the Senate approved their recommendations despite the objections of the Pulcher brothers.

It gave us all the deepest satisfaction to see the workmen commence the reconstruction of our Palatine mansion. The work began within days of the Senate's decree on a clear, mild, sunny late September day. The workmen's first task was to dismantle and dislodge the marker that Clodius had had erected after his operae had razed the house. This they accomplished despite the menacing presence of Clodius and his operae who raucously demonstrated against the demolition of the Libertas shrine. However, they made no attempt to interfere as Milo's and Sestius' gangs were on site and ready to take them on.

There was but one personal drawback to this progress—Terentia. She refused to live with me at the Carinae house because she could not bear to inhabit the same house with Pomponia. In all fairness, she acknowledged that Pomponia was also loath to share the house. Alas, she even cited Atticus' frequent admissions over the years that Pomponia had an unbearably mean, dyspeptic temper. No matter how I tried to persuade, to cajole, to reason, I could not dissuade Terentia.

So, during the whole time that the house was under reconstruction, I lived with Quintus and his family in the Carinae. Though I visited Terentia and saw you, my son, every day at the Vestal Residence, there was no possibility of conjugal relations with my wife, your mother. She was also so abstemious that she would not consent to an assignation with me at either Atticus' or Servius' house. During this enforced celibacy, my peculiar problem, first manifested during the exile, was exacerbated in the months after my return. Terentia's refusal to live with me until the house was completed was a rejection that cut me to the core. Looking back, her refusal was a significant turning point in our marriage, ultimately contributing to our later estrangement.

The smashing of the Libertas marker distracted me from further considerations of my own spousal problems. It had become a tangled, twisted waste heap. Was it not possible, I mused, that the triumvirate, for which Clodius was a formidable weapon, could be similarly demolished and discarded? Deadly, destructive musings these were; yet, in my public statements, I was all praise and laudation for Pompeius and Caesar.

When I thanked the Senate for the restitution of my land and for the generous grant with which to rebuild the house, I clearly demonstrated an appreciation of Caesar's goodwill by proposing a twenty-day thanksgiving in honor of his victories of the last two years. The Senate unanimously sanctioned it.

Publius Clodius used this opportunity to hope, ever so facetiously, that the citizens would not be too hungry to celebrate the festivities. At the time, Pompeius and Quintus had gone down to Sicilia to buy grain for the City rabble, lest their hunger pangs should provoke them to commit violence in the streets. Now, Clodius cast barbs at the continuing grain shortage. He also hit on Milo's continued obstruction of the aedilician election when he announced, "Though there's not enough food, we at least have aediles to direct the games and celebrations Marcus Cicero proposes. But when the New Year begins, we'll not even have *them!*"

Everyone knew that Clodius was still covetous of the aedileship, and though out of office, he was still a formidable gangster. He and his operae were standing ominously about the Capitoline summit, heckling and cat-calling when the Consuls' attendants took down his bronze tablet containing the banishment law. It was thrown down to the ground. Using hammers and axes, workmen pounded it into scraps as Clodius' mob screamed and bellowed in protest. Fortunately, Milo's men were on hand to keep them in check.

Ironically, this incident turned out to be a source of friction with Marcus Cato. Returning to Roma from his Cyprus annexation mission after an absence of nearly two years, Cato was hailed and congratulated by all. Though he could boast of his honesty in resisting any and all opportunities for personal gain, it was clear from his ruddy, swollen face and inflamed eyes that he had not mended his drinking predilection. After reporting on his mission before the Senate, he privately took issue with me over the banishment tablet's removal.

"Do not think, Marcus Cicero," he qualified, "that I'm not pleased at your recall. Do not think that I don't rejoice in the restitution of you properties. But, if you have any intentions of deposing more of Clodius' tablets, then bear in mind that were it not for his bill, I would not have been entrusted with the task of annexing and organizing a new addition to Roma's imperium. You can have any of them pulled down as far as Hades; but *not* the one commissioning me to annex Cyprus. If anything happens to that one, I'll take it as a personal affront!"

I did not bother to answer him, for I was certain that he was speaking either through some physical indisposition or perhaps through his *wine*.

At about the same time, Atticus also returned to Roma. Of course, he was glad to see me returned from exile. He told me that his business affairs in Picenum had gone very well. On the subject of business, I asked him to arrange for the payment of the arrears to Crassus. He was surprised at this and asked about the source of the funds. "So then, Marcus, you profited somewhat during your banishment," he quipped after I told him of the *sealed jars* of Macedonian revenue. With this, I finally paid off Crassus. Old *Bald-Pate Money-Bags* was duly impressed.

Atticus had his own financial news to confide. He told me that a consortium of equites, headed by a prominent banker, Gaius Rabirius Postumus, had advanced large sums of money to Auletes. "And so with Roman money did Egypt's King buy his crown yet again from the Senate," my friend said with a financier's acumen. "Naturally, I'm part of the consortium, but Caesar and Pompeius hold the mortgage on Egypt and all its treasures."

Egypt—her King and her grain; Clodius and Milo and their rival gangs; Caesar and Pompeius and Crassus and their ambitions in the face of a newly emergent Senate were the Republic's new battleground.

BY EARLY OCTOBER, THE FOUNDATIONS and the outer walls of the house were completed, a remarkable feat in view of the fact that Clodius' ruffians harassed the workmen with vile words and sometimes even with swiftly thrown pebbles and rotten fruit and eggs.

One day, Tiro, Alexio, and I were returning from an inspection of the construction when the riffraff began to assail us with these same missiles. The closest place for us to seek shelter was Clodia Pulchra's house, only a short remove from my site, though I was reluctant to go there. Tiro pulled me in that direction probably because he believed that even *Juno Medusa's* abode was preferable to being pelted with stones and refuse. Alexio tried to cover our flight. By the time we reached the door, I realized why Tiro had chosen this sanctuary.

There at the door, where a porter should have been on duty, stood Marcus Caelius. My former pupil and protégé and young friend looked like a man who had traded in his youth for experience, his virtue for wantonness.

"In here! In here!" he called to us. As soon as we had cleared the door, he closed it behind us. "Marcus Cicero, hail and welcome!" he saluted me excitedly. "I'm glad… I'm so glad…." He could not continue for he broke down into remorseful, guilt-ridden tears. I embraced him like a forgiving father and thought back to the time when he had lived under my roof. When he had become Clodius' friend and then Clodia's lover, he dissociated himself from me. He had given me neither help nor sympathy when I was banished, and in the weeks since my return to Roma, he had made no attempt to contact me. But from the depths of my being, I forgave him.

Yet there was irony in my forgiveness, for Caelius was still with Clodia, no doubt living with her.

A slave appeared and told us that her mistress invited us into the atrium. Upon entering it, we saw Clodia. Her dark eyes focused on me with her greeting. "Marcus Cicero, we are honored and, in all truth, very surprised to see you." She smiled that same captivating, enigmatic smile.

Aside from having put on a little weight, which she carried remarkably well considering her rather small frame which was adorned with a saffron stola, she had not changed very much since the day of her brother's acquittal. The same abundant raven black hair framed her face and fell upon her shoulders.

"They were being attacked by Publius' thugs," Caelius commented, "and I had them come in."

"Good," she said so amiably.

I was not sure if she was referring to Caelius' assistance or to the fact that I had been under attack.

"Once, not so long ago, Cicero," she sighed, "I warned you against antagonizing my brother. How deeply you paid for ignoring my warning. You were even more foolish to oppose Caesar. He was willing to share power with you, but instead you made yourself his rival. What a pity! More's the pity since he and Crassus betrayed their partner so that you could reap fame and glory by destroying him."

"Catilina," I whispered almost inaudibly. But she heard me.

"Yes—*Catilina!* Do you imagine that it all happened by accident? No, my darling, it was all by design and by calculation. Catilina was too bold, too impetuous, too radical. He wanted a revolution. Caesar and Crassus wanted to grow into power. So when they could no longer control Catilina, they put Publius up to inform against him. Fulvia and I were links in the chain that connected you to my brother. In exposing Catilina's plot, in destroying him, you did Caesar and Crassus a great favor. And they were willing to compensate you. But you, you my darling, were too lofty to join them. Then you crossed my brother and still Caesar was willing to protect you had you gone with him to Gaul. Even *that* you refused!"

Clodia's dark eyes gleamed with an intense glow as she spoke. Her lips and chin were taut, and she inclined her head toward me as though her words were for me alone. I was mesmerized as much by her as I was by her words. "When men in power go beyond their offices and call it *political necessity*, they had better be sure to have powerful friends. But you rejected the friendship of men who could have spared you and your loved ones so much suffering."

I took Clodia's words to heart as Caelius and several of her slaves escorted us back to the Carinae. Even Caelius seemed troubled.

DURING THE LAST THREE MONTHS of the year, the food shortage was considerably alleviated by Pompeius who brought twenty grain barges up from Sicilia. At about the same time that the precious cargo was being unloaded at the Ostian docks, a very special dignitary disembarked from an Egyptian vessel. This was Dion. He had been sent to petition the Senate against restoring the deposed Auletes.

Though the emissary's arrival was anticipated, he never made it to Roma. News came to the Senate that Dion had been assassinated by unknown assailants. An investigation was immediately decreed, and with it the hope that the murder of an Egyptian envoy on Roman soil would not jeopardize the flow of Egyptian grain. Three senators of praetorian rank volunteered to serve on the investigative panel: Marcus Valerius Messalla, Quintus Arrius, and Gaius Pomptimus. All three were of unimpeachable probity. In particular, Pomptinus had assisted me during the Catilinian crisis.

The Egyptian question—grain and politics—was becoming more complicated. Meanwhile, the reconstruction of the Palatine house continued despite Clodius' persistent harassment of the workmen. His ruffians were kept from inflicting serious injuries and delays by Milo's men who kept the Clodians in check.

However, with the end of Milo's and Sestius' tribunates in early December, there was no longer any effective barrier to the aedilician election. At last, Publius Clodius was elected to his coveted office. When he entered office in Januarius, he immediately began an extravagant round of games and shows for the City rabble's entertainment. Both the Great Circus and the Flaminian Stadium were packed with the foul, vulgar mob, cramming and jostling for hours in advance of gladiatorial contests and chariot races. Even during inclement weather, Clodius' games went ahead. Besides entertainment, Aedile Clodius feasted the mob on the grain reserves that Pompeius had just brought to the City.

During one day of such raucous celebration, loud underground rumblings resonated throughout Roma, terrorizing the crowds. The noises reverberated intermittently over several days. Also, it was reported that lightning had struck and defaced the statue of Jupiter on the Alban Mount. Alarmed, the Senate called in soothsayers from Etruria. Known as Haruspices, these seers were believed to be capable of interpreting such phenomena, unlike the augurs, whose divination simply indicated favorable or inauspicious signs.

The four old men in their multi-colored togas, their heads banded with fillets, bore themselves with a dignity that contrasted with their ludicrous attire. They announced that each specialized in one of the four essential elements of nature—air, earth, fire, and water.

The earth seer pronounced, "Fathers of Roma, when the bowels of the earth rumble, it betokens the gods' disfavor at the violation of sacred places, the murder of sacred persons among you, and the laxity in the worship of the gods and the negligence of all rites due them."

The air seer interpreted the lightning strike on Alban Jupiter to indicate the same divine disfavor.

As de facto Princeps Senatus, Lucius Lucullus was the first to respond. "Conscript Fathers, we all know that envoys and emissaries of foreign states have always been sacrosanct. Yet, men who were ambitious to keep the Egyptian Dion from addressing this body did plot to murder him almost the moment he set foot at Ostia. Who are these men, if not the same who took Auletes' money for his crown, and took his money again so that he could be restored despite his subjects' rejection?"

The allusion to the triumvirs was unmistakable, but Pompeius and Crassus sat in stone-faced silence as the senators murmured around them. Lucullus showed both remarkable courage and a complete lack of tact in making the charge.

Then, Clodius was on his feet, out of order of course, and ready to reply ever so irreverently. "Senators, the lightning bolts on that old, ugly effigy of Alban Jupiter could only be an improvement!" There was laughter from certain equally, irreverent senators. "These earth tremors," Clodius laughed, "are probably from my brothers-in-law, Metellus Celer and Marcius Rex, engaged in *farting* contests in Hades!" There was an even greater eruption of laughter.

Then he turned serious and looked directly at me. "By its own decree the Senate has impiously desecrated a sacred place when it ordered the restoration of land that had been consecrated to Libertas. As for the games—well, since I've been aedile, the people have been treated to such prodigious spectacles that there's hardly been standing room."

"But Clodius," I interrupted, "*you* needn't worry about standing room as you can always lie with your wife, *and* your *sister!*"

Thunderous applause and raucous laughter erupted among the senators. Even Pulcher's older brother, Gaius, the praetor, seemed to be amused.

"*You* have the effrontery to speak of the desecration of sacred places!" I declared. "*You*, who violated with impunity the Good Goddess rites, *you* dare to speak of impiety!"

My words, like a hurled javelin, pierced him and pinned him back to his seat. Then I proceeded to impugn his entire life, both private and public, as a shameful desecration of Roman morality. No one seemed to care that I had changed the meeting's entire agenda so as to hurl my spite against Clodius.

At a subsequent Senate meeting, Lucullus threw a virtual Jovian thunderbolt into the entire Egyptian issue. Upon the Haruspices' interpretation, he had had recourse to the Sibylline Books, the archaic prophetic volumes whose custodianship was the responsibility of a collegial Board of Fifteen. One of the Fifteen happened to be Consul Marcellinus. Lucullus invited him to announce a relevant passage from the oracles. With haughty aplomb, the Consul rose and announced with his stentorian voice, "The sacred books forbid the restoration of an Egyptian king with a *multitude!*"

There, in the sublimely vague language of divine prophecy was the thunderbolt that struck at the triumvirs' plans for putting Auletes back on his throne. *No multitude* meant: *no armed forces—no legions, no cohorts—not even a century.* Without such Roman military might, the Alexandrian mob and whatever forces Auletes' enemies may have assembled, could not be overcome, and the King could not be restored to power. No other inferences were possible.

While some senators listened to reason, with or without remuneration, and clearly appreciated the practical necessity of Auletes' restoration, most of them, believers as well as agnostics like myself, heeded the oracular directives. The Senate voted to rescind their earlier decree on the King's behalf. Couriers were sent to convey these tidings to Proconsul Spinther.

I wondered whether he would be disappointed or relieved at not having to bring Roman might into Egypt.

Religious scruples and Roman superstition often affected the Republic's policies whether for broad or narrow purposes. The optimates had marshaled a vague prohibition from an ancient set of prophecies in order to hamper the triumvirs' arrangements concerning Egypt. In doing so, they seemed oblivious to the real likelihood of Egyptian political instability disrupting Roma's grain supplies when the need was particularly acute. I knew not what other expedient they may have had in mind.

However, religion and superstition could also be used in a broader sense for the Republic's benefit. When the Pontiffs ruled in my favor concerning the Palatine property, they had opened the door to unraveling the entire triumvirate. If Clodius' consecration of my land was nullified because his tribunate was invalid, invalid because his plebeian adoption was implemented in violation of Bibulus' consular auspices, then just as invalid and for the same reason was Caesar's entire legislative program.

This convergence of politics and official religion presented a breach within the triumvirate. If aggressively exploited, the breach could become the undoing of Caesar and Pompeius and Crassus. It was up to the Senate to do this, and it mattered not if they or I took the lead in this endeavor.

Omniscient Narrative

"*Damn him! Damn him to Hades!*" Clodius Pulcher denounces his inveterate foe. The wine from his cup splatters onto the marble table, a direct consequence of his fist pounding upon it.

"Has *Chick-Pea* so unnerved you, Publius?" Fulvia, propped up by several pillows, reclines at table opposite her agitated husband. She is several months pregnant, but otherwise her features remain unchanged. Her red hair and her red-brown complexion and her amber eyes contrast with Clodius' dark eyes and his black beard and black hair and his olive skin tone.

"I banish him, and they bring him back so he can be a scourge once again."

"There's no getting rid of *Chick-Pea*, I suppose," Fulvia replies.

Clodius snorts an abrasive laugh. "That's where you're wrong, *Fulvy-plum*. I could arrange it just as easily as I arranged the Egyptian's removal."

"*Shush!*" Fulvia interjects. "Don't speak of that in the house!"

"But I could have Cicero killed by the same assassins!" Clodius whispers emphatically.

"No, no, Publius! Don't even think of it!" Fulvia is equally emphatic. "They'll know it to be your doing, and such a deed will surely compromise you with the triumvirs, certainly with Caesar and Pompeius. I'm not sure that even Crassus would be willing to protect you."

"I'm sick of doing their bidding! It disgusts me having need of them, or even any *one* of them. They wanted the envoy removed, and I delivered. But they treat me like a puppet, pulling me here and there—the *Cock-Eagle* pulls in one direction, then *Duxie Magnus* pulls in another, while *Bald-Pate Money-Bags* expects me to kiss his rich *ass!*"

Fulvia extends her hand across the table and takes him by the forearm. "Be patient, Publius. Remember, every great man rises with the help of powerful patrons."

Clodius rolls his eyes and throws back his head in annoyance. "No, please, not again! Don't tell me about your grand-father and your grand-uncle—the *Gracchi*. They didn't have a triad like Caesar-Pompeius-Crassus to contend with or a thorny-tongued fox like Cicero snapping at their buttocks."

Fulvia withdraws her hand and places it on her swollen belly. "There's no convincing you, is there, Publius? Well then, I'm sorry you don't share my confidence in the *Big Three*. They'll take care of Cicero, in their own way, and just as with the exile, they may use *you* as their instrument." She lowers her voice to a seductive whisper. "And you'll do as they direct because you—*we*—*need* them. In time, your services will pay off. You'll see. Trust me."

If Clodius trusts anyone, he trusts his wife, for Fulvia is as shrewd as she is satisfying.

Marcus Porcius Cato enjoys the distinction of having added a new piece of territory to Roma's Eastern imperium. The strategic island of Cyprus has been annexed without war or bloodshed or loss of Roman lives. The only casualty was the Ptolemaic ruler, the brother of Egypt's deposed Auletes, who took his own life in protest at the seizure of his island kingdom.

Seated at his dining table, he has described with justifiable pride his annexation mission. His guests, the former consul, Marcus Bibulus, and Lucius Domitius Ahenobarbus, the former praetor, have listened attentively and even tolerantly. They know Cato well enough to realize that digressive details become the norm when he has over-indulged in wine. They cannot help but laugh hearing him relate how, while during a regimen of emetics, he had received Cypriot Ptolemy while sitting on a commode, and he had stiffly apologized for not rising to receive the King.

Eventually, the Cyprian stories are exhausted, along with Bibulus' tales of the Italian cattle trails and forests. Domitius directs their attention to the current political affairs in Roma. While they agree that Lucullus and Consul Marcellinus used a clever stratagem to block the Egyptian king's restoration, in the long term, for the sake of the people's welfare, the Senate must intervene in the Nile kingdom.

"Egypt is not Cyprus," Bibulus points out. "Whoever restores the King could easily become a powerful dynast with Egyptian wealth to support him."

"Yes, that's what Crassus wanted years ago when he was Censor," Cato reminds them, "and Catulus foiled him."

"Lentulus Spinther is just as honest as you, Cato," Domitius says. "You didn't profit from Cyprus—at least *not* publicly—and I don't think he would have exploited Egypt for himself."

"Perhaps you're right," Cato slurs. "But here's the thing. How to undermine the *three-headed beast*? What else can be taken from them that would weaken them? We've frustrated their promises to the Egyptian King, but what else would directly hurt them, eh? I think we all know."

Domitius speaks up. "Curtail Caesar's proconsulate over the Gauls. I want those provinces. They've been governed by Domitii ever since my grand-father conquered the Transalpina."

Then Bibulus joins in. "I want revenge upon Caesar. He humiliated me during my consulate. I want him stripped of his powers, his legions and provinces. I want him reduced to nothing."

Cato nods. "You two have much in common. Let's add to the mix. Marcus Bibulus, give me your hand." Bibulus complies, though for what he does not know. "Domitius here has been married for years to my sister. Bibulus, will you take my daughter as your wife? Let our personal enmity toward Caesar be matched by a personal bond." Cato exploits the former consul's availability—he recently divorced his wife of many years, alleging her infidelity.

"I would be honored to marry Porcia," says Bibulus. He firmly shakes hands with Cato and then asks, "What about *your own* nuptials?"

Cato is at first surprised, but then he remembers. "Marcia? Of course, Marcia! Hortensius will divorce her by spring, and then we'll marry in the summer. She's a good woman, and she's been a good mother to my children. She's nearly made them forget about Atilia, and that's no small task I assure you. And Hortensius! He's taken good care of Marcia. A good man Hortensius is!" He laughs inanely, but then quickly recovers his serious mood. "About the triumvirate, knock down their land commission and we hit them hard—hit them in the *balls!* And then, in every way, at every turn, split them apart like a slaughtered carcass on a butcher's block!"

Drunk though he is, Cato knows of what he speaks. His alter ego, Bibulus, appreciates this, and bronze-haired, broad-framed Domitius knows that once set upon a course, Cato will not be swayed or deterred. Both men also realize that Cato's ambition is to be the new voice, the new force directing the Senate's optimates.

Cicero's Respublica

OVER THE NEXT SEVERAL WEEKS, the optimates found their voice and mustered the strength to challenge the triumvirs' other arrangements. Cato's brother-in-law, Lucius Domitius Ahenobarbus, the former praetor who had been one of the first optimates to discuss my recall, spared no energy in attacking Caesar's proconsulate. He insisted that the Senate curtail Caesar's command because the Assembly had conferred it in violation of Bibulus' consular auspices. But many senators knew that, privately, Domitius coveted the Gallic provinces for himself as his prospective propraetorian command. So often he reminded us of his noble ancestor who had conquered the Transalpine tribes. He therefore considered the governorship of the Gauls to be his birthright, and Caesar's continued tenure was an irritating obstacle.

Then, Tribune Publius Lupus attacked on a different front. Totally contrary to most tribunicial initiatives, he proposed that the Senate discuss the legality of Caesar's agrarian laws. Later, at a convention of the Tribal Assembly, he invited public discussion of the same issue. He declared that if the Senate and the People found the legislation or the mode of its passage irregular, then the agrarian commission was to be dismantled. In this event, further allotments would be blocked, especially for the urban poor.

"What's Pompeius up to?" Quintus asked one night at supper. "He utters not a sound when the Senate kills the Egyptian decree. His friend, his partner, his father-in-law's in danger of having his provinces pulled out from under him and he sits as though he were posing for his portrait. Now, one of his own men, whom he helped to the tribunate, has threatened those Campanian farmsteads."

"But you know," Servius offered, "if the land commission is broken up, Pompeius needn't fear being out of a job. He's still got the grain curatorship. That puts him one up on Crassus. And should it matter to him if no further allotments are made? Why should it? His veterans are all comfortably settled."

Atticus took a deep draught of wine before joining in. "The way Clodius is going through the grain reserves, Pompeius had better prepare to go shopping again."

"You know, brother," Quintus said to me reprovingly, "you ought to be more cautious about tweaking *Pretty-Boy's* nose. He's still dangerous, and the *'Big Three'* are still behind him."

"But Caesar's up at Ravenna preparing for a new spring campaign in Gaul," I countered, "and his two partners are feuding with each other. Clodius has only his gang to back him up and the optimates have Milo to check *Pretty-Boy*."

"It's no surprise that the Senate has found its backbone," Servius agreed with me. "If they take away any part of Caesar's provinces and hamper the land commission, it'll be the beginning of the triumvirate's crack-up."

"Just so!" I happily announced. But Quintus was visibly perturbed at my enthusiasm. He looked squarely at me, dismay registering on his face.

Philologus, my brother's steward, appeared in the doorway to announce that Marcus Caelius Rufus was in the atrium requesting to speak with me. Quintus told his steward to escort Caelius into the dining room, but Philologus demurred. "Marcus Caelius desires to speak privately with Marcus Cicero," the steward replied obsequiously. I was very pleasantly surprised by Caelius' visit. Without hesitation, I rose from the dining couch and after a slave assisted me with my shoes, I proceeded out to the atrium.

"Welcome to my former home, Marcus Caelius," I greeted him.

"Marcus Cicero," he replied, clasping my extended hand, "I'm sorry to have imposed on you." He looked ill, pale, and drawn as though he had not slept in weeks, and he seemed to be consumed with dread and self-loathing.

"But you've never been an imposition, and I've sorely missed you."

He stared sadly into my eyes and said, "I've had my fill of them. I'm through with them for good. The Pulchers were suffocating me. Clodia's an insatiable wanton. She's exhausted my body and drained my spirit."

I listened in stunned silence, believing every word, and my heart ached for him.

"The whole family's depraved! She told me outrageous tales about her brothers and sisters. If I was inclined to doubt them, I learned differently very soon. Publius and Fulvia visited and...." He turned away from me for an instant. When he faced me again his face was full of horror and revulsion. "We had several pairings and we... exchanged partners. Even after Fulvia became pregnant, she serviced me with her mouth like an *irrumatrix*; and Clodia and her brother... *disgusting*."

There had always been rumors and gossip about the Pulcher siblings' incest, but I had never heard an eye-witness account of any of their couplings. I could not help but share his disgust.

"When I told her I was leaving, she became a veritable tigress. She accused me of taking her money and using her. Yes—she'd given me money and gifts—yes, I accepted them—it was my pay for servicing her like a stud slave! And she said *I* was using *her!* What a brazen *lupa!* And Publius expected me to do *his* dirty work!"

Suddenly, he paused and looked away from me again as though he were concealing something that he had inadvertently touched upon. After such intimate disclosures, there was yet something he wished to keep hidden.

Caelius shook his head as if to clear his thoughts, and then he reverted to Clodia. "She told me, 'No man leaves Clodia Pulchra until she's finished with him.' If I've learned anything about her, I know she'll not let go easily. I'm expecting reprisals. Marcus Cicero, will you be my friend and patron again? Will you help me?"

Clutching his shoulders and looking directly into his eyes, I said to him, "You needn't have asked." Then, I insisted that he partake of some food with us in the dining room.

CAELIUS WAS ENTIRELY CORRECT TO expect recriminations from his jilted lover. Within a week after we had spoken, Clodia Pulchra went before Praetor Gnaeus Calvinus in the Court of Public Violence and accused Caelius of attempting to poison her. But that was not all. She also accused him of stealing money from her so that he could hire assassins to murder the Egyptian emissary, Dion. A spiteful, vindictive charge to soothe her ruffled pride was coupled with a politically explosive accusation. Perhaps this was what he could not confide in me.

As I had promised him my help, I undertook his defense against the charge of attempted murder while *Money-Bags* Crassus handled the assassination charge. Crassus' interest in the case stemmed from his and his triumviral partners' commitment to the Egyptian King's restoration. Apparently, it was in their interests to quash any charge of conspiracy to murder any of Auletes' enemies.

The prosecution team was comprised of Hortensius and Gaius Pulcher. Appius would surely have been on the team as well had he not been governing Sardinia as propraetor.

The trial was held in the Aemilian Basilica. The spectators' stands were packed with Pulcher's friends and retainers. Clodius' riffraff held the Forum ground about the courthouse. Though out of office, Milo was on site with his own operae to deter any trouble.

Hortensius' prosecution waxed ever so eloquently on pure theory. There were so many holes in his argument that Crassus had an easy time refuting any connection between Caelius and Dion's murder. Hortensius must have been getting old, for I could not believe that he sincerely expected to nail Caelius on a conspiracy charge without knowledge of the assassins and without any corroborative proof. I couldn't believe that he would have taken the case at all given its inherent weaknesses. Either the Pulchers had persuaded him with appeals for patrician solidarity or old Hortensius must have thought that a successful prosecution would have restored his former pre-eminence in the courts.

From Hortensius' accusations and Crassus' defense, I inferred a reasonable scenario concerning the Egyptian's murder. Who would have benefitted from the murder? Clearly, the deposed King. Who were his supporters? Obviously, the triumvirs. Theoretically, they or their retainers could have hired assassins. Caelius had mentioned doing Clodius' "dirty work". It was a reasonable deduction that Clodius and Caelius—brother and lover of Clodia Pulchra—could have directly conspired to kill Dion.

If my inferences were correct, no wonder that Caelius was so beside himself. His complicity in the deed chained him both to Clodia and to Clodius. Fortunately, Crassus had eloquently argued against any Clodian chain linking Caelius to any murder conspiracy. The jurors would ultimately decide.

Gaius Pulcher attempted to portray his sister as a wronged patrician lady, seduced and exploited by an up-and-coming younger man about town. Caelius was made out to be the rapacious rake, the aggressive outsider, the unscrupulous social climber using an affair with a mature, patrician lady to advance himself. He accepted gifts from Clodia, and what she did not proffer, he took. And so, Pulcher concluded, Caelius wanted to poison his lover and benefactor because it was the most secure way to silence her about his murder plot.

Speaking in defense of Caelius, my strategy was to impugn Clodia Pulchra's reputation and depict her as a predatory exploiter of young Roman manhood. Rising to speak, I looked assuredly at Caelius, who was seated at the defense table between Crassus and me. "Citizens of the jury," I began as I surveyed the fifty some senators and equites who were seated on stone benches to the right, "it's generally known that often times young men need to sow their wild oats. Though I must confess I was a rare exception to this general tendency, Marcus Caelius was very much an exemplar; and Clodia Pulchra was a most willing partner."

Now I turned from the jury and faced the dark-haired, dark-eyed plaintiff. Clodia returned my gaze, holding it on me while smiling her inimical, enigmatic smile. "Clodia Pulchra, you shared your house and your bed with Marcus Caelius. How often did you cavort in the Claudian gardens on the Tiber's far side? How often did you traverse the great highway built by your illustrious ancestor? How often did you frolic by the seashore at Baiae and Antium? But when your lover tired of you, when you had exhausted him with your insatiable appetite, when your lustful excesses had revolted him, you tried to bind him to you with money and gifts. When he broke from you instead of waiting to be discarded, you spitefully took him to court and charged him with attempted murder. To further ensnare him, you accused him of conspiracy to murder the emissary of Egypt—a charge as outrageous, as bogus, as ludicrous as that of attempting to poison you!"

Jurors and spectators laughed at the phrase, "waiting to be discarded." But then, at the mention of the murdered Egyptian emissary, an uproar from outside was commenced by Clodius' mob. I recognized Clodius' nasal voice asking, *"Who's starving the people of Roma?"*

The mob chanted back, *"Gnaeus Pompeius! Gnaeus Pompeius! Gnaeus Pompeius!"*

Clodius would ask, *"Who's his partner?"*

The mob replied, *"Marcus 'Chick-Pea'! Marcus 'Chick-Pea'! Marcus 'Chick-Pea'!"*

Then Clodius would bellow, *"Who should feed the people?"* With perfect timing, the mob would respond, *"Marcus Crassus! Marcus Crassus! Marcus Crassus!"*

The instigator would then demand, *"And who should restore Egypt's King?"* The mob screamed back, *"Marcus Crassus! Marcus Crassus! Marcus Crassus!"*

The litany continued throughout my speech. With smug satisfaction, Crassus nodded and grinned each time his name was called out. He chuckled at the mention of "Chick-Pea" and smirked at Pompeius' name. In fact, Pompeius was not then present in Roma.

I did not allow the chanting to interrupt me. Speaking above the outside din, I became even more abusive of Clodia. "You put on the airs of an outraged lady. But you are too well known for what you really are—an insatiable wanton, a 'quadrantaria' selling yourself for a mere quarter of an *ass;* the 'Palatine Medusa' turning all men who look upon you to stone because of your promiscuous excesses!"

Clodia's dark eyes flashed with anger, her face flushed with embarrassment, and her smiling lips parted as her tongue teasingly played over her teeth.

"You exploited this young man for your own sensual pleasure. Must you now ruin him because your lascivious appetites have driven him to revulsion? There are plenty of other men in Roma ready and willing to service you. You will find them without much effort."

Turning to the jury, I delivered my conclusion. "Citizens of the jury, by your verdict, extricate this young man from the jaws of a vindictive 'lupa.' You will not regret it. Marcus Caelius has a brilliant future ahead of him. Do not deprive him of it and in so doing deprive the Republic of his dutiful services."

Before resuming my seat, I noticed Gaius Pulcher peering angrily at me from the prosecution table while Hortensius smiled and nodded admiringly. Sitting between them, draped in a mauve stola and blue palla, Clodia Pulchra regarded me hatefully.

The jury's deliberation was brief. A vote was taken and a solid majority voted for Caelius' acquittal. Crassus and I congratulated each other and Caelius. All the while, Clodius' mob persisted in its clamoring.

Our Republic always extended broad latitude to free expression. The mob could howl and jeer or applaud and cheer whoever was under their fickle scrutiny. Likewise, barristers and advocates and candidates for public office could with impunity heap abuse and calumny upon defendants, witnesses, and rivals. Public vilification was the life-blood of Roman politics and jurisprudence.

Caelius' acquittal freed him from the onus of condemnation and exile. But the assassins of Dion were still unknown, though it was widely assumed that pro-Auletes agents must have arranged the murder.

Even so, the optimates prided themselves on having succeeded in using religious obstruction to thwart the triumvirs' intention of restoring the King to his throne.

Now there was a renewed impetus to hack away at the triumvirate's arrangements. In the Senate, I spoke in favor of Consul Marcellinus' proposal for a discussion of Caesar's agrarian legislation on the Kalends of Maius. The Consul was following up on Tribune Lupus' earlier proposal on the same issue. The difference was that Marcellinus was targeting a specific date which was less than a month away.

A substantial majority approved the proposal. There was no misunderstanding of the ramifications involved in the Senate's vote. In less than four weeks, debate and discussion would pick apart Caesar's land laws, the agrarian commission that had been functioning for three years, and ultimately the rest of Caesar's consular acta.

Domitius Ahenobarbus beamed at the prospect of curtailing Caesar's provincial command and possibly acquiring one or both of the Gallic provinces for himself. The door had been left ajar when the Senate had overridden Clodius' tribunicial law in order to restore my land and my house. Now, the Senate had taken steps to pull the door off its hinges. I was proud to have had a hand in the endeavor, but Quintus looked askance at me.

Pompeius and Crassus had been present, but they had abstained from the vote, all the while regarding each other coldly. Afterwards, Pompeius told me that he was leaving for Corsica to buy more grain. As his legate, I offered to go with him, but he told me he was taking Quintus instead. They were going to take ship at the port of Pisa after first stopping at Luca.

Oddly enough, Crassus was said to have left the City for parts unknown only a few hours after Pompeius and my brother had departed. Even stranger was the exodus of more than two hundred senators and some three hundred equites.

When I called on Atticus, his steward told me that he had left Roma on business. It was unusual for Atticus not to tell me of his comings and goings. Something most strange was happening. Yet, no one seemed willing to speculate on what it could be—*except* for Consul Marcius Philippus.

Philippus' neutrality had been compromised by his marriage to Caesar's widowed niece. This marital connection made him privy to at least some of the triumvirs' schemes. Narrowing his small, squinty eyes and inclining his bald head toward me so that it almost touched mine, he confided what would prove to be a disaster for the Republic. "Caesar is coming down from Ravenna. He ought to be going the other way to start his new spring campaigns. But instead he's going to meet Pompeius and Crassus at Luca." He paused long enough to pull his head back and look at me sideways as though making sure his words had registered. "Their friends and clients among the Senate and equites have gone up there too. There's to be a big meeting. We'll hear soon enough!"

"Is this generally known?" I inquired of him.

He frowned and shook his head stiffly. "Mostly hearsay; many think they know, but no one wants to think out loud." Then he looked at me, grimaced sourly and asked, "Surely your brother must have known? And what about his brother-in-law? You mean to tell me *neither* one of them said anything about it to you?"

I felt irritated, not so much by the Consul's questions as by a ponderous sense of betrayal. Indeed, why had neither Quintus nor Atticus told me anything about a triumviral conference at Luca? Perhaps Quintus was duped into believing Pompeius' story about a grain mission to Corsica; but certainly if Atticus had gone north with the equites, then he must have known about it. Was my exclusion their way of protecting me?

Omniscient Narrative

Luca bestrides the Cassian Road in northern Etruria some twenty miles west of Pistoria, where Catilina's rebel army had been obliterated. The green hills and colorful meadows of Etruria surrounding the town are vibrant under the April sun. Farmsteads worked by retired soldiers extend for miles in every direction from the old highway, Roma's main artery into the Gallic provinces. Nature thrives in the Italian spring, and Luca is alive with the sounds of its citizens plying their crafts and pursuing the business of life in a small town.

Luca has been chosen as the site of the triumvirs' conference. Pompeius and Crassus have come up separately from Roma, as have several hundred senators and equites. Caesar and his proconsular entourage have come down from the Cisalpina. Technically, he should not be out of his province, especially with legionaries. But it is urgent that he meet with his partners and plug up certain holes and gaps in their alliance. So urgent is their need to meet that he comes to them on Italian soil rather than having them come to him at Ravenna, the Cisalpina's capital city. Luca's chief officials, the duumvirs, offer their offices to the Romans, for it is an honor to host the triumviral conference.

Seated at a large oak table, like three points in an isosceles triangle, they get to business immediately. "I need an extension of the Gallic command in order to complete Gaul's subjugation," Caesar states, "for another five years, with additional legions and legates, no Senatorial interference, and then a second consulate. For this consulate, I want special dispensation from the Senate to canvass in *absentia*. I can't risk becoming a *privatus* because then my enemies will pounce on me and do everything in their power to destroy me. After the second consulate, another long proconsulate will be in order."

Pompeius and Crassus agree. Then, they submit their own demands. They both want a second joint consulship for the ensuing year, meaning that they will need to canvass in the current year. "Afterwards, I want the two Spains as my proconsulate," Pompeius asserts, "and I want to remain in Roma while my legates govern on my behalf. Yes, it's unprecedented, but someone's got to remain in Roma to oversee conditions."

Caesar and Crassus acquiesce. "I want to govern Syria as proconsul," says Crassus, "and in that capacity I want to restore Ptolemy Auletes to the Egyptian throne."

Crassus' partners quibble about the second item. They hold that the political situation in Egypt, upon which Egyptian grain for Roma is so crucially dependent, cannot be put off until Crassus' proconsulate.

"Well, I'd be willing to accept a special commission immediately," Crassus smugly counters them.

"Not acceptable," Caesar maintains. "You and Pompeius want next year's consulates, no? If so, you'll both have to be in Roma to canvass together. Marcus, if you go off to Egypt now, you'll need the better part of a year to restore Auletes and to stabilize conditions, especially the grain supply. No, the King's restoration cannot wait. It must be effected *now,* but *not* by *you!*"

Pompeius nods thoughtfully. "Aulus Gabinius, Proconsul of Syria, should do it, and the Senate's obstructive decree, fueled by Lucullus' oracular scruples, must be ignored."

Caesar has been thinking of Gabinius all along. He assumes that Gabinius will be pleased to accept the task and to face whatever consequences the Senate might subsequently lay upon him.

"Of course, Ptolemy is to be charged appropriately for the use of Roman arms to reinstate him," Caesar adds.

"That's reasonable," Pompeius concedes.

However, Crassus still wants the Syrian proconsulate. "Look, as a trade-off for relinquishing the Egyptian restoration, I want a free hand to deal with the Parthian kingdom, even to the extent of invading it and subduing their territory."

Both Caesar and Pompeius are taken aback by the proposal. To invade Parthia is to endanger the eastern borders of Roman imperium, they both tell him. Pompeius is particularly emphatic on this point because his Eastern campaigns had stabilized the entire border after years of flux.

But Crassus is equally emphatic. "Gnaeus, you were in too great a hurry to return home so you could display your triumphal laurels instead of reducing Parthia to a client-kingdom of Roma."

The two men—naturally antipathetic to each other—are jockeying to get into their respective high horses, especially when Pompeius insists that his pirate campaigns and his Eastern settlement together kept him away from Roma for nearly five years. As has been his wont through many years of association with Crassus and Pompeius, Caesar brings them to an accord. Crassus gets his Syrian proconsulate and the authority to wage war against Parthia, an enterprise that could extend Roman imperium far beyond Babylon's ancient rivers.

They further agree that Pompeius' and Crassus' proconsulates are to run concurrently for five years, after which they are to be followed by yet another consular term. Caesar will send one of his legates, Gaius Trebonius, to Roma to be elected tribune so that all enabling legislation will be presented to and passed by the Concilium Plebis, the single most pliable of all of Roma's citizen assemblies.

"Speaking of tribunes, what about Clodius and *his* future?" Pompeius asks.

Caesar shrugs as Crassus considers him with careful scrutiny. "Give him his due," says Caesar, "but see to it that he doesn't overstep himself. If he does, we may have to deal with him as we did with Catilina."

Crassus proposes, "Will we need to use Cicero again?"

"I think not," replies Caesar. "All I want from him is his cooperation or his silence. I'm equally prepared to be generous or severe, and I'll have Quintus Cicero convey my sentiments to his brother. By the way, Gnaeus, if you could spare him from your staff, I could use Quintus up in Gaul for the next campaign. Decimus Brutus has supervised the building of a fleet for use against the Veneti. The sooner we complete our business here, the sooner I can join my legions."

Pompeius nods his assent. "What about the others?"

"Nothing at this time, but watch Milo and his gang; and Domitius Ahenobarbus, who's so anxious for my command, must be kept out of the consulate for as long as possible."

Crassus asks about Cato, which gets a hearty laugh out of Caesar. "Make sure he'll always have something to rail against," Caesar suggests. "That should keep him drunk and buried in his wife's bosom. *Poor Marcia!* Between Hortensius and Cato she's been sorely deprived of entertainment."

The triumvirs snicker at Caesar's quip. Then Caesar turns serious. "I'll speak with my senators while I feast them. Do the same with yours; and the equites—assure them of good business and sound profits if they know which way the wind is blowing. By the way, Gnaeus, take care of my daughter! Marcus, you should be very proud of your sons. They're both excellent and exemplary soldiers."

"I know," says Crassus. "If you can spare Publius, I'd like him to be my chief of staff when I govern Syria."

"Fair enough, and *done!*" Caesar agrees.

Thus, the triumviral conference ends as the three partners rise from their chairs and clasp their right hands across the table.

Cicero's Respublica

"We'll hear soon enough," Philippus had said.

He was right. Several days after we had spoken, I received a short, curt note from Quintus. He wrote that there had been a conference of the "Big Three" at Luca. They had patched up the petty differences between

Pompeius and Crassus and they had renewed their pact. Quintus closed by saying that he had much more to tell me after returning to Roma. He said he was setting off only hours after dispatching the letter.

Quintus arrived just two days later. He was agitated and fatigued, and he reeked of sweat from hard riding along the Cassian Road. He refused to eat, drink, or bathe until he had spoken with me. As we sat in the small library of the Carinae house, I saw on my brother's harried face an intensified version of the dismay and disapproval that he had shown when I spoke of dismantling the triumvirate and reviewing Caesar's legislation. He was in a most foul temperament, so much so that he snapped at young Quintus for innocently running into the room. Pomponia tried to defend the child, but then she wisely retreated with the boy in hand.

"Marcus, I want you to listen. Don't say anything. Just listen. *Understand?*" Brother Quintus was commanding, and I assured him I would comply. "Pompeius and Crassus are to run together for next year's consulate. They expect to win. They *will* win! And once in office they or their hirelings will push through a new batch of laws for the triumvirs. Caesar's command is to be extended. He's to have more legions and more officers; and at the end of it, he'll have another year as consul to be followed by another province. He won't even have to come to Roma to canvass. His partners agreed that he'll be allowed to canvass in *absentia* while he's governing Gaul. *Yes, I know what you're thinking!*"

I was thinking: *What a travesty! He's holding a provincial imperium, legions under his command, and at the same time standing for the Republic's highest office. It was unprecedented!* But I dared not interrupt him.

"When Crassus and Pompeius complete their term, they're to have provinces—both Spains for Pompeius and Syria for Crassus, each for five years; and Pompeius is to govern his through legates while *he* remains in Roma to monitor the Republic's affairs."

This too was an unprecedented arrangement, though it was obvious that the triumvirs saw the need for at least one of them to be present in the City. I was glad that it would be Pompeius who would have the run of things.

Quintus paused and sighed impatiently as though he were exhausted with the telling. He pursed his lips and nodded at me as he began again. "There's more that directly affects *us*. They want *our* complete cooperation, or at least *your* total abstention from any interference in their plans. When we were trying to cancel your banishment, I guaranteed your good behavior. Now, they want me to make good on my promise. I'm to be transferred to Caesar's provincial staff. I'm expected to report to him at his headquarters in Ravenna. I'm to bring him your answer. Are you prepared to cooperate—yes or no?"

I was absolutely dumbfounded! My brother was to be a virtual hostage of Caesar's as a pledge, a guarantee of my loyalty. How insidiously, cruelly calculating! My world was crashing down about me. How could I compromise my brother's safety—in fact, his *very life*? It would have taken no great effort—nor would it have pained Caesar's conscience—to arrange his demise in a pitched battle against the Gauls. There was no real option but submission and accommodation.

"They consented to your recall," Quintus reminded me. "They allowed the return of your properties, *but* they won't brook your interference. It's that simple."

"Brother," I finally said to him, "I wish you'd been less ambitious in your pledge on my behalf."

"Marcus, what's said and done cannot be unsaid or undone!" Quintus snapped at me. "What answer do I bring to Caesar?"

I winced at the piercing tone of his voice, and then I nodded, turning away from his sour, embittered gaze.

That night, I did not retire before composing a letter for Quintus to bring to Caesar. In it, I pledged my loyalty and cooperation in any ventures beneficial to Roma, and my neutrality in any initiatives which were purely motivated by his and his partners' self-interest. *To my very depths, what a bitter draught this was to swallow!* When I spoke with Terentia about this, she reproached me for compromising myself and Quintus and the entire family. "Did you really think they consented to your recall so that you could return to disrupt their plans?" she boiled over at me. "Now, Marcus, you've been warned again. This time, if you challenge them, Quintus will be the first to feel their anger; and when they get around to you, it won't be banishment they'll inflict on you. No… not *this* time! As for myself, I don't want to be hounded and driven out of house and home a second time! So put your high-minded politics aside and do what's expedient! Think of *us* this time!"

A short time later, Servius reiterated Terentia's sentiments, but with far less fire and wrath. "Marcus, you know these optimates. They're so thoroughly fickle and self-serving. They'll not stand together if Caesar's and Pompeius' and Crassus' men unite against the Senate. Their men are too resolute for the optimates to withstand them. Don't sacrifice yourself for them. They're not worth it!" Then, almost as an afterthought, he added, "Don't delude yourself that any debate on Caesar's laws will occur on the Kalends of Maius. It's just as likely that the Tiber will dry up!"

Servius was directly on target. I knew from personal experience how fickle the optimates and their leaders could be.

When Atticus returned to Roma, I chided him for failing to tell me about the Luca conference. He could not come up with a plausible defense except to say, "I didn't want to speculate in advance." This was an ironic answer from a man whose occupation *was* speculation. But he recovered his confidence sufficiently after I had told him of my predicament. "Of course, Marcus, you made the necessary choice, the choice based on wisdom and self-preservation. You could not do otherwise. Now before you castigate yourself on a rack of remorse and disloyalty, consider what's in store for you if you adhere to your pledge. The triumvirs have guaranteed us new, lucrative opportunities in Spain, in Syria, and in Caesar's newly conquered lands in Gaul. Marcus, your stock could double, even triple, within a single year; and Caesar's not remiss about granting bonuses to his preferred friends."

First, it was a matter of personal survival. Now, there was a pecuniary inducement to accommodate myself to the "Big Three." How well Atticus knew me to understand that I would always exploit a proffered opportunity to increase my resources. After all, the optimates put great stock in their fish-ponds and parks and thought nothing of political expediency. So, why should I have been above acquisitiveness as I was suborned to the Republic's de facto ruling council? The bitter draught of my recantation was mollified by the prospect of profit-sharing in the equites' tax-farming.

AT THE SENATE MEETING ON the Kalends of Maius, I spoke in glowing terms of Caesar's proconsulate. I proposed the appointment of additional legates for him and his authorization to recruit three new legions for his new campaigns. Moreover, I urged the Senate to reject consideration of any motion to curtail his proconsular imperium. Militarily, this made perfect sense. "It is not the Alps and the Rhine," I declared, "but the arms and generalship of Caesar which I account our true shield against the barbarous tribes of Gaul and the wild hordes of Germania."

The optimates received my speech with a frigidity that could have come from the coldest Alpine peaks. But a succession of Caesar's and Pompeius' and Crassus' senators spoke in support. In the end, Caesar had his new legions and extra legates, and Domitius Ahenobarbus, Marcus Bibulus, and Marcus Cato bolted from the Curia in a huff.

As Servius had predicted, there was no mention of Caesar's consular laws, not on the Kalends of Maius or any subsequent day. Word of the Luca conference deflated the optimates' will to resist the triumvirs. As they had planned, Pompeius and Crassus announced their candidacies for the consulate.

Though the outcome was inevitable, the campaign was marred by chronic street fighting between the triumvirs' supporters and the optimate candidates' men. Domitius Ahenobarbus was in the forefront among the optimates. Milo, running for the praetorate, loaned his gang to Domitius' service. Publius Clodius' gang supported Crassus while shouting slanders against Pompeius. The Magnus himself resorted to using cohorts of his discharged legionaries.

I wondered what the triumvirs had decided about Clodius' future. He was becoming an important power broker in his own right. From all appearances, he was serving Crassus' interests more so than he was advancing the three dynasts' agenda.

Marcus Caelius canvassed for the quaestorate under my sponsorship, thereby beginning his public career.

At the same time, another young man came under my mentorship. This was Publius Cornelius Dolabella. It was Caesar's specific request that I take him under my wing, and I dared not refuse. Dolabella was an extremely handsome patrician. Built sturdily like a professional athlete, his features appeared to be almost sculpted, and his eyes were as blue as the Bay of Neapolis in summer.

He was married to a somewhat older woman named, ironically, Fabia. She was an heiress, and I suspected he had married her for her fortune. They had an infant son. I could not imagine at the time the impact that Dolabella would have on our lives, especially my daughter's life.

In taking on Dolabella, I was performing the first of many services for Caesar and his partners. For several years, I remained at their beck and call while my brother fought in Caesar's Gallic wars. As he was a hostage in Caesar's legions, I, in Roma, became a prisoner of my own accommodation.

Omniscient Narrative

Publius Clodius Pulcher cradles his infant namesake son in the crook of his left arm. He is sublimely ecstatic over the baby, born only several days ago. This tiny bundle of infant manhood has the dark hair and olive and rose complexion of the Claudian Pulchers, and Clodius is unabashedly proud. Standing on the balcony of his Aventine house, Clodius surveys the bustling panorama of Roma sprawled before him while cooing to the baby in his arm.

"Yours my son, all of it will be yours for the taking; the streets, the temples, the Forum and the Seven Hills, the vulgarity and the glory of Roma; and the mob—the dirty, coarse, blood and sinew of Roma will follow you and hail you as they do me."

Clodius brings the sleeping infant to his lips and kisses him on the forehead. The baby wrinkles his brow and squirms, disturbed by his father's beard, but he sleeps on contentedly. Clodius too is content, for he now has a son.

Fulvia and her sister-in-law, Clodia Pulchra, are in the bedroom. Clodia has come to visit her brother's family, especially the newest arrival. While waiting for Clodius to come in from the balcony, she fondles her little niece, two-year old Claudia. She is very partial to her brother's first born, perhaps because the child so strongly resembles the Claudians. One might almost take the little girl to be Clodia's rather than Fulvia's daughter. The same ebony hair and dark eyes with the rose and olive hue to her skin are shared by the aunt and her niece.

The little girl's nurse stands quietly in a corner of the room, waiting to be summoned by Fulvia. However, Fulvia enjoys seeing Clodia fuss over the child. She is very relaxed, reclining on her bed, wearing a diaphanous, pale green gown through which her full, melon-like breasts are visible. "She grows more Clodian every day!" Fulvia remarks about her daughter.

From the Mauretanian carpet laid over the tiled floor, Clodia looks up from the cherub in her lap and smiles at her sister-in-law. "Her *looks*, yes, I grant you her *looks*; but what about her temperament?"

"Well, that's a mix of different elements; some Clodian to be sure, but also Fulvian and Sempronian." Fulvia smiles back at Clodia.

The two women hold each other in view. Their visual exchange today is different, far different from what it has been before. Fulvia senses Clodia's attention to her bosom. She has seen it many times before today. Yet now, having delivered a second child, Fulvia's aspect is different for Clodia. Fulvia notes the curves in Clodia's own bosom as she nestles little Claudia on her lap. For her as well, the bosom is enticing, welcoming, promising delights not yet realized.

Nearly a moment passes before Fulvia says, "I'm *not* going to nurse the baby."

Clodia responds in mock outrage, "You're *not* going to nurse Publius' son! *Shameful!* That could be grounds for divorce." She laughs and her dark eyes gleam.

Fulvia smiles dreamily. "It was quite taxing to nurse that *one*, and I don't think a son will be less demanding. Publius understands. We don't want *these* turning to sacks." As she says this she cups her breasts and feels a momentary surge when Clodia looks at them. "So, we've purchased a wet nurse. She's got virtual *cow udders*. I'm sure little Publius will be… *satisfied*."

Suddenly, little Claudia bolts from her aunt's lap and runs to her nurse. Fulvia commands, "Mara, see if she needs to relieve herself."

The nurse takes up the little child in her arms, and little Claudia's pink stola rises above her tiny buttocks. She carries the child from the room as Fulvia and Clodia titter affectionately.

Clodia stands up and walks to Fulvia's bed. She is beautiful and elegant in a blue stola draped over her ivory-colored palla. A leather belt is coiled around her waist while another crisscrosses her bosom. As always, the abundant black hair frames her oval face and descends upon her supple shoulders. She stands at the bedside looking down at Fulvia. They are locked in each other's eyes.

Fulvia's nipples have hardened. They are conspicuously pressed against her pale green gown. Almost breathlessly she says, "Publius is busy with the election canvassing. He's not running this time, but he's committed to Crassus. Besides that, he has to prepare for this summer's Apollonarian Games."

"*Men!* Their elections! Their games! And these hot, stifling Roman summers!" Clodia plops down on the bed next to her sister-in-law. "Oh, Fulvia! Let's get out of here! Let's go down to my place at Antium. We can take the children with us… *unless*… you think you can leave them here with their nurses?" Clodia's lips part invitingly as she speaks and they remain parted when she has finished.

Fulvia hesitates. She touches her breast as if to steady her pounding heart. Clodia touches her sister-in-law's flame-red hair and then strokes the line of her cheek. Fulvia tenderly kisses Clodia's hand. "We'll take the children *and* the nurses with us," Fulvia decides. She cannot utter another word before Clodia's moist mouth locks upon hers.

Cicero's Respublica

It was not only my political freedom that was imprisoned, but the very life force within me was bound into inertia.

My newly reconstructed, handsomely refurbished Palatine house became the prison of my accommodation. Upon its completion, we moved back in, expecting our lives to resume as they had been before my exile. But we were sorely mistaken. I had longed for Terentia throughout the months of banishment. Though wounded and frustrated by our continued separation—a separation imposed by her own willfulness—I had wanted her all during her sojourn with the Vestals. Yet, on our first night together in over two years, my manhood deserted me.

Terentia was patient and compassionate, even after several thwarted attempts to make love to her. Did she understand my humiliation at having become subservient to the triumvirs? Could she fathom the void in me where once there had been the honor of service to the Republic? Was she capable of understanding that my sexual impotence was a manifestation of my own political paralysis?

In my fitful sleep after each failed amorous endeavor, I saw the luminous, dark eyes and the enigmatic smile of Clodia Pulchra, mocking and teasing me. Victory was upon her face as truly as defeat was embedded in my soul.

Liber III Bellum (War)

Marcus Tullius Cicero to Titus Pomponius Atticus in Buthrotum, Epirus; Written from Roma, fourteen days before the Kalends of Martius, in the Year DCCX from the Founding of the City.

Greetings to you, dear friend. I hope all is yet well with you and your estate. Here in Roma, the trappings of dictatorship daily metamorphose into the regalia of monarchy, albeit without the dreaded title. The obsequious Senate continues to heap honors and titles upon the Great Man. It is expected that he will soon embark upon his campaign against the Parthians in order to avenge the annihilation of Crassus' legions nine years ago.

I'm sure you'll remember that today was the Feast of Lupercalia. Among the scantily-clad runners was none other than the Great Man's colleague, Marcus Antonius. This bull in wolf's skins took delight at the swooning girls salivating at his oiled, muscular torso. His new wife, Fulvia, appeared to relish the girls' adulation of Antonius, but she was certainly not oblivious to the handsome flesh exhibited by the Consul's fellow runners, clad as immodestly as was Antonius.

With each lap about the Forum's perimeter, the runners struck out with strips of wolf pelts at women who deliberately stood in their path. In this way, according to the old myth, would fertility be bestowed upon barren wombs. Our Great Man's wife was in this way and for this reason struck several times, most conspicuously by Antonius. I wonder if he's ever used his rod on her. (Very well, I know how my vulgarities annoy you!)

If Calpurnia could bear him a son, we'd have a dynasty for certain. The young Egyptian Prince's legitimacy is questionable, at best. The gods alone, if they exist, know who fathered Queen Cleopatra's bastard, and this certainly doesn't mean that the Great Man is beyond reproach. He was in Egypt long enough, in fact, more than long enough!

As for our Brutus, though he's been rumored to be one of the Dictator's heirs, his relationship to Caesar is still the focus of much speculation, and in the right circles, of many vulgar jokes.

Whoever Caesar's son may be, or ever will be, is not of particular importance to me. "Why then," you are probably saying to yourself, "*are you* expending so much time and space on his progeny?" It is because, my dear Atticus, I'm still enough of a Republican to be cognizant, and alarmingly so, of our drift to monarchy. Read on, and you will understand.

No sooner had the races ended when Antonius, sweating and winded as a stallion, approached Caesar, seated on his curule chair. Antonius held aloft a coronet fashioned of copper or bronze. Three times he attempted to place it on Caesar's already laurel-crowned brow, and three times Caesar pushed it aside as the mob roared its approval. Certain of his parasites called out to him, *"Rex! Rex!"* The Great Man shot back, "My name is *Caesar, not Rex*! Then, his face became ashen, his hands began to tremble, and he appeared about to collapse. After a few moments, he regained his composure sufficiently to descend the Rostra and depart from the Forum with his lictors and other attendants.

I don't doubt the genuineness of Caesar's illness. Indeed, I'd seen him like this on an earlier occasion. However, the whole incident of the proffered crown reeks of a theatricality better suited for Pompeius' Theatre than the Forum. With his colleague's collusion, the Great Man was testing the public's sentiments on the notion of monarchy. I cannot help but wonder what the outcome might have been if the mob had *protested* rather than approved Caesar's refusal of a regal crown.

Ironically, as Caesar was on his way back to the Regia, he ordered the arrest and the suspension from official duties of Tribune Flavus and Tribune Marullus. Their crime? Removing coronets from Caesar's statues. This is a sorry business, a harbinger of much distress to come.

Where personal matters are concerned, there's still no movement from Dolabella about the dowry. Also, Publilia and her family have of late left me alone, though I'm certain I've not heard the end of them. By the way, you should know, in the event that an interested party should inquire of you, that an endowment, a most generous one at that, has been established for young Marcus.

Incidentally, I'm still at work on *Respublica* for his benefit. I only hope he'll find it a worthy testament. So far, I've written about the Catilinian conspiracy and Caesar's combination with Pompeius and Crassus. I revisited the trauma of my exile, the joy of my restoration, and the humiliation of my enforced silence under the triumvirs. I've yet to write about the civil war and my frustrated neutrality, culminating with the Great Man's dictatorship.

The writing is a slow, laborious task fraught with painful reminders of my steady decline from pre-eminence. Quintus and Servius have assisted me with opinions and recollections. As always, I look forward to having your insight about this project. So, please write as soon as possible. Better yet, please endeavor to return to Roma before I depart for Athens. In the interim, stay well.

Pax, salus, et vita.
Marcus Tullius Cicero

Caput XI Cicero's Respublica

CAESAR AND POMPEIUS WERE UNITED in ambition and allied in their domination of the Republic. Then they were joined in sorrow upon the sudden, tragic death of Julia, daughter and wife of two of Roma's triumvirs. It happened in the summer of the year following the consulate of Pompeius and Crassus, two years after my accommodation.

Street fighting and election riots had been endemic. First, the optimates tried but failed to prevent the triumvirs' election. Returning home from one such battle, his toga bloodied and torn, Pompeius had so shocked Julia that she fainted and fell to the floor of their atrium. At the same time, she had been with child, and the trauma of Pompeius' bloodied appearance and her collapse had caused her to miscarry.

Two years later, Julia was again with child. Amid continuing street fighting between rival electoral gangs, Pompeius was reported to have been killed. The news caused Julia's labor to commence prematurely. The weak, sickly son that she delivered died within hours after his birth. But poor Julia, exhausted by the trauma and travails of childbirth, physically and emotionally drained at the loss of her child, succumbed and died soon afterward in Pompeius' arms.

Julia's funeral procession progressed from Pompeius' house on the Palatine and then down through the Forum. It was very much a public, state ceremony including senators and equites, friends and allies of the triumvirs, clad in the gray and black garb of mourning, plebeians and soldiers, and musicians and hired mourners whose dirge and lamentations were altogether pathetic. I walked among the senators as the procession wound through the Forum bound for Mars Field where, at Pompeius' expressed request, I was to deliver the eulogy.

As we were passing the Rostra, Consul Domitius Ahenobarbus protested against these public rites for a private citizen, a woman, but Pompeius ignored him. The procession continued on its way.

In Mars Field, near the magnificent temple-theatre complex that Pompeius had had built during his consulate, Julia's corpse was set upon a pyre of elm and myrtle wood. The triumvir and proconsul stood to one side, stiff, reserved, impassive in black toga and tunic. His sons and daughter and their spouses, handsome young adults, grieved with dignity. The senators and equites faced the pyre as the mourners and musicians circled it three times. Then, they halted before the young woman's corpse. Upon a signal from the prefect of rites, I ascended a wooden podium adjacent to the pyre and prepared to deliver the eulogy. The twilight's descending sun bathed Mars Field in an eerie light.

"Gnaeus Pompeius Magnus, senators and citizens," I addressed them, "we honor with these rites the young woman who was in life the daughter and wife of the Republic's most illustrious citizens. Gaius Julius Caesar has extended Roma's imperium into far northern Gaul. Gnaeus Pompeius Magnus has cleared the seaways of piracy and has pacified the entire East. We have honored the achievements of both men. We have saluted them both for services to the Republic. Now, we must commiserate with their sorrow, with the husband who grieves for his deceased wife, and with the father whom duty keeps from being here, among his countrymen, to mourn for his daughter."

Earlier in the year, I had delivered the eulogy for Caesar's mother. I had mentioned then that duty had kept him from his mother's rites.

"May the gods grant that Julia's spirit will continue to sustain the concord between Gaius Caesar and Gnaeus Pompeius. Their harmony is the foundation for peace within the Republic."

I went on to describe the violence that had disrupted the elections during the last years, and I attributed Julia's premature death to recent political upheavals. Concluding the eulogy, I called for all citizens to put aside strife and factionalism, to persevere in the pursuit of peace with dignity, and to labor for the attainment of a new concord of the orders.

The pyre was set aflame immediately after I descended the podium. The flames consuming Julia's remains shot up toward the dusky sky. At that instant, I felt an intense premonition of loss. It was as though my own daughter were being consumed in the holocaust.

A few days after the funeral, I called on Pompeius at his Palatine residence. I found the man drenched in his own sorrow. Yet, he quite surprised me with his openness.

"She was so very dear to me," he sighed so pathetically. "This child, who was my wife, my companion, my bond...."

Yes, I thought, Julia had been as obedient to her father's will as I had been at their beck and call since my accommodation.

"Gnaeus, you cannot bury yourself in your own grief." I tried to comfort him, not realizing at the time how ironic my advice would later prove to be. "The Republic needs you! We're drifting into anarchy. With Caesar in Gaul and Crassus in Syria, the only expedient that can save us is a dictatorship!" It was fortunate for the Republic that Pompeius' Spanish proconsulate had been entrusted to his legates, Afranius and Petreius, while he remained in Roma.

He suddenly looked up at me with those red, swollen eyes, and replied, "*Theirs? Or mine?*"

Without hesitation I answered, "You heard me speak of a *concord* of all good citizens."

Pompeius shook his head and demurred, "The extremists on both sides will *never* accept it! The new oligarchs, Cato, Ahenobarbus, Bibulus and their crew, will never accommodate."

The word "accommodate" stung me like a scorpion's sting, but I feared Pompeius was right.

By this time, the old oligarchs, those men who had steered the Republic during my consulate and for so many years before, had departed from the political arena.

The first recent departure was Lucius Lucullus. Only months after obstructing the Egyptian restoration, he had become ill with a debilitating condition that attacked his mental faculties. My physician, Metrodorus, had opined that Lucullus' dementia was the result of his over-indulgence in the curious berries from the Pontic Sea that he had cultivated in his luxurious gardens. There was even malicious gossip connecting his second wife, Servilia, to Lucullus' death. In any event, his young son was placed under the custodianship of Lucullus' younger brother, Marcus. However, with Marcus' death during the year of Pompeius' and Crassus' consulate, the child was relegated to his mother's care.

In the same year in which Caesar's mother and daughter died, the Caecilius Metellus clan suffered a great loss with the death of Metellus Nepos. Only lately returned from his Spanish proconsulate, Metellus, who had been consul in the year of my recall, succumbed to a stroke. With his passing, the only significant Metellus left was Metellus Scipio, an optimate and a pontiff in place of Marcus Lucullus, and a most ambitious pursuer of the consulate.

Now, the only remaining oligarch was my erstwhile rival advocate, Hortensius. But he was living in retirement, and in frail health, at his estate at Bovillae.

During my accommodation, I had refrained from active, independent political activity. Instead, in my semi-retirement, I devoted my energies to researching and writing treatises on oratory and rhetoric, on philosophy and divination, and on law and politics. In reaction to the chronic strife of those years, I harkened back to the golden age of Scipio Aemilianus and composed the dialogues, *De Re Publica* and *De Legibus*.

However, I did make an occasional appearance in the Curia for Senate meetings. Also, I was always ready to undertake a legal brief for the triumvirs' men.

The sting of the word *accommodate* from Pompeius' mouth subsided only after I took a few swallows of watered wine.

"Then there's the other side," Pompeius added, "Clodius and his rabble. He ignores my warnings. Ever since your recall, he's been at war with Milo, and Milo's just as recalcitrant as Pulcher." He took a long, deep draught of wine before speaking again. "Strange though that Crassus always had a stabilizing effect on him, rather like a stern, reproving father. If he were here now, perhaps he could keep Clodius in line. Instead, he has to pursue glory in the East! He has to make war against the Parthians so that he can match or even surpass Caesar's Gallic conquests and my own Eastern victories. More's the pity! With all his wealth, Crassus was always insecure. At Luca, he told us he'd not renew our compact unless he was given a free hand in Syria."

I mustered enough courage to speak about Crassus' expedition. "I don't recall a proconsulate that began under such opprobrium as had Crassus'." There had been much rumor and speculation that he was going to invade Parthia on the pretext of securing the Cilician-Syrian frontier. When he was attempting to pass through the Appian Gate, Tribunes Aetius Capito and Aquillius Gallus planted themselves and an incense chaffing pan in the path of Crassus' large entourage of attendants and lictors. Heaping denunciations and imprecations upon Crassus and his son, the tribunes invoked the gods' maledictions upon an unjust, unwarranted war, a war whose only objective was to feed Crassus' ambitions.

Pompeius looked askance at me. He may have thought that he alone could criticize Crassus' vanity, but I was not to be deterred.

"But that was not all. There were two women by the gate. They called out to Crassus. No one is sure what they said to him or even who they were. Strange, you know. I wonder if these were Catilina's wife and step-daughter. They had accosted me when I returned from exile. Well, whoever they were, after a moment's hesitation, Crassus and his son led their troop out the gate and down the Appian Road, while the two tribunes, burning incense in the pan, continued to curse their expedition." I paused as Pompeius' eyes remained fixed on me. "I suppose if one doesn't believe in the gods, then curses and imprecations have no power. Still, it was an inauspicious departure."

Pompeius shrugged his shoulders. "The latest reports are that he's massed forty thousand men plus auxiliaries on the Euphrates frontier."

Then, he shook his head in disgust, took another deep swallow of wine, and mumbled, "Damn foolish, bloody business!"

That night, as I settled in to sleep, I thought of my visit to Pompeius. It did not escape me that he had been evasive on the issue of a dictatorship to save the deteriorating situation in Roma. Yet, it was ironic that he could berate his partner's governorship of Syria as a springboard for an invasion of Parthia.

The previous year, Crassus' predecessor, Aulus Gabinius, had launched a military expedition to Egypt to restore King Ptolemy Auletes to his throne, in direct contravention of the Senate's decree. Gabinius' campaign was successful; the King was once again securely enthroned. Leaving a sizeable, but motley garrison of Roman, Syrian, and Gallic soldiers, Gabinius then returned to Syria. With the termination of his proconsulate, he returned to Roma, where he was promptly impeached on charges of inciting war without the Senate's authorization.

Pompeius had asked me to defend him. Realizing that the request was actually an order, I undertook the defense of the man who had refused to help me when I had first been targeted by Clodius.

There had never been any doubt in my mind that Gabinius' action in Egypt was ordered by the triumvirs and spurred by money that Auletes had had to borrow from Roman financiers. Even Atticus could confirm this latter point. But in defending Gabinius, I had had to tread carefully. I could not name Caesar, Pompeius, and Crassus as the real instigators, even though their culpability was widely assumed. Instead, my strategy was to justify the restoration as a positive good for the Republic in that Auletes would stabilize Egypt's internal affairs and guarantee the annual grain shipments to Roma.

In the end, the jury accepted my argument, but for whose benefit? Obviously, the interests of the men for whom Auletes' return to Egypt's throne far outweighed the prosecuting Consul Appius Claudius' contention that Gabinius' action was tantamount to treason against the Republic. I had no doubt that the jury had been well-compensated.

However, on the heels of Gabinius' acquittal came another prosecution, this time for extortion upon the Syrian provincials. Here, my arguments did not prevail; nor did the triumvirs' bribes. The prosecutor, my former protégé and junior senator, Marcus Caelius, secured the jury's majority for conviction.

Gabinius and his wife, Lollia, went into exile at Massilia. I wondered if a similar fate awaited Crassus because of his Parthian adventure. It was surely impossible for me to realize at the time that the Fates would prove to be even less merciful to him and to his son.

THOUGH I HAD FAILED TO achieve a second acquittal for Gabinius, I was successful in other briefs. Clodius Pulcher and his allies prosecuted the men who had aided me either in my consulate or during my exile. Publius Sestius, Gnaeus Plancius, Gaius Pomptinus, Lucius Flaccus, even Lucius Piso, were fair game for suits alleging provincial malfeasance. When I achieved acquittals for these men, I considered it a triumph over "Pretty-Boy" and his henchmen, the likes of whom included Fufius Calenus, Ventidius Bassus and Sallustius Crispus.

Clodius even attacked Pompeius' former legate, Marcus Aemilius Scaurus. The charge was the same yet again, but the accused was a unique target insofar as he was connected to the triumvir. In fact, Scaurus had married Pompeius' divorced wife, Mucia, probably with the triumvir's consent. Mucia remained close with her children by Pompeius, attending each of their weddings. For her new husband, she had borne a namesake son who was said to be adored by his older step-siblings.

My defense of Scaurus was successful. He and Mucia were both most appreciative of my efforts. Pompeius was so grateful that I received a noteworthy reward.

An equite, one Lucius Publilius, a former client of mine and an acquaintance of Pompeius, died shortly after Scaurus' trial. In his will, I was named as the guardian of his only daughter. At the time, Publilia was about twelve. Upon meeting her, I discovered her to be a most comely child. However, her mother and her elder brother were an equally matched pair of intolerable bores. Despite them, guardianship of Publilia made me trustee of her substantial fortune until such time as she should marry.

I surmised that Pompeius had had something to do with these arrangements.

Another windfall came to me from another quarter. Atticus told me that Caesar had advanced a sum of eight hundred thousand sesterces for the purchase of properties and land in areas north and west of the Forum and the Comitium. Caesar had various urban renewal projects in mind including a new, enlarged forum and a new basilica. I was expected to head the consortium of equites, along with Atticus and Roma's leading bankers, Balbus and Oppius, in purchasing the desired properties.

I accepted the commission with avid enthusiasm.

However, I had less enthusiasm for another development. Publius Dolabella, the young man whom I was obliged to take under my wing, became enamored of Tullia and she with him. The barrier posed by his wife, he said, would be removed by an expedient divorce. This smacked of a mercenary insensitivity that I found loathsome, especially as he had a child. While I could not prevent his divorcing his wife, I nevertheless told him that I could not presently sanction his marriage to my daughter. Dolabella deferred to my decision, but the combination of Terentia's machinations and Tullia's filial persistence was nearly insurmountable.

Terentia insisted that Tullia was too young and too lovely to remain a widow. Tullia affirmed that she loved Dolabella, that he was a good match for her. He was handsome and talented and ambitious, and as he was a Caesarian, we could not afford to reject him.

"So that's *it!*" I declared. "My beloved *Tulliola* has to be mortgaged as part of my pledge to Caesar?"

"Tata, please!" she implored. "Do this for me. He fills the void in my life. Please accept him. *Please.*"

As much as it pained me to deny her, I remained opposed to the marriage, at least then; but the world changes.

Not long thereafter, another new member joined our circle. This happened when Atticus forsook his bachelorhood and, in his early fifties, married Pilia, a handsome, graceful young woman of equestrian family. I was happy for them both. We celebrated their nuptials in the early summer, shortly before the elections were scheduled to take place. Pilia was good for Atticus, far better for him than I believed Dolabella would be for my Tullia.

The election canvass season sparked a renewal of civil strife as the candidates mobilized their gangs of operae and ruffians to do battle in the Forum, the Comitium, and all the streets leading into these assembly areas. Repeated attempts to hold the elections were disrupted by gang fighting.

Adding to the disorder was a widespread bribery scandal involving many consular and praetorian candidates. The current consuls themselves, Appius Claudius and Domitius Ahenobarbus, were believed to be implicated. Claudius maneuvered to avoid investigation and impeachment by setting off for his proconsular province of Cilicia before the end of the year and without first having been invested with the proconsular imperium.

Before his departure, Claudius paid me a surprise visit. However, my true sentiments were more of *shock* than surprise. Since my consulate, I had not been on very cordial terms with the entire Pulcher clan. Claudius wanted to put all this behind us. He extended his hand to me, and without hesitation I took it in my own, promising to put aside all enmity toward him. I made no promises regarding any of his siblings however, especially my neighbor, Clodia Pulchra. Claudius assured me that they would in time make their own peace with me. In fact, he added, he was going to visit his sisters and bid them farewell, starting with the *Palatine Medusa* (*my* words, not his).

Touching on another family item, he mentioned that his son-in-law, Marcus Brutus, was accompanying him to Cilicia. Brutus had been quaestor in that year, but he had refused a posting under Caesar in Gaul. So, he was to serve as proquaestor on the island of Cyprus, which had been placed under the aegis of the Proconsul of Cilicia.

We did not discuss politics or even allude to the bribery scandal. However, he did not regret that his colleague, Domitius, did not have a proconsular province. Domitius still coveted the Gauls, but all discussion regarding a successor to Caesar was banned in the Senate and in the People's Assemblies. Domitius would have the Gauls or no province at all.

Summer passed into autumn, and Father Tiber flooded his banks, bringing extensive destruction and death to multitudes of people who lived in the low-lying areas of the City. Relief efforts were hampered by acrimonious debates in the Senate, while intermittent gang warfare precluded the holding of the elections. Inevitably, the New Year began with no magistrates in office. In such circumstances, as had happened before Crassus' and Pompeius' consulate, the Senate appointed *interreges* to serve both provisionally and expeditiously as stop-gap chief executives in place of the missing consuls. The first interrex was Metellus Scipio, who served for a month. In the continuing absence of elections and therefore new magistrates, the Senate appointed Valerius Messalla as the second interrex.

All during this crisis, Pompeius remained sequestered at his Tibur mansion. As the Senate tried to provide some semblance of government, rampant rumors called for a dictator, and Pompeius was the favored choice.

When at last the consular elections were held, the interrex Valerius Messalla and a neutral partisan, Gnaeus Domitius Calvinus, were elected. After the praetors were elected, Pompeius wasted no time in returning to Roma and insisting on the legal prosecution of the consular candidates who had been implicated in the bribery debacle. The foremost culprits were Gaius Memmius and Aemilius Scaurus. Pompeius had so much clout that the prosecutors and the presiding praetor virtually suborned the jurors to return guilty verdicts. Both men went into exile.

Omniscient Narrative

Mucia Scaurus rightly assumes that she does not need an appointment to call upon her ex-husband, Gnaeus Pompeius Magnus. The porter on duty at the Palatine residence admits her without question as though she still lived there. Then Pompeius' major-domo conducts her to the atrium as a mere formality.

Mucia looks about the spacious room, structurally familiar to her but so completely changed in its décor. No doubt this is the design of her replacement, Julia, Caesar's daughter and Pompeius' recently deceased wife. They say that he was supremely happy with her, she muses, and that Julia adored Pompeius. It had been that way for them as well, she recalls, in their marriage of almost twenty years. But Mucia and Pompeius had both been young when they began their life. Could Julia have reminded him of Mucia at age seventeen? Julia and Pompeius had not been together long enough to reach the threshold where love's ardor becomes an ember that glows ever so weakly.

"Welcome, Mucia!" Pompeius' voice interrupts her reverie.

"Gnaeus, you look well." Mucia is polite, but not entirely truthful. Despite Pompeius' robust physique, his handsome, well-defined features, even with more pronounced jowls, there is a gray, sad melancholy about him. Reluctantly, she extends her hands to him, and with equal reluctance he kisses her on both cheeks. These are polite gestures of civility in respect of their years together and the children they begat.

"You also look well, Mucia." Pompeius is sincerely observant. Mucia's figure is fuller and rounder but no less becoming, though it is wrapped in somber gray stola and palla. However, the application of dyes and modest cosmetics render her well-coiffed hair and lovely face in a beauteous light.

There is an awkward tension between them stemming not so much from their terminated marriage as from the most recent development. Mucia alludes to this when she says, "I've already bid farewell to our children. Now, for whatever benefit you may derive, I've come to bid *you* farewell also."

Pompeius does not need to ask for details, for he easily surmises that Mucia is joining her husband in exile. "I see," is all that he can manage to say.

"Marcus has already left. In a few days, I'll take *our* son—*his* son and *mine*—and we'll go after him."

"A safe journey, Mucia; may Fortuna smile on you."

"He was consistently loyal to you, Gnaeus. You know that. Yet, far from helping him, you let it be known that he was to be *convicted!* Why Gnaeus?"

"It is best that we not quarrel about political matters that are beyond your understanding." Pompeius is obnoxiously aloof and patronizing.

"But I understand *you*, Gnaeus Pompeius!" Anger rises in Mucia's voice. "I know the self-serving creature that you are. It's always been about *you! Your* elevation to glory! *Your* pursuit of fame! You were so busy with yourself that you forgot and forsook everyone else, especially your *wife!* Yes, you abandoned me long before you divorced me. This is why I took a lover. Yes, all during your Eastern campaigns I had a most charming, most promising, most ambitious lover. Shall I name him? Or can you infer who he might have been?"

Pompeius' face flushes with anger and intense anticipation. Mucia knows that she has him tangled in her web spun of innuendo and suspicion. She could walk out now victoriously, leaving him to stew in his own inferences. Instead, she decides on a final flourish.

"It was the *father* of your beloved *Julia!* It was *Caesar!* Caesar was my lover! Now... hail and farewell, Pompeius *Magnus*... forever!" Mucia turns and walks out of his life.

Stunned, Pompeius cannot fully realize how his life and his politics will be from this time on irrevocably altered.

Cicero's Respublica

The Consuls were well-meaning men, especially as Pompeius once again kept aloof from the political storm, but they were unable to hold the elections for the ensuing year. Political gang fighting bloodied the streets of Roma and turned Mars Field into a virtual battlefield. As a result, when the New Year began, only the new tribunes were in office. Again, the Senate had to appoint an interrex, Marcus Aemilius Lepidus, to preside provisionally over the Republic, a state drowning in chronic civil strife.

Lepidus' term expired without any abatement of the violence. The elections were still not held. The Senate then honored Servius Sulpicius Rufus as the next interrex. My dear friend accepted the post with grave reservations. His erudition in matters of Roman jurisprudence was beyond comparison, but he was lacking in the political pragmatism necessary to address the deteriorating situation. Consequently, he was no more successful than Lepidus.

The third appointed interrex was Marcus Valerius Messalla, an experienced senator who had been selected in two previous years. He presided over the Senate when, in the midst of continued disorders, it received news of a fiasco that brought black clouds upon Roma.

The legate Gaius Cassius Longinus had sent a dispatch reporting the defeat and annihilation of Crassus' legions at Carrhae, beyond the Euphrates River, deep in Parthian territory. Both Crassus and his son, Publius, had been treacherously captured and killed. Out of forty thousand Romans, barely ten thousand battered, demoralized men made it back to Syria. Cassius pledged to hold the Syrian-Cilician frontier against an almost certain Parthian incursion. He implored the Senate to send reinforcements.

Ex-Consul Domitius Ahenobarbus proposed that the Proconsuls Caesar and Pompeius, as the two commanders with the greatest armies, should each donate one legion for service in the East. Pompeius consented to this, and it was so ordered by the Senate. At the time, Pompeius was still maintaining an absentee proconsulate over the Spanish provinces, administering them through legates while he remained in Roma. His legates were veterans of the Eastern wars, Lucius Afranius and Marcus Petreius.

Aside from sending two legions to reinforce Cassius, no one seemed to know what ought to be done. No one proposed that either of the previous year's Consuls, Domitius Calvinus or Valerius Messalla, should be sent out to Syria, and neither one of them volunteered. The East needed a commander with a sufficient army. Unless the elections for new consuls and other magistrates were held immediately, and one of them was dispatched to the critical region, I saw no alternative but to appoint Pompeius to the task. The new oligarchs might even have welcomed the opportunity to get him out of Roma. But Pompeius gave no indication of wanting the job.

Meanwhile, the competition among the three most prominent consular candidates intensified with unparalleled ferocity. Pompeius' former legate, Publius Plautius Hypsaeus, was up against Titus Milo, and a prominent optimate, Metellus Scipio. Among the praetorian candidates, Publius Clodius, as usual, was the loudest and the most brazen. He and his operae lost no opportunity to intimidate his rivals and to provoke Milo's men to violence.

While the Senate groped for a policy against the Parthians and improvised the day-to-day-administration of the Republic, Quintus returned to Roma after three years as Caesar's legate. He looked leaner than when he had left, strong and fit, but there was an unsettled aspect to his disposition that he wore to mask some deep wound.

"I haven't been totally discharged," he said over a light supper with me. "Actually, I've been transferred back to Pompeius' service. I don't know if he's going to send me out to Spain or if he'll use me to help him with the grain supply. By the way, judging from your appearance, Marcus, there doesn't appear to be a food shortage here in Roma!"

I laughed at the barb aimed at the weight I had gained since we last saw each other. "The perils of inactivity, brother," I replied sardonically in my own defense.

We talked long into the night, briefing each other on familial and political matters, and in the process draining a fair amount of wine. Quintus observed, "So, old 'Money-Bags' allowed his greed and ambition to overcome his judgment and strategy. I've heard those barbarous Parthians are expert archers, especially when mounted on swift, armored horses. Crassus' men couldn't hold up against them or their heavy cataphracts."

I shook my head, still appalled at the monstrosity of the disaster. "Thirty thousand men killed! A score of legionary eagles and standards captured. The whole East in danger of invasion! Crassus and his son butchered!" My throat became tight. "It's said that they poured molten gold down his throat; a horrible and yet ironic death for Crassus." I grimaced with the mention of such barbarity, but I recovered after a momentary pause. "You remember when Publius came for lessons in oratory and law? What a quick, alert mind he had!"

"Yes," agreed Quintus, "but you know his younger brother's very sharp too. He's been Caesar's quaestor for two campaigns. Young Marcus Crassus can do no wrong, at least none worthy of an official reprimand. But if you dare show some independence, some initiative at seizing the moment... well... never mind!"

There was a tinge of resentment in Quintus' description of young Marcus Crassus' exemplary service. However, I failed to persuade him to elaborate on his own fall from Caesar's grace. He said only that it was because of a tactical error on Caesar's part that my brother had attempted to cover. Apparently, the Proconsul could not brook being upstaged by his subordinates.

"When he learned of his daughter's death," Quintus began to explain, "Caesar didn't shave his face or trim his hair, what little he has left, for an entire campaign. He led us on a vengeful pursuit of a rebellious Belgic chief named Ambiorix. We went from Belgic territory and across the Rhine into German lands. We plundered and burned their farms, villages, and shrines in pursuit of the elusive bugger. We all knew that it wasn't military necessity that drove him as much as it was the pain of his own grief."

"There can be no greater sorrow," I sighed, "than the loss of one's own child. But Julia was the bond between Caesar and Pompeius. For the time being, they're united in their mutual grief for her loss. But how long might that last?"

Quintus snorted, "They've plenty of other relatives they can mix, match, and marry."

"Perhaps, but you know, with Crassus dead, there's a gap in their coalition that no one can fill. There's a rumor floating around that Pompeius has donated one of the two legions that he'd lent to Caesar last year."

Quintus laughed sardonically. "Marcus, that's more than rumor. I know for a *fact* that Caesar will send back *both* legions, the *First* and the *Third*, for duty against the Parthians. When he does, he'll personally reward each man with a generous bounty. Caesar's no fool."

INTERREX VALERIUS MESSALLA CONVENED THE Senate on a cold, inclement day late in Januarius to hear the latest news from the far frontiers of Roma's imperium. Sitting on the president's curule chair, the Interrex read a dispatch from Gaius Cassius. For the time being, the Eastern frontier was quiet as the expected Parthian invasion had not occurred. However, Cassius would not rule it out completely. Again, he implored the Senate to send reinforcements.

The former interrex, Lepidus, reluctantly stood. At the time, he was well over fifty, and he had not yet served as praetor. Surveying the senators, he appeared timorous and diffident, and his small, spare figure accentuated his nervousness. It was most remarkable that the Senate had earlier chosen him to lead because for all practical purposes he was a nonentity. After being recognized, Lepidus asked about the legions donated by Caesar and Pompeius. *Were they not to be sent to Syria?*

Metellus Scipio replied that they would be sent to Brundisium to await favorable winds in order to make the crossing to Macedonia and thence to Syria. However, there was something in Metellus' voice that smacked of insincerity. My sense was that upon their arrival, the two donated legions would be kept in Italia for Pompeius' immediate use, though for what purpose I could not ascertain.

Pompeius had withdrawn from the City and was hibernating at his Tibur mansion. *What a time to quit Roma!* No magistrates in office. Gang warfare was rampant. The Eastern frontier could flare up at any time; and from the north, there was more disturbing news.

Messalla took up another dispatch. This was from Caesar. He reported that a massive uprising had broken out among the Arverni. Led by a chieftain named Vercingetorix, the revolt was spreading rapidly among the disaffected and hostile Gallic tribes. Caesar reported his fear that the allied tribes in the Transalpina might be induced to join the rebellion.

My thoughts flashed back to the Allobroges, the Transalpine tribe that had received assurances and promises of improved treatment from Roman authorities. The Allobroges expected as much because of their envoys' assistance to the Republic in thwarting Catilina's conspiracy during my consulate. But they were disappointed in their hopes, and so they had rebelled the following year. Propraetor Gaius Pomptinus had fought an arduous campaign to suppress them. He had been allowed to triumph for his victory, but Allobrogian anger and resentment of Roman cupidity was still simmering. They and their fellow Transalpine tribes could easily be induced to join the Arverni to throw off the Roman yoke.

The optimates voiced the common opinion that Caesar had overstepped his authority in conquering vast new territories. They said that his ambitions had provoked this uprising as surely as Crassus had upset the tranquility and security of the Eastern frontier. As Crassus had suffered an ignominious death at the hands of the Parthians, so too should Caesar at the hands of the insurgent Gauls. Marcus Bibulus, Domitius Ahenobarbus, Marcus Cato and then speaker after speaker among the optimates voiced these sentiments in sharp, caustic language.

Attempting to calm their vindictive, bellicose ardor, I reminded them that if Caesar were to suffer in Gaul what had befallen Crassus in Parthia, the Transalpina and the Cisalipina could not contain the hordes that would descend upon Italia, bringing death, pillage, and destruction in their wake.

Suddenly there was a loud commotion from the Forum. The sounds of thousands of voices, chanting, shrieking, bellowing, stilled and silenced all debate, all movement within the Curia. It was as though a great enemy host had invaded the city. Senators left their places and went out to the portico to see what was happening. Servius, Quintus, and I followed.

A multitude of plebeian riffraff had surrounded the Rostra. A draped corpse lay upon it. Atop the steps stood Fulvia, her red-brown hair disheveled, her gown bespattered with blood. She was haranguing the mob. "They've killed my Publius!" she frantically screamed at them. "They've murdered him! Milo and his swine! Cicero and all of them! Look! Look at him!" With that she pulled the bloodied, lacerated toga from the corpse, revealing it to be Publius Clodius Pulcher.

My nemesis was a bloodied, soiled heap of carnage. From my vantage point, I could not distinguish details. Perhaps this was because I was too far away; or perhaps death had robbed "Pretty-Boy" of his delicate, feminine beauty.

The mob of Clodius' thugs, gladiators, and operae shouted curses and obscenities at Milo, at the Senate, and at me. Weaving through their midst, Tiro came running up to the portico from the Forum pavement.

"Dominus!" he exclaimed, panting and wild-eyed. "I've heard them say there was a battle on the Appian Road near Bovillae. Milo's and Clodius' men tossed insults at each other. The insults and taunts gave way to arms. Someone among Milo's men threw a javelin at Clodius. He was pinned down and then hacked by the others. The dead and wounded lie right up to the City walls!"

Tiro coughed for breath, but before I could speak, Fulvia screamed from the Rostra, "My husband loved you! You were his children, as dear to him as our very own. Men of Roma, avenge him! Make *them* pay for his life!"

Like a ferocious beast, the mob roared its approval. "Take him up!" Fulvia commanded. "Up there!" She gestured toward the Curia. As though they were one body, the men closest to the dead man took hold of him and carried him down the Rostra's steps, across the Comitium, and then up the Curia's steps. Tribune Gaius Sallustius was in their van. He was gesturing to the senators congregated on the portico to disperse. We gave way without the least opposition.

"What are they about?" Servius could only wonder aloud as Clodius' bloody corpse was borne past us. I saw his black-bearded face besmeared with blood and sweat, his head, like a child's doll, shook from side to side. There had to be at least a thousand men snaking their way up the steps and pouring into the Curia. At least a score of them were brandishing torches.

Once inside, they began to dismantle the wooden benches where senators were wont to sit when in session. Their shouts and curses could he heard above the din of the chopped and hammered wood. Erecting a funeral pyre in the middle of the floor, they laid their dead demagogue upon it and ignited it. They cursed the Senate and all who had ever been at odds with Clodius. Milo's and my name were most prominent among their deprecations.

"Let's get out of here!" Quintus urged, pulling at my arm.

We and other senators abandoned the Curia where we were to debate and deliberate. For our own safety's sake, we fled from the flames that engulfed it in a mighty conflagration. Clodius' riffraff came storming out, pitching themselves down the steps and assaulting the most vulnerable senators.

Servius, Quintus, and I and our attendants moved out of harm's way as quickly as our feet would carry us. We made our way to the nearby Temple of Concord. But as we passed the Rostra, Fulvia, like a woman possessed by all the Furies of Hades, shouted at me, "You'll pay for him, Marcus Cicero! You'll pay!"

True as it was that Clodius had been my enemy and I held him accountable for so much of the misfortune that had befallen me, I had had nothing to do with his death. At the time, however, I had no remorse over his demise. Publius Clodius had initiated violence and in the end he fell as a victim of it.

I pondered the dead demagogue's hostility as we stood on Concord's portico watching the Curia turn into a burned shell of an edifice. Other senators had sought shelter with us. The fiery spectacle of Clodius' cremation within the hallowed chamber filled me with dismay. It was as though we were seeing the funeral of the Republic itself. I saw Cato, Domitius Ahenobarbus, Bibulus, and Metellus Scipio and other optimates hobnobbing in an agitated state with much gesticulating, head-shaking, and fist-clenching.

After several moments, Cato and company approached us, hard resolution showing on all their faces. "Marcus Cicero," he said, "will you come with us to see Gnaeus Pompeius?"

GNAEUS POMPEIUS GREETED US IN the atrium of his Tibur mansion. He had been apprised of Clodius' death, the rioting in the Forum, and the burning of the Curia. Doubtless, he knew the reason for our visit.

"Roma in these last four years has been nothing if not an arena where hired gangs of gladiators have fought so that this or that candidate might prevail," Cato announced in his usual direct, no-nonsense manner. "You, Gnaeus Pompeius, have contributed to this violence in the past when you sought the consulship and most recently by your own inactivity."

Pompeius regarded him coldly, even malevolently. He sniffed as though Cato were giving off a foul scent. The triumvir looked harried and weary. That grief had marked his face was obvious, but there was something else too. There was an edge about him, an uneasiness reined in with deliberate effort.

"The mob sets fire to the Curia," Cato continued, "and has the run of the City. A tribune leads them in their incendiarism! Gangs are at large. Milo's, Clodius', and other candidates besides them have wreaked havoc. If the Republic is to survive this turmoil, something must be done. So, Gnaeus Pompeius, we have recourse to you. You are the only responsible citizen to whom we can turn. The Senate appoints you Sole Consul of the Republic. Will you accept this commission and restore order?"

Pompeius looked from Cato to me and then to Bibulus, to Domitius, and then to each of the eight others. He understood, as we all did, the implications of his appointment. The words *"Sole Consul"* in the absence of a second consul, clearly gave him the dictatorship. Though Cato and the others had not included me in their counsels, I agreed now with their choice. Truly, there was no one else with soldiers at his beck and call who could have been trusted.

After a long, silent moment, Pompeius nodded and said to us, "Gentlemen, I accept the Senate's charge."

Pompeius was as good as his word. Assuming the consular fasces, he at once set out for Campania to raise an army from among his settled veterans. I thought it strange at the time that he would not wait for the donated legions from Caesar. Perhaps he reasoned that Caesar would need all of his forces to suppress the Gallic revolt, or he may have regarded the chaotic situation in the City as too desperate for any delay.

Quintus opined that in the time it would take for even one legion to reach Roma, Pompeius could have a veteran force recruited from nearby Campania. My brother was right. Within a week after receiving his consulate, Pompeius marched on Roma with a legion force of veterans. Additional cohorts were expected as well.

Occupying the Forum, the Comitium, and Mars Field, his soldiers dispersed the gangs and gladiator troops that had had the run of the City. But this was far from a bloodless restoration of order. Roma ran with blood and the carnage was frightful. Those who would not disperse were either killed or taken prisoner. They were confined under guard in the Circus Maximus, converted by Pompeius into a huge detention center for the dregs and thugs.

When sufficient order had been restored, trials in the Court of Public Violence were held for the principal gang leaders and perpetrators of disorder. In the absence of praetors, as none had been elected, Pompeius appointed *"quaesitores,"* senatorial inquisitors, to preside over the court. Domitius Ahenobarbus and Marcus Favonius were the first two appointees.

The tribune Gaius Sallustius was condemned, notwithstanding his inviolable office, and banished. The consular candidate, Publius Plautius, despite his former service as Pompeius' legate, was also convicted and exiled. But to the general surprise, Metellus Scipio was acquitted, though his use of armed operae had been no less violent than that of his rivals.

When Titus Milo was brought to trial for the murder of Clodius, I consented to defend him, especially because of his invaluable services in my recall. But I must sadly admit that I disappointed him. On the day of his trial, the whole Forum and Comitium, and in particular the area immediately adjacent to the Rostra, were ringed with Pompeius' armed soldiers. Their bronze helmets and armor and weapons glinted in the winter sun. The sight of them unnerved me so that I could not speak effectively. Though I had prepared an excellent oration on Milo's behalf, defending his actions as in the best interests of the Republic, my delivery was flat, timid, and shamefully diffident.

Seated on the Rostra, Milo saw my discomfiture. His big, square face flanked by dark hair, his cleft chin, the lines creasing his cheeks, and his piercing light eyes portrayed a strength and defiance which I altogether lacked as his defense counsel.

When the guilty verdict was announced, he stood erect, his firm, tough build giving no semblance of fear or disappointment. Upon hearing the sentence of banishment and the confiscation of his properties, he turned sharply and strode off the Rostra. The soldiers and spectators parted a path for him.

I looked after him, feeling utter remorse that I had failed him. Though his methods had matched Clodius' in their violence and militancy, Milo had sought to bolster the Senate's authority against popularist demagoguery. His politics may even have been reflected in his choice of a wife, for he had married Fausta, the daughter of the late dictator, Sulla. His opportunism also showed because he had quickly snatched her after Gaius Memmius, the exiled consular candidate, had divorced her.

Some time after the trial, I tried to compensate for my failure by writing my oration as I would have wanted to deliver it. Atticus' copyists published it. The speech read better, far better, than it had been delivered. I sent a copy to Milo, and even *he* was pleased with it. Writing from Massilia, he told me that had I actually delivered such a fine defense, he and Fausta would not then have been enjoying *in exile* the superb oysters of the Transalpine coast. Apparently, exile and oysters contributed to his sarcastic irony.

At the public auction of Milo's house and movable property, I arranged with Terentia for her freedman, Philotimus, to bid for the properties as my proxy. The wily Greek was successful in outbidding the competition. Of course, I was happy about this, as I did not want Milo's property to fall into the hands of his foes. But I was perturbed by Philotimus because, in his bidding, he surpassed my strict limits by some twelve thousand sesterces. This was an unexpected drain on my finances at a time when I was attempting to augment Tullia's dowry in preparation for her inevitable, new marriage; for Dolabella did not desist in his attentions to her.

When I discussed this matter with Terentia, she obstinately defended her freedman, denying any impropriety on his part. "And yet," she countered, "*you* commit the impropriety of buying up the properties of a man whom *you* failed to save from banishment!" Recoiling from her distemper, I let the matter drop.

Terentia had grown ever more imperious and intemperate in recent years. Though she showered boundless affection upon you, my son, and even upon Tullia, she was increasingly aloof and detached from me. My physical limitation persisted through this time, and we had both given up any attempts at conjugal intimacy. We both distracted ourselves by directing our energies into other endeavors. For Terentia, it was her bank accounts, her rent collections from at least fifteen insulae situated across Roma, and the income from rich Italian forest lands that were the focus of her attentions. For me, it was my activity in the courts, though hardly distinguished, my limited role in the Senate, my treatise writing, and my engagement, albeit discreetly, in various business consortia.

Quintus was almost always complaining about Pomponia. Arguments between them were chronic and bitter. Even Atticus, quite happily married to Pilia, was finding it increasingly difficult to mediate between his sister and my brother. It seemed that the Republic's stresses were mirrored in our own family.

AT POMPEIUS' URGING, THE SENATE sanctioned Metellus Scipio's appointment as co-Consul. Pompeius expressed his full confidence in his new colleague's ability to help him restore complete order in Roma. Confidence was not all that Pompeius had in him. The two Consuls negotiated a marriage contract, Pompeius marrying Scipio's daughter, Cornelia. She was young, pretty, and widowed by the death of Publius Crassus. It was ironic that Pompeius should marry the former daughter-in-law of his deceased triumviral partner.

Pompeius' new marriage produced heated speculation that he was engineering a political alliance with the optimates. His sons had already taken brides from optimate families. Gnaeus had married a Claudia, one of Appius Claudius Pulcher's daughters. Sextus' wife was a daughter of Lucius Scribonius Libo, an up-and-coming optimate senator. Likewise, Pompeius' daughter had married Faustus Sulla, son of the late dictator, twin brother of Fausta, and brother-in-law of the exiled Milo. Rumor had it that Pompeia's marriage had been arranged by the Magnus as a cold rebuff of Caesar's proposal that he marry Pompeia in order to replace the bond that had been dissolved with Julia's untimely death. *What was going on in Pompeius' mind? What was he calculating?*

Ironically, as Publius Crassus' death helped to create a marital bond between Pompeius and Metellus Scipio, it also brought me an appointment to a prestigious religious post. The College of Augurs named me to succeed to young Crassus' vacancy. As Pompeius was an augur, I surmised that he had something to do with it. Though I accepted the appointment obligingly, my agnosticism remained irrevocably intact. *Marcus Tullius Cicero the Augur?* On appropriate occasions I would have to don the spiked skull-cap and the multi-striped toga. If not, how could *I* possibly take the *auspices*? I wondered how two augurs, in their ludicrous attire and brandishing their divining wands, could possibly pass each other in the street without bursting into laughter. Yet, there were serious, inauspicious signs to consider.

WITH SUFFICIENT ORDER RESTORED, POMPEIUS deemed it safe to conduct the elections for the following year's magistrates. The consulate was secured by an optimate, Marcus Claudius Marcellus, a virulent anti-Caesarian, and by my own dear friend, Servius Sulpicius Rufus. However, the new tribunicial board was dominated by men believed to be staunch Caesarians.

No sooner had the elections been concluded when Consul-elect Marcellus announced his intention of terminating Caesar's proconsulate, and at least four of the tribunes-elect were equally emphatic in their commitment to protecting Caesar's interests. The new oligarchs, especially Domitius Ahenobarbus, still covetous of the Gallic provinces, reinforced Marcellus' rhetoric.

There had been no news from Gaul for months. Then, not long after the elections, word arrived that Caesar had cornered the rebellious Gauls at a stronghold called Alesia. But another great host had surrounded Caesar's position so that he was obliged to face an enemy on two fronts. The uncertainty of Caesar's situation caused Pompeius to assume that the two donated legions were retained in Gaul as they could not then be spared.

While Pompeius had brought law and order back to Roma, he could not address our apprehensions about the future. He announced in the Senate a comprehensive agenda of legislation intended to safeguard the status quo and to mitigate the unbridled competition for public office and proconsular commands. However, the precarious situation up in Gaul and the uncertainty on the Parthian frontier played upon men's fears and misgivings.

My sleep was visited by macabre visions. In one, I saw the Roman she-wolf snarling over busts of Caesar and Pompeius. Between them was a pedestal with the label *Marcus Licinius Crassus*, but without his bust upon it. Blood poured forth from the Lupa's breasts, covering the triumvirs' heads. In another dream, I saw a field on which soldiers attired in Roman armor and equipped with Roman weaponry waged mighty battle with each other.

One night, Tiro awakened me from one such strife-ridden dream. He told me that Clodia Pulchra wished to see me. She was waiting for me in the atrium. Fortunately, Terentia, and I had been sleeping in separate rooms, so she would not have been awakened by Tiro. Rising from bed, I threw on a robe, put sandals on my feet, and headed out to the atrium. On the way, it occurred to me that I did not have to receive her at that late hour. *Why then had I not told Tiro to make excuses for me?*

The sight of Clodia was almost like one of my nightmarish visions. She was clothed head to toe in black. Evidently, she was still in mourning for her murdered brother. But it struck me how, with her long, black hair, so dark that it seemed to have blue highlights, and black raiment, she resembled a raven, a bird of ill omen. Her face was hard and severe in the dim oil-lamp light. She looked at me, her eyes glistening with tears as she seemed to be studying me before she spoke.

"Marcus Cicero," she hoarsely whispered almost inaudibly. "Are you satisfied by my brother's death? Does it please you?"

I could not answer her, for in all truth, I did not know what to say. She would not have believed my refutation, and to give her the satisfaction of being correct was dangerously unthinkable.

She took a few steps forward. "His blood is mine, Cicero; patrician, Claudian blood. May his blood, his *death* be on you; may you and all whom you love be stained by it!" With that, she produced a small dagger from her palla. I was too petrified with fear to move. Holding out her left hand, she cut the palm quickly and deeply with one slash. Then she hurled the dagger at my feet. Her blood on the blade splattered onto my sandaled feet and unto the hem of my robe.

Clodia cast me a venomous glare, hateful, malevolent, yet pathetically tearful. I almost wanted to comfort her, but I knew that would be impossible. She made for the door with steady, purposeful steps like a black specter blending into the night and vanishing.

Caput XII Cicero's Respublica

By late summer of Pompeius' and Metellus Scipio's consulate, word arrived from Gaul that Caesar had crushed the great revolt. Vercingetorix had surrendered. Here and there, Caesar's legates were stamping out the last embers of rebellion. I proposed and the Senate optimates grudgingly sanctioned a twenty-day thanksgiving to the gods for Caesar's victory.

Consul-elect Marcus Marcellus suggested that with the pacification of Gaul, the time had come for the Senate to consider terminating Caesar's command and appointing a successor. The optimates supported this notion, claiming that Caesar's relinquishment of his provincial imperium would be a necessary pre-condition for his expected candidacy for another consulate. Domitius Ahenobarbus was particularly outspoken because he still coveted the Gallic provinces for himself. Bibulus and Cato relished the prospect of Caesar as a *privatus,* a private citizen without the protection of imperium to shield him from criminal prosecution for his consular and proconsular illegalities.

Pompeius said little to counter their demands, except to remind the optimates that the entire tribunicial board had secured passage by the Tribal Assembly of a law validating Caesar's prerogative to canvass for the consulate in *absentia* while retaining his proconsulate. The optimates bristled at this.

"But Consul," Cato fumed, "your own sponsored legislation requires that *all* candidates for public office *must* be physically present in Roma in order to canvass. If a precedent of exception is made for Caesar, then why not for any other provincial governor?"

Over the hubbub of comments, Pompeius replied, "Marcus Cato, the answer to that resides within the tribunicial board." Pompeius smiled coyly. His meaning was certainly understood. However much the Senate optimates might complain and maneuver against Caesar, the tribunes committed to his interests would interpose their vetoes to thwart them.

Yet, there was something contrived about Pompeius' statements on Caesar's behalf. His apparent lack of conviction did not *inspire* conviction among the senators. But where he was peculiarly lethargic, almost indifferent to his partner's interests, Caesar's friends, and even many neutrals, extended much energy in their insistence that the tribunes' dispensation law should be upheld.

The optimates backed down, at least for the time being. I was certain, however, that during his consulate, Marcus Marcellus was bound to raise again the issue of Caesar's command; and I was less certain about Servius Sulpicius' disposition. Would he attempt to block his consular colleague? In any event, I would not be present in Roma for most of their consular term.

The Senate decreed that, in accordance with Pompeius' recent legislation approved by the Tribal Assembly, Marcus Bibulus and I were to be sent out to administer the respective provinces of Syria and Cilicia. Based on an earlier senatorial resolution, Pompeius' law specified an interval of five years between the holding of a public office and the imperium of a provincial command. It was a sound measure intended to rein in excessive competition for public office—in recent years the prime cause of the Republic's civil strife. The law further stipulated that those senators of consular and praetorian rank who had never held provincial governorships were to be given priority over all others.

I cannot speak for Bibulus, but I was nonplussed by the assignment. I was not particularly desirous of going out to a provincial governorship. It seemed like a second banishment, albeit this time in the service of the Republic. Also, the most dangerous part of Roma's imperium was the Eastern frontier, for Cilicia and Syria were most vulnerable to an expected Parthian invasion. I was flattered to be chosen for the task, and in all probability Bibulus was as well. Yet, I could not help but suspect that my absence from Roma was desired by some in the Senate.

Pompeius assured us that as soon as the two donated legions—his own and Caesar's—arrived in the City, they would be sent out to reinforce the Cilician-Syrian frontier. So Bibulus and I accepted our respective postings.

The last item on the Senate's agenda that day was the appointment of Faustus Cornelius Sulla as official curator of the Curia's reconstruction. Consul Pompeius spoke glowingly of his son-in-law's qualifications for the job. "His father, Lucius Sulla, restored peace, and law and order to the Republic after years of civil war. The Senate's ascendancy was validated by Sulla. Now, his son will continue the Dictator's legacy by rebuilding the devastated Curia Hostilia, the time-hallowed meeting place of the Conscript Fathers of the Senate."

Pompeius wisely did not mention the terror of Sulla's repression, the proscriptions and the confiscations that accompanied the Senate's restored supremacy in the Republic; nor did he mention his own subsequent efforts in undermining the Sullan settlement.

Nevertheless, the Senate approved Sulla's appointment, and he was allocated generous funds for the Curia's reconstruction. Young Sulla was a walking example of the power of a name among the optimates. Pompeius' gesture of nepotism was well founded. By the time of my departure for Cilicia in the following spring, Sulla had supervised the dismantling of the Curia's charred ruins and the laying of an expanded foundation for the new edifice. In the interim, the Senate would continue to convene in various other venues such as the Temple of Concord and the Portico of Pompeius' Theatre out at Mars Field. On that particular day, Consul Pompeius had convened the Senate in the Portico of his temple-theatre complex, an appropriate meeting place as he was, at the time, the Republic's savior. Statecraft, the gods, and theatrical dramatics are so often entwined in the Republic's service.

MY LATE DEPARTURE FOR CILICIA was partly attributable to contrary winter winds. I used the weather delays to arrange my affairs. Quintus was to accompany me as my chief legate. We agreed that you and your cousin would come out with us, the first time that the two of you had ever been abroad from Italia. Education and travel go hand in hand. Leaving Alexio at home for Terentia's and Tullia's protection, I planned on taking Tiro and Metrodorus from the household servants. So that you and your cousin could keep up with your lessons, I arranged for your tutor, Dionysius, the old Stoic disciple, to accompany us.

We were taking the newly elected quaestor, Lucius Mescinius Rufus and the military tribune, Quintus Fufidius. Besides your Uncle Quintus, there were three additional legates, Gaius Pomptinus—a former praetor from my consular year—Lucius Tullius, and Marcus Anneius. Complementing these capable men, there were two prefects, Quintus Lepta and Quintus Volusius.

Speaking with them, I outlined my intentions for an effective and honest provincial administration. However, by the comments and questions offered by each of them, even by my brother, I discerned that they had peculiarly acquisitive intentions toward the Cilicians. I surmised that I would need to be most circumspect.

Servius agreed with me. I asked him and Atticus and Caelius to write me regularly as I wanted to be kept apprised of developments in the Capital. Also, I insisted that Terentia and Tullia keep Dolabella at bay. They were not to enter into any semblance of a betrothal agreement without my approval or during my absence. Terentia fumed and Tullia was crest-fallen at this, but at least they agreed, albeit reluctantly.

By Maius, our entourage departed from Roma, but our journey to Brundisium was delayed because of Pomptinus' dalliance with a certain lady of easy virtue. Then the passage to Dyrrachium was quick and uneventful. Traveling overland, our party arrived at Athens, where I called upon various friends of Atticus.

It troubled me little to delay our arrival in Cilicia for the sake of philosophical discourse. Among the philosophers with whom I met was Patro, the head of the Athenian Epicurean society. Over an extravagant repast, we discussed the masterly poem, *De Rerum Natura—On the Nature of Things*—by the recently deceased poet, Lucretius.

An ardent follower of Epicurus, Lucretius had eloquently set these principles to verse. Several lines at the opening of Book II had a particular bearing upon the threatening situation between Caesar and Pompeius:

Men lost, confused, in hectic search for the right road; the strife of wits, the wars of precedence, the everlasting struggle, night and day, to win towards heights of wealth and power.

Patro asked me to use my influence in a particularly sensitive matter. The exiled politician, Gaius Memmius, the former patron of Lucretius, was at the time in possession of the dilapidated house which had once belonged to Epicurus. Memmius was believed to have had plans to demolish the house, but the Epicurean society wished to purchase it as a memorial to their founder.

I sent a letter off to Memmius. Though he may have had little regard, as I did for Epicureanism per se, notwithstanding that Lucretius had dedicated his poem to Memmius, I implored the exile to consider Patro's request. Unfortunately, I did not remain in Athens long enough to learn of the final disposition of the disputed house.

WE RESUMED OUR JOURNEY TO Cilicia, though the ominous words of Lucretius resonated in my thoughts. By mid-Quinctilis, we arrived at Laodicea, in the province of Asia. I arranged with the governor, Propraetor Minucius Thermus, for you and your cousin and Dionysius to be housed comfortably there. The uncertainties of the Eastern frontier caused me to reconsider my original intention of taking all three of you to Cilicia. Your uncle agreed that it was safer for you to remain in secure Roman territory. Though you and your cousin bristled at this change in plans, my word as Father, Uncle, and Proconsul prevailed.

Next, we traveled into the allied-kingdom of Galatia. King Deiotarus received and entertained us *regally*. Concerned about a probable Parthian invasion, he agreed to furnish about twelve thousand foot soldiers and horsemen to augment the two legions already garrisoned in Cilicia. I was grateful for his assistance.

Likewise, King Ariobarzanes, ruler of the adjacent client-kingdom of Cappadocia, met us as we crossed the frontier from Galatia into his own domain. The King paid his respects to the new Proconsul of Cilicia. He too was concerned about the security of his kingdom in the event of a Parthian invasion. However, he admitted that he was unable to make significant military contributions because his kingdom's finances were severely strapped.

Hearing this, I could not help but notice the shabby appearance of the King's retinue. Ariobarzanes explained that his plight was the result of indebtedness to various Roman financiers, especially to the previous quaestor of Cilicia, namely Marcus Brutus. The King was prepared to make a small payment toward the debt to Brutus, and I agreed, fully appreciating the fact that his pledge to respect Brutus' interests might preclude the use of the King's money for purchasing military stores and mercenaries. In all decency, given these circumstances, I could not anticipate from Cappadocia anything approaching the aid that King Deiotarus had pledged.

By the end of the month, with our arrival at Tarsus, the provincial capital, my official tenure as proconsul began. Inspecting the two legions stationed there, I was disturbed at their laxity. To remedy this, I instructed Quintus and the other legates to implement a vigorous program of military drill that lasted well into September.

In the meantime, I met with the town's leading citizens and familiarized myself with the records left by my predecessor, Appius Claudius. He and most of his staff had quit the province well before my arrival. In and of itself, this was not an unusual occurrence. However, he had left a legate, one Marcus Scaptius, to wait upon me. This man, of equestrian lineage, had a cunning fox's demeanor and a visage that went well with it. I consented to his request for a private meeting. What he had to tell me made me fully realize the complexities of a provincial proconsulate. Fairness and justice for the provincials would have to be tempered with circumspect diplomacy for the interests of Roman equites and officials.

Under the previous governor, Appius Claudius, Scaptius had tried to collect a debt from the people of Salamis, a town on the island of Cyprus. Since the island's annexation, it had been incorporated under the province of Cilicia for administrative purposes. Employing a troop of horse, Scaptius had besieged the town council within the walls of their curia. After several councilors had died of starvation, the council voted to make good on their obligation to Scaptius.

Repulsed at this brutal use of force to exact payment on a loan, I reprimanded Scaptius, and I forbade him to return to the island. He was willing to comply, but he told me that his cavalry troop was still in place in Salamis.

"Quintus Volusius!" I abruptly called for one of my prefects from an adjoining room. The prefect entered, his highly burnished doublet catching the oil light of the room. Closing the door behind him, he snapped to attention.

"You and Tribune Fufidius will take a cohort to the town of Salamis on the island of Cyprus. You will integrate into your command any forces you will find there. You will offer any and all assistance to the townspeople and, most particularly, to the town council. *Understood?*"

"Yes, Proconsul."

"Good! Leave on the earliest favorable tide. Now go." Yet, the prefect remained standing where he was, waiting for my attention. "You have questions, Volusius?"

"No, Proconsul. But while you were speaking with Marcus Scaptius, two representatives arrived from Salamis. They beg leave to speak with you."

Scaptius' face blanched. Assuming that the Salaminians had their own side to relate, I told Volusius to admit them.

The two men introduced themselves as Demetrios and Nestor. They were members of the Salamis town council. They spoke in *koine* Greek, while I responded in the polished, formal Greek that I had studied since my childhood. Their attire was clearly Greek. Each wore a linen *chiton* over which was draped a light *himation* and a *chlamys* of purple, indicative of their rank.

"Tell me about the loan that your people owe this man." Saying this, I indicated Scaptius, and the councilors recognized him.

They told me that their people were hard-pressed to repay the loan at the excessive interest rate of *forty-eight percent*. Incredulously, I asked them to repeat the figure, which they did. I was appalled at this rate because it was four times the norm, which I had intended to decree later in my tenure.

"Well?" I turned to Scaptius. He proceeded to explain that the loan had been originally contracted not in Salamis, but in Roma, in fact, during the year of my consulate. "That's quite unlikely," I retorted, "since, at the time, the Senate, in an attempt to halt the flow of gold and silver from Italia, had prohibited all loans to foreigners."

With smug satisfaction, Scaptius admitted, "Of course; that is why the interest rate was set at forty-eight percent and *not* twelve."

I was growing ever more suspicious about this bizarre story. Who was this Scaptius that he could finagle a loan in violation of the Senate's decree? Turning to Demetrios and Nestor, I asked, "What is the total of your debt?"

"One hundred six talents!" Nestor said.

"Actually, somewhat *more*," Scaptius interjected. "It's closer to *two hundred.*"

The Salaminians produced documents that confirmed their figure. Exasperated, Scaptius declared his willingness to drop the whole business. But I saw through this immediately. "You hope to have more success with my successor?" My challenge discomforted him. "Moreover, the interest owed will have increased by the time my tenure expires."

To prevent this, the Salaminians offered to deposit a portion of the loan in a temple in Tarsus. "I'll not allow that," I told them. "Your debt was illegally contracted at an exorbitant interest rate. Your case will be adjudicated by the Senate, but I will note that your offer to make a payment constitutes a legal tender."

Satisfied with my decision, the councilors thanked me and then departed. I reminded Volusius of his mission to Salamis. As Scaptius and I were again alone, he presented me with a scroll bearing the seal of Marcus Brutus. "This is addressed to you, but the quaestor left it in my charge. I was to give it to you *if* and *when* it should prove necessary." Scaptius was regaining his confidence.

Such a necessity has apparently presented itself, I thought as I broke the seal and began to read the revealing letter. Scaptius was merely the agent of Marcus Brutus; Brutus had originally negotiated the loan to Salamis. Cato, Brutus' uncle, and other leading men of the Senate, had given the Salaminian loan special and secret consideration, including the allowance of the forty-eight percent interest rate. Brutus urged me to do everything possible to further his interests, especially insofar as they were represented by Scaptius. The letter concluded with his certainty that I would remember my own partisanship with Cato and my renewed friendship with the former governor, Appius Claudius, Brutus' father-in-law. So much then, for Cato's probity, for Brutus' integrity, and the proffered friendship of Appius Claudius. I put the letter aside in utter disgust.

"Marcus Scaptius, you will return to Roma on the first available ship. You will tell Brutus and Cato and Appius Claudius that I will *not* be their agent to fleece the Salaminians. Upon my return, I will move that the Senate investigate this entire putrid business." He attempted to interrupt. *"Please! No protests. No recriminations.* This is my last word on the matter. Now get out of my sight!"

Without a word, Scaptius withdrew from my quarters.

I wrote to Atticus about the Salaminian business. When he wrote back, he criticized what he called my *temporizing posture*. He found my indulgent concern for the Salaminians to be sharply inconsistent with my proxy purchase of Milo's properties.

I suspected that the Milo affair was probably a matter of general knowledge among the Roman business community. Apparently, the freedman, Philotimus was too closely linked with the Cicero household to make a real estate purchase without arousing suspicions of my own involvement.

LETTERS FROM SERVIUS AND CAELIUS satisfied my hunger for political news from Roma. The elections had been held without delay or interruption. The anti-Caesarians scored a victory with the election of Gaius Claudius Marcellus to the consulate. He was a cousin of Marcus Marcellus, the incumbent Consul, and he was equally committed to thwarting Caesar's plans. His colleague was Lucius Aemilius Lepidus Paullus, older brother to the former interrex, Marcus Lepidus. Paullus' sympathies were said to be favorably disposed to Caesar. Servius could not speculate on how successful either man would be in checking the other. However, as in recent years, most of the newly elected tribunes were pro-Caesarians. So, it seemed that the New Year's political maneuvering would follow the same pattern: consular proposals to discuss terminating Caesar's command would be offset by tribunicial vetoes.

One of the newly elected tribunes was Gaius Scribonius Curio, whose eponymous, deceased father had once been a leading optimate. As young Curio had been a legate of Caesar, it would not be difficult to gauge his political stance.

Nevertheless, there was a new twist. A censorial year would begin in Januarius, and the two elected Censors were Appius Claudius Pulcher, my proconsular predecessor, and Lucius Calpurnius Piso, my deceased son-in-law's kinsman. Pulcher had been most outspoken in his intentions to purge the Senate of all men too fervently aligned with Caesar.

Concerning Pompeius, Servius wrote that the Magnus was again in his inimitable Olympian aloofness, sequestered at Alba Longa. At the same time, his and Caesar's donated legions, having finally arrived earlier in the year, were encamped near Brundisium. There was no movement in the Senate to send them off to the Eastern frontier. Servius speculated that Bibulus and I would have to fend for ourselves in gathering troops. Apparently, the two donated legions were purposely being detained in Italia.

Caelius' letter repeated much of what Servius had written, except that he added the news of his own election to the aedilate. Intending to sponsor spectacular games during his term, he asked me to hunt down and capture as many panthers as there were in Cilicia and then ship them off to Roma. *Could he have had any notion that I had far more important matters at hand?* Namely, the Parthians.

Dispatches from Proconsul Bibulus reported that while he confined himself to his headquarters at Antioch, all military field operations were left to his legate, Gaius Cassius. It had been Cassius' resourcefulness that had secured Syria against a Parthian invasion in the aftermath of Crassus' disaster. Now, it appeared that, with minimal forces, Cassius, in the mold of classical Roman commanders, had checked the Parthians from making inroads into the Eastern provinces—at least for the current campaign season.

I wrote to the Senate complaining that the legions in Syria and Cilicia were in dire need of reinforcements in order to safeguard the precarious frontier. As a further precautionary move, and to season the Cilician legions, I undertook a campaign against various tribes of brigands who had fortified themselves in the Amanus Mountains east of Issus. We besieged their mountain fortress called Pindenissus. After several weeks they capitulated. The legionaries saluted me with the honorary title of "*Imperator*." I remarked to Quintus, who had distinguished himself in the campaign, that Issus was the site of a crucial victory won by Alexander of Macedon some three hundred years earlier. "He was a far better general than either *you* or *I*," I flippantly quipped.

The captives from the campaign were sold into slavery, the proceeds amounting to two and a quarter million sesterces. I deposited this sum and a part of the campaign booty in my name and in Quintus' in the hands of Roman bankers at Ephesus. The rest of the spoils were divided among the legionaries, the officers, and the Galatian auxiliaries.

With the end of the campaign season, I had Quintus and Pomptinus billet the legions in winter quarters near Tarsus. After sending Anneius to administer Cyprus, I took Tullius, Mescinus, and Tiro with me as I conducted a tour throughout western Cilicia, holding assizes and dispensing justice. Quintus discharged the same duties in the eastern half of the province.

I reported our campaign to the Senate, rather immodestly, and requested the honor of a triumph. It had come to my attention that Bibulus had also submitted claims for a triumph, and he, as in the days of his consulate, had never even ventured forth from his quarters.

The first half of my proconsular term ended as December gave way to Januarius. I was anxious to return home, but I had at least six months ahead of me.

Omniscient Narrative

THE CHARCOAL EMBERS GLOW HOT in the brazier, and the heat it gives is comforting, pervading the dining cubicle on a cold, damp January night. Gaius Scribonius Curio rotates his cup, watching the watered wine swirl about as the scent of cinnamon and cloves ascends to his nostrils.

"Roman winters, with all their wind and rain, are nothing like the ones up in Gaul." Curio takes a swallow of wine. "Ah, that's better! It takes the chill away."

He is reclined on a dining couch, and the table before him is well appointed with a rich assortment of preserved meats and pickled fish, various cheeses and olives. The years of military service in Gaul have hardened him so that he no longer has the appearance of a male plaything.

The two women, who recline on couches to his left and right, might well wonder if he is still on intimate terms with Marcus Antonius. If so, it is as an equal partner. Curio is muscular in a compact way. His hazel hair is close-cropped, and his hazel eyes are like candle flames in the oil-lamp light of the dining room. He has grown handsomer in the years since Fulvia and Clodia Pulchra had last seen him. Despite the winter chill, he has discarded his toga. His crimson tunic reveals well defined, muscular legs and arms and a broad, sinewy neck.

Curio had been one of the *cubs* in Clodius Pulcher's *wolf pack*, just below Marcus Antonius in prominence. Both women remember this.

"I know how dear Publius was to both of you," Curio says without the least trace of the irony that would have rung in Cicero's voice had he said the same. Fulvia and Clodia nod in acknowledgement. "When the news reached us, we were hard pressed by the great revolt. You know, for a time, I seriously doubted that I'd ever see Roma—or either of you again." Curio takes another swallow of wine.

"Was it *Roma* or *us* that you were more anxious about, Gaius?" The question teasingly comes from Clodia.

Curio is diplomatic. "Can there be a Roma without Clodia Pulchra and Fulvia Bambalio?"

"Ah, well said, Gaius!" Clodia titters. "But be candid. *Which* of us were you more anxious to see? The *widow*? Or the bereaved *sister*?"

"Oh, Clodia! Stop!" Fulvia interrupts. "You're embarrassing him; and it's much too early for any guest of ours to be embarrassed."

"Very well then, Fulvia. No embarrassing questions for Gaius Curio, at least not until he's had more wine." Saying this, Clodia beckons to a slave to refill Curio's cup. Curio notices the ease with which Clodia commands in Fulvia's house; Fulvia is altogether complacent about it.

"Gaius, I'm convinced that your visit is for more than just socializing with old friends." Fulvia teasingly bites into a date. "Is there not some political purpose that brings you to Roma?"

Curio coughs over his refilled wine cup. "A shrewd observation, Fulvia, well said!"

Clodia reinforces her sister-in-law's question. "No doubt, there *is* a political purpose in your visit. Forgive me if I embarrass you, Gaius Curio."

Curio sighs and puckers his lips thoughtfully. "You're both right, and Clodia, you've *not* succeeded in embarrassing me. You see, Caesar has sent me for a special mission. I'm to assess the general mood and sentiment toward him. I've been elected Tribune of the Plebs, not just for *their* benefit, but more importantly to safeguard Caesar's interests. That's my political purpose."

"But you're not telling us everything. What *else* is there?" Clodia looks at Curio in a sideways glance.

Fulvia speaks before Curio can reply. "You want to be Tribune of the Plebs for Caesar's benefit. In recent years he's had to have many tribunes oversee his interests."

"But the most famous, or some would say, *infamous,* was Publius Clodius Pulcher." Curio knows that he has hooked the two women. "Don't imagine that I would want the tribunate entirely to serve Caesar's purposes. I want it for myself as well. I want the mob in my grip; I want to be able to wield it against the Senate. Now, Publius Clodius was well connected—three Pulchra sisters, the most prominent being in our present company." He nods in Clodia's direction, and she smiles graciously at him. "And he was well married to Fulvia Bambalio, granddaughter and grand-niece of the Gracchi, the People's martyred heroes." He pauses enough to observe both women beaming in delight. Then, with tongue-in-cheek, he adds, "I hope I'm not *embarrassing* either of you."

Fulvia and Clodia exchange a jaded smirk. *Can Curio know of or even infer the bond that has grown between them?* They readily infer that their guest has offered marriage and that he sees both of them as equally desirable for his political purposes.

As if hearing their thoughts, Curio says, "It's a pity that we Romans espouse monogamously. Otherwise, you'd both be more than suitable for me and my designs. But as it is, though you both value your independence, you, Fulvia, have young children who would benefit by having a step-father; and you, Clodia, widow of the highly esteemed Metellus Celer, would you consider marriage an *endowment* or a *hindrance*? Well, neither of you needs to answer now. I propose that you both think about it, and perhaps over the winter we all might reminisce about our beloved Publius."

Clodia and Fulvia laugh, fully realizing that Curio is in earnest. Composing herself, Clodia says to him, "Have more wine, Gaius Curio."

"Yes," Fulvia agrees, "for the night is yet young."

Cicero's Respublica

The winter at Cilicia passed uneventfully. There were no crises from within the province or challenges from without. In particular, the Syrian frontier remained quiet as the dreaded Parthian invasion failed to materialize. My letters to Servius, to Marcus Varro, to Lucius Piso, and others were full of entreaties for them to prevent the extension of my tenure and to expedite the appointment of a successor by summer. By that time, I would have completed one year of provincial service. I deemed it an adequate term.

In response to Caelius' urgent requests for Cilician panthers, I sardonically wrote that conditions in the province were so tranquil that all the panthers had fled to neighboring Caria and Lycia because they alone were being preyed upon. In all truth, I was loath to organize any hunting expeditions as they would have been an unnecessary burden to impose upon the provincials. Not only in this, but in all other logistical matters it was my policy to impose no requisitions beyond the basic minimum for food and shelter. More often than not, we slept out in the open rather than quarter ourselves in private homes, even though it would have been our prerogative to do so.

With the coming of spring, I had Quintus and the other legates put the legions through conditioning drills and maneuvers. The change in season could very well bring with it a Parthian attack. However, Proconsul Bibulus wrote me that the Syrian frontier was quiet. In fact, he passed on to me the rumors he had heard about dynastic strife within the Parthian royal family. If there was any truth to these, it could account for their military inactivity on the borderlands.

I received news that a quaestor, Coelius Caldus, would be assigned the province effective on his arrival by mid-summer. Relieved though I was, remaining in Cilicia until Junius or Quinctilis proved to be interminable. Quintus emphatically insisted on returning with me. So, as soon as Caldus arrived, I left my quaestor, Mescinus and the legate Tullius to brief him. Writing to Anneius and Volusius, I charged them to remain in Cyprus until Caldus ordered otherwise. As Gaius Pomptinus had already departed in Martius with my consent, our return party consisted of Quintus, Fufidius, and Lepta, Tiro and Metrodorus, my twelve lictors with their cumbersome fasces, and various attendants who served my officers.

Before starting out, I had written you and your cousin, informing you to expect our imminent arrival in Laodicea. I paid my respects to King Deiotarus when we passed through Galatia. Then, after a brief sojourn in Laodicea, we traveled on to Miletus. From there we sailed across the Aegean Sea, disembarking at Athens. We continued overland to Patrae on the Corinthian Gulf.

There Tiro, who had been ailing since our departure from Tarsus, fell ill with some form of ague. He was confined to bed, and I remained with him, hoping that he would quickly recover, especially as Metrodorus was so exacting in his ministrations. However, an anxious impatience to return to Italia soon overwhelmed me.

Making every possible arrangement for Tiro's convalescence, including leaving my physician to care for him, I continued the homeward voyage. While waiting at Dyrrachium for a ship to take us across to Italia, I wrote to Tiro. Inquiring after his health, I urged him to make no attempt to travel until he had sufficiently recovered. It was during this time that I resolved to manumit him once we were all in Roma.

Due to our delay at Patrae, we did not set foot on Italian soil until two months after quitting Cilicia, landing at Brundisium by mid-September. I immediately dispatched letters to Roma to announce my return. Though it was my intention to remain at Gaius Maenius' house and await responsive letters, I gave leave to my officers to return to Roma. Fufidius and Lepta were gratified by my indulgence. Quintus, however, was reluctant to return to Pomponia and renewed quarreling.

The familial letters that I had received while in Cilicia were static and perfunctory. Terentia complained about her pains in the joints, while Tullia pined for Dolabella. Pomponia's letters to Quintus, however, were another matter. My brother had shared these with me. They were filled with recriminations against Quintus for *these, those, and sundry other* slights and offenses. No wonder he was not anxious to return to Roma, though he had been so adamant against remaining in Cilicia. How painful it must have been for him to be so torn.

Returning to Roma or remaining with me for awhile in Brundisium—I left the choice up to him. After about a week, he decided to return. I saw him and his son off from Maenius's house.

Within a day or so after their departure, letters began to arrive from Roma. *What tidings they brought!*

"Tata, I've married Dolabella."
Almost the first item in Tullia's letter was her marriage! Fates be damned!
"I know Mother and I promised to wait, but I could not help myself."
Oh Tullia, had I known that you were so weak, I would have taken you with me to the East and left you with Marcus and Quintus in Laodicea.
"Please forgive me, Tata, for going back on my word to you. Can we come down to visit you at Brundisium? Or will you be returning home soon?"
So much for Tullia. Now Terentia was almost philosophical about it. *"They love each other, Marcus. What's done is done and you must accept it as I have."* She offered no apology or defense for disregarding my warning and my insistence about forestalling Dolabella until my return. Writing to them, I told them to meet me at Tusculum in a week's time. Hopefully, my journey up the Appian Road would not take long; as I was anticipating a triumph for my victory over Cilician brigands, I dared not enter Roma, preferring instead to remain at Tusculum.

Gaius Maenius attempted to comfort me in my angst, but not having marriageable children of his own he could not fully relate to my plight; and you, my son, you held your peace and kept your distance from me. No doubt you must have feared that my umbrage against your sister and your mother might be directed at you. My memory fails me, but if I targeted you, I was wrong, and I now apologize for it.

The political news distracted me somewhat from my domestic worries. Servius related that before becoming my son-in-law, Dolabella had attempted to prosecute Appius Claudius for extortion during his Cilician proconsulate. This prosecution was certainly justifiable, especially in view of the Salaminian affair. But at a time when the Pulchers and I were attempting a rapprochement, it would have been highly impolitic for my then prospective son-in-law to have prosecuted my predecessor, especially as Appius was then Censor-elect.

Fortunately, the whole business had come to naught. Appius' friends in the religious collegia persuaded Dolabella to drop the suit.

Their inducement was Dolabella's appointment to a vacancy on the Board of Fifteen Custodians of the Sibylline Oracles. Religiously, Dolabella would have little use for this post, but, if my assessment of his mercenary character was accurate, he would exploit it for all it was worth politically.

Concerning Appius Claudius, Servius almost anticipated my question. His letter went on to describe Appius' draconian efforts to expel Caesarians from the Senate on the grounds of moral or financial turpitude. The expulsions would have been even more severe had he not been checked by his censorial colleague, Lucius Piso.

All men and all initiatives associated with Caesar were fair game. As Censor, Claudius attempted to purge the Senate, and Domitius Ahenobarbus continually called for Caesar's proconsular termination. In a demonstration against Caesar's prerogatives, Consul Marcellus ordered the public flogging of a Gaul from the colony of Novum Comum who claimed to have been granted Roman citizenship by Caesar. The victim was the Senate's surrogate for Caesar himself.

Consul Lepidus Paullus was generally ineffective in checking his colleague's militancy. This was probably due to his ceaseless energies directed at restoring, no doubt with funds from Caesar, the Aemilian Basilica, which had been constructed by the Consul's ancestors. This project and Faustus Sulla's reconstruction of the Curia Hostilia were the Forum's major building projects, Servius observed ironically, as the optimates vigorously sought to deconstruct Caesar's power.

The proof of this could be clearly seen in the results of the consular election. Two staunch anti-Caesarians were elected: Lucius Cornelius Lentulus Crus and another of the Claudii Marcelli, Gaius, brother and cousin to consuls of the last two years. The new tribunicial board included three prominent members: Marcus Antonius, the nephew of my consular colleague, and Quintus Cassius Longinus, cousin of that Cassius who had secured the Syrian frontier. While these two were ardent Caesarians, Lucius Caecilius Metellus was committed to the optimates.

In an odd post-script, Servius mentioned that Hortensius, the last of the oligarchs of my consular year, had passed on. He had lived in ailing retirement for several years. Now, as the Republic teetered on the brink of a new crisis, the Fates consigned him to an ultimate retirement. I was saddened by his death, and yet I envied him.

Atticus reported on himself, on his wife, and on my ward, Publilia. He remarked that Publilia was growing into a lovely, nubile young woman.

On financial matters, he reported that my affairs were well in order, though I would have to arrange a dowry for Tullia. Generally, however, credit and the money supply were beginning to tighten. This, he felt, was an ominous indication of the business community's anticipation of civil war.

Not since my consulate had conditions been so conducive to civil war. The developing crisis in the Republic was well expressed by Marcus Caelius. In his letter, he observed that the basic issue was that Gnaeus Pompeius and his optimate friends in the Senate were determined to prevent Gaius Caesar's election to the consulate unless he first surrendered his army and his provinces. But clearly Caesar realized that he could not survive if he relinquished his imperium.

Caelius characterized the triumvirs' relationship as a love affair, a scandalous union, degenerated into covert backbiting and edging inexorably to civil war. Caelius was uncertain, as he surmised that I was, as to which course to take. He had ties of obligation and friendship with the Caesarians, particularly with Curio, Antonius, and Dolabella. Yet, while he loved the Republic, he hated the oligarchs and their optimate minions.

Displaying a political sophistication far beyond his years, Caelius reasoned that in such circumstances as then confronted the Republic, it behooved a man to take the more respectable side so long as the struggle was purely political and not by force of arms. However, if it should degenerate into actual fighting, then he should choose the stronger side and reckon the safer course the better.

The stronger side? The safer side? In the present crisis, Caelius inferred that Pompeius would have the support of the Senate and the propertied citizens, while those who were fearful and had small hope for the future will espouse Caesar, whose legions were incomparably superior.

I read and re-read these letters and pondered them as we made our way to Tusculum. What were we going to as our coaches bounced along the Appian Road? You and I and half the lictors were in one coach and the other six were in the second coach. I had spent a year in Cilicia bracing for a Parthian invasion that never came. Now, I was journeying so close to the Republic's seat of power where ceaseless debates and intrigues appeared more and more ominously to be portents of an irrepressible armed conflict.

In the event of civil war, I knew that I would support the Senate, and therefore Pompeius. However, during the senatorial debates and during all public discourse, what posture was I to assume? After all, I was under obligation to both Caesar and Pompeius.

Arriving at Tusculum, I decided to use my proconsular status and my expectation of a triumph to absent myself from Roma, from the Senate, and from the raging controversy.

Omniscient Narrative

"This measure will force them to line up—the warmongers against the olive-branch bearers." Gaius Scribonius Curio is explicating the tribunicial proposal that he is preparing for presentation to the Senate. He paces the tiled floor of the atrium of Fulvia's Aventine house. Having married her earlier in his term, he had decided that her house, renowned as the former residence of her grand-father, the popularist hero, Gaius Gracchus, ought to be their primary residence. As Tribune, he could not have desired a more fitting domicile.

Marcus Antonius and Quintus Cassius, tribunes-elect for the ensuing year, sit at a marble table where they have been listening to their host. Neither man is comforted by what he hears.

"The oligarchs won't accept it," Antonius offers bluntly, "and I don't think that Pompeius will be willing to make any such concessions."

"Yes, I agree," Curio admits, "but the majority *will* accept it because they're the ones who don't want war."

Quintus Cassius, hard, lean, chiseled-face elder brother of Gaius Cassius, hero of the Syrian border, savior of Crassus' decimated legions, snorts, "What about the minority that won't accept it?"

Curio leans in toward both men. "Let them be seen for all of their intransigence. Something's going to break and *soon!* If not during the few weeks left of my term, then it will surely happen during yours."

Publius Dolabella sits a few paces away from the table. He is positioned in such a way that a slight turn of the head will take the sight of the men from his eyes and instead fill them with the image of Fulvia and Clodia reclining on couches on the other side of the atrium. So far he has not heard anything touching upon his particular concerns, and with increased frequency he has turned to Curio's flame-haired wife, large with child, and her raven-haired companion who has been taking his measure with her ebony eyes.

Clodia Pulchra smiles her forever imperceptible smile. She wonders if Dolabella is happy with Cicero's daughter. Is he still philandering with Antonius' wife? Dolabella has a son, she remembers. Well, the child is better off staying with his mother. She looks to her side at her sister-in-law.

Fulvia has been methodically rubbing her pregnant belly, all the while watching Marcus Antonius. Several times, she has caught his eye. She has seen him smirk, no doubt at her hardened nipples showing through her soft stola. Of all the *cubs* in Publius Clodius' *wolf pack*, she remembers Antonius had always been the handsomest, the most desirable. Marrying Curio had been a gesture of surrogate-paternal security for her children by Clodius—Claudia was now seven, and young Publius was almost six. Curio had realized her motive from the outset, as she had known that his was entirely politically self-serving. Even so, she had dutifully submitted to his conjugal embraces, pleasurable and satisfying as they were; unshielded, unprotected, she had promptly conceived.

Dolabella turns back to the men. Attempting to turn the discussion toward his concerns, he asks, "Does Caesar have a definite policy about debts?"

The men look at him stunned, for his question is a non-sequitur to their discussion about protecting Caesar's imperium and avoiding civil war.

"If—or rather, *when,* Caesar enters into a second consulate, no doubt then he'll address the debt issue." Curio is tolerant. No doubt Dolabella's question, reflecting his own insolvency, was raised to distract his own attention from the women. "We might better ask if Caesar has an alternative to my proposal." Curio addresses this to the tribunes-elect.

"Yes," Antonius replies, "he has what he's calling an *ultimate compromise*. Quintus and I will present it in the Senate after the first of the New Year—that is, Curio, if your proposal is voted down." Antonius smiles and winks at his former lover.

Clodia is thinking: *If war comes, my brothers will be on opposite sides. Appius will go with the Senate, and Gaius will stay with Caesar. Great Mother of the gods, protect them both. Publius, beloved Publius, which side would you have joined?*

The child in Fulvia's womb stirs and stretches. The mother grimaces in discomfort and pats her belly in circular motions, thinking all the while: *What an uncertain time to be with child.*

"SEMPRONIA, DO YOU REALLY BELIEVE your son will remain loyal to Caesar if it comes to civil war?" Servilia sponges the beads of perspiration from her ample bosom. A towel is draped upon her chair.

Sempronia replies, "Most assuredly. He's invested so much of his time and energy in these last nine years. He's made his name and his fortune with Caesar." Seated across from Servilia, she pats the sweat from her supple arms and legs.

"His *fortune* perhaps," Aurelia Orestilla interjects, "but he already had his name. He owes that to his father, *not* to Caesar." The widow of Lucius Catilina lies prone on a low, towel-draped stone shelf. Beads of perspiration cover her body from shoulders, down the back, over her buttocks and legs.

Orestilla's daughter, Flavia, sits against the warm wall near her mother. Her eyes are closed in seeming indifference to their conversation. She breathes deeply of the myrrh scented steam and pours a ladle of warm water over her taut, supple torso. Seated next to her on the same shelf and leaning against the same warm wall is Pompeia, the former wife of Gaius Caesar. She too is lulled into a thoroughly relaxed state by the scented humidity of Servilia's commodious bathing chamber with its jets of warm water alternating with steam. The very tiles on the floor and on the walls retain the room's enervating warmth. The women have become intimately attached over the last several years. They are linked by their noble blood, by their marriages to prominent senators, and by their varying degrees of antipathy to Gaius Julius Caesar.

Servilia, blonde beauty in her early fifties, had been his mistress until their falling-out on the eve of Caesar's departure for Gaul. Pompeia of the bronze-colored hair, her pale complexion now rendered pink by the sultry air, is in her mid-forties. She had been his second wife, even while his affair with Servilia consumed him. She had been the expedient victim, Caesar's cast-off wife because she had not been above suspicion in the Good Goddess scandal.

Orestilla had been wife to Catilina, Caesar's former associate, before Caesar betrayed him. She is in her early fifties; her complexion is fair, and her reddish-gold hair has been treated to forestall the graying effects of aging.

Sempronia, a sturdy, big-boned beauty in her late forties, with hair like golden wheat, had once been wife to the oligarch, Decimus Brutus, and mistress to Lentulus Sura, a co-conspirator of Catilina. Caesar had tried but failed to save Lentulus from execution. Disciplined by her tradition-bound husband, Sempronia, with her son's connivance, had had her revenge upon the elder Brutus.

And Flavia—in her late twenties, she is the youngest of the women. Daughter of Orestilla and step-daughter of Catilina, she is very pretty with a voluptuously full figure. Her oval face is framed with long, dark hair. She is quiet and serene, but internally there is a seething passion born of memories of things that her mother has suspected for many years. Like Orestilla, she hates Caesar for betraying Catilina.

Pompeia rouses herself from her lethargy and says, "Titus has quit Caesar for good. He says his services were never fully appreciated. Caesar is selfish and capricious in his rewards."

Orestilla raises her head and looks at Pompeia. "As Caesar's former wife, you could certainly attest to his selfishness."

The barb, as intended, hits a nerve with Pompeia. The Good Goddess affair and its aftermath had been a monument to Caesar's expedient selfishness. But she recovers sufficiently to offer, "My husband has ties with Pompeius that far outweigh his services to Caesar."

"Of course he does, dearest," agrees Sempronia, "that's why Titus Labienus will stick with the Senate as long as Pompeius does." Then turning to Servilia, she asks, "Servilia, what about your sons?"

"Marcus Brutus hates Pompeius, as you all know, and you also know why. But my Marcus sees beyond personal antipathies and personal loyalties. For him, and for Marcus Silanus, it's the Republic that matters."

Orestilla now sits up and modestly covers her large, pendulous breasts with a towel. "Servilia dear, can the same be said of Cato? I'm sorry, I did not mean to mention...."

"But of course you did!" Servilia snaps. "Yes, my obnoxious half-brother hates both Caesar and Pompeius. He's crafty and cagey, though. He'll use Pompeius as indeed will the entire Senate so that in the Republic's name and for the Republic's good Caesar will be destroyed."

Pompeia's interest is piqued. "What about your daughters' husbands? Where do they stand?"

Servilia's daughters, born of her second husband, Decimus Junius Silanus, have contracted good marriages with the Republic's noble families. "Gaius Cassius will hold with the Republic," Servilia confidently asserts, "despite his cousin, the tribune-elect, who's supporting Caesar. About Lepidus and Vatia, I can't be sure. From what my daughters have told me, they'll try to remain neutral, if the oligarchs afford them that luxury."

Orestilla offers a compliment. "All of your children have made good marital alliances. They're a credit to you."

"Yes, I believe that's true." Turning her attention to Flavia, Servilia asks, "And you, my dear, is there not some young man upon whom you've set your eyes?"

Sullenly, yet politely, Flavia responds, "Servilia, my step-father's notoriety has overshadowed me; neither the optimates nor the popularists are desirous of marrying their sons to Lucius Catilina's step-daughter; to the optimates, he was a renegade patrician; to the popularists, he was an abysmal failure."

"*Bah!* Your step-father and the man I loved were partners in a bold enterprise that could have been for Roma's benefit," Sempronia impulsively asserts. "I don't care a fig about Catilina's or Lentulus' detractors. He wanted to break the Senate's strangle-hold on offices. It's the very thing Caesar is aiming for."

Servilia is irritated and Pompeia grimaces in discomfort at this laudation for Caesar. Sempronia speaks on. "Aurelia Orestilla, if you agree, your daughter would bring honor and beauty to my son as his wife. Flavia, he would be good for you, and good *to* you. Well, what do you think?"

Orestilla and Flavia look at each other coyly. The mother asks, "But Sempronia, would Decimus be agreeable?"

"*Agreeable?* You needn't concern yourself about that, Orestilla. You see, my son has always been respectful of his Mother's wishes." Sempronia smirks, remembering what she dares not mention.

"I know Decimus," Flavia admits, "but will he be more *your son* than he would be *my husband?*"

Sempronia laughs. Rising from her couch and wrapping a towel around herself, she stands between Flavia and Orestilla. "*That's* up to you, my dear. I'm sure your mother and I could both advise you on that score." Sempronia smiles cunningly.

"Amazing, isn't it?" Orestilla opines. "We may well be on the verge of civil war; yet here we are planning our children's marriage."

Sempronia extends her left hand to Orestilla and her right to Flavia. The mother and daughter clasp hands with her. The three women nod and smile at each other.

Servilia raises a cup of watered wine and toasts them, "To marriage, and the *power* to be gained by it!"

Pompeia also raises her cup as well, but her toast is laced with sarcasm. "In view of developing conditions, Flavia, I hope you'll not become a *widow* before you become a *bride*."

Cicero's Respublica

When Terentia arrived at Tusculum she was accompanied by Alexio and three maidservants. During my absence her joint pains had so increased in their intensity that she had to walk with a birch cane. I was very sorry for her discomfort.

She was happy to see me safely home from my proconsular sojourn. We kissed and embraced most affectionately, and our conversation was quite pleasant. But it turned sour and noisy when Tullia's marriage came up. Terentia offered no apologies for failing to delay the nuptials until my return. This, far more than her unreliability, unnerved me. Our conversation was an in-person replication of what we had written in our exchange of letters, and it would serve no purpose to replicate it here.

We parted in anger, Terentia returning to Roma, while I remained at Tusculum.

A few days later, Tullia and her new husband arrived. I lavished fountains of affection upon her, despite my continued annoyance with her rash entry into this marriage. Toward Dolabella I was reservedly polite, even when I expressed my disappointment at his inability or unwillingness to hold off the marriage until my return. Naturally, we discussed the dowry. He was pleased with what I offered, but disappointed that it would have to be rendered in installments.

Over a light supper, we discussed his future plans—domestically and politically. He avowed that he was totally devoted to Tullia. I pondered if he had ever had such devotion to his first wife. About his son from that marriage he said little, except that little Publius and Tullia were quite fond of each other. Touching on political matters, he was committed to Caesar, even if matters escalated to civil war.

"But for you, Father," he assured me, "you need have no concern. My loyalties should not compromise you at all."

I was dubious about this as I inwardly cringed at being addressed by him as "Father." When they left to return to Roma, I gave them both my blessing, though my reservations remained unmoved.

Several days later, Atticus and Servius visited. In the Senate, Servius told me, there was no discussion at all about a triumph either for my Cilician or for Bibulus' proconsulate. The issue towering over all was Caesar's Gallic command and how or when or if it was to be terminated. Something was in the offing from Tribune Curio, just what Servius was unable to say.

Atticus had visited clients in the northern municipalities, and he had conferred with Caesar's chief money men, Balbus and Oppius. There was bedrock support for Caesar's interests among them. Though these communities did not want war, they also were not prepared to antagonize Caesar.

These developments did not bode at all well for the Republic's peace or stability. To my great surprise and pleasure, Gnaeus Pompeius visited me. His opinion was that Bibulus and I waited in vain for triumphs that would never be celebrated.

I said to him, "Gnaeus, what if Caesar refuses to relinquish his command and insists on standing in absentia for the consulate?"

He looked at me as an ominous, foreboding darkness came upon his strong, handsome face. "What if my son tried to beat me with a stick? Law and tradition bear heavily on the rights and prerogatives of the fathers, do they not, Marcus Cicero?"

Pompeius' answer was pregnant with meaning. He saw himself, probably because of his senior age, as a father figure to Caesar. If Pompeius could not brook a junior partner who had become his equal, if not indeed his superior in conquests and in fame, then it was utterly unrealistic that Caesar should cling to a subordinate status that he had unequivocally outgrown.

This was the crux of the issue dividing them, and on it the war-mongering optimates hoped to use Pompeius to bring Caesar to heel. Apparently, it mattered not to them if the Republic were rent by civil war.

Pompeius and many in the Senate were unquestioningly receptive to Titus Labienius' appraisal of Caesar's legions. The erstwhile tribune who had defiantly enjoined me from addressing the people on the last day of my consulate, had recently returned to Roma, having served as Caesar's chief legate since the beginning of the Gallic proconsulate. Both in and out of the Senate, Labienus berated his former commander and spoke disparagingly of Caesar's legions. They were worn out after nearly ten years of rigorous, incessant campaigns. The legions would most likely, in Labienus' opinion, *not* follow Caesar if he challenged the Senate's authority.

Labienus' defection from Caesar and his return to his first commander and patron, Pompeius, was a significant loss for Caesar and a noteworthy gain for the Senate. This and his negative pronouncements fueled the optimates' ire against Caesar and encouraged them in their resolve to terminate his command.

"But Gnaeus, has not Caesar been given by law an extended imperium and the right to canvass in absentia?" I asked this question fully anticipating his answer.

"True enough, Marcus," he smugly responded. "But remember, during my emergency consulate, the Senate and the People's Assembly extended my Spanish proconsulate for five years. Caesar's extension, on the other hand, was contingent upon the completion of his subjugation of the Gauls. Many in the Senate, notably Domitius Ahenobarbus and

Marcus Cato, are making the case that Caesar's work is completed. So, it's time to appoint a new proconsul, and Caesar should therefore return to Roma, as a *privatus*, and then canvass for a second consulate."

"You fully realize, of course, that he'll never reduce himself to a private citizen and expose himself to the optimates' prosecution?" Again, I posed the question anticipating his answer; but instead he kept silent. "What are you prepared to do?"

"Again, Marcus, what would you expect me to do if my son tried to beat me with a stick?"

There was nothing to infer except that Pompeius would act in concert with the Senate in attempting to curtail Caesar's power.

I reviewed this conversation with Caelius when he visited me. Caelius observed that there was a growing sanguinary attitude among the optimates, while the popularists were becoming militantly entrenched in their defense of Caesar's interests. Senators were being driven to take sides, and the number of neutrals was diminishing rapidly.

"Marcus," I said to him so despondently, "if civil war comes, no matter which side wins, the Republic will lose. We'll have either a dictatorship of the optimates or a tyranny of the popularists with proscriptions and confiscations following upon them. The horrors of Marius and Sulla and Cinna will afflict us yet again. You'll see as an adult what you were too young to remember happening when you were a child."

The weeks passed into December as I waited out events at Tusculum. Here I insulated myself from the swirling vortex of political strife. Yet, my villa was close enough to Roma for me to be kept promptly informed of the latest developments.

Omniscient narrative

"Conscript Fathers of the Senate, to break this impasse that threatens to divide the Roman people into warring factions, I offer for your consideration this proposal."

Tribune Gaius Scribonius Curio has the Senate's complete attention. Not a sound is heard in the cella of the Temple of Concord where the Senate has convened. Presiding Consul Gaius Claudius Marcellus sits sternly on the raised curule chair.

"To facilitate Gaius Caesar's relinquishment of his proconsular imperium and to forestall any hostile movement against him, I propose that both he and Proconsul Gnaeus Pompeius Magnus relinquish command of their legions and their provinces at the same time"—an outraged hubbub emerges from the diehard oligarchs—"by a date to be set by the Senate."

The presiding Consul recognizes various dissenters; the oligarchs' trio of Ahenobarbus, Bibulus, and Cato are the most prominent among them. Each in turn inveighs against the Tribune's proposal. They are followed by reasonable men who insist on putting the question to a vote. Marcius Philippus, Lentulus Spinther, Lucius Piso, Servilius Vatia, and Marcus Lepidus convince Consul Marcellus to call for a division.

The resulting tally shows the Senate to be heavily dominated by moderation—three hundred and seventy senators approve the tribune's proposal. But the bellicose minority of twenty-two obstinate die-hards remonstrates against the vote as an illegal abrogation of Pompeius' legal proconsulate.

Leading them are the consuls-elect for the New Year. Only a month away from their inauguration, Gaius Marcellus and Lentulus Crus behave as if they were already in office. Bolting from the temple, they march across the Forum and up to the Rostra where Pompeius has been awaiting the outcome of the Senate's meeting.

From the folds of his toga, lividly red, beefy faced Lentulus Crus draws a sword and offers it hilt first to Pompeius. "Gnaeus Pompeius Magnus, I authorize and charge you to take this sword and defend the Republic against those who would subvert it! Will you accept this charge, Gnaeus Pompeius Magnus?"

With cautious dignity, the Magnus takes the sword, placing its hilt against his togated breast. "In the name of the Senate and People of Roma, I accept this commission and I will discharge it loyally." In dramatic hyperbole, he declares, "I need only stamp my foot and legions of veterans and levies will muster to the Republic's defense."

From the pavement below the Rostra, a strident voice of protest sounds off. "Consul-elect though you are, Lentulus Crus, you have no authority to charge or commission any one to do anything!" Tribune Curio looks up at Lentulus and the Magnus.

Cries and shouts are exchanged between the Tribune's followers and the minority dissenters. Consul-elect Marcellus faces down the obstinate Tribune. The sagging jowls of his pock-marked face appear to break as he declares, "The time is fast approaching, Gaius Curio, when the Senate will silence all, *all* who would obstruct the Republic's business for Caesar's benefit!"

"*You—you* have subverted the Senate's vote for your own self-serving purposes! And now you threaten the tribunes of the people!" Curio's assertion is defiantly spoken.

Standing among Curio's followers are two tribunes-elect, Marcus Antonius and Quintus Cassius. Committed to safeguarding Caesar's interests, they note well the implied threat to the tribunes' inviolability that has been issued by Marcellus' bold pronouncement. Their term will begin in a few days, time enough to consult Caesar again.

IN THE INTERVAL BETWEEN THE new tribunes' assumption of office on December tenth and the consuls' and other magistrates' inauguration on January first, there has been lively speculation concerning Caesar's offer of a compromise. Pessimists among both optimates and popularists are calling it his ultimatum.

Speculation ends in the Senate, again meeting in the Temple of Concord on New Year's Day. Recognized, albeit grudgingly, by presiding Consul Lentulus Crus, the new Tribunes, Marcus Antonius and Quintus Cassius, attempt to read Caesar's offer. Though they do not get very far with their presentation, rumor has it that Caesar proposes to give up *all* his legions *save one* and to retain his imperium *only* in Illyricum if the Senate in turn will allow him to canvass in *absentia* for the consulate.

First, Tribune Lucius Metellus vetoes the reading of Caesar's offer. Antonius and Cassius protest, but to no avail. They honor the veto, a temporary setback, but they try again the next day. This time, a full-scale debate ensues for ten consecutive days. The optimates hold their tribunes in check, and they take the floor, denigrating any compromise with Caesar.

Firm and unyielding, Cato demands, "What makes Caesar believe that he can dictate terms to the Senate? Does he believe that because he lords it over the Gauls, he can also lord it over the Republic's august body? The Senate is not in the habit of negotiating with proconsuls. The *Senate* will decide *what* Caesar *should* or should *not* retain and *when* he shall do so!"

The optimates applaud madly, and their throats burn with cheers for Cato. He is encouraged to continue. "Are we to believe that Caesar asks only for justice? Yet, we all know he fears justice, the true justice that he deserves. Caesar has completed his illegal conquest of Gaul. There is no need for his imperium *not* to be terminated? There is *no* reason for a successor *not* to replace him. Yet, the tribunes—last year Curio, and now Marcus Antonius and Quintus Cassius—would have us believe that if we revoke the law on which Caesar's future ambitions hinge, then we of the Senate shall have initiated civil war."

The optimates cry out, *"No! Never!"* Over their uproar, Cato declares, "Conscript Fathers, by the great god whose Eternal Mind guides the Cosmos, let Caesar and all his creatures here know that if *he* dares disobey the Senate's decree then the onus of civil war lies solely and irrevocably upon *him!* Upon *Caesar!*"

Cato's sentiments are echoed by a score of optimates, the same stubborn minority that had opposed Curio's proposal only weeks earlier.

The Caesarians provoke angry catcalls, clenched fists, and obscene gestures when they demand that the tribunes be allowed to read Caesar's offer.

Among the neutrals, Marcius Philippus, Servilius Vatia, Praetor Marcus Lepidus, and Aurelius Cotta urge moderation. Servius Sulpicius reflects Cicero's sentiments.

"Conscript Fathers, let your patriotism be pure and unalloyed by self-serving resentment and vindication. Uphold the laws, the constitution, and all the traditions which are and have been the foundation of the Republic."

"Sulpician platitudes!" Bibulus sneers *sotto voce* to Cato and Ahenobarbus.

Servius continues. "Within the living memory of most of us here is the horror, the infamy, the wantonness of civil war. *Can* we, *shall* we prefer war to conciliation? Shall we countenance the wholesale destruction of Roma and the devastation of Italia in place of compromise and concord? Shall we in this very temple dedicated to concord fuel the fires of discord when within our reach is the path that will lead to peace?

"Conscript Fathers, think well on what Caesar would offer. Put your love for Roma and your constancy to the Republic above petty personal resentments. Let us strive for peace while yet we may."

Consul Marcellus rises from his seat. Without waiting to be recognized, he calls out, interrupting Servius, "Only Caesar can be the guarantor of peace by fully complying with the Senate's decrees. We have had enough of speeches. Therefore, I propose that Gaius Julius Caesar shall relinquish his proconsular imperium by a specific date which the Senate will designate. I further propose that Caesar and all who follow him will be declared to be public enemies, if they refuse compliance. And finally, I propose that the Senate declare a state of emergency and that it issue the Ultimate Decree, empowering the Consuls to see that the Republic suffers no harm!"

"*Veto!*" Tribune Antonius bellows over the mounting crescendo of approving and disapproving murmurs.

"*Veto against all the Consul's proposals!*" Tribune Cassius reiterates.

"In the name of the People, we enjoin the Senate from considering any of Consul Marcellus' proposals!" Antonius again bellows; his big-headed, thick-necked Taurus demeanor is lacking only a pair of horns to complete his *bull-on-hind legs* appearance.

Presiding Consul Lentulus Crus barks at him, "You are out of order, Tribune! The Senate *will* vote on the question!"

"Beware Consul!" Antonius warns. "Would you ignore the veto of the People's Tribune? Would you put aside what has been the law of the Republic for more than four hundred years?"

Consul Lentulus springs to his feet, announcing, "If you persist in your obstruction, Tribune Antonius and Tribune Cassius, then *you* and *all* others who would oppose the Senate's decree will be regarded as traitors to the Republic! Go! Go to your master! Go to your Caesar! Your safety in Roma cannot be guaranteed! You have been warned!"

Undeterred, Antonius holds his space on the floor. "Consul and Conscript Fathers, by what you've done, you have made civil war a certainty." Then turning about, he, Cassius, Curio, and Marcus Caelius tramp out of the temple. Scores of Caesarian senators file out after them. Their footsteps are like ominous drumbeats.

With the optimates firmly in control, the Senate now votes to approve all of Consul Marcellus' motions. A militant minority of optimate extremists has set the stage for civil war, or possibly Caesar has pulled the right ropes to provoke his desired response from them.

AN INCONSPICUOUS, GENTLY FLOWING STREAM called the Rubicon separates Italia proper from Caesar's Cisalpine province. Well dined, well rested, and well informed by his fugitive tribunes of the Senate's ultimatum, Caesar stands on the riverbank and looks across at Italia. He is arrayed in the battle armor of a Roman proconsul—scarlet military cloak fastened at the shoulders of his burnished bronze and leather coat, sword and dagger fixed to his heavy metal belts, bronze greaves on his shins joining his boots at the ankles. His thinning hair is meticulously dressed.

The sky above him is pale with a few low, heavy clouds. He is uncertain about the season—early January by Roma's traditional calendar with its inherent flaws and inaccuracies, but quite possibly late November by a more accurate reckoning. The calendar needs reform and revision, yes, someday soon perhaps; but not now, not today.

Looking behind him he sees his favorite comrades-in-arms, the Tenth Legion. Their helmets, shields, and weapons catch the early morning sun's rays. The neighing and whinnying and snorting of horses break the eerie silence.

Go forward across Italia and make war upon the Roman Republic; either this or an ignominious collapse into oblivion. Those are his options. Caesar has thought well on them. The men behind him, girt in bronze and leather and iron, standing like silent automatons, will do his bidding. He is certain of this. They await his orders.

Mounted near him are his legates, hardened, seasoned officers—Marcus Antonius, Gaius Curio, Decimus Brutus, and Quintus Cassius. Marcus Caelius and young Publius Dolabella, Cicero's current son-in-law, are with them as well. Twelve mounted lictors with Caesar's proconsular fasces slung over their left shoulders vigilantly await the order to advance.

Caesar has always claimed descent from Venus, Roman goddess of Love and Beauty—good propaganda to have the gods in one's lineage. But this is now an occasion for war, not for love or beauty. This is the season of Mars and Bellona. To them, if they exist at all, Caesar commits his enterprise.

"The die is cast!" Caesar says to the Italian side of the Rubicon. Raising his hand, he signals the bucinators, cornucens, and the trumpeters to sound the advance. Shrill, piercing ululations resound along the legion's column. Caesar spurs his horse forward, splashing across the Rubicon River. The Tenth Legion, with hearty, throaty shouts, follows after him. He is flanked by mounted standard bearers. One carries his scarlet vexillum emblazoned with his name. Another holds aloft the silver eagle, once the ensign of Gaius Marius and then of Lucius Catilina, but now Caesar's talisman.

The die is cast for Caesar—for good or for ill. His course is set. There is no turning back. *"Forward, men of the Tenth Legion!"*

Caput XIII Cicero's Respublica

MARCUS ANTONIUS HAD WARNED THE optimates, *"By what you've done, you have made civil war a certainty."*

And so it fell out. Caesar invaded Italia, sweeping down the Adriatic coast and the Apennine passes of Etruria. The towns of Ariminum, Ancona, Arretium, Faesulae, and Cingulum opened their gates to him.

Pompeius and the Consuls and the die-hard optimates panicked with fear at Caesar's lightning celerity in advancing so close to Roma, and without opposition. It seemed that Pompeius had forgotten how to stamp his foot, for there was no great mustering of veterans or fresh levies to defend the Republic. His credibility damaged, the Magnus advised a tactical withdrawal to Luceria, far south of Roma and within a few days' march of Brundisium.

Metellus Scipio, recently appointed Proconsul of Syria, had already set sail from Brundisium, but the two donated legions supposedly earmarked for service in Syria remained behind. Domitius Ahenobarbus, finally appointed proconsul of Cisalpine and Transalpine Gaul, was aghast at Pompeius' abandonment of Roma and likely withdrawal from Italia. He boasted that he could raise at least three legions of veterans and recruits from among the Picenes, the Aequi, the Marsians, and the Paeligni. With these Italic men, he proposed digging in at Corfinium and making his stand against Caesar. After defeating him, he would then proceed triumphantly all the way up to the Cisalpina.

The division in their counsels did not bode well for the optimates or for the Republic. Servius Sulpicius, ever the voice of moderation, urged them to send emissaries to Caesar to negotiate a truce and to preclude the spilling of Roman or Italian blood.

"*Negotiate!*" Cato snapped. "Negotiate with a proconsul in arms against the Republic? He's committed an act of war by leading his legions into Italia. We *all* know *this*! And Caesar knows it all too well. So – we fight him and destroy him, or he will surely destroy us and the Republic! That's all!"

The Consuls and the optimates concurred with Cato, but Servius drew Pompeius aside. He urged the Magnus to be receptive to any peace overtures that Caesar might initiate. "For the sake of the Republic," Servius implored him, "and for the sake of the woman, his daughter, who was your wife."

In reply, Pompeius brusquely snorted, "Servius Sulpicius, you would do better to contribute *actions*, rather than words!" Then, turning to Quintus, he sneered, "Convey my respects to your brother, and remind him of his duties."

Quintus responded without hesitation, "We *both* know our duties, Gnaeus Pompeius."

THERE WAS A MASS EXODUS from Roma as the optimates, with their families, their retainers, and any and all movable property, clogged the Latin and Appian Roads making south for Luceria, the concentration point designated by Pompeius. The Republicans, as they called themselves, left in so great a hurry that they, or specifically the Consuls, forgot to take the state funds out of the Treasury of Saturn's temple. In addition, they left behind a skeletal, bewildered Senate consisting of neutrals and other men who hoped they could remain neutral.

All of these developments were reported to me by Quintus at Tusculum. On our prospects, he offered, "We can stay in Roma, like Servius and Figulus and Philippus and a score of others and await Caesar's arrival – two, three days at the most; or, we can join Domitius on the Valerian Road and get bottled up in Corfinium; or, we can follow the Republicans to Luceria. What do you think, Marcus?"

"I'm taking the fourth option," I countered. "Let's go to Arpinum. It's far safer than staying here, and Corfinium and Luceria are out of the question if we hope to remain neutral."

Quintus mulled it over. "I hadn't thought of the farmstead."

"Yes, Arpinum; besides, you've been saying young Quintus wants to don the *toga virilis*. Well, so does Marcus. We could have the ceremony there, after acquiring a priest or augur from the town." I sighed deeply before adding, "I would never have expected the boys to have their initiation in the midst of a civil war."

Quintus agreed with me. He returned to Roma to collect his family and close down the Carinae house. He also brought my tidings to Terentia. I wanted her to close the Palatine house, bring Tullia, and all the household servants down to Arpinum. I hoped Atticus and Pilia and Servius would join us, but they chose to remain in Roma.

While waiting for them, I was made happy and relieved by the arrival of Tiro and Metrodorus. My secretary was thoroughly recovered, strong and fit. I embraced them both and thanked Metrodorus profusely for taking good care of Tiro. They had gone directly to Roma, but upon being informed that I was at Tusculum, they made haste to report to me. I told them of my plans about sojourning at the Arpinum homestead. They both appeared relieved at my decision to remain aloof from the escalating conflict.

Tusculum became our rendezvous point and from there we traveled via the Latin Road down to Arpinum. All during the journey, a heavy sense of foreboding enveloped me, an unshakable feeling that I would not see Roma for some time and that our lives would be irreversibly changed.

Before setting out from Tusculum, I dismissed my lictors, directing them to return to Roma and store my fasces in Saturn's temple, the official repository for all official axes and rods of authority. I was glad to be rid of them, especially as I now had Alexio. My burly manservant was as reliable and as formidable as all twelve lictors combined. In dismissing them, I was relinquishing both my imperium and any expectation of a triumph. These were now utterly unimportant if I were to be neutral in the incipient civil war.

My worries about the future were compounded by Tullia's news. She was pregnant, two months gone with child, while her husband was on the march with Caesar. *O Tullia! How bittersweet the news was, tempering my joy for you with uncertainty about all our lives.*

THE BRICK AND STONE FARMHOUSE at Arpinum and the adjoining buildings were in fine condition. The caretakers who rented it in our absence had done a commendable job of keeping the place and the grounds in good order. They had put in a plentiful supply of wood for the fireplaces and the braziers. Ample food had been stockpiled, particularly milled grain, olive oil, and wine and water.

Terentia, Tullia, and Pomponia and several women attendants checked the supply of linen and bedding. Tiro brought my books, tablets, and parchments to the study. He knew to make sure that there was sufficient lamp oil and tapers for my late night reading and correspondence. Metrodorus busied himself by inspecting the quality of the stored provisions, particularly the pantry's stock of spices and herbs from which he might need to prepare medicinal recipes for us.

Having sent Alexio and Quintus' steward, Philologus, into Arpinum to negotiate for a priest to officiate at our boys' imminent initiation, I took a leisurely walk, a tour of inspection about the grounds. Since my return from exile, I had visited the farmstead rarely and briefly, preferring my more fashionable country villas over my ancestral estate. It struck me how little the place had changed over the years. But I had, and so had Quintus. The great old oak, Marius' oak down by the gently flowing Liris River, looked like a bucolic deity, its dark, thick, naked limbs spreading out in every direction. Enormous cumulous clouds hung in the sky, so low they almost seemed to touch the earth. What was waiting to pour out from those clouds, I wondered.

"Father, may I speak with you, please?"

I recognized the voice even before I turned around. You, my son, stood before me, a veritable picture of myself at age fifteen. How you had grown! You were my height, not that I was ever particularly tall, more of medium stature. Your eyes were somewhat darker than mine, but just as deeply set. A routine of regular exercise in Mars Field showed in your firm, fit body. I was and remain proud of you. You were a good youth, and I loved and yet love you dearly.

"Of course, Marcus. What is it, son?"

"I wanted to tell you...well, I appreciate your allowing me to don the toga even though I'm not quite sixteen." You paused, picked up a pebble, and cast it into the river. It plopped into the water with a wet thud. *What an arm you had!* "You see, I wanted to make, that is, I wanted to be able to make my own decision, even if it is not the same as yours."

"Decision?" Of course, I knew what you meant, but I wanted to hear it directly from you.

"The *war*, Father. To go with the Senate and Pompeius or to remain neutral as I know you wish to be."

"You do not mention Caesar?" I asked.

"Going to Caesar is not an option, father. How can it be for any citizen who loves Roma and wishes the Republic to survive?"

I smiled admiringly at you. "My son, life should be, but unfortunately is not that simple. And putting on the citizen's toga does not make it simple." We walked by the river bank, all the while discussing the ambiguities of adult citizenship.

When the day of your initiation arrived, you and your cousin stood before the altar of our household gods. The local priest from Arpinum solemnly intoned that the omens were favorable for the two youths to enter officially into the order of citizens. *Favorable omens, indeed!* What irony, I thought, with civil war having broken out in the land. I swallowed hard and looked at my brother. Judging from the cynical expression he wore, he may have been thinking the same thing.

You and your cousin removed the *bullae*, your childhood lockets from about your necks and placed them upon the altar. Then, assisted by household servants, you and he removed your purple-bordered togas of youth. These were carefully folded and given to Terentia and to Pomponia, a ritual signifying that their sons, standing before them in their cinctured, broad-striped tunics, were forever discarding boyhood. Terentia held it tenderly against her breast as tears began to well in her eyes. But all through the ceremony, Pomponia and my brother appeared severe and strained.

"Quintus Tullius Cicero," the priest intoned again, "are you prepared to put on the toga of Roman manhood and to assume your place in the civic community?"

Young Quintus replied in a low, grave monotone, "I, Quintus Tullius Cicero, am prepared to put on the toga of Roman manhood and to assume my place in the civic community." Having thus consented, Quintus draped himself with the white woolen toga of the Roman adult. In accordance with custom, his father assisted him.

My nephew was seventeen years old. He stood as tall as you, but in his appearance, he favored his mother, the same protrusive mouth and sly, conniving aspect about the eyes. He had Pomponia's dark olive complexion as well. Robed in the virile toga, he looked almost embarrassed.

The same formula and procedure was replicated with you. I felt a swelling paternal pride in you as I draped the virile toga over your broad shoulders. Felicitations were exchanged all around. Then we retired to the dining room to partake of the celebration meal. The tables and couches were all in order and the room was festooned with holly and strips of white, woolen cloth in token of the plain, white, woolen adult's toga.

All was ready for what should have been a convivial meal. But Pomponia appeared alarmed and perturbed. Looking from the dining couches to me and then to Terentia and finally to Quintus, she fumed, "Well! You've seen to *every* detail and *without* any word from *me!* My son is part of this celebration too, you know!" With this, she stormed out of the room and headed for her bedroom.

Quintus threw up his arms in disgust. "You see what I must put up with! *You see!*" Then, muttering profanities and imprecations under his breath, he tramped out toward the paddock. Dumbfounded, I exchanged perplexed glances with Terentia, Tullia, and our two new citizens. In stupefied silence, we partook of the evening meal.

From Roma, letters from Atticus and Servius brought the news of the war into our insular world at Arpinum.

Caesar's march through Italia continued relentlessly southward. By-passing Roma, he made straight for Corfinium where his scouts had undoubtedly told him that a large army was concentrating. Caesar invested the place with siege works, intending to starve the defenders into submission. But within days, Corfinium fell into his lap in yet another bloodless conquest. Domitius' officers and the leading citizens surrendered him and his son, Gnaeus, to Caesar, and threw open the town gates to the rebel proconsul.

Rather than exact reprisals upon his opponents, Caesar pardoned both father and son and allowed them to go their way on the single condition that they abstain from further fighting. The two Domitii promptly disappeared, and Caesar allowed their recruits to enlist in his own legions.

Now with the fall of Corfinium, the Republicans despaired of holding out against Caesar. Pompeius might not have trusted the loyalty of the two legions donated by Caesar. If Domitius' legions had deserted to Caesar, Pompeius must have reasoned, then what likelihood was there that the legions that had served under Caesar would stand up to him in a pitched battle. So, Pompeius and the Consuls ordered a withdrawal to Brundisium. Commandeering every sea-worthy vessel, they packed themselves on board and crossed the Adriatic to Dyrracchium before Caesar could prevent their escape.

Unable to pursue as he was lacking ships, Caesar headed back to Roma. But on the way, he broke his journey at Arpinum. Evidently, Dolabella, having been informed by Tullia of our whereabouts, had told Caesar where I could be found.

It was late Januarius. The bone-chilling winter rains had been afflicting us for many days before Caesar's arrival. Poor Terentia, chronically suffering from her pains in the joints, was especially indisposed during the winter months. She complained bitterly about the rustic accommodations at the farmstead and with good reason. I wished we all could have been back in Roma, in the comfort of the Palatine house. But we had come out to Arpinum so that we could insulate ourselves against the warring factions. How ironic it was that the leader of one faction would have sought me out and then found me.

We sat in the study, warming ourselves near a brazier and sipping heated wine. I was sure he was studying me all the while that I scrutinized him. We had not seen each other since his consulate, ten years before. He looked quite fit, leaner actually, and his hair too was considerably thinner. He wore the armor and military cloak of a proconsul. His face was lined, harder than before, severe yet weary, no doubt showing the toll of his exertions in Gaul over the years and the marks of personal sorrow.

I listened patiently and in silence as he related his reluctance to wage war on the Republic. The intransigence of the Senate, he declared, had forced his hand just as it had forced Pompeius to take up arms against him. "I stood on the bank of the Rubicon and looked across at Italia," he recalled, "and I knew that by crossing that little stream I was taking a step from which there could be no retreat. I said aloud, *'the die is cast,'* and so we marched across. In all the towns that received us, I announced that I had come with my legions to defend the sacrosanctity of the Roman People's tribunes against attacks from an entrenched oligarchy within the Senate."

He went on to describe his aborted attempts to send negotiators to Roma, and he berated the optimates for their intransigence. "At Corfinium, I granted Domitius Ahenobarbus and his son clemency, knowing full well that they'll not quit. Domitius will show up somewhere else with a sword in his hand."

Then, he spoke of his frustration in failing to prevent Pompeius' departure from Italia. "If we could have spoken, face to face, we could have resolved matters. But the last thing the optimates would allow is such a meeting. When I looked out at their departing ships, all I could think to say was, *'Now I must turn away from an imperator without an army and face an army without an imperator'.*"

I understood all too well his allusion to Pompeius' legions in Spain.

"Marcus Cicero," he said to me almost imploringly, "I need your help in effecting a reconciliation with Pompeius."

I agreed. "What would you have me do?"

"Come then to the Senate. I'll convene the few who haven't fled. Servius Sulpicius, Lepidus, my niece's husband, Philippus, are all yet in Roma. Come Marcus, and urge peace!"

I looked at him suspiciously. "On my own convictions?"

Caesar replied, "Am I to prescribe to you?"

"Then I'll urge the Senate to disapprove of your going to Spain to subdue Pompeius' legions."

He snapped at me, "This I cannot allow!"

"I assumed as much! And so if I cannot speak by my own convictions, then I cannot attend the Senate. You invade your country and claim to be defending the People's Tribunes. Yet, you would forbid a free, open discussion of a truce. Had you wanted peace, you would not have invaded Italia; you would not have seized any ground, let alone a dozen towns, even if they opened their gates to you. If you want peace, how then can you even contemplate going to Spain, a move full of bellicose intention. No, Caesar, what you've done, like everything else in your career, is predicated on your own aggrandizement of power and control. That is all that matters to you."

Caesar looked at me for a long moment, all the while nodding his head as a crooked grin played upon his lips. Then he said, "Truly, I hope you'll remain aloof and detached if you cannot help me to restore peace." With that, he took his leave and departed for Roma.

I was glad to have stood up to him. Discussing the interview with Quintus, I expressed no remorse for my candor.

"Yes, of course," Quintus agreed, "but it's all too plain that he *must* go to Spain. If not, then Pompeius could order those legions to invade Italia, and at the same time, once he's raised an army in the East, he could return. Caesar is too smart to be trapped, and his legions are already spread pretty thin. Besides what he's taken with him, he's had to leave a sufficient military presence in his provinces – all three of them. Believe me, Marcus, Caesar *must* conquer or win over the Spanish legions before he faces Pompeius."

With consternation etched on his face, Quintus shook his head, looked into my eyes, and added, "*We* too are in danger of being trapped, Marcus. Caesar may allow us neutrality, but I doubt that Pompeius and the optimates will be so tolerant."

"I know, Quintus, but I must wait at least until after Tullia is delivered of her child. I couldn't bear to leave her now – not in her present condition."

My brother did not appear satisfied with my answer, but it was the only one I could have rendered at that moment.

Omniscient Narrative

Motherhood has become second nature to Fulvia. Her two children by Publius Clodius now have an infant half-brother, little Gaius, fathered by Fulvia's second husband, Gaius Scribonius Curio. The happy, proud father holds his infant son gingerly against his bronze cuirass. He takes every precaution that its hard, metallic surface does not chaff the baby's tender cheek. The baby sleeps and moves his mouth as if he were nursing, and Curio smiles affectionately. Only children, especially new-born infants, can be totally oblivious to the strife and turbulence of an enraged, divided land.

Fulvia sits upon a cathedra chair. She is flanked by her other children, young Claudia, age seven, and young Publius, almost six. They are good children, loving and respectful, and physically they are living portraits of their father and his Claudian forebears. Their aunt, Clodia Pulchra, is a virtual surrogate mother to them, as well as Fulvia's ever present companion. She sits on a divan opposite her sister-in-law.

"How much time are you allowed?" Fulvia's question distracts Curio's attention from his infant son.

"Hardly any." Curio walks toward the women, all the while cradling the baby.

"At least you'll wait for Caesar's arrival." Clodia's statement is hopefully spoken, though it is actually more of a question.

"No, Clodia. Caesar's on his way back from Brundisium. But he's already sent my orders."

"So where are you off to, if we're privileged to know?" Fulvia asks coyly.

Curio laughs. "I'm to secure Sicilia. Once that's done, I'm to cross over to Africa and hold it. The grain supply is vital. We know it, and the Pompeians know it. Blockading the sea lanes and starving out Roma and Italia would be their first offensive. Caesar cannot allow that to happen."

"And you cannot risk disappointing Caesar," Fulvia emphasizes. "What are Antonius' orders?"

"Which one?" Curio's question tickles the women into a giggle.

"Don't be silly, Gaius," Clodia playfully reproves him. "We know that Gaius is holding Illyricum and Lucius is still out in Asia. So, obviously your wife is asking about *Marcus!*"

"Of course! I knew it all the time!" Curio laughs. "Well, I'll tell you. I don't really know about his orders. But my guess is that Caesar will leave him to look after things here in Roma when he goes off to Spain. If I'm right, and if I know Marcus, he'll make the time to look in on you. That'll be something else for me to worry about while I'm away." Curio renders a wounded grimace that quickly changes to a sardonic smile.

Clodia's giggles now become hearty laughter. "Curio, your worries will be well matched by Antonius'." She looks playfully over at Fulvia. "If Dolabella is also kept at home he may prowl around Antonia."

Fulvia acknowledges this with a bogus clucking of her tongue and a disapproving shake of her head. "Poor Antonius! But perhaps you could help, Clodia."

"*I?*"

"Why yes, of course. Perhaps you could distract Dolabella from Marcus' wife. After all, with Tullia ensconced with her parents, he'll need some diversion, and we both know what a diverting creature you are."

Such bantering is inappropriate in the presence of the children, Curio thinks. "Publius, Claudia, why don't you go fetch the wet nurse." The baby in his arms has started to fuss, ramming his tiny hand into his mouth and sucking his fingers. "I think your little brother wants to eat – something or *someone*!"

The two children obediently go off on their appointed errand. The mood in the room becomes serious. Curio looks from the baby to Fulvia. "Take good care of my son." Then he pauses and looks back at the infant. "My son, I hope this bloody business will not keep me away from you very long."

The wet nurse appears at the hallway entrance to the atrium. She is an attractive, buxom young woman. "Domina?"

Fulvia gestures to the baby. "He may need to be fed."

The wet nurse takes the infant from Curio's arms. "Farewell, my son," Curio says tenderly.

Fulvia senses a queer resignation in her husband's voice. Clodia notes it too. *Men and their wars,* she thinks with tearful disdain.

Cicero's Respublica

Arpinum became our insular world, far from the strife of civil war, unless one were to count the numerous flare-ups between Quintus and Pomponia and between my brother and his son. Most of our news came in letters from Servius and Atticus.

Upon arriving in the environs of Roma, Caesar observed a constitutional nicety in remaining outside the City because of his status as a Proconsul with imperium. He arranged for the Senate, of whom less than two hundred remained, to go to his encampment in Mars Field and meet with him. The senior magistrate left in Roma was the Urban Praetor, Marcus Lepidus, who was entirely cooperative.

However, the Senate tried, as I had, to dissuade Caesar from going to Spain to eliminate Pompeius' legions. Not only did Caesar insist on the necessity of his going, but he also demanded money from the Treasury to finance the campaign. The senators quibbled about this, insisting that the Treasury reserves could not be allocated for civil war.

Abruptly, Caesar dismissed them. The next day, he came into Roma with a cohort of legionaries. Making straight for Saturn's temple treasury, he found Tribune Lucius Metellus barring the doors. The Tribune insisted that the Treasury reserves, by tradition, were expendable only for the purpose of bribing Gallic invaders. Caesar countered that as the conqueror of the Gauls, he was certainly entitled to the money.

Undaunted, the Tribune persisted in his obstruction, whereupon Caesar warned him that he would have his soldiers remove him bodily. He even added that the threat was harder to pronounce than actually implementing the deed. At this, the Tribune moved from the entrance, and Caesar appropriated all the funds he needed.

Upon reading of this incident, I remarked to Quintus, "So, this is how Caesar defends the sacrosanctity of the Tribunes!"

Shortly after this, Caesar started off for Spain, leaving Marcus Antonius as his designated propraetor to oversee Roma and Italia in conjunction with Praetor Lepidus.

Atticus informed me that Dolabella had been commissioned to build a fleet of transport galleys in the port of Brundisium. No doubt Caesar was anticipating crossing over to Macedonia once he had secured the Spanish provinces.

Even before Caesar's arrival in Roma, another of his legates, Gaius Curio, the former tribune whose disarmament proposal had failed to prevent civil war, had set off with three legions to secure Sicilia and Africa against any disruption in Roma's grain supply.

However, the *money* supply was growing ever tighter, and rents and interest rates were spiraling to such exorbitant levels that, in Atticus' opinion, the prospects for a debtors' revolt seemed dangerously real.

IT WAS ABOUT MID-FEBRUARIUS WHEN I received Atticus' and Servius' letters describing these events. I wrote back to them in deepest sorrow over my *"Tulliola"*. She had miscarried just before the Ides. Metrodorus, who had tended to her during her ordeal, assured us that she would regain her strength and vigor, but I saw a disturbing change come over Tullia since losing the baby. Gone from her face was the youthful, vivacious glow of the girl-woman, and in its place was a somberness that I had never seen before in her.

Terentia told me that Tullia had been that way immediately after the murder of her first husband, Piso. "It's fortunate for you," she mentioned, "that you were away in banishment, or you would not have endured the pain of seeing her so depressed."

As soon as I was permitted, I entered Tullia's room. She looked at me pathetically through glassy eyes and whispered hoarsely, "I'm sorry, Tata."

I shook my head in denial. "No, no, my Tulliola, you've nothing to be sorry about. Nature must have its way." I took her into my arms and cradled her as I had when she was but an infant.

That Februarius of Tullia's miscarriage was a dark, austere time, fraught with enveloping uncertainties. If Dolabella had been with Caesar near Roma, he made no attempt to contact Tullia, nor did he write to her from Brundisium. His apparent lack of concern for his wife, my daughter, distressed and angered me. I could not believe that it was impossible for him to get even a short note to her, and Tullia wanted so much to tell him of their loss. Anger against him precluded my sending any messengers to seek him in Brundisium.

By Martius, letters from Atticus and Servius brought us up to date on the latest developments. These added to my general sense of uncertainty. A major reversal for Caesar was being heralded in Roma. Having secured Sicilia, Curio had crossed over to Africa. There, he was lured into a trap by King Juba's Numidians in the Bagradas Valley. Curio and his entire army were annihilated.

It surprised me that the optimates had made an alliance as far afield as Numidia. I wondered by what inducements they had persuaded King Juba to support their cause. Hopefully, they had not surrendered the province of Africa or any part of it to them.

On another front, the allied, free city of Massilia on the Transalpine coast had revolted against Caesar. Its recalcitrant Greek citizens had necessitated Caesar's expenditure of valuable time and effort investing the city with siege operations. Leaving a contingent under his legate,

Decimus Brutus, to press the siege, Caesar had then marched on to Spain.

With the African debacle and the Massilian revolt, Caesar had suffered reverses in two vital areas. Though they did not betoken the eventual outcome of the war, they did cause Quintus and me no end of concern. Then by Aprilis, Atticus and Servius were reporting rumors of Caesar's entrapment in Spain. Even if there was any truth to the rumors, Quintus speculated, Caesar had extricated himself from many traps during his Gallic wars.

Notwithstanding this, I was further distressed by reports that Pompeius and the Republican Senate were building up a tremendous power in Macedonia. They had issued a decree that was just beginning to circulate in Italia – all senators and equites who remained in Roma and Italia were to be regarded as traitors to the Republic. The Republicans were allowing no tolerance for neutrals.

Despite this, Servius wrote, he was going to remain in Roma. As far as he knew, so would Lepidus who, as Praetor, was the only legitimate magistrate left in the City. Other neutrals, like Piso, Philippus, Figulus, and Aurelius Cotta, were also remaining. But I could not share their confidence or recklessness.

Though obligated to both Caesar and Pompeius, I was inclining toward the latter, especially since he was on the side of the optimates. Their decree concerning neutrals had much to do with pointing me in the direction of the government in exile. The last thing I wanted was to be reckoned as a traitor and to fall victim to the optimates' wrath. Surely this would have happened if indeed Caesar were defeated in Spain. We and all neutrals, as well as Caesarian partisans, would be liable for vindictive retribution at the hands of the Republicans. Such a prospect filled me with tremendous fear.

However, I did not get a sense of fear or misgiving from Atticus. He seemed confident in his ability to survive the storm. How typical this was of him. He always had the astute equite's knack of connecting with all parties while surmounting any and all commitments. He could always manage to be *"in with every one and out with no one."* I knew of his business connections with Balbus and Oppius and other pro-Caesarian bankers. I was not certain, though, of the extent of his investments among the optimates. For his and for Pilia's sake, I hoped that his good fortune would not be reversed by the ultimate outcome of the conflict.

Omniscient Narrative

Marcus Antonius, legate of Gaius Caesar, propraetorian Tribune of the Plebs, is loath to discharge an extraordinary but necessary duty. As his valet helps him on with his cuirass and his military cloak, he wonders if he should bring his wife along on this special mission. Antonia could be an important asset.

As cousins, they had known each other for years before they became espoused. Theirs has been a good marriage. He loves and reveres his uncle and father-in-law, Gaius Antonius, now living in exile on the island of Malta. Antonia loves and reveres her aunt and mother-in-law, Julia, widow of Marcus Antonius Creticus and then widow of Lentulus Sura, the executed Catilinian conspirator. So typical of noble Roman marriages, theirs is saturated with politics. All the more reason to take Antonia with him, for his mission is laden with political purpose.

She has matured both physically and emotionally during their marriage. The child has blossomed into a comely and formidable woman with none of the Antonian porcine or bovine features. Fortunately, she resembles her mother in her delicate mouth and chin; her neck is like a slender column of alabaster mounted upon a broad, expansive chest. Her hair, meticulously layered upon her head, is the color of ripened chestnuts with russet highlights. Her figure is thin and well-toned, motherhood having come to her early in marriage. Little Antonia is her parents' pride and joy.

Antonia and Antonius travel from the Carinae to the Aventine district by way of a two-horse chariot. Pedestrian and vehicular traffic yield to Caesar's legate as Antonius steers his team through the narrow, paving-stone covered streets. Antonius' attendants, burly soldiers and veteran gladiators, help to clear his path.

It is not long before they arrive at the house of Fulvia, widow of Publius Clodius. Ironically, Antonius' task is to inform her that she has again been widowed.

Fulvia receives her visitors in the atrium. Clodia Pulchra is with her. Salutations and greetings are exchanged amicably.

"You are always welcome, Marcus Antonius and Antonia," Fulvia says, extending her hands to them. She sees by his demeanor that something is amiss.

Between Clodia and Antonia there is an unspoken communication, a meeting of their eyes as the two women appraise each other. Antonia is not naive. *It is good that she has you, Clodia, especially now,* Antonia reflects.

"Fulvia, I'm sorry," Antonius says, "but I come here today bearing sad tidings."

Intuitively, Fulvia responds, "It's Curio, isn't it? He's dead, isn't he, Antonius?"

Antonius nods. "In battle...in Africa...against the Numidians. Most of his command was wiped out. We've had word only from a few survivors."

Fulvia is silent and reserved, her head erect with pride. Antonius admires her as never before. Clodia and Antonia are quick to notice.

Cicero's Respublica

The great oak of Marius had sprouted its mass of green leaves, the leaves that in my youth had seemed like the face of eternity. I had known such tranquility looking up at them with the sun's rays shining through, so long ago.

Now, the tranquility of my youth was displaced by torrential doubts and fears. Each day, you and Quintus and his son assailed me with entreaties and questions concerning our course. The three of you looked to me to determine our future, and I grew resentful at being made the arbiter of our fate. Tullia was enveloped in a cloud of depression and my heart ached for her. Quintus and Pomponia snapped at each other more ferociously with each passing day. And Terentia badgered me to put off any decision at least until after definitive news of the Spanish campaign had been received. Each day I saw myself sinking ever more deeply into the optimates' disfavor – *Marcus Tullius Cicero – traitor to the Republic.*

Thus assailed from without and from within, my doubts and fears, my indecision and vacillation literally sickened me. I don't recall for how many days I was ill with severe abdominal pains and delirious with fever. In my delirium, I saw visions of Fabia tending Vesta's sacred fire; of Clodia Pulchra and Fulvia reproaching me for Clodius' death; of Caesar demanding that I speak for peace on his terms; of Pompeius ordering me to report to the Republican encampment at Thessalonia; of Tullia screaming in the pain of miscarriage; of you, of Quintus and his son imploring me for a decision and of Terentia urging me to wait, to wait....

I vomited black bile. Then, thanks to Metrodorus' ministrations, I began to recover slowly. And with my recovery came resolution. I decided to go to Macedonia and join the Republicans, but I did *not* urge you or your uncle or your cousin to follow suit. Yet, each was of a mind to join me in this course. It was as though each of you had previously decided to go, but you were waiting for me to concur with you.

Anticipating that Brundisium would be garrisoned by Caesar's troops, we planned a circuitous route. We would travel to Circeii on the Tyrrhenian coast and then take ship from there. The spring time currents would be in our favor all the way down to the Straits of Messina. Negotiating them, we would sail across the Ionian Sea, plotting our course for Dyrrachium. From thence, we would travel overland to Thessalonica.

As preparations were underway for our departure, Terentia came to me. "You know I'll not go with you," she bitterly announced.

I would never have expected her to share my decision, and not just because of her chronic malady.

"I don't believe you're doing the right thing, and certainly not the practical thing," Terentia went on, "and so I cannot go with you, though I'm sure many other spouses have. But I will pray for you, for all of you, and no matter the outcome, I hope all of you will return...." She was trying so hard to suppress a sob.

I took her into my arms and kissed her tenderly on the mouth, but instead of passion I found in her only sorrow, even recrimination. Pulling back from her, I saw tears streaming down her cheeks. "Stay here then," I told her, "as long as you can, as long as the food holds out. If you need to, if you can, then go back to Roma."

Terentia stared at me, her face hard with anger and wet with her own tears. Her face and that of my *"Tulliola"* alternated in my mind's eye all during the journey to Macedonia. With each swallow, I tasted the salt of my own tears and Terentia's and Tullia's.

I left big, brawny Alexio to look after them. Tiro, Metrodorus, and Quintus' steward, Philologus came with us. In my mind and soul, I commended them all, Terentia, Tullia, Pomponia, to a higher, unknown power, the very same power whom I hoped was guiding our way.

The Republican camp at Thessalonica was a beehive of martial activity. A mighty host of nine legions had been assembled. Five of these were of Roman and allied citizens transported from Italia. These were the First and Third Legions that had been donated by Caesar for service against the Parthians, plus the remnants of the three legions that Ahenobarbus had had at Corfinium. One legion had been recruited from settled veterans in Crete and Macedonia, and two had been raised in Asia by Consul Lentulus Crus. Another legion was comprised of auxiliaries collected from Thessaly, Boeotia, Peloponnesus, and Epirus. There were about three thousand archers from Crete, Sparta, Pontus, and Syria, and some twelve hundred slingers and seven thousand horsemen had been conscripted from the Greek city-states, the Eastern allied kingdoms, and even the barbarian tribesmen of the Balkan regions. Five hundred men of the occupation force that Aulus Gabinius had left in Egypt, following Auletes' restoration six years earlier, were now in camp. These so-called *"Gabinians"* were commanded by young Gnaeus Pompeius.

In Syria, Proconsul Metellus Scipio had recruited two legions of provincials to defend the frontier against the ever-present threat of a Parthian invasion. However, internal discord among the barbarians rendered their expected incursion unlikely. So, it was anticipated that Scipio would bring his legions to Macedonia to augment Pompeius' army.

All told, Pompeius and the optimates could count eleven legions and substantial auxiliary forces at their command. I had much time to walk about the encampment to observe the splendid martial panoply. This was because neither Pompeius nor the Proconsuls had given me any commission or assignment. However, Quintus and his son and you, Marcus, were given charges befitting your rank and your respective ages.

Upon our arrival at the camp, after several weeks of uneventful travel, we were at first received with reserved civility. Before long though, we were generally shunned by the leaders. Cato chided me for relinquishing what he called my *"potential status as a mediator,"* a role I might have assumed had I remained in Italia. I reminded him of how he had once denigrated any and all negotiation with Caesar. Lentulus Crus and Gaius Marcellus sarcastically congratulated me on finally turning my head in the right direction. I replied in turn, alluding to the divided counsels of Pompeius and the optimates, "Too many helmsmen obscure the course."

At one point, Pompeius irritably demanded of me. "*Where* is your son-in-law?"

I replied with cool aplomb, "With *your father-in-law!*"

He became further annoyed at my flippant reference to Caesar, his former father-in-law. Pompeius was the one man in the camp whose favor I did not want to lose. Eventually, I came to an understanding with him, a monetary arrangement to placate him and to restore myself to his good graces. However, I made the mistake of omitting Quintus from the deal, and this indiscretion would compromise me later.

During my sojourn at Thessalonica, sarcasm became my defense, my refuge against a growing sense of alienation as the optimates shunned me, seeking neither my counsels nor my companionship. I made caustic remarks against all their plans, particularly their negotiated alliances with the barbarian kings, Cotlys of the Thracians and Burebistas of the Dacians. It was an outrage that Romans should enter into pacts with barbarians against other Romans.

The optimates' mood became more sanguinary with the arrival of Pompeius' legates from Spain. Afranius, Petreius, and Varro reported the loss of the Spanish legions and provinces to Caesar's conquering arms. Then Proconsul Domitius Ahenobarbus, arriving at the camp a few days later, reported the capitualation of Massilia and his failed attempt to install himself as governor of the Transalpina. For a second time, he and his son had received Caesar's pardon, but the Domitii were all the more infused with belligerent ardor despite Caesar's clemency.

Pompeius and the optimates were dangerously divided on what strategy to follow. He wanted to concentrate their strength in the East and await Caesar's initiative in moving against them. Despite the onset of autumn and the formidable Republican fleet patrolling the Adriatic, Pompeius was certain that Caesar would attempt a crossing against contrary winds. He reckoned that Caesar was rash and bold enough for such an endeavor. In doing so, he risked destroying his army and this, Pompeius reasoned, would play into the Republicans' interests.

Lentulus Crus, Gaius Marcellus, and Cato voiced the optimate objection. They favored exploiting the favorable east-to-west winds and taking the offensive against Caesar by invading Italia with their tremendous host.

With neither consensus nor compromise forthcoming, they therefore took no action at all. The weeks passed slowly, miserably, and I remembered the months of exile I had spent at Thessalonica eight, nine years earlier. At least then, I had been apprised of news from Roma via letters from family and friends. But the Republican naval blockade now precluded the reception and delivery of correspondence.

Instead, there were only bits and pieces of news, hearsay, and rumors: Caesar had been named Dictator, and then he had been elected Consul. If either were the case, then the outlaw commander might have acquired some degree of legitimacy in his war against the optimates.

The year was drawing to a close. Winter set in, turning the blue Aegean into gray slate. From the Adriatic side of the Balkan Peninsula we heard reports of naval skirmishes. It seemed that Pompeius had correctly guessed his opponent's intention. Caesar was actually attempting a winter crossing. This was confirmed by Marcus Bibulus, the once *"sky-watching Consul"* who had been Caesar's colleague. As commander of the Republicans' Adriatic fleet, he reported extensive ship-building and naval preparations in Brundisium's harbor.

The optimates prevailed upon Pompeius to move the army west. He saw the wisdom in this, for military necessity dictated that Dyrrachium, the Republicans' supply base on the coast, be secured against a likely assault by Caesar. Should Caesar succeed in his bold endeavor to cross the Adriatic against contrary winds, should he succeed in eluding the Republican fleet, then he would be compelled by military logic to seize his opponents' chief supply base.

Pompeius assembled all the women and children of the optimates, including his daughter and his wife, Cornelia. For their own security, he was having them ferried across the Aegean to the island of Lesbos. He put a cohort under the command of his younger son, Sextus, and commissioned him to escort the non-combatants and remain with them. When they set sail, he sent couriers to Metellus Scipio, urging him to bring his legions to Macedonia with all haste. Then, he put the army on the march. For miles and days, the Egnatian Road was clogged with the mighty, winding snake of Pompeius' legions, the cavalcade of horses, and the caravan of his draft animals.

Despite the inherent dangers of a winter crossing, made all the more precarious by Bibulus' naval squadrons, Caesar managed to ferry his legions across the Adriatic. They landed on the Epirot coast, not far from Dyrrachium. For several weeks, Caesar's and Pompeius' legions maneuvered as each commander tried to gain the more strategically advantageous positions. There was even a Caesarian peace overture which Titus Labienus, Pompeius' fiery legate, aborted with the unbridled severity of a barrage of arrows, javelins, and sling-shot missiles.

Ultimately, Caesar interposed himself between Pompeius and Dyrrachium. Both sides dug in. Caesar's entrenchments formed a seventeen-mile arc which denied Pompeius land-access to the town. Pompeius' inner circuit, fourteen miles of redoubts, earthen ramparts and palisades, secured a wide expanse of seacoast.

As the siege wore on, we learned that Bibulus had died from exhaustion and exposure due to his unsuccessful efforts at preventing Caesar's crossing. I could not resist a caustic observation alluding to Bibulus' ineffective consulate. "He'd have done better to stay indoors and observe the weather!"

Cato, Pompeius, and the optimates did not appreciate my irony. In particular, Cato's daughter, Porcia, sequestered at Lesbos with the optimate women and children, was rendered a widow by Bibulus' death.

The long siege probably took a greater toll on Caesar's men as they were denied access to the sea by the Republican lines. However, ships from Dyrrachium kept Pompeius' legions well provisioned, while Caesar's men had to forage from the scarce resources of an inhospitable locality.

But upon me the siege was an unmitigated ordeal. I had never been partial to the military life, and I was still being shunned by the optimates. My alienation was made all the more insufferable because I was separated from my loved ones. I ached to see Tullia and Terentia, to embrace them and to smother them with kisses. I was starving for news of Servius and Atticus, to break bread with them, and talk politics and business. You, my son, and your cousin were aflame with a bellicose excitement that I could neither tolerate nor contain, and my brother grew each day more laconic and forlorn.

I repented of having left Italia. I almost preferred death rather than my virtual imprisonment among the war-mongers. Again, I was afflicted with the same abdominal pains and fever that had visited me at Arpinum.

During this delirious illness, I was confined to my tent. Metrodorus ministered to me with all of his art and skill. Though I cannot explain his ministrations, I am certain that once again he saved my life. But he could not save me from horrifying visions as the cacophony of battle swelled all along the siege lines. Blood, assaults, and counter-assaults between the Pompeians and the Caesarians merged in my delirium to conjure scenes of butchery, death, and dismemberment. Where in those battles were my son, and my brother, and my nephew? Would they survive? Or would they fall victim to civil war? And I could not free myself from the debilitative bonds of my illness.

In the caverns of my mind I saw a fair-haired youth, younger than you and Quintus. He crossed the Roman Forum to Janus' temple whose open portals betokened a state of war. A voice like the clanging of hammers on bronze announced: "Romans, behold the pacifier of your imperium. Look not for an end to your discord without his Providence!"

Each time I had this dream, a pervasive sense of calm came over me, bringing me some respite from pain and inner turmoil.

It was not long after my fever broke that Pompeius visited me. He was most solicitous for my complete recovery, and he asked if there was anything he could provide for me. He seemed flushed with some measures of success. "Caesar tried to break our lines, but we held, and we forced him to retreat. All along his lines, his legions are in retreat. They're heading south, toward Thessaly. If my men had not been exhausted from the rigors of the siege and the battle, I'd have gone after them immediately and annihilated them. That's what they're blaming me for not doing!"

I inferred that he meant the optimates. Weakly, faintly, I managed to ask him what he was going to do.

"I'm reinforcing the garrison at Dyrrachium; Cato will be left in command; with the bulk of the army, I'm going after Caesar. I expect to link up with Metellus Scipio very soon. He's landed at Thessalonica and I've sent word for him to meet us in Thessaly."

Pompeius' confidence was belied by a queer sadness. He looked from me to a flickering oil lamp by the side of my cot. "This business could have been finished here, but it didn't happen that way. Now we take it to Greece. Somewhere on the plains of Thessaly — yes, that's where it will be decided."

Facing me again, he commended me to the care of the Dyrrachium garrison. We clasped hands and stared for a long moment into each other's eyes. It was the last time that Pompeius and I saw each other.

Later that same day, Quintus and you and your cousin visited me. You inquired after my health and then gave me the same battle report as had Pompeius. Then Quintus told me that you were all moving out with the legions.

"We're going after Caesar to finish him off and end the war," Quintus said with smug resignation.

I struggled to rise, but I was too weak. You and your cousin embraced me. You both promised to do your duties as Roman citizens. How ironic, I thought. When was it ever a Roman's duty to kill his fellow citizens? I cursed my own weak, immobile condition. This alone kept me from going with you.

"Execute your duties," I told the three of you, "but don't sacrifice yourselves. Not for *this*!"

You were stunned at my injunction. Then I turned to my brother and said, "As much as you can, Quintus, look after them, and guard yourself as well. Don't even think about imitating the Spartans. Carry back your *own* shields rather than be carried on them!"

Quintus took my hand. "We'll try brother; for now, hail and farewell, Marcus."

Leaving behind a legion, including the wounded and sick, Pompeius and the rest of the army left Dyrrachium near the Ides of Quinctilis. I was moved into fairly comfortable quarters in the town. Gradually, over the next several weeks, despite the oppressively hot summer, I regained my strength under Metrodorus' watchful eye.

The entire garrison, under Cato's command, anxiously awaited news from Pompeius in northern Thessaly. The optimates now had an effective strength of ten legions to fight Caesar's forces, said to be undermined by battle losses and supply deprivations. Yet, most of Caesar's men were tough veterans, whereas most of the Republican troops were provincial levies, untried by battle, except for the recent fighting in Dyrrachium, and generally unaccustomed to the rigors of the march.

The days and the weeks passed. We waited.

Omniscient Narrative

THE THESSALIAN TOWN OF PHARSALUS occupies one end of a plain watered by the Enipeus River. The scorching summer heat of what the Romans call the month of Sextilis afflicts the multitudes of warriors in their bronze and iron helmets, metal-studded leather and ring-mail coats assembling in battle formations.

Caesar's eight legions, some twenty-two thousand men, have suffered defeat at Dyrrachium. Their tactical withdrawal into Thessaly has not dampened their ardor, but the refusal of towns and villages to succor them with provisions has infuriated them. One town in particular, Gomphi, by Caesar's orders has been sacked.

Their food replenished, their frustration vented, the legions have pushed on deeper into Thessaly with Gnaeus Pompeius pursuing them. The two armies have now encamped on opposite sides of the plain near Pharsalus, with the Pompeians situated nearer the town.

For days, Caesar has offered battle, but Pompeius has refused to engage the enemy. Then, one night, soldiers on both sides behold a bright, flaming light in the sky that passes over Caesar's camp and falls into Pompeius.' Many of the Caesarians take it as an ill omen portending victory for the Pompeians. The superstitious among Pompeius' officers and men divine it the same way. But Caesar goes about his encampment, encouraging his legionaries. On his authority as Chief Pontiff, he tells them that the falling star betokens a victorious thrust from their forces against the enemy. Caesar's augurs confirm his interpretation.

The next day, under pressure from the optimates, Pompeius orders his ten legions, some forty thousand strong, into battle formation. Each legion is drawn up in the regular tripartite configuration – four cohorts, then three more, and finally the remaining three as a reserve line.

Pompeius' right flank brushes the river bank. Its Cilician legion and Spanish cohorts are commanded by Lucius Afranius. The Pompeian center is held by Metellus Scipio with his Syrian legions. Pompeius concentrates most of his might on his left flank. Here, under Domitius Ahenobarbus' command are the Legions I and III – those donated by Caesar ostensibly for service against Parthia – plus all of Pompeius' seven thousand horsemen under Titus Labienus. Archers and slingers are formed up to support them. The Magnus positions himself here.

Pompeius sees victory in pushing back Caesar's right flank with his massive cavalry and then swinging behind Caesar's rear and rolling up the whole line. It is a perfect plan, almost foolproof – on parchment.

Caesar appreciates his foe's strategy, and he makes provision to counter it. His left flank, held by Legions VIII and IX under Marcus Antonius' command, is positioned on the river bank. His center is held by three legions under Domitius Calvinus. Three legions, including Caesar's favorite, the Tenth, hold the right flank. To command them, Caesar has appointed a new member to his staff, Publius Cornelius Sulla, a former Catilinian conspirator and fugitive who has lived for years in exile in Macedonia. Service under a victorious Caesar is his anticipated path to a rehabilitated political and civic life.

Also on the right flank, Caesar has massed his few hundred horsemen, knowing full well that they will not hold against the imminent onslaught of Pompeius' cavalry. The master strategist takes precautions against the enemy's attempt to turn his flank. He passes the order down through legates and tribunes and centurions – one cohort from each legion is withdrawn from the battle line and moved into position on the right flank, out of view and hidden by the Tenth Legion and by the cavalry. The men of this fourth, hidden line are given special directions from Caesar himself. They acclaim him with the battle cry, *"Venus Victrix!"* and they pledge themselves to do their duty.

Placing himself between the center and the left wing, Caesar, astride his war-horse, orders the buccinators and trumpeters to sound the advance. The entire front line and the second line move forward at a steady pace; the legionaries hold their javelins at the ready and their big oblong shields are held aloft on their left forearms.

At one hundred paces from the enemy, the buccinators sound the charge and the legionaries break into a run. But the centurions see that Pompeius' lines remain immobile, awaiting Caesar's charge. Lest the attackers should exhaust themselves before making contact with their foes, they are ordered to slow their advance. Then, at fifty paces from the Pompeians, Caesar's front rank explodes with the guttural battle cry, *"Venus Victrix!"* They discharge their javelins at the enemy's front lines, and then they charge forward, swords drawn for the kill. At the same time, the second rank directs its javelin volley at the Pompeian rear ranks.

The deadly iron shafts, with their sharp barbs and heavy wooden stocks, find their targets. While some of the Pompeians parry the incoming javelins with their shields, scores and hundreds of others are pierced, transfixed to the hot, dry earth which is soon drenched with the blood of the wounded and the dying and the dead. Within minutes, the front ranks of both armies are engaged in hand-to-hand combat. Caesarians and Pompeians thrust, stab, parry against each other, all the while striving to maintain their formations. The legionaries on both sides hold their ground. They stand shield to shield and shoulder to shoulder, but those who fall are methodically replaced by legionaries moving up to the combat line.

From his position on the left flank, Pompeius decides to activate his envelopment. He orders his aquilifer to raise the standard and wave it aloft. Seeing the signal, the cavalry commanders order their *ala* and *turmae* units forward at the gallop. The mass of seven thousand horsemen charges across the field, shouting their battle cry, *"Hercules Invictus!"* They crash into Caesar's right flank, scattering his cavalry and pushing back the men of the Tenth Legion as the Pompeian archers and slingers assail them with arrows and stones and lead balls.

But their charge and their engagement with the enemy have broken their formation; they have become an amorphous assemblage of men and horses, enveloped in the heat and swirling dust of the battlefield. They do not have time to regroup before Caesar's hidden eight cohorts are upon them. The charging legionaries wield their javelins like spears, stabbing and thrusting at horses and riders alike. Hundreds are killed and toppled from their mounts in only minutes. As their deficient saddles lack stirrups, for Roman technology has yet to develop them, the

Pompeian horsemen cannot resist the ferocity of this surprise attack, and this unconventional mode of combat unnerves them. Panic-stricken, the Pompeians turn and wildly flee from the field, leaving the defenseless archers and slingers to be slaughtered like sheep.

Caesar observes the action from his command position on the right flank. His tactic has succeeded in thwarting Pompeius' envelopment. Now, he takes the initiative. He orders his shock troops and regrouped cavalry to join with the recalled Tenth Legion and charge around the enemy's exposed left flank. At the same time, he sends couriers to his legates; the second and third lines, up to now held in reserve, are ordered to advance *en masse*.

The Pompeian lines cannot withstand the onerous onslaught, while the Caesarian envelopment of their left wing is total. Pompeius is first to leave the field. Frantically, he rides back to his camp.

All along his lines, there is wild, panicked flight, and the pursuing Caesarians make bloody work of them. Though spent by the oppressive heat and the deadly rigors of the battle, the victors yet press on, chasing the fugitives to their camp. They storm the ramparts like waves crashing over a mole. The defenders are beaten back and butchered. Pompeius' camp is overrun and captured. But there is no sign of Pompeius, for the Magnus and a group of horsemen have precipitately fled the camp.

Caesar crosses the bloody, corpse-strewn field, followed closely by his legates and aides. They hear the legionaries salute him as Imperator as they have hundreds of times before when he had vanquished the Gauls. But this, perhaps his greatest victory, is a triumph over his own countrymen.

Caesar's path from the Rubicon to Spain and to Macedonia, from Dyrrachium to Pharsalus on the plains of Thessaly has been a quest for the ultimate, yet evasive resolution, for the victor's mind resounds with the question: *Where is Pompeius Magnus?*

Cicero's Respublica

At about the middle of Sextilis, we received news as black as death. Pompeius had been soundly defeated near a Thessalian town named Pharsalus. Refugees brought in conflicting, fragmentary reports. Among them were Metellus Scipio and, to my great relief, you and your uncle and your cousin. You were all bloodied and shaken but whole and alive.

Your wounds were dressed, and after you were fed and afforded some time to rest, Cato asked Scipio to report on the battle.

"We were camped on a plain opposite Caesar's position," Metellus began. The recounting of the event creased his lined face with new evidence of pain. "For days, Caesar arranged his legions offering us battle. But Pompeius won't budge. Then, after five days of this taunting and much criticism from Lentulus and Marcellus, he ordered the legions to deploy for battle. Immediately, Caesar met our challenge."

Metellus paused long enough to take a swallow of wine. The veins in his temples and thick neck throbbed as he drank. "I held the center with the two legions from Syria. Our right flank held the steep banks of a river. What was it? The…yes, they called it the Enipeus. Lentulus Crus and Domitius were in command there. Pompeius and Marcellus held the left. That's where the legions, the First and the Third, the ones from Caesar, were placed along with all our cavalry, archers and slingers."

My brother interrupted, "I was in command of a cohort in the Third Legion." Then, indicating you and your cousin, he added, "They were among the cavalry." You and your cousin appeared uncomfortable, almost ashamed at the mention of your part in the battle.

Metellus grimaced at the interruption and then continued. "Pompeius wouldn't give us the order to advance. The whole line stood motionless when Caesar began to attack. They hurled their javelins at our whole front at one and the same time. Our men shielded themselves as best they could, but many fell under that hail of missiles. Then Caesar's whole front line charged us with drawn swords. Our men held and this may have been part of our undoing. We should have met their charge on the run rather than standing still for it. Anyway, the fighting was fierce, neither side giving nor receiving quarter. And the *heat*! Good gods! I don't remember a hotter day in my whole life. We nearly melted under that sun."

Impatiently, Cato demanded, "What was Pompeius' plan – to fight standing still?"

Again, Quintus cut in. "We had some seven thousand horses, far more than what we could see Caesar had…."

"The *plan*," Metellus annoyingly announced, "was to sweep around Caesar's right wing with our cavalry. Once this was accomplished, our entire line would charge. It was a brilliant plan...."

"Yes!" Quintus declared. "But totally transparent to someone as sharp as Caesar. "He must have guessed what Pompeius was up to, and he prepared for it. After an hour of fighting, Pompeius ordered the cavalry and archers and slingers to charge. They moved forward in a great mass pushing back Caesar's right. But suddenly, out of nowhere, a force – I'd say about six cohorts – attacked our horsemen, making mincemeat of them and slaughtering the archers and slingers."

Cato turned to you, my son, and to young Quintus. "The two of you were with the cavalry?" When you both hesitated to respond, he snapped at you, "Well?"

"Yes!" You shot back. "We were among them. We went as far as we could, but, well...."

"Those legionaries," young Quintus cut in, "they came from behind Caesar's lines. They charged at us like...like savages. Instead of hurling their javelins, they thrust at our horses and even into our faces. We... we had to fall back."

"Afraid of getting your dainty faces scarred, eh?" Metellus sarcastically asked.

I felt my blood starting to boil, and at the same time I was pained by your mortification in having to admit that you had run. Then, with a hard edge to his voice, my brother continued the battle narrative.

"Those hidden cohorts – they were murderous. Not only did they push back our horse, they also charged around our left flank. Caesar did to us what Pompeius had intended doing to him. The only difference – Caesar's stratagem worked! At the same time, he must have ordered his second and third lines into action. Charged from the front by fresh troops and our flank turned, our whole line collapsed into a wild, frenzied retreat."

"But Caesar gave us no respite," Metellus put in. "You'd think his men would be worn out by the fight and the heat. No! They chased us all the way to the ramparts of our camp. With the few cohorts that had been left to guard it, we tried to make a stand. But Caesar's men broke through, scaled the earthworks, surmounted the palisades, and overran the camp. We were lucky to get out."

Now young Gnaeus Pompeius, left behind by his father, asked a crucial question. "And my father?"

Metellus answered, "He fled for the coast, in the direction of Larissa. Lentulus Crus was with him. So was Marcus Favonius. They had some forty horsemen with them."

Cato asked, "What about the legions?"

Metellus shook his head. "They're finished. We lost thousands in the battle, more thousands captured by Caesar's men. Among the dead are Ahenobarbus, Lentulus Spinther, and Claudius Marcellus. Any who survived will be coming back here – except for Labienus. He's supposed to have made for Africa. Perhaps others may follow him."

Cato looked about the town square where we had been meeting. Heavy storm clouds were piling up over the whole coast. With the dusk, torches were being lit and within a few moments, the whole square was illumined. There were at least thirty men present, senators of praetorian and quaestorian rank and military officers.

Cato announced, "Comrades, the first thing we must do is appoint an interim leader until we can join up with Pompeius." Then he looked directly at me, and I thought: *Oh no, Marcus Cato – no, not me!* "As senior consular, Marcus Cicero should be entrusted with the command. Marcus Cicero, will you accept?"

I declined the proffered command. Then, I made the mistake of giving my reasons. I told them that the issue was lost. "Give up all intentions of continuing the war," I urged them, "and let us accommodate ourselves to the fact of Caesar's victory."

Cato implored me to desist from such defeatist expressions as the men began to murmur in an ugly, reproachful undercurrent. Then, young Gnaeus Pompeius, infuriated at my pronouncements, came at me with his drawn sword.

"I'll show *you* how the fight is lost for *you* and all *traitors* like you!" he growled. I heard cries of *"Traitor!"* from the assembly as they all began to close in on me. Their blood was up and they wanted a scapegoat.

Fortunately for me, Cato and Quintus, and you and your cousin interposed yourselves and saved me from being killed on the spot. For our own safety, we were obliged to withdraw from the assembly. Subsequently, we learned that they named Metellus Scipio as commander in my stead. They resolved to regroup in Africa and reinforce their remnants with new recruits and with the forces of their Numidian ally, King Juba.

WITHIN A FEW DAYS, WE crossed over to the nearby island of Corcyca. There, Quintus and I had a tempestuous quarrel. We were just getting settled at an inn when he asked me, "Is it true that you gave Pompeius a draft on the money at Ephesus?"

I was taken aback that he knew about my arrangement. "Yes," I replied. "When Pompeius lamented his cash deficits, I offered to help."

"Very generous; yes, my brother, you are generous." Quintus was seething behind a placid exterior. "Pompeius alluded to your generosity the night before Pharsalus. Of course, he was under the impression that I knew of the exchange. That I *knew* of it!" With this last utterance, he exploded in self-righteous wrath. "You drag me into this bloody business, into the *losing* side yet! And behind my back, *you* decide to lend *our* money! How long, Marcus? How long were you going to keep this from me?"

I turned on him with equal vehemence, "*I* dragged you? Let me jar your memory, Quintus. You badgered and pestered me about what we ought to have done. You were not obliged to follow me. You don't remember you had your reasons for going against Caesar...."

"*You* were the cause of my difficulties with Caesar as surely as you squandered my share of the money. As surely as Pompeius is lost, just as surely is the money lost. You had no right to sign over any part of it without my knowledge – without my agreement!"

"Quintus picked up a wax tablet and hurled it against the stone wall. "But it's always been this way. You've always overshadowed my life. You made it to the consulate, but I rose only as far as praetor. Then my career stagnated because I had to be the guarantor of your good behavior. I had to be the bondsman between you and Caesar and Pompeius. I was always wrapped up in the folds of your toga. Even Pomponia said so, and we had many an argument because of *you* and your accursed control. But I've had enough. I'm taking Quintus and Philologus and we're getting out of here! You can stew on your own in this mess. You'll not trip me up any more. Farewell, Marcus – and good riddance!"

Quintus must have been storing up his anger for many years. I had never had any reason to imagine that he bore me such resentment. It wounded me to the heart to hear all of his recriminations, especially in those troubled circumstances.

Quintus was determined to extricate himself from his difficulties. He was not about to partake of the calamities of what he undoubtedly believed was my misplaced loyalty. Accompanied by his son and his slave, he set out in search of Caesar and Caesarian clemency.

Not long after their departure, we – you and Tiro and Metrodorus and I – hired a ship to take us across to Brundisium. We took up residence in the house of Gaius Maenius, Atticus' business client, who had hosted me at the time of my exile. How ironic that now, as a civil war refugee, I was obliged to avail myself of the equite's boundless hospitality in the very same house where I had spent part of my exile.

As I dared not move deeper into Italia, I sent Tiro to Arpinum with letters for Terentia and Tullia. I told him to go on ahead to Roma if he did not find them at the farmstead. Lest I should antagonize Caesarian legionaries on garrison duty, I kept a low, inconspicuous profile. Then, we waited.

Sextilis gave way to September. The heavy, humid air of Brundisium lightened somewhat, dissipating the fetid odor of the harbor. My thoughts were of Quintus and his son.

I hoped they were well and safe. But my brother's recriminations still resounded in my ears. The argument came down to money and politics and loyalty. I was not responsible for my brother's choosing to go over to Pompeius and the optimates, however much he could claim that he had followed my lead. But the money matter was different.

In the years since my accommodation to the triumvirs, I had drawn from the *"sealed jars"* of the money at Ephesus to pay off the arrears on the Palatine house. Then, Quintus and I had reaped significant dividends from our investments in several equestrian consortia. Additionally, the profits from selling captured brigands into slavery during my Cilician proconsulate had augmented our joint account at Ephesus. I had *never* had any notion that the accumulated funds – close to four million sesterces – were exclusively mine. Yet, during my sojourn at the Thessalonica camp, alienation and desperation had caused me to assume a singularly possessive attitude. In lending the money to Pompeius, I had hoped to improve our damaged relations and at the same time bolster the Republican war chest.

Looking back, I may have assumed their victory as a foregone conclusion and as a certain repayment of the loan. Pharsalus, however, totally negated my calculations. Also, in the aftermath of my falling out with Quintus, I realized that I had blundered by not consulting him about the loan.

Over the years, had I expected too much of him? His loyalty to me had been without limit and conditions. Had I hampered him? Had I truly given him cause to reproach me?

Money, politics, and loyalty – how deeply they cut. I was estranged from my brother because of them. I had chosen to forego my neutrality and I had backed the losing side in the civil war because of misplaced political loyalties, and inappropriate use of money. Now, as I waited for the next set of events to play out, I realized that a new period of exile had descended upon me, and yet again I was tortured on the rack of uncertainty.

Caput XIV Cicero's Respublica

WITHIN A FORTNIGHT AFTER OUR arrival at Brundisium, Tiro returned. He brought with him Tullia and Alexio. To see my *Tulliola* again after more than a year was like returning from the dead. We wept as we embraced each other. She looked so much healthier and stronger than when I had last seen her. She appeared well recovered from the miscarriage, at least outwardly.

Tullia seemed unwilling to talk about her mother, except to say that she was well. When I asked why Terentia had not come down with her, she told me that there was so much about which I needed to be brought up to date.

Alexio gave me letters from Atticus and Servius. Indeed, so very much had happened during my absence. First of all, the government in Roma was headed by Publius Servilius Vatia, Caesar's consular colleague. He regretted that as Consul, he could not sanction my return to Roma. So, I was advised to remain at Brundisium until such time as Caesar could review my situation.

My friends' letters pieced together the threads of political events since we had gone to Macedonia.

When informed of Caesar's victory in Spain, Praetor Marcus Lepidus had urged the Senate, packed with Caesarian supporters and neutrals, to name Caesar dictator. Upon returning to Roma, Caesar had entered upon the dictatorship so as to implement certain administrative acta, namely to secure his and Vatia's election to the consulate. However, after only eleven days, he had resigned the dictatorship, all the while preparing to cross into Macedonia to attack Pompeius.

Then, in the wake of the news of the Pharsalus victory, the Senate, at Vatia's motion, proclaimed Caesar dictator for a term of one year. Servius believed that Caesar would probably maneuver at retaining the dictatorship indefinitely.

Atticus explained his involvement with the Caesarian bankers, Balbus and Oppius, in formulating war-time monetary policies. During Caesar's emergency eleven-day dictatorship, money hoarding had been prohibited. Creditors had been legally bound to accept land in place of money for payment of debts. Land values were to be assessed at pre-war rates. Caesar had decreed that in all cases of debt, interest already paid should be deducted from the principal. By Atticus' reckoning, this measure would amount, ultimately, to a reduction of indebtedness by as much as one-fourth.

Though Caesar's financial program was designed to placate both creditors and debtors, Atticus believed that extremists would find the plan objectionable because it did not go far enough to ease the burdens of debtors or to protect the interest of creditors.

Touching on political legislation, Servius explained that at Caesar's direction, the Centuriate Assembly had recalled many political exiles, with the notable exception of Titus Milo. Also, Caesar attained a goal that had been on his agenda for about fifteen years: Roman citizenship was extended to the inhabitants of Cisalpine Gaul. Through this measure, he broadened the base of his political clientage, particularly because the Cisalpina had proven to be a reliably fertile recruiting ground for his legions.

But while Caesar was fighting Pompeius in Macedonia, dissension within his own party had emerged. My former pupil and protégé, Marcus Caelius, had been elected praetor. He used his office to agitate for a greater reduction of debt. One of his colleagues, the Urban Praetor, Gaius Trebonius, a staunch Caesarian, and Consul Servilius Vatia had had to resort to force to drive Caelius' volatile supporters from the Forum. Then the Senate had suspended Caelius from office when he refused to desist from his demands.

Utlimately, Caelius had departed from Roma, ostensibly to seek out Caesar. However, neither Servius nor Atticus, or anyone else for that matter, was quite sure of exactly where Caelius had gone. My friends shared the view that there was bound to be more trouble from him and the debtors, of whom there were thousands all over Italia.

Relating to personal matters, Atticus wrote that he and Pilia had had a child, a little girl whom they named Caecilia Attica. (The name Caecilia was derived from Atticus' curmudgeonly, adoptive uncle, and Attica was the feminine form of his own assumed cognomen.) She was a healthy child, and Pilia was a loving mother. However, his sister, my sister-in-law, Pomponia, was, as usual, loud and impossible.

Atticus was looking out for the property of my young ward, Publilia. She was becoming a lovely, nubile young woman. The girl's mother and older brother were very protective of her, fearing, no doubt, the advances of fortune-hunting suitors. Atticus mentioned that Publilia often questioned him about me and our family.

Concerning my own accounts and properties, Atticus assured me, they were in order and untouched by the Caesarians. Finally, he advised me to remain as tranquil as possible while awaiting Caesar's return, and he promised to keep me informed as he would use his influence on my behalf with the Caesarians in Roma.

As a post-script, he advised me to be attentive to Tullia. He thought it inappropriate to relay certain developments touching directly upon her. These, he wrote, should be better spoken of by Tullia herself.

"Tullia—what is it, my child?" I questioned her that night after supper at Maenius' dining room, but her reply was evasive. "Is it your mother?"

Again, Tullia said that her mother was well, though her pains in the joints had flared up so acutely that they had had to leave Arpinum and return to Roma last winter.

"Then what is Atticus referring to?"

"Please, Tata, don't press me about it. Not now."

I could not breach her resistance and so I gave up trying, at least for the time being. Besides, Tullia was adept at changing the subject when it suited her. Lovingly and indulgently, I allowed her to do so on several occasions. In this way, I learned about the minutiae of Aunt Pomponia's chronic constipation and Aunt Fabia's and Mother's differing theories on how best to alleviate it.

With each passing day, I expected Terentia to arrive, but she did not come. Instead, she wrote to me, and her letters were full of concern for my welfare. Though she frequently proposed coming to Brundisium, she also gave this or that excuse for not coming. In my letters of reply, I told her not to trouble herself in coming to me, all the while hoping that she would lovingly disobey me. I was hurt that she did not come, and soon, my pain turned to anger. Tullia noticed my annoyance, and before long we were discussing Terentia.

"Tata, while you were away, Mother complained, but she didn't mean what she said. She was so upset. We were both upset."

"About *what* did she complain?" I asked. But Tullia was reluctant to continue. "Tell me truly, child."

She swallowed hard and then admitted, "Mother said you had a penchant for choosing the wrong side and the wrong cause. She said your misjudgments strained our family, especially our finances."

Again—*money*! "What else, Tullia? What else did your mother say?"

She shook her head and looked away from me. Even so, I saw tears filling her eyes. "Mother complained about… she said she'd probably have to use her own money to save you from… from whatever might happen if Caesar defeated Pompeius and the Senate."

"Your mother actually said *that*?" I asked incredulously.

"Please, Tata! Don't hold it against her. Mother was overwrought when she said these things. She didn't mean any of them."

Tullia was unwittingly confirming certain impressions that had begun to take shape in my mind. I was fully aware of the real possibilities of Caesarian reprisals against me because, after my aborted early neutrality, I had gone over to Pompeius and the optimates. I surmised that, at the least, my properties, some anyway, would be confiscated. If so, then I did not want to be in a position of financial dependence upon a spouse who would probably tighten her own purse strings and thereby inhibit my monetary freedom, and perhaps even my future political freedom. *Future?* Did I even have one?

I was beginning to doubt that Terentia and I had one. I yet loved her and hoped that she loved me. But so much had happened to batter our lives into an empty and purposeless marriage. I was unwilling to allow her to constrain me financially or politically in such a void.

When I confessed these sentiments to Tullia and to you, my son, you both became very upset. Tearfully, your sister implored me to take no drastic measures against Terentia until I had met with her and discussed our differences face to face.

THE WEEKS PASSED, SEPTEMBER GIVING way to October. Still, Terentia did not come to Brundisium. But others did.

One day, the harbor was filled with galleys and transport ships. Tullia, and you and I and Alexio watched them from the docks, a magnificent mass of brown hulls and white and crimson sails emblazoned with the Roman eagle and the Roman lupa.

A small skiff was put out from one of the galleys. As it rowed closer to the dock, I recognized the two figures in it—Marcus Antonius, standing at the prow, and my son-in-law, Dolabella, seated further back. Dolabella recognized us as well, and he waved and smiled at us, calling out, "Tullia!" and "Father!" Even recalling how he used to call me *Father* irritates me. However, Antonius stared at us without any gesture of greeting.

When the vessel had docked, they both came to us. Dolabella and Tullia kissed and embraced each other, but there was a peculiar restraint about their greeting. He warmly shook hands with me and then with you; Antonius followed suit, and he bowed politely to Tullia. Both men wore military uniforms denoting their elevated rank as Caesar's legates. In particular, Antonius was a veritable Hercules, resplendent in his burnished armor and scarlet cloak. He was a magnificently handsome bull, not quite forty years old, and he was totally devoted to Caesar.

Dolabella's prettiness was gone and replaced by a chiseled virility and tanned, weathered cheeks, but the eyes were still sea-blue. "We've brought most of the army with us!" he exclaimed indicating the ships. "Caesar took only two legions and some horse to go after Pomepius. You probably know Caesar's been named Dictator."

"Yes, I know," I quickly put in.

Then, he turned to Antonius and added, "Caesar appointed Antonius as his Master of Horse, and I'm his legate." Dolabella's enthusiasm was met by Antonius' sullen, heavy demeanor.

I replied almost dryly, "You're both to be congratulated. You owe your exalted rank to Caesar's beneficence. Remembering this, I trust you'll be deterred from abusing his power."

Antonius smiled sardonically. "Marcus Cicero, as Caesar's deputies we are empowered to be his eyes and ears and the instruments of his authority. We are charged to maintain order in Roma and throughout Italia and to be vigilant against any and all dissent and opposition." Again, the same sardonic smile crossed his broad mouth. He knew that I had comprehended his warning.

I said to him, "I'm here as a refugee and as a suppliant. With your permission, I'll remain here until I've had an opportunity to state my case before Caesar."

Antonius nodded his assent.

"But I ask that my son be permitted to return to Roma." You were taken by surprise. Antonius looked at you and smiled pleasantly.

"Very well, if young Marcus Cicero desires to return to Roma, he may do so," Antonius offered.

Dolabella patted you on the back. "You can travel with us!"

You objected. "Father, but are you sure that you don't want me to remain here with you?"

"Your mother longs to see you, son. Go to her. It's very unlikely she'll be coming here. So you'd better go to her."

"As you wish, Father."

Then Dolabella turned to Tullia. "Will you return with me to Roma, Tullia?" he asked rather sheepishly.

"No, Publius. I'm staying here with Father."

My daughter's response stunned me as much as it gratified me. I sensed that something was not right here, especially because Dolabella did not seem surprised by her refusal to leave with him. But he was certainly displeased.

"Very well then," he bitterly conceded. "Stay. Stay as long as you wish." Then he pulled me aside and we walked a few paces away from the others. "Father, you know I'll do all I can to intercede for you." He drew in closer to me as though we were hatching some sinister plot. Again, at hearing him call me *Father* I cringed. But this was not all. It unnerved me that I should be dependent upon his influence with the Caesarians.

"Very good of you," I managed to say with sardonic aplomb.

"You see, I'm planning to run for the tribunate."

"*Tribunate?!?!* But you're a *patrician!* Surely you know that's strictly a plebeian office."

"*Adoption,* Father," he said without missing a beat. "Adoption by a willing plebeian; it shouldn't be hard to find a willing adoptive father."

I remembered that Publius Clodius had trod the same path. "But why would you want to be a tribune of the plebs?"

"Father, as tribune I could be very useful to you. But the canvass is an expensive undertaking and I'm rather short of money just now." He looked at me sideways.

Beware! Here it comes, I thought, another assault of *pecus.*

"You know, it would truly help me if I could have another installment…of the dowry. I realize all too well that your present predicament may, well, shall we say, make a payment… difficult. But if you could see your way…."

What rubbish! I thought. He was totally insensitive to my plight. It was easy for him to be insensitive because he did not know that I owed Caesar eight hundred thousand sesterces plus interest; or that I had lost close to four million sesterces that had been lent to Pompeius. I was toying with the idea of divorcing Terentia, and I knew that this would entail repayment of her substantial dowry. On top of all this, my son-in-law was demanding dowry payments in an insipid, fawning, minced speech. I wasn't even certain that I would *live* after Caesar returned to Italia!

Notwithstanding all these considerations, I told Dolabella that I would contact Atticus and arrange a payment. This seemed to placate my avaricious son-in-law.

The galleys and transports had begun to discharge their soldiers and cargoes. The entire harbor heaved and swelled with toil and activity. We were obliged to move out of the way. However, before departing, I invited Dolabella and Antonius to join us for refreshment. They graciously thanked me, but politely declined, saying that they had to oversee the disembarkation and the billeting of the legionaries.

"But if it is not inconvenient, Marcus Cicero," Antonius suggested, "could you offer us a late supper this evening?"

"Of course," I agreed. "We're staying at the house of Gaius Maenius. Everyone in Brundisium knows it. We'll see you at the ninth hour?"

Antonius smiled amicably. "Agreed."

On the way back to Maenius' house, I attempted to question Tullia about Dolabella. "Why did you refuse to go back to Roma with your husband?" I inquired of her.

"Because I'm needed here," she smiled in reply. But when I looked into her eyes the smile vanished.

"My *Tulliola*, is that the only reason?" My daughter's eyes held heavy tears.

We walked on in silence to the house through crowded, narrow streets. Burly Alexio preceded us, clearing our path. Once we had arrived, Tullia opened up to me. "After Caesar had returned from Spain, Dolabella learned that we were at Arpinum. He was so tender to me. He was sorry about the baby. It was almost winter; the rains were about to begin, and Mother was complaining about her joints. So, we agreed at Dolabella's urging to return to Roma. But he went back ahead of us because he said he was needed by Caesar.

"Well, this bothered me and Mother, but, as we had Alexio with us, we thought we'd be safe returning on our own. We had no trouble going back and we found the house in good order. But on the day we arrived...." Tullia's voice cracked and she sobbed.

"What happened, child?" I implored.

"*Oh, Tata!* He betrayed me!"

I was not surprised. After all, this *was* Dolabella. "With whom, Tullia?"

"With Antonius' wife, though I'm not entirely sure about it." Tullia managed to speak between sobs.

"Then why do you suspect Antonia?"

"That's what Atticus and Servius told me. They said Antonius had complained to them, suspecting Dolabella was trying to seduce Antonia. They said Antonius was capable of killing him were it not for Caesar's authority. But about the *other*—I've no doubt!"

"The other?" I hoped she could tell me without breaking down into another crying jag.

"Mother and I saw him going into Clodia Pulchra's house late in the afternoon."

"*Clodia Pulchra!*" The name stabbed me like a legionary's sword. "Will we ever be free of those ubiquitous Pulchers?"

"He must not have known that we were at home," Tullia continued. "Night fell, and he did not come out until the following day, almost at noon. Then, he must have discovered we were at home because he called on us.

"I asked him about his visit to Clodia. He didn't deny it. He said he had gone to her to borrow money, for she was very generous. He said this so facetiously, so casually, that I began to lose my temper. 'Your father is so tight-fisted about paying your dowry,' he complained, 'I've had to borrow money from anyone willing to lend it, and Clodia's certainty willing to put out.'

"'*Did* she *put out* for you?' I asked him as my heart ached and broke within me. Dolabella threw back his head and laughed. 'Where should I have gone? With civil war, the money lenders are charging ridiculous interest rates, while your father slips off to Pompeius!'"

Hearing all this, my own heart broke apart like a shattered clay vessel. *Dolabella! Shameless cad!* I was aghast at how he treated my daughter. His behavior was deplorable and with all people, *Clodia Pulchra!* She was probably mounting and riding him to spite me and, through Tullia's anguish, contriving to wound me.

Yet, between sobs, Tullia admitted that despite his infidelities, she still loved him, loved him too much to terminate their marriage. She hoped Dolabella would reform his behavior with the end of the war. Indeed, the war should have ended at Pharsalus; but Pompeius was a fugitive pursued by Caesar, while the optimates mobilized new legions; it could be sometime before my son-in-law could be expected to settle down. *How* she could have loved him I could not understand!

"What has your mother had to say about all this?" I asked.

"She *despises* him!" Tullia admitted. "She said *this* is yet another proof of Pulchra's promiscuity. She even has the wild notion that you and she...."

"Never mind that! That's your mother's nonsense. What has she advised you to do?"

Tullia shrugged. "Mother said that there's hardly a marriage in all Roma that's not been tainted by either partner's infidelity. But according to the law, if I divorce him, he'd be entitled to keep whatever portion of my dowry that you've paid."

So true, and how exacting it was of Terentia to point that out. Dolabella was sharp enough to realize this as well. That's why *he* didn't divorce Tullia, for then *he* would have to repay the dowry. He probably had already gone through the money I had paid him. So, he was borrowing from *Medusa of the Palatine* and bedding her as a bonus. Strange though, I saw my own predicament reflected in Dolabella's callousness. Yet, I would rather have lost the money than see my *Tulliola* hurt and manipulated by such a blackguard.

"Then bear with him, daughter," I advised her, "*if* you wish to stay in this marriage. But if he ever broaches the subject of divorce, don't discourage him. Understand?"

"Yes," she nodded. "Tata, I love you so!"

I WAS BEGINNING TO REGRET that I had invited Antonius and Dolabella for supper, for just then I could not abide the sight of my rakish churl of a son-in-law, or for that matter *anyone* of the Caesarian party. Whence I summoned the tact and reserve to be hospitable to them I cannot say. I must admit, however, that Dolabella was polite and deferential. Actually, so was Antonius. Though Dolabella's affectionate attentions to Tullia unnerved me, I gave no outward sign of annoyance. Unfortunately, I was not as successful in concealing my dismay at hearing Antonius' narrative of the Pharsalus battle. While his account did not differ markedly from Quintus' and Metellus Scipio's, Antonius added certain details that filled me with a deeper despair for the Republic.

"The optimates lost the heart of their faction," Antonius recalled. "That Lentulus who had pulled off your recall was found among the dead in Pompeius' center. The proconsuls Claudius Marcellus and Domitius Ahenobarbus fell defending their camp. And their camp! It was decked out with laurel and oak as if they had already won! When we got to Pompeius' tent, Caesar found a satchel of letters, notes, what-not. He knew full well he'd discovered names of friends, allies, supporters of Pompeius."

At that instant, Antonius shot me a suspicious glance before pausing long enough to take a drink of wine.

"Well, we'll never know. Caesar ordered the whole bag to be burned. And it was, right in front of him too. He said he wanted no recriminations against those who'd taken up the sword against him. *Clemency.* That's what Caesar's all about. That's his policy."

If that were actually the case, I wondered if there would be any clemency available for me and for all the men of the Cicero family.

"We must have captured well over twenty thousand legionaries," Antonius crowed. "He allowed them to join his own ranks or to go back home in peace. But he warned them not to make war on him again; well, we'll see about that. If and when he catches up with the fugitives, with Lentulus Crus, the other Claudius, and Pompeius himself, he'll doubtless extend the same leniency to them. But we've had reports that Cato, Scipio, and others are putting together a new army in Africa with their Numidian allies. I don't know that they'll ever come to terms with Caesar."

I interrupted him to dare to ask about Pompeius.

"We heard he'd gone to the coast, and Caesar surmised that he might make for Ephesus. We were given our orders to take the bulk of the army back to Roma." Then, almost facetiously he added, "I'm sure Pompeius will turn up somewhere before long."

Returning to a serious tone, Antonius mentioned a staggering casualty count among the optimate forces. "I was with Caesar when he rode across the field. We saw the dead in heaps, the wounded and dying vomiting blood, crying aloud like so many orphaned children. The field was strewn with lopped-off arms, legs, and heads. I heard Caesar say, as if he were thinking aloud, '*They* wanted it so, not I'. It took three days to gather and stack, burn and bury their dead and ours. But our losses were minimal compared to the optimates. They sacrificed some fifteen thousand men."

All during Antonius' recitation of these gruesome details, you and your sister sat in stunned silence. Dolabella's eyes furtively darted from Tullia to Antonius and then to me. I almost felt dizzy and a hard dull pain attacked my bowels.

"Yes, Pharsalus was a slaughter," Antonius concluded. "Such is war. Whether or not there are other such fratricides depends on your friends, Cicero. I hope they'll learn to be as prudent and as... *accommodating...* as you've been."

You and your sister and I exchanged glances. You both must have noticed the umbrage registered on my face just as I saw the pain showing on yours. Sensing my irritation, Dolabella suggested that the hour was late. As they had to get an early start in the morning for Roma, he and Antonius thanked us for our hospitality and graciously took their leave. Tullia once again refused her husband's invitation to return with him to Roma.

Over breakfast the next morning, I bade farewell to you, my son. However, Tullia insistently refused my suggestion that she go with her husband. How loyal and devoted was my *Tulliola*.

NEAR THE END OF THE year, with the December rains pelting the earth, we had been in Brundisium about three months. The major talk in town was about disturbances at Thurii in Brutium on the far side of the Italian arch. Thurii had become the rallying point for a debtors' revolt. I remembered Atticus' letter describing Caelius' abortive debtor agitation in Roma.

A new letter from my business friend related yet again that, all things considered, my financial affairs were in relatively sound condition, barring of course, my indebtedness to Caesar and the insecurity of the Ephesian account.

Generally, however, the same observation could not be made elsewhere. Atticus reported that Pompeian properties were being seized without payment by Antonius, Dolabella, and other Caesarians.

Dolabella had indeed canvassed for the tribunate, all the while making public pronouncements against Caesar's debt program. Atticus acknowledged the pocket of debtor insurgency down in Thurii. He even noted that its reputed leader was none other than my former protégé, the suspended praetor, Caelius. Rumor had it that Titus Milo, my former benefactor, had returned illegally from exile and had joined the insurgents. How many were there? Atticus could not say. But the Master of Horse, Marcus Antonius, and Consul Servilius Vatia were preparing to take action against them.

While Titus Milo had returned illegally, other exiles availed themselves of Caesar's clemency. These included my consular colleague, Gaius Antonius, and Aulus Gabinius, who had been convicted and banished because of his illegal but successful restoration of Ptolemy

Auletes. While Antonius kept a low profile, Gabinius accepted a military commission under Caesar. But his tenure was short-lived. Atticus reported that he had been killed fighting Pompeian forces in Illyricum.

I learned that you were with your mother, and she and Pomponia, Fabia, and Pilia were in good health, despite their distress over the general uncertainty of the times. So much of Pomponia's anxiety was the result of letters she had received from Quintus. Atticus conveyed their essence, and I found the news very distressing.

After parting from us at Corcyca, Quintus and his son had caught up with Caesar at Ephesus. Caesar had gone there from Pharsalus because he had been informed that Pompeius was in the vicinity. Two other Pompeians had also been looking for Caesar. Marcus Junius Brutus, Cato's nephew and, by ribald rumor, the love-child of Caesar and Servilia, had abandoned the optimate faction after its defeat at Pharsalus. Caesar was delighted to see him. Not only did he pardon Brutus, but at the latter's urging, he also pardoned Gaius Cassius, the other defector from the optimates.

During the fighting around Dyrrhacium, Cassius had commanded a naval squadron in the Adriatic. This may have been something of a demotion for the man who had salvaged the remnants of Crassus' shattered army and had secured the Eastern frontier against Parthian invasion. His defection made perfect sense for a man who knew how to survive. Cassius and Brutus were not only comrades-in-arms and recipients of Caesar's clemency; they were also brothers-in-law, for Cassius had married the youngest of Brutus' half-sisters, Junia Tertia.

When Quintus begged Caesar's pardon, he attributed his joining the Pompeians to my persuasion. I could not imagine how much credence Caesar attached to this preposterous claim, but he did extend a conditional pardon to my brother and his son. They were both required to remain at Ephesus until such time as Caesar saw fit to allow them to return to Italia. I saw this as Caesar's way of allowing Quintus to calm his umbrage against me.

Caesar also exacted monetary guarantees of good faith from Brutus, Cassius, and Quintus. These were cash withdrawals from their accounts in the Temple of Artemis in Ephesus. I wondered if my brother appreciated the irony in having to fork over to Caesar the very money that had provoked our quarrel.

Though I was happy to know that Quintus and his son were safe and well, it wounded me to realize from a third-hand source that my brother had had to vilify me in order to obtain Caesar's conditional pardon.

By mid-Januarius, another letter from Atticus confirmed reports that the Brundisium authorities were getting from Thurii. The debtors' revolt there had been bloodily suppressed by troops commanded by Master of Horse Antonius and Proconsul Vatia. Among the casualties, Atticus sadly reported, were Caelius and Milo. How it pained me to read these words, but my pain turned to outrage when Atticus related that among the agitators was my son-in-law, *Dolabella!* His role in this fiasco was certain to compromise further my already poor position with Caesar and his entire faction.

Among other things, the debtors demanded the remission of house rents for one year and a complete cancellation of debts. There had been similar debtors' outcries during my consulate—fifteen years earlier. But I would never have suspected that my former pupil and protégé, or my benefactor, or my own son-in-law would have followed in the footsteps of Catilina!

Servius wrote that elections for new magistrates had never been held under Vatia's consulate. As a result, the New Year had begun with Master of Horse Antonius as the only legitimate authority actually present in Roma. Caesar, the absent Dictator, was said to be in Egypt, where he had gone in pursuit of Pompeius. No one knew when, or even *if* he might be returning to Roma. So, upon Marcus Antonius' broad shoulders would fall the task of restoring some degree of order in the Capital and in Italia.

But Servius was not convinced that the Master of Horse was up to the task. Antonius was far too concerned about indulging his own pleasures, particularly with the twice-widowed wanton, Fulvia. He was virtually living with her, scandalizing whatever was left of conservative morality in Roma, and forcing his compromised wife and cousin, Antonia, to seek solace in her father's house.

At the same time, Dolabella rivaled him in licentiousness. Atticus reported that, despite my son-in-law's house arrest, he was regularly visited by Clodia Pulchra. The gossip-mongers had much grist to grind. How utterly shameless he was! It was not enough that he had transgressed the Dictator's decrees, and in so doing had further compromised me, but he was also pursuing his affair with the *Palatine Medusa*.

I was grateful that at least Tullia was with me rather than in Roma as her husband mocked their marriage.

Omniscient Narrative

Gaius Antonius Hybrida, former consul and recently returned from exile, has purchased a small house in the Subura, a Roman neighborhood that ordinarily would have been spurned by the magisterial class. The house is sparsely furnished, for Antonius has brought few possessions with him. However, his most prized possession is a wax life mask of his deceased wife, the mother of Antonia.

Antonia and her child have come to live with her father because she can no longer bear the calumny of her husband's reproaches or the indignity of his infidelities. She studies her mother's image, set on a pedestal in the dimly lit atrium. Her memories of the woman have been strained by the passage of time since her untimely death. Yet, the life mask's wide mouth and high cheek-bones reflect Antonia's own face.

In her reverie, she senses that she is not alone. Gaius Antonius has entered the atrium, his heavy shoes slapping hard on the stone floor. "What are you doing, daughter?"

"Just having a few words with Mother. I'm glad you've kept this after so many years."

The porcine-faced consular agrees. "Yes, your mother's image gave me much comfort when I was down at Malta. Had she lived, I'm certain she would have joined me in exile."

Antonia approaches her father. "What would she have told me to do about Marcus?"

Antonius presses his lips together in a frown. "Antonia, I believe she would have agreed with my advice—let your husband make the move."

"He's using me, Father."

"Yes, I know."

"Using me as an excuse to lock up Dolabella and take up with that flame-haired lupa. She's got her claws so deeply imbedded in him that...."

From the street is heard the neighing of horses and the grinding of wheels against the cobbled street. A familiar voice barks orders to his escort and to his horses.

"It's Marcus!" Antonia murmurs in alarm.

Not a moment passes before the Master of Horse has entered the house and stands with them in the atrium. His dark, curly hair, bull-like face, and muscular neck dominate his burnished cuirass as though he were a moving statue. He throws back his crimson cloak over his right shoulder. His bronze-trimmed leather boots reach to the knees of his muscular legs. He smiles broadly, yet briefly to his cousin-wife and to his uncle-father-in-law. "Greetings, Antonia. Greetings, Uncle Gaius."

They return his greeting with polite reservation. Gaius Antonius asks him, "Have you had news of your brothers?"

Marcus Antonius walks half-way about the small atrium. "Lucius is still holding Asia for Caesar. Gaius was taken prisoner in Illyricum. I've had no word about his whereabouts." He looks about the atrium, arches his eyebrows, and adds, "Uncle Gaius, I could have arranged for a better house for you."

"Thank you, Marcus, but we're comfortable here, for now."

Marcus Antonius catches the plural in his uncle's reply and smiles. "Well, I'm happy to hear that." He approaches Antonia and places a scroll in her hand. "This will make it official."

Realizing that she has just been presented with a notice of divorce, Antonia passes it to her father. "Are you sure this is what you want, Marcus?"

As his uncle-father-in-law peruses the scroll, Marcus Antonius raises his head imperiously. "Our marriage is unsalvageable. I cannot maintain it as you might have been the lover of a man who has flagrantly betrayed and attempted to subvert Caesar's interests."

"And what of *your own betrayals*, my husband?" Antonia dares to challenge him.

Marcus Antonius' face flushes to the same color as his cloak. But before he can speak, Gaius Antonius interjects, "You *will* make full restitution of Antonia's dowry?"

"Just as I've written," Marcus replies while glaring at Antonia, "but not until things settle down. There's much to attend to in Roma and in...."

"What a hypocrite you are, Marcus Antonius!" Antonia sneers at him. "Just like Caesar's wife, so too must Antonius' wife be above suspicion. That's it, isn't it, Marcus? Your Imperator's hypocrisy has now become your own. But I'll not dignify your suspicions by either *admitting* or *denying* anything! Go and discuss them with *your* mistress—*Fulvia!*"

Marcus Antonius exhales deeply. "Take care of our daughter. If either of you need anything.... Farewell!" He turns and stamps out of the house. Only moments later, the street echoes with the sounds of his departing chariot and mounted escort.

Gaius Antonius rolls up the scroll and taps his left palm with it. Having only recently returned from exile, he is in no position to oppose his nephew's wishes. Neither is Antonia, and she knows it well.

Cicero's Respublica

Accompanied by Tiro, I was in the habit of taking daily walks from Maenius' house to the harbor. Though the foul odors of the docks were utterly repugnant, I was always looking for arrivals, fugitives from the broken optimate forces. I hoped that one day Quintus and his son might be landing and that we might reconcile our differences. However, there was no sign of them. I even expected Caesar to put in so that I might make amends to him and one way or another end my dreadful uncertainty; but there was no triumphant Caesar disembarking.

Instead, at the beginning of Februarius, a small flotilla of Greek ships docked in the harbor. A large number of women and children came ashore. By their dress, I could see that they were Romans. Strange though, I saw no men among them, aside from some slaves and attendants, most of whom appeared to be tutors for the younger children. The arrivals checked in at a booth manned by a team of centurions and armed legionaries.

For about an hour, I stood and watched this process, until I saw a man who, judging from his clothing, was not a slave but a Roman citizen. Walking beside him, holding his forearm for support, was a Roman lady. From my vantage point, I could not recognize either. Yet, I had the overpowering sense that I knew them.

I approached the centurion's check-point and heard the man identify himself; "Marcus Favonius, former legate of Metellus Scipio, Proconsul of Syria." Then, indicating the woman, he said, "This is Lady Cornelia, wife of Gnaeus Pompeius Magnus."

Yes, of course! Metellus Scipio's daughter! The widow of Publius Crassus! The once vivacious widow was now a harried refugee. No wonder I didn't recognize her by sight alone, and the man with her—I was only remotely acquainted with him. Marcus Favonius had been Cato's protégé. He was a small, spare man, veined like marble, not at all imposing. But circumstances had rendered him the protector, the guardian of Pompeius' wife.

The centurion was incredulous about their identity. He was questioning them for proof, and he was even skeptical when Favonius showed his signet ring. I intervened, "Centurion, I can vouch for them." The centurion was well acquainted with me.

"Very well, Marcus Cicero," he agreed, "if you say so."

"With your permission," I said addressing Favonius and Cornelia indirectly, "I can provide them with lodgings."

The burly soldier humphed his assent. Favonius and Cornelius and their attendants followed us back to Maenius' house. Favonius gratefully acknowledged my intervention, but Cornelia was stone silent.

During our supper, she remained silent, and she hardly picked at her plate. Tullia and I both sensed some deep shell of pain and remorse that enveloped her. Favonius suggested that she might retire. Tullia accompanied her to a spare room where she would spend the night.

I did not have to invite Favonius to tell me what was amiss with the woman, for during the meal we had avoided speaking of the war and of Pompeius. But no sooner had Tullia and Cornelia left the room when Favonius grimaced and bowed his head in dismay.

"She's had a very brutal time, more so than most women experience in a lifetime," Favonius said plaintively.

"What happened after Pharsalus?" I asked, already sensing that some tragedy other than defeat in battle had to have befallen Pompeius.

"The Imperator didn't want to be caught in Greece," Favonius began. "So I led him and a party of horsemen to the port of Larissa. We hired several ships and made directly for Mytilene, on the island of Lesbos, where he had sent all the women and children. He was afraid we might be overtaken by Caesar's ships or any ambitious men out to collect a bounty on him. But we made it safe and sound. When Cornelia saw him, she fell weeping into his arms, reproaching herself that she should live to see him defeated and in flight.

"Pompeius took hold of her and held her at arms' length from himself. He reprimanded her for her self-reproach. 'We must deal with whatever fortune has been allotted to us,' he told her. 'For now we must seek refuge. In time, we'll gather a new army and carry on the fight. But I'll not stand for self-recrimination from my own wife.'

"Young Sextus asked his father where they should go. Proconsul Lentulus Crus, who had fled with us from Pharsalus, suggested Parthia. Pompeius' name was revered among the Parthians. They'd be honored to receive him and succor him. So Lentulus argued. But Pompeius objected. 'They are treacherous. Before I'd put our lives into their hands, I'd rather abase myself before Caesar himself. No, we've only three viable alternatives. We can go to Numidia or to Mauretania, or we can go to Egypt. Egypt is closest. Its ruler owes me much, and he's named me guardian of his children.'

"So it was that we sailed for Egypt after taking on about ten more ships, enough to transport the women and the children, and the cohort commanded by Sextus.

"We had known for some time that the 'Flute-Player' Ptolemy had died and that his kingdom was being jointly ruled by his eldest son and one of his daughters. But it was not until we had landed at Pelusium that we learned that the Egyptians were having their own civil war. The faction supporting the Boy-King had driven the King's elder sister into the desert. A certain minister to the King, a horrid-looking eunuch named Pothinos agreed to allow Pompeius and Lentulus to come ashore. I had misgivings about this, but I could not convince the Imperator to decline.

"In particular, he saw two old comrades-in-arms in the little Egyptian vessel. These were Lucius Septimius, a tribune, and a centurion, one Salvius."

"What were they doing in Egypt?" I interrupted to ask.

"They were in the occupation army that Aulus Gabinius had left in Alexandria, but they had served under Pompeius years ago in the pirate war. When they saw Pompeius, they saluted him as Imperator, and he was put at ease by them. But I still distrusted that freakish-looking Pothinus. Along with him there was a Greek-Egyptian general. He called himself Achillas when he introduced himself in Greek to Pompeius. He had four soldiers with him in the boat. I didn't feel comfortable about him either.

"Cornelia and Sextus implored him not to go with them, but he wouldn't listen. Quoting from Sophocles, he said to them, 'Whoever takes his way into a tyrant's court becomes his slave, although he went there a free man.' He kissed them and embraced them both. Then he and Lentulus descended into the Egyptian vessel, and Achillas extended his hand to assist them.

"The oarsmen began rowing toward the shore as seagulls flying overhead made a deafening cackle. Suddenly, the Roman officers and Achillas and his soldiers drew their swords and attacked Pompeius and Lentulus. Cornelia let out a blood-curdling scream and collapsed onto the deck of our ship.

"Thus it was that great Pompeius and Lentulus Crus, a proconsul of the Republic, were treacherously murdered by the Boy-King's ministers and within our sight."

I was completely stunned and revolted by such barbarism. "But why?" I wondered aloud. "After all that Pompeius had done to secure Egypt's autonomy! What purpose was served by murdering him?"

Favonius shook his head and sighed remorsefully. "They murdered him to curry favor with Caesar, I suppose. A bloody, barbarous gesture calculated, no doubt, to please the victor and win new concessions from Roma. We didn't linger there to speculate. Fearing we'd lose the tide and be captured by the Egyptians, I gave the order to weigh anchor and we sailed away. But Sextus and I looked back to see their butchered bodies dumped onto the beach. They hacked off Pompeius' head and carried it off with them like a gruesome trophy." He shook his head in disgust. "Gods!"

Favonius and Cornelia remained with us for several weeks. Cornelia would not or could not emerge from her own psychic prison built of the walls of memory and the undying image of a murdered husband. Favonius told me that Sextus and the cohort were still at large. For them, the war was not over.

Strangely, a letter from Antonius allowed Favonius and Pompeius' widow to return to Roma. Favonius said he would take her to Pompeius' Alban estate, assuming it had not been appropriated by Caesar's men.

Their departure and my reflections on the terrible news of Pompeius' end cast me into an abysmal depression. My ideal of the Republic's rector, moderator, and gubernator, was dashed and never to be seen again.

I did not know how many more months of exile lay before me at Brundisium, although I was deeply relieved to have my *Tulliola* with me. However, despite her presence, the future, both mine and the Republic's looked perilously bleak.

Nine months later, I walked along the seashore to Tarentum. Caesar's ships and legions had already disembarked. My meeting with him was as inevitable as it was necessary, and I was not going to put it off. Having left Alexio with Tullia back at Maenius' house, I took Tiro and Metrodorus with me.

The October sunshine was brilliant, and a cool, misty breeze wafted over us from the sea. The sand beneath our feet was firm, teasing the incoming waves to assail it. But they crashed far from where we walked. Tiro and Metrodorus were speaking in their native Greek, about what I do not recall. My thoughts dwelled on the months since Pharsalus. Several times, Atticus and Servius had come to visit, each visit lasting several days. We had talked and speculated and reminisced and commiserated. But Terentia had made no attempt to come, and her letters, and my own, had become briefer, even curt, and cold and far less frequent.

As we drew nearer to the town, we saw a large war galley moored in the harbor. I guessed it was Caesar's. There was much activity on the dock and on the ship's deck. Orders were being barked and repeated. Cargoes were being unloaded. Wagons and carts, pulled by sturdy draught animals, were lumbering every which way through the port. Over and above all this commotion, a strident, piercing voice called out, *"Cicero! Marcus Cicero!"*

Straining to see more clearly, I beheld a figure in military attire, a scarlet commander's cloak billowing in the breeze. He was coming toward me on the beach. His head was bare, and I made out his face, the deeply set eyes and aquiline nose, the thin black and gray hair strategically combed over a balding pate. It was Caesar!

"Marcus Tullius Cicero!" he called out to me again. With outstretched arms he came upon me and embraced me as the waves crashed on the seashore and seagulls cackled overhead. "My dear friend, how are you?"

"Relieved at your safe return," I offered.

"I too am relieved at *your* safe return, Marcus." He swung his arm over my shoulders and started us off on a stroll away from the town. I looked over my shoulder, to see Tiro and Metrodorus standing still with Caesar's lictors and attendants.

"Once, I asked you for your help, Marcus. You refused me. Yet, I honored your decision. But then you made common cause with those who opposed me and who were so determined to destroy me, and with me, the Republic."

My eyebrows arched and my head jerked to hear him equate himself with the Republic's welfare. Just then, I became conscious of my clothing, for I was dressed in the garb of mourning, gray, sordid toga and tunic, covered with a coarse, hooded cloak. This was the raiment of an exile such as I had worn when I was pleading for official aid against Clodius' persecution. As though he had been reading my thoughts, Caesar observed, "Why this suppliant's costume, Marcus?"

"It's appropriate so that I may plead for my life," I answered dryly.

Caesar smirked and stopped us both. "Could I give you less than what I've given to men who were more adamantly my foes than you ever were?"

"You are merciful, Gaius," I replied. Then, inhaling the sea air for courage, I asked, "And what is the price for my life?"

Throwing back his head, he laughed winningly. "How very sharp you are, Marcus! Your brother has already made arrangements. Judging from the things he said about you, the two of you have not been in touch."

Of course, I knew exactly what he meant. Yet, though I wanted to hear from him directly about the Ephesian account, I was fearful to ask about it. Instead, Caesar told me of his meeting with Quintus and his son. Quintus had said *this* and Quintus said *that* and Quintus had pleaded for Caesar's clemency. And the upshot was my brother's signing over to him our joint account—my former "sealed-jar" money—as an unofficial penalty for our having joined Pompeius.

"Your other properties and accounts are yours, as is your life. You have my word," Caesar assured me.

Even as he said this, I realized that the loss of the Ephesian money was a relatively small price to pay for my life, and my liberty, and my overall financial security.

"If you wish," he said to me as he started us walking again, "you may return to Roma, or anywhere else you may wish to go."

"Thank you, Gaius Caesar." My humility was genuine.

Once again, he halted as a pained expression clouded his face. "I'm told that Roma is in shambles. I'm going to need help, all I can get, and from all quarters." He looked squarely at me. "Your help, Marcus, to set Roma back in order. No, you needn't answer me now, so don't look so distressed."

Actually, Caesar looked more distressed with each spoken word. He turned and faced out to the gray-green Adriatic Sea. "When I arrived at Alexandria, hoping to find Pompeius and at last settle our differences and put an end to all strife, they showed me his head and gave me his signet ring." He seemed to be choking back tears as he spoke. "Eight years I fought in Gaul. Defeated hundreds of tribes, sacked and looted scores of towns, slaughtered upwards of a million Gauls. But the sight of Pompeius' head revolted me. I wept openly. Yes, he was my enemy because he was used and persuaded by Cato, Bibulus, Ahenobarbus and others to become my enemy. But he'd been my friend, my ally, my daughter's husband. She died trying to give him a child."

He bowed his head and looked down at the beach. "Pompeius is dead. His sons and the optimates still defy me. Even young Marcus

Crassus died in Gaul, nearly two years ago. Did you know that, Marcus?"

I nodded sympathetically.

"There's no one left of the old days whom I can trust; only you, Marcus." He turned from the sea and looked at me closely. "You, Marcus Tullius Cicero. At least think about it. No blame will attach itself to you. On that too you have my word."

We continued to walk along the beach. Caesar told me of his activities following Pharsalus. Failing to find Pompeius in Asia and learning that his rival had fled to Egypt, Caesar had promptly followed. Once there, he had become embroiled in the Egyptian dynastic civil war. His intervention elevated Ptolemy's daughter, Cleopatra, to the throne after her brother and rival had perished in battle. After dallying with the young Queen, Caesar had then marched through Judaea, Syria, and Pontus to reinforce Roman authority. In Pontus, he had defeated the upstart Prince Pharnaces, the son of our late, bitter foe, Mithridates. The Prince's attempt to recover his ancestral kingdom had been decisively checked by Caesar's victory at Zela. His victory message to the Senate, relayed to me by Servius, had been pithy: "Came, saw, conquered."

As I listened, I felt an immensely heavy burden lifted from my spirit. For the second time, I had been rescued from exile by Caesar's dictate, the very same dictate that was to be the foundation of the new order in which he wanted my participation. But first, there were personal matters that needed my attention.

I HAD RESOLVED TO DIVORCE Terentia. This was not an easy decision, but it was necessary because I was unwilling to compromise my political status with a spouse who would attempt to frustrate my financial independence. But this was only the surface. Something had happened to us, something neither Terentia nor I could pinpoint. It may have been the war. It may have been the stresses and hardships of my exile and our separation. Perhaps she had had enough of the vicissitudes of my faltering career. For my part, I was exhausted by her incessant back-biting. I could not have said that I no longer loved her, but during my sojourn at Brundisium, without her solicitude, my affection for her was tempered and diluted by resentment and rejection.

I sent Tiro to Roma with instructions to present Terentia with a notice of divorce. She was permitted substantial time to pack her possessions and vacate the Palatine house. I intended to take up residence at the Tusculum villa, and I arranged for Tiro to open up the house,

About a week after Tiro had started for Roma, Tullia, Alexio, Metrodorus, and I departed from Brundisium. I thanked Gaius Maenius for all of his selfless, abundant hospitality, and he wished me all of Fortuna's favors.

I found myself remembering my triumphal progress to Roma when I had been recalled from exile. This time, however, the trip was different. There were no adoring crowds or laurel-bedecked temples and shrines welcoming me. Instead we passed military outposts garrisoned by Caesar's legionaries.

We made good time and arrived at Tusculum in less than a week. The white-washed, red-tiled house was a refreshing sight. I had not had occasion to visit it since before the war. Tiro was waiting for us. As usual, he had followed my directions to the letter. The house was in a remarkably well-ordered state. I commended Tiro for his efficiency and exactitude. When I questioned him about Terentia, he told me that she had received the divorce notice with calm, quiet reserve.

"Did she say anything?"

"Only that Domina Terentia will comply with your wishes," he replied. "Also, Domina Terentia said that she would contact Titus Pomponius Atticus."

Of course, I thought, she'll arrange for Atticus to collect her dowry. That was the law. Atticus later asked me to reconsider the matter, if only for the sake of my strapped finances.

"Are you quite sure," he asked, "that you want to end this marriage of over *thirty years*? Is this really what you want?"

"Atticus, I've had more than enough time to consider it. Yes, I want to do it. Just make sure that Philotimus doesn't approach me. I want nothing to do with that creature!"

"Very well then, Marcus," Atticus agreed with an abject air of resignation. "But be warned, old friend, this is going to cripple your finances."

Even as he spoke, I saw a remedy to my problem, and I was not slow to seize the opportunity.

Not long after arriving at Tusculum, I was visited by my ward, the young maiden Publilia, and her mother and older brother. Publilia had just turned sixteen. She was a beautiful, young nubile girl-woman. And she was extremely wealthy. As her guardian, I was responsible for managing her fortune until such time as she should marry. The idea of marrying her and securing her money and property as a new dowry for my use was an appealing and most expeditious tactic toward extricating myself from my monetary woes.

Servius and Atticus pooh-poohed the idea of a sixty-year old man marrying a sixteen-year old girl. I answered them with a brazenly vulgar witticism: "Publilia may be a girl today, but in time, she will be a woman."

The girl and her mother and brother were quite enthusiastic about the proposal. In short order, a marriage contract was drawn up, followed by a betrothal, and then the wedding which was held at Tusculum. Tullia was adamantly against the marriage. "It wasn't enough that you divorced my mother," she bitterly protested, "but you've given me a step-mother young enough to be my baby sister!" Publilia was fully aware of Tullia's disapproval. In time, I became the battle-ground of wills between these two headstrong, possessive young women.

However, on the wedding day, Tullia was there and, much to my surprise and discomfort, so was Dolabella, apparently released from house arrest. At first, I thought he had come for another dowry installment. But during the nuptial banquet, Tullia explained that she was moving back to Roma with her repentant husband. I resigned myself to her decision, though my heart ached for her.

You, my son, offered no objections to the marriage. So I assumed that you approved. I noticed that during the ceremony and during the banquet, you could hardly keep your eyes off Publilia. I found it amusing how the two of you, only a few years apart, frequently exchanged furtive smiles.

The wedding banquet was a relatively small, intimate gathering. At least it was intended to be until, completely unexpectedly, Caesar and an entourage of about one hundred soldiers and attendants arrived. As his escort encamped on the grounds, I made room for Caesar on my dining couch. It was almost comical the way he nestled in between Publilia and me, all the while displaying such self-effacing graciousness.

"Felicitations, Marcus Cicero, and Lady Publilia!" Caesar toasted us as he raised a cup of watered wine to his lips. Everyone at the adjacent tables followed suit.

"We thank you, Caesar, for your good wishes." Looking about, I noticed how inebriated Servius was. He drank deeply from his cup and then looked at Caesar drunkenly under drooping lids.

The only political reference from Caesar was to his earlier invitation to contribute my advice and counsel to his regime. "Of course," he qualified, "only after you've tended to matrimonial obligations." Saying this, he cast a quick teasing glance at Publilia. My young wife blushed in response. The rest of the conversation touched on light, banal topics.

Caesar was the first of our guests to leave. He had stayed less than two hours. Before departing, he confided his satisfaction in Dolabella's reformed behavior. "I insist upon uprightness in all my officers. Well then, hail and farewell, Marcus Cicero and Lady Publilia." At the sight of their Imperator, Caesar's lictors and soldiers snapped to attention. He and his aides mounted their horses and then the entire entourage started off for Roma.

Within the next few hours, the guests made their farewells until only Servius was left. His slave helped him so that he could safely descend from the dining couch. Servius waved him away and leaned precariously toward me, reeking of wine. In all the years I had known him I had never seen him in such a state.

"Shall I tell you a secret, Marcus?" His speech was slurred and he hiccupped loudly.

"I didn't think there were any between us, Servius."

He giggled like a naughty child. "A little wine reveals all confidences, all secrets. This one I've kept from you, from my children, from everyone. But now I'll tell you." He looked about the room to make sure there were no eavesdroppers. "Do you know why Caesar chose me to be Proconsul of Greece? No? Shall I tell you? Well then, it wasn't because I was neutral—something you tried and failed at!" He half laughed and half coughed into my face, spraying me with his drunken saliva.

"It wasn't because I had been Consul before the war. No!" His voice now became a slurred, tremulous whimper. "He offered it to me as a tribute to my Postumia. My beloved wife—*he'd* had *her*! Caesar had bedded her—years ago, when I was off—wherever I was. Years ago, she told me, on her deathbed she told me." He shook his head at me. "You don't believe me, do you? That I should be chosen Proconsul of Greece because my wife had serviced Great Caesar! Well, how do you think Gabinius got his command in Illyricum? How do you think he won Caesar's trust? They're saying that he put up his wife for security! That's right! A long time ago, Lollia, loveable, lucky Lollia had laid him. That's how Gabinius, just returned from exile, got his command, and that's how I became proconsul-designate! Now you know. And I reproach myself that I've not the stomach to kill him, much less oppose him. So Marcus, don't punish yourself for coming to terms with a tyrant who can take our lives and our wives. *Wives?* You'd better go to yours!"

He laughed aloud, a drunken stupor of a laugh, called for his slave, and made his way to the door. I called after him and insisted that he stay over-night and sleep off his condition. Without waiting for a reply, I ordered the slave to bring Servius to a spare bedroom and see to his comfort.

I was not so much surprised at what he had told me as I was by the fact that he had kept his sorrow to himself for so long. Postumia had died several years before my consulate. He had never given any indication that he was carrying such a secret. As for Caesar, his lovers were said to be innumerable, restricted neither by age nor gender. There was no clearer sign of his dominance over the Republic than the power to have and to take pleasure of whomever he chose. But *Postumia*—what could have impelled her to become one of Caesar's conquests?

DESPITE MY VULGAR REPLY TO objections to our winter-to-spring marriage, I took no nuptial liberties with my young bride. If anything, I regarded her more as an adopted daughter than as a wife. How accurate it was of Tullia to refer to Publilia—seventeen years my daughter's junior—as her baby sister." Besides, I was at the time, and remain even now, afflicted with that peculiarly male sexual handicap which parallels my political impotence. Having begun during my exile, it became more pronounced after my recall and subsequent accommodation.

However, I fear that my paternal attitude to Publilia was a source of annoyance and frustration for her. No doubt, the arrangement could not have served to gratify the young woman's appetite or to have quenched the fires of youthful passion. The marriage was based on unilateral self-serving motives—entirely my own—with Publilia deriving no conjugal benefit from it. At the very least, the marriage connected her with a consular noble, albeit one of advanced age.

While I remained at Tusculum, I gave her leave to go back to Roma. Strangely, despite my general neglect of her, Publilia remained. Soon, I found her presence a hindrance.

Developments in Roma were relayed to me by letters from Servius. Upon Caesar's return, he had assumed the dictatorship that had been conferred upon him after his victory at Pharsalus. There was much to do that only dictatorial powers could redress. Caesar had little time for administrative politics. He was not oblivious to the revived optimate cause in Africa. Their gathering strength demanded his prompt attention.

Presiding over the elections, Caesar secured the consulate for two of his legates, Quintus Calenus and Publius Vatinius. Their term would be short however, as there were only four months left in the year. Either one might be assigned to Illyricum to replace Aulus Gabinius, whose recent, sudden death had created a vacancy in the province's administration. Caesar himself and the neutral senator, Marcus Lepidus, were elected consuls for the ensuing year.

Marcus Antonius and Publius Dolabella, as well as other presumptuous Caesarians, were forced to pay pre-war prices for the Pompeian estates they had confiscated during Caesar's absence. Also, because of their high-handed behavior, they were relieved of all duties and functions in the Dictator's regime. Lepidus became the new Master of Horse.

Servius speculated that Antonius took comfort from the humiliation of his demotion by marrying his mistress, Fulvia. The two-time widow of Clodius and Curio thus acquired a third husband.

More titillating news came from Atticus. He took particular glee in reporting a notable exception to Caesar's iron-clad policy of maintaining pre-war real estate values, at least according to the latest rumors. The Dictator's mistress, or former mistress, Servilia, was buying up the properties of deceased optimates at bargain prices. As insipid rumors held that Servilia had made her youngest daughter, Tertia, available to Caesar, I wrote back to Atticus, and described Caesar's generosity as *Tertia deducta,* a one-third discount.

Atticus related that he and Balbus and Oppius had met with Caesar to discuss the recent debtors' disturbances and to plan feasible programs of amelioration. As Caesar was expecting to depart for Africa to deal with the Pompeian insurgency, he could not risk the outbreak of another debtors' revolt during his absence. So, he decreed rent remissions of up to five hundred denarii in Roma and one hundred twenty-five denarii thoughout Italia. Also, interest paid on debts from the beginning of the war was to be remitted. Atticus inferred Caesar's hope and expectation that these measures would constitute a compromise to the debt issue, a solution that would placate both creditors and debtors.

No sooner had these arrangements been concluded when Caesar was confronted with a mutiny of the Tenth Legion, his preferred unit. These legionaries had fought in Gaul, in Macedonia and Greece, in Egypt, and in the Pontic campaign. They were demanding either the immediate payment of their bounties or their discharge from active duty. In their truculence, they had driven Caesar's negotiator, Gaius Sallustius, the recently returned exile, from their camp in Mars Field, and they had marched to the very gates of Roma.

Both Atticus and Servius witnessed what happened next. Fearlessly, Caesar mounted a podium and stood above the raucous soldiers. At the sight of their Imperator, they fell silent. Caesar addressed them with the condescending appellation "Citizens" instead of the customary military designation "Comrades." At this, the soldiers were ashamed and then further mortified when Caesar declared them to be discharged.

Forgetting their earlier insolence, they implored the Imperator to take them back into service. They clamorously pledged to serve him unflinchingly, especially in the African war. Remarkably, here was a leader who could turn mutineers into devoted soldiers. What chance did the Pompeians have against such an opponent?

During this time, despite Caesar's invitation, I abstained from politics. It was not my wish to appear as a collaborator in the eyes of the insurgent Pompeians and optimates. However, living at Tusculum, I endured the domestic squabbles that ensued whenever Tullia visited us. She and Publilia, both headstrong women, were most incompatible in their temperaments and dispositions. Publilia resented my fondness for Tullia and she was especially jealous of Tullia's harmonious marriage while ours had never even been consummated. For her part, Tullia still resented her young step-mother as an intruder in our family. Indeed, she may well have resented me for divorcing Terentia.

Where Terentia was concerned, all was relatively quiet. I had repaid her dowry from Publilia's dowry. So she had no reason to complain. No wonder then, I received no correspondence from her. However, Atticus told me that she had bought a house in the revamped Aventine district and she had vacated the Palatine. You were with her.

Also, from Publilia's dowry, I paid Dolabella the penultimate installment on Tullia's dowry. He was very appreciative of this, but I still harbored doubts about the longevity of my son-in-law's reformation. It was unclear to me whether he had dropped Clodia Pulchra or she had discarded him. My general impression, however, was that they had not completely finished with each other. I only hoped that Tullia would not be hurt again.

I OCCUPIED MY TIME AT Tusculum with literary pursuits. I began but soon abandoned a poetic history of my life and times. Then, I sketched a monograph on my consulate. However, most of my completed writing consisted of treatises on oratory and rhetoric and law and politics. These were slated for publication by Atticus' firm.

While engaged in these preoccupations—it must have been late November—I was surprised by my estranged brother, Quintus. Though Atticus had found out from Pomponia as early as September that Quintus was on his way home, I had had no idea that my brother would be dropping in on me. Obviously, either Pomponia or Atticus must have told him that I was residing at Tusculum.

At any rate, Quintus arrived unexpected and unannounced, but not at all unwelcome. He stood in the atrium, with the grave, reserved bearing of a soldier standing guard duty at an official funeral. As his clothing was covered with dust, it was obvious that he had ridden on horseback instead of being borne in a litter. Without speaking, I rushed over to him with open arms and embraced him heartily for a long moment. Then pulling back from him, I saw that his face was flushed, his eyes tearful. So were mine.

"Quintus...." I began, but I could not finish.

"It's been a long time, Marcus," my brother filled in, "a long time, but not a good time." He rubbed the dampness from his nose and coughed. "I caught cold during the crossing."

I motioned him to an adjacent table where there was a beaker of wine. He took hold of my arm. "I said some things on Corcyca and at Ephesus when I met Caesar. I can't retract them. I can't unsay them, but...."

"Forget it, Quintus," I cut in. "The whole world's been upside down; no telling when, if ever, it'll be right side up again."

We shared a cup of wine and seated ourselves by a brazier to kill the November chill.

"I was sorry to hear about the divorce," Quintus said between swallows. I shrugged and waved off his commiseration. "But I'm just as sorry about your new marriage." He could not help but giggle before completing the last statement.

"Yes, I know, and so others have told me. But it's had its advantages—for me anyway."

Quintus laughed into his cup as he took another swallow. But when he took it away, his face was somber and pained. "Brother, I'll probably go down the same road. Pomponia and I..., it's impossible. It's more impossible than it ever was! She's never agreed with anything I've ventured. She's never backed me on anything, especially if it concerned Quintus. Now she's saying that he should join the Caesarian party if that's what he wants. He's of age, so Pomponia says he should make his own decision. Then she goes on to say I ought to do the same—if I had any common sense at all! For once, she said, don't do what your *brother* does."

My blood began to boil hearing Pomponia's reproach through Quintus' words. But I contained my anger as there would have been no point in raking up old issues that had caused the rupture between us. I kept silent for a moment to give myself an opportunity to calm down.

Then I said to him, "Quintus *is* an adult, and with or without your consent, he'll do what he wants. He'll probably join the Caesarians even if you disown him. Truly, I hope I'll not have any of this from Marcus."

"I hope not, brother," Quintus agreed.

"About Pomponia, you know best the viability of your marriage. But I'd caution you against any hasty action. You can trust Atticus. He knows all too well what a shrew his sister can be. Let him look into your finances. Don't strap yourself with dowry restitution if you can avoid it."

Quntius thanked me for my advice. Then, quite unexpectedly, he said, "Don't you think you should introduce me to my young sister-in-law?" We both laughed.

Meeting Publilia, Quintus was polite but circumspect. His demeanor toward her was more avuncular than one would have expected from a brother-in-law. Publilia was also polite, deferential, and hospitable. But she grew tiresome with her persistent inquiries about the younger Quintus and, in particular, about you. Quintus tolerated her questions with good humor, often looking at me sideways and winking.

Upon departing, he said to me, "What an exceptional man you are, Marcus, to relinquish a wife and in her place gain another daughter." He surmised so accurately the peculiar nature of our marriage.

I replied, "We do our best with what life gives us."

Before the end of the year, Quintus sent Pomponia a notice of divorce. I was sorry for my brother, my nephew, and for Pomponia.

Omniscient Narrative

Leaving Master of Horse Lepidus to oversee Roma, Consul and Dictator, Gaius Julius Caesar sets out for Africa and a new campaign. His legions are ferried in shifts from Rhegium across the straits to Sicilia. There, they regroup and then march to the southern coast to await the ships to sail around from Rhegium. It is not a favorable time to venture southward, for it is late December, and the winter winds are not in Caesar's favor.

Caesar's calculations make Sicilia and Africa Provincia vital for his regime's stability. The grain lines from Egypt cannot fall prey to the optimate forces concentrated in Africa. But Caesar also remembers the disaster that had befallen Gaius Curio at the beginning of the war.

He will not allow for its repetition upon the legions under his direct command.

Even before departing from Roma, Caesar has sent couriers to Publius Sittius, an Italian freebooter whose mercenary army has served Mauretania's kings. He trusts the mercenaries and King Bocchus to invade Numidia and thereby hamper King Juba's support for the optimate-Pompeian legions.

Caesar's nine legions are anxious to complete the war by subduing this new bastion of opposition. Caesar has had to make promises, offer encouragement, and elevate his rhetoric in order to forestall further mutinies like that of the Tenth Legion outside Roma and that of the Twelfth against his legate, Publius Sulla. The loyalty of the legions is essential. To mollify the legionaries of the Twelfth, Caesar has relieved Sulla of his duties. Now, the former Catilinian conspirator and nephew of the late dictator will slip into oblivion, joining Autronius Paetus and Lucius Cassius.

Caesar resorts to stratagems to bolster the legions' bellicosity. Upon landing on Africa's coast, the Consul-Dictator is overcome with fatigue or illness and he collapses. But then he recovers sufficiently to grasp the seashore sands and exclaim, "Africa! I hold you fast!" An inauspicious incident is repaired.

When superstitious legionaries feed the rumor that no Scipio can ever be defeated on African soil, Caesar responds in kind. The Pompeian commander is Metellus Scipio, a descendant of the Scipio Africani who had defeated Roma's ancient enemy, Carthage. Combing the soldiers' rosters century by century, Caesar discovers one Scipio Sallutio and quickly promotes him to the rank of junior centurion. Now, even in Caesar's legions, the name of Scipio betokens ultimate victory for their Imperator.

The heavens and the elements intrude upon the invading Romans. The arms and armor of Caesar's legionaries glow with an eerie luminescence of fire as though Jupiter's thunderbolts and Vulcan's flaming shafts have jointly landed upon them. Caesar hails the luminous prodigy as an omen of the gods' favor, especially of his ancestress, Venus Victrix.

The African war is marked by serpentine maneuvering as Caesar's legions seek adequate provisions while the Pompeians and their Numidian allies attempt to thwart the invaders at every turn. There are intermittent, indecisive skirmishes in which Titus Labienus effectively employs the Pompeians' cavalry superiority to harass the Caesarians. Caesar resorts to having his legions march *expedita*—without heavy packs—in order to increase their speed and flexibility.

After a half-year of such tactics, a decisive battle is fought at the coastal town of Thapsus. Here, Caesar succeeds in dividing the Pompeians and maneuvering them onto, what is for them, unfavorable, marshy ground. When certain of his legions, especially the Tenth and Twelfth, take the initiative in commencing the battle, Caesar cannot do otherwise but order an attack. The Consul-Dictator's initial hesitation might be attributable to another onset of illness. According to strict military discipline, the legionaries' behavior is clearly insubordinate, but apparently Caesar takes their ardor to be motivated by the supply privations they have had to endure. No doubt, Caesar shares in their desire to vanquish the foe and complete the campaign as expeditiously as possible.

Caesar's archers and slingers wreak havoc upon the Numidian war elephants positioned on the enemy's flanks. The formidable, yet clumsy beasts are assailed into hysterical panic; they trample upon the Pompeian infantry and scatter the cavalry into disorganized flight.

Their forces divided and forced to fight on terrain not conducive to the deployment of either their cavalry or the Numidian war elephants, the Pompeians and their allies are routed. Caesar's hardened legions make butchers' work of them. Labienus and the Pompeius brothers escape the rout, but Lucius Afranius is captured. Caesar has spared him once before, in Spain; this time there is no clemency for him. He is executed on the spot. Later, the chief Pompeian commander, Metellus Scipio, will perish by his own hand.

King Juba of Numidia, his kingdom overrun from the west by King Bocchus' Mauretanians and Publius Sittius' mercenaries, and his army obliterated at Thapsus, enters into a suicide pact with Marcus Petreius. After dispatching the Roman, Juba then turns his dagger upon himself.

However, there were others who surrender and Caesar readily extends his clemency to them. Chief among these is Pompeia, the Magnus' daughter, whose husband, Faustus Sulla, has been killed at

Thapsus. She and hundreds of others are given safe conduct back to Roma.

Pompeia brings with her the ashes of her husband and those of Metellus Scipio. Scipio's will be given to his daughter, Cornelia, to be placed honorably beside the ashes of Pompeius, which Caesar had retrieved from Egypt.

Yet, Caesar's clemency and magnanimity are not valued by Marcus Cato. Commanding the Pompeian garrison at Utica on the African coast, he refuses to surrender after receiving the news of Caesar's victory. Yet, he is wise enough now to realize the utter futility of further resistance. So, despite the entreaties of his family, he clumsily stabs himself—*almost* to death. Attempts to bind his wounds and stanch his bleeding prove futile. The implacable foe of Caesar dies. His daughter, Porcia, recovers the book he had been reading prior to his suicide. The committed Stoic had probed the soul's immortality as expounded in the "Vision of Er," the final book of Plato's *Republic*.

Arriving at Utica, Caesar learns of Cato's suicide from Cato's son. The Consul-Dictator pardons the young man and all of his followers, including the entire community. Respectfully, he visits Cato's grave marker by the sea. He solemnly intones: "Cato, I grudge you your death, as you have grudged me the preservation of your life."

Caesar remains in Africa for some time for there is much to be settled. The neighboring client-kingdom of Numidia is annexed because of its ruler's folly in supporting the losing side. The western portion is given to Caesar's ally, King Bocchus of Mauretania in return for his support and probably in appreciation of the monarch's wife, Queen Eunoe. The eastern portion is organized as a new province, Africa Nova, and assigned to Gaius Sallustius as proconsul.

Another Caesarian ally is also rewarded for his services. By Caesar's dictate, Publius Sittius, the expatriate Italian equite and former Catilinian accomplice, is restored to full Roman citizenship. Moreover, he is awarded the exclusive franchise to lucrative business prospects in both African provinces as well as in the two Mauretanian kingdoms.

Sittius is gratified by these honors coming to him after eighteen years of commercial and military enterprises. He is a survivor, unlike three other Romans in his mercenary band who have succumbed to disease or war. The Catilinian conspirators, Lucius Vargunteius, Porcius Laeca, and Gaius Cornelius will never see Roma or Italia again.

Thus, Caesar vanquishes his enemies in battle, extends clemency to those who have surrendered, and rewards his faithful allies and friends. But there is a voice of dissent, a discordant note, a vehement reproach to nullify his African victory. Porcia Cato agrees to return to Roma as per Caesar's dictate, but she warns him that she will do all in her womanly power to extol her dead father's name and his sacrifice for the Republic. Lest Caesar think that the war is over, she tells him what he already must surmise: That the struggle will go on as long as Titus Labienus and Gnaeus Pompeius the Younger and Sextus Pompeius have the defiant will to fight.

The news of Caesar's African victory precedes Porcia's return to Roma. The Consul and Master of Horse Marcus Lepidus goads the Senate into naming Caesar Dictator for the unprecedented term of ten years, but with the proviso that his tenure should be annually renewed.

It will be late summer, after an absence of nine months, before Caesar will return to Roma and assume the extended dictatorship. Power, once attained, may weigh too heavily upon him.

MARCUS ANTONIUS AND FULVIA ENJOY living at Pompeius Magnus' former mansion at Tibur. This had been a prime property seized in the aftermath of Caesar's victory. The house is larger and far more ornate than Antonius' old house and Fulvia's Aventine domicile combined. The inlaid floors, the frescoed walls, the spacious atrium with its broad, deep impluvium pool and high compluvium sky-light all bear the distinct marks of the late owner.

Since acquiring and then, by Caesar's dictate, paying for the house, Antonius has implemented certain remodeling in accordance with his own tastes, or more specifically with Fulvia's preferences in mind. New apartments have had to be added to accommodate her children by Clodius and by Curio, and a nursery is currently under construction, for Fulvia is yet again with child.

In her sixth month, she reclines in the opulent, tree-shaded garden, but not entirely comfortably. This pregnancy is different from the others. Perhaps this is because she is older now, but her belly and her innards feel heavier, more ponderous, more cramped than before. She has not yet told her husband what her household midwife, the very same who tended to her with the three previous births, has divulged to her. After an examination, as thorough as Roman gynecology could permit, the midwife has told Fulvia that her womb houses twins, just as Rhea Silva of old had borne Romulus and Remus.

Elated at the news, she has come to believe that her twins have a special destiny. They will initiate a new era, a new foundation for Roma, one that will rival the City's original founding by the ancient twins. Fulvia had desired to share this extraordinary development with Antonius, but his foul mood has him nervously pacing and bemoaning his enforced retirement from Caesar's service.

"He wins new laurels in Africa," he complains, "while I sit here and stew. To Lepidus goes the honor of proposing a new dictatorship. Master of Horse Lepidus has the run of the City and of the Senate, while I speculate day in and day out about my future."

"But Marcus, this is only a temporary setback," Fulvia assures him, "a minor inconvenience. Once Caesar returns from Africa you'll be restored to his good graces and to a prominent office yet again." She has conveyed such encouragement to him on many occasions, but she adds something new this time. "At the very least, my dear, I hope you've learned to exercise some moderation in …."

"*Moderation?!?!*" Antonius erupts, his bull neck pulsating with passion. "I put down traitors who would have wrecked his arrangements. Caelius and Milo could have surrendered, like *Dolababy* but they preferred to die fighting. Many others also refused to surrender. Moderation? Every one of them ought to have been killed, especially *Dolababy*! He agitated against Caesar's debt and credit laws and what's *his* punishment? He's stripped of office and relegated to Caesar's dung pile. Just like me! But the difference is: I quashed the revolt, and then *I* was unhorsed as Master of Horse and put on the same dung pile!"

"Patience, Marcus! All will be set right when Caesar returns. I guarantee it. You needn't aggravate yourself needlessly."

Antonius swallows a hearty draught of wine and smacks his lips. "Dolabella! I should've killed him years ago. He'll always be an ugly shadow between me and my ambition."

Fulvia smirks. "Marcus, you needn't concern yourself about either. Soon enough, he'll be too exhausted to hamper you.

Antonius laughs. "Clodia?"

Fulvia chuckles. "Clodia! Cicero and his daughter will have far more reason than you, my Taurus, to worry about Dolabella." Fulvia is amused at her husband's gratified laughter. Over it, she adds, "He visits her whenever Tullia goes to Tusculum to visit her father." At that instant, the twins stir in her womb, one plunging down and the other pushing up. Fulvia places one hand on the dome of her belly and the other on her swollen bosom. "Clodia has a thing about the men of the Cicero household. I'll wager that one day, if she doesn't seduce 'Chick-Pea' Junior, she'll have Senior firmly lodged in her loins."

DOLABELLA LIES SUPINE ON THE sturdy, firmly padded couch in Clodia Pulchra's bed chamber. His chin is uplifted and the smile that curves his lips is wet with anticipation. From his broad chest to his muscle-sculpted abdomen and into his naked loins a surge of passion flows. His male member, engorged and erect, its prepuce retracted, is as rigid as a rod in a lictor's fascis.

He sees Clodia Pulchra's nude torso from the rear: the supple shoulders caressed by her glistening raven tresses; the broad, yet slender back tapering into a trim waist that crowns her curvaceous, voluptuous buttocks and the sensuous olive and rose-hued legs. The outer edges of her melon-like breasts are visible below her upraised, sensually defined arms. Her oval face is in alternate left and right profiles, and a lasciviously teasing smile plays upon her full curved lips as she gauges her lover's arousal from the corners of her eyes. He stirs from the couch and approaches her, his member having further swollen in erotic anticipation.

Clodia knows from rich and varied experience that he is hers, and she relishes the power of her will over him even as he thrusts inside of her, pouncing upon her flesh, smothering himself in her bosom and ultimately inundating her with the nectar of his released passion. It is her power and will to bring him up again and yet again until her own passion is gratified and spent. And in her climatic culmination, her mind's voice reverberates: *"Marcus Cicero, what a fool you are!"*

Caput XV Cicero's Respublica

I HAD COME TO ROMA to visit Tullia and to see you, my son. Publilia insisted on coming with me and reluctantly I consented. Obviously, she wanted to visit her mother and brother. This was perfectly understandable. But whenever you came to the Palatine house, she became inseparably attentive to your every word and gesture. It was rather curious to see the flirtatious bantering that went on between the two of you. Publilia seemed to be the younger sister that you never had. You even accompanied her when she called upon her mother and brother.

About your mother, you said little except in answer to my specific questions regarding her health and overall well-being. It distressed me to learn that Terentia's joint pains had become almost insufferable.

It distressed me even more to see a marked coldness between Tullia and her husband. Dolabella was sullen with her while showing me a modicum of courtesy. He complained about his continued exclusion from Caesar's regime—certainly a reasonable penalty for having helped lead a debtors' revolt. Unhappily, there was something amiss with them, and though Tullia and I were not afforded an opportunity to speak privately, I sensed that my son-in-law may have resumed his infidelities.

I HAD HAD NO IDEA that my sojourn in the City would have coincided so neatly with Caesar's return from Africa. He thrilled the mob by celebrating four successive triumphs, not over Romans but over foreign enemies: Gaul, Egypt, Pontus, and Numidia.

At the conclusion of his Gallic triumph, as Caesar was offering sacrifice to Jupiter for his victories, the Arvernian chieftain, Vercingetorix, who had spent several years as an honored hostage of the Republic, was conducted to the Carcer and garroted. The mob went wild with cheers of approbation when his corpse was exhibited, but I was sickened by the morbid spectacle.

During the Egyptian triumph, Arsinoe, the seditious half-sister of Queen Cleopatra, walked in chains behind Caesar's chariot. Not since Pompeius' triumph over Mithridates had royal females graced a triumphator's parade. The Egyptian Princess bore herself with a proud, regal demeanor, and the mob, much to my surprise, cheered while I would have expected them to jeer at her insolence.

Arsinoe was subsequently banished to Ephesus where she lives to this day in a sanctuary of Artemis. She is either another example of Caesarian clemency, or she is being used as a sharp political ploy to tighten Cleopatra's bond with Roma, lest her ambitious sibling should try to establish a royal court in exile.

In the Pontic triumph, an effigy of the vanquished Prince Pharnaces was exhibited. The populace went wild with denunciations against him just as they had years earlier against his regal father, King Mithridates. Pharnaces' little domain of the Cimmerian Bosporus had been given over by Caesar to another member of the royal family, Mithridates Pergamenos—a fitting reward for the princeling who had brought reinforcements to Caesar at Alexandria. Numerous placards were inscribed with Caesar's victory message from the Pontic campaign: *"Veni, Vidi, Vici."*

During the Numidian triumph, a most inauspicious incident occurred when the axle of Caesar's chariot wheel broke, throwing him to the pavement. As though atoning for this bad omen—which may have been the work of either pranksters or assassins—he then walked on his knees up the Capitoline ramp, flanked by a column of war elephants captured in the campaign.

Naturally, there was much speculation about this freak accident, and rumors began to circulate that Caesar had contracted an illness in Africa, or at least that the first indications had been seen there. It was said that he had fallen on the African seashore and that he had regained his composure sufficiently to invalidate what would otherwise have been interpreted as a bad omen. He is said to have clutched the sands and cried out: *"Africa! I hold you fast!"*

Despite his impressive improvisations on these two occasions, there is guarded speculation that Caesar suffers from the falling sickness, known to some as the *Divine Illness* and to the Greeks as *epilepsy*.

Not long after these triumphs, Queen Cleopatra arrived in Roma with great pomp and spectacle rivaling even Caesar's extravagance. She took up residence in Caesar's mansion on the west side of the Tiber. Among her retinue were her thirteen-year old half-brother and co-ruler, Ptolemy XIV and her infant son, Caesarion. The child was alleged to be the offspring of the Queen's affair with Caesar.

Officially, it seemed that the purpose of the royal visit was to complete a new treaty validating the integrity of the Egyptian kingdom. However, according to prevalent gossip, passion had taken priority over politics. Ironically, another of Caesar's reputed regal mistresses, the Mauretanian Queen Eunoe, was also visiting at the same time, and apparently Cleopatra was not one to be upstaged.

Cleopatra and Eunoe were the rulers of countries on the opposite ends of Africa. The former was descended of Greco-Macedonian stock allegedly without a drop of native Egyptian blood. She was not particularly beautiful, but she did possess an alluring attractiveness that could easily render her desirable. The Mauretanian was an amalgam of Moorish-Berber and Negro as evidenced by her dark, wooly textured hair and her honey-brown complexion. Eunoe was several years older than her Egyptian counterpart.

Both Queens, as well as Roman womanhood in general, had been the inspiration for ribald verses chanted by the soldiers parading in Caesar's triumphs. I recall one that went something like this:

Hail the mighty Conqueror! Home at last from field afar;

Into Roma's enemies we plunged our swords and brought their lands under Lupa's teats;

While royal queens of desert dunes and fertile valleys his mighty rod did probe.

Romans, Romans, near and far, lock up your women, young and old,
Lest our bald war-whoremonger ravish them for sport upon the
Seven Hills and along the Tiber's banks.

Though Cleopatra outdid Eunoe in distributing extravagant gifts to various senators in exchange for their support, she failed to make anything but a negative impression on me. In spite of her attractiveness and ready charm, she was also willful and capricious, the very epitome of Hellenic-Oriental queens. Animosity between us was precipitated when the Queen, either sincerely or spitefully, claimed that I had made improper advances on her.

In all truth, all that I had requested, through her ministers, Ammonius and Sara, was her assistance in obtaining certain ancient philosophical manuscripts believed to be extant in Egypt. After this, I deliberately avoided all contact with her.

MEANWHILE, CAESAR PRESIDED OVER THE elections. As expected, his supporters filled the major offices, and he was elected consul—sole consul—for the ensuing year. Implementing the powers granted him as Dictator, he embarked upon a rapid, comprehensive reform program which the Senate and the assembly perfunctorily approved.

The first of these was directed at reforming the calendar. With the assistance of Sosigenes, Cleopatra's royal astronomer, Caesar replaced the troublesome and archaic lunar calendar with a solar calendar containing three hundred sixty-five and one quarter days. However, to bring the current year into alignment with the solar year, it was necessary to intercalate two extra months between November and December. As one intercalary month had already been inserted earlier in the year, the current year would have had the extraordinary length of four hundred forty-five and one quarter days!

Many senators were irritated at Caesar's presumption in tinkering with the calendar, although for years there had been a general consensus that it was desperately in need of reform. In fact, one of the prerogatives of the Chief Pontiff, by custom and tradition, was periodic calendar adjustments. However, Caesar's innovation was all-encompassing. Writing to Servius Sulpicius, who was administering Greece as proconsul, I sarcastically noted: "Even the heavens conform to the Great Man's will."

One day, I was taking my exercise, walking through Mars Field with Marcus Varro and Publius Figulus. Varro was one of many Pompeians pardoned by Caesar. In addition, he had been entrusted with the commission of compiling books for what was to be Roma's first public library. He mentioned certain archaic texts on astronomy in the course of our conversation about Caesar's new calendar. When Figulus asked if the constellation *Lyra* would be visible on a given night, I replied: "Of course it will, for it has been commanded to appear!"

Only moments after this, I had a startling experience. Among the young men taking their exercises—riding, discus and javelin throwing, wrestling—there was one who appeared mysteriously familiar. I inquired about him, and Figulus told me that the golden-haired youth was Gaius Octavius Caepias, the great-nephew of the Dictator. I estimated that he could not have been more than seventeen years old. Varro added that he had been born in the year of my consulate. I had seen him before, but I could not place him.

As I studied the youth's small, slender frame, Varro was speaking further about him. "He's Marcius Philippus' step-son. His mother, Atia is Caesar's niece, the daughter of one of his sisters. Philippus married her only a year or two after the elder Octavius' death."

Then Figulus interjected further details. "The Octavii are originally from the hill country of Velitrae. Curiously, there's even a legend, some three or four hundred years old, that when the town's walls were struck by lightning, soothsayers prophesied that the world's ruler would come from Velitrae."

I heard all of this as I tried to discern where and when I had seen him before. As the clouds of my memory began to lift, a queer chill came over me, despite the warmth of that September day. *I knew him!* He was the youth who had appeared in my recurring dream where a divine voice designated him as Roma's peace-maker. He was unmistakably the same youth!

Then Figulus mentioned to us that in a moment of oracular inspiration on the occasion of the boy's birth, he had told the elder Gaius Octavius: "The ruler of the world has been born among us!" Figulus the Pythagorean savant, always clad in black toga, did not often divulge his visions or inspirations.

The youth in the dream was now running about Mars Field; the ancient legend of Velitrae seemed to dovetail with Figulus' prophecy at the boy's birth. Whether or not these things added up to anything I could not say. But I stored them deeply in my memory.

FIGULUS' PRONOSTITICATIONS ABOUT YOUNG GAIUS Ocatvius concerned the Republic's future. Another voice recalled its past. This was Porcia, the widowed daughter of Marcus Cato. She and her brother, Marcus, pardoned by Caesar at Utica, had returned to Roma in advance of the Conqueror. As her father's and her husband's houses had been appropriated by Caesarians, Porcia established herself in her cousin, Marcus Brutus' house. There she held court, extolling the virtues of her father, now called by the honorific title *Cato Uticensis*, to all who cared to offer their condolences and to commiserate over the Stoic fire-eater's death.

I was one of many who came for these purposes. Porcia regarded me with steely-eyed reserve for several moments. Just when I was certain that she would not speak to me, she hissed her venomous spite. "What do you want here, Marcus Cicero?" She was like a female manifestation of her late father, the flashing eyes and the proud, upturned face. "My father had to save you from young Pompeius' sword when you urged them to surrender. *You* returned to Italia to *beg* mercy of the tyrant, but my father and others of his ilk continued the fight. Even when defeated again, he would not give in. He would not grovel. If he could not live in a free Republic, he chose to die by his own hand. Even my brother and I could not stop him."

The color in her cheeks and neck turned scarlet with anger. I wanted to reply, but wisely I refrained.

"So what do you want here?" she asked again. "The children of Cato Uticensis do not need or desire your sympathy." She rose from her chair, her eyes swollen with tears. "There's nothing here for you. *Go! Go back under the tyrant's wing and live out what's left of your useless life! Go!*"

I gave her no argument but quickly took my leave.

Porcia had elevated her father to martrydom—Cato Uticensis, the Champion of the Republic. Feeling obligated to honor his memory, and moved by Porcia's rebuke, I wrote, and Atticus published for me, a panegyric treatise entitled *Cato*. At great length, I extolled his uncompromising Republican virtues, even though his obdurate resistance to compromise had often been impossible to brook.

The *Cato* was widely read and discussed. Not to be outdone, Caesar eventually wrote and published a rebuttal to my work which he entitled the *Anti-Cato*. In it, Cato was denigrated as a warmonger whose truculence and unyielding, uncompromising politics had torn the Republic asunder with civil war. Even in death, Cato was a controversial statesman.

However, the *Anti-Cato* was not the only piece of Caesarian propaganda making the rounds among Roma's literati. While governing the Gallic provinces, Caesar had sent regular dispatches to the Senate describing in detail each of his campaigns. Now, they were collated and published as Caesar's *Commentaries on the Gallic Wars*. The story of Gaul's conquest was clearly laid out as the Dictator's self-aggrandizement, a military chronicle describing how he had surpassed Pompeius Magnus in adding vast new territories to Roma's imperium.

Additionally, a companion piece appeared in *The Civil War*. In this work, Caesar not only described the campaigns in Italia, Spain, Massilia, Macedonia, and Greece; he also attempted to justify his actions against what he termed a selfish, intransigent oligarchy. I shuddered to think what would have happened if Catilina and his rebels had had such propaganda to service them.

FOR THE TIME BEING, THE unequivocal ruler of the Roman world pressed on with his reforms. By his dictate, praetorian and consular governors were to serve terms of one and two years respectively. Obviously, the Dictator intended to forestall the emergence of another powerful military presence in the provinces. Caesar also legislated out of existence the all-too-often disruptive workingmen's *collegia* which had been revived during Clodius' wild tribunate. Sumptuary laws were passed limiting expenditures for private and public banquets. The use of litters and wheeled vehicles in the City during daylight hours was banned so as to reduce traffic congestion.

Massive construction projects were advanced, namely the Julian Basilica on the Forum's northeastern side, and the Julian Forum with its planned central Temple of Venus Genetrix, Caesar's adopted ancestress. Though these structures were officially dedicated with all civic and religious rites, they remain to this day incomplete, like Caesar's own political edifice. However, a new Rostra was nearly completed, and a new Curia, begun by Faustus Sulla before the war, was slowly rising. Designated as the Curia Julia, Caesar probably expected that with its completion, his Senate would no longer have to meet in substitute chambers like the Portico of Pompeius' Theatre.

These construction projects provided employment for thousands of the urban mob, at least for those who were skilled stone masons and builders. In addition to employment, public welfare also occupied Caesar's attention. The number of citizens on the public dole—recipients of free public grain—was cut in half as a direct result of the establishment of numerous overseas colonies in such far-flung locales as Carthage and Corinth—once destroyed by Roman legions, but now to be rebuilt by Roman citizen-colonists—and Narbo, as well as sites throughout Italia and Spain. In addition, thousands of discharged legionary veterans were similarly and strategically assigned to these overseas colonies. In time, they would become active agents of *Romanization* and reliable sources of emergency recruitment.

By Caesar's dictate, sanctioned by the Senate and legislated through the Assembly, the excess urban population, the idle, chronically troublesome rabble, was drained off into public works projects and colonies that implanted Roman culture in remote sectors of the Republic's imperium.

In truth, Caesar did much for the health and stability of the Republic. Yet, I could not countenance his power because it was acquired through war on his fellow citizens; and the exercise of that power was not *with* the Senate and the People, but *over* them with his loyal, battle-hardened legions backing him. Those legions were anything but expendable.

Caesar was becoming a prisoner of his own entrenched power. He showed this in a subtle, but significant way. Seated on a curule chair while observing the work on the Temple of Venus Genetrix, he did not rise when a delegation of senators approached him. Instead, he remained seated like an ancient potentate receiving a group of groveling suppliants. The senators, particularly the young Pontius Aquila, were quite perturbed.

But the irritated sensibilities of senators were, if anything, a minute concern for Caesar; for in the midst of his whirlwind of administrative acta, he was also preparing for yet another campaign. The Pompeian remnants, led by the Pompeius brothers and Titus Labienus, had regrouped in Spain, exploiting an already volatile situation.

Late in the previous year, Caesar's appointed governor, Quintus Cassius Longinus, had become overly zealous in his management of the Spanish provinces. He had provoked several mutinies among the very same Pompeian legionaries who, two years earlier, had gone over to Caesar. Even the Spanish auxiliary troops had become insubordinate. With the Pompeii and Labienus posing as champions, the legions had defected to them after killing Longinus and some of his officers.

Virtually the entire province of Further Spain was in Pompeian hands. Caesar had to extinguish this flame of revolt before the disaffection spread to the neighboring province of Nearer Spain.

IN AN EFFORT TO PRECLUDE disaffection within Roma and Italia, Caesar extended clemency to many senators and equites who had dared not return since Pharsalus. Among those recalled was the optimate consular, Marcus Claudius Marcellus. He was the elder brother of Gaius, the consul who had done much to precipitate the civil war and who had been killed at Pharsalus. Marcus had a cousin, also named Gaius, who had succeeded in remaining neutral, probably because he was married to Caesar's grand-niece. This family connection may have been instrumental in persuading Caesar to recall Marcus Marcellus to Roma.

Caesar had convened the Senate in the Temple of Concord, a most appropriate setting from which to decree the recall of his countrymen. As I was yet in Roma, I attended the meeting, impelled more by curiosity than by any sense of obligation.

Seated on a curule chair, the Dictator wore the victor's laurel crown and the triumphator's purple toga—two flattering concessions from an obsequious Senate. He noticed me when I entered and seated myself among the senators. By his smile and his nodding head, it was apparent that he was happy at my presence.

After Caesar promulgated his recall decree, the senators applauded it. Their applause was even more clamorous when he singled out Marcus Marcellus for recall. Then, at Caesar's invitation, I broke my self-imposed silence to deliver a brief, extemporaneous oration.

I praised Caesar for his clemency and moderation, commended him for his reform initiatives, and saluted him for victories over Roma's foreign foes. But I segued into dubious terrain when I urged him to negotiate a settlement with the Pompeians in Spain rather than wage war upon them. "There need not be another Dyrrachium, another Pharsalus, or another Thapsus," I declared. Hearing these battle sites, Caesar's hands began to shake. "Romans need not spill each other's blood in further civil war." Finally, I recommended that, having pacified the Roman imperium—with the exception of the Spanish revolt—he should resign the dictatorship, as had Sulla more than thirty years before, and restore the free operation of the Republic. "Caesar would leave no finer legacy to the Roman People than the return of government by the Senate; of magistrates *freely* elected by the unhampered comitia; of laws *freely* sanctioned by the Senate, approved *without* coercion by the citizens, and adjudicated without bias by *free* courts." I deliberately emphasized the words "*freely*" and "*free*."

There was a startled hush in the Senate in response to my bold suggestion. Their silence was broken only by stirrings and murmurings when Caesar, as though in a trance, dropped various documents he had been holding. The Dictator suddenly appeared to be ill. His pallor became ashen, and his forehead and temples below his laurel crown were wet with perspiration. My words had apparently unnerved him.

At the conclusion of my oration, I was given polite, though restrained applause. But Caesar precluded any subsequent discussion by adjourning the Senate.

I had spoken my peace, availing myself of Caesar's proffered invitation to contribute to the re-ordering of the Republic. No doubt, he did not approve of my contribution. Though I had hoped he would abdicate his dictatorship, I knew in my heart that he would not. I was not even sure that he could even if he had wanted to do so. Yet, I did not see his entrenched power as a perdurable good for the Republic.

Soon after this, I returned to Tusculum, determined to refrain from further public statements and to concentrate on my books and my writing. However, my return was bittersweet. *Sweet*—because Tullia had just discovered that she was pregnant again—the result of Dolabella's rekindled love. My happiness about this news was, however, somewhat guarded. *Bitter*—because I saw Tusculum as a new abode of banishment from a political situation that excluded me.

There was a peculiar post-script to my Senate oration. Early in December, Servius Sulpicius, Proconsul of Greece, wrote from Athens about the strange fate that befell Marcus Marcellus, the recalled exile. Upon being informed of his pardon and recall, he was preparing to depart from the island of Cos when he was mysteriously murdered. There was subdued speculation that this may have been arranged either by the Dictator or by those close to him.

It was ironic that Marcellus, pardoned by Caesar, should then have been marked for assassination—a rare exception to Caesar's policy of clemency. The murder remains a mystery to this day.

By year's end, the news of Marcellus' murder reached Roma. At the same time, Caesar departed for Spain, leaving Master of Horse Lepidus to administer matters in his absence. Caesar took with him a select group of aides, some veterans, some neophytes. The former included Gaius Pollio, Gaius Trebonius, the Dictator's nephew, Quintus Pedius, and my son-in-law, Dolabella. Among the latter were Caesar's grand-nephew, Gaius Octavius, the youth whom I recognized in Mars Field, and my nephew, your cousin, Quintus, who went over his father's strenuous, but ineffective objections.

A surprising omission from Caesar's staff was Marcus Antonius. Apparently, he was still on the Dictator's list of *personae non grata*. Still, Caesar had a task for him, albeit a non-combative one. Antonius was entrusted with overseeing the establishment of a veterans' colony at Narbo in Transalpine Gaul.

Omniscient Narrative

Fulvia says, "Did I not tell you, Marcus?"

Antonius, attired in military garb, beams with satisfaction. "I only wish you could come with me."

"You know that's not possible." Fulvia motions with her uplifted chin to the opposite side of the nursery. "The twins are too young and fragile to make the trip, and I can't bear to leave them." She is strong, vigorous, well recovered from delivering twin boys. Her complexion is the same red-brown hue, and her flame-red hair is pulled back into a chignon at the nape of her neck. Though showing evidence of years and recent childbirth, her figure is yet full, well-defined; the bosom is firm and high, and her back and shoulders are straight. The mauve gown she wears delineates her figure most flatteringly.

"I know," Antonius admits. He turns to the pair of wet-nurses who are suckling the weeks-old-infants. He goes to the one, a buxom Sicilian whose left breast is being milked by the infant she holds. He leans over and kisses the baby's head. "Eat well, Antyllus, and grow strong." Teasingly, he pinches the wet nurse's delectable breast, causing her to give out a startled chortle. Turning to the other woman, a lithe but well-endowed Umbrian, he leans over and kisses the head of the baby suckling energetically on the woman's exposed breast. "And you too, Iullus, eat well and keep up with your brother." Again, he affectionately pinches the nurturing breast, but the Umbrian shoos him away with her free hand. Her annoyance causes Antonius to laugh.

"Should I procure a pair of wet-nurses for you too, Marcus?" Fulvia liltingly asks.

Without missing a beat, Antonius replies, "Oh no! I'll see what's available up at Narbo." He looks back at the wet nurses shifting in their chairs as they re-position the infants to alternate breasts. Tickled by the sight of the copious teats, he asks his wife, "On what farm did you find them?"

But Fulvia becomes serious. She walks over to him and cautions, "Be careful, Marcus. How you handle this commission will determine where you go next."

"Frankly," Antonius nods, "I wish it were to Spain with Caesar."

"Caesar knows your valor in battle. He's given you the more important duty of administering the veterans' colony. Do it *well!*"

Antonius takes her in his arms and her breasts and hips press against his cuirass and the leather straps of his doublet. He kisses her passionately on the mouth, oblivious of the wet nurses.

"Sweet leave-taking?" Clodia Pulchra enters the nursery herding in Fulvia's three older children, pre-adolescent Claudia and Publius, and little Gaius, now almost four years old.

Disengaging from Fulvia, Antonius sweeps little Gaius up into his arms. He saunters over to the other two, smiling affectionately at them. All three children adore their step-father. Antonius loves them and treasures the memory of their fathers, the strapping friends of his youth, Publius Clodius and Gaius Curio. "Mind your mother—and your Aunt Clodia—while I'm away. And look after your baby brothers." Antonius kisses little Gaius on the cheek before setting him down. Then he embraces Claudia and Publius. "Day by day they grow and grow! By the time I return we may need an even grander house!"

Clodia Pulchra has come to Fulvia's side. She looks longingly at her sister-in-law. Fulvia returns her gaze. The two smile at each other and unspoken affection passes between them. The amber eyes of the one and the ebony eyes of the other meet and accentuate what the two women have known and shared.

Their reverie is broken by Antonius' voice. "Was your leave-taking with Dolabella as sweet? No rumbling undercurrent of guilt or self-recrimination?"

Clodia looks at him obliquely. "I've no time or tolerance for anyone possessed of those vices."

Antonius laughs sardonically. "I'll leave the two of you alone to conspire." To the children, he exhorts, "Come with me, little legionaries. Let's see if we can steal some sweetmeats from the pantry!"

Giggling delightfully, the children go off with their step-father. Fulvia directs the wet nurses, "If they're asleep, put them in their cradles."

"Yes, Domina," they reply in unison.

Fulvia conducts Clodia into her adjacent bedchamber. Clodia remarks, "You know, I'd have thought that since this time you had twins, you'd nurse them yourself."

"Just like the old *Lupa*, eh?"

Clodia giggles. "But wasn't it the shepherd's wife—what's her name?—*Acca?* Yes—*Acca Larentia!* She's supposed to have suckled Romulus and Remus. But myths and legends are so twisted and warped about. Perhaps *she* was the actual *Lupa* whose teats nourished them!"

"Whichever! No—I had no intention of emulating either the Lupa or old Acca. Marcus and I even crossed over this, but *I prevailed*."

They have entered the bedchamber and have seated themselves on a commodious couch. "I'm happy that you're not nursing them," Clodia coos as she caresses Fulvia's breast. Her own bosom rises against the folds of her fuchsia gown. Fulvia strokes Clodia's cheek and neck, and Clodia kisses her hand tenderly.

"Do you think Dolabella will insist that Tullia nurse their child?" Fulvia wonders aloud as her face draws closer to Clodia's.

"I don't know. He's never confided that in me." Clodia's whispered reply lands on Fulvia's mouth. Their kiss is deep and long and ardent. Their gowns, Fulvia's pale purple and Clodia's vibrant red-purple, meld when their arms wrap around each other. Their entwined bodies on the couch are like a wild, vivid, exotic flower.

Cicero's <u>Respublica</u>

Shortly after Caesar's departure, you came to see me at Tusculum. You wanted to go to Spain and serve in Caesar's legions. "If I'm going to advance in the regime, I can only start with military service," you asserted. "Then my political career will advance under Caesar's direction."

"*No!*" I insisted. "I won't tolerate that! After I've spoken in the Senate against Caesar's new war, *you* want to go off and fight in it!"

Just then, Publilia came into the study. You and she greeted each other pleasantly, but I was annoyed that she had to intrude just then. "We were discussing Marcus' plans," I said, hoping she would take the hint and leave. But she did not. Instead, she sat down near you. Your eyes were fixed on her, and she returned your gaze.

Becoming impatient, I pressed on. "Marcus, your way of embarking on a public career is not only erroneous, but it shows poor judgment."

"*Poor judgment!*" You snapped insolently and looked again at Publilia. "What other choice do I have? Should I retire as you have before I've had any career? Or should I follow Uncle Titus into business and banking?"

I could not abide your sarcasm, and the exchange of glances between you and Publilia unnerved me. "That's enough!" I ordered. "You'll *not* follow your cousin to Spain. That's a certainty! That's carved in bronze just like the Twelve Tables!"

Abruptly, you rose from your chair and faced me directly. "I only came here out of respect, Father. If need be, I'll go without your consent."

"And you'll go without any allowance from me!" I knew that was what you really wanted. You would not have come to me if Terentia had been willing to give you money for this Spanish venture.

You turned and made for the open door. "Where are you going?" I demanded.

"Does it matter?" You sneered over your shoulder as you walked out toward the vestibule.

"Marcus! Wait!" Publilia shot up from her chair and ran after you. I remained seated, stunned at my young wife's emotional intervention. She caught up with you in the vestibule. I saw you both through the open door, talking so closely, though I could not hear what you were saying. Publilia held your forearm, her voice and gaze apparently calming you. You looked away from her after a moment before nodding and then reaching down to kiss her hand. She reached up quickly and kissed you on the lips. I could not believe what I was seeing.

The kiss was not a maternal one, and how could it be? Yes, legally she was your step-mother; but in age, she could have been your younger sister—or your *lover*. But no! I refused to believe this. I refused to believe what I had seen. *I could not!* I blotted from my mind the sight of Publilia kissing my son furtively and ever so passionately on the mouth.

You left, probably bound for Roma. I would not discuss the episode with Publilia; nor did she broach the subject of your desire to go to Spain. She became a sullen, sour, lovesick child.

WHILE CAESAR BATTLED THE POMPEIANS in Spain, I suffered the most crushing loss of my entire life. A month after I had quarreled with you, Tullia, distraught and conspicuously pregnant, came to Tusculum.

"What is it, *Tulliola*?" I asked her.

"Tata, it's over!" she wailed. From her gown, she produced a small parchment and handed it to me. "It's over!"

What I had feared, what I had known would eventually happen but had hoped would not, was within my hand. Dolabella had sent her a notice of divorce all the way from Caesar's camp in Spain. After quickly reading it, I looked up at Tullia. She was sobbing pathetically, but in between sobs she told me what I was too afflicted to ask.

"Tata after you left, Publius again consorted with *that* woman"— Tullia nearly choked when saying the name—"Clodia Pulchra. I demanded that he stop. He said he would do whatever he wanted with whomsoever he wished. Right up until the time he left for Spain, he was seeing her. He spent so many days and nights with her and away from me." A new torrent of tears gushed out.

I held her in my arms, trying to comfort her. "Why didn't you tell me before?"

Tullia shrugged and stammered, "I hoped I could win him back. He was so happy about… about the baby. I didn't know what to do. When he went to Spain, he told me he'd write." She burst anew into tears. "*That!* That is what he sent me." She indicated the divorce note that I still held in my hand.

I had paid Dolabella the final dowry installment before returning to Tusculum. So, I could not figure out why he had chosen this time to initiate the divorce. He was not stupid. He knew he would have to refund the dowry. What had poisoned him against Tullia? Despite what she had said, was Dolabella displeased about the child that he had fathered? Or was he simply but irrevocably bewitched by the wiles of the *Palatine Medusa*? Whatever it was that turned him into such a reptile, I loathed and hated him now more than ever because he had wounded my *Tulliola* beyond healing.

She wanted to remain with me until the baby's birth, and I would never have allowed her to go elsewhere. But Publilia went out of her way to show her displeasure at Tullia's presence, while at the same time rendering no sympathy at all for her plight. Tullia was as antipathetic to my sullen, sour young wife as you, my son, were attractive and appealing to her.

You visited several times after Tullia moved in. You commiserated with your sister's predicament, but you still wanted to go to Spain. I remained adamantly opposed. At every meal we shared, between arguing with you and observing Publilia's increasing flirtation with you—which you did nothing to discourage—my bowels were under chronic attack by the united forces of indigestion, cramps, and dyspepsia.

When Metrodorus ministered to me, he indicated that Tullia was declining in health. This was obvious. She was losing weight, and she looked so wan and so fragile. She hardly touched any food. Metrodorus believed that she would not successfully carry the pregnancy. I feared he was right.

Early in February, two notes came within a few days of each other. Dolabella wrote that the divorce was necessary, though he did not explain why. He was sorry for any grief he had caused Tullia and me. How utterly false! Was he just as false when he assured me that he would repay the dowry? On this issue, Caesar's note assured me that he had accepted Dollabella's word that he would make all necessary restitution. This promise had been elicited, Caesar wrote, as a condition for Dolabella's continued service in the Spanish campaign.

I appreciated Caesar's concern, but I rued the day that Dolabella had ever come into our lives.

Tullia's anxiety and depression, her severe heartache and ague, induced an early labor and the delivery of a sickly, poorly developed baby. Metrodorus confessed that he could do nothing for him. We named him Lentulus as this was a common name among his father's gens. He died within hours after his birth.

For several days, my beloved *Tulliola*, weakened beyond recovery by the ordeal of labor and the subsequent death of this, her second son, lingered in a twilight realm between life and oblivion. Holding her in my arms, I saw her life ebbing away. She died. My precious child died, and with her passing the light within me was extinguished.

Now Publilia, far from commiserating with my grief, had the insensitivity, the heartlessness to announce her satisfaction that the burden of Tullia had been removed. All my pent-up anger and sorrow exploded at her in a denunciatory rage. I ordered her out of the house and out of my life. You consented to accompany her back to her mother's house in Roma. So absorbed was I in my sorrow that I did not heed her parting words of reproach and recrimination. I was even oblivious to the financial implications of putting her out. The loss of Tullia virtually numbed me to all reality, so great was my sorrow for her, like nothing I had ever known before.

Tullia's funeral and that of little Lentulus was a brief, relatively unceremonious affair totally arranged by Tiro. Terentia attended, as did Pomponia and Fabia, but our sorrow as well as our private rancor precluded any lengthy exchanges between us. Likewise, Pomponia said little to Quintus. Then, Fabia, lovely, almost ethereal Fabia, expressed her tearful condolences. She even told me that within Vesta's sacred fire she had seen Tullia's face, tranquil and sublime, transcendent and eternal.

But the words meant nothing to me at the time. Even the consolatory attention of Atticus and Pilia could not register within me.

Following the funeral, you offered to stay with me, but I declined your offer. Instead, I urged you to return to Roma and stay with your mother.

I desired nothing but solitude. Abandoning Tusculum, I went to another country estate, the one at Astura, taking with me only Tiro, Alexio, and Metrodorus. For weeks, I interred myself in sorrow. I found little if any solace in my books or my writing, although I did devote some attention to a treatise entitled *On Consolation* that I addressed to myself.

The deep, dark woods surrounding the house were a visual metaphor for the darkness enveloping my mind and soul. Atticus and Quintus tried but could not penetrate its depth with even the slightest light. Still, they were supportive, even though my brother had problems of his own.

Having failed to prevent his son from accompanying Caesar to Spain, he was now contending with Pomponia's unreasonable demands for the immediate repayment of her dowry. Even Atticus told me that Publilia's mother and brother were pestering him about my restitution of the girl's dowry. But I blotted this out of my mind, for it intruded on the dark vacuum of my sorrow.

Consolatory letters came to me from all quarters. From Spain, in the midst of war, Caesar wrote me. Truly, he knew all too well the pain of losing a daughter. Lepidus, the Master of Horse, wrote from Roma on behalf of the entire Senate. Marcus Antonius wrote from Narbo, and even my ex-son-in-law had the decency—or the hubris—to send his condolences, but not the courage to own up to his culpability.

The most poignant letter came from Servius Sulpicius who was still administering Greece as Caesar's appointed proconsul. He urged me to bear my sorrow with the same dignity with which I had borne the honors of my political career. In his view, Tullia's death was equated with the demise of the free Republic. However, he differentiated the two insofar as the one is part of the cycle of life, while the other was the inevitable result of a historical process that predated both of us and transcended our efforts to forestall it. Finally, Servius reminded me that there is no grief that time cannot mitigate or diminish.

Writing back to Servius, I thanked him for his counsel during my sickness of soul. How I wished I could have seen him! My grief over Tullia's passing was so profound, I explained, because there were no avenues of civic activity open to me that might have assuaged my sorrow. The free Republic indeed was gone. So, I could not divert my sorrow into service in the courts, in the Senate, or in the Assembly because these institutions had become shams under Caesar's power. Notwithstanding this, I acknowledged Servius' liberality and his genuine concern for my welfare and his sincere friendship.

I closed by expressing my hope that upon his return from Greece we might together plan how best to live quiet lives under the political status quo.

MY GRIEF WAS NOT ALLEVIATED until I underwent a spiritual experience. One day, several weeks after Tullia's passing, I was contemplating the urn containing her ashes, the last physical reminders of her life. At the same time, I noticed the cold, damp winter giving way to the first signs of another spring. New leaves and buds were sprouting on trees and bushes. The meadow's yellow-brown hue became a vibrant, verdant carpet. The songs of larks and hummingbirds filled the air as though heralding the rebirth of creation. The death of winter was giving way to the new life of spring.

I thought of the old oak tree of Marius back at Arpinum. Its massive, dark limbs, naked in winter, became clothed in summer with infinite green leaves. The sun's rays poured through them giving to any thoughtful observer a glimpse into eternity. I remembered my youth and my student days in Athens when I was initiated into the secret rites of the Elysian Mysteries. These rites celebrated the myth of Persephone's annual release from Hades so that she could briefly be with her mother, Demeter, and thereby renew all forms of life on earth.

There are myths for virtually every occurrence in life, but I had never paid much attention to any of them for anything other than scholastic purposes. Now, Persephone became connected in my mind with Tullia, and I hoped for my daughter's release from the Underworld.

However, I went beyond the expectation of a periodic rebirth or renewal. In perusing my own writings, particularly the final book of *On the Republic* which I entitled *"The Dream of Scipio,"* I re-discovered a common Greek belief in the immortality of the soul in a celestial abode. Again, I realized a truth that I had only faintly perceived when viewing the grave of my first son-in-law, Piso: That there is an infinite life of the soul above and beyond the physical enclosure of life in this world.

I came to believe with all my heart and consciousness that Tullia was not really gone, that she would never be lost to me, for she was part of my soul.

So strongly did this realization take hold that I conceived the idea of building a shrine to memorialize Tullia. Atticus and Quintus assisted me in trying to locate a suitable piece of ground for it. We spent many hours discussing it and sketching its shape and design. Atticus favored a replica of the Vestal Temple in Roma because it housed the eternal flame safeguarding the City. Quintus leaned toward my idea of a solid stone orb signifying the infinite, everlasting, transcendent nature of the soul.

In the end, the project came to naught as our search for an appropriate site was interrupted by squabbles with my estranged in-laws. Atticus suggested urgency in finding some saleable property or consolidating some book royalties so that Publilia's family could be placated with at least an installment on her returned dowry.

At the same time, you were starting up again about going to Spain. This time, however, your mood was very different. There was no sarcasm, or sneers, or attitude of assertive self-reliance. You seemed strangely troubled as though some great weight were upon you. Some inner torment of guilt or remorse wreaked havoc with your conscience.

"Must it be Spain?" I had resolved to bargain rather than argue with you.

"I don't understand," you admitted with confusion playing upon your guilt-ridden face.

"Look, Marcus, let's be fair. You want to leave Roma for reasons that you're unwilling or unable to divulge. I hope there's nothing criminal or immoral that impels you." I noticed you wince at the word *immoral*. I thought—*No! Not Publilia! Not Marcus!* Taking a deep breath, composing myself, and blotting out what was too painful to contemplate, I went on. "Not Spain where there's only civil war and death, but Athens...."

"*Athens?*"

"Yes," I continued, "Athens." It's time you broadened your education"—you winced again as though education implied something sordid—"in rhetoric and philosophy. Cratippus is still one of the finest teachers in Greece, and Servius Sulpicius is still governing the province. It can all be very easily arranged."

You were almost convinced, but not quite. Now, I resorted to my ultimate inducement. "Marcus, how does a stipend of fif... *uh, forty* thousand sesterces per year appeal to you?"

Of course, that clinched the discussion. The necessary letters were sent. You were expeditiously packed and shipped off to Athens. Deep within me, I hoped that, besides succeeding in your studies, you would find healing for your troubled spirit. Also, I hoped there would be no repercussions from whatever mischief you may have committed.

As of this writing, Marcus, you have been away for seven months. Your stipend and the repayment of Publilia's dowry have tied my revenues so that I have had to abandon plans for Tullia's memorial. But Cratippus has written that you are more interested in wine and debauchery than you are in rhetoric and philosophy. Not an admirable way for my money, your stipend, to be spent, especially when I considered that Tullia's shrine—both the land and the monument—would have required less money than what you were apparently squandering.

Omniscient Narrative

Decimus Junius Brutus is, by Caesar's nomination and the Assembly's vote, Praetor of the Republic. By his mother's wrangling, he has married Flavia Fimbria, the daughter of Aurelia Orestilla, widow of the infamous Lucius Sergius Catilina. Grudgingly and resentfully, he has entered into this marriage. It is not his wife whom he resents, but instead his mother, Sempronia, for pressuring him into it. There is sufficient resentment as well for his mother-in-law for her part in arranging the marriage. Like two conspiratorial harpies, they had talked and agreed that Decimus and Flavia should marry. All of these arrangements had been made while he had been up in the Transalpina holding the province so that Caesar could battle Pompeius and the optimates.

Over dinner in his modest home in Roma's Caelian district, Decimus ponders his situation, eating meagerly as his wife and mother and mother-in-law busily chatter away. He is in a peculiarly unenviable position. He is politically powerful as Caesar's man and as Praetor, by Caesar's selection. Yet, he remains subject to his mother's over-bearing influence. Probing his own psyche, Decimus has the Oedipal guilt of a son who, albeit *knowingly*, became incestuously entwined with his mother and who knowingly assisted her in poisoning his father, the elder Decimus Brutus. His guilt and shame render him Sempronia's virtual pawn and puppet. He knows his mother is capable of divulging their complicity. Sempronia does not fear the law, where bribery can secure acquittals; nor is she fazed by social ostracism. But for himself, Decimus knows that at the very least, he would be thrown out of favor with Caesar and his political career would be relegated to the trash heap.

So Sempronia, wielding the proverbial sword of Damocles over his head, has tenderly maneuvered and manipulated him into marrying the daughter of the renegade, Catilina, whose co-conspirator, Lentulus Sura, had been Sempronia's lover.

Decimus looks at his wife, reclining on the dining couch next to him. She is beautiful, alluring and fetching, a younger manifestation of her mother. She was just as beautiful when she had admitted to him that her step-father, Catilina, had been her lover, and that Orestilla has long suspected their relationship. Decimus had laughed at the sick irony of the whole sorry, warped business. Consumed with guilt, shame, and self-loathing over his relations with his mother and his connivance in his father's death, he has been pressured into this marriage with a woman who had been her step-father's mistress—just as his own mother had been mistress to Catilina's confederate. How decidedly bizarre that their lives and fates should be warped within such dark, perverse irony!

The women's conversation focuses on their mutual friends, Mucia, Pompeia, and Servilia. Their questions and ruminations are filled with speculation. How might the Magnus' ex-wife and Caesar's ex-wife fare in Spain? Will Caesar treat them favorably after his inevitable victory over the Pompeian remnants? Could Mucia really have been Caesar's mistress while Pompeius was engaged in the Eastern war? Did Pompeia, she whom Caesar divorced because *she* was not above suspicion, ever suspect that he and Mucia were lovers?

Sempronia and Orestilla laugh at their recollections of the Bona Dea affair some eighteen years earlier. "It could have been Publius Pulcher's undoing," Orestilla opines. "Now the Claudii Pulchri are finished. All the men folk have died—Publius before the civil war, and his older brothers during it. Their sisters will probably fade into oblivion."

"But not the *youngest*," says Flavia, "not the one who's lately been Dolabella's mistress."

The women laugh and agree. "She reminds me very much of a friend, long gone," Sempronia recalls.

"Who might that be?" Orestilla asks, her bow-shaped mouth puckering with the question.

"Praecia. Certainly you remember Praecia?"

"Yes, yes, of course," Orestilla recalls. "She was involved with Gaius Cethegus when my husband...."

"And before him—with his brother, Publius; together, they once had a lot of clout in the Senate, a long time ago."

"She's the one who hanged herself, no?" Flavia presses her fingers against her throat as she speaks. "Clodia Pulchra reminds you of Praecia?"

"Yes," Sempronia admits. "Like Praecia, Clodia is also a rebel. She too wants a niche in the Roman political order, and to get it, she competes with her sister-in-law, except where Fulvia marries up-and-coming men, Clodia merely beds and then discards them!"

Orestilla mentions Appius Claudius' two daughters. One is probably in Spain with her husband, the younger Gnaeus Pompeius. "But the other, the one married to Marcus Brutus,"—here, Decimus Brutus becomes especially attentive at the mention of his kinsman's name—"well, rumor has it that Servilia may soon have a new daughter-in-law."

SEATED ON A CATHEDRA CHAIR in her bedchamber, Servilia harangues her son. "This is not a good move, Marcus. Your cousin is the daughter of Caesar's implacable enemy. How can you hope to rise in Caesar's regime if you're espoused to Cato's daughter? Don't you see that it's a politically risky marriage? It sends the wrong message. Despite Caesar's pardon and his fostering of your career, you'd espouse the old oligarchy that he's fought and all but obliterated. Not to mention that you'd alienate the Claudii Pulchri by divorcing Claudia. Truly, you can see this, no?"

Brutus has been leaning languidly against a pillar. Now he springs away from it and stands rigidly before his mother, his hands extended to her. "But the Pulchers are finished. There's no hope of gain for me in continuing my marriage to Claudia. In so many words, she's told me the same thing."

Servilia shakes her head in dismay. "If you're thinking about a marriage that will advance your career, how can you imagine that Porcia's right for *you*? She hates Caesar, perhaps as much as Cato hated him."

"And I share that hatred with her. Yes, Mother. I hate him because he rejected you after all the years he had used you!"

Servilia's pained expression darkens her lovely face. She well remembers her rejection by Caesar, when he had said to her that Caesar's wife had to be above suspicion.

"He rejected me," Brutus continues, "so that his daughter could marry the murderer of my father—my *father, your husband!*"

Thoughtfully, sadly, Servilia warns, "Marcus, cross him now and you may as well forget about the urban praetorate next year."

Brutus is undaunted. "I'll take whatever office I can get. It's my birthright. And I'll divorce and marry whom I please! He'll not stop me! Nor will you, Mother!"

Cicero's Respublica

During my bereavement and spiritual awakening, Caesar conducted a relentless war in Spain. Young Quintus wrote his father regularly, and in this way we were kept informed. From my nephew's letters, I inferred that this Spanish campaign, in its ferocity, ruthlessness, and brutality, surpassed Caesar's previous wars against his fellow Romans. Both the Pompeians and Caesarians inflicted barbaric reprisals on each others' supporters and prisoners.

Caesar's legions captured town after town before decisively defeating the Pompeians at Munda. Here, the tide of battle seemed to be going against the Caesarians, and in desperation, Caesar snatched a sword and shield from a fleeing legionary. Advancing into the heat of battle, Caesar cried out, "You would send your commander to his death!"

Shamed by this pronouncement, the troops who had been retreating turned about and returned to the fight. Simultaneously, there must have been some tactical confusion in the Pompeian ranks, for their formation broke in wild flight to the safety of Munda's walls.

Titus Labienus was killed trying to rally the retreating soldiers. His corpse was recovered from the battlefield and brought before Caesar. Sextus Pompeius was believed to have escaped, and even now his whereabouts are not known for certain. His elder brother was not so fortunate; he was hunted down by Caesar's Gallic horsemen, captured, and beheaded.

Omniscient Narrative

GNAEUS POMPEIUS THE YOUNGER STARES blankly from dead eyes forever paralyzed in terror. The lips are curved downward and the chin is splattered with blood. The severed neck bleeds onto the Gallic spearhead that holds the head aloft for Caesar and his officers to see it.

There is no revulsion for Caesar as there had been three years before when, in Egypt, he had beheld the Magnus' severed head. Exhaustion from endless wars and anger at his enemies' intransigence have driven revulsion and compassion from Caesar's sensibilities. He looks at the ground on either side of the spear holding the Younger Pompeius' head. The slashed, bloodied corpses of Titus Labienus and Marcus Aemilius Scaurus lie on legionary shields. Both had once been the Magnus' legates, serving under him valorously, and Scaurus, by Pompeius' arrangement, had married Mucia after she had been divorced by the Magnus. Labienus had fostered Caesar's interests as plebeian tribune. Then, for eight years he had been Caesar's chief legate in Gaul before defecting to Pompeius on the eve of the civil war. He also had married Caesar's divorced wife, Pompeia.

Caesar may well remember all of this as he stares at the two corpses laid at his feet. But there are other corpses, hundreds, thousands of them, his casualties and those of the Pompeians. The protracted fighting has taken its toll on Caesar's will and spirit. He knows all too well that Pompeian resistance will never be terminated as long as one of them remains at large. Can clemency or negotiation win over Sextus Pompeius to Caesar's side? Rather than magnanimity, will terror move the obstinate defenders of Munda to surrender?

"Find Sextus Pompeius!" Caesar orders his Gallic horsemen. "Bring him to me—alive if possible. If he resists, kill him!"

The Gauls comprehend their Imperator's Greek words and his sanguinary intentions. Saluting, they gallop off, scouring the countryside in search of their quarry.

"Gather up their dead," he tells his officers, "and stack them around Munda's walls. Let them *rot* and *stink* to the high heavens!"

The officers, Dolabella, Pedius, Pollio, Rebilus, and Fabius Maximus, and Caesar's grand-nephew, Gaius Octavius, offer no dissent to their Imperator's orders, though they are nonplussed by their barbarity. For many days thereafter, they supervise the legionaries in stripping the Pompeian dead of their arms and armor. Iberian, Celtic, and Italian corpses are piled up to form macabre, putrid walls of rotting flesh, and their stench and the simmering summer heat assail both the Caesarians and Munda's defenders.

But it is the besieged whose spirits break. The soldiers and townspeople of Munda wisely and unconditionally surrender. Caesar's legionaries salute him as victorious Imperator when he enters through the town's gates, and the starving, terrorized, leaderless populace watches him impassively.

Just inside the gate, a group of veiled women confronts him. Recognizing them, Caesar reins in his horse. Staring at him defiantly are Mucia, the ex-wife of the Magnus and his own former lover; Pompeia, Caesar's ex-wife and now the widow of Titus Labienus; Claudia Pulchra, Appius' daughter, and now widow of Gnaeus Pompeius the Younger; and Scribonia Libo, wife of the fugitive, Sextus Pompeius.

Caesar says to them, "Your sons and husbands made relentless war upon the Roman People...."

"They fought to restore the free Republic," Mucia defiantly interrupts him.

"... and their rightful leader," Caesar imperiously continues. "But I do not make war upon women and children. You...."

"But you make war upon the *dead!*" Pompeia declares against her ex-husband.

"You and all others are free to return to Roma or anywhere else you might desire to go." Caesar moves his horse closer to the youngest of the women, the small, round wife of Sextus Pompeius, and intones menacingly, "Scribonia Libo, if you can contact your husband, you should persuade him to make peace with me, before my men find him."

Scribonia is undaunted. "He'd do better to fight to the death, Caesar. We've all seen the shallowness of *your* clemency!"

Sitting astride his horse, Caesar begins to feel ill, dizzy, and weak. He manages to order an aide, "See to their comfort!" Then, spurring his horse forward, he leads his retinue deeper into the town, but the women's defiant words resonate in his mind's ears.

Caesar remains in Spain for some time administering the newly re-conquered province. He visits Gades on the coast facing the great, outer ocean. Many years before, when he had been quaestor, he had visited this ancient Phoenician town. Standing before a statue of Alexander of Macedon in the Gadian Temple of Hercules, Caesar had openly wept upon considering that, at the same age as the great conqueror, he had achieved nothing of importance for himself or for his country. Now, remembering the incident and reflecting on his own military victories over both foreigners and his fellow Romans, and recognizing his unchallenged pre-eminence in the Republic, Caesar is overcome with a nauseating vertigo that pitches him to the temple's stone pavement. Fortunately, his companion kinsmen, young Gaius Octavius and Quintus Pedius, succeed in catching him and preventing him from cracking his skull.

SATISFIED THAT SPAIN HAS BEEN set in order, Caesar sets out to return to Italia. En route, he stops at Narbo in the Transalpina. Marcus Antonius conducts him on an inspection tour of the newly established citizen-soldier colony. Caesar is overwhelmingly impressed by the neat, precisely laid-out farmsteads. Antonius is commended. Some seven thousand legionary veterans and five thousand of Roma's idle citizens have been established on their very own farms.

"You've done well, Marcus," Caesar says to him, "very well indeed. The Narbo community will be even more productive now with so many hands working the land."

Caesar and his retinue have arrived back in town. Marcus Antonius sees to their comfort in his headquarters near the town square. His office is spacious and well illuminated. Slaves distribute cups of wine from several large beakers. However, Marcus Antonius and Publius Dolabella eye each other venomously, even though both men know that their recent commissions have restored them to Caesar's favor. Caesar's grand-nephew, Gaius Octavius, notices the umbrage tossed between the two men. Quintus Pedius and Gaius Pollio are attentive to their Imperator's words and observations.

"Well, Lucius, what would you guess about Narbo's future now that all these colonists have been settled?" Caesar's query is addressed to a tall, swarthy man wearing a plain, white woolen toga. He has as many years as Caesar. His face is large, angular, and creased with world weariness. He is Lucius Cornelius Cinna, the brother of Caesar's first wife, his beloved, deceased Cornelia.

Cinna has lived in exile in Narbo for the last thirty-three years, ever since he had fled Roma and Italia after the failure of the abortive popularist rebellion against the Sullan regime. Caesar had wisely held aloof from the debacle, choosing instead to work against the optimates by attaining political office through the course of advancement. However, Caesar has kept in regular contact with Cinna. During his Gallic proconsulate, when his legions were in winter quarters, Caesar often called upon his brother-in-law in Narbo, assuring the exile that he would someday restore him to his home country.

Caesar has kept his word, issuing a dictatorial decree recalling all political exiles, with few exceptions. Yet, Cinna remained at Narbo, probably to avoid choosing sides in the civil war. Now, fresh from his Spanish victories, Caesar hopes that the civil war is finally at an end, and Cinna will certainly return to Roma.

Cinna replies to Caesar's question. "Gaius, you know as well as I that the produce of these new colonists will not only enrich Narbo, but their surplus will also help to feed Roman mouths."

"So then, Lucius, why not return with me to Roma? You've been away far too long." Caesar notices that Cinna is still not convinced. "Banishment has kept you out of politics; most regrettable. So, come back with me and I'll nominate you for one of the praetorships in the next election. Well? What do you say?"

Cinna shrugs, casting his gaze to the stone floor in resignation. "If you must have me in Roma, well, I suppose I'll have to tear myself away from Narbo."

Wrinkling his nose and furrowing his brow, Caesar lays on another calculated inducement. "Pompeius Magnus' daughter became a widow with her husband's death in Africa. Faustus Sulla was a good man, and I wish he'd been among my own. But, more to the point, Pompeia is yet an attractive woman. She'll probably re-marry, and I'd like her to be connected with me. Catch my drift, Lucius?"

"If she'll have me," Lucius says amiably.

"Excellent! Excellent!" Caesar raises his cup. "Gentlemen, let's drink to the return of Lucius Cornelius Cinna!"

"To Cinna!" Caesar's officers salute him in unison and then drink deeply.

Caesar swallows hard, pursing his lips. "Now, some other business; Marcus, I want you to be my consular colleague. Are you up to it?"

Antonius is elated, and relieved. "Yes, Imperator, I'm at your service!"

"Good!" Caesar turns to Dolabella. "Before I leave for Parthia, I'll relinquish the consulate. I want you to be Suffect Consul. You accept?"

Dolabella too is elated. Rendering the military salute of fidelity—clenched fist upon his breast—he proclaims, "Your servant, Caesar."

"Now, Antonius and Dolabella, I trust you'll resolve whatever issues remain between you—as expeditiously as possible." Caesar takes a turn around the wooden table and looks up at the compluvium; he sees thick, high clouds through the sky-light. "When I relinquish the consulate, Fabius Maximus and Gaius Trebonius will assume it and finish out the year." He looks down at his officers, his face grimacing in discomfort. "Gentlemen, I'm tired. Dictatorship and Consulate weigh too heavily and I must...."

Pausing, he notices Gaius Octavius. "No, I haven't forgotten you, young man. You'll accompany me to Parthia."

"Thank you, Uncle," says the golden-haired lad.

"But first you'll go to Apollonia to study. You've had your taste of warfare. Now, it's time you delve into philosophy and rhetoric. Agreed?"

"Of course, Uncle; thank you."

Antonius cannot help but smirk at the youth's enthusiasm. Dolabella catches sight of this and grins sardonically.

Caesar says to Pedius and Pollio, "There will be offices and provinces for both of you, as well as for all Caesar's loyal officers." Gaius Octavius observes that Caesar speaks in the third person as though he were writing a new edition of his *Commentaries*.

Before returning to Roma, Caesar will go to his estate at Lavinium, to rest, to recover from the rigors of the recent campaign, and to plan for the future.

Cicero's Respublica

In September, hearing that Caesar had returned to Italia, and inferring that Dolabella might also have returned with him, I reluctantly left the peace and serenity of Astura and traveled to Roma. It was my intention to speak with my erstwhile son-in-law and delicately, but clearly, remind him to return Tullia's dowry.

Not long after settling in at the Palatine house, I realized that speaking to him would be difficult at best. Yes, he was back in the City, living a short remove down the Hill, at Clodia Pulchra's house. He had moved in with his consort. *Well and good*, I thought, rather than the *Juno Medusa* moving into the house that Dolabella had shared with my daughter. *Tullia! My Tulliola!* What a mistake you—we all—made with him.

I refused to approach him, to speak with him in the company of *Juno, the Black-Eyed Medusa*. As Atticus was then away from Roma on business, I had no intermediary on whom I could rely. So, I waited and fumed with anger and frustration, yet mourning for Tullia.

Marcus Antonius was also back in the Capital, having completed his colonizing duties in Narbo. He and his wife, Fulvia, frequently called at Clodia Pulchra's. *And why not?* The two women—the raven-tressed Clodia and the flame-haired Fulvia—were sisters-in-law and companions in sensual pursuits. And the men—the Herculean bull, Antonius, and the narcissistic Roman Apollo, Dolabella, were both Caesar's officers and apparently slated for important offices. The four of them, like a team of prize horses, were frequently seen in public, in the Forum, at Pompeius' Theatre, and at the Circus Maximus. They were always wildly acclaimed by the numerically reduced but still foul City rabble.

The Master of Horse Lepidus convened the Senate at the Portico of Pompeius' Theatre. I attended because I had hoped to encounter Dolabella. Ironically, he did not attend. Neither did Antonius. So, all eyes focused on the small, spare, insignificant man shouldered with the responsibility of serving as Caesar's eyes, ears, and voice.

From his suburban estate at Lavinium, Caesar had sent a letter to the Senate which Lepidus duly read. In it, Caesar resigned the Consulate—but *not* the Dictatorship—and nominated Fabius Maximus and Gaius Trebonius to complete the remaining three months of his term. Caesar also authorized Lepidus to conduct the elections for the following year. He nominated himself and Marcus Antonius for the consulate. It was a foregone conclusion that the Assembly would implement the Dictator's dictate.

The Senate did its part too. After Lepidus had completed Caesar's letter, proposal followed proposal conferring numerous titles, honors, and privileges upon Caesar. He was named *Perpetual Dictator* and granted the permanent title *Imperator*. This implied not only his overall command of the legions, but also his complete authority over the Republic and the entire imperium. Ironically, he was given the innovative post of *Prefect of Public Morals*—the Senate could not have named a more inappropriate candidate. He was given the dubious titles of *Father of the Country* and *Liberator* and he was named to the college of Augurs—so that now he could read the omens any way he chose.

The Senate reaffirmed Caesar's unique privilege of wearing the triumphal garb of purple and the laurel crown on all occasions. I knew this would appeal to his vanity, for his hair had become so thin that the laurel crown afforded some protection and concealment for his balding pate. His privilege of sitting on a golden curule chair when presiding over the Senate and the Assembly was also reaffirmed. Caesar's effigies and statues, also adorned with coronets, were permitted to be placed on the newly completed Rostra and in various temples.

It was totally unprecedented that any Roman statesman, however distinguished, should be so honored in his own lifetime with the erection and coronation of statues of himself. As revolting to Republican sentiment as all these honors and privileges were, by far the most excessive and the most repugnant was Caesar's *deification* by the Senate! Beyond his Chief Pontificate, he was now divinely sanctified, elevated to the status of the gods of the Roman state, to be hallowed and revered as one of them. Adding insult to injury, Marcus Antonius was named *Priest of the God Julius*. Disgusting!

Lepidus wasted no time in holding the elections. The voters, properly instructed, chose Caesar and Marcus Antonius consuls for the ensuing year. Among those elected to the praetorate were Marcus Brutus and Gaius Cassius, respectively Urban and Foreign Praetor. Their nomination, no doubt, had been Caesar's reward for their abandonment of the optimates after Pharsalus. Caesar's nominees, Fabius Maximus and Gaius Trebonius, were chosen by the Centuriate electors to finish out the remaining months of the Dictator's relinquished consulate.

It was amusing but at the same time degrading for all who loved the Republic that Caesar should trifle with magistrates and offices as though they were *his* personal possessions to be held, surrendered, and given over to others by *his* whim; and the Assembly, in blind obedience, did his bidding.

WHILE CAESAR TIGHTENED HIS GRIP on the Republic, squeezing into nothingness its remaining liberties, I implemented an idea that I had considered since returning from my Cilician proconsulate on the eve of the civil war. I drafted documents of manumission for Tiro, my faithful slave and secretary since the time I had donned the virile toga.

On the Kalends of November, I brought Tiro before Praetor Decimus Junius Brutus at his tribunal in the Forum. Presenting him with a copy of the prescribed documents to be filed in the archives of the Tabularium, I conferred upon Tiro, now my freedman, the name, Marcus Tullius Tiro, and declared that his status as a slave of my household was officially at an end. This was done, according to law, before witnesses—my brother, Quintus and his son. Donning the customary *Liberty Cap* and holding his manumission certificate, Tiro was congratulated by us and by Praetor Brutus. Tiro pledged his continued attachment and loyalty to me and to our entire family.

Lest there should be any resentment on their part, I assured Metrodorus and Alexio that they too would be manumitted in the foreseeable future. I reminded them and Tiro that by Roman law, a freedman's descendants would enjoy all the privileges of Roman citizenship. Yet, I wondered of what good these would ever be to them in a state that was becoming increasingly autocratic.

Despite my happiness for Tiro, my disgust and disillusionment with the political situation reminded me of how sorely I missed Tullia. She would have distracted me and filled the void in my life with her light. But I remembered that her travails had afflicted me as much as the sham of Republican government under Caesar. I wanted to speak with someone who could have been a surrogate for my *Tulliola*. So, I visited my sister-in-law, the Vestal Fabia.

I waited for her in the same large atrium where, so many years before when I was Consul, Caesar had tried to enlist my support in exchange for his cooperation in destroying Catilina's conspiracy. Looking about the room I saw the same statues of former Chief Vestals, standing in their appointed niches and staring through vacant eyes. From the inner side of the atrium, the heavy twin doors were pushed open by female attendants, and Fabia, veiled in white wool, gracefully entered.

"Marcus! Marcus!" She said my name as she extended her hands to me. I took them tenderly into my own. We kissed each other chastely on the cheek. "What a sublime surprise!"

"*Sublime?*" I repeated incredulously. "I fear I can never measure up to being sublime. That's a word better applied to you, Fabia. You were always sublime, and will always remain so."

Fabia was still beautiful. The years had not diminished her beauty even to the slightest degree. I remained silent for a moment, taking in her exquisite, graceful loveliness. Looking back at me, she began to blush. Even in the dimly oil-lit room that was obvious.

We talked freely and ever so amiably. I inquired after Terentia, and Fabia told me that aside from more acute attacks of her joint pains, she was in good health, ever busy with her accounts and properties. "She stays purposely busy so as not to grieve about Tullia," Fabia confided.

"I envy her that pre-occupation. Tullia was my favorite. Terentia always favored Marcus."

"You're wrong, Marcus," she demurred. "You and Terentia love them equally, but differently." Fabia was very perceptive for a woman who had never conceived nor borne a child.

I confided in her my recent unhappiness concerning you and Publilia, honestly admitting my neglect. Fabia gave no indications of surprise or disturbance. She did not attempt to controvert my suspicions; nor was she in any way judgmental about the Publilia affair or my divorce of Terentia.

"So often it happens," said Fabia "that children afflict their parents in life and in death." She looked at me and smiled knowingly.

"Yes, Fabia. My children have given me much pain. Even Quintus has his problems."

"His son is back from Spain?" she inquired.

"Yes, he's back. But they've created a veritable monster in that boy." I felt ashamed to speak disparagingly of my nephew before Fabia. Begging her pardon, I explained that from my brother's own account, the Spanish war had calloused and poisoned young Quintus to an extent that went beyond his twenty years.

"I'm sorry for him," Fabia admitted, "and for your brother and Pomponia too." She clasped my hand and added, "Marcus Cicero, you've endured much sorrow and suffering. I'm afraid the Fates are not yet through with you. There's more you will yet endure."

"Greater sorrow than losing a beloved child?" I mused. Then I began an account of Tullia's loss of the baby and her own death and my own bereavement and spiritual experience. Certainly Fabia knew the circumstances surrounding my daughter's passing, for no doubt Terentia had told her the abbreviated version that I had written her. As one committed to religious service, Fabia was enthralled at hearing of my realization of Tullia's eternal existence.

"I'm happy that such an experience came to you, Marcus," she said looking at me with those radiant, luminous eyes. "The gods have their way. They afflict, but they give the means to healing. They'll do this for you to ease the grief of Tullia's loss. A long time ago, they also brought me to healing."

I was intrigued. "Fabia, could… would you tell me of your healing experience? If that's presumptuous of me, then I…."

"No, Marcus, not at all. Besides, you know the public part of the story. Of course you remember. It happened in the first year of the great slave revolt. You and Terentia had been married only a few years…."

Yes, I was thinking. I do remember, Fabia. With much pain and resentment I remember.

"I was only a novice," Fabia recalled, "when I had a spiritual crisis. I felt drawn to Lucius Catilina. He and Marcus Crassus had visited the Vestal House because Crassus was interested in buying some property owned by the Chief Vestal, Licinia. She recently retired, but she was kin to Crassus, a fine woman, virtuous, abstemious beyond all doubt.

"Each time they visited, Catilina spoke to me. He stirred my emotions. Though he never made any disrespectful or indecent advances, I detected something disquieting in the way he looked at me. Soon, I began to question whether I truly belonged in Vesta's service; and my mind was racked by doubt, even when I tended the sacred fire.

"Then there was the investigation, prompted by Crassus' enemies. They accused him of attempting to seduce Licinia because they were jealous of his wealth and fearful of his ambition. They even went so far as to accuse Catilina of being his accomplice and of having the same intentions toward me."

"Yes, Fabia, I remember the trial. I cannot exonerate Catilina of shameful, licentious designs on you. But Crassus had the highest respect for Roma's religious collegia, especially the Vestals, despite his shameful bribery at the Good Goddess trial."

"I know, Marcus, and that is why he and all of us were acquitted and spared the horrible penalty of being buried alive. I'm sure you know that's the punishment for unchaste Vestals. But for so many years afterward, I was tormented by the accusation of unchastity. And I could not deny having feelings for Lucius Catilina. He had tapped something primal, something instinctive within me; something that we Vestals take a solemn oath to deny. Yet, I wanted him. I wanted him."

I was shaken to realize that my lovely, pristine, beautiful sister-in-law was once in love, or at least infatuated, with the subversive rebel, Catilina.

"I prayed to Mother Vesta for direction," Fabia glowed. "Each day when it was my turn to tend the sacred flame, I concentrated all my energies, all my thoughts on it and on the deity for whom it burns. Soon, I was seeing visions within the fire. I saw Catilina's conspiracy years before you uncovered it, Marcus. I saw that he would come to a bitter end. I saw that out of his defeat there would come to Roma a new order, but one that not all Romans would accept."

Fabia's visions had proven to be accurate. I was one of the Romans who grudgingly assented to Caesar's regime.

"This sight of things yet to be, this was the fruit of the spiritual healing that Mother Vesta granted me. Mind you, I don't always see things in the Holy Fire. It's only when the goddess allows me to see them."

"For one who doesn't believe in the gods," I confessed, "I've always been fascinated with divination. I'd like to write a book on it, and I've already begun to gather materials for it. That's all there is for me now—read, research, digest, and write. Caesar's new order, the very one you probably foresaw, Fabia, allows me no other occupation. Oh yes, there's one other. *I remember. I remember.*"

"Marcus Cicero," Fabia smiled at me, "Roma will have need of you. It is your destiny to serve the Republic."

Fabia's words registered in my mind with a prophetic gravity. I could not imagine a destiny other than one of exclusion and exile and accommodation such as had been the bane of my existence for so many years. But Fabia may have seen something in her fiery visions about which I dared not ask.

Just then, she moved in closer to me, inclining her head and holding my hand even more securely. "I'll confide something in you, Marcus, but please keep this to yourself. A few days ago, a courier from Lavinium brought us a document from Caesar. It was his last will and testament to be stored here in the Vestal archives. *Why now, Marcus? What's in Caesar's mind?*"

I could only reply, "My dearest Fabia, I'm not at all privy to Caesar's intentions."

As I was unable to approach Dolabella on the matter of the dowry, I decided to go on an inspection tour of my rural estates. Tiro, my new freedman, and Metrodorus and Alexio accompanied me, along with a handful of domestics. We went down to the villa at Putoeli. It was early December, and the Italian winter was dampening the earth and my mood. To my shock and utter amazement, Caesar and a large retinue—some two hundred soldiers, attendants, and lictors—paid me an unexpected visit.

How he knew I was at Putoeli I had no way of knowing. Though I was considerably put out to receive, feed, and entertain such a large group, I dared not complain. While his escort encamped on the grounds, I hosted him in the house.

My conversation with Caesar was lively and amiable, but completely lacking in political import. When I told him about your sojourn at Athens, he mentioned that his grand-nephew, Gaius Octavius, was at Apollonia pursuing his studies.

Though he gave no hint of illness or fatigue, he still had not returned to Roma since coming back from Spain. I asked him when he might return; he smiled and merely said, "Soon, Marcus, fairly soon." I was chagrined that he did not take me into his confidence even in a small matter. Writing to Atticus a short time later, I remarked: "He's not the sort of visitor to whom I would say, 'Please call again'."

Caesar could not and would not confide in me because, as his power became all the more entrenched, he became more aloof and isolated from the Senate, from the citizens, and from his friends and acquaintances. That he held Republican institutions in contempt was already obvious, but it was all the more conspicuous on the last day of the year during his Spanish triumph. Upon the sudden death of the Consul, Fabius Maximus—the very same man who, at the time of the Catilinian conspiracy, had been my intermediary with the Allobrogian envoys—Caesar appointed Gaius Rebilus to the vacant consulate for the remaining fourteen hours of the day and of the year.

My disgust at the political situation was encapsulated in a caustic witticism: "I'll wager that no crimes will be committed during Rebilus' short term, for he's bound to be so vigilant in his fourteen hours that he'll not have time to eat, drink, sleep, or even relieve his bladder or bowels!"

MY RECOLLECTIONS HAVE NOW RETURNED to the point at which they began. Reflecting on myself, on Marcus Tullius Cicero, I see a man who loved his country and his family. Through his own efforts and merit, he attained promotions through the course of offices and reached the pinnacle of his career with his election to the consulate. He saved the Republic from a dangerous conspiracy, and then he fell from power and influence because of the machinations of a handful of powerful men and because of the fickleness of the senatorial aristocracy.

Though I loved and yet love Terentia, insurmountable circumstances precluded the harmonious continuation of our marriage. I could no longer abide her interference in my politics. Deprived of my political independence—as well as the life-force of my virility—I endeavored to obtain my personal independence; so I terminated our marriage.

Tullia's death, less than a year ago, has indelibly scarred me. I cannot find the words to express how dear she was and remains to me.

My finances, as usual, are in a state of flux. I need to retrieve Tullia's dowry from Dolabella. The sooner I do, the sooner I can expedite the repayment of Publilia's dowry, and then I can dissociate myself totally from Dolabella and Publilia and her family—all of whom I cannot abide.

Marcus, my son, your teachers, particularly Cratippus, have reported that you shirk your studies and devote an inordinate amount of time to wine and debauchery. Even allowing for youthful indulgences, you should not have lost sight of why you are in Athens. In that cradle of democracy and philosophy, you have the opportunity to delve into the wisdom and learning of a civilization predating Roma by at least a thousand years. If you must squander your time, your energies, and *my* money, then you would do better to return home where there are myriads of pleasures to satisfy every whim and vice. I have conveyed these sentiments in several letters to you, hoping you would heed my advice.

As for myself, I live in the shadow of an entrenched dictatorship, ruminating upon my thwarted ambitions and domestic failures without any hope of redeeming a failed career, and longing for the light that Tullia's passing has extinguished in my broken life.

I have deposited *Respublica* for safe-keeping in the Vestal Mansion. Fabia has assured me that I can easily retrieve it should I need to have copies made of it. Whatever may happen in the days ahead, I am certain that it will be there, safe and secure for you, Marcus, my son.

Your devoted Father—Marcus Tullius Cicero.

Liber IV Elysium

Caput XVI Cicero's Elysian Voice

There is a sure place in Heaven for those who have served their fatherland, preserved it, aided it, and contributed to its growth: a place where they may enjoy eternal life in everlasting bliss. There is nothing more acceptable to the chief of the gods who rules over the Cosmos, of all things that happen on the earth, than the councils and gatherings of men who associate together in respect for law and justice; that is, the organizations called states. Their rulers and preservers have come from Heaven and will return there.

I wrote these words in *"The Dream of Scipio"* segment of *De Re Publica*, describing the dialogue between Scipio Africanus and his adopted grand-son, Scipio Aemilianus.

But here, written words are non-existent. Instead, thoughts, memories, voices permeate the air like the shafts of light emerging through open portals and penetrating swirling mists, dissipating and evaporating them. Like the rays of sunlight that would shine through the leaves of Marius' mighty oak at Arpinum, falling upon my face so that I might foresee Eternity long before I would come to know it; so it is here, far from the strife and contention of the world's madness.

Notwithstanding the songs of poets and the musings of philosophers, here there is no oblivion of the past, of one's earthly life and struggles. Perhaps this is so only for those who, like me, are newly arrived. Nevertheless, I yet can see and hear and feel what transpired in cosmic measure but moments ago.

During the last two years of my temporal life, the Roman Republic was convulsed with murder, civil strife, war, and the terror of proscriptions. For a while, it almost seemed that the free Republic of old could be restored under the Senate's direction and will. Loyal Romans looked to me for guidance, and I did not shirk the role of senatorial Princeps that Fate thrust upon me. But other men were perverse and self-seeking. Putting their personal ambitions above loyalty to the Republic, they used the military, both veterans and new recruits, to bring a new tyranny to Roma. How sadly familiar it all is now.

Omniscient Narrative

Terentia hobbles into the Vestal Atrium, leaning on her thick, oak cane. Her half-sister, the Vestal Fabia, greets her, extending her arms and embracing Terentia ever so affectionately.

"Welcome, Terentia," the Vestal coos. "Haven't those joint pains subsided at all? Even after you've availed yourself of the warm baths I've often recommended?"

The two women kiss each other's cheeks. "Oh, Fabia, these pains are almost nothing compared to the heartache that's afflicted me." Terentia sits at a chair that Fabia indicates and places her cane across the adjoining table.

"What is it, Terentia?" Fabia sits in an adjacent chair. "What heartache are you talking about?"

"It's Young Marcus. I was relieved that Cicero had persuaded him to go to Athens and study rather than join the Caesarians in Spain. When he came to me before departing, he was awfully troubled, as though he were carrying some grave secret that impelled him to flee. I wondered if it could possibly concern a woman."

Fabia braces herself, for she has already heard from Cicero what Terentia is very likely about to say.

"That child that Cicero married, well, it seems she's not such a child after all, but not through Cicero's doing. It was a ludicrous marriage from the outset, and I knew it wouldn't last. A child married to an old man! Yes, I know it was only for money, of which Publilia was well endowed. Quintus didn't remarry after divorcing Pomponia, though I don't envy him his recalcitrant son. The young man is determined to make his own destiny in total disregard of its impact on his father or his uncle. At any rate, *Publilia's* mother's written to me. She says that… she says that Marcus, my son, Marcus has had an affair with Publilia! But more than an affair—Publilia's gotten letters from Marcus, all the way from Athens, and he's pledging his undying love for her! Can you believe it? How shameful for our family! Can you believe it, Fabia?"

Ever so delicately, Fabia replies, "Yes, Terentia, I can believe it because Cicero himself had his suspicions about their relationship. He told me as much when he visited back in December."

"What did he say he was going to do?"

"He didn't say because he didn't know. What would you have him do? Discipline Marcus? Disinherit him? Punish the girl whom he's divorced?"

"Oh, Fabia! The whole mess stinks! Had we not divorced, that little *lupa* would never have come into my son's life."

Fabia shakes her head. "You can't be sure he wouldn't have had her. After all, she *was* Cicero's ward for years before he married her. Tell me, Terentia, do you believe that Marcus is in love with her?"

"Well, Publilia's mother seems to think so. What's more, she says that her daughter admits to being in love with *him*. Oh, Fabia, I've not known such pain since Tullia…. My heart will never mend because she's gone—and now *this!* I know she was Cicero's favorite, and I'm embarrassed to admit that I envied their closeness, especially after he returned from exile and from Epirus."

Terentia breaks down into tears and sobs. "Perhaps I was remiss… in holding back expressions of my concern for him, but he didn't seek them. I loved him, bore him two children… endured, shared with him the ups and downs of an erratic political career, and now, in all truth, I find that I still love him."

"Why, of course you do," says Fabia, as she reaches over to comfort her sister. "And I know that he still loves you. The fact that neither of you can abide living under the same roof with the other will not vanquish the love you have for each other."

Having recovered somewhat, Terentia admits, "I've made some arrangements for Marcus, a testament and an endowment. Cicero should do the same, but I dare not approach him directly about it. So, when Atticus returns, I'll have him discuss this matter, for I know Cicero would turn Philotimus out unheard and unseen. Still, someone should talk to him about Marcus and Publilia. Fabia, what's to become of them?"

"I wish I had an answer for you, Terentia, but I don't. Nor have I had any visions concerning them." Fabia notices the look of disappointment on her sister's face. "They'll need to work this out for themselves, and I'll pray that Vesta may guide them. We'll all need her guidance in the days ahead. Even our Chief Pontiff has requested special prayers and supplications from the Vestals for the success of his upcoming campaign against the Parthians. However, our Chief Vestal has confided in me the crucial concerns that haunt Caesar's mind."

Terentia is intrigued and distracted from her preoccupation over her son's lover. Seeing this, Fabia moves closer and speaks in a hushed, secretive tone. "As you know, the weather this winter has been unusually severe. Hail storms have afflicted us, and fires have broken out in various districts of the City. Violent wind storms have torn down at least a dozen flimsy insulae, killing scores of people. Certain wards have even reported earth tremors. Several augurs to whom the Chief Pontiff has been more than politely attentive have interpreted these occurrences as portending some imminent disaster. I remember, and no doubt Caesar is aware, that similar prodigies were reported prior to Crassus' expedition against the Parthians."

"Another catastrophe!" Terentia interjects.

"But that's not all. The Chief Vestal has also confided in me the disturbing report submitted to Caesar by his secret police. Certain legionary veterans, who had been colonized on land adjacent to the city of Capua, were cultivating the soil. In the course of their labors, they uncovered what appeared to be the tomb of Capua's legendary founder, Capys. A mysterious Greek inscription found in the tomb read: *'Disturb the bones of Capys, and a man of Trojan stock will be murdered by his own kindred, and later avenged at great cost to Italia'*."

Terentia is bemused. "*Trojan stock?* I don't follow."

"This inscription bears a profound relevance for our Pontiff because he has always publicly claimed descent from Venus and from Aeneas, the legendary Trojan warrior, reputedly the founder of the Roman state, long before Romulus and Remus were ever born."

Fabia looks about the atrium, ascertaining that there are no eavesdroppers. "Terentia, there have lately been rumors of plots and intrigues against Caesar. That's what makes the Capuan inscription particularly ominous. Of course, the Chief Vestal admitted that Caesar is not oblivious to the probability that certain persons could very well have planted the inscription. Perhaps these same individuals are responsible for graffiti on the Rostra and on the Praetorian Tribunal addressed to Marcus Brutus. Whoever wrote this knows of the Brutus of old who overthrew the dreaded Tarquin monarch. These messages call upon Marcus Brutus, a reputed descendant of the tyrannicide, to emulate the example of his patriotic forbear."

Terentia objects, "But truly he owes his post of Urban Praetor to Caesar's favoritism. What's more, Brutus has always had over him the shadow of Caesar's paternity. For years, his mother was said to be Caesar's mistress...."

"I don't know what's in Brutus' mind, Terentia. However, the totality of these reports, rumors, and omens has cast Caesar into a deep melancholia, so the Chief Vestal has confided in me. But that's not all, Terentia. The Dictator's wife has visited us several times within the last week. Poor Calpurnia, who was never more than a pawn of her husband's and her father's political ambitions, is a nervous, frightened wreck. Since the Lupercalia, her sleep has been disturbed by frightful dreams."

"Has Calpurnia divulged these to the Chief Vestal?" Terentia's innate fascination with dreams and their latent messages piques her deepening interest in Fabia's litany.

"Yes, and she in turn told me."

"Well then," Terentia observes, "with all you've told me, it seems that Vestals are not reliable confidants."

Feigning annoyance, Fabia complains, "If you'd rather not hear more, then…"

"Oh, Fabia, come, come. About Calpurnia's dreams?"

"Very well! Calpurnia has dreamed that the honorary pediment that the Senate had decreed for the Regia was crumbling and crashing down. Amid the rubble and debris, she sees herself holding Caesar's bloodied, lifeless corpse. She awakens screaming from this terrifying vision.

"She also told us of strange phenomena that have occurred since the Lupercalia. The Regia's doors and shutters flew open as though some great supernatural force had exhaled into the house. The arms and armor of Mars, traditionally kept in the Chief Pontiff's mansion, were knocked to the floor and broken. And household servants reported seeing the statue of Caesar's alleged ancestress, Venus, sweating blood.

"Calpurnia has told the Chief Vestal that each morning's auspices have been found to be unfavorable. The entrails of each sacrificed animal were found to be riddled with worms and cankers. And the augur, Spurinna, has thrice warned Caesar to beware the Ides of Martius."

"The Ides of March?" Terentia wonders. "Why, that's only three days hence."

"True." Fabia sighs deeply and looks at Terentia with her head slightly bowed. "I must tell you one last thing, and this is from me, not from the Chief Vestal or Calpurnia. One evening, after Calpurnia's last visit, I was tending the sacred fire when I saw in the flames visions of a bust of Cicero at which many ravens and crows were ferociously pecking. I needn't remind you that these are birds of ill omen. Beyond this, I can't interpret what I saw. But, touching on Calpurnia's dreams and the strange occurrences in the Regia, I'm certain that they betoken some imminent disaster for Caesar and perhaps for all of Roma."

"And for Cicero as well?" Terentia is alarmed by Fabia's vision.

Fabia is now silent, as silent as the silent statues of former Chief Vestals that line the atrium's walls.

Terentia muses, "Once, we were a family, but now we are broken, detached, scattered. I'm happy, though, that at least we have each other." Terentia leans over to Fabia and kisses her on both cheeks. "Remember me, Fabia, and pray to Mother Vesta for my son and for the man who was my husband."

The two sisters peer into each other's tearful eyes. Terentia fears the future, and Fabia wishes that she were not endowed with visions of things yet to be.

Cicero's Elysian Voice

"What do you think, Servius? Should I have refused her invitation?" I always valued Servius' opinion, even if I disagreed with it. He had been for two years administering Greece as Proconsul, and I had written him frequently about this and that and the other. I wished he could have been with me when Tullia passed. He had returned in the autumn of the year in which her passing had afflicted me. Atticus however, was still away on business.

"As you've said, Marcus, if that's the only way you'll get to Dolabella, then you must go." Servius was showing the wear of his years. He looked older than his sixty-four years, and his health seemed compromised. "But are you sure you can tolerate the company—the *Medusa* and her red-haired *lupa* sister-in-law? They're very close, as you well know, attached at the hip as it were!"

We both laughed at the allusion to current rumors alleging their Sapphic intimacies. "Strange though, Marcus, that you would attend Clodia Pulchra's banquet honoring Caesar, yet you're loath to attend the Senate on the Ides. The whole city is in a frenzied state anticipating the Dictator's imminent departure for the East."

"Yes," I agreed. "It seems Caesar's always coming or going, and his arrivals and departures are always heaped upon with various and sundry honors."

"You've heard the latest rumors, I take it?"

"Of course I have, Servius. But they're more than rumors. I have it on a most reliable authority that the Great Man's kinsman, old Aurelius Cotta, has been preparing the unthinkable—a proposal conferring a regal title upon him which is to be employed only in the East, where such titles are appreciated because they're part and parcel of the political heritage of those lands and peoples. Caesar will probably be occupied there for some time."

Servius nodded in agreement. "And who is your *reliable authority*?"

"Marcus Varro," I replied.

"Indeed!" Servius chortled. "Just because he's been commissioned to compile a public library he knows for certain what's to happen when the Senate meets at Pompeius' Portico."

"Not quite," I admitted. "You see, our superstitious Dictator and Chief Pontiff wants to bolster his upcoming Parthian expedition with every conceivable auspicious omen. So, he's been rummaging through numerous ancient writings for references or prophecies relating to Roman arms overcoming the Parthians. He's asked Varro to look for such references among the books compiled for the new library. Varro tells me that even Dolabella, one of the curators of the Sibylline oracular books, was entrusted with a similar task. I'm surprised that I, as a member of the Augural College, was not asked for input."

Servius laughed. "I suppose it's because your agnosticism and skepticism, though well accepted, conflict with what Caesar seeks. Certainly, he knows better than to expect you to discover an oracle justifying his power and his foreign adventures."

"Even so, Servius, Varro has told me that he found a neat epigram in the Sibylline Books, one sufficiently vague and yet regally potent for Caesar's purposes. It's recorded that we Romans must recognize a *king* in order to be *saved*."

Servius threw back his head, his face beamed with uncanny delight. Before he could speak, I went on. "You may well say that this prophecy could relate to any time and to any situation. *Most assuredly!* And from what or whom are we to be saved through recognizing a king?"

"I think kingship is something Caesar desires not so much for his own personal aggrandizement as for purposes of military success against the Parthians," Servius explained. "At the Lupercalia, he already tested the popular sentiment about it. Soon enough, through his kinsman, he may venture to have a regal title from the Senate."

"Quite so," I agreed, "and that's why I won't attend the Senate tomorrow. I'm satiated with Caesar's honors. To see him granted the title and crown of *Rex*, even if only in the East, is beyond my endurance."

All Servius could do was frown and grimace and gesticulate with resignation.

"Ah, Servius, what a shameful pass we've come to! It's unconscionable that here in Roma, before the Senate, an elder statesman of the Republic should propose crowns, sceptres, and titles, even if they're to be borne outside of Italia. But Caesar's been advancing toward this omnipotence for the last twenty years! To speak of Republic or Respublica is to bandy about antiquated words so totally alien to our circumstances. Such words, diluted by the blood of fratricidal warfare, are the painful stuff of old men's memoirs and reminiscences."

IN HER INVITATION, CLODIA PULCHRA had written that the dinner party was to be an intimate gathering. But she had an exaggerated sense of intimacy. Including myself, there were eleven guests. I must admit, however, we were all comfortably accommodated on some luxuriously plush couches. Truly, Clodia *knows* her couches.

Our guest of honor, the Great Man himself, attired in purple tunic and toga and crowned with the triumphator's laurel, greeted me most cordially. His wife, though, was not present; he apologized for Calpurnia's indisposition as he took his place on the hostess' couch, reclining with Clodia to his right while I was to his left. At the far right end, next to his mistress, was my ex-son-in-law, Dolabella. Polite and deferential, he was not in the least embarrassed at my presence.

On the left hand couch, Marcus Antonius, Caesar's co-Consul, was with his wife, Fulvia. The flame-haired *lupa*, in teal stola and palla, reclined lasciviously next to her husband and regarded me with sullen suspicion. Next to her were Junia and then her husband, the Master of Horse, Marcus Lepidus.

The right hand couch had the Urban Praetor, Marcus Brutus, nearest me, and then his new wife, Porcia, daughter of Marcus Cato, the Republican martyr. She looked at me with haughty disdain throughout the dinner. Next to her reclined Tertia and then her husband, Praetor Peregrinus, Gaius Cassius. Brutus and Cassius, once Caesar's foes, were now his trusted officers and dining companions.

While I wore a plain white toga, Caesar's men all wore the official purple-bordered toga of magistrates. Of the women, Junia and Tertia were two of the three daughters of Caesar's former mistress, Servilia. It was said that Caesar was quite partial to Tertia. No one seemed the least bit fazed at the ease with which the women *reclined* on *couches* rather than *sitting* at the *table*. New mores were affecting even Roman dining habits, and Clodia was an unabashed innovator.

In different ways, the two sisters resembled their celebrated mother, both had fair complexions and fair hair, but their physical comeliness could not match Servilia's, at least not as she had been in her younger years. This may have been the effect of their father, the late Junius Silanus. At any rate, their bantering behavior and posturing attitudes rendered them insipid to my sensibilities.

Still, I affected the demeanor of one exhilarated by the sophisticated company. To what muse of the theatrical arts I should attribute my performance I cannot readily admit.

Clodia spared no expense in the dinner. The raven-haired "Medusa" had arranged a veritable cornucopia of meats and fishes, cheeses and delicacies, and wines from nearly every province of the imperium. Of course, Caesar's favorite, the Falernian, was in abundant supply. An Epicure's delight! Were it not for certain of the guests, I almost wished that Atticus had been there. Given Caesar's sumptuary laws, I almost marveled at how Clodia could have evaded them to provide such an extravagant repast. But on second thought, why should the Great Man not have made an exception for her? After all, the dinner was in *his* honor.

Between courses, an actor, one Bracchus, recited poetry from Hesiod, Sappho and our own Valerius Catullus to the accompaniment of a lyre. Clodia and Fulvia were enraptured by Sappho's pieces. They looked at each other longingly. But in response to the verses by Catullus, Clodia was especially attentive, as she should have been. After all, she had helped to destroy him by her own predatory fickleness.

By now, Clodia must have been about forty-five. Yet, she was still an alluringly beautiful woman. Her hair, though most likely treated, was yet thick, a luminous blue-black; her olive-rose complexion seemed to glow in the room's oil-lamp light. Clodia's figure was full, voluptuous, and her bosom was accentuated by the linen bands crisscrossing her saffron-colored stola. Leaning against her bolster, her left arm was long, fleshy, sensuous, fetching. Each time I stole a glance at her, her ebony eyes met mine and held on me. Noticing our frequent eye contact, Fulvia smirked and tapped her husband's elbow.

I had not been so close to Clodia in years, not since the day of her brother's riotous funeral. She had come to me overflowing with anger and hate; after cutting her hand, she had thrown the bloody dagger at my feet. Why had she thus wounded herself? I had pondered this for years without finding a satisfying answer. Yet, in her invitation, there had been no trace of hatred or vengeance—just the opposite. Extending an "olive branch," she hoped for civility and harmony between us. Her words had intrigued me. She had always intrigued me while at the same time repelling me. Strangely, this evening, as a guest in her house and at her table, I was further intrigued but *not* repelled.

The guests complimented the actor's recitation, and Clodia announced that he was currently appearing in a new play about a tyrannicide that was being performed at Pompeius' Theatre. Servilia's daughters interjected with enthusiastic praise for the drama.

"We saw it a week ago," Julia beamed. "We were so afraid the foul weather would have cancelled the performance. It was so moving. In fact, the dark, heavy clouds and the rumbling thunder seemed to be perfectly timed to accompany the old king's murder."

Something in her words struck a chord within me.

Porcia looked from Brutus to Caesar and asked, "Does art imitate life or does life imitate art?" Her dark brows curled in anxious anticipation of an answer. You could almost feel a collective cringe emanating from each couch but Caesar's.

The Great Man sipped his wine, dipped his fingers into a cleansing bowl, and then began to speak about his dictatorship. "Can any of you deny that peace, law, order, and stability have been restored to Roma after decades of turmoil, disorder, and civil strife?" He paused momentarily as though waiting for a response. "Well then," he began again, "if I'm to infer that you rate me a tyrant, then measure what Roma has gained."

Porcia challenged him. "Yours was a forced peace imposed by way of civil war. Your order, your stability was built upon the corpses of Romans who died to save the Republic!"

"There will be no end to civil war so long as Sextus Pompeius refuses to make peace and remains at large." Caesar spoke ever so calmly, but Porcia became more emphatic despite Brutus pulling at her arm.

"How could he be expected to make peace with the murderers of his father and his brother?" she demanded.

The room was charged with tension. The mosaics of nymphs and satyrs on Clodia's walls seemed paralyzed with fear. Even Caesar appeared to be moved by Porcia's outburst.

"The Pompeii and Labienus," he recalled, "what a horrible, bloody business they made in Spain! They were so intransigent in their protraction of a war that they could not possibly have won. They must have had enough sense to realize this. In Egypt, I wept publicly at the Magnus' death. But in Spain, I could have no remorse over Gnaeus' execution." Caesar was blunt and direct as though he were dictating a military dispatch.

Endeavoring to change the subject, Antonius interjected with the observation that Caesar was certain to win new glories against the Parthians and to avenge Crassus' disaster of nine years before.

"Venus willing!" Caesar shifted easily onto the new topic while turning his gaze away from Porcia. "I anticipate a year's campaign against them, and I won't make the same mistakes that Crassus made."

At this, Gaius Cassius, lean-faced and of angry mien, perked up his ears; he had been Crassus' quaestor on the ill-fated expedition. After the disaster at Carrhae, it had been Cassius who regrouped the scattered Roman elements and led them safely back to Syria.

"I'll use the Gallic and Spanish cavalry to guard the legions' flanks as we advance into open country." Caesar, pleased with his tactics, nodded and reached for his goblet. "My legions won't become butchers' meat for those accursed Parthian cataphracts."

Caesar drank and Cassius opined, "You may be disappointed, Caesar, in the effectiveness of your horse against Parthian mounted archers. Crassus learned that lesson, much to his tragic dismay."

"Perhaps you should accompany me, Gaius Cassius." Caesar set down his goblet and grinned sardonically at the praetor. "Once the Parthians are subdued, all I want from them is the restoration of the legionary standards captured from Crassus, the release of all Roman prisoners, and the surrender of several royal hostages as a guarantee of their good faith."

Turning to Antonius and Lepidus, he directed, "The Consul and Master of Horse will manage things here in Roma. See that you do so with all circumspection." Then, looking past Clodia he addressed Dolabella. "You'll become Suffect Consul after I've resigned the consulate."

Caesar now looked at each of his men. "Next year, Vibius Pansa and Aulus Hirtius will hold the consulate. According to my plans, in that year I'll subdue the Dacians and the Thracians and stabilize the Macedonian frontier."

Antonius interjected, "By that time, I'll be Proconsul of Macedonia...."

"And I'll rely on you to push up against the Thracians," Caesar added.

Their conversation reminded me of Gaius Antonius' campaigns at the time of my exile. Presumably, Caesar and Marcus Antonius would be more successful.

"I thought I was to have Macedonia as propraetor," Marcus Brutus complained.

Marcus Antonius, quipped, "Proconsuls outrank propraetors."

Caesar then intervened, "Have no fear, Marcus Brutus. Caesar will decide justly."

"*Caesar* will decide!" Porcia exclaimed utterly disgruntled. "He decides on officers, on commands, on provinces!"

"Porcia! Enough!" Brutus tried to placate his irate wife.

"This is why my father took his own life, instead of surrendering and living under this tyranny. I'll always honor my father's memory. I'm proud to be the daughter of Marcus Porcius Cato!" As Porcia spoke she glared vindictively at me.

I inferred her unspoken accusation: *You deserted the Pompeians; you deserted the Republic; you have accommodated yourself to Caesar's dictatorship.* I was tempted to reply to Porcia's implication, to defend my own policies, to speak about the expediency of accepting the reality of what could not be overcome. But I kept myself in check because I knew I had to tread very carefully. Though I hated the very idea of Caesar's dictatorship, I still recognized my personal and financial obligations to him. So, I quietly chewed on an artichoke and kept my peace.

Perhaps it is more accurate to say that I tried to keep my peace. Clodia and Fulvia would not let me off so easily.

"Marcus Cicero, what do you think of Cato's suicide?" Clodia asked.

And Fulvia put in immediately, "Why, Marcus Cicero, have you not lately contributed your unique talents to the Republic?"

"Yes," Tertia echoed their inquiries, "why have you retired from politics instead of giving Caesar the benefit of your counsel and your years of political experience?"

My answers to these questions could easily have been construed as impolitic. The three shrews knew what they were about, but I was determined not to satisfy them.

"Clodia, I'll be happy to provide you with a copy of the *Cato*. You may read for yourself what I think of Cato's suicide." In this way, I bypassed the *Medusa's* trap. To Fulvia and Tertia, I summoned even more diplomacy. "I've always been prepared to render service, advice, and counsel whenever I've been asked to do so."

Caesar appreciated this. He chuckled and winked at me. Then, he issued his own bit of advice. He announced to his officers—Antonius, Dolabella, Lepidus, Brutus, and Cassius—that they should rectify any irregularities in their affairs before his departure for the East. Saying this, he looked directly at Dolabella and then to me. I took this as an indication of Caesar's dictate that Dolabella was to repay the dowry without further delay.

Perhaps it may have been presumptuous of me to infer that the Great Man set such importance upon my financial affairs. But where they concerned one of his officers, one who was to become Suffect Consul following Caesar's departure, and especially in view of Dolabella's high-handed behavior after Pharsalus, I believe it was entirely reasonable of me to draw conclusions favorable to my interests.

"Father," Dolabella said, "why don't you come out to Syria with me when I take up my proconsulate?" He still used this annoying, even insulting address. *Father indeed!* He could *not* have been serious. "You could be one of my legates. I'll give you a free hand with the province's revenues and I'll clear things up with you this way. Fair, isn't it?"

Yes, he *was* serious, serious in his mockery of Tullia's dowry, and shamelessly careless in speaking before Caesar of how he would administer his province. Though I graciously declined his offer, telling him that my age precluded any further provincial work, I privately considered the advantages of such a commission. But if I were to go abroad, my first stop would have to be Athens so that I could see Young Marcus.

Soon, the dinner conversation reverted to the play about the tyrannicide. Caesar was saying that he did not fear death despite the recurring rumors of plots and conspiracies against him and the reports, albeit exaggerated, of inauspicious phenomena and signs. "Is there better proof of my confidence," he asked, "than the dismissal of my troop of Spanish bodyguards? You see, my friends, how I trust you and all the men I've favored to rise to offices with my support. Those foolish enough to assassinate me would plunge the Republic into civil war."

Then, he turned to Porcia and said, "All too often, art doesn't truly reflect life because art and the theatre must always simplify, perhaps even *over-simplify*, in order to dramatize. Life is too complex to be contained within the proscenium of the theatre."

Porcia seemed ready to reply, but Clodia broke in. "Life alternates between pleasure and pain, joy and sorrow, but it always ends in death." She looked from Caesar to me. "If we could choose the manner of our death, would it not be less foreboding? What is the best way to die?"

This was hardly a polite or genteel topic for a dinner's conversation, but apparently none of the guests wanted to offend our hostess. So, in response to Clodia's suggestion, each of us related our preferred circumstances and means of dying.

The round began with Fulvia and proceeded in a haphazard manner. "The best death for me," she declared, "would be in the arms of Antonius—*or* some other passionate lover!" She giggled like a child, and the others politely laughed at her childish witticism. Affecting the umbrage of a cuckold, Antonius said he preferred to die in battle against Roma's enemies.

Then, from the opposite table, Porcia spoke, reiterating what she had said earlier. "I would be honored to die as my father had died, in defense of my principles, even if I were to die by my own hand as he had died." Echoing this sentiment, Brutus opted for death with honor, a death that would enshrine him in the memory of his countrymen. Porcia spoke again, even more emphatically than before. "Gnaeus Pompeius Magnus and his son may have died as fugitives," she declared so vehemently to Caesar's face. "But I would die as they died—I'd gladly offer my neck to resist a tyrant!"

Caesar did not appear to be amused.

Servilia's daughters wanted to abstain from the discussion. However, when pressed for her opinion, Junia replied, "Death and dying should not be a preoccupation of the living." Then Tertia concurred, saying that only those who pursue death would concern themselves about how to die. "It is far better," she said, "to be thoughtful of how one should live rather than how one should die."

Then Cassius, like Antonius, preferred death in battle against the Republic's foes—typical for a boorish soldier. Dolabella's preference was also quite characteristic—to die wealthy and debt-free.

Lepidus wanted to die in the peace and comfort of his own bed; he added the qualification that death should come after having learned the truth of all existence. Amazing! I had never taken spare, insignificant Lepidus to be to any degree a philosopher.

Clodia was even more profound. "Death should reconcile pleasure and pain, the flesh and the spirit, the erotic and the ethereal." She looked at me and smiled that enigmatic, captivating smile, the smile that had not changed at all through the years. Then she added, "I would want to die as though I were awakening from a beautiful dream."

When my turn came, I said I would prefer to die as a respected statesman in the service of the Republic. I heard Fulvia mutter, "Who *needs* him?"

Finally, it was Caesar's turn. He looked at every face, stared with particular intensity at his officers, and then intoned, "Quick and sudden!" His face betrayed such pain, a world-weariness that seemed to cry out for release from a life of travail and turmoil. For a long moment, everyone was silent, but I noticed that Brutus and Cassius and their respective wives exchanged ominous glances.

After this discourse on Thanatos, the conversation resumed with gossip and banter. I politely made my farewells and took my leave. I was glad to depart, although I had not been able to settle the dowry affair with Dolabella. All evening, he and Clodia had fawned over each other, and their flirtations had become utterly tiresome. There would be no meaningful discussion with him then and there about anything of a serious nature. I regretted accepting Clodia's invitation. Why had she invited me in the first place? To taunt me perhaps, by showing me how she had Dolabella wrapped up in her wiles and curves? So much, I reckoned, for her "olive branch."

On the way home, I remembered that the next day was the Ides of March. Caesar was to preside over the Senate meeting in Pompeius' Portico. This would probably be his last presidency before setting out for the East. Evidently, he preferred a new war against foreign enemies over remaining in Roma and administering an obsequious, complacent Senate. He was trapped in his own omnipotence; he was pressured by his own limitless ambitions, and I was afflicted by my own thwarted ambitions; he was convinced of his own invincibility as I was resigned to my own vanquished state. And yet, despite all appearances and his expressed confidence, he wanted out of his perpetual dictatorship.

I did not plan to attend the Senate; nor did Quintus. I would probably hear about it from Servius or Varro or Figulus. They would certainly tell me if Aurelius Cotta would succeed in proposing a regal title for Caesar. I did not think that I could bear to see such a play.

As I drifted off to sleep, the dinner's conversation replayed in my mind—the tragedy about the tyrannicide, the talk of death—and Clodia Pulchra.

Omniscient voice

Clodia Pulchra's guests have departed, except for Fulvia and Marcus Antonius. He lies supine on his couch, head nestled against the bolster. He is sound asleep, overcome with food and wine, especially wine. He snores loudly, rhythmically, his throat and chest rising and falling in regular undulations. Fulvia watches him and alternates between smirks and sneers.

The Consul's snoring resonates with Dolabella's dormant fanfares, for he too has been bested by an over-indulgence in wine. He lies prone on the couch, one arm stretched across Clodia's lap while the other hangs toward the tiled floor. Clodia looks from him to Fulvia reclining at the adjacent couch.

"Even in their cups, they compete," Clodia sighs. "No harm done, though, I suppose. Caesar wouldn't chastise them for being drunk, so long as they're not on duty."

Fulvia chuckles, "But they're both expected to attend tomorrow's Senate meeting. I wonder if they'll be up to it."

"Tomorrow has come, Fulvia. We've arrived at the Ides of March."

Fulvia is alarmed, not having realized the late hour. She reaches for Antonius' chest. "I should wake him."

"No, no!" Clodia objects. "Let him sleep awhile longer." Turning to Dolabella, she frowns. "Let them both sleep. We'll have a chance to talk. How are the children?"

"They're fine, and the twins thrive. I'm so amazed how the older ones get along, considering they're from different fathers."

"But they have *one* loving mother, and that matters more than anything else."

Antonius' snoring almost seems to validate Clodia's words. The two women giggle.

Fulvia says, "It was a lovely dinner; the recitations—*moving*; the conversation—*exhilarating*." She rises gingerly from her couch and goes over to sit next to Clodia.

The two women have been speaking in hushed tones. Now, almost instinctively, they lower their voices to mere whispers. Clodia repeats the words, "*Moving… exhilarating*." She and Fulvia kiss hard, passionately on the lips. When their lips part, Clodia asks, "Did you like the company?"

"How could I *not*? Porcia gave us a fine show of political oratory. Cato would have been so proud of her. Caesar was delightful in all of his pomposity. But those two sisters! *Gods!* What a pair of bovine bores!"

Clodia giggles. "Fortunately, we were spared their sister. The three of them together might have been far more obnoxious than any two of them at one time. They're totally unlike their mother. Servilia's still a vivacious, captivating woman for her age—so fit, still so beautiful. How I envy her! Regrettably, she wasn't able to attend our little party."

"You invited her? Knowing that there's a rift between her and Caesar?" Fulvia is incredulous.

"Of course! I thought it would have been so fashionable to have had in one room, at one table, Caesar's wife, and his long-time mistress, and his two royal consorts. Alas, Calpurnia could not attend, but I don't believe her illness to be genuine, and the two Queens were otherwise engaged."

Fulvia quakes with laughter. "Clodia, that's *monstrous*."

"Perhaps. Still, it would be… what was it you said, oh yes, *exhilarating*? Well, I think the combination would have been *scintillating!* You think Porcia was political? Well, I had invited Cinna, Caesar's first wife's brother, and his wife, the Magnus' daughter, Pompeia. Imagine what *she* would have thrown at Caesar!"

"They declined?"

Clodia nods. "Interesting man, Cinna is. He comes out of years of banishment. Caesar makes him praetor and fixes him up with Pompeia.

Yet, he's very aloof to Caesar's regime. He wrote that he could not attend out of respect for his wife's feelings. Imagine *that!*

"A man who respects his wife's feelings?" Fulvia muses. "How utterly *un-Roman!*"

"So true! Roman men usually treat their wives like chattel, using and abusing them as they will. Only their mistresses fare better." With her uplifted chin, Clodia indicates the snoring, sleeping Dolabella. "Two wives divorced, but with me nothing but the most affectionate attentions."

"Your brother was as affectionate and caring with me, both before and after we married," Fulvia remembers. "I miss him, but so often I see him in Claudia and in Publius." Fulvia stops herself from descending into maudlin ruminations, especially as Clodia tries to change their conversation.

"You know, we might have had *two* Brutuses here tonight." Clodia points to the couch where Marcus Brutus and Porcia had dined. "I had invited Decimus Junius and his wife, but he declined because of an important prior engagement. I so wanted to see Flavia because I was sure that Caesar would get a rise at the sight of her, the daughter of the man he betrayed. Come to think of it, Marcus Brutus and Cassius had also originally declined with the same excuse. Then they both sent word that they would come after all. I can't help feeling that the two Brutuses and Cassius have something in the works. Something… I don't know, perhaps my own intuition is running rampant."

"Rumor has it that Flavia gets on better with her mother-in-law than she does with her husband," Fulvia relates, "and she and Sempronia and Aurelia Orestilla are a veritable *triumvirate*. Poor Decimus Brutus! It's bad enough to be hen-pecked by a wife, but in his case both his mother and mother-in-law have been at work on him."

Clodia moves in toward Fulvia's face so closely that their noses almost touch, and her whisper is such that she is almost mouthing the words. "I've heard more brazen rumors, Fulvia." She cups her sister-in-law's ear and whispers into it.

"*By great Priapus!*" Fulvia nearly chokes with amazement. "Just like Oedipus and Iocasta? But it can't be! *God!* I'd try to seduce Decimus just to pry the secret out of him."

Clodia shrugs indifferently. "I'll share another secret with you, sweet Fulvia. One day, I hope to discover Cicero's secrets, his fears and ambitions, though we may well wonder if he is worth the bother. Perhaps, he's outlived the usefulness of his own life. We'll see. I think he's about sixty-two or sixty-three, and in all truth, he's still quite handsome. The once chestnut brown hair is now all gray, but no less thick. His face is strong, full, yet chiseled by time and experience into lines and angles of pain and sorrow. It seems to show such intelligence and an enlightenment that could almost be divine. His eyes, those deeply set brown eyes, still fill me with longing as they did when I was young. Though he's grown somewhat stouter with age, his body appears to be still firm and supple, that body that once I desired but never had."

Even as Clodia opens her heart to Fulvia about Cicero, an internal reverie reviews her past with the retired statesman.

I hated him because he became my brother's enemy. Do you still hate him, Fulvia? Do you still want vengeance? I don't know what I want of him. Once, I wanted him to suffer for Publius' death, but my wrath has diminished over the years because I know that Milo was directly responsible for his murder, and the murderer has paid with his own life. Yet, I want Cicero to be under obligation to me so that I can manipulate him to my every whim and wile. If you have such designs on him, Fulvia, then perhaps we could make common cause in this endeavor? Does he hate me ruining his daughter's marriage? Dolabella was already a rake and a philanderer before I took up with him, and I only did it to spite Cicero. I had seduced Caelius for the very same reason. Am I unjust to hate him because I've wanted him since my youth and I've not been able to have him? Or am I merely frustrated because he's the only man whom I ever wanted and yet never had?

Fulvia breaks in upon Clodia's thoughts. "Cicero is finished, a mere cipher, a complete nonentity. Why you waste your breath and your energy upon him, Clodia, is completely beyond me. My Antonius and your Dolabella, even in their drunken sleep, have more potency in them than *Chick-Pea* can ever dream of."

Clodia nods in agreement. "But Fulvia, you know that, despite all outward appearances, the political situation is far from certain. Forget all the rumors. Forget all the signs and portents. You must try to hold

Antonius in check while he administers Roma in Caesar's absence. Power goes to most men's heads the way blood rushes to their penises to make them erect. But Antonius drinks the draught of power to its very dregs. So watch him! As for Dolabella, all he wants is money and pleasure. Political power for him is secondary. I'll keep him under restraint in ways that he'll find so titillating. Lepidus and Cinna are mere followers who'll fall in line behind any man who appears to be in charge. Decimus Brutus might be formidable, if he can find his way out of his mother's enveloping loins. But Marcus Brutus and Gaius Cassius bear watching. They've confided in me their resentment and envy of Caesar's power. Brutus, in particular, hates the shadow of Caesar's paternity. For that matter, Cassius also has a personal axe to throw because Caesar may have had Tertia. If Brutus and Cassius receive provincial commands in the East, they could disrupt Caesar's Parthian war."

Fulvia has listened intently, taking in all of Clodia's prognostications. "And what of Caesar?"

"Caesar will always be Caesar: ambitious for power; grasping for supremacy; avaricious for wealth; desirous of love on demand. Will he ever be sated? Only if he were dead! And then, just as Caesar had foretold, his men and his foes would fight each other for control of the Republic."

"Oh, Clodia, you're making my head spin!"

"Let me help you set it right," Clodia laughs. "You know, Fulvia, it seems to be in the nature of powerful men to want to be dominated by their lovers. This was true of our Caesar. The few times I was with him I obliged by mounting and riding upon him. The more powerful the man, the more exalted his rank, so the more pronounced his need for domination. They have in them an inherent weakness, and they dread anyone discovering it."

Fulvia motions to Dolabella and Antonius. "These two certainly have their weaknesses. We need look no farther than their cups."

Clodia demurs, "No, with Caesar it's another kind of weakness. When Dolabella returned from Spain, he told me of Caesar's illness at Gades. He was visiting the Temple of Hercules and admiring a statue of Alexander the Great. Suddenly, he swooned and collapsed to the temple's marble floor. Hearing this, I was reminded of an incident

Caesar had related to me years ago. When he was quaestor in Spain, when he was a young man, he had visited the very same temple in Gades. He wept upon beholding Alexander's statue because the Macedonian ruler at Caesar's age—he was then thirty-three—had conquered lands on three continents. But Caesar, up to that time, had achieved nothing of importance."

"Marcus has told me the same story," Fulvia admits. "So Caesar's weakness is jealously or insecurity?"

"Hardly. Caesar also confided in me that, at the time, he had been having bothersome dreams of incestuous relations with his own mother. After visiting Hercules' temple, he had spoken with a seer who interpreted the dreams as foretelling that Caesar would one day possess the whole earth. When Caesar told me this, I could not imagine how accurate the seer's interpretation would prove to be."

"So then, our Caesar fears his own destiny, or its fulfillment." Fulvia looks across at Marcus Antonius, still in deep slumber. "Since the Lupercalia, the augur Spurinna has cautioned him to beware the Ides of March. Well, they've come. How does the augur's warning touch on Caesar's destiny? What's the warning mean for us, for you, for me, and for these two? Oh, Clodia, my head's spinning again!"

Clodia replies, "Then let's set it all to rest." Gently she removes Dolabella's arm from her lap and rises with Fulvia from the couch. "Come with me Fulvia. We've talked enough."

The two women embrace; Fulvia's hands go to Clodia's curvaceous buttocks while Clodia's are planted on Fulvia's voluptous hips. They join their lips in a long, ravenous kiss. Then, arm in arm they leave the atrium and walk to Clodia's bedroom, leaving to Morpheus the snoring, slumbering men.

Cicero's Elysian Voice

CLODIA PULCHRA BECKONED TO ME. I approached her without knowing why she was here, of all places, in the Temple of Vesta, in the very sanctuary where the goddess' sacred fire burns under the watchful eyes of an attendant Vestal.

"Come, Marcus. Come with me," she called to me alluringly as that enigmatic smile played on her mouth, her dark eyes glistening in the dim oil-lit chamber. "Come and look into the flames. Fabia will let you look. Come see the great and mighty fall, bloodied and despised and abandoned."

Clodia stood behind kneeling Fabia. "May we look too?" she solemnly asked of the Vestal. But in asking she merged with, disappeared into, and became Fabia.

And Fabia shrieked, "Great Mother Vesta! They murder him! They murder Roma! Great gods take counsel!" She pulled off her veil in distraught anguish. Her plaited hair became undone, falling in copious waves upon her shoulders and back. She turned from the fire to face me, her face streaked with blood. It was no longer Clodia or Fabia, but Fulvia. She laughed and cried out maniacally. And her cry stirred me from sleep. I awakened in a cold sweat.

Judging from the sunlight streaming into my bed chamber, it had to have been at least two hours past dawn. I rose slowly from the bed and sat on its edge. I had not told Tiro to awaken me, as the days of the early morning callers occurred less and less frequently. My nightshirt was soaked with perspiration from the frightful dream. I made my way to a nearby washbasin where I washed the remaining sleep from my eyes. I removed the dampened nightshirt, replacing it with a linen robe. The tiled floor sent shivers from my bare feet up my back to my shoulders. A cold, damp day—this was the Ides of March.

"Dominus! Dominus!" Metrodorus was calling from the corridor and knocking frantically on the door. There was much agitation in his voice. I gave him leave to enter.

"Dominus, I've just come up from the Forum," Metrodorus blurted with frenzied breathlessness. "They're saying that Caesar's been killed! Only this morning, not more than half an hour ago! The people are scared. They're angry. They're in an ugly state. They're...."

"Caesar's killed?" I shouted over his babbling. "When? But how?"

Metrodorus panted, "At the Senate meeting this morning at Pompeius' Portico near the Theatre. In the Forum I heard certain names thrown about—Marcus Brutus, Decimus Brutus, Gaius Cassius, Publius Casca, even Marcus Antonius. But no one knows anything for certain. There's a multitude streaming into the Forum from Mars Field...."

In my shock at the news I managed to move toward the balcony. Throwing open the doors, I hurried out onto it and looked down at the Forum. Yes, as Metrodorus had said there was an enormous mass of people, the Roman riffraff, pouring into the Forum from the northwest, from the direction of Mars Field and Pompeius' Theatre. From my vantage point, I could see the Jovian Temple atop the Capitoline Hill. Something was stirring there as well, the movement of men, about one hundred, maybe more, wearing helmets and bearing arms – swords, shields, spears and pikes – which glinted in the morning sun. There were senators, judging from their white togas, about as many as the armed men, moving quickly to occupy the Arx, the ancient fortress situated between Jove's and Juno Moneta's temple on the Capitoline's opposite spur.

All morning and into the afternoon, the Forum crowds swelled. Armed legionaries, at least a thousand, ringed the Capitoline's slope, occupying all approaches to it. It seemed that a battle was about to be fought between the soldiers and the Capitoline occupants.

By mid-afternoon, a messenger brought a note from Servius Sulpicius.

Marcus Cicero, we are entering a catastrophe. Caesar is murdered— cut to pieces as if he were a sacrificial beast. What a bloody mess! What a frightful scene I witnessed in Pompeius' Portico. Almost the moment Caesar arrived, daggers appeared in scores of hands. They surrounded him, cutting and slashing at him like a trapped animal. Besides those who attacked him, there were many others who shouted encouragement to the assassins. The rest sat paralyzed with shock and fear, except for Calvisius Sabinus and Marcius Censorinus. They tried to shield Caesar as the assassins hacked away at him. How they were not killed in the fray, I cannot explain.

So, our Dictator no longer rules and no longer lives. Be ready, dear friend, to lend your voice and your counsels for the Republic's welfare. We will surely have need of you. Do not begrudge us.

Servius Sulpicius

The confusion reigning in Roma brought to my mind's vision images that had pointed to this day's events. I remembered Fabia telling me that the Republic would again require my services and that it was my destiny to serve Roma yet again. All the talk at Clodia Pulchra's about death quickly played in my mind, culminating with Caesar's "quick and sudden" remark. The rumors, the speculations of plots against his life were now all well founded. Had Caesar ever heeded Spurinna's advice to *Beware the Ides*? Or was he truly convinced of his own inviolability and indestructibility? He had said that civil war would be the inevitable result of any attempt against his life. I was convinced of Caesar's accuracy on that score as dusk descended upon the gathering forces in the Forum. I was also convinced of the accuracy of the dream I had had before the Great Man was struck down. Could Fabia have foreseen these events just as she was seeing them in my dream?

Well after night had fallen, the Forum was ablaze with hundreds of torches. Bundled up against the night's chill with two tunics, a toga, and a heavy woolen over-cloak, I continued to survey the Forum and the Capitol from my balcony. Tiro came up to announce that a delegation of senators was waiting for me in the atrium I was at first alarmed, but then he told me that they were led by Servius Sulpicius, Marcus Varro, Lucius Piso, and my brother, Quintus.

I went down to them and saw that there were about thirty of them, some Caesarians, some Pompeians, and some, like Servius and Piso, neutrals.

Servius spoke first. "Forgive this intrusion, Marcus. But we need you. Will you come with us to the Capitol? If we don't endeavor some conciliation, there's bound to be civil war here in the City."

"The assassins are up at the Arx," Marcus Varro put in. "The Brutuses, Marcus and Decimus, Gaius Cassius, and the others, they've got their retainers and a troop of gladiators. They'll fight off any assault that Antonius might send against them."

Then Piso added, "It shouldn't be necessary for Romans to kill Romans again. If you'll help us, Marcus Cicero, we can prevent this."

Naturally, I agreed to help, though I wasn't certain about the feasibility of any truce. Accompanied by the senators and by Tiro and Alexio, I went down to the Forum. I found it and all approaches to it occupied by Consul Antonius, Master of Horse Lepidus, and Suffect Consul Dolabella commanding about three thousand soldiers of the Thirty-Fifth Legion. As I spoke with Antonius, the interplay of torchlight and shadows made grotesque designs upon his hard, handsome face.

"I've acquired Caesar's body," he said with an air of contemptuous triumph. "We carried it out on a litter, and his limp right arm was dangling pitifully over the ground upon which he'd trod so triumphantly. I noticed a small unopened scroll in the folds of his torn bloodied toga. I opened it and read it. It was a warning against all those who conspired to kill him."

Antonius abruptly turned from me and looked up at the Capitoline. For an instant in the torchlight, I noticed his brothers, the praetor Gaius and the tribune Lucius standing on either side of him. "They're up there now, priding themselves on having killed Caesar." He turned back to me. "Lucius and I obtained his papers and effects, and his money from Calpurnia. At first she was reluctant to cooperate, but Piso convinced his daughter that it was for the good of Roma. I also have Caesar's will." Antonius smiled almost menacingly. "The Vestals at first were loath to deliver it, but your sister-in-law, your Fabia, convinced them to do so. Very wise of them! I'll see that his acta are ratified and implemented."

It had been politically astute of both Piso and Fabia to intervene, for I had few doubts that Antonius would have brusquely seized what was not willingly turned over to him.

"A public funeral will be held for him with all attendant honors. And those who murdered him must surrender and stand trial for treason. Go tell them, Marcus Cicero. These are my terms. If they reject them, then I'll storm the Capitol and slaughter them all."

There was no question that Antonius was securely in charge of the Caesarians as neither Lepidus nor Dolabella offered any dissent or other input to the Consul's terms.

I started up the Capitoline steps on the southern slope with Quintus, Piso, Varro, Servius, and Tiro and Alexio. Two of Antonius slaves accompanied us with torches to light our way. The ascent was tiring for one of my age—some three hundred steps for a man of sixty-two years. The night air was cold, and ominously heavy clouds hung overhead against a sky bereft of stars.

Half-way up the steps, voices called down to us to identify ourselves. When I responded, we were told to proceed upward.

Reaching the summit, we were admitted to the Arx, a foreboding, stone relic of a fortress. There we conferred with the assassins, a group of about twenty men whose togas were splattered with blood. There was little unity of thought and purpose among them. Decimus Brutus and Gaius Trebonius appeared to be spokesmen for several of them, while Marcus Brutus and Gaius Cassius held rein over the others.

"We'll not put ourselves into Antonius' hands!" Marcus Brutus protested. Brutus' earth-colored hair was matted with sweat and it was impossible to distinguish between the blood smears and the pockmarks on his cheeks and neck.

"Did we kill a tyrant only to make ourselves victims of Antonius' vengeance?" Cassius demanded. His sinuous neck and long, tight, almost canine face rendered him a hideous figure in the glaring torch light. "Or hold a public funeral for him? Like all tyrants, his body should have been dumped into the Tiber. That's what we were going to do and then seize his papers; yes, until pandemonium broke."

Trebonius and Decimus Brutus also opposed surrendering. However, if granted amnesty, they said they would be willing to descend the Capitol and agree to Caesar's funeral.

"Antonius will attack you," I warned them. "Don't imagine that he'll sit down there forever."

"Then let him come!" Decimus bellowed. "The tyrant is dead and Antonius is merely...."

"Antonius is merely ambitious enough to pick up Caesar's fallen laurels and place them upon his own brow," I rebuked him sternly. "Had you included me in your enterprise, I'd have insisted that Antonius be removed along with Caesar." *Why? Why had they excluded me? Had they anticipated that I would negotiate on their behalf after the deed was done?*

We haggled in this way for the better part of an hour. Nothing that I or any of my colleagues proposed met with the assassins' agreement. Exasperated, I at last suggested that Marcus Brutus and Cassius should respectively and individually meet with Antonius and Lepidus. With a tinge of sarcasm, I added that they ought to share a conciliatory meal. My sarcasm, however, did not register with them.

Much to my surprise, Brutus and Cassius agreed to my proposal on the condition that their safety would be guaranteed. I was later even more surprised when Antonius, after a moment's hesitation, agreed to a conciliatory supper with Marcus Brutus. Lepidus followed suit, agreeing to dine and negotiate with Cassius. And so, later that evening, the Consul and the Praetor met at Servius' house, while the Master of Horse and Cassius supped at Piso's. Quintus and I hosted Decimus and Trebonius. We talked long into the night.

Tilting his long, equine face toward me in a conspiratorial slant, Decimus related the day's events. He and a party of senators had arrived at the Regia to accompany Caesar to the Senate. "But Calpurnia insisted that he should not venture out of the house. She said that each time the morning auspices were taken they were found to be unfavorable. She said she'd not slept well because of the violent over-night storms and her own nightmares. Caesar was about to send word to the Senate that he would not attend—a husband placating his wife's superstitions. But I prevailed upon him to disregard the signs and Calpurnia's forebodings, to trust in the Senate's good intentions, and to attend them without further delay. Caesar was still vacillating, but with Antonius' arrival, he was sufficiently encouraged to set forth."

What cold-blooded calculation! I thought.

"On our way to the Pompeian Portico, an aged scholar, a former teacher of Marcus Brutus, one Artimidorus, handed Caesar a scroll and implored him to read it at once. Caesar, however, merely held it, but did not even look at it. As we were entering the Portico, Spurinna the Augur warned Caesar—and not for the first time—to beware of the day. Caesar jokingly returned: 'The Ides of March have come.' Then Spurinna replied ominously: 'And they have yet to pass.'

"As planned, Trebonius here, feigning a desire to speak with Antonius, drew him aside from Caesar and detained him outside."

Trebonius interjected, "Some men, not of our party, told me of their wishes for the success of our endeavor. I was unnerved that rumor of the plot may have spread, and I feared that Caesar had taken counter-measures to thwart us."

"Once inside," Decimus continued, "Caesar was startled to find that his gilded chair was missing. I explained that perhaps the custodians had removed it, thinking that he would not be presiding over the Senate. While he was still bothered and distracted by this, Tillius Cimber, one of our confederates, petitioned Caesar to recall his brother from exile. This was the signal we'd agreed on. We crowded around Caesar supposedly to press for Cimber's entreaties. Publius Casca came up behind Caesar and plunged a dagger into the back of his neck. Recoiling, Caesar managed to inflict a small wound in Casca's arm with his stylus before the rest of us, brandishing our previously concealed daggers, closed in. We hacked away at him. So closely did we press him that when Censorinus and Sabinus tried to defend him, they couldn't get close enough to be at all useful. Marcus Brutus struck the mortal blow, stabbing Caesar in the groin—fitting retaliation for all the years that Caesar had been his mother's lover."

"I was close enough to hear him speak his final words," Trebonius recalled. "With his dying breath, he moaned almost facetiously, *'Even you, my son?'*"

Decimus took a long drink of wine, swallowed hard, and then continued the narrative. "We'd pushed and slashed at him as far back as Pompeius' statue. There, he fell. Curious, isn't it? Mighty Caesar dropped dead beneath the image of his rival. Just then, Marcus Brutus held aloft his bloodied dagger and called on you, Cicero. Yes! I wish you'd been there! He called on you and all Republicans to witness the restoration of the free Republic. Suddenly, the frightened, shocked senators revived themselves sufficiently to flee the Portico. Within moments, there was pandemonium in Pompeius'Theatre as the first news of Caesar's death was given out."

"You know, they were performing that play about the regicide," Trebonius told us with an awkward twist of his ruddy, bald head, "a play about a regicide—*what irony!* Hearing of Caesar's death, the spectators stormed out of the theatre and into the adjacent walkways, bemoaning the murder of their beloved Caesar and cursing his assassins, though they did not yet know who they were."

"We had a troop of gladiators stationed at the theatre's rear. With them as a buffer, we made our way to the capitol. And now here we are, Marcus Cicero, enjoying your hospitality while waiting for the outcome of our deed." Decimus Brutus took another long draught before adding, "What will it be, Cicero, a compromise, or civil war?"

"That depends ultimately on what your confederates arrange with Marcus Antonius and Lepidus," I replied cautiously. "But in all truth, it's *Antonius'* word that will matter. Then of course, the Senate will have to ratify whatever they arrange. It's a pity the Senate has forgotten how to deliberate autonomously."

"They'll learn again," Decimus opined, "now that Caesar's no longer around to dictate to them."

I could only shake my head in dismay as I thought: *Fools! Don't discount Antonius.* Then my curiosity got the better of me. Here were two officers of the Dictator. Yet, they had conspired against him and assassinated him. "Why did you undertake this deed?" I asked them. "Decimus, you served under him for years in Gaul. You attained the praetorate by his nod. And Trebonius, you were one of his trusted legates. You owe so much of your advancement to him. Brutus and Cassius were both pardoned by him. Yet, you and a score of others killed him. Was it entirely for the good of the Republic?"

They were both rendered uncomfortable by my questions, and they shifted nervously on their couches. Quintus and I looked at each other during a momentary lull in the conversation. But then Trebonius spoke. "I've always been against dictatorship. My father opposed Sulla's regime. Our family spent years in exile because of it. Yes, I gained from Caesar's favor. He encouraged me and sponsored my career. But when I saw his power become that of a *king*, I had to put aside personal feelings and loyalties. I had to put the Republic's welfare above all else. I joined with like-minded men to plot his assassination so that a free Roma could live again."

Then, Decimus regained his tongue. "I was his legate in Gaul from the beginning of his proconsulate. I served faithfully and staunchly, putting my life in peril in so many campaigns. But Caesar guarded his glory the way a miser hoards gold. He was jealous lest anyone cast a shadow on his victories."

Again, Quintus and I looked at each other. I remembered and no doubt he remembered his similar complaints about serving under Caesar.

"*I* should have been designated Suffect Consul," Decimus complained, "but instead men less worthy than I, Dolabella, for example, were promoted over me. In this, I saw the foulness of dictatorship. I could tolerate it no longer. So I and the others acted."

Decimus Brutus was the progeny of conspiracy. His mother, Sempronia, had been one of Catilina's conspirators. Rumor had it that she had been instrumental in the *natural* demise of her husband, the elder Decimus Brutus. Now her son was justifying his participation in the plot to kill Caesar. Clearly, his motive was not purely patriotic; nor was it entirely familial, in spite of his kinship to Marcus Brutus. No, there was something else gnawing at him, though I could not discern it. Perhaps he had been impelled by his wife, Flavia, Catilina's stepdaughter; by his mother-in-law, Aurelia Orestilla, Catilina's widow; perhaps by his own mother, Sempronia, who had been the mistress of Lentulus Sura, one of Catilina's chief conspirators. These three women may have wanted revenge against Caesar, the man who had betrayed Catilina. Using their feminine wiles in different ways, they could have been the agents who put the dagger in Decimus Brutus' hand.

"We all had some personal motive that moved us against him," Decimus admitted. "Gaius Cassius was jealous and resentful. So were the Casca brothers. And Marcus Brutus lived his entire life in the shadow of Caesar. Yet, he was convinced, as we all were, that Caesar was the only obstacle to the return of the free Republic."

Trebonius leaned forward. "Listen, Cicero, you'll need to keep something in mind when you negotiate with Marcus Antonius." He paused and looked sideways at Decimus Brutus as though he were expecting either encouragement or a rebuke. "I solicited him for our plot."

"What? Caesar's right arm?" I could not believe what I had heard.

"Last summer, when he was at Narbo, he wasn't the 'right arm', and he bore many grudges against Caesar. I had returned from Spain ahead of Caesar and I met with Antonius at Narbo. He was interested, but he declined to join us. Then, he and Caesar were reconciled."

Decimus Brutus then put in, "That's why we wanted to kill Antonius, but Marcus Brutus wouldn't hear of it. Apparently, he trusted Antonius to keep silent about our plans."

"And we rewarded his silent complicity," Trebonius continued, "when I detained him outside the Portico. He seemed willing enough *not* to be pulled into the fracas."

"Antonius knew when you would strike?" I asked.

"It seems that our conspiracy was a poorly guarded secret," Decimus mused.

For a moment, I thought, *What if they had included me in their plot? Would I have had the courage to act? Would I have had the will to disregard my personal obligations to Caesar and murder him? Would my resentment of his power, of his overshadowing of my life, have impelled me to kill him, to kill him for the good of the Republic?*

They had not made me privy to their plot, and this rankled me, especially because rumors and gossip had leaked out, complementing what certain good people reported as omens of ill fortune. Even Brutus' old teacher knew what was afoot. Yet, I was kept out of their counsels. Perhaps, they had done this for my own protection, or perhaps they had doubted my reliability.

It did not matter now. I had a task at hand—to reconcile the two parties, the assassins and the Caesarians, and to prevent renewed civil war.

THE NEGOTIATIONS BETWEEN ANTONIUS AND Marcus Brutus produced agreement on a Senate meeting scheduled for the seventeenth in the Temple of Tellus. The general mood and atmosphere was laden with tension and hostility as the Caesarians and the assassins presented and debated their conflicting terms for defusing the crisis. In the debates, Marcus Brutus and his confederates referred to themselves as *Liberators*, a term that did not endear them to the most hard-core Caesarians.

At my urging and in the interests of peace and concord, a compromise was hammered out that basically resembled what Decimus Brutus and Trebonius had proffered on the evening of the Ides. Antonius grudgingly assented to a decree of amnesty for the Liberators, though he referred to them as assassins. All of Caesar's acta—decrees, proposals, appointments—were to be maintained and implemented. In this, every one gained, for lucrative provincial commands and political offices were at stake.

Their compromise also included a public funeral for Caesar on the twentieth. This was to be held with all appropriate honors in Mars Field with Consul Marcus Antonius delivering the eulogy. However, both Marcus Brutus and Gaius Cassius were to address the populace before Antonius.

Then, the Caesarians, the Liberators, and the neutrals concurred in Dolabella's appointment as Suffect Consul for the remainder of the year. He was to have served in this capacity during Caesar's Parthian campaign. However, the question of this expedition, whether to cancel it, postpone it, or appoint new commanders, was temporarily tabled.

Instead, a more vital issue was addressed when the Senate appointed Antonius and Dolabella to head a commission of inquiry into Caesar's unpublished memoranda. This was to forestall any irregularities in the implementation of the late Dictator's plans. However, as Antonius already controlled Caesar's papers, effects, and funds, he was in an enviably advantageous position to dictate all of Caesar's plans, both genuine and bogus.

Though I had been instrumental in brokering the compromise, I was wary of its longevity. As we were leaving the temple, I turned to Quintus and Servius, and in response to their inquiries, I remarked, "We've laid the foundations for concord, but I wouldn't build a temple on them. Everything hinges on Antonius, and I fear he'll abuse his power."

THE TWENTIETH OF MARCH WAS a raw, overcast day. The Forum was packed with the urban mob, the coarse, vulgar, turbulent riffraff that not even Caesar had been able to remove totally from Roma. From the Regia, Caesar's purple-draped corpse was borne on a golden bier through the Forum and placed on the Rostra. The late Dictator's lictors, bearing the official fasces, accompanied the corpse. Consul Antonius and Master of Horse Lepidus led cohorts of Caesarian veterans who comprised an honor guard. A score of trumpeters and bucinators blared a military dirge during the entire funeral procession.

The praetors Marcus Brutus and Gaius Cassius each spoke in succession, delivering eloquent but unmoving addresses to the populace. Both attempted to justify their tyrannicide as an act of Republican patriotism. But the mob had been so conditioned by years of Caesar's dictatorship that they could not conceive of a patriotic endeavor encompassing the murder of their beloved Caesar.

Sporadic heckling interrupted the praetors so that they may have spoken more briefly than they had originally planned. They descended from the Rostra and stood around its steps with those senators and equites who had been in the procession. Servius, Quintus, and I were among them.

Solemnly, Antonius proceeded to deliver the eulogy. He reminded the populace of Caesar's many services to them in the course of his career. "Caesar has provided you with bountiful largess and games and entertainments of unsurpassed grandeur. Caesar has added vast new territories to the Roman imperium by his conquest of Gaul, his expeditions to Britain and the German lands, and his victories in Egypt, Pontus, and Numidia. Had he lived, Caesar would have carried Roman arms into Parthia, Scythia, Dacia, and Thrace."

Antonius reminded them of Caesar's constant clemency and moderation. "Where power in most men brings their faults to light, in Caesar power brought into prominence his talents and virtues. Rather than make him insolent, power and prosperity gave him a sphere that corresponded to the clemency and moderation of his nature."

Then, Antonius held up Caesar's blood-stained toga. The spectators' outraged shock was surpassed only by their horror at the subsequent sight of Caesar's nude, bloodied, hacked body. Antonius heaped on the pathos, declaiming on Caesar's inbred goodness. "Caesar was constant. He was never carried away by anger and never spoiled by success. He did not retaliate for the past. He never tried by severity to secure himself for the future. He consistently sought to save all who would allow themselves to be saved, and he always endeavored to repair old acts of injustice."

Antonius lauded Caesar as a founding father of the Roman people. "You loved him as your benefactor. You made him chief of state, though he was not desirous of titles. To the gods, he was Chief Pontiff. To the people he was Consul. To the legions, he was Imperator. To the enemies of the Republic, he was Dictator. In all, he was Father of the Country. Yet, this did not spare him the cuts and slashes of the assassins' daggers!"

With each demonstrative hyperbole, the mob cried out its collective denunciation. Antonius was working them with the utmost rhetorical finesse. As though brandishing a weapon, he held aloft a scroll and identified it as Caesar's will. He told them they were among Caesar's beneficiaries. When the mob cried out for the will to be read, I knew that Antonius' master stroke was about to be loosed. Brutus, Cassius, and the others surely must have regretted consenting to the public funeral that Antonius was endeavoring to turn into a riot. The Liberators began to disperse.

Despite Antonius' feigned reluctance to promulgate the will, the mob cried out all the more boldly, demanding that he read it, and so he began to do so.

To each citizen on the public dole, Caesar had bequeathed the sum of three hundred sesterces. In addition, to the whole citizenry, Caesar had donated his gardens on the Tiber's west bank as a public park.

Antonius announced that Caesar's chief heir in the first degree was his grand-nephew, Gaius Octavius, to whom three-quarters of the Dictator's estate, said to be worth seven hundred million sesterces, had been bequeathed. Also, Gaius Octavius was to be posthumously adopted as Caesar's son and he was to bear Caesar's name.

The other heirs in the first degree were announced as Caesar's nephew, Quintus Pedius and his other grand-nephew, Lucius Pinarius, who were each to receive one-eighth of the estate. In the event that Calpurnia should have borne him a son, Caesar had named several men to be the child's guardians. Ironically, these men were among Caesar's assassins. One of them was Marcus Brutus. Angry murmuring could be heard from the crowd when Antonius read that portion of the will. Finally, Antonius announced that he and Decimus Brutus had been named among the heirs in the second degree.

Frequent cries of outrage and lamentation spread across from the rabble, punctuating the reading of the will. Now, they acclaimed Caesar. They refused to allow his body to be taken outside the City, even though a funeral pyre had been set up in Mars Field. Some clamored for the body to be taken up to the Capitoline, while others demanded that it be burned there on the Rostra.

At that instant, I feared that I was about to see a re-enactment of Publius Clodius' riotous funeral that had burned down the Curia. But the most vociferous and aggressive of these dregs of Romulus assaulted the Rostra, pushing us, the senators and equites, out of the way. They took up the corpse and carried it to the relatively vacant eastern end of the Forum, flanked by the Regia and the Vestal Mansion. There, where the funeral rites had begun, the frenzied mob erected a makeshift pyre of broken chairs, benches, and tree limbs. Upon this, Caesar's corpse was set, and then it was set aflame.

The fire consuming the Dictator's remains was fed and augmented as the mourners tossed upon the pyre whatever flammable items they could readily grasp. Legionary veterans and Caesarian idolizers seized firebrands and ran off in search of the assassins. Through the rest of the day, Caesar's pyre was dwarfed by isolated fires as the houses of Brutus, Cassius, and Decimus and the others were torched. Out of necessity, the Liberators and their families fled Roma.

Thus, Marcus Antonius made his bid for power. By deftly playing upon the emotions of the mob, and without leveling any direct accusation against the assassins, he subverted the compromise constructed in the aftermath of Caesar's assassination. The conspirators, assassins, liberators, patriots became political outcasts. Now, the Caesarians were firmly in control of affairs—Antonius at the helm, flanked by Lepidus and Dolabella, and supported by a fanatical mob and several thousand Caesarian legionary veterans.

I had thought that I might have had a part in re-constituting the state after Caesar's removal. But now a new usurper had subverted the accords. Though the Dictator was dead, the dictatorship yet thrived. There was no purpose in my remaining in Roma. I did not even feel safe staying indoors at the Palatine house.

So with Tiro, Alexio, and Metrodorus, I retired to the villa at Antium for yet another session of waiting out events. By the time Atticus returned to Roma, he found circumstances very much changed. I was certain that Quintus and Servius would bring him up to date as well as keep me informed of any subsequent developments.

Caput XVII

*THERE IS A SURE PLACE in Heaven for those who have served their fatherland...
a place where they may enjoy Eternal life in everlasting bliss.*
From "The Dream of Scipio" in *De Re Publica*
CICERO'S ELYSIAN VOICE

THIS BLISSFUL ABODE ALLOWS FOR no return to the strife and turmoil of political contention. But such was not the case in my temporal life in the Roman Republic. State crises, the entreaties of friends, and my own sense of duty pulled me back into the fray.

ANTIUM WAS BASKING IN THE warm, spring sunshine of early Maius. The waters of the Tyrrhenian Sea sparkled in blue majesty beneath the veranda of my villa. Its white-washed stone walls were decorated with crimson and blue-bordered windows below the terra-cotta tiled roof. It was a perfectly idyllic existence, far removed from the strife, the uncertainties of Roma. Roma under Marcus Antonius' regime was like old Mount Vesuvius further down the coast. Its gray-black smoke billowing into the sky was sometimes carried up to Antium by southerly winds. Like a dangerously seething volcano whose violent eruption could at any time pour forth the molten lava of repression and murder, Antonius held the Republic in his consular grip. Though the Dictator was dead, the Dictatorship yet thrived.

In the weeks since Caesar's riotous funeral, I had lived at Antium. Every other day, news reached me from Roma conveyed by couriers from Quintus and Servius. Consul Antonius orchestrated the Tribal Assembly through a series of laws, ostensibly based upon Caesar's memoranda. Provinces were assigned both to the Liberators and the Caesarians.

Decimus Brutus was designated Proconsul of Cisalpine Gaul and his co-conspirators Tillius Cimber and Gaius Trebonius were respectively allotted the proconsulates of Bithynia-Pontus and Asia.

Among the Caesarians, Gaius Pollio had been appointed Proconsul of Further Spain where once again Sextus Pompeius was fomenting rebellion. Titus Plancus was named Proconsul of Gallia Comata, "Gaul of the Long Hairs," the Gallic Territory that Caesar had conquered. The provinces of Africa and Africa Nova were assigned respectively to Quintus Cornificius and Titus Sextilis.

Special arrangements were made for Marcus Lepidus. Relinquishing the office of Master of Horse, since Antonius had secured the legal abolition of the dictatorship, Lepidus was then nominated to the vacant post of Chief Pontiff. In a reactionary bit of politicking, Antonius transferred the election of Chief Pontiff from the Tribal Assembly back to co-optation by the Pontifical College, a move that reversed what Caesar had achieved during my consulate. There was no reason to suspect that the Pontiffs would be loath to choose Lepidus as the new Pontifex Maximus, even though he would soon have to be absent from Roma; Lepidus had been appointed Proconsul of Transalpine Gaul and Hither Spain.

As Antonius went to considerable lengths to secure Lepidus' loyalty, he gave equal attention to my erstwhile son-in-law, Dolabella. He arranged his own and Dolabella's exclusive appointment to the commission to review and validate Caesar's memoranda. The two Consuls now had no reason to fear Senatorial interference, especially in regard to getting their desired provinces—Macedonia for Antonius and Syria for Dolabella.

Also, with Antonius' connivance, his brother, Gaius, had assumed the duties of Urban Praetor since Marcus Brutus had fled the City. Strange though, that Antonius should appoint some of the assassins to proconsulates while ignoring Brutus and Cassius in this regard.

Roma was a dangerous City for Caesar's assassins and for anyone even suspected of being of their party. In the chaos ensuing upon Antonius' provocative eulogy, the mob had mistakenly seized a tribune of the plebs, Gaius Helvius Cinna, and, as he bore the same cognomen as Caesar's former brother-in-law, they lynched him despite his pathetic protests that he was *not* one of the assassins. No wonder then, that Praetor Lucius Cinna not only fled the City, but he also relinquished his office, claiming it had been bestowed upon him by a tyrant.

So dangerously uncertain had conditions become that two distinguished visitors had been obliged to quit Roma. The Egyptian Queen, Cleopatra, and the Mauretanian Queen, Eunoe, hurriedly departed to their respective realms. Since Caesar's death, they could not have been preoccupied any longer with personal matters. Whether or not they had completed their official business was uncertain. No doubt, the political climate was no longer agreeable to them.

For all practical purposes, a new triumviral triangle held the Republic in its grip: Marcus Antonius at the apex with Marcus Lepidus and Publius Dolabella at the bases dominated the Senate and the People's Assembly.

THE SIGHT OF GRAIN BARGES bound for Ostia caused me to hope against vain hope for a part in reconstituting the Republic in the aftermath of Caesar's assassination. I wondered what lay ahead for Roma.

Looking down the coast, I could see the promontory of Circeii with its domed, colonnaded shrine to Apollo. Apollo—the Roman god of prophecy: what intelligence did he have of the Republic's fate? If any at all, how much would the god divulge about the outcome of our present state of affairs?

I passed the time at Antium reading various monographs on religion and divination. One day, shortly before the Nones of the month, my studies were interrupted by an unexpected group of callers. Lucius Marcius Philippus arrived with his step-son, Gaius Octavius, and the youth's companions, Marcus Agrippa, Gaius Maecenas, and Quintus Salvidienus. Also with them was Gaius Claudius Marcellus, Octavius' brother-in-law.

Philippus and Marcellus were both Senatorial neutrals. Philippus had been consul the year after my recall. Prior to that, he had married Octavius' widowed mother, Atia, Caesar's niece; Marcellus was married to Atia's daughter, Octavia. However, this had not prevented his or his like-named cousins' virulent opposition to Caesar. Through three successive consulates, their antagonism had precipitated civil war. But when it came, Marcellus joined the neutral faction. Subsequently, with one cousin killed at Pharsalus and the other pardoned by Caesar but then mysteriously murdered, he could have commended himself for an astute change of allegiance.

The two consulars had met the young men at Brundisium a week earlier. Octavius and his friends had returned from Apollonia because his mother had relayed the news of his adoption and the bequests willed by Caesar. The six of them, with their attendants, were on their way to Roma via the Appian Road, but they had turned off for Antium so that Philippus, knowing that I was sojourning there, might present his step-son.

I remembered seeing Octavius taking his exercises in Mars Field. It was then that I had recognized him as the young man of my recurring dream, the dream in which he was designated as the one to bring final peace to Roma. He had been born in the year of my consulate, which put him at nineteen years of age. A comely young man, he was small of stature, and in his general appearance and coloring he strongly resembled his mother, Atia, a living mirror of the Caesars. He was intelligent, perceptive, and thoroughly polite and deferential.

Octavius' companions were quite different from him as well as from each other. Marcus Agrippa, I learned later, was the descendant of a freedman. Tall and burly, he had that aspect of roughness about him that one would associate with rustics; yet, it did not render him obnoxious. Gaius Maecenas, of noble Etruscan stock, had an unctuous, agile urbane demeanor. Oddly, he did not inspire my trust or confidence. Quintus Salvidienus appeared to be the oldest of Octavius' companions. As his name denoted, he belonged to the Vestini, a people of the Picene hill country. He was of humble stock, but he had risen to the rank of Military Tribune under Caesar. It was not at all surprising that he possessed a stiff, reserved, military bearing.

The four of them appeared to be inseparable. Since Caesar's return from Spain, they had been studying at Apollonia, with what diligence or success I could not gauge. But where fulfilling his ambitions was concerned, Octavius did not appear to lack determination.

Though his testamentary adoption had yet to be formalized, he fashioned himself as Gaius Julius Caesar Octavianus. However, both Philippus and I refused to acknowledge him as anything other than

Octavius. I don't think this annoyed him because he respectfully addressed me as "Father."

"Did you know, Father," he flattered me, "that during the Spanish war, Caesar had spoken so highly of you? Referring to you, he said, 'It is better to have extended the frontiers of the mind as has Cicero than to have pushed back the boundaries of imperium'."

Emboldened by my obvious pleasure at this flattery, Ocatvius asked to speak with me in private. Excusing ourselves from the others, we withdrew from the veranda and went into the library.

"I admired Caesar's literary and rhetorical talents," I admitted as we seated ourselves at a table. "It is regrettable that he abused these talents, as well as other qualities, in subverting the Republic. In lording over Roma and the Roman People and the Roman imperium, he hastened his own destruction." My candor was unbridled.

Octavius listened intently with a serene composure characteristic of more mature men. Then he said, "Father, am I worthy of reproach for my loyalty to my murdered kinsman? Am I less than a Roman because I grieve for his death while others hold that our country's freedom is preferable to a relative's life?"

Well reasoned, I thought. I replied carefully, "Your esteem for your adoptive father is worthy of all praise. But, you know, Caesar had been living on borrowed time. During my consulate, when the Senate was debating the punishment of subversive conspirators, he had almost been attacked when he persisted in advocating life imprisonment for them. He even tried to obstruct the Senate's vote."

"The Catilina crisis," Octavius put in. "I've studied your orations, Father. How brilliant they are!"

I nodded appreciatively, but continued about Caesar's transgressions. "Then, during his consulate, he violated the very basic institutions of our Republic and made civil war inevitable." Just then, I realized that I was getting carried away, and so I reined in my comments. "Hopefully, when your grief has passed, you will come to realize the necessity of Caesar's removal."

Abruptly, Octavius changed the subject. "Father, will you come with me to Roma and help me to obtain my legal inheritance?"

I was stunned at this, but again I was flattered.

"You're the senior consular, and if you spoke on my behalf, the Senate and the magistrates would heed your words."

I did not bother to correct Octavius; in fact, I was *not* the senior consular since Caesar's kinsman, Aurelius Cotta, consul two years before me, was still active in the Senate. Again I was flattered that he should request my help, but my reply was non-committal. I explained that Antonius was indisputably in control of the political situation in Roma, especially as a considerable bodyguard of veterans from the Thirty-Fifth Legion was always in attendance upon him. "Nothing is likely to be achieved as Antonius controls Caesar's treasury and papers. Even if I could influence Dolabella to support your adoption and inheritance, Antonius could exercise his consular prerogative and veto his colleague's measures." In the end, I advised Octavius to wait at least until the new consuls entered office.

"Thank you for your advice, Father," he replied while rising to his feet. "I hope that I may call on you again."

I assured him that he could do so at any time. Undeterred, Octavius, with his friends and relatives, set out for Roma.

WHEN I WROTE TO ATTICUS about the interview, I speculated that the young man would bear careful watching, and not only because of his inherited name. I wondered if Antonius would use or abuse him. Would Caesar's money-men, Balbus and Oppius, have anything to do with him? I warned Atticus not to be surprised if Octavius were to contact him for financial assistance.

Octavius' visit occurred when I had been gathering materials for two religious treatises, *On the Nature of the Gods* and *On Divination*. Letters from Varro and Figulus had given me much encouragement to undertake these works. However, my agnosticism, despite my membership in the Augural College and my spiritual experience in the wake of Tullia's passing, remained fundamentally unchanged, at least as far as the deities of the Greco-Roman pantheon were concerned.

I was intrigued by the business of Lucius Cotta supposedly having planned to propose the title of *King* for Caesar. A prophecy in the Sibylline Oracles apparently postulated that we had to recognize a king in order to be saved. I wondered about the time and the person that such a prediction might have indicated, as well as from whom or what we were to be saved.

Figulus had a typically Pythagorean viewpoint on this. Having conferred with Varro on the *king* prophecy, he interpreted it not in a political or military sense, but instead in a metaphysical dimension. He contended that the Greeks of old expected the *Logos* or the *Universal Wise Man* about whom Socrates and Plato had taught. In *Prometheus Bound*, Aeschylus had referred to the *Logos* when he wrote:

Look not for any end, moreover, to this curse until God appears, to accept upon His Head the pangs of thy own sins vicarious.

There are other prophecies pointing to a divine visitation for mankind, particularly the ancient Hebrew Scriptures that predicted a *Messias*, or as he is reckoned in Greek, *Christos*, which is rendered "the Anointed One." If there is any connection at all between the Sibylline Oracles, the Greek and Hebrew prophecies, and my own recurring dream concerning Octavius' destiny, I would have been hard-pressed to describe conclusively. However, of this I was certain: Nearly all prophecies, by their very ambiguous nature, can be accommodated virtually to any time, any situation, and personage.

My immersion into these metaphysical concerns did not totally distract me from certain mundane and pecuniary matters. I hoped that some royalties could have been applied to expedite the dowry reimbursement to Publilia, at least partially. Dolabella continued to evade his obligations to me regarding Tullia's dowry. Perhaps he seriously expected me to go out to Syria with him when he took up his proconsulate. And the political situation in the City, though I had fled from it, still weighed heavily on my mind. At least, I was certain that Quintus and Servius would write often enough to keep me abreast of developments.

Omniscient Narrative

"You are welcome to our home, Gaius Octavius Caepias," Consul Marcus Antonius formally says in welcoming his young guest. His wife, Fulvia, stands next to him in the atrium of their Aventine house. The Consul wears a purple-bordered toga of office, and Fulvia, her flame-colored hair ornately dressed, is attired in a white stola and green palla.

"Thank you, Consul, but I've actually assumed my adoptive name: *Gaius Julius Caesar Octavianus*." The young visitor speaks without the least temerity. In fact, he proudly pronounces his new name, causing Antonius and Fulvia to be momentarily taken aback. They look at each other somewhat bemused.

"You are to be congratulated on your good fortune," the Consul says turning back to Octavius.

"Please, come and sit." Fulvia gestures to several couches arranged near the impluvium. She is not sure how to address him.

"Your assumption of Caesar's name is a bit premature, don't you think?" Antonius asks as he sits down.

"It's about that that I've come to see you, Consul." Octavius also sits down opposite Antonius. "As Consul, you have the authority to confirm and validate my adoption by Caesar and to endow me with his bequests. Is that not so, Consul?"

Antonius is surprised and irritated by his visitor's self-assurance. "That's quite true, Octavius, or should I say *Octavianus*."

"Actually I prefer *Caesar*, and I would appreciate your help in effecting my adoption and in turning over to me my adoptive father's money and papers." The young man's cool, assertive self-assurance remains unrattled.

But Antonius' temper has been piqued. "You *would* indeed! Well, my young friend, let me remind you that just now there are other matters, more pressing than your *adoption* that must take priority. Caesar's assassins must be brought to justice; Roma and Italia must be stabilized; and Caesar's planned Parthian campaign..."

"Respectfully, Consul, you drove my adoptive father's assassins from the City, and while two of them are lingering at Antium, several of the others have been assigned provincial commands. Is this how you bring murderers to justice? By...."

"How dare you!" Antonius erupts. "You dare to question my dispositions! Listen, *boy*...."

"Don't call me *boy!*" Octavius objects.

"Listen *boy*—while you were on your ass studying in Appolonia, *I* took matters in hand in Roma when all hell had broken out. Think about *that*! Whether they're governing provinces or stewing in their own feces, those murderers will pay for their treachery, but according to *my* plans! As for your adoption, you'll have to grow and mature into Caesar's name before you can have it!"

Fulvia has sat quietly between the two antagonists, taking in their arguments. She is well acquainted with her husband's explosive temper, but she is intrigued by the youth's unruffled, unflappable demeanor as Antonius harangues him.

Octavius rises from his couch. "I've learned from my own father, from my step-father, and from my adoptive father to be respectful of my elders. I've asked for your help, and you've answered me with insults; very well then. While I wait, I'll let the people and the veterans know who I am. They'll know I'm Caesar's adopted son and heir."

Having said this, Octavius bows to the Consul and his wife and then takes his leave. Antonius glares after him, fuming in outraged anger. Fulvia looks after him also, impressed but also alarmed.

LATER, AT CLODIA PULCHRA'S, FULVIA relates the interview to her sister-in-law and companion. "Why, he's just a child. I'd wager he's never even ridden or been ridden, and sensing this, I felt an itch and a tingle in my loins and my nipples hardened so that I thought they'd pierce my gown."

Clodia sniggers jadedly. "No wonder you couldn't say anything if he had you so aroused!"

"Though he may lack years and experience, he doesn't lack presumption and fortitude. Imagine it! This boy, eighteen, maybe nineteen, calling himself Caesar and demanding of Antonius, who's twice his age *and* Consul, the formalization of his adoption and the transference of Caesar's money to himself! Not even a word of thanks or acknowledgement to the man whose courage and constancy have driven the murderers from Roma! Antonius deserves more respect than this *Caesar-Boy* showed."

"What's Antonius going to do about him?"

Fulvia shrugs indifferently. "For the moment—nothing; but he'll continue to postpone the formal adoption and he's not about to surrender Caesar's money. By the way, he's told me that he must have spent four hundred thousand talents for his own purposes."

"Good Goddess!" Clodia exclaims. "Was there ever such a sum in the whole Treasury!"

"*Caesar-Boy* said he'd take his cause to the citizens and to the veterans. Just how he expects to do this with no money and no patron escapes me!" Fulvia sighs deeply.

"Well, my sweet, it seems the stage is being set for a confrontation between Caesar's right-hand man and his adopted son and heir." Clodia purses her full lips into a pout. "There have already been noisy demonstrations in the Forum for *Caesar-Boy*."

"And no doubt they were organized by him or his agents." Again, Fulvia sighs. "Still, Antonius plans to depart for Campania to inspect the veterans' colonies."

"Are you going with him?"

"Of course, Clodia. I only hope that Dolabella can contain this nuisance. I told Antonius that he should not have allowed Lepidus to go off to the provinces."

"You don't trust Dolabella to handle *Caesar-Boy*?" Clodia asks tongue-in-cheek.

Fulvia giggles. "Well, perhaps if you'll back him up." The two women laugh, inclining their heads toward each other so that they touch, raven tresses meshing with flame-red locks.

"I'm going down to Antium, partly for myself and partly to deliver a message from Dolabella to his ex-father-in-law. Please, Fulvia, drop in when you finish with the inspections. Perhaps we might together visit the *Chick-Pea*. That should enliven his dry, sterile existence."

Fulvia smiles whimsically and passes a forefinger across her painted lips. "Clodia Pulchra and the seashore at Antium—an unsurpassable combination," she whispers to her sister-in-law.

"It lacks only your presence, my sweet. You *will* come, won't you?" Clodia's whisper is even more subdued than Fulvia's, and so thoroughly inescapable.

Cicero's Elysian Voice

The summer heat of June came upon us at Antium just before the Ides. It was a perfect setting for a heated family conference I attended at Servilia's villa. Marcus Brutus was there with his wife, Porcia. One of his half-sisters, Tertia, was also present with her husband, Gaius Cassius, Brutus' partner in patriotic tyrannicide. Young Marcus Silanus, Servilia's son by Decimus Silanus, sat quietly by his mother's side along with her adolescent nephew, Marcus Lucullus, the son of the late oligarch and Servilia's estranged sister. Porcia's brother, young Marcus Cato, the very image of his illustrious father, stood with Brutus and Cassius.

"Am I to believe that Caesar had marked me to be grain curator in Crete," Brutus complained, "instead of proconsul?"

Canine-faced Cassius put in, "By the re-writing of Marcus Antonius—yes! And by his re-writing I'm to go to Cyrenaica for the same purpose."

"First he drives us from Roma, has the mob burn down our homes," Brutus spoke again, "then he takes away our offices and reduces us to grain merchants. More than insulting, it's degrading."

"Be patient, my son." Servilia tried to placate him. "I'll be returning to Roma soon. When Antonius returns from Campania, I'll have a few words with him."

"Mother," Brutus objected, "*this* is Marcus Antonius, *not* Julius Caesar."

"You doubt me? There was nothing I could not obtain from Caesar or any of his underlings."

For her fifty-some years, she has the beauty, charm, grace, intellect, and above all, the will to get practically anything from Antonius. After all, Antonius is the kind of man who would have had much regard for her extensive intimacies with Caesar.

"It's unfortunate that you need to negotiate with Antonius," I commented. "You see, if you had included me in your counsels, I would have advised you to eliminate him and perhaps even Lepidus at the same time. Then, there would have been no deterrent to your seizure of power. But instead you...."

"Enough!" Servilia abruptly turned on me. Her face was flushed with anger. The once golden hair, now streaked with silver, seemed to stand on end. "My son and son-in-law were not out to seize power. By killing Caesar they had one goal—to restore the Republic. Had they included you in their plot, your vacillation and indecision would have weakened their resolve and nothing would have been achieved. Kill Antonius? Why? He was only Caesar's pawn, despite what he's lately become. They weren't trying to commit a massacre! So there was no need to strike at any of Caesar's officers. What's more, what purpose is served by dredging up what *should* or should *not* have been done? We must deal with things at hand. Granted—Antonius is a factor that no one foresaw. But as I said before—*I'll* deal with him."

Then she turned from me to Brutus and Cassius and assured them, "Your commissions will be upgraded from curators to proconsuls!"

Besides their annoyance over their titles, Brutus and Cassius were anxious to quit Italia rather than risk their lives against Antonius' power. "Every praetorian edict we've issued against his actions, he's ignored," Brutus announced. "Why should we remain?"

"We collected a considerable fleet of small but seaworthy vessels along with sufficient provisions," Cassius added. "We've had much support from the money-men, especially your friend, Atticus." Cassius turned his canine face to me as he mentioned my friend.

"Atticus is shrewd, I observed. "He's made private contributions to defray the loss of your homes, but he refuses to head the equites who've publicly assisted you."

Yes, I thought. Atticus is ever shrewd and so utterly politic. Yet, I hoped my friend would continue to be careful lest he compromise himself. I already knew that he, and Balbus and Oppius, had loaned money to Gaius Octavius.

Just then, as though he were reading my thoughts, Brutus said, "There are rumors that Octavius' agents have been distributing money and promises among Caesar's veterans in Campania. He hasn't gotten as much as a copper from his inheritance because Antonius is holding on to Caesar's money like a miser. So, who's supplying him with money?"

I chuckled to myself and again thought of Atticus. He should not want to incur Antonius' disfavor by being too generous to someone who was becoming a nuisance to the Consul.

So much, then, for the family conference; I declined Servilia's invitation to dinner and returned to my villa, a short remove down the coast. That Brutus and Cassius were in such earnest preparation to leave Italia weighed heavily upon my mind. Perhaps, I thought, so should I. After all, the news from Marcus' teacher, Crattipus, continued to be discouraging. My son's neglect of his studies and his reckless debaucheries demanded my attention. Yet, I vacillated.

Omniscient Narrative

The dinner conversation at Servilia's villa continues to focus on the Liberators' plight.

"I think Cicero was right," Porcia opines.

"What about?" her husband asks.

"About killing Marcus Antonius." Porcia is not fazed by the startled expressions on her dining companions' faces. "However sanguinary I might sound, I'm also being practical. All of Caesar's closest officers should have been killed: Antonius, his co-Consul; Lepidus, his Master of Horse—even though he's also your son-in-law, Servilia; and Dolabella, his Suffect Consul. They're far too loyal, too attached to him to have been expected to compromise with us. That they did so was only a pretense."

Tertia concurs. "Yes, as things turned out since the funeral, the accords that Cicero negotiated *were* a sham."

The women's husbands chew their food silently, ruminating on the women's words.

"And Cicero should have been killed as well," Porcia adds decisively.

"And why Cicero?" Servilia asks of her daughter-in-law.

"Because he's an accommodator. He deserted my father and all who would have died for the Republic. He lived in silence under Caesar's dictatorship; and after the Dictator was killed, did he espouse the brave tyrannicides? *No!* He played *mediator* between them and the Caesarians! Mark me well, all of you, it would not at all surprise me if he were to sponsor Caesar's nephew, the adopted one."

"*Cicero* support *Octavius?*" Cassius chortles. "Not likely!"

Brutus adds, "My dear, Cicero's a champion of the old Republic. He accommodated himself, as have many of us, because Caesar's power overshadowed all of us. But now that Caesar's removed, Cicero will direct the Republic."

But Porcia is wary. "Marcus, in time you'll see that I'm right. Cicero's not to be trusted."

Praetor Decimus Brutus has ambivalent feelings about departing from Italia. For weeks after Caesar's wild funeral, he has kept himself as inconspicuous as possible even to the neglect of his official duties.

Roma within the iron fist of Consul Marcus Antonius allows for none of the dead Dictator's assassins to remain in the City, much less discharge their offices.

So, Decimus Brutus has resided at the town of Sutrium, a few miles north of Roma on the Cassian Road overlooking Lake Sabatinus. His quarters at a hostelry have been barely comfortable, but they have at least afforded him a safe refuge from harassment and possible assassination; for that he is grateful. Still, he is anxious to depart for his Cisalpine proconsulate, a posting that Caesar had arranged for him and about which Marcus Antonius has thus far not meddled.

Beyond the Antonian regime in Roma and his incommodious quarters at Sutrium, Decimus is hounded by three women who have become increasingly like a trio of harpies, hovering over him, criticizing him for all that has gone amiss since the fateful Ides of March. His mother, Sempronia, with whom he has shared forbidden intimacies and colluded in shameful parricide, contrives through subtle, manipulative coercion to control his psyche. His wife, Flavia, as always, cold, remote, and aloof, consistently provokes his barely suppressed revulsion. His mother-in-law, Aurelia Orestilla, widow of the renegade, Lucius Catilina, is a constant reminder of his own mother's infidelity and subversion.

The man who is himself dominated by a feminine triad is now setting out to command a northern province and its legions. He expects the task to be easier than contending with the women who have come up from Roma to see him.

"Good fortune to you, my son," Sempronia wishes him in a haughty tone matching her beauteous, conceited demeanor. "Guard yourself well. Though now you go out to your province like a fugitive, see that you return triumphantly."

Flavia chimes in, "Decimus, may Fortuna smile upon you." She politely kisses him on the cheek that he reluctantly offers.

Orestilla then says to him, "Go safely, Decimus, and return safely."

Decimus has had enough of them. A queer sense of foreboding elicits his honest response. "Whatever may happen up there, whatever may happen in Roma, I hope I don't see any of you again this side of Hades!"

Flavia and Orestilla chortle jadedly, but Sempronia is taken aback. "Decimus, how dare you speak to me so!" she reprimands him.

"That I should speak with you at all is beyond all reason," Decimus shoots back. "I can't stand to have your bloody claws in me any longer! Now get out of here, the lot of you!" To Orestilla, he hollers, "Take your trollop of a daughter and find her a new step-father to *copulate* with! While they're at it, *you* could sit on his face and let him see your *true* worth! *To Hades with the lot of you!*"

After the women have set out in their coach to return to Roma, Decimus and several attendants begin their ride up the Cassian Road to Cisalpine Gaul. Decimus hopes for a new life. He cannot know what awaits him. The Fates and the intrigues of ambitious men will show him.

Cicero's Elysian Voice

As I was engaged in my writing, letters from Servius and Quintus reached me. Servius complained about a persistent cough and frequent fatigue. Still, he was up-to-date on political developments. He reported that the designated consuls for the next year, Aulus Hirtius and Gaius Pansa, had recently returned from the Gallic provinces. They confided in Servius their consternation over affairs in the City, most especially the fact of Caesar's assassination. But regarding Antonius' consulate, it was difficult for him to read their sentiments. Conversation with them was hardly a stimulating experience, Servius reported, as they were both woodenly boring military types.

Meanwhile, this year's consuls had promulgated and pushed through the Tribal Assembly an agrarian bill empanelling a board of seven. Antonius' brother, Tribune Lucius, was appointed board president, and to no one's surprise, two other board members were the Consuls themselves, Marcus Antonius and Publius Dolabella.

Quintus wrote, "What was attempted but blocked during your consulate has now become reality. This agrarian board of seven is empowered to buy up and distribute all remaining public land in Italia."

However, the bill created a rift that Servius believed could not be repaired. The Consuls' attempts at popular favoritism among the urban and rural poor and the as yet unsettled veterans attracted the support of large numbers of equites. But the large landowners, of whom Servius numbered us, stood opposed, fearing confiscations and seizures. Even some of the Caesarians were beginning to turn against Antonius.

Still, he held sway over the Senate. With unbridled haughtiness, he juggled the provincial commands of Cisalpine Gaul, Macedonia, and Syria. Having originally secured the proconsulate of Macedonia for two years, Antonius then cowed the Senate into changing his command to Cisalpine Gaul for five years and having his brother, Praetor Gaius, appointed to Macedonia in his stead. Now the problem was that Decimus Brutus was already governing Cisalpina. Would he be willing to relinquish it? If not, then the inherent seeds of discord could produce a harvest of civil war.

Farther afield, Antonius had the Senate extend Dolabella's Syrian proconsulate from two to five years. Then, he manipulated the legions, using the Tribal assembly to transfer to himself the command of four of the six legions stationed in Macedonia. These were the troops that Caesar was to have led against the Parthians.

There was hardly any subtlety to Antonius' moves. The Cisalpina had been a fertile source of levies for new legions, and it is much closer to Italia than is Macedonia. Whoever governs the Cisalpina is in a far better position to control Roma. Caesar taught us that lesson. Hence, Antonius logically preferred Gaul over Macedonia.

The most intriguing development was Antonius proposing in the Senate that the provincial commissions of Marcus Brutus and Gaius Cassius were to be elevated from mere curates to official proconsulates. There was token objection from Antonius' friends and sycophants, contending that the Praetors had abandoned their duties when they had fled the City. Nevertheless, presiding Consul Dolabella called for a vote, and the senators, as though on cue, approved the proposal.

This slight show of favor for the principal tyrannicides seemed out of place for Antonius. I remembered Servilia's assurances that she would influence Antonius so as to upgrade Brutus' and Cassius' provincial assignments. Apparently, she had succeeded. No doubt her influence also secured the appointment of her son, Marcus Silanus, as legate to her son-in-law, Marcus Lepidus.

Antonius was fishing for allies as he faced threats from both far and near. The renegade, Sextus Pompeius had just bested Proconsul

Pollio in Further Spain, while Proconsul Lepidus in Nearer Spain had yet to come to grips with him. Potential trouble could also have come from those tyrannicides already established in their provinces. Just why Antonius had countenanced their placements remained a mystery to me.

Within Roma and its environs, young Gaius Octavius continued to be a festering sore for Antonius. An apt rabble rouser, he provoked numerous incidents that his inflammatory speeches escalated into near riots. Antonius even accused him of tampering with the Caesarian veterans in Campania.

It must have unnerved Antonius and his brothers to have had to use cautious restraint in dealing with these Octavian disturbances, if only because the young man, as Caesar's relative and heir, was beloved of the mob and the veterans. He indulged the mob by putting on games and shows and by distributing Caesar's bequests to the citizens. The last gesture was something that Antonius, as executor of Caesar's will, had never attempted to do. As fickle as the mob was, it was possessed of an exemplary memory where donatives were concerned.

THOSE TWO OVER-PAINTED, OVER-ADORNED BIRDS, Clodia Pulchra, ever like a raven, and Fulvia of the flaming hair, had nothing better to do than to drop in and divert me from my reveries and writing. They contrasted with and yet complemented each other like a pair of exquisite vases—Fulvia's red-brown Arrentine hue and Clodia's rose and olive complexion. As before, Clodia attracted and repelled me at the same time. She was utterly beautiful and desirable. Yet, she aroused in me something primeval, contrary to social convention, and altogether unsettling. But Fulvia, like a hawk, had an aura of danger about her, and she filled me with acute uneasiness. In fact, I feared her as Antonius' wife far more than I had ever feared her when she had been Clodius' mistress and then *his* wife.

Their vivacious conversation was clever, witty, and filled with praise for the beauty of the countryside and seashore. However, neither of them let slip an opportunity to make some oblique, enigmatic remark as though they were sharing, to my exclusion, a private joke between themselves.

"Antonius and I spent nine days touring the veterans' homesteads throughout Campania. Those men are very fortunate to have been so well provided for. But in various communities we encountered surly malcontents, hard-headed, mean-spirited barbarics who scoffed at us." Fulvia spoke disparagingly while partaking of the wine, fruit, and sweet cakes I had laid out for them. "Can you imagine it, Cicero? We should have had to suffer such rude behavior from men who owe so much to Caesar *and* to Antonius!"

"Typical soldierly behavior," I agreed, "yet there is a modicum of respect that they owe to a Consul of the Republic *and* to his *wife*."

"Antonius made inquiries of a score of them. Each told us the same thing. One Quintus Salvidienus, a friend and agent of the *Caesar-Boy*, has been stirring them up, telling them to expect this and that and the other from Caesar's heir."

It's an old story, I thought. All it takes is a troublemaker exploiting uncertain conditions and before the veterans can bring in a harvest, they're ready to foment revolution. I asked her, "What does this Salvidienus—or should I say, Gaius Octavius—want from them?"

Fulvia asserted, "Their help in getting his adoption formalized. That *Caesar-Boy* is far too impatient for his own good, and for Antonius' comfort."

I sighed and shrugged. "Antonius would do well to stave off trouble by giving Octavius his due. But then again, I suppose your husband has his own agenda."

This did not sit well with Fulvia. Her face took on a harder aspect. She seemed ready to speak, but Clodia cut her off.

"The times are so uncertain because you men, as usual, have to play your power games." She glanced at me sideways and probably saw Fulvia peripherally as well. "Cicero, Dolabella has asked me to remind you of his offer of a legateship on his proconsular staff. He really wants you to go out to Syria with him. He's leaving by late summer. You should go. You *know* why you should go, don't you?"

Clodia had purposely hit a nerve. I coolly replied, "Clodia, you know it all too well. Naturally, Dolabella has told you about my daughter's dowry."

"Aside from the dowry, Cicero," she advised, "Consider your own situation. You don't want to be needlessly dragged into a new political storm, not at *your* age."

Clodia was an adept archer with her words. Within seconds, she had hit another nerve. She smiled seeing my reaction to her barb about my age. "But a legateship under Dolabella, well, that's another matter that your age should not preclude, despite your misgivings about it."

I composed myself enough to ask her, "You say he's leaving by summer's end?"

Clodia nodded while chewing on a grape and then stole a glance at Fulvia. "What is it with some of our magistrates quitting Roma well before the end of their terms and prematurely going out to their provinces?"

"Well," I replied, "there have been precedents. No matter! Thank Dolabella, but tell him to make the offer himself." I hoped that would be the end of it, but I was wrong.

"He already has, Cicero," she peevishly answered. "Remember? At the banquet for Caesar, or did you think he was jesting?"

"I know Dolabella quite well, though perhaps not as *you* know him, Clodia." In her own jaded way, she grimaced in response to my verbal barb. "Very well, perhaps he *was* serious. I'll reconsider it. Thank you, Clodia, for conveying his tidings."

Fulvia stood up from her chair. "Come, Clodia, it's time we left so that Marcus Cicero can tend to his affairs."

"Fulvia, please convey my salutations to Antonius when you return to Roma." I even offered to have Tiro and Alexio accompany them anywhere—just so they'd leave.

"You're most gracious, Marcus Cicero," Fulvia purred. "Actually, I'll be staying with Clodia for a few days." The two women exchanged mischievous glances. Then they made their farewells and departed. Their litters bore them down the coastal path to Clodia's villa.

I was relieved at their departure, for being in their presence unnerved me, just as it had many years before when they informed me of Catilina's conspiracy.

Omniscient Narrative

A SMALL OIL LAMP CASTS minimal light in the bedroom of Clodia Pulchra's Antium villa. Just outside the open window, the waves can be heard crashing in on the seashore. A gentle breeze stirs the window's curtains and wafts over Fulvia's naked back and buttocks and legs as she caresses and fondles and kisses Clodia who lies nude below her. Her black tresses are splayed upon her pillow as Fulvia's mouth descends upon her tender, supple breasts, kissing and licking the nipples into stiff arousal. Both women are in ecstasy.

Clodia gives voice to her thoughts while Fulvia's mouth and tongue give them mutual pleasure. "The *Chick-Pea* looked so forlorn, though he politely received us. I still think he was interested in my offer, but of course, he wouldn't give me the satisfaction of accepting or rejecting it unless he's sure it's really from Dolabella himself." Clodia moans in delight, twisting her head back upon the pillow. "*Satisfaction!* Yes, we'll see! I don't feel he was uneasy in our presence, unless he imagines that we—*ooh, Fulvia*—or you bear him ill will because of Publius. Perhaps he may have felt some stirrings or imbalance of his inner self."

Fulvia looks up from Clodia's navel that she's been plying with her lips and tongue. "Must we have *him* in bed with us, Clodia?"

Clodia giggles as her hands gently coax Fulvia's head back to her belly. "Do you think he keeps any one for his recreation, perhaps someone from among his household slaves? Do you think his faithful Tiro services him? Freedman though he is, he's always clinging to his former master. Perhaps, like us... *don't stop, Fulvia*—they need the seclusion of Antium for their intimacies. I wouldn't mind having a tryst with him if he were briefly released from Cicero's charge."

Pausing again, Fulvia looks up, her flame-red locks straddling Clodia's belly and hips. "So now we have to have *Tiro* with us, too?"

Clodia caresses Fulvia's hair. Flexing her buttocks, she spreads her legs apart. Responding to the invitation, Fulvia descends into the dark delta, her mouth and tongue probing. Clodia's hands clasp Fulvia's hands as they manipulate and tease Clodia's berry-like nipples. Still in the throes of passion, she goes on with her verbal reverie. "Tiro's an attractive man: the figure of an Apollo, with the face that could entice a Vestal, and perhaps, an organ crafted by Priapus himself. *Fulvia... Fulvia... ooh, Fulvia!* Perhaps, some day, we'll see about that too!"

The gratification giver and the receiver climax simultaneously, moaning and sighing and panting. Fulvia's head rests upon Clodia's moist pudendum. Regaining her breath, Clodia speaks again. "Could Cicero be celibate? If so, by his own will? Perhaps he's given up the pleasure of a woman's flesh because Terentia had so thoroughly henpecked him. His experience with Publilia may also have turned him off. He may even be impotent, and so he immerses himself in his books, his writings, and his own meditations as though he were seeking to fill a life devoid of purpose."

Clodia feels a stirring sensation in her loins. Fulvia has resumed her lingual attentions. Clodia looks down to see her lover's flame-red hair entangled with her own ebony pubes. "Sometimes, the company of men bores me to the point where I need to withdraw from them. I've even grown tired of Dolabella. When that happens, I seek new diversions." Clodia caresses Fulvia's head, gently pressing it downward. "Then, I have recourse to you, my delicious Fulvia. Your charms are a delightfully satisfying diversion. You fill me in ways that many of the men I've known could not begin to imagine... *mmm, Fulvia.*" Clodia shudders in delight as her lover's hands press against her ribcage.

At the same instant, Fulvia too arrives at her own ecstatic climax. After a few moments' respite, she rises, kneeling on the bed between Clodia's outspread legs. The two women smile at each other and then break into giggles. Fulvia says, "As delicious as Picene figs in summer. *Quid pro quo, Clodia?*"

"Of course, darling." Clodia and Fulvia exchange places and again commence their ritual.

THE VESTAL FABIA TENDS VESTA'S sacred fire, for it is her turn on this night. She prays to the goddess to protect Roma, but she also offers her own private intentions, particularly for her family.

Staring intently into the flame, she sees a vision. It is Cicero advocating a young man whose face she cannot discern but whose head is adorned with a laurel crown. After several moments, the vision changes, and Fabia sees the Rostra bleeding. Her heart pounds furiously within her breast. She feels faint and nearly collapses.

The next morning, Fabia writes a quick, short note to her sister, Terentia. She relates the visions, and she admits to having told Cicero that the Republic would again require his services, that it is his destiny to serve Roma. Yet, she is frightened by what she has seen. *If, as Atticus has said, Cicero is going to Syria as Dolabella's legate, he should go soon and remain abroad for some time. Conditions in Roma will only worsen, and there is much potential danger for him if he remains here.*

THE APOLLONARIAN GAMES HAVE BEEN in progress for several days. This year's celebration is different, however, because they are presented in honor of Julius Caesar's birthday on the day before the Ides of Quinctilis. In the absence of the Urban Praetor Marcus Brutus, Praetor Gaius Antonius has assumed the presidency of the games, while the late Dictator's adopted son and heir, young Gaius Octavius, has underwritten their expenses.

The Great Circus has been packed to capacity as the mob clamors to honor the dead Dictator just as they had hailed him in life. They have come to know the presumptive Caesar for all his speeches and donatives among them, and equally well they know his constant companion and friend, Marcus Agrippa. They identify with him, for he is a commoner, the descendant of a freedman.

The equites in the Circus stands also have come to know Octavius and Agrippa. The money-men have loaned them funds directly as well as indirectly through Octavius' friend, the Etruscan dilettante, Gaius Maecenas. The veterans of Caesar's wars, still waiting for land allotments, have been charmed by the young man and his companions, especially the former Military Tribune, Gaius Salvidienus.

Urban mob, equites, and legionary veterans have been thunderously appreciative of the races, gladiatorial combats, and shows that they have seen over several days. But nothing has prepared them for what they witness on the games' penultimate day, the anniversary of Caesar's birth. At dusk, a bright light, similar to the one that many veterans claimed to have seen before Pharsalus, darts across the sky. Amid widespread, awestruck murmuring, the superstitious spectators proclaim the heavenly portent to be the soul of the Divine Julius ascending into Heaven.

The mob's acclamation is reinforced by Caesar's heir, and then validated by the Pythagorean savant, Nigidius Figulus, and finally sanctified by Augur Spurinna, he who had forewarned Caesar to beware of the Ides of March.

At the conclusion of the games, Praetor Gaius Antonius, basking in the afterglow of the comet, proposes that the Senate decree that henceforth the month of Quinctilis be designated as *Juleus* in honor of the slain Dictator's birth month. "What better proof can we hope for of Caesar's divine status," Gaius Antonius postulates, "than the sight of his spirit flying across the heavens?"

So, it happens that the Dictator, whose assassination had been spoken of by some as an act of patriotic tyrannicide, is not only elevated to the Divine Pantheon, but his name, by the Senate's decree, is enshrined forever among the months of the Roman calendar.

A new divination paradigm has been formulated. The mob and the veterans, a would-be Caesar, and an ever obsequious Senate are empowered to interpret heavenly phenomena. Agnostics and skeptics could speculate that, if they exist at all, the gods might well be laughing.

Cicero's Elysian Voice

By the Ides of Sextilis, I had been at Rhegium for about two weeks. In vain, I waited for favorable winds to make the crossing to Messina. Each day, I watched the waves crashing against the twin promontories, Scylla on the Sicilian side of the Messina Straits and Charybdis on the Italian side. As I watched, I could not help but see an analogy to my own storm-tossed situation, buffeted by the waves of indecision and vacillation. Should I have returned to Roma from Antium? Should I perhaps have tarried longer at Antium? Could I call myself a patriot if I considered my own welfare above that of the Republic? How damnable it had been of me all during my career to be afflicted with this malady of irresolution!

At the time, I believed there was no reason for me to remain anywhere in Italia, let alone Roma. Marcus Antonius continued to lord it over the Republic, and Dolabella, my erstwhile son-in-law, was his fully cooperative partner, biding his time before going out to his province. Marcus Brutus and Gaius Cassius had already departed, ostensibly for their respective provinces of Crete and Cyrene.

Atticus, Quintus, and Servius encouraged my departure. In fact, my brother was particularly insistent in urging me to go abroad, sensing that there was bound to be a major rupture between Consul Antonius and young Gaius Octavius. Why then not remove myself from an increasingly volatile situation?

Had conditions permitted, I would have been content to remain in any of my country estates and pass the time by reading, contemplating, and writing. Atticus had visited me at Antium to tell me that my published treatises, *On Divination* and *On the Nature of the Goods*, were well received among Roma's literati. In particular, Varro and Figulus told him that the books' timely appearance came on the heels of the comet that many seers have postulated to be Caesar's divine soul ascending to the heavens. Appearing during the Appolonarian games, the comet was as good a reason as any for the Senate to change the name of Quinctilis to its new name of Juleus in honor of the assassinated Dictator.

The honors for this tyrant are ceaseless, even in death. This contributed to my desire to leave Italia, so that I might be spared hearing or seeing further insipid, posthumous honors for one who bestrode and subverted the Republic. So, I decided to accept Dolabella's proffered legateship in Syria.

Enroute to Syria, I planned to stop off at Athens and visit Marcus. However, rather than cross over from Brundisium, the most direct port for all Eastern bound travel, I had decided to go by way of Sicilia and thereby avoid the Macedonian legions, summoned by Antonius. Elements of these legions were already disembarking at Brundisium.

Unfortunately, I had not anticipated such stormy, contrary winds. As I waited for a break in the weather, I was completely surprised when a courier from Roma found me and brought me a letter from Servius Sulpicius. "Reconsider, my friend, your decision to leave Italia," he wrote. Unless I was fully resolved to participate in Dolabella's proconsulate, I should return to Roma and contribute to what could have been an opportunity to reconcile the feuding parties of the state.

Of late, Antonius was appearing to be conciliatory, and there was to be a Senate meeting on the Kalends of September to reconsider the recent provincial assignments implemented by the Consul. "Return then to Roma," Servius urged, "so that you can attend the Senate."

The delaying winds may have weakened my resolve to leave Italia, or perhaps it was weaker than I had thought it was when I had departed from Antium. Atticus, Quintus, and Servius had come down to Antium to bid me farewell. While they all supported my decision to leave, Quintus and Servius did not agree that Dolabella's provincial staff was an appropriate or fitting pretext for me. Servius had even told me that I was better off remaining at Athens rather than serving under my profligate ex son-in-law.

At any rate, after reading Servius' letter several times over the waves crashing against Scylla and Charybdis, I decided to forego the legateship and the trip to Athens, at least for the time being. Writing to Marcus, I explained this abrupt change in plans as a conflict between paternalism and patriotism. I urged him to be diligent with his studies and to forego the youthful indulgences that too frequently distracted him. By next spring at the latest, I wrote, I would cross over to Athens.

Then, packing our belongings, Tiro, Alexio, Metrodorus, and I paid our innkeeper at Rhegium and then started back to Roma. All during the journey home, I hoped I'd arrive in time for the September first meeting. In fact, we made very good time, arriving at the Palatine house at dusk on the thirtieth of Sextilis. Shortly after we had settled in, Quintus arrived.

"I thought you'd arrive between today and tomorrow," he explained. "You must have winded your horses to get here, and for *what?*"

"What are you talking about?" I asked him.

"The word being passed around is that the Senate is to discuss further posthumous honors for Caesar; *that and nothing more!*"

"What? What about the provincial commands? Servius wrote that...."

"A change in agenda," Quintus interrupted, "by the Consul's order."

I felt utterly exhausted. The rigors of travel had taken a severe toll on my almost sixty-three year old body. "Well then," I sighed, "I won't attend. I've not the strength, the stamina, or the will to endure such trivialities. I'm going to rest and catch up on the latest news, unless it's nothing but the same Antonian usurpatious and Octavian rabble-rousing."

Quintus shrugged. "As you wish; I'm sure Servius and others will be disappointed not to see you."

What an understatement this turned out to be. The Senate met at Jupiter's Temple on the Capitoline. Presiding Consul Antonius, upon noticing that I was absent, launched a vehement tirade against me. He demanded that I be dragged from my home and conducted under guard to the Capitoline. The senators sat in horrified silence until Antonius imperiously dismissed them.

"Why could my absence make any difference to him?" I inquired of Servius and Quintus.

"Antonius wants no dissenters," my brother replied. "Your absence spoke volumes. He knows you're in Roma. Had you been elsewhere, perhaps he wouldn't have been so perturbed."

The next day, I attended the Senate, intending to explain my absence from the previous day's session. Ironically, Antonius was absent and Dolabella presided in his place. (I was surprised that he had not already left for the East.) At Dolabella's invitation, I addressed the Senate.

"Conscript Fathers, I departed from Roma in the wake of the disorders attendant upon Caesar's funeral. From that time until now, the Consul Marcus Antonius has completely changed his policy from conciliation to usurpation. However, when told that the Consul was willing to cooperate with the Senate, I abandoned my plan of going abroad and returned to Roma. Then I learned that the Senate was to propose more honors for Caesar, honors that are nothing less than impious.

"While I supported the ratification of all of Caesar's acts, I cannot abide the implementation of mere promises and casual memoranda as though they had the force of law. In this, lay Antonius' major offense."

I turned and directly faced Dolabella who sat on the presiding consular chair. "Both Consuls would do better to see and pursue genuine civic virtue rather than dominion over their fellow citizens. As for myself, I have already proved my constancy. I will not fail to do so in the future."

My remarks were quite restrained. I had attacked Antonius only in the context of his public acts. In doing so, I purposely left open the possibility of an accommodation with the Consul.

The next day, Dolabella set out for Syria. He stopped off to see me, and he tried to persuade me to accompany him. But I was adamant in my insistence on staying. I felt both proud and apprehensive of my stance. About Dolabella himself, I still could not forgive him for his abuse, for his shameless treatment of Tullia. He warned me to beware of Antonius.

After Dolabella's departure for the East, a curious power vacuum developed. Antonius was said to have retired to his suburban estate of Tibur—the one he had appropriated after Pharsalus. The final decree of protest issued by Brutus and Cassius before departing for their province was making its rounds. They condemned Antonius's usurpations and declared that in the interests of peace they were going off to the provincial tasks assigned them by the Senate. But cautious speculation had it that their true destinations and intentions were far broader than procuring grain in Crete and Cyrene, even with the rank of proconsuls.

Strangely, little had been heard or seen of Gaius Octavius. I decided to withdraw from Roma and return to Antium.

Omniscient Narrative

Enroute to Brundisium and the East, Proconsul Dolabella detours off the Appian Road, and he heads for Antium. He cannot quit Italia and attend his proconsular duties without bidding farewell to Clodia Pulchra.

She is as beautiful, as fetching, and as alluring as mortal woman can be. Her olive and rose complexion is luminescent, and her copious ebony hair is like a regal crown. She exudes charm, flattery, enticement with subtle persuasion so that Dolabella is tempted to tarry awhile in Antium.

But Clodia does not wish him to stay longer than an evening's meal and a night of coital passion, which she knows will be their last. It is her way; Dolabella has served her needs, and now it is time for him to move out of her life.

Sensing that she's terminating their union, Dolabella drinks in her voluptuous beauty: her full, high breasts, tender and supple like the ripened fruit of summer, her hips and pubic mound, sensuous, succulent fleshy treasures.

Clodia nonchalantly bids him farewell and good fortune. Strangely, she senses that he will not return from the East. The Fates often coalesce with a woman's intuition; she had suspected that Cicero would not go with Dolabella after all; and she was proven to be correct.

Consul Marcus Antonius drinks heavily as he writes. He pours himself cup after cup of wine, and onto the parchment pages spread out on the mahogany table in his library he pours bitter invective into his words.

It is near dusk on a mid-September afternoon at Tibur. However unconventional it is for a Consul of the Republic to be absent from Roma, Antonius nonetheless has sought the peaceful, restful refuge of this suburban villa. Here, he believes, he may best think and remember and write a scathing reply to Marcus Cicero's speech delivered on the second. His own over-indulgence in wine the night before had prevented his attendance. Just as well, Antonius thinks, for had he been there, he might very well have torn the old *Chick-Pea* apart.

Antonius remembers and blames him for the execution of Catilina's men, so many years ago. One of them, Lentulus Sura, was Antonius' step-father, and there had been a mutual fondness between them. He blames *Chick-Pea* for the disrepute that befell his Uncle Gaius, who had been *Chick-Pea*'s consular colleague. He lays upon *Chick-Pea*'s hands the murder of their beloved Publius Clodius, Antonius' bosom friend and his wife's first husband. Antonius accuses *Chick-Pea* and Milo of conspiring to kill Clodius. In Antonius' catalogue of accusations, *Chick-Pea* had even contrived at Caesar's murder, even though he had been too cowardly to attend the Senate and participate in the deed or even witness it. What better proof of his cowardice than his retreat back to his seashore villa at Antium.

There have been many interruptions to Antonius' writing. At every opportunity, he plows away at Fulvia who regularly teases and cajoles his coital attentions. Fulvia enjoys having her husband so worked up, for he's truly in his element when he's in battle mode. He's all the more the Taurus when he has someone to gore, and she is convinced that *Chick-Pea* will inevitably discover this if he's foolish enough to return to Roma.

When not in the throes of passion, Fulvia and Antonius dote on their twins as well as on Fulvia's children by Clodius and Curio. They are good children, though somewhat spoiled. Yet, they are obedient and respectful, knowing when to leave their parents alone. The household nurses and pedagogues are ever vigilant and painstaking in their duties.

When the children have been retired to their own quarters, their parents host glittering dinner parties populated with actors, dancers, and other performers of uncertain talent—and gender. One of their regular guests is the notorious actress, Cytheris. Fulvia tolerates and yet resents her, for she knows that the over-painted wanton has been Antonius' infrequent lover. Fulvia will not back down from her, and she is confident that her husband will honor her ultimatum to break off all ties to the sensual thespian. Fulvia has always managed to have her way; Cytheris will be no exception.

Antonius and Fulvia may well have lost track of the days, but they have been at Tibur for nearly a fortnight. The next meeting of the Senate at which Antonius will preside is scheduled for the nineteenth. He and his speech will be ready.

Consul Antonius storms into the Capitoline Temple dramatically arrayed in battle uniform. He spews at the convened Senate, inveighing against Cicero's entire career: an upstart "new man" from Arpinum who climbed his way to office; political murderer of the Catilinians, especially the praetor Lentulus Sura; traitor to his consular colleagues, Gaius Antonius; the agent behind the murder of Publius Clodius; the impetus of the rupture between Caesar and Pompeius; the villainous contriver of Caesar's assassination. His invective attempts to unite all parties—Pompeians, Caesarians, Republicans—in an alliance against Cicero.

He is so enraptured in his oration that he is oblivious to those senators who, in pairs or trios, slip quietly out of the temple's cella. Quintus Cicero and Servius Sulpius are among the dissenters. Within minutes, others join them: Calpurnius Piso, Terentius Varro, Nigidius Figulus, and Marcius Philippus.

Most of those who remain seated are overcome with dismay and foreboding. They cannot fathom that the assassination on the Ides of March has foisted upon them this iron-fisted despot.

"Marcus Tullius Cicero would do well to stay far from Roma!" The Consul warns at the conclusion of his oration. Then, dismissing the Senate, he stamps out as imperiously as he had stormed in.

Cicero's Elysian Voice

Letters from Quintus, Servius, Piso, and Varro included excerpts from Antonius' September nineteenth address. I read and studied them thoroughly. Then, I wrote a rebuttal to his invective.

Against his charge of political murder in that I had executed his step-father, Lentulus Sura, and the other Catilinians: I wrote that they were conspiring to overthrow the state, to burn down Roma, and with the aid of Gallic mercenaries, to murder citizens and magistrates of the Republic. Authorized by the Senate's Ultimate Decree, I took decisive steps to forestall rebellion and arson, murder and pillage that the conspirators had planned.

Against his charge that I had plotted with Milo to murder Publius Clodius: I wrote that Antonius should consider whether or not *he* would have assassinated the demagogue if Caesar had so ordered it. It was widely believed that Caesar had wanted Clodius eliminated because he had become too truculent for the triumvirs' interests.

Against his charge that I had incited war between Caesar and Pompeius: I wrote that his own arrogance as Caesar's envoy had prompted the Senate to issue the Ultimate Decree and forced the Senate's mobilization for war.

Against his charge that I had conspired to murder Caesar: I wrote that had I been privy to the plot, I would have insisted on Antonius' removal so that we would not have had to suffer his tyranny. I accused him of having knowledge of the plot against Caesar, and yet he failed to protect its target. Did Antonius *want* Caesar killed so that now he could lord it over us?

Then, I attacked Antonius' private life. Though his grandfather had been a distinguished orator, consul, and censor, his father died, without attaining the consulate, while unsuccessfully conducting a campaign against the Cretan pirates. The Senate ridiculed rather than honored him with the dubious title of *Creticus*.

Antonius grew to manhood in poverty, a poverty of both material welfare and moral integrity. His mother used extremely poor judgment of character in marrying Lentulus Sura, a profligate renegade whose debts and debaucheries had caused him to be expelled from the Senate and then driven into the fatal intrigues of Lucius Catilina.

His Uncle Gaius had also been expelled from the Senate for his debts. But he managed to make a comeback with his election to the praetorate and then to the consulate as my colleague. I had had to buy his defection from Catilina.

In his young manhood, Antonius became the companion and intimate of Clodius Pulcher and Scribonius Curio, who serviced him as his catamite. Through them, he made the acquaintance of Fulvia, whose charms and ill-repute tore him away from his loving cousin-wife and their child. And so, on the pretext of Antonia's alleged infidelities with Dolabella, Antonius divorced her and took up with Fulvia immediately after Curio's death in Africa.

But even while married to Fulvia, Antonius persisted in his infidelities and gratified his lust and passion in debaucheries with courtesans, actresses, dancers, and all manner of riffraff as though not even Fulvia's warped sensualism, the Lupa with her twin sons, could satisfy his depraved appetites.

This then, was the character of Marcus Antonius, the Consul who would have discredited me and surpassed Caesar in his rape of the Republic. I concluded that he would do well to profit from the example of Caesar's murder.

Though I doubted that I would have occasion any time soon to deliver the oration, I hoped to publish it. I realized full well, however, that once it was published, there could have been no accommodation between Antonius and me. Inevitably, one or the other of us would have had to forfeit his life.

MY SON WROTE TO ME conveying the news that Marcus Brutus had arrived in Athens. Far from Crete, he was recruiting troops and gathering funds for his operations in Macedonia. Brutus would have to dislodge the official governor, Antonius' brother, Gaius, who had been appointed proconsul. Clearly, civil war was about to erupt in Macedonia. At the same time, Gaius Cassius, far from Cyrenaica, was likewise operating in Syria, and just as surely he would encounter opposition from Dolabella, the official Proconsul.

Writing to Brutus, I told him of my feud with Antonius, and I enclosed copies of my two speeches against him, the one I had delivered on September second and the other which I had just completed. I thought of them as my *Philippics* because in their tone and purpose they were similar to the orations delivered by Demosthenes of Athens against Philip of Macedon over three hundred years earlier.

I urged Brutus to judge for himself if I had properly named them. Certainly it was presumptuous of me to equate myself to the renowned Athenian orator whose speeches warned his countrymen against Macedonian aggression. But parallels run throughout history as the struggle against tyranny is ongoing in every polity that wants freedom for its own citizens. A redundant theme was the uncertainty of the times. No one knew what to expect under the incoming consuls, Hirtius and Pansa. No one knew what Decimus Brutus would do if Antonius attempted to dislodge him from the Cisalpina. And the most mysterious cipher of all was young Gaius Octavius. All through the spring and summer, this designated heir of Caesar had provoked numerous demonstrations against and confrontations with Antonius, all for the purpose of securing his adoptive name and inheritance which the Consul had thus far prevented. Out in Spain, Sextus Pompeius had defeated Gaius Pollio and was maneuvering against Marcus Lepidus.

I reminded Marcus Brutus that when he and Cassius and the others had struck down the Dictator, they fulfilled what the Great Man had predicted concerning his own demise, that his murder would only provoke civil war. I urged him to be prepared to follow through on all the consequences of their patriotic deed.

If there was to be civil war, as seemed likely in various parts of Roma's imperium, then there would be no reticence on my part. The foe was clearly recognizable, and there could be no accommodation with him; then Marcus Brutus, Decimus Brutus, Gaius Cassius and their compatriots should come to the Republic's assistance as expeditiously as possible.

I CONTINUED MY SOJOURN AT Antium, reading, writing, reflecting and anxiously anticipating news from Roma, especially if it was news of improved conditions.

Letters from Atticus, Quintus, and Servius reported an incident that clearly manifested Antonius' tyrannical disposition. On the day after the Kalends of October, Tribune Titus Cannutius convened a public meeting of the citizens in the Forum. Atop the Rostra, this brave fellow inveighed against Antonius' consulate. The Consul had the effrontery to attend, but his presence did not in the least intimidate the Tribune. In fact, by a clever rhetorical stratagem, he even induced Antonius to declare publicly his enmity to Caesar's assassins. Thus, the Liberators' friends and sympathizers, together with all true Republicans, were alerted. Any lingering doubts as to Antonius' true intentions were dispelled when he announced that Marcus Brutus, Gaius Cassius, and the others should be tried for the murder of Caesar. So, yet another crack undermined the compromise of March seventeenth. Men who had been given official amnesty were now to be tried as murderers and traitors.

Notwithstanding Antonius' announcement, one of the Liberators, Publius Casca, had defied the Consul by remaining in Roma instead of fleeing to some province as had the others, including his brother, Gaius the Tribune. Publius Casca, Tribune-elect, was to enter office in December, and he may have realized that in quitting the City he would forfeit his office.

Remarkable as it was that one of Caesar's assassins should have been elected to the plebeians' tribunate, it was equally unrealistic to hope that Antonius would respect his office. Quintus suspected that Casca and Cannutius were in league with another tribune, Decimus Carfulenas. If only others could have combined to oppose Antonius.

GAIUS OCTAVIUS, ACCOMPANIED BY HIS ever-present friends, Agrippa, Macenas, and Salvidienus, paid me an unexpected late night visit in mid-October.

"Forgive the intrusion, Father," he apologized as Tiro escorted the visitors into the atrium. Household servants were lighting additional oil lamps. "But there is urgency in my coming here, and secrecy forces me to come at night."

"You are welcome here at any time," I assured them. I invited them to sit down, which they did, and to partake of some wine which they politely refused. Octavius leaned forward from his chair and proceeded to divulge a bold plan which in audacity and ambition rivaled even the designs of Lucius Catilina.

"The despotism of Marcus Antonius is insufferable," he began. "He has not only denied me my inheritance, but he's also used my esteemed adoptive father's papers and treasury to lord over the Republic. Right now he's headed for Brundisium to receive the legions that he stole from Macedonia. I've raised a legion of veterans from the farmsteads in Campania. These men served under Caesar in Gaul and during the civil war, three thousand tough, loyal soldiers." He paused and looked intently into my eyes. "With them, I'll march on Roma. Then, with Tribune Cannutius, we'll demand the impeachment of Marcus Antonius. Father, this enterprise will succeed if *you* will accompany us."

Again, he was trying to embroil me in his schemes! Why would this youth not leave me alone?

"If you were to address the people they would listen. The Senate would rally to us. And Antonius would be brought down!" Octavius' hazel eyes held on me squarely.

I sighed deeply and swallowed hard. "What you propose is nothing less than revolutionary, and totally unprecedented. Beyond that, it's totally bizarre!"

Octavius' eyes narrowed and his body stiffened. His companions regarded me suspiciously.

"You're a private citizen and legally under age to hold any civic office. You would march on Roma with your own private army and attempt to impeach a Consul of the Republic? However tyrannical he may be, he's still a public magistrate and you're still a youth without office and legal authority."

"Father," Octavius calmly replied, "Gnaeus Magnus was not much older than I when he recruited three legions for Sulla. And like me, he too was without office and legal authority."

Yes, it was true. How many times had such revolutionary designs succeeded? Here was another would-be adventurer casting his future on an armed march on the City. And he wanted me along for the sake of legality and respectability!

Then Gaius Salvidienus put in, "We've already been active among the cohorts that have landed at Brundisium. They're committed to Octavius. In fact, when we were at Apollonia we made it our business to fraternize regularly with all ranks. So, you shouldn't think that Antonius is assured the loyalty of the Macedonian legions just because Caesar was to have led them on a new campaign."

Octavius placed his hand on Salvdienus' wrist to silence him, and then I said to him, "Octavius, I've advised you before to wait until Antonius leaves office. I still urge you to...."

"I *cannot* wait!" he insisted. "I've expended too much time and money already! I've borrowed from friends and relatives, and I've sold off some of my own property. I've bought the loyalty of the veterans and the favor of the City mob. There can be no turning back for me now, or *waiting*. If I back down from Antonius, I'm finished for good."

The youth's impetuosity matched his determination. I remembered his grand-uncle's determination in crossing the Rubicon in the pursuit of his own destiny.

In the end, I declined Octavius' offer, but I could not dissuade him from his purpose. After he and his friends departed, I sat alone in the atrium, thinking about the young man's antagonism with Antonius. I wondered how efficacious it might be for the Senate to exploit their antagonism, to play off Octavius against Antonius, to use him as a weapon as they had used Pompeius against Caesar. Like Pompeius, Octavius, I was sure, would be steadfast in his duties and purpose.

I thought of my son, wishing he could be equally steadfast. I wrote to him.

...While a host of reasons would impel me to leave Italia, at the same time I'm prompted to remain, though as yet I know not why. Perhaps in these uncertain times there is some duty that the Fates have reserved for me. I've had much time to contemplate my duties and services to the Republic. For you, my son, I've written a book entitled On Duties. *I'm enclosing a copy for you so that you will be encouraged to be diligent, steadfast, and conscientious in following a dutiful course in these troubled times.*

I implore you to pursue the four cardinal virtues that comprise moral goodness—justice, wisdom, courage, and temperance. Beware of the conflict between moral goodness and expedience. Read carefully the examples I've cited from the Academic, the Stoic, and the Epicurean schools. Into these schools of Greek philosophy, I've woven illustrations from Roman history so as to render the Greek ideas comprehensible to the Roman mind, yours, my son, and your peers.

More than anything else, I hope On Duties *will convince you of the necessity of service and devotion to one's country. Marcus, my son, you are all I have left. If you love your father, then please reform your life. Put* behind you the licentiousness of youth. Remember you are a Roman, the son of a consular. If you are considering enlisting in Marcus Brutus' forces, or if he has offered you a position, then I urge you to accept it. Serve well our beloved Republic.

After you've read On Duties, *please write. I'm curious to know what you think of it.*

Pax, salus, et vita
Your loving Father

Omniscient Narrative

Consul Marcus Antonius and his wife, Fulvia, with their escort of the Thirty-Fifth Legion, twelve lictors, and various and sundry attendants, are proceeding down the Appian Road toward Brundisium on a sun-drenched, vibrant afternoon in late October. Antonius has had no qualms about his many absences from Roma during his consulate. He trusts his brother, Tribune Lucius and his friends and supporters in the Senate to manage affairs in the City. This trip to Brundisium is entirely for official business; elements of the four Macedonian legions have landed at the busy port. The Consul has come to commandeer them, especially since there have been disturbing reports that Octavius' agents have been tampering with their loyalty.

Five miles distant from Brundisium, Antonius sees the legions' encampments. Straddling the roadway are neat, orderly rows, seemingly endless rows of canvass and leather military tents. Riding closer, he can discern the banners and eagle standards of the Second, the Fourth, the Martian, and the Alauda, or *Crested Larks,* Legions.

Upon passing through the encampments of the Martian and Fourth Legions, the Consul finds the soldiers in a rambunctious and insolent mood. They laugh contemptuously at Antonius' promises of generous bounties because Gaius Octavius, the accursed *Caesar-Boy's* agents, have lately visited them. Antonius now realizes that there is substance to the rumors. The legionaries have taken the adopted son's money; they have listened to sensational promises, and they have been incited to mutiny.

Antonius cannot allow the disease of disaffection to spread. He must resort to severe measures. Using cohorts from the two loyal legions, the Alauda and the Second, whose men apparently have not been sufficiently manipulated by *Caesar-Boy's* bribes, the Consul seizes three hundred mutineers, including a score of centurions and decurions, from among the trouble-makers. Approaching Fulvia's litter, which the mutineers have assailed with missiles of dung and other refuse, Antonius directs her, "Fulvia, you should withdraw."

Peering out from the litter's curtains, the Consul's wife will not hear of it. "Do what you *must*, my husband," Fulvia emphatically declares. "I'll *not* withdraw!"

"It's *not* going to be pretty, Fulvia. Don't cross me in this. *Withdraw!*"

Through clenched teeth, her face turning almost as red as her hair, Fulvia sneers, "I *will not*!" To her attendant major-domo, she commands, "See that the litter-bearers do not stir from this spot, and keep it aloft so that I can see the punishment!"

"Yes, Domina!" the slave humbly replies.

Exasperated and livid with anger, Antonius turns back to the assembled mutineers. "For insubordination and disrespect, these men, in accordance with ancient military discipline, will be *decimated!* Proceed with the punishment!"

Every tenth legionary from among the mutineers is pulled out of line, stripped naked, and then clubbed to death by the loyal soldiers supervised by officers of the Thirty-Fifth Legion. Atop her litter, Fulvia is close enough to the grisly scene for the soldiers' blood to splatter onto her face and bosom. She is repulsed and yet aroused by the spectacle. A warm, moist, sensual rapture envelops her breasts and thighs. Her heart pounds as though it would break free of her chest. She perspires as the sight of the battered and bruised and bleeding torsos of the soldiers brings her up and makes her shudder in ecstasy. Coming down from her climax, she almost swoons, for the decimation has moved her far more than anything she has ever seen in the Circus.

The object lesson is completed; Antonius and the officers of the loyal Alauda and Second Legions believe that sufficient order has been restored among the surviving mutineers. He orders the Alauda Legion to march with his escort back to Roma via the Appian Road. The other legions are to march northward along the Adriatic coast. With them, Antonius will assume the proconsulate of Cisalpine Gaul. There, he will face an enemy, the resident governor, Decimus Brutus, who may refuse to relinquish his command. But in Roma, he must deal with an insidious foe, Gaius Octavius and his agents. Unless they are eliminated, he cannot be certain of his legions' loyalty. Antonius knows this all too well.

Cicero's Elysian Voice

The crisis in Roma escalated from mid-November to early December as relayed to me in letters from Quintus and Servius.

"Confusion reigns," Quintus reported, "and we are surely on the precipice. Even the most haphazard nudge will topple us into civil war." He went on to relate that Gaius Ocatvius had entered Roma with his private army of Caesarian veterans and occupied the Forum. Antonius and his bodyguard were away at Brundisium, otherwise there would surely have been a battle.

Tribune Cannutius introduced Octavius to the crowd, who appeared to be quite bewildered by the entire situation. But when Octavius himself addressed them, the people recognized him and responded with greater enthusiasm.

Pointing to an equestrian statue of Caesar—actually more of a work in progress—that Antonius had ordered erected near the Rostra, Octavius read aloud the inscription carved on its base: "Best Deserving Parent." Octavius reminded the people of his own devotion to his revered, adoptive father. He reminded them of his recent generosity in paying them Caesar's bequests.

The bold young man was most politic. Lest he should alienate the men variously called Liberators or Patriots or Tyrannicides or Republicans or whatever else they might be deemed, he declared his hope for a rapprochement with Caesar's assassins in accordance with the March compromise. The proof of this came when, alluding to one of them, the Tribune-elect, Publius Casca, he admitted no objection to the fellow's assumption of office.

Amazingly, Octavius, though younger than my son and my nephew, used a statecraft far exceeding his years. In his address to the people, he exploited the breach within the Caesarians, trying to merge the moderates with the conservative Republicans into a new political coalition against Antonius. Despite their reduced numbers, these hardcore remnants of the old optimate faction had suffered the exactions of Antonius' agrarian board.

As Octavius continued with his harangue denouncing the Consul, there were sudden outcries that Antonius was within three days' march from Roma. The crowd began to disperse, some in fear, others in complete satisfaction. Even the veterans showed a marked disinclination to fight Antonius.

Realizing that his revolt had failed, Octavius wisely decided not to force the issue. He withdrew his army. Quintus wrote that according to public speculation, they had retreated to the environs of Arretium.

There was also much speculation about his next move. According to Atticus, Octavius was not yet finished; Atticus would have known because he and various other financiers had underwritten much of the young man's activities.

It was ironic that Octavius should bide his time and wait out events up at Arretium while I did the same at Antium.

Then Servius' letter reported that Marcus Antonius, after he had entered Roma and again made himself master of the City, called the Senate into an emergency session. Before some one hundred twenty senators, hardly a quorum, he accused Gaius Octavius of plotting to murder him. Though claiming to have the paid assassins in custody, he did not present them for interrogation. In view of this assassination attempt and the public outrage perpetuated by the armed march on the City, Antonius declared it imperative that the Senate issue an injunctive decree against Octavius.

However, before any debate or vote would ensue on the Consul's motion, couriers brought him reports of the defection of the Fourth and the Martian legions. It was said that these two legions had been decimated at Brundisium, but now they had totally mutinied and were reported to be proceeding by forced marches to Octavius' camp at Arretium.

Antonius peremptorily dismissed the Senate and then dashed off to Tibur, apparently to reaffirm the loyalty of the Second and the Alauda legions. Servius wrote that he was most eager to go after him and see first-hand whatever might happen at Tibur. He speculated that the legions might mutiny or Antonius might need to decimate them as well or perhaps these men might be totally loyal to Antonius. Servius even wanted to go up to Arretium and look in on Octavius.

Yet, his neutrality prevailed, and he did not venture anywhere. He mentioned that his persistent cough produced some traces of blood, and he was feeling more fatigued of late. Servius wished he had the same confidence in his own physician as I had in Metrodorus.

The general consensus of opinion was that with Antonius' imminent departure for his province, the Cisalpina was bound to become a battleground if Decimus Brutus refused to relinquish command. Between Roma and the disputed province was Gaius Octavius with a legion-strength force at Arretium.

SEVERAL DAYS LATER, ANOTHER LETTER arrived from Servius. "What a shameful spectacle I witnessed today! The convening of the Senate, of course at Antonius' bidding, resembled more a dress rehearsal of an actors' company than a meeting of the Republic's august body. There were even fewer senators present than there had been on the twentieth. Antonius marched in, sweating in his battle armor like a warrior just returned from combat with a vicious foe. Rumor had it that he had had to make exorbitant promises to maintain the loyalty of the two legions at Tibur. To some tribunes and centurions it was said he issued substantial donatives to quell their restlessness."

However, Antonius did not attempt to buy the Senate. Bullying the few who had heeded his summons, he cowed them into making a new round of provincial assignments. His brother, Gaius, was confirmed as Proconsul of Macedonia, and Calvisius Sabinus, one of Caesar's defenders, was named propraetor of Africa Vetus in succession to Quintus Cornificius. The most disturbing revision affected Marcus Brutus and Gaius Cassius. They were officially relieved of their proconsulates of Crete and Cyrene because these provinces, at least ostensibly, were slated for autonomy in the New Year. But Antonius' real purpose—stripping these two main assassins of their provinces—was all too transparent.

Antonius directed the Senate to decree a thanksgiving in honor of Marcus Lepidus because he had secured a truce with Sextus Pompeius. For the time being at least, there was a tenuous peace in the Spanish provinces.

Concerning this, Servius conjectured, "Antonius seeks to further ingratiate himself with Lepidus. He must appreciate the likelihood of having to drive Decimus Brutus from the Cisalpina by force. In this event, Antonius may need to call upon Lepidus for assistance. And of course, he must prevent an alliance between Lepidus and Decimus."

Antonius' last outrage upon them was the exaction of an oath of allegiance—totally meaningless, of course—from the senators and from his officers. Oaths can only be valid if they are freely given and only from a valid session of the Senate, when at least a quorum is present.

Leaving in Roma a frightened, disorganized Senate and a confused, demoralized populace, Antonius set out for his province. Ahead of him in Arretium lay Octavius, whose private army had been augmented by the mutinous Martian and Fourth legions. Further north in the Cisalpina, Decimus Brutus was entrenched in his headquarters at Mutina.

Servius concluded, "If I had religious sentiments, I'd wish for an oracle to foretell the magnitude of the tragedy that lies before us."

Omniscient Narrative

The bodyguard of Consul Marcus Antonius, some one thousand strong, occupies the streets and alleys adjacent to his Aventine house. They stand at attention as Antonius' twelve lictors line up on both sides of the entrance. Their fasces are held high on their left shoulders as the Consul walks through their formation and passes into the vestibule. The porter on duty bows respectfully, but Antonius hardly notices. He makes straight for the atrium where his family awaits him.

The first to be acknowledged is Julia, his mother. The formidable and elegant dowager offers her cheeks which he dutifully kisses. "My son, are you coming from the battlefield or are you going to it?" Julia alludes to her son's military garb, the bronze cuirass, the greaves on his shins, the officer's belt holding the gladius and pugio. He carries his scarlet crested helmet in the crook of his arm.

"We'll see soon enough, Mother," he answers her before moving on toward Fulvia. Without formality, he kisses her deeply on the mouth, embracing her with his free arm. Fulvia reaches up to his broad, armored shoulders and hugs him. She and her mother-in-law lock frigid eyes for an instant. "Can you stay for a while?" she asks her husband.

"The legions are already on the march," he says, looking into her hard, beautiful face. "They're taking the Flaminian Road to Ariminum and then the Aemilian to Mutina. I know it's indirect, but I can't afford to get entangled with Octavius at Arretium."

"I should go with you," his brother Lucius says. "I'm ready!" Lucius' plebeian tribunate has ended only two weeks earlier. Like his older brother, he is robust and bull-like, dark and dangerously handsome. He thrives on action, be it military or political.

"Not yet," Antonius disagrees, clasping his brother's right forearm. "I'll need you in Roma to keep an eye on my men in the Senate, especially the new consuls. If I get stymied up in Cisalpina, then I may need you there, or you may have to take on *Caesar-Boy* so that he won't harass my lines of communication with Roma."

"As you wish, Marcus."

"Uncle Gaius, how good of you to come!" Antonius embraces his uncle and former father-in-law. "But where's my daughter!"

Gaius Antonius minces words. "Well, ah, she's at home... she's with her mother."

Antonius' face darkens with annoyance. "Why didn't you bring her so I could see her before I leave?"

"Well, her mother... you see.... Antonia would not allow her to come."

Antonius exhales impatiently, remembering the animosity between Antonia and Fulvia. "Very well, I'll stop by the house. You know, Uncle, if you could manage some authority over your daughter, I might be inclined to sponsor you for the censorate two years hence. That's a plum post, don't you think?"

"Of course, Marcus, and I'd be honored."

"I'm sure you would." Antonius tosses his helmet to Lucius and then stoops to sweep up his sons into his strong, muscular arms. The two boys, now two years old, cackle with delight, pulling at his ears and pinching his large nose.

"Tata! Tata!" The twins coo at their father.

"Let's see the rest of my *treasures*!" Antonius swings about to see lovely twelve-year old Claudia and pugnacious, almost eleven-year-old Publius—Fulvia's children by Clodius. Five-year-old Gaius, Curio's child, is standing with them, contending with his step-brother for a place closer to Antonius. "And how are my gems today, eh? Behaving, I trust!" Antonius beams at them and they return their step-father's affection. The three of them embrace Antonius on every available side. "Mind your mother while I'm away, hear?"

"Yes, Father," Publius responds.

"We will, Tata," Claudia says, gathering little Gaius into her arms.

"I'll bring you back some Gallic wolf cubs to play with!" Antonius promises with arched eyebrows and a sardonic smirk.

"*Not* to this house you will!" Fulvia objects. "Bring *yourself* back—in one piece."

Antonius turns to Julia. "Mother, as long as Fulvia and the children will be in the City, why don't you stay with them?"

Fulvia grimaces, and sour glances are exchanged between the two women.

"Thank you, son," Julia replies, "but if Fulvia needs me, she'll let me know."

I'd sooner you'd go to Gaul, Fulvia thinks.

With Antonius' departure, everyone is left with something to consider. Lucius will not fail to safeguard his brother's interest in the Senate, while anticipating a possible provincial legateship. Uncle Gaius' political appetite has been whetted. A censorate would restore him to office in the Republic and crown a somewhat erratic career. The children, especially the older ones, will miss their step-father as he is likely to be away for some time.

And the two women—Julia has one son in possible harm's way in Macedonia. Now, her eldest sets out for a proconsulate fraught with peril, and not from the natives, but from another Roman governor. Lucius, her youngest, may well be in danger both within the City and in Cisalpina, should he need to go there. For Fulvia, Antonius' absence poses a danger that no one in their family has voiced. Should Cicero end his sojourn at Antium and return to Roma, what might he do to subvert Antonius' power? Her feminine intuition is alarmed, especially because young Gaius Octavius *Caesar-Boy* is still at large.

TERENTIA IS BORNE IN A litter to the home of Titus Pomponius Atticus. She keeps the litter curtains closed against the City's fetid, foul smells and the curiosity of many passersby. The eight study bearers make good time from her home in the Aventine to Atticus' house in the Carinae district.

Memories flood her mind—memories of the years she and Cicero had lived in the Carinae house that had once belonged to his father. In her recollections, it seems their lives had been happier then, perhaps because Cicero had not yet risen to the consulate and all the crises that had ensued from it. Quintus Cicero, she remembers, still lives in the Carinae house, perhaps with greater tranquility since his divorce of Pomponia.

Arriving at their destination, the litter bearers are directed by Philotimus, Terentia's officious freedmen, to set down the litter. She parts the curtain and looks out at the imposing brick and stone house, recently over-laid in travertine. Yes, she thinks, this is it. This is Atticus' house, a monument to his successful business enterprise.

Terentia waves away Philotimus' proffered hand. She emerges from the well-padded, well-cushioned litter on her own strength, assisted by her sturdy oak cane, a necessary weapon in the war against her chronic, debilitating joint pains. Leaning on it she proceeds slowly to the vestibule door while Philotimus and the litter bearers remain outside in the damp, December mist.

The porter easily recognizes Terentia and admits her. Despite the handicap of her joint pains and her all too obvious limping gait, she remains an attractive woman in her early fifties. Matronly stoutness and graying hair have failed to diminish her comeliness, though the somber colors of her palla and stola would seem to betoken an aggrieved woman.

Escorted to the atrium, Terentia is met almost immediately by Pilia, Atticus' wife. She is a handsome woman, tall, slender, with a square head, unconventionally bobbed hair, full eyebrows, light, round eyes, and a rather large, long nose. She and Atticus have been married for twelve years, and she is about as many years her husband's junior. They have a daughter, now about ten years old. A minute reflection of her mother's attractiveness, Caecelia Attica trails behind her into the atrium.

Mother and daughter greet their visitor almost simultaneously. "Terentia! Welcome! How good it is to see you." She kisses Terentia's cheeks, and indicates a set of chairs flanking a marble table. "Welcome, please sit down."

"Aunt Terentia!" The little girl calls as she reaches up to kiss her as well. "Can you tell Tata to let me in to his office so I can play secretary with him?"

The women laugh as they seat themselves. "I've told you, Caecilia, your father is busy with clients. You cannot play in his office just now." Pilia smiles affectionately at the child.

Terentia intervenes. "Dear, why don't you tell him that I'm here and that I need to speak with him for just a few moments?"

The child looks to her mother for approval. "Alright, Caecilia, go on, but don't pester your father."

"Mother, I'm not a *pest*," the child says before running off on her errand.

"Gods, the December chill is ruinous for my bones," Terentia says, extending her hands over a charcoal brazier on the tiled floor.

"I'm so sorry," Pilia commiserates. Rising, she takes a woolen throw from a chair next to her and places it across Terentia's lap.

"Oh, yes, that's better. Thank you, dear."

In the few moments that the women have with each other, they speak politely and haltingly about family concerns and they partake of heated wine sweetened with cinnamon and cloves. Terentia's health and joint pains are reviewed. Pilia says that they had been recently visited by Pomponia, and she had succeeded in unnerving Atticus. Apparently, Atticus' patience with his sister's boorishness has grown thin over the years. Briefly, Tullia is mentioned, and Terentia is moved to tears recalling her deceased daughter.

Atticus joins them and distracts the women from sorrowful recollections. He is both happy and surprised to see Terentia.

"Business must be thriving," Terentia says to him. "You look stouter than when last I saw you!"

Atticus pats his togated paunch and laughs. "Fortunately, Terentia, we equites no longer need to ride horses; otherwise they'd have to be very broad."

Terentia considers that he must be doing quite well judging from the ornate frescoes on the walls, the exquisite tile work on the floor, and the finely wrought oil lamps whose aromatic scents pervade the room. But by now, Terentia's joint pains start to annoy her, so she comes right to the point of her visit.

"I had a letter the other day from Marcus, my son, Marcus," Terentia begins. "He's joined Marcus Brutus, who has ambitious preparations under way in Athens. He's getting ready to invade Macedonia. I know I can't control my son's life anymore, especially when he's so far away, but my heart aches for him. I've not been able to sleep for worrying over him."

"So many fine young men will be choosing sides," Atticus opines, "in Greece, in Syria, even here in Italia, and perhaps even men who are not so young."

Terentia glares at him for stating in so perfunctory a manner the reality that has torn her heart asunder. Her tone becomes severe. "In his letter, as in all his letters, he's asked about Publilia. Have you had any news concerning her that's worth my son's knowledge?"

Atticus shrugs, shakes his head, and replies, "Since I took care of the dowry business, I've not heard from her or her family."

Terentia's tone is still more severe. "Atticus, you've told me Marcus is still at Antium. Though you've advised him to stay clear of the City, I know him far too well. In these aching bones I know that he won't detach himself from the current crisis. Now that Antonius has left, Marcus is sure to return. He should have gone to Athens to be with Young Marcus, or to Syria with that blackguard, Dolabella, or anywhere far from Roma. Instead, he returned to the Capital and provoked an unnecessary argument with Antonius; why, rather than retire again to Antium, why did he not leave Italia altogether?"

"So typical of Marcus to change his mind—*frequently*," Atticus remarks almost sardonically.

"Atticus, I implore you to dissuade Marcus from becoming embroiled in these struggles. He'll heed your opinion and your caution more than he will mine. Though I'm so pained on his account, I can't bring myself to write him directly, and these bones couldn't take the trip down there. Besides, I doubt he'd appreciate my solicitude."

Pilia is moved to tears by Terentia's entreaty. She looks at her husband, becoming annoyed at his silent, unmoved stiffness.

"Atticus, unlike my ex-husband, you've always managed to have an 'in' with *all* parties, especially since Caesar's murder and with all the contention that has ensued. I know you've expended loans to the assassins and you've been generous to Caesar's would-be heir. I'm sure you've kept Antonius mindful of your pecuniary services to Caesar throughout his dictatorship. No matter who emerges from this latest power scramble, it would be hard for anyone to cast aspersions on your political and financial acumen."

Atticus grimaces and sighs before replying. "Terentia, I'll convey your sentiments to him. I don't know that I'll have an opportunity to go down to Antium any time soon, so I'll write to him. For his own good, I too hope he remains far from Roma." Then Atticus inclines his head toward the house's interior, toward his office, and says, "The men I was just speaking with have told me that credit is tightening up and people are hoarding their money. I've seen these signs before. People are afraid. Civil war is looming and...."

"I don't care a *fig* about credit or money!" Terentia exclaims. "It's my son and my... the man who was my husband... I care about *them*! I don't want them to become victims if your *civil war* comes!"

The hard, practical man of business, of money and stocks and credit, is unnerved by Terentia's passionate outburst. The last time he had been as disturbed by a woman had been on the occasion of his own sister's visit. At that time, Pomponia, like Terentia, had sought his intervention to keep Quintus Cicero, her ex-husband, and young Quintus, their son, from following Marcus Cicero into a new fiery abyss of blood and havoc. Atticus knows that when family and politics intersect, it is difficult to curry favor with all contending parties.

Cicero's Elysian Voice

On the Ides of December, I was remembering that the Great Man had been killed exactly nine months before, struck down by assassins who anticipated the immediate return of the free Republic with the Dictator's death. Instead, a new dictator had come to power, trampling upon the terms of amnesty and compromise. Soon thereafter, Antonius was challenged by Caesar's grand-nephew and adopted heir. In the ensuing confusion, the Republic's Liberators were forced to flee. While Marcus Brutus and Gaius Cassius built up their power in the East, young Gaius Octavius, with three legions, sat astride the Via Cassia at Arretium provoking much fearful speculation as to his ultimate designs. In a few weeks, the new consuls, Hirtius and Pausa, were to take office. Would they truly support the Republic, or would they become Antonius' pawns?

Two letters reached me. The first, from Atticus, urged me to stay put in Antium or go abroad for some time at least until the uncertainties were resolved, one way or the other. He mentioned Terentia several times; she had professed her heartfelt concern for my safety.

Though Antium, with the entire Tyrrhenian seashore, was lovely and exhilarating in spring and summer, one would be hard-pressed to imagine a drearier locale in winter. Yet, as much as I would have quit the place, I could not fathom going outside Italia. Something, some unknown force, kept me locked at the villa.

In the midst of my indecision, a second letter came to me. Enclosed in it was a copy of a proclamation from Decimus Brutus Albinus, Proconsul of Gallia Cisalpina. It had been sent to the Senate and was written from Mutina on the Kalends of December.

Conscript Fathers,

Having been named by the Senate and People Proconsul of the Cisalpina for a term of two years and having received the imperium, I will not relinquish command because of the capricious whims of Consul Marcus Antonius. I will retain my command and I will resist any attempt by the Consul to dislodge me. This I pledge to the Senate and People of Roma on my honor as a citizen and magistrate of the Republic. Decimus Junius Brutus Albinus
Proconsul of Gallia Cisalpina

Then, the letter specifically addressed to me read:

Marcus Cicero, your friends and colleagues in the Senate have sent you this copy of Decimus Brutus' edict. We urge you to read it carefully and to consider its implications. We hope you will correctly infer our intentions. We await your decision. The Republic needs you. Do not fail us.
Servius Sulpicius Rufus
Marcus Terentius Varro
Lucius Calpurnius Piso
Publius Nigidius Figulus
Aulus Hirtius – Consul-Designate
Gaius Pansa – Consul-Designate
Written from Roma on the Nones of December in the Year DCCX
From the Founding of the City.

A fervent hope thrived in me that our Republic could be saved from tyranny. If Decimus could hold out; if Octavius' private command could be legitimized and utilized by the Senate, and if the new Consuls remained loyal to the Republic, then could not Antonius be destroyed?

From Greece, Marcus Brutus had earlier written me, urging that I be wary of Octavius. He urged me to cross over to Epirus and then travel to Macedonia which he expected to control early in the New Year. Atticus had also repeatedly urged me to wait out events, to avoid committing myself to a fight against Antonius. But for how long could I have waited in self-imposed exile, in shameful inactivity?

Even the *Medusa Quadrantaria*, the *Black-Eyed Juno of the Palatine*, had an opinion and advice for me. She visited me, as usual, totally unexpectedly. Her excuse was to wish me a felicitous Saturnalia, as the holiday season was fast approaching, but I saw through this immediately.

"Why have you come here, Clodia?" I asked her almost curtly. "What do you want?"

"*You,* Marcus Cicero; I want *you.* Surely, that doesn't surprise you." She smiled and her ebony eyes glowed. Her raven-black hair hung about her shoulders, falling upon the folds of her gown, a garment of the peculiar color of nearly ripened olives. "Come with me to the East," she urged. "Together, we can flee from this madness. We'll lose ourselves among the Aegean isles, some of them so small they're not even charted."

"*Why, Clodia?*"

"I want you. I need you. Come with me!"

I shook my head in disbelief at her incredible proposition. Yet, I believed that she truly expected me to consider it.

"What's to keep you here, Marcus? You really think you'll make a difference? You will keep from happening what's meant to happen? Antonius will destroy or he'll be destroyed. You think you will help or hinder this? Decimus will fight or he'll surrender. What of it? Octavius will get his inheritance or he'll die trying. So what? Why should you care—for the Republic?" She laughed contemptuously. "Have you not learned that this Republic is a sick, enfeebled old harlot crying out for destruction and a merciful death? That's what Caesar knew! That's what he was trying to do. But they killed him. They thought they were going to revive the harlot, make her strong, vibrant, and beautiful again. What idiotic dung!"

She moved in closer to me and I could smell the perfumed scent of her ardor. "Marcus Cicero, if you thrust yourself into this fight, there will be no Caesar to pardon you at the end. There will be no banishment. There will be only *death!* Come with me! Forget all this! *Come with me!*"

Her arms encircled my neck and she pulled my face down to hers. She kissed me hard, passionately on the mouth, and I responded in kind. Her mouth was moist, warm, her tongue sweet, strong. The core of my life, of my being, for the first time in many years was aroused. It was an effort to pull myself from her. "I cannot go with you. I'm a senator, a consular. I can't abandon my… I cannot." The passion that I felt at that moment I had not felt since my exile.

"*Why?* What can you not abandon?" she demanded. "Your country… your destiny?"

"Can you understand what I'm seeking, Clodia? Is it preferable to undertake an uncertain journey with you than to accept the proffered leadership of the Senate? I know both alternatives are fraught with peril."

"You'll not stop what's meant to be," she warned me again.

"I could flee with you into obscurity and safety, preserve my life and let the Fates take their predestined course. *Or,* I could seize this opportunity…."

"*To die!*" Clodia interrupted.

"… to *redeem* myself. That's what I've longed for. This is my last chance to defend the Republic and redeem my life from the ignominy of defeat, compromise, and accommodation."

Clodia's eyes filled with tears, but her enigmatic smile was constant. She shook her head in dismayed resignation.

I WAS RESOLVED TO RETURN to Roma and take up the leadership of the Senate in its fight to save the Republic and liberate it from the tyranny of Marcus Antonius. *The die was cast.*

Caput XVIII

There is nothing more acceptable to the chief of the gods who rules over the Cosmos, of all things that happen on the earth, than the councils and gatherings of men who associate together in respect for law and justice; that is, the organizations called states.

From "The Dream of Scipio" in *De Re Publica*

Cicero's Elysian Voice

Returning to Roma, I learned that two of the new tribunes, Publius Appuleius and Publius Casca, in the absence of the consuls and praetors, had called the Senate to convene on December twentieth. We met in the Temple of Concord. I could not help but recall the crucial debate that had taken place there so many years before when I led the Senate in crushing the Catilinian menace. Now, a new menace bestrode the Republic.

At first, attendance was slight, but apparently the news of my arrival encouraged the reticent to follow my example. Caesarians, optimate remnants, and neutrals filed into the temple's cella, seating themselves on the wooden benches.

The tribunes were implacable foes of Marcus Antonius. Short, bald-pated Casca was like a satyr with dark eyes and thin black whiskers framing his swarthy cheeks and chin. He was the only one of Caesar's assassins to remain in Roma. Appuleius was of medium stature, round, stocky build, and ruddy complexion. His face was dominated by heavy apple-like cheeks that shook when he spoke. He proposed that the Senate nullify the last round of provincial assignments ordered by

Antonius. Then he moved for the assignment of an armed guard for the protection of the incoming consuls Hirtius and Pansa.

As the senior consular present, I was the first to speak. I regretted the delay in taking action until January first, by which time the new consuls would have entered office. Hirtius and Pansa should have been assigned a bodyguard immediately instead of having to wait until the commencement of their term. I also proposed that Octavianus and the Martian and Fourth Legions be commended, for by their actions they had prevented Antonius from massacring those citizens who would not submit to his authority.

I referred to Caesar's grand-nephew as Octavianus rather than as Octavius, and in so doing I was extending oratorical recognition to the young man's adoption although it had yet to be formalized. Hopefully, the moderate Caesarians could be consolidated in the Senate's battle against Antonius.

I extolled Decimus Brutus as a worthy descendant of his ancestors who had expelled the dreaded Tarquin kings, and I denigrated Antonius as a tyrant surpassing them in villainy. I proposed that the Senate confirm Decimus Brutus' initiative in holding Cisalpine Gaul.

Next, I proceeded to attack Antonius' entire consulate as a subversion of the fair accords negotiated in the aftermath of Caesar's assassination. In particular, his provincial assignments were arbitrary and capricious and deserving of the Senate's annulment. He had usurped the Dictator's power, aiming at the supremacy of the state. Even his brothers, Gaius and Lucius, were no less reprehensible.

"A consul who behaved as Antonius has behaved should not be regarded as consul. Therefore, the legions and Ocatvianus and Decimus Brutus have not acted criminally, but *patriotically* in their opposition to him. With Brutus and Caesar Octavianus as their champions, the Senate must seize the opportunity and act with vigor.

"The Roman people, born to be free, can now achieve freedom. This day, and my exertions and pleading, for the first time brought to the Roman people the hope of the recovery of their liberty."

There was little dissent from my motions. Following the senatorial session, I mounted the Rostra and, introduced by Appuleius and Casca, I addressed the citizens in the Forum. The equites and senators were huddled closely about the Rostra, serving as a barrier against the fractious, vulgar dregs who had no conception of liberty.

I announced that measures had been taken for the protection of the new consuls; that honors and commendations had been voted to Octavianus, to Decimus Brutus, and to the soldiers of the Martian and Fourth Legions, and to the loyal provincials of Cisalpine Gaul, and that the provincial assignments of November twenty-eighth were nullified.

"Citizens, these measures implicitly declare Marcus Antonius to be an enemy of the Republic. This struggle against the tyrant, with whom no conditions of peace are possible, is to decide not only the liberty of the Roman people, but whether they shall be permitted to live at all. Citizens, show that valor of your forefathers that made the Romans the conquerors of the world!"

The applause of the senators and the equites went in tandem with the catcalls and heckling of the insolent mob.

QUINTUS WAS WITH ME AT the Senate as well as on the Rostra. I was proud that his son was also there with us. Young Quintus, it seemed, had forsaken the Caesarian party and had returned to his father's counsels. Both my brother and I were most gratified by his change of direction.

Tiro began copying these two orations, my Third and Fourth Philippics. They were soon to be published, along with my Second Philippic, which had never been publicly delivered. Atticus' copyists were busily engaged. He assured me with sullen gravity that by the next Senate meeting on the Kalends of Januarius, all who would have read the orations would understand how committed I was to ridding the Republic of the Antonian menace.

On the first day of the New Year, the new Consuls were inaugurated. Both were stolid, no-nonsense military types, but all good men of the Republic hoped that their patriotism was keen and energetic. Hirtius, the elder of the pair, was tall, broad, and brutish looking, almost like a veteran gladiator. By his appearance one would hardly have expected him to have had any literary inclinations. Yet, he was credited with the authorship of the final book of Caesar's *Gallic War Commentaries*, as well as the chronicles of Caesar's Egyptian, Asian, African, and Spanish wars.

The other consul, Pansa, looked like a rustic goatherd from Apulia. He was a short, broad-framed man with a head seemingly carved from a block of oak and topped by coarse russet and gray hair. His face was lined and weathered.

They convened the Senate in the Capitoline Temple of Jupiter immediately after their inauguration and laid before them the state of public affairs. Since the Senate's last meeting, Marcus Antonius had invested Decimus Brutus in Mutina, and Gaius Ocatvianus was on the march toward the Cisalpina.

Pansa first called upon his father-in-law, Quintus Calenus, to deliver his opinion. This leader of the Antonian faction had the face of a predatory hawk and the sly demeanor of a lurking wolf. He advised the Senate to avoid the extremity of war against Antonius. Instead, he proposed that an embassy, consisting of neutrals, be sent to Antonius to instruct him to raise the siege of Mutina and submit to the Senate's authority.

It was supreme folly for Calenus to expect Antonius to be mindful of the Senate's counsels, for the renegade was attacking a proconsul in his own province. Antonius had trampled on the Senate when he was Consul. Were we to believe that with an army at his back and while making war on a fellow magistrate he would be reasonable? Nevertheless, many of the moderates spoke in support of Calenus' motion. These included the Valerii Messalae, Lucius Piso, Marcus Varro, Publius Figulus, and, much to my own amazement, even Servius Sulpicius. Despite the events of the recent past, these men believed that negotiation, however futile, was preferable to war.

When I spoke, I deprecated any attempt at negotiation with Antonius. At the December twentieth session, the Senate in effect had branded him a public enemy by commending Octavianus and the Fourth and Martian Legions that had deserted Antonius. Octavianus and the legions were presently en route to the relief of Decimus Brutus in Mutina. It was therefore inconceivable that the Senate could treat of peace with a virtual public enemy.

I reminded the senators yet again of Antonius' consular improprieties and illegalities. By virtue of his siege of Mutina, a colony of the Roman people, he was actually prosecuting war on his own countrymen. To send an embassy would only delay the war and weaken the universal indignation.

To Decimus Brutus for resisting Antonius, and to Marcus Lepidus for persuading Sextus Pompeius to desist from further aggression in Spain, I proposed a vote of thanks. Furthermore, I proposed that a gilt equestrian statue of Lepidus to erected on the Rostra or elsewhere in the Forum. (By this gesture, I was gambling that Lepidus might detach himself from Antonius.)

Then, I proposed that Caesar Octavianus, whom I pledged "would always prove such a citizen as the Senate ought most to wish him to be," should be elevated by the Senate's decree to propraetorian rank; he should have a seat in the Senate, and he should be allowed to stand, despite his young age, for the consulate.

My advocacy of Octavianus was the most controversial element of my speech. After all, he was the murdered Dictator's grand-nephew and designated heir, and he had never held any of the elective offices because he was legally under age. I had even told him this when he had requested my help for his "March on Roma." But, he had an army under his command, and for the Republic's sake I was trying to legitimize his position.

FOR THE NEXT THREE DAYS, the Senate was torn by fierce debate over Calenus' motion and my counter-motions. Among the Antonians, the new praetors, Marcius Censorinus and Ventidius Bassus, were the most emphatic speakers on behalf of an embassy to Antonius. My brother and the ex-tribune Cannutius spoke against it, but in support of my proposals. Piso, Varro, and Servius also spoke in support of them, but they also favored the embassy to Antonius.

How I wished others of my circle could have been present for the debate. Sadly, men like Gaius Pomptinus and Lucius Flaccus, who had helped me crush Catilina's conspiracy, were among the casualties of Pharsalus. They would certainly have supported my proposals and denigrated any embassy to one behaving like another Catilina. So would Publius Sestius and Gaius Plancius, who had helped me during my exile. But they too had been killed during the civil war. Good, reliable friends and allies, struck down in fratricidal strife, Roma's renewed curse.

On the third day, Antonius' mother, Julia, and his wife, Fulvia, and her children appeared before the Senate, having been brought in by Tribune Salvius against ancient custom and tradition which banned women and children from the Senate's deliberations. Attired in the gray and black garb of mourners, they beseeched the senators with pathetic supplications to negotiate with Antonius. Catching sight of me, Fulvia glared venomously as she spoke. "Senators, do not heed the calumnies that have been written and spoken against my husband and our family. Instead, remember Antonius' services to Roma. Do *not* make war upon him! Instead, send men of honor to deal with him. I know my husband better than *all* of you. He will not disregard the Senate's envoys. I and my children and my husband's mother *implore* you, Conscript Fathers!"

The debates ended the day before the Nones. Escorted by Quintus, Servius, the moderates, and a large number of equites, I went down to the Forum and ascended the Rostra. Tribune Appuleius called the people to order and bade them give ear to me.

After summarizing the conflicting proposals and the ensuing debates, I told them of the Senate's final disposition. "The proposed honors for Decimus Brutus and Caesar Octavianus have been carried, and Calenus' motion for an embassy, thanks to the intervention of Tribune Salvius, has also been approved. The appointed envoys are: Servius Sulpicius Rufus, Lucius Calpurnius Piso, and Lucius Marcius Philippus. They have been charged to order Antonius to submit to the Senate; to abandon the siege of Mutina; and to withdraw his legions to the Italian side of the Rubicon River, but not nearer to Roma than two hundred miles. They are to convey to Proconsul Decimus Brutus the Senate's approval of his actions and of the legions defending Mutina."

I attributed the Senate's leniency to some hope or other, but I knew not what. Despite the futility of sending an embassy—for I predicted that Antonius would not submit to the Senate's will—the Roman People had to wait patiently for the envoys' return. In the interim, I pledged to watch over the interests of the Republic. "Other nations can endure slavery," I told them, "but the Roman People's peculiar possession is Liberty."

Returning home, I reflected on the Senate's choice of envoys. It was all too apparent that they were striving for diplomatic balance. Servius' selection was no doubt based on his legal expertise and his friendship with me. Marcius Philippus' inclusion was motivated by the fact that he was Octavianus' step-father. Lucius Piso, as Caesar's father-in-law, was acceptable to both Caesarians and Antonians. In the wake of that fateful Ides of March, Calpurnia, Piso's widowed daughter, had vacated the Regia and was now living with her father. I speculated that Piso's selection was, in part at least, a tribute to Caesar's widow.

Tiro began immediately to transcribe the orations of early January which I designated my Fifth and Sixth Philippics.

On the sixth of the month, I realized that it was my birthday; I had turned sixty-three. Servius Sulpicius wished me felicitations when he stopped by before leaving for the Cisalpina. Since my return to Roma, I had noticed that he looked ill. During the Senate meetings, he struggled to stifle his persistent cough. When he spoke, it was with difficulty as his voice lacked the power that it had had of old. He looked so wan and fatigued, and he complained of difficulty breathing.

"Servius, don't go!" I begged him. "You're ill, too ill to make such an arduous journey for a task laden with so much peril. The winter's raw winds and rains will weaken you. They say the Cisalpina is having immoderate snowfall that will only impede the embassy."

"No, I must go," he insisted in a tremulous, raspy voice. "The Senate has charged me to go with Piso and Philippus."

"Someone can go in your place, any one of the moderates who believes in negotiating with that *monster*. This whole embassy is a fool-hardy enterprise. It will only result...."

"Marcus, I've not the strength to debate with you." Servius put out his hand to me. "Farewell, Marcus. Farewell, good friend."

An eerie foreboding came over me as I clasped his hand in mine. I fought back a choking sensation in my throat. "Hail and farewell, Servius. Return soon and safely."

The weeks passed slowly as we waited for the embassy's return or for news of its progress. Though I still believed that it would accomplish nothing but to dampen the Senate's ardor in its war against Antonius, I could not help but admire the courage, the fortitude, and the patriotism of the envoys in accepting their mission.

While waiting for their return, the Senate wisely made contingency provisions. Consul Hirtius was commissioned to conduct military levies throughout Italia. It was decreed, for our own security, that we wear the military garb of leather and mail coats and cloak instead of the civic garb of toga and tunic at all sessions of the Senate. In Hirtius' absence, Consul Pansa was to have the sole duty of presiding over the Senate. However, he deferred to me in most matters, so that most of the senators began to regard me as *Princeps Senatus*—First Senator of the Republic. This was a far different situation from that of the previous year. Fortune is fickle.

Calenus began circulating letters purportedly from Antonius. Rumor had it that Antonius was inclining toward compromise on the question of his Cisalpine proconsulate. I addressed these developments in an oration in the Senate.

"Conscript Fathers, preparations for war are continuing in Roma and throughout Italia despite the attempts by the embassy and by Antonius' friends to quench the public's bellicose spirit. I too am for peace, but there can be no peace unless we first wage war; if we shrink from it, we shall never have a secure peace. There is nothing I dread more than war disguised as peace.

"Peace at this time would be dishonorable as it would show inconsistency and vulnerability on the part of the Senate when it has, in effect by its decrees, branded Antonius an enemy of the Republic. Peace would be dangerous because it would lead to Antonius' unmerited holding of a consular seat among the Conscript Fathers. Peace is impossible between Antonius and the municipalities; between Antonius and Caesar Octavianus and Decimus Brutus; between Antonius and the Roman people.

"Antonius must yield, for if he does not, then he has declared war upon the Roman People, whose liberty hangs in the balance. Consul Pansa must lead the Senate in freeing the Republic from this beguiling danger of a bogus peace. Antonius must yield or be destroyed!"

Lucius Antonius replied to my oration. "Marcus Cicero, how long will you persist in your antagonism to my brother? *You* are the most obdurate barrier to peace. *You* opposed the embassy. Now *you* deprecate overtures from Marcus Antonius that could lead even to a truce. Beware, Marcus Cicero! *Your* calumnies will redound upon *your* own head!"

The Antonian faction, headed by Calenus, Bassus, and Censorinus, applauded Lucius Antonius' remarks. But I was satisfied to have blocked any discussion of peace, at least pending the embassy's return.

Omniscient Narrative

The publishing house of Titus Pomponius Atticus is located in the Caelian district just within the City walls. In a large, well-illumined room, one hundred copyists are seated at a score of pine tables and engaged in painstakingly copying Cicero's orations against Marcus Antonius.

Atticus goes from table to table, inspecting the work. The copyists, for the most part, are slaves. They work with reed pens, dipping them into small pots of resinous, lampblack ink, and then transcribing Cicero's words from his original manuscripts onto parchment rolls. Atticus considers the profits he will gain from the sale of these *Philippic* orations. Cicero's royalties should be impressive as well, though his choice of subject matter is laden with danger. The *Second Philippic*, though never delivered, has found life, through Atticus' publication, as a vitriolic political manifesto against Marcus Antonius and his entire family. Even his wife, Fulvia, has been the target of Cicero's vituperation. Atticus has heard from her, and the *Lupa's* blood is hot for revenge.

His reverie is interrupted by Pomponia's loud, boisterous voice. "*Titus!* They told me I'd find you here," his sister announces.

"Pomponia—what an *unpleasant* surprise!" Atticus looks at her, grimacing without apology. "Please lower your voice, lest you disturb my scribes."

Pomponia leans over the nearest table and recognizes Cicero's words. "*The Seventh Philippic of Marcus Tullius Cicero Against Marcus Antonius*," she reads aloud as a sour, dyspeptic expression covers her hard, painted, lined face. She stands up as straight as her short, doughty frame, draped in brown stola and yellow palla, will allow her. "He's at it again! He's at his *Big Brother's* elbow—there to nudge, or take notes, or to coach if *Big Brother* forgets a name or place or date."

"You're speaking of Quintus?" Atticus queries.

"Yes, my Quintus, or should I say my *former* Quintus? He always twitched under his brother's toga. But he did little to get out from under it and make his own mark. It always had to be Marcus Tullius Cicero and little brother, Quintus. *God's piss!* If he doesn't get out of his brother's toga folds soon, he'll be dragged down the Cloaca Maxima in them as surely as Marcus Antonius jumps and mounts and rides!"

Pomponia slaps a parchment roll to the stone floor. "They've even dragged my son into it! It's not enough that his uncle and his father must play *Heave the Tyrant and Save the Republic*. Must Young Quintus follow them into perdition? I've written to him; I've begged him not to sacrifice himself. He's so young! He's plenty of time to make his political ties when this storm passes. I've offered him money. I've offered to send him to Athens where he could stay with his cousin until this stew has finished brewing...."

"You don't know, Pomponia," Atticus interrupts her, "that Marcus is no longer studying at Athens? He's joined Brutus, and by now they're probably on the march into Macedonia."

Pomponia is dismayed. "Titus, for god's sake, *talk* to them. Tell them to quit this foolishness if they want to live."

THE WIND-SWEPT WALLS AND RAMPARTS of Mutina are hard, impenetrable obstacles to Marcus Antonius' ambitions. Bitter cold assails both the town's defenders and its assailants. Armored and draped in a scarlet military cloak, Proconsul Antonius walks in a rapid, fervent pace along the southern arc of his circumvallation lines. The envoys from Roma are hard-pressed to keep up with him. In particular, Servius Sulpicius is painfully winded trying to follow behind the Proconsul's vigorous gait.

Antonius proudly shows them his assault ramps of timber and stone rising and advancing closer and closer to Mutina's walls. Ballistae and catapults hurl deadly, destructive missiles against the besieged. The cold, heavy air is thick with the cracking and whirring reverberations of these war machines. Mutina's defenders answer in kind, assailing Antonius' defenses with their own projectiles of propelled death. The envoys duck and dodge to avoid the incoming missiles.

Piso does most of the talking, conveying the Senate's terms. Antonius listens contemptuously, feigning attentiveness to them but concentrating his attentions instead on the progress of his siege works. At last, the Proconsul speaks, rejecting the terms out of hand. His counter-terms are that all of Caesar's memoranda, which Antonius had implemented, are to be upheld.

"For my part," Antonius demands, "I'll give up Cisalpina in exchange for the Transalpina with Decimus Brutus' legions augmenting my own for a five-year term. To make sure my exact words are conveyed to the Senate, Tribune Popillius Laenas will accompany you back to Roma."

"Proconsul, we'd hoped that you would allow us to pass through to Mutina so that we may bring the Senate's tidings to Proconsul Decimus Brutus." Piso's request darkens Antonius' insolent visage.

"*This* I will not allow. Your embassy was to *me*, not to Brutus. You accomplished your mission, and now you may return to Roma. I'll send my own tidings to Brutus." With a wave of his hand, Antonius signals for a new volley of ballistic and catapulted missiles to be shot at and over Mutina's walls. Stones, iron spikes, and flaming balls of pitch arc across the clear, hard winter sky.

The envoys' spirits sink into despair as they realize the utter futility of their embassy. Cicero had been right to oppose it, for it has served no purpose. After a quick military meal and a few hours' rest, they start on their return journey in the midst of snow, wind, and cold which impede their progress. Servius Sulpicius, ailing and fevered, does not disclose to his companions that he is coughing up blood as though his innards were mangled.

Piso prevails upon the sick man to be carried in a litter, and this further slows their journey home. Couriers are dispatched to Roma with the news of their imminent arrival. By the time they arrive at Arretium, Servius is too ill to continue. His companions confine him at an inn. Their intention is to leave him with several aides and then press on to Roma in the morning. However, during the night, Servius expires.

Cicero's Elysian Voice

"The embassy has suffered an irreplaceable casualty in the death of Servius Sulpicius Rufus." With these words, I began my address to the Senate when the envoys returned on the third of Februarius. "It is calamitous that the aged and infirm consular should have consented to make the difficult winter journey in so futile a cause. But Servius Sulpicius performed his duty as he saw it.

"*Duty*. What is the duty of the Senate? To play with words? To warp and distort them into oblivion? Only yesterday, Consul Pansa and Calenus proposed that Antonius be designated *adversary* rather than *enemy* of the Republic; that a *tumult* rather than a state of war be declared.

"Conscript Fathers, I urge you to remember that all of Antonius' conduct and all of the martial preparations in Italia vividly show the renegade Proconsul to be nothing less than a public enemy, provoking war against the Republic!

"Conscript Fathers, has there ever been a tumult without a *war*? If not war, then what is the meaning of the levies throughout Italia? Of the siege of Brutus in Mutina? Of the operations of Consul Hirtius and of Caesar Octavianus against Antonius? If indeed a state of war does *not* exist, why then has the Senate decreed military garb in place of the civic toga?

"We who have seen the futility of the embassy which cost the life of Sulpicius, can we treat of sending a second embassy, as some have proposed? What will it accomplish? Will not Antonius press on with the siege of Mutina? Will he not demand again that we grant land and money for his legions? That we leave intact his consular acta and decrees supposedly based on Caesar's memoranda? That we accept his forfeiture of Cisalpine Gaul so that he may wrest the Transalpina and with an even stronger army lord it over the Republic?"

Undercurrents of approbation and dissent rippled across the Temple of Concord's cella. I did not attempt to assess their exact nature as I pressed on with my oration.

"Antonius' terms are intolerable! We will not suffer to hear these terms from a second embassy, nor will we tolerate in our presence a second agent from Antonius to complement his first, Tribune Popillius, who had the effrontery to set these shameful outrages before the Senate.

"I propose that the Senate decree an amnesty for all those with Antonius who should lay down their arms before the Ides of Martius. Any man who should join Antonius after this decree shall be deemed a traitor."

After several senators had spoken both for and against my proposals, the Senate adjourned for the day without taking a vote, leaving us in an unofficial state of war against a proconsul who, in fact, was an enemy of the Republic, but who in name was merely an *adversary* and even that was unofficial. I feared Antonius' friends, especially that that *quadriga* of Lucius Antonius, Calenus, Censorinus, and Bassus, might push for a second embassy, anything to temporize and buy time for Marcus Antonius. This had to be prevented!

The next day, the Senate voted on proposals regarding a public funeral for Servius. The Lupercalia festivities were set aside so that his rites could be held on that day. I was honored to deliver the eulogy.

From atop the Rostra, where Servius' corpse had been set with his son and daughter standing on either side of it, I looked upon the Forum crowded with senators, equites, and plebs. "As we condemn those who raise arms against the Republic," I proclaimed, "let us honor those who have raised a voice of conciliation. Citizens, I could wish that the immortal gods had allowed us now to be returning thanks to Servius Sulpicius in life rather than devising honors for him in death."

I reviewed the circumstances of the embassy to Antonius. "Sulpicius' health was so fragile when the embassy set out that he had small hope of ever returning. I could not dissuade him from going, for so dedicated was he in his patriotism. He has been brought to death by the embassy, no less than those envoys in olden times, who had been slain by treacherous foes."

The Senate had decreed the erection of a pedestrian statue to honor the memory of my dear friend. "The honor of this public funeral," I announced, "the assignment of a burial place for him and his posterity, have been decreed for this citizen who gave his life for the service of the Republic. May these honors, particularly the statue, serve as perpetual memorials of the villainy of Marcus Antonius."

Young Servius and his sister, Sulpicia, both committed to literature and philosophy, accompanied the funeral procession out to Mars Field where their father's remains were rendered unto ashes and charred bones. I prayed to his spirit: *Farewell, good Servius. You made the ultimate sacrifice. You will be remembered. But you will never be replaced.*

That evening, in the privacy of my home, I wept bitter tears for him.

Late in Februarius, the Senate received dispatches from Marcus Brutus. They told us of his virtual domination over Illyricum, Macedonia, and Greece, and the confinement under siege of Gaius Antonius in Apollonia.

Naturally enough, Calenus and his partners condemned Brutus' actions as illegal. They reminded the Senate of the latest provincial assignments made by Marcus Antonius back in November. At that time, Brutus had been stripped of any and all proconsular powers. Therefore, Brutus' actions were totally unauthorized, and Calenus urged that Brutus should be ordered to desist from any further aggression against Gaius Antonius.

In opposition to this, Consul Pansa proposed Brutus' appointment to the legitimate command over the provinces that he already effectively controlled. The ensuing debate had the Senate divided between the conflicting proposals of Pansa and his father-in-law. I contributed to the debate in support of Brutus.

"Quintus Calenus, why do you perpetually declare war against the Brutuses? Had it not been for Marcus Brutus and his defiance to Gaius Antonius, the Republic would have lost Macedonia and Greece, and these provinces would either serve as sanctuaries for Marcus Antonius or as embarkation points for an invasion of Italia. Gaius Antonius plundered and wasted the provinces that his derelict brothers contrived to obtain and then forfeited. But Marcus Brutus, denied this province which should rightfully have gone to him, has brought with him security and order through all the provinces east of the Adriatic.

"The legions in Greece and Macedonia have realized this, for they have abandoned Antonius and have rallied to Brutus. Calenus has said that Caesar's veterans will be offended if we accept Brutus' command in the East. Calenus, if this be true, then it is time that we choose *death* instead of military despotism.

"Through the actions motivated by his counsel, Marcus Brutus, with his army, has become a bulwark against the *Antonii*. Marcus Brutus should be commended. By the Senate's public decree, he should retain his command; he should be ordered to protect Macedonia, Illyricum, and Greece with full authority to levy public funds and to make all necessary requisitions."

These proposals were subsequently carried, but by a narrow margin. Couriers were dispatched to bring these tidings to Brutus in Apollonia. But the Antonian faction was livid. They clustered together in an agitated circle of conspiratorial intrigue. I wished we could have recruited an informer from within their group so that we might have learned their plans. Why, for example, did the Praetors, Censorinus and Bassus, leave Roma after the vote for Brutus' command? Where could they have gone? To Antonius, whose siege of Mutina had stalemated—or elsewhere? For what purpose? For what mischief against the Republic?

Omniscient Narrative

The atrium of Fulvia's Aventine house is well lit by four large oil-lamps and heated by three charcoal braziers that ward off the winter chill of a Roman February. This evening, Fulvia is entertaining guests. They are seated on rich, mahogany chairs while she and Clodia Pulchra recline seductively on plush couches facing each other. Clodia's languid posture is at odds with Fulvia's agitated state.

"Can you believe the audacity of that *Chick-Pea?* He's forever tearing down my Marcus in every Senate speech, and even in the speeches from the Rostra!" She reaches toward an adjacent table and lifts a scroll, and then tosses it toward Clodia. "He calls this rubbish his *Second Philippic.*"

Clodia has caught the scroll, and she begins to examine it. Fulvia proceeds with her denunciations. "Is this supposed to be funny? Well, what he's written about Marcus and me and our family *isn't* at all funny. He's even written about me as Roma's new *Lupa* suckling her twin sons. How dare he disparage me and my children! He's low and cowardly. He wouldn't dare say such rubbish in public, and he didn't have the guts to publish it until after Marcus had left the City. The cowardly bastard should have his tongue pulled out and his head and hands chopped off!"

Fulvia and Clodia regard each other sullenly. The guests are taken aback by the violence of Fulvia's words. Calenus smirks, inhaling deeply. "Every motion I make for conciliation is talked down by Cicero. He's committed to having the Senate war against Antonius with *Caesar-*

Boy marching around as a propraetor. But the youngster still hasn't been able to break through Antonius' lines."

Lucius Antonius leans forward in his chair and offers, "Cicero wants Antonius and all with him declared as public enemies. So far, Calenus and I and others have thwarted him. But he'll not lord it over us much longer." He and Calenus exchange knowing glances. Lowering his voice to a barely audible whisper, he admits, "Bassus and Censorinus are recruiting Caesar's veterans in Picenum to reinforce Marcus."

"Excellent!" Fulvia purrs.

"And I'm going up to Cisalpina to help my brother," Lucius admits.

"What?" Fulvia objects. "You would leave now? Just when I might have to become a refugee? Things are becoming too hot here for me...." She looks quickly at her mother-in-law's disapproving grimace. "And for *all* of us. We may have to leave Roma altogether. Tibur is too close, and I don't want to take the children up into the war zone."

"Fulvia, you can stay with my family if the City becomes too dangerous for you," Calenus suggests.

Shaking her head, Fulvia demurs. "The way things are moving, you too may soon have to flee. Besides, your son-in-law, Pansa, may object."

Gaius Antonius, the aged consular, former colleague of Marcus Cicero, uncle and former father-in-law of Marcus Antonius, offers the protection of his house.

Fulvia laughs this off. "Thank you, Uncle Gaius, but your daughter would not countenance her ex-husband's wife living under the same roof with her." The look she gives the old man seems to suggest the obvious fallacy of his idea.

"Why not stay with Atticus?" Clodia has nonplussed all of them. "He's not politically aligned with anyone."

Fulvia shoots back, "He's *Chick-Pea's* intimate friend!"

Gaius Antonius nods thoughtfully. "And the creditor of anyone who needs financial support."

"All the more reason you'd be safe, Fulvia, and you wouldn't even have to leave the City. His house is but a few paces on the other side of the hill."

The mother-in-law now puts in her two coppers worth of advice. "He's a shrewd man. He'll tally up marks of gratitude with Marcus by sheltering us. Though I hope we'll not have to have recourse to him."

Fulvia braces herself, thinking—*What a meddling, old dowager cow you are!* However, she manages to say, "Look, old woman, you're free to leave any time and go back to your own home! It's one thing to be the mother of an almost public enemy, but quite another to be his wife and the mother of his children."

"Whatever affects my sons," Julia coldly responds, "affects me as well. You would do well to remember that, Fulvia."

The two women glare insolently at each other as the men anticipate a mother-in-law and daughter-in-law verbal clash. Clodia tries to defuse the room's tension. "Perhaps if I'd been more successful in keeping the *Chick-Pea* at Antium, we would not now be so hounded by him."

The quip succeeds. Julia and the men laugh gleefully, but Fulvia remains obdurate. After the laughter passes, she turns to her brother-in-law and Calenus and hisses malevolently, "I want his head and the tongue that waggled his calumnies and the hands that wrote his hateful words." Then Fulvia turns to face Clodia. Their eyes lock in yet another sullen exchange. No one in the room laughs now.

Cicero's Elysian Voice

With the beginning of Martius, I received an anonymous note. Addressed to Marcus Tullius Cicero, Leader of the Senate, it read: *You are in grave danger if you persist in your antagonism with Marcus Antonius. His friends are plotting your assassination. Withdraw from Roma—quit Italia—before it is too late. Be warned! One who knows.*

The note reminded me of the conspicuous absence of Ventidius Bassus and Marcius Censorinus from the Senate meetings since the debate over Marcus Brutus' Macedonian command.

Only hours after receiving this mysterious note, I received one from Terentia. She wrote:

On the few occasions during our life together that you took my advice, you did so grudgingly. I don't presume that you will follow it now, and yet I implore you again, if not for my sake—for I'm sure I'm of little or no importance in your life—but for Marcus' sake and especially out of love for the memory of our beloved Tullia, please desist from your private war against Marcus Antonius.

Atticus has repeatedly given you the same advice and so has Fabia. Of late, she has had frightening visions in Mother Vesta's flames. She told me that she saw an unidentified young man wearing a laurel crown turning away from you as though he were abandoning you. Then there were three successive images of women. I was the first, tearful and distraught. Then, there was an image of a dark woman attired in a dark, olive-colored gown, so dark it was almost black, and it exposed her right shoulder. Fabia could not determine her emotions, for she seemed to convey none. She was like a statue in her posture and composure. Next, there was an image of a flame-haired woman removing a hairpin from her hair. As she did so, her hair fell in cascades of fire upon her neck and shoulders, and she laughed spitefully and maliciously. Finally, Fabia saw the Rostra covered with blood.

Marcus, she is sorely afraid for you. You justify your actions as service to the Republic in its hour of need. In so doing, you're risking your life for a cause you believe in. However commendable and patriotic your efforts may be, have you considered that whatever's going to happen is going to happen with or without the forfeiture of your own life?

I implore you, Marcus, leave Roma, leave Italia; go to the East and be with our son. Stay well out of harm's way.

Once your wife, and always the mother of your children.

Terentia

I sadly noted the pathos in Terentia's words. Ironically, her rationale for my own withdrawal from the struggle echoed Clodia's sentiments back at Antium.

GAIUS ANTONIUS, THE COLLEAGUE OF my consulate, visited me to offer a remarkable proposition. I had not had occasion to speak with him in all the years since his return from exile. He had grown heavier, his gait was slower, probably from his chronic gout, and his features had become more porcine.

"A long time ago, Marcus Cicero, you made me an offer of a lucrative province in exchange for my dissociation from Lucius Catilina," he reminded me. "Of course you remember, no?"

"As I recall, you did not need much coaxing," I replied. "Catilina has cast a long shadow on all our lives."

"Well, I've come to make you an offer that should prove as beneficial to you." He paused to make sure that his hook had secured itself into my attention. "My nephew—Marcus Antonius—has all but guaranteed a censorate for me next year."

"I would not count on your nephew's ability to deliver on that," I cautioned him.

Antonius shook his porcine face. "Don't discount him, Cicero. Remember, all the veterans in this strife—what you insist on calling a *war*—are *Caesar's* veterans. In the end, they'll make common cause with whoever will offer them the most in the way of rewards. Marcus is just now fighting on two fronts, besieging Brutus in Mutina and holding off Octavianus...."

"And soon enough, Hirtius and Pansa will bring new levies to reinforce Caesar Octavianus," I interrupted.

Antonius chuckled and smiled sardonically. "It's curious how you've taken to calling him by his grand-uncle's name." Then he became quite earnest. "Look, Cicero, here's my offer. Give up this *war* against my nephew and next year you'll share the censorate with me. Think of it: *the Censorate of Antonius and Cicero!* What a capping off of our political careers; and how appropriate! Once we were praetors together, and twenty years ago we were consuls, even though in both offices you overshadowed me. But no matter! Cicero, what do you say, eh? Have we a deal?"

I studied his excited but still porcine face as I wondered whether the offer came from him alone or from Marcus Antonius as well; not that it mattered in the least.

"I don't even need to consider this, Gaius Antonius," I responded after a brief pause. "My course is set. There's no turning back. I'll not live in a state controlled and ravaged by Marcus Antonius or anyone allied with or even following him."

Antonius shook his head, dismayed and disgruntled. "Why are you so bent on destroying yourself, Cicero?"

"Perhaps you cannot understand. There's nothing else that matters now but the liberty of the Republic. If I'm destroyed securing it, or even striving to secure it, then so be it. The die is cast."

Again, Antonius shook his head, this time fully exasperated. "Marcus Cicero, you may well find that the die is not in your favor. May Fortuna smile on you, at least enough to enlighten you."

After saying this, he took his leave. This proved to be the last time that I would speak with him. He would soon thereafter commit himself to the Antonian faction.

WHEN THE IDES OF MARTIUS rolled around again, I remembered that it was the first anniversary of the Great Man's assassination. Our crisis was the legacy of his death and of the assassins' failure to strike down Antonius as well. What if Dolabella, my ex-son-in-law, had also been marked for removal? The Senate would not then have had to hear about his transgressions.

Dolabella, Proconsul of Syria, thanks to Antonius' machinations, had invaded the province of Asia which was governed by the Caesarian assassin, Gaius Trebonius. Upon Dolabella's orders, Trebonius was captured and brutally executed.

This was a major reversal for the Republic. At the same time, the news from Mutina was painfully discouraging. With winter abating, Antonius was pressing the siege of Mutina ever so vigorously. At Bononia, some thirty miles south, Consul Hirtius was still training his recently levied troops. Octavianus' legions had been unable to inflict significant damage upon Antonius' siege lines owing to the severe weather which had impeded his movements. Besieged within Mutina, Decimus Brutus had not been able to send any dispatches to the Senate.

However, Hirtius and Octavianus forwarded to me a letter that Antonius had sent them. I read it and then shared its contents with Quintus and Atticus. We were appalled at Antonius' knavery, but we agreed that the letter should not be publicized until it could be most effectively used to undermine the usurper.

Other dispatches came to the Senate. From the once free, allied city of Massilia on the Transalpine coast, Sextus Pompeius sent his salutations. With them came his offer to bring his army of expatriates and freedmen to Mutina to relieve Decimus Brutus' beleaguered forces. He admitted, however, that he would not do so unless directly charged by the Senate to intervene, for he was loath to offend the veterans.

The *veterans!* By what perversion of civic rule should they have the authority, the influence to approve or preclude the services of a loyal patriot to the Republic?

The proconsuls of the Western provinces were influenced by the same perversity. Plancus, Proconsul of Gallia Comata, and Lepidus, Proconsul of Transalpine Gaul and Nearer Spain, sent dispatches to the Senate urging negotiation with Antonius. They warned that they could not guarantee the loyalty of their veteran soldiers who were unwilling to cross swords with Caesar's former right-hand officer.

These developments made it imperative that Antonius be defeated, completely and irreparably.

The contagion of dishonorable peace with a tyrant and the subversive disloyalty of his parasites merged with Calenus' devious offerings. First, he proposed that Dolabella be declared a public enemy because of his invasion of Asia and his unlawful execution of the legitimate provincial governor. Second, the Senate should appoint Consul Pansa to the command of Asia with the responsibility of destroying Dolabella's power. Third, the Senate should order Sextus Pompeius to remain at Massilia and *not* to intervene at Mutina. Fourth, the Senate should commend the Proconsuls Lepidus and Plancus for their peace initiatives. Finally, and based on these initiatives, the Senate should send another embassy to negotiate with Antonius.

Calenus named himself to the embassy because he was Antonius' friend and supporter; he named Lucius Piso because of his neutrality and because he had been Caesar's father-in-law; Lucius Caesar, a kinsman of the late Dictator, and the consular, Servilius Vatia, brother-in-law of Marcus Brurus, were also designated because of their neutrality; and I was suggested as a counter-weight to Calenus himself. However, I would not have put it beyond Calenus to plot my murder if I had undertaken to go.

As senior consular, I spoke first on Calenus' motion. "For once, Calenus is to be congratulated on his vigorous motion against Dolabella. But while condemning Dolabella, the Senate must be on guard against successive measures which will extinguish the ardor of the Republic in its war of liberation against the twin usurpers, Antonius *and* Dolabella."

I warned against commissioning Consul Pansa to the command in Asia. "Soon, he will leave for the north, bringing new levies to Mutina's relief. The enemy closer to Roma demands the attention of *both* Consuls. But the war against Dolabella requires a general already equipped and in the vicinity. No man is so well prepared or so well placed as Gaius Cassius. He is already there, and no decree of the Senate could deprive him of the command of his devoted army. Therefore, I propose the appointment of Gaius Cassius as Proconsul of Asia and Syria with full authorization to make war upon Dolabella and to vanquish him."

The Antonians among the Senate grew restless at my proposal on behalf of one of Caesar's assassins. Undaunted, I pushed ahead with my speech. "Cassius will act for the best interests of the Republic, even without the Senate's authorization. So will Sextus Pompeius, whose offer of assistance is an undeniable proof of his patriotism. This surviving son of Gnaeus Pompeius Magnus has acted agreeably toward the state with the disposition and zeal of his father and ancestors, and with his own accustomed virtue, energy, and good will. His offer should be welcomed and accepted by the Senate and the Roman People, for it will redound to his honor and dignity. Furthermore, the Senate should restore to him his father's, the Great Pompeius' estates.

"Judge for yourselves, Conscript Fathers, the nobility and loyalty of Sextus Pompeius, who hesitates to act lest he should offend the veterans. *Why in the name of mischief is the name of the veterans always introduced to prevent every good undertaking?* We must attach ourselves to those veterans whose patriotism puts them on the Republic's side; but those who put on airs and espouse Antonius' cause, we will *not* tolerate!

"If the Senate is to be governed by the nod of the veterans, and if all our words and actions are to be referred to them, then it is time to wish for *death!* True Romans have always chosen it over tyranny. The day of the veterans is passing, for the youth of Italia, in their devotion to liberty, are everywhere enlisting. While the loyal veterans will be rewarded for their patriotism, they are not to be feared. The Republic's ultimate victory now depends on the young soldiers."

I saw Calenus smirk and shake his head in a cynical reproof of my denigration of the veterans. Yes, I was gambling on their loyalty to the Republic. Perhaps he surmised just how reliable they would prove to be.

"Neither the veterans nor their commanders must dictate policy to the Senate. Lepidus and Plancus should be acknowledged and thanked for their desire for peace. But their urgings *cannot* and *must not* be used to justify a second embassy to Antonius."

I knew that Calenus was seeking to play for time favorable to Antonius and his siege operations against Mutina.

"The previous embassy accomplished nothing but the death of Servius Sulpicius Rufus, my beloved friend and the Republic's loyal servant. To send another embassy would dampen the ardor of our Republican patriotism. As we can make no concessions, no terms of peace are possible; and if peace were possible, can we countenance the readmission of so many criminals to Roma?

"I myself should have been the last person to have been nominated as an envoy, for I have been from the first the most committed foe of Antonius. I will not shrink from the personal dangers inherent in such an endeavor, but the embassy is unwarranted. There is no evidence of any change in Antonius. Far from that, his despotic villainy has outdone itself."

From the folds of my military cloak, I pulled out the scroll of Antonius' letter to Hirtius and Octavianus. Unrolling it, I held it aloft with its author's seal dangling at the bottom. "Behold the seal of Marcus Antonius," I intoned. "Let all know that this is the actual writing of the Proconsul who would destroy our liberty."

Loud murmuring spread among the senators. Several even came forward from their seats in the Capitoline Jovian cella to examine the scroll and its broken seal.

"Consul Pansa, Conscript Fathers, by your leave, I will entrust the reading of the letter to Quintus Cicero."

My brother stepped forward and looked at presiding Consul Pansa. The Consul nodded and gestured toward me. I handed Quintus the scroll and he began to read it. His voice was at first tremulous, but soon he recovered its natural power and sonorous clarity.

Antonius' letter began with a reprimand against Hirtius and Octavianus for their ingratitude to Caesar's benefits and for their aid to Decimus Brutus. He went on to describe the Caesarians as two armies of one body fighting each other like gladiators. Then he compared me to a *lanista*, a trainer of gladiators, who had deceived them with flowery speech into mortal combat.

Asserting his loyalty to his veterans and to his allies, Lepidus and Plancus, he affirmed that he would suffer no insults to himself or to his friends; nor would he give in to the Pompeian party whose resurgence was a certainty if Caesar's partisans fought each other.

Finally, he declared his solemn oath to avenge Caesar's murder. He hoped that all loyal Caesarians would join with him in this oath. Completing the letter, Quintus rolled up the scroll, handed it back to me, and then resumed his seat.

The senators had listened intently to the reading without a single murmur. Except for Quintus' voice, the Jovian temple had the severe stillness of an undiscovered tomb. Before anyone could venture to comment, I tore into the arrogant, pompous renegade.

"From the beginning of this war, Conscript Fathers, a war undertaken against disloyal and abandoned citizens, I feared lest some insidious negotiation for peace should quench our zeal for the recovery of liberty, for indeed the very name of peace is alluring. But can any of us believe that peace is possible with the whole crowd of Antonians? You have heard the very words by which he attempts to subvert the loyalty of the Consuls and of Octavianus and through which he would destroy our faith in Plancus and Lepidus.

"Do the words of Antonius bear the aura of nobility and loyalty? *No!* But in Octavianus we see no phantom of his adoptive-father's name beguiling the young man to forsake the greatest duty of a son, which is the preservation of his fatherland.

"Antonius speaks of parties, of vanquished Caesarians and resurgent Pompeians. But what parties are here when, on the one side, the authority of the Senate, the liberty of the Roman People, and the safety of the Republic are set as ideals; on the other, the massacre of good men and the partition of Roma and of Italia? You have seen Antonius' treacheries laid bare. Would Lepidus, if he saw this letter, make peace with such a man? Sooner would fire and water come to terms; and better were it should Roma be shifted from her place, and then migrate, if it were possible, to other lands where she should not hear of the deeds or the names of the *Antonii*.

"Conscript Fathers, I urge you to reject Calenus' proposed embassy. Instead, this war for the recovery of our liberty and the defeat and destruction of Marcus Antonius must be prosecuted with the utmost energy. I urge you, Consul Pansa, to set out with all possible speed to Mutina. Bring the weight of your levies, together with the forces of Consul Hirtius and Caesar Octavianus, to bear against Antonius' army. Raise the siege of Mutina and liberate Decimus Brutus!"

Above the increasing hubbub resonating in the cella, I concluded, "As for myself, Conscript Fathers, it is my destiny to win or lose, to stand or fall, to live or perish with the Republic and with the liberty of the State."

With the exception of the Antonian faction, the senators stood and applauded my oration. However, despite their enthusiastic response, the senators of all factions – neutral, Caesarian, Pompeian, and Antonian – debated, temporized, and voted on what amounted to a compromise. The embassy was rejected; Sextus Pompeius' proffered assistance was declined; and Gaius Cassius was denied the official proconsulate of Asia and Syria. Instead, the Senate decreed that the Consuls, after the relief of Mutina, would be assigned these provinces and the joint command against Dolabella.

As Quintus and I left the temple, I stopped and surveyed the ocher Roman panorama spread out below the Capitoline Mount. "You know, Quintus," I mused, "liberty is too precious an ideal to be compromised. We might as well hurl ourselves from the Tarpeian Rock. Death is preferable to life under tyranny."

A FEW DAYS LATER, PANSA set off with his levied troops for the Cisalpina. He left one legion of new levies, encamped at Mars Field, to guard the City, and the Urban Praetor, Marcus Cornutus, to preside over the Senate. We remained ever vigilant.

OMNISCIENT NARRATIVE

GALLIC AND MAURETANIAN CAVALRY RECONNOITER across the marshes and bogs flanking the Aemilian Road south of Forum Gallorum. The Gauls, helmeted and clothed in mail coats, and the Mauretanians, their long hair thickly braided, their torsos in leather doublets, are headed south toward Bononia. Their commander, Proconsul Marcus Antonius, has received intelligence that Consul Pansa is leading four legions of raw recruits up from Bononia toward Mutina to relieve the beleaguered Decimus Brutus. The Proconsul's plan is to intercept and destroy these legions before they can augment the forces of Consul Hirtius and Octavianus.

Through the damp, drizzly mists of a mid-April morning they see columns of legionaries marching up the Aemilian Road, perhaps two thousand paces distant. The cavalry prefect, Publius Decius, recognizes their eagle standard and vexillum as belonging to the Mars Legion. Decius is alarmed, for he and his commander had assumed that this battle-hardened, veteran legion was still entrenched at Mutina. Now, he speculates that the Martians are in the vanguard of the Republican relief forces and that Pansa's recruits are probably further down the road.

At the same time, the Martians' commanders, Servius Galba and Decimus Carfulenus, spot the cavalry and correctly identify them as Antonian auxiliaries. The word spreads through the ranks that contact has been made with the enemy.

But Decius' orders are to avoid clashing with the Republican troops; so he orders the cavalry to withdraw. Now, the rank and file of the Mars Legion take the initiative. The men remember how their comrades had been decimated at Brundisium upon Antonius' orders. They hanker and thirst for revenge and there is no military discipline that can restrain them.

They deploy into battle formation. Eight cohorts in triple lines—three in front, two in the middle, two in the rear—take up positions to the right of the road under Galba's command. The remaining two cohorts, under Quintus Salvidienus, and Consul Hirtius' praetorians deploy to the left. Octavianus' praetorian cohort, commanded by Carfulenus, holds the center on a causeway elevated above the surrounding marshland.

As the cavalry withdraws, the Antonian Thirty-Fifth Legion is sighted by the Martians. Officers of the Thirty-Fifth had supervised Antonius' decimation upon the Martians. They rush upon their former comrades and join battle in a ferocious fight.

On the left flank, Hirtius' praetorians and Salvidienus' two Martian cohorts are set upon by the Antonian Second Legion. Marcus Antonius' praetorian cohorts assail Carfulenas' cohort on the causeway. The Republican troops are sorely outnumbered along the entire battle line, but their center on the causeway is particularly hard-pressed.

Former comrades under Julius Caesar, but now foes, the legionaries stab and thrust and parry at each other. All the while they struggle to maintain their footing and formations in the treacherous, marshy fields of the Cisalpina. Swords clang against swords, and they thud upon bronze-covered wooden, oblong shields. Battle cries and curses accompany each thrust and counter-thrust. The wounded fall back to be relieved by comrades from the rear. The dead litter the soft, damp earth enshrouded by a pervasive mist that the April sun struggles to dissipate.

Further down the Aemilian Road, Consul Pansa is alerted that the Mars Legion is under attack. Decisively and quickly, he appraises the situation. He orders two legions to fall out and to construct and fortify a camp. Then, he orders the two nearest legions to discard their marching packs. They are to quick-march with him up the road toward Forum Gallorum.

Their arrival is propitiously timely. Having beaten back the Thirty-Fifth Legion, Galba and his Martians behold the Antonian cavalry attempting to envelop their flank. Unaware of the battle's progress on the left, Galba orders a withdrawal which Pansa's newly arrived recruits succeed in covering. However, Carfulenus and his cohort are overcome by Antonius' praetorians and slaughtered to the last man; their corpses are thrown off the causeway and into the bogs on either side. The Republican center ceases to exist. Proconsul Antonius and his junior legate, Marcus Silanus, only recently seconded from Proconsul Marcus Lepidus, congratulate each other, valiant comrades-in-arms, on breaking the Republican center.

Antonius' Second Legion succeeds in pushing back the cohorts of Hirtius and Salvidienus as the Gallic and Mauretanian cavalry begins to outflank the Republican left. However, the soft, marshy ground hampers the heavy-hoofed Gallic and Spanish horses. The cavalry is therefore unable to prevent the Republicans from making a safe, orderly withdrawal.

The Aemilian Road and the surrounding marshlands are clogged by the retreating Republican troops. Pansa's recruits afford them some degree of cover from the Antonians and they manage to limp back to the newly built camp. However, in fighting a delaying action, Pansa is severely wounded and then carried from the field by his aides. Before succumbing to unconsciousness, he orders a retreat.

Flushed with victory, Marcus Antonius orders his legates, Popillius Laenas, Lucius Varius, and Publius Decius, to regroup their cohorts and cavalry squadrons. He will not repeat Pompeius' tactical error at Dyrrachium in allowing the enemy to escape. No—despite the strain of the battle and the late hour of the afternoon, Antonius orders his victorious but spent legions to proceed down the Aemilian Road to destroy the retreating Republicans.

But by the time Antonius' forces catch up with them, the Martians and Pansa's recruits are impregnably entrenched in their camp. Undaunted, Antonius orders his exhausted legions to assail the enemy camp's earthen, palisaded ramparts. However, each successive attack is beaten back with disastrous results. The Martians have their revenge, decimating in battle both the Second and the Thirty-Fifth Legions.

Antonius' legates prevail upon him to forego the attack and retreat back to the sanctuary of their siege lines at Mutina. As the remnants of the briefly victorious Antonian legions withdraw, they must own up their present defeat.

Consul Hirtius exploits the enemy's vulnerability. He leads twenty-two cohorts of recruits in harassing the retreating Antonians all the way back to the battle site near Forum Gallorum. The Antonians lose two legionary eagles and sixty standards, and Publius Decius, the cautious cavalry commander, is captured by the Republicans.

Returning to camp, Consul Hirtius sees to the comfort of his wounded colleague before sending Servius Galba to Roma with the news of their victory.

Cicero's Elysian Voice

Several weeks had passed since Pansa's departure. We in Roma waited anxiously for news from the north. But there was none. Instead, rumors ran rampant in the City: rumors that Antonius had captured Mutina after defeating the Consuls' forces; rumors of the Praetors Bassus and Censorinus preparing to march on Roma with legions they had recruited among Caesarian veterans throughout Italia. Fear, foreboding, and suspicion hung over us like ugly, black storm clouds.

I had received numerous threats against my life as well as anonymous notes warning me of imminent danger. Terentia, in particular, urged me to leave Roma and even Italia and to go to the East. Ironically, her reasoning echoed Clodia Pulchra's when, back at Antium, she had offered to accompany me to the Aegean. But now as then, I set my mind to stay the course and fight, even if it was to the death, for the Republic's liberation from tyranny.

Quintus and his son feared some rash attempt on my life by the Antonian faction. So, without the Senate's authorization, they organized an armed bodyguard of sixty young equites. They accompanied me every time I set forth from the house to attend the Senate or to go to the Forum. While the bodyguard fended off would-be assassins, it also fed the fears and suspicions of the Antonians. They gave out that I was planning to seize the fasces and proclaim myself Dictator.

On April twenty-first, Tribune Salvius, a staunch Antonian, called a public meeting in the Forum. Atop the Rostra, he denounced me before a howling mob of plebeian riffraff. "Marcus Cicero deprecates all proposals for negotiation," the Tribune declared, shaking his clenched fist at me. "His enmity toward Antonius is so vile that he would commit the young manhood of Italia, as well as the veterans, to fratricidal civil war!"

The mob howled its approval. There were outcries of "Down with Cicero!" and "To the Tiber with Cicero!" Satisfied with their boisterous response, pale, pasty Salvius pranced about the stone deck of the Rostra between the short, pillared balustrades flanking the opening that faced the Forum.

"He would have you believe that the destruction of Antonius will ensure the Republic's liberty," Salvius railed on. "People of Roma, believe him *not!* Marcus Cicero wants the supremacy of Roma! He'll stop at nothing to get it. He'll murder Roman citizens as he did when he was Consul. He'll ignore and dispose of the laws and rights of citizens. He'll attack the People's Tribunes as he attacked the People's beloved Publius Clodius!"

With each denunciation, the mob howled and shrieked ever more malevolently. I was standing toward the Rostra's back, near the seven commemorative columns, with my brother, my nephew and Alexio and the bodyguard of equites. We braced ourselves for a likely assault.

When I faced front again, Tribunes Appuleius and Casca were going up beside Salvius. Holding up his hand as if trying to silence the mob, Appuleius called out over the hubbub. "Citizens! Citizens! Citizens!" The mob settled down, at least momentarily. "Do not allow yourselves to be deceived by unfounded fears and rumors instigated by Calenus and his confederates. Cicero's words have always been for the People's welfare. Neither by word nor by deed has he aimed at domination over you. But it is rather *Antonius* who would enslave you! Salvius knows the tenure of peace initiatives made on Antonius' behalf. He's been in the Senate as I have and as Publius Casca…."

At the mention of Casca's name, the mob exploded into outcries of "Assassin! Murderer! Villain!" Casca tried to speak to them but they cried out all the louder. Even Salvius joined in the chorus and with gesticulations he encouraged them like a clown bating a wild beast.

Some of the mob rushed around to the Rostra's curvilinear steps. They were shouting, "Away with them! Down with Appuleius! Down with Cicero!" At that instant, the equite bodyguards formed a protective ring around me. Some of the mob began to scale the Rostra's front wall, using the ornamental ships' prows as footholds and supports. Once over the balustrade, they menacingly advanced like wolves on the attack. Summoning all the strength of my voice, I called out to Appuleius and Casca, beckoning them to take refuge within the equite barrier. They hurried to us just as several ruffians lunged at them.

Quintus drew the sword from his scabbard. "Well, Marcus," he said with a grimly set countenance, "the Senate was wise to have us wear military garb." He winked at me as I drew my own sword.

Suddenly, a troop of horsemen, about forty, came galloping through the Forum. The pounding of the horses' hooves on the stone pavement startled the mob. Those ruffians who did not give way were knocked down and trampled. Panting and covered with the dust of travel, the horsemen reined in at the Rostra's steps.

One of them removed his helmet and announced, "I am Servius Galba, Legate of the Martian Legion." A hush and stillness fell over the boisterous mob. "Where is the first Senator? Where is Marcus Tullius Cicero?"

Reluctantly, I stepped forward from the equites and walked over to the horsemen. Quintus and his son and Alexio flanked me. "I am Marcus Tullius Cicero."

The man who called himself Servius Galba looked up at me, noting my drawn sword and military cloak and leather coat. Then he cocked back his head and announced, "We come from Forum Gallorum." Raising his fist triumphantly, he bellowed, "Marcus Antonius is defeated! The Republic triumphs!"

A general shout went up from senators and equites, echoed by the ever fickle dregs within the populace. "Servius Galba"—saying his name brought to mind my late, beloved friend—"come to the Capitoline and report to the Senate."

My bodyguard cleared a path for us as we made for the Capitoline ramp. The senators, equites, plebeians, and soldiers escorting us hailed me as "Savoir of Roma." At such a moment of triumph—like the one during my consulate when I had crushed the Catilinians—using the triumphal ramp was altogether fitting.

ABOUT THREE HUNDRED SENATORS ENTERED the Jovian temple and seated themselves on the stone benches lining the cella's walls. I noticed that Calenus and a score of Antonians were among them. As the senior magistrate left in Roma, Praetor Cornutus called the Senate to order. Then, he gave leave to Galba to make his report.

The old warrior gave us a vivid account of the battle at Forum Gallorum; how the veteran Martian Legion and two praetorian cohorts took on Antonius' Second and Thirty-Fifth Legions and then made an orderly withdrawal covered by Consul Pansa's levies. He beamed with pride as he related how they had beaten back Antonius' attacks on their camp before Consul Hirtius led a counter-attack on Antonius' retreating column.

"We captured two of their legionary eagles along with sixty standards. Consul Hirtius captured Antonius' cavalry prefect, Publius Decius. Those two legions—the Second and the Thirty-Fifth—they're just about wiped out." Then Galba's tone became somber. "But we too had many casualties. An entire praetorian cohort, the one belonging to Caesar Octavianus, was killed off entirely with its legate, Decimus Carfulenus. We lost hundreds of the levies, under-strength and undertrained as they were." He paused for an instant and looked at the stone floor. "I regret to announce that Consul Pansa has been seriously wounded."

There were brief murmurings of commiseration which then gave way to applause from the senators after Galba concluded his report. Some senators cried out in my direction, "Savior! Father! Defender! Liberator!" Galba seemed dumbfounded that they should acclaim me instead of the soldiers. He could have had no idea of my diligent efforts to keep alive the Senate's bellicose spirit.

Though this was my golden hour of acclamation, I knew that my labors were far from completed.

Old Lucius Cotta was given leave to speak. This kinsman of Caesar's and otherwise silent member of the neutrals proposed a public thanksgiving for the victory at Forum Gallorum. Besides this, he proposed that the Senate put aside military garb and resume the civic toga.

I detected some mischief in the old senator's motions. To gauge the Senate's position, I allowed men junior to myself to speak ahead of me. While the Antonians were strangely silent, except for Calenus, who again urged negotiation, the Republicans and some moderates were convinced that the war was over.

When I decided to speak, I shook their complacency with the reality of our situation. "Conscript Fathers, the abandonment of military garb is premature as long as Decimus Brutus remains besieged in Mutina; and if there is any substance to the rumors that Bassus and Censorinus are poised to attack Roma, then indeed civic garb is unthinkable at this time. I marvel that Calenus remains among us rather than joining the Praetors. But if he were not here, who else would advocate negotiation and peace?"

A wave of laughter swept across the cella. Even Calenus looked amused by the remark.

"On the motion of a public thanksgiving, consider, Conscript Fathers, that there has never been a thanksgiving proclaimed for victories over fellow citizens. If we acknowledge and grant this motion, then, in effect, we are branding those defeated by our commanders as enemies. Our legions have steeped their swords in the blood that was shed in battle. If that blood was the blood of enemies, the devotion of our soldiers was supreme; but a monstrous crime if it was of citizens. How long, then, shall he who has surpassed all enemies in crime be without the name of *enemy*? Should we wish the weapons of our soldiers to waver in doubt whether they should be plunged into a *citizen* or into *an enemy*? Truly welcome will be our thanks, welcome our sacrifices to the immortal gods when there has been slain a multitude of *citizens* rather than of *enemies!* It is now imperative that those who are enemies in *fact* should be branded in plain terms, and declared by our votes to be *enemies!*

"Therefore, the Senate should proclaim a thanksgiving for the unprecedented period of fifty days. The Consuls Hirtius and Pansa and the Propraetor Caesar Octavianus should each be designated *Imperator* in accordance with ancient custom which granted this title in conjunction with a public thanksgiving.

"It is also my proposal, Conscript Fathers, that to the soldiers of the Martian Legion, and to those who, fighting by their side, have fallen, there be raised a monument in the noblest possible shape as an eternal memorial to their divine valor. The rewards we had promised to give the soldiers should be fully paid with interest to the survivors of the fallen, for in death these men have become victors."

There was additional debate after I had concluded my address; but ultimately the Senate accepted all my proposals except for the motion to have Antonius and his followers declared public enemies. Against this measure, Calenus and the Antonians, despite their dwindling numbers, were able to exert their obstructive influence. But the military garb remained, and with it the state of undeclared war against a man whose enmity to the Republic the Senate was so reticent to declare formally.

By the end of April, however, new developments in the Mutina campaign would bring the Senate to its full sense of reality.

Omniscient Narrative

At dusk on April twenty-six, Consul Hirtius and Propraetor Octavianus surreptitiously move five legions in a seven-mile arc from their camp on the south side of Antonius' contravallation defenses around to the northern extremis. For days, scouts have reported that Antonius' fortifications at this point are the least formidable of his outward-facing defenses. Heavy forests west and north of Mutina shield the marching legions.

Within the contravallation ring of palisaded earthen ramparts, spiked trenches, and redoubts fortified by war engines, slingers, and archers, there is yet another cordon of defenses facing inward toward Mutina. This circumvallation envelops the entire town with similar fortifications. Ballistae and catapults have regularly hurled their deadly missiles at and over Mutina's walls. On the cordon's southern and eastern sides, Antonius' engineers have constructed siege ramps to facilitate the legionaries' assaults against the beleaguered town. Thus far, Decimus Brutus' soldiers have held the attackers at bay. However, Brutus' legions are exhausted from months of siege, privations, and assaults. Brutus knows that they cannot hold out indefinitely. Yet, he hopes that the relief forces will ultimately succeed in raising the siege.

Antonius' forces, split by the onerous task of maintaining circumvallation and contravallation lines around Mutina, and depleted by their losses at the battle of Forum Gallorum, are dangerously stretched. Antonius has managed to send out couriers to Proconsul Lepidus in the Transalpina and to Proconsul Plancus in Gallia Comata urging their support. But he has had no word from either. He is aware of the possibility that one or both of the Proconsuls could join the relief forces. Such a contingency would be utterly disastrous for him.

Consul Hirtius and his wounded, ailing colleague, Pansa, have taken stock of their situation with young Octavianus. Their questions have prompted heated debate among them. Is there any likelihood of coming to terms with Antonius? Does Decimus Brutus, an assassin of Caesar, deserve to be liberated from Antonius' siege? Which of them, Antonius or Brutus, is the more dangerous foe? Are they themselves in danger of being trapped should the legions of Lepidus and Plancus arrive to reinforce Antonius?

There are no easy answers, but there is a consensus among the leaders: They must break Antonius' grip on Mutina and they must do so as expeditiously as possible. For this reason, they have gambled on Antonius' weakest point—the northern rim of the contravallation line. Though they cannot communicate with Decimus Brutus, nevertheless they hope that he will simultaneously order an attack on Antonius' circumvallation at the point parallel to the outer cordon.

All through the night, Hirtius and Octavianus position their legions. The soldiers are afforded a few hours of rest, perhaps time enough for short naps or a quick and meager breakfast of bread and vinegar, the soldiers' sour wine, before commencing their deadly business.

As the first streaks of dawn's light cross the eastern sky, Consul Hirtius orders the bucinators and cornucens to sound the attack. The blaring ululations resonate from the woods across the defenses and onto the defenders atop Mutina's battlements. In broken but determined formation, the attackers pour out of the woods and move toward the shallow trenches immediately before the contravallation's low ramparts. Both Hirtius and Octavianus are in the van of their advancing cohorts.

The attack is launched early enough in the day and against what is already a poorly fortified target. If the Antonian defenders are too few and too heavy with somnolence, and if Decimus Brutus will attack in tandem, then the relief forces could sweep over the outward-facing defenses and then attack the circumvallation cordon from the rear. So many *ifs*, so many contingencies, and on them all does victory hinge.

The Antonian defenders on the northern rim are indeed surprised. Compared to other points along the outer cordon, the defenders are fewer in number, no more than three cohorts at best. But their defense is valiant. They hurl at the attackers every missile at hand—javelins, spears, arrows, slingshot lead balls and pebbles, though they are bereft of war engines at this position.

Stalwart as their defense is, it is not unyielding. After an hour of resistance, the Antonians give ground as the Hirtian and Octavian cohorts, bloodied and wounded, surmount the defenses and pour into the space between the outer and inner cordons.

At the same time, Decimus Brutus, having watched the battle from a tower on Mutina's northern wall, decides to act. He orders his three praetorian cohorts to attack the circumvallation defenses directly parallel to the point of the relief forces' attack. His soldiers have been tried and tested by months of privation, but their aggressive spirit is not diminished. They advance in neat, orderly battle formation against Antonius' inner cordon, an area almost as weakly fortified as the northern outer ring.

In his command tent, Antonius receives word of the attack. He hastens to the battle site with his own praetorian cohorts. If the northern rims are breached, his entire cordon will be compromised. Before Antonius' cohorts complete the four mile march to the critical area, decisive deeds are played out.

One of Brutus' legates, Pontius Aquila, a former plebeian tribune and a Caesarian assassin, is beset by three legionaries of the Fourth Legion. He thrusts and parries with consummate skill, but one of his assailants aims a mortal blow at the right side of his exposed neck. Pontius Aquila instantly drops to his knees, blood effusing from his wound, and then he falls forward, flat on his face, his left hand still clutching his shield. After Gaius Trebonius in Asia, he is the second of the tyrannicides upon whom death is visited.

Several Antonian legionaries recognize Consul Hirtius by his conspicuous scarlet military cloak and the high crest atop his helmet. Retrieving discharged javelins from their dead comrades' corpses, they pause long enough in their retreat to take careful aim as Hirtius urges his men forward. After hurling their missiles, they turn and run after their comrades-in-arms. Whizzing through the damp early morning air, the javelins find their targets with deadly accuracy. Pierced in the throat, abdomen and groin, the Consul falls backward upon the bloodied ground. His corpse is a macabre sight in the melee of battle, a mound of mail-coated flesh, like a hunted beast, with three upright javelins protruding from it and waving ominously in the air.

Propraetor Octavius and several legionaries fight off Antonian soldiers bent on scavenging the corpse for souvenirs, the Consul's signet ring, his sword, his baldric, his helmet, his caliga. Sheathing his sword and discarding his shield, Octavianus pulls out the javelins from the body. Then, half-carrying and half-dragging it, he takes it away from the field and back beyond the attack point. Over his shoulder, Octavianus calls to his attendant bucinator, "Sound the retreat! Sound the retreat!"

The bucinator exhales into the long-necked bronze bugle wrapped under his left arm and curving high above his helmeted head. The retreat signal is sounded, high-pitched and eerie over the field.

Bewildered in their moment of triumph, the legionaries begin a cautious retreat from Antonius' inner cordon. Seeing this with equal bewilderment, Decimus Brutus similarly orders his cohorts to retreat.

By the time Marcus Antonius arrives at the battle site, the fighting has ceased. He sees the relief forces retreating back into the woods and Brutus' troops scurrying back into Mutina. His first instinct is to attack the woods, but he holds back lest a trap awaits him there. Instead, he reinforces both the outer and inner rings. And he thinks about his next move.

Octavianus takes the legions back to camp, all the while studying Hirtius' corpse as it is borne on shields by several legionaries. He remembers how only days before the two Consuls had questioned whether they were fighting the real enemy.

Back in camp, the troops dress their wounds and rest. Octavianus orders the surgeons to clean the Consul's body and prepare it for delivery to Roma. Then he informs Consul Pansa of the day's events, of the battle whose outcome is now in doubt.

Pansa struggles to speak. Lying supine on a military cot, his body bound in bandages to stop the bleeding from his multiple wounds, his breathing is labored. His words, however, register volumes of intention and purpose in Octavianus' heart and mind. The young man listens and absorbs the wisdom of a dying man. He stays by his side long after the Consul stops speaking, and still longer after he ceases to live.

Now, not *one*, but *both* Consuls' remains will be sent to Roma along with Octavianus' report of the battle on April twenty-seven. The young Propraetor will also include in his report the news that Marcus Antonius has withdrawn from Mutina.

Since the battle, Antonius has taken counsel with his brother, Lucius, and with his other legates. Their consensus is that they should not allow themselves to become entrapped before Mutina, an eventuality almost certain to occur if either Lepidus or Plancus should arrive to reinforce the relief troops. They cannot be certain about what either of these Proconsuls will do; nor can they know that both Hirtius and Pansa are dead. But retreating into the Transalpina toward Lepidus is the favored option.

Taking with him the shattered remnants of the Second and the Thirty-Fifth, and the nearly full-strength Alauda Legion and most of his cavalry, Antonius sets forth unopposed and unobstructed along the Aemilian Road. Gallic Alpine mountain ranges rise on his right flank and the seacoast shimmers on his left. He has gambled with Fate at Mutina and lost. Now, he will gamble again in the Transalpine vastness, confident that his erstwhile ally, Lepidus, will remain steadfast, or that he can at least be won over. Marcus Antonius thus begins a new phase in his determined bid for power.

In Mutina, Decimus Brutus' relief is boundless. He cannot realize, however, that one raised siege is about to lead to another.

Cicero's Elysian Voice

The Senate's joy upon receiving the reports of Marcus Antonius' retreat and of the relief of Mutina was nearly vitiated by the simultaneous delivery of the Consuls' remains. Aulus Hirtius and Vibius Pansa had given their lives in the Republic's war against a usurping tyrant. Public funerals were decreed for them.

At last, the Senate unequivocally declared Marcus Antonius, his brothers, and all who followed them enemies of the Republic. Their properties were forfeited to the State. Decimus Brutus was directed to assume complete command over all forces in the Cisalpina, including the sick and the wounded legionaries that Antonius had abandoned along with some cavalry.

The Senate also conferred comprehensive military powers upon Marcus Brutus and Gaius Cassius for the purpose of destroying Dolabella. Sextus Pompeius was named Admiral of the Republic for his expressed loyalty, and in recognition of his formidable fleet, some fifty war galleys and half as many transport vessels. He was formally commissioned to bring his forces to the Republic's service.

In the wake of the victory reports, with all the attendant measures against Antonius and in favor of the tyrannicides, Calenus and his faction slipped out of Roma. Good riddance to them!

However, in retrospect, we erred with respect to Octavianus. We assumed that he would be subordinate to Decimus Brutus, when he may have wanted to share command. Adding insult to injury, the Senate awarded Brutus the honor of a triumph, while the secondary honor of an ovation was decreed for Octavianus; and when a decemviral committee was empowered to reform the entire political situation, again the Senate blundered foolishly in assigning neither Brutus nor Octavianus to it.

I shared in the consternation of many senators that Marcus Antonius had been afforded an opportunity to flee rather than be captured or destroyed. Was this a blunder, or an intentionally calculated risk on Octavianus' part?

On the eve of the Kalends of Maius, the deceased Consuls were honored with a public funeral in Mars Field. Delivering the eulogy, I praised Hirtius and Pansa for their devotion to the Republic, their patriotism, and their self-sacrifice. Out of respect for their memory and in recognition of the prevailing political realities, I reminded the senators and citizens that the struggle was not over as long as Antonius remained at large. The commanders of the Republic's legions had to be supported, respected, and encouraged. In particular, I urged that Caesar Octavianus be flattered, promoted, and *exulted* to the clouds.

As the flames of the Consuls' funeral pyre consumed their remains, I realized the inherent ambiguities in my remarks on behalf of Octavianus.

Caput XIX

THERE IS A SURE PLACE in Heaven for all who have cared for their fatherland. . . . There is nothing more acceptable to the chief of the gods who rules over the Cosmos, of all things that happen on the Earth, than the councils and gatherings of men who associate together in respect for law and justice; that is, the organizations called states. Their rulers and preservers have come from Heaven and will return there.

From *The Dream of Scipio*

Cicero's Elysian Voice

The events that directly brought me here were the last acts played out in the tragedy of my own and the Roman Republic's demise.

The success we had achieved in Aprilis began to unravel during the Month of Maius. In the wake of the Consuls' deaths, Urban Praetor Marcus Cornutus remained as the senior magistrate. A sallow-faced, bent-backed, spent relic of a man, he presided over all Senate meetings. At one session late in the month, I was availed an opportunity to read a letter from Decimus Brutus.

The Proconsul reported that his legions had been generously resupplied by Octavianus after the siege of Mutina had been raised. However, Octavianus refused to pursue the fugitive, Marcus Antonius.

Brutus was disturbed by the regular fraternization of the relief forces and his own troops since the siege had ended. They soon became of one mind in their obedience to Octavianus—who insisted on calling himself *Caesar*—and in their recalcitrance toward Brutus. They even demonstrated against him as one of the Dictator's assassins.

Desperately, but unsuccessfully, he had appealed to the legions to remain loyal to the Republic. Not only did they refuse to place themselves under Brutus' overall command and pursue Antonius, but they also clamored for the immediate payment of their bounties. Their contention was that the war was over, despite the Senate's insistence that Antonius must either capitulate or be destroyed. Moreover, Brutus reported that the soldiers appeared to share Octavianus' resentment over a remark attributed to me, to the effect that the young man should be honored, promoted, and *carried off* to the heavens.

In point of fact, I had said that he should be *exulted* to the heavens, but my words could have been misconstrued to mean *done away with*.

Nevertheless, the veterans, both Brutus' and Octavianus', were comrades-in-arms of the late Dictator. They had fought under him in Gaul and in the war against Pompeius Magnus. Brutus warned that they were not likely to fight against Antonius, the Dictator's foremost legate and former Master of Horse.

Brutus admitted that he feared for his life. Thus, having commandeered several newly recruited Cisalpine cohorts, he had departed from Mutina. He was on the march into Gallia Comata, hoping to link up with Proconsul Titus Plancus, whom he assumed was yet loyal to the Republic. Once their legions had merged, Brutus intended to move into the Transalpina to seek out and destroy Antonius, unless Proconsul Lepidus should have already accomplished this.

Hoping that the Fates would keep Lepidus loyal to the Republic, Brutus further hoped that his decision would meet with the Senate's approbation. What he endeavored was for the Republic's welfare and his own safety.

In a post-scriptum, Brutus mentioned his annoyance over Octavianus' release of Publius Decius, Antonius' cavalry prefect who had been captured at Forum Gallorum. It did not bode well that he should have been given leave, as well as encouraged, to return to Antonius.

THE SENATE HAD NO CHOICE but to condone Decimus Brutus' actions. Yet, we were all alarmed that the Republic's forces were now split. What was Octavianus up to?

"He sits on his ass at Mutina like a sulking child!" Quintus exclaimed back at the Palatine house. "He ignores all of your entreaties and the Senate's orders to move and complete the task. And all we've accomplished goes for nothing if Antonius slips away. That's where we are."

Quintus put the situation so concisely for Atticus. With an expression of smug resignation, the ursine money-man shook his head and looked at me.

"My efforts to defend Octavianus in the Senate have been in vain," I admitted sadly. "Cornutus and the other praetors have swung the majority to the view that the war's over and the youth is no longer needed. They simply will *not* understand that only Antonius' complete destruction will end it."

"There's something poisoning them," Atticus speculated. "Something is sapping their energy. What about Antonius' friends?"

"His *triumvirate* of Calenus, Censorinus, and Bassus? Their whereabouts are unknown. The legions they're supposed to have raised are not near Roma. We've sent out scouts in every direction to look for them." I wished that I knew more.

Quintus added, "They may have gone north to attack Octavianus, or more likely to join Antonius." A quizzical expression came to his face. "It was good of Pansa to leave behind a legion. But I've inspected them, and I tell you truthfully they're neither combat-ready nor of unimpeachable loyalty. We'll need more and better men than these."

"What about Marcus Brutus?" Atticus inquired. "Surely, he must realize how urgently he's needed here."

I sighed in dismay. "I've written him, urged him to bring his army to Italia. Each time, he's written back with a different excuse. First, he insisted that the siege of Apollonia demanded his immediate attention and all of his resources. Then he pleaded lack of preparation, and then he protested against the unstable conditions in Italia. *Great Jupiter's balls!* It's those very conditions that require his legions! Finally, he inveighed against my patronage of Octavianus, warning me not to trust the *Young Caesar*. You know, I've even asked Servilia and Porcia to pressure him to come. What could be more persuasive than a mother's entreaties or a wife's badgering? But the mother is haughty and aloof, and the wife is acutely ill. They've both told me that Marcus Brutus knows what he's doing. They've also reprimanded me for sponsoring Octavianus."

"The victory we won in April has turned out to be hollow, at best." Quintus gestured with his hands, forming a circle with his fingertips. "We've been celebrating a thanksgiving without laurels. In their place, we've had entreaties from Lepidus and Plancus. *'Negotiate! Accommodate! Make peace!'* Make peace with a public enemy?"

"The Senate has talked at greater and greater length about their petitions," I put in. "But the consensus remains that they should not interfere in the Senate's deliberations."

Just then, Quintus laughed facetiously, while I remained unaffected. "The Senate has its back against the wall."

"As Leader of the Senate, I wrote to them of the Senate's position, reminding them of their duties to intercept Antonius and neutralize his forces."

Atticus placed his hands on his knees and mused, "For your sake, Marcus, and yours too, Quintus, I hope they regard *that* as their duty."

"There's something you can do for us, and for the Republic," I said to him. Atticus looked at me curiously, his head turned toward me, and his brow furrowed. "Your house guest may have some visitors or correspondence that I and the Senate should know about."

Atticus smirked and then cocked his head, looking at me with his pale eyes half-closed. "That's quite indelicate, Marcus. You would have me *spy* on Fulvia, on her mother-in-law, on her children?" He shook his head disapprovingly. "They came to me and asked for sanctuary…."

"Which you did not refuse," I interjected.

"*Which I did not refuse.* And now I must refuse to violate the hospitality that I've extended to them. Sorry, Marcus, but I cannot help you with this."

His refusal irritated me, but it did not surprise me. Informing and spying was below Atticus, and when he gave his hospitality it was without reservation or contingency. All the same, his houseguest was the wife of an enemy of the Republic. His refusal to inform on her was probably motivated more by business considerations than by patriotism or social courtesy.

Unbeknownst to him, I had arranged for Alexio to keep an eye on who visited his house in the Aventine district. Alexio told me that a frequent visitor was Clodia Pulchra.

Omniscient Narrative

"Nearly two months since it all happened, and I still marvel at how quickly it was done." Fulvia remembers when she and her children and her mother-in-law had been forced to vacate the Aventine house, the house that had once belonged to her grand-father, Gaius Gracchus. She is telling her visitor, Clodia Pulchra, the full measure of her angst. "They took away Antonius' house in the City and his Tibur place. Then they even booted us out of my grand-father's house. Atticus allowed us to stay here. He and his entire household have been so hospitable and solicitous."

Indeed, Atticus' house in the Aventine district has been home to Marcus Antonius' family since the Senate decreed him a public enemy at the end of April. The house is spacious enough to afford ample, separate quarters for the children, for Antonius' mother, Julia, and for Fulvia. Each time Clodia visits, she and Fulvia retire to this well-appointed room to exchange confidences and for other intimacies.

"You shouldn't be surprised, Fulvia," advises Clodia. "All of you are his latest investment. He's wise enough to realize that Marcus Antonius is far from finished, though he's on the run." Clodia is especially vibrant today, adorned in a cream-colored stola and saffron palla. Her luminous blue-black hair cascades upon her straight shoulders. Her ebony eyes glow in the oil-light of the room, and her oval face and bow-shaped mouth beckon invitingly.

Fulvia leans in ever so closely, taking in her visitor's spikenard scent. Her own flame-colored tresses grace her neck and shoulders, complementing her violet stola and mauve palla. She whispers, "The other day, I received a note from Calenus. He and his partners, Bassus and Censorinus and their troops were allowed safe passage beyond Mutina. Can you believe it? They had expected to have to fight their way to the Transalpina, but *Caesar-Boy* let them pass unmolested. How bizarre! What's that kid up to?"

Clodia purses her lips thoughtfully. "He's hedging his bet, no doubt, making overtures to Antonius toward a possible accommodation."

Fulvia nods in agreement. "Perhaps. Almost two months since Mutina's relief and still no word from Marcus. What could have happened to him? Should I assume that no news is good news? I don't know, but each day, I grow more apprehensive, especially as the *Chick-Pea* continues his verbal assault on my Antonius. Imagine it! My Antonius declared a public enemy! *Chick-Pea* must pay for this in an exemplary way!"

Pulling back from Clodia, Fulvia turns her head slightly, looking at her guest sideways. "Have you lately looked in on your neighbor? Have you succeeded in working your charms on him? Were I you, I'd smother the old bugger with his own pillow after he'd spilled out whatever putrid seed he might yet have in his aging loins."

Clodia smiles. "How passionately spiteful you are, Fulvia – Fulvia *Vulva*."

Fulvia has understood the invitation. She removes Clodia's palla and caresses her neck. "But never mind," she coos. "I'll have my revenge in my own way – with or without your help." Fulvia kisses her hard on the mouth, drawing Clodia close to her so that their bosoms touch. While nibbling on Clodia's long neck, she sighs, "My Clodia, your touch, your very nearness arouses me. Your mouth is so deep, warm, and moist. Your neck is like an alabaster column." She slips off Clodia's stola from her shoulders.

Clodia arches her back, her nipples are aroused, and her breasts point enticingly at Fulvia. "Your breasts are like two tender, young doves," Fulvia murmurs as her lips and tongue ply Clodia's breasts and nipples. Clodia lies back on the couch upon which they have been sitting. Her back is supported on a plush pillow, and her legs rest securely upon her heels as her knees spread wide apart. Fulvia raises the hem of Clodia's stola and manipulates her exposed pudendum. "Your thighs, your *labia*, are like ripened figs from Picenum."

In response, Clodia raises her arms above her head, her long, slender fingers are buried in her copious black hair, and she murmurs, "You raise me up higher than the Aventine. Oh, Fulvia, lets' forget, for awhile anyway, let's forget about Antonius and the *Chick-Pea* and the *Caesar-Boy* and all the other personae of this insanity."

"My sweet pomegranate, more than anyone else you've carried me through this ordeal." Fulvia descends—lips, mouth, and tongue—upon Clodia's fragrant, moist delta.

Clodia moans in rapture. Her body shudders in ecstasy. She arches her back, pushing her loins forward and upward toward her lover's ministrations, and her hands cup her own breasts in climactic ascent. Through her rampant reveries, a face comes clearly into view; the face of the man she wants ever so desperately, but who has thus far eluded her. *How long, how long will you hold me at bay? How long, how long Marcus Tullius Cicero? How long?*

Cicero's Elysian Voice

More dire news for the Republic came from Proconsul Lepidus. Writing to the Senate, he informed us that his legions had made contact with the forces of Marcus Antonius. The soldiers on both sides had laid aside their weapons and embraced as comrades-in-arms in peace and friendship. Before this encounter, his tribunes and senior centurions had warned him that the legionaries were so strongly disaffected toward the Senate that they could not be relied upon to fight Antonius.

On several earlier occasions, Lepidus had written the Senate to urge peace with Antonius, but his entreaties were rebuffed. Now, the legionaries had forced him to make his own peace. So, emulating the soldiers' example, he had clasped hands, in full sight of the legions, with the Proconsul whom the Senate had declared to be a public enemy.

Now that their legions were united, Lepidus admitted that he deferred to the counsels of Marcus Antonius.

With the defection of Lepidus, he too was declared a public enemy and his properties were confiscated. Our only hope appeared to be Octavianus, who was close at hand in the Po Valley, and at a greater distance, Marcus Brutus in Macedonia. By the Ides of Junius, his dispatches told us that he had captured Apollonia and had Gaius Antonius in custody. Immediately, the Senate sent couriers to Brutus ordering him to bring at least a part of his forces to Italia.

While we waited, Octavianus sent a delegation of soldiers to the Senate with his request that he be allowed to stand in absentia for election to one of the vacant consulates. He wanted the other vacancy to be filled by his elderly kinsman, Quintus Pedius.

Cornutus and the other praetors insisted that Octavianus' request was illegal and unconstitutional. Though the Senate had elevated him to propraetorian status during the Mutina war, Octavianus was barely twenty years old and he had held none of the prerequisite offices. The praetors would not follow through with what had been previously sanctioned. Moreover, they refused to recognize any political canvassing in absentia.

I criticized the dangerous inconsistency of conferring upon Octavianus a lofty office when it suited their purpose, but then denying him the consulate because of strict legalities. And of course, the rationale was simple. Though Antonius had joined forces with Lepidus, he was not considered a viable danger, especially since Plancus, Pollio, and Decimus Brutus remained loyal to the Republic. Also, as the Senate put so much stock in Marcus Brutus' recent victories in Macedonia, their rebuff of Octavianus was meant to bring him to heel.

Though I expressed these sentiments publicly in the Senate, privately I too had reservations about a youth becoming consul. Then again, expediency should have taken priority over strict legalities.

The centurion in charge of the delegation was Gaius Herennius. Upon hearing the Senate's denial, he clutched his sword hilt and sneered, "If you will not make him Consul, then *this* will!"

After the delegation had departed, the Senate voted to recall the legions of Proconsul Cornificius from Africa. Luckily, Cornificius had refused to relinquish his governorship to Antonius' appointee, Calvisius Sabinus. The Senate hoped that they could rely on his aid, for they were uncertain and fearful of Octavianus' motives. I was beginning to share their sentiments. What kind of game was he playing? If the Senate thought Cornificius would prevent any rash moves by Octavianus, I doubted that he could bring his forces to Italia soon enough.

While in the midst of this reverie, I looked over at the colossal image of Capitoline Jove majestically looking down upon the senators in their military garb. Then, I caught sight of the statuette of Minerva that I had placed on the goddess' pedestal before setting out for exile so many years earlier. Yet, there she remained, by the foot of Wisdom's larger than life-size statue.

THROUGH THE MONTH THAT USED to be Quinctilis and which was now honorifically named Juleus, Atticus implored me to leave Roma and to go to the East, to Athens or to Appolonia. He said, as had others, that I had relied too heavily on Octavianus, even though his step-father, Philippus, and his brother-in-law, Marcellus, had consistently vouched for the young man's loyalty and reliability. Admittedly, my patience with Atticus had grown rather short. I replied to his entreaties by asking why he did not advise the Antonius family to flee instead of sheltering them. He had even extended his protection to Lepidus' household since the Senate had declared him a public enemy owing to his defection to Antonius. I wondered if he would do the same for Plancus' family.

By mid-month, Plancus wrote to the Senate of his falling out with Decimus Brutus. He reported that Brutus had wanted their combined strength to seek out and destroy Antonius. However, Plancus tarried and delayed because most of his soldiers were untried recruits unlikely to stand up against Antonius' seasoned, but depleted, veterans. Plancus intimated that Antonius had sent him messages reminding him of the benefits they both had received from Caesar. The very province that Decimus governed had been subdued by Caesar.

As his loyalty to the Senate wavered and faltered, disaffection spread through his legions and those of Brutus. The Proconsuls argued before their soldiers, Brutus insisting that they march south into Transalpina to hunt down Antonius, while Plancus refused and insisted on waiting for further developments.

When his soldiers mutinied, Brutus fled to the Illyrian city of Aquileia. Plancus surmised that Brutus would endeavor to proceed from there to Macedonia and then join forces with Marcus Brutus. But the fugitive's plans came to naught. Decimus Brutus was hunted down and killed by Gallic auxiliaries, probably at Antonius' instigation.

Brutus' body was delivered to Plancus, and he in turn was sending it down to Octavianus at Mutina. Plancus concluded his report by stating unequivocally that, as his legions had declared for Antonius and would otherwise have mutinied, he would acquiesce to their demands.

Yet another defection from the Republic shook the Senate's resolve, though their decree declared Plancus a public enemy and confiscated his property.

At about the same time, Sextus Pompeius wrote from Massilia, yet again professing his loyalty to the Republic. But he dared not move from his base despite the Senate's earlier commendation and commission. I was starting to have my doubts about him as he progressively became more of an enigma.

Then, a second delegation arrived from Octavianus to present his second request for election to the consulate. They also delivered the remains of Decimus Brutus, doused in olive oil and soldiers' wine and wrapped in his scarlet military cloak.

In answer to the petition, the Senate remained steadfastly negative. The Proconsul's body was given over to his family. I proposed the honor of an official funeral for Decimus Brutus. The Senate decreed it, but with far less enthusiasm than I would have expected. The strain of war and uncertainty weighed upon us all.

Omniscient Narrative

Upon a long, rectangular marble table in the atrium of his mother's house, the corpse of Decimus Junius Brutus is laid out. A white gown has covered his washed body. The marks of the stab wounds and gashes on his torso are concealed, but those on his throat and shoulders are plainly visible.

In gray and black mourning attire, Decimus' mother stands at the head of the table near her son's head. Her face, once so beautiful in its vivacity and allure, is now hard and distraught with grief. Around the table are six women, friends and acquaintances of Sempronia. They have come to pay their respects to Decimus Brutus on the eve of his official funeral.

Directly to Sempronia's left is her daughter-in-law, Flavia, whose beautiful countenance betrays no emotion. Next to her is her mother, Aurelia Orestilla, as hard in her beauty as a precious, polished gem. At the end of the table is Servilia, not only friend to Sempronia, but also kin by marriage to Decimus' deceased father.

Sempronia, Orestilla, and Servilia are a formidable trio encompassing beauty, carnal and political experience, and exuding unbounded notoriety. They have been mothers widowed by various circumstances, and they have had politically prominent lovers who have met violent deaths. However much they may deny it, their time of influence is waning.

Such may not be the case with the younger women on the opposite side of the corpse-bearing table. To Sempronia's right is Junia, Servilia's first daughter and wife of Marcus Lepidus, the Proconsul only lately declared an enemy of the Republic. Next to her is Tertia, Servilia's third daughter and wife to the tyrannicide, Gaius Cassius Longinus. At the end of the table stands Porcia, wife of Servilia's first son, the prime tyrannicide, Marcus Brutus, and daughter of the Republican martyr, Marcus Porcius Cato.

Servilia is distressed at her daughter-in-law's presence. She has been ill for several weeks. Wan and ashen, Porcia supports herself on a birch cane, her hand trembling on its hilt. Though her body is wracked by fever and pain, her spirit is indomitable. Cato would have been proud of her.

Besides their marriage ties, the young women are also cousins by virtue of the half-sibling kinship of Servilia with Cato. Porcia is a feminine variant of her late father's long-faced, long-necked features. Junia and Tertia reflect in opposite but hardly commensurate ways their mother's silver-haired beauty.

Sempronia had insisted that her son's body be transported from his house to her own. In this, she had surmounted Flavia's spousal rights, but the young woman had respectfully acquiesced, prompted by Orestilla's intervention.

Looking at Decimus' rigid corpse displayed upon the marble table, Servilia thinks of her own sons. She knows of Marcus Brutus' recent successes in Macedonia, his subjugation of the province, and the formidable power he has built up there. But she knows nothing about Marcus Silanus, except that he has fled with Antonius into Transalpina.

Of her sons-in-law, there has been no recent news from Syria concerning Gaius Cassius' movements; like all of Roma, she knows that Marcus Lepidus has joined with Antonius and has thereby fallen afoul of the Senate. Within her family, the divisions of Roman civil war are manifestly evident. Another son-in-law, Publius Servilius Vatia, a senatorial neutral, that rare and diminishing faction, is married to

Servilia's middle daughter, Junilla. She has not attended the rites because Vatia expressly forbade her.

Servilia's reveries are interrupted by Sempronia's voice. "Friends, women of Roma, thank you for coming here tonight to share in these humble rites. Tomorrow, my Decimus will be honored with an official state funeral." She pauses momentarily, looking down at her son. Then, raising her tear-swollen eyes to all the women, she continues. "But for *myself*, I ask for nothing beyond a simple cremation outside the walls."

The women are shaken by this strange utterance. Turning to her daughter-in-law, Sempronia asks, "Flavia, will you manage this for me?"

Orestilla answers for her stunned daughter, "My daughter will render all respect and obedience." But even Orestilla does not understand. Servilia and the other women exchange furtive, puzzled glances as though they are all wondering: *What is she about?*

"It is my wish to join my son among the shades of the dead," Sempronia announces in a hushed, steady voice, "and I implore all of you—do *not* try to dissuade or restrain me in carrying out my intention." Again, she looks down at her son's body. "My Decimus died a Roman's death, at the hands of Roma's foes. His mother, too, will die a Roman's death—by her own hand."

On either side of the table, the women are gripped with tension, but none dares to speak. New tears begin to stream down the aggrieved mother's face, and her voice quavers. "My son did his mother's bidding in all things. I know, and all of you know of rumors and innuendoes about my husband's death so many years ago. Now, before all of you, I freely admit that he died at my own hands."

As though struck by bolts of lightning, the women are paralyzed with shock.

"I need not justify what I did to him, for he deserved it. But I procured an ally—in my own son, my Decimus." Here, Sempronia smiles pathetically at the corpse and passes her hand over his matted hair. Her voice is choked with emotion as she admits, "I seduced my son and made him my partner in murder. This womb..." she touches her own belly, "this womb from which he was born became...."

"*Enough, Sempronia!*" Servilia's shrill, outraged voice interrupts. The women's shock has now turned to revulsion. Cupping their mouths,

Servilia's daughters retch. In utter disgust, Porcia shakes her head as though to dislodge the revelation from her mind. Flavia and her mother regard each other ominously, for they both remember that Catilina had been the apex of their own peculiar triangle.

"... the chamber of our dishonor." Completing her statement, Sempronia removes from her black palla a lethal dagger. "I'll not live in this world without him!" She brandishes the long, slender blade well above her head for all to see before bringing it down and plunging it into her own groin. Several times she repeats the ritual, and with each stab her blood splatters upon her son's corpse and upon the nearest women.

Horrified, the younger women scream like the Furies of Hades. Orestilla and Servilia, like two marble statues, are too shocked to move, much less to intervene.

Her face ashen, her loins bloodied and torn, Sempronia collapses to the tiled floor into a pool of her own blood. Her dead eyes seem to stare upward toward her son's corpse on the table above her.

Sempronia—the once great beauty; the widow of the optimate oligarch, Decimus Brutus, the mistress of Lentulus Sura, co-conspirator of Lucius Catilina; and the jaded mother of young Decimus Brutus, murdered in Roma's latest civil war—lives no more.

Cicero's Elysian Voice

SEVERAL DAYS AFTER DECIMUS BRUTUS' funeral, the Senate received victorious news from Gaius Cassius. He reported that the province of Syria had been secured for the Republic. After a three month siege, his legions had captured Laodiceia, in large measure because Dolabella's soldiers deserted him, and the citizens surrendered the city. Cassius had allowed no pillaging, but he replenished his depleted resources from the city's reserves of grain, oil, and wine.

Deserted by his soldiers and betrayed by the townspeople, Dolabella had taken his own life. One of his aides directed Cassius to Dolabella's body. Cassius assured us that he would provide funeral honors commensurate with Dolabella's rank and status.

Cassius and his officers had now a full agenda to administer: secure the grain lines from Egypt; guard Syria's borders against the Parthians; and to confirm the loyalty of the client-rulers nearest Asia before moving into the province and removing Dolabella's legate. We knew that Cassius had been in regular contact with Marcus Brutus. Between Brutus' conquest of Macedonia and Cassius' victory in Syria, large areas of Roma's Eastern imperium had been secured for the Republic. Cassius promised that their combined forces would soon come to Italia. He expressed the hope that Antonius was being kept at bay, if he had not yet been destroyed. His further hope was that the Proconsuls of the Western provinces remained steadfast in their loyalty to the Senate.

Finally, Cassius warned us against putting any stock in Gaius *Octavius*, for Cassius was convinced that the young man's overriding ambition was to be another Caesar, both in name and in fact. He even refused to acknowledge the adoptive form of his name.

The Senate formally named Cassius as Proconsul of Syria and Asia. We who were loyal to the Republic hoped that he and his partner, Marcus Brutus, would persevere in their efforts to hold the East intact.

My former son-in-law, my beloved Tullia's ex-husband, had died an honorable Roman's death as though to mitigate and to atone for the recklessness and profligacy of his life.

THERE WERE RUMORS THAT OCTAVIANUS was on the march—not in pursuit of Antonius, but toward Roma! Would the legions from Africa arrive soon? Could they be counted on to be loyal? Our one legion had been deployed in and about Mars Field to check any hostile advance from the north.

It was so tempting to consider Atticus' advice to flee to the East. Though Quintus and I discussed it, we remained undecided. Even more tempting and unsettling was an offer from another quarter.

Clodia Pulchra visited me. She was magnificently beautiful and supremely alluring. "How long will you tarry here, Marcus Cicero?" Her words were more an entreaty than a question. "Your *Caesar-Boy* has proven to be unreliable. Marcus Antonius has been joined by men whom you were certain would have destroyed him. Should they all unite their forces do you imagine there will be any clemency for you?"

"You're so well apprised, Clodia," I observed. "It comes from being so intimate with Antonius' wife, I suppose."

She bypassed my flippant remark. "I care about you, as insane as that may sound to you. Evil will befall you if you don't leave while you can."

"Why, Clodia, why do you care what happens to me?"

She smiled that notoriously enigmatic smile. "If not just desire, then love; if more than love, then obsession. These are the three racks you've tortured me on, Marcus." Her dark eyes held on me. "Come with me, Marcus. Come with me to the Greek isles. We'll make our own Elysium. Come with me, even now."

Not Elysium, but fire was in her embrace as her arms enveloped me. Her mouth pressed against mine as though she would swallow me. I could not, I *would* not, pull away from her. Instead, I took her into my arms. My own lips were on hers and we breathed moist, warm breath into each other's mouths. I was irreversibly charged, impassioned as I had not been in years. My heart pounded in my chest like an assaulting battering ram. I wanted her and I could have had her then and there in the privacy of my own atrium. Fleetingly, I remembered, as though from a dream, the night, so many years before, when I almost had taken her. But now, if I were to take her, I would have had to go away with her. There could not have been any life without her.

Suddenly, she stopped. Breathlessly, she said to me, "Then you will come with me, Marcus?"

It was then that my composure returned; my ardor was suspended in abeyance. Seeing the change in me, she spoke again. "You're not yet ready, are you? Well, soon Marcus, soon you'll be ready, won't you? Don't stay here any longer, darling Cicero."

Then, she left, but her words and her aura remained with me, penetrating to my heart, to my very core.

HEAVEN AND EARTH WERE IN tumult at the beginning of Sextilis. Heavy, violent rains poured down upon Roma and the immediate environs. Even hail stones, large enough for slings, assailed the City. Winds from the north and from the Tyrrhenian Sea buffeted the walls, wreaking havoc upon the flimsiest insulae. The Tiber flooded its banks, inundating those who lived in Roma's low-lying districts. Publius Figulus reminded me that there had not been such foul, inclement weather since the eve of that fateful Ides of March which brought death to Caesar. "Some calamity," Figulus intoned, "some great reversal of our present status is at hand. Through such unseasonable weather, the gods make known our fates."

Yes, it was unseasonable weather for summer, and it persisted well past the Ides. Tempestuous winds had knocked down several monuments in the Forum, including one to Atius Regilus, a hero of Roma's first war with Carthage nearly three hundred years before. Once Roma's mortal foe, Carthage had been laid waste after more than a century of intermittent warfare. And Carthaginian territory had been organized into the province of Africa.

It was from Africa that we anticipated the arrival of the legions that the Senate had hastily summoned. How ironic it was, then, that the first cohorts should have landed at Ostia in the wake of the windstorm that had toppled Regilus' monument. At least, the ships that carried them had had favorable winds at their backs.

The Urban Praetor, Marcus Cornutus and one of his colleagues, Quintus Gallius, a lean, unassuming stick of a man, hurried down to the Roman seaport to assume command of the troops and bring them to the City. However, they returned only with their lictors and other attendants.

Having pitched their camp in and around Ostia, the African cohorts refused to advance into Roma. Their tribunes and centurions said they were waiting for the remaining forces to arrive. The soldiers' refusal to be inducted under the Praetors' command augured ill for the Republic.

The Praetors inspected the legion encamped at Mars Field. These young recruits had grown surly and disaffected. The boredom and monotony of camp life, especially under the hardships of incessant rain and wind, had sapped their youthful patriotism, such as it may have been. Cornutus and Gallius were as displeased with them as they had been with the African cohorts encamped at Ostia.

During the night of the eighteenth, while vicious winds and rain pelted Roma, the young recruits deserted their posts in Mars Field. Crossing over the Milvian Bridge, they headed north toward Etruria. The officers who had apparently tried to dissuade them from deserting were killed.

The next day, a delegation of senators, of which Quintus and I were members, went out and beheld their bodies strewn over the camp grounds. Through the drizzle, vultures could be seen flying overhead. Our spirits crushed, we arranged for the officers' burial before returning to the City.

Praetor Cornutus convened the Senate in the Capitoline Jovian Temple. As the senators were ascending the Capitiline ramp and the Gemonian Steps, exultant outcries were heard from the Forum below. The resonance of marching feet on hob-nailed soldiers' boots filled the Forum from end to end. Standing next to me, Quintus strained his eyes to recognize the standards of units of the Second and the Martian Legions.

"Could it be?" I wondered aloud. Just then, I recognized Gaius Octavianus riding a gray, dappled horse at the head of a troop of horsemen. His head, that fair-haired head, was uncovered as he bore his helmet in the crook of his arm. He wore a brown, leather cuirass studded with bronze and iron. Coming up behind him were his constant companions, Agrippa, Maecenas, and Salvidienus, also mounted and attired in military uniforms.

The people in the Forum were calling out to him: *"Caesar! Caesar! Vindicator! Hero! Victor!"* His legionaries fanned out, positioning themselves all along the Forum's perimeter and even atop the temples' steps and upon the Rostra. His horsemen pushed aside the cheering crowds, containing them. Those young, raw recruits, who had deserted us the night before, had gone over to Octavianus. They assisted the horsemen in improvising a barrier against the mob which called out all the more vociferously each time they were pushed, shoved, and manhandled.

Octavianus looked up to the Capitoline and spotted the train of senators arrayed along the Mount's staircase and ramp. Beckoning to his companions and to several horsemen, he made for the triumphal ramp so as to ascend more quickly to the summit. The senators were obliged to move out of the way of the ascending cavalcade.

Turning to Quintus, I remarked, "Before today, he sent delegations. Now, he comes in person, not to petition, but to *demand*." The senators resumed their ascent to the temple. At the summit, Octavianus remained mounted, watching impassively as the senators filed past him, walked up the temple's steps, and entered it. Cornutus and the other praetors, so adamant in their refusal to allow him to stand for the consulate, bowed nervously in his presence.

By the time we were seated, and Cornutus had called us to order, Octavianus entered the cella. He was flanked by his companions and several lictors in respect of the propraetorian status that the Senate had decreed for him.

One of his companions was his elder cousin, Quintus Pedius. He was a frail, sickly specimen of a man who looked considerably older than his mid-forties. His gait was halting, probably from the afflictions of gout, and even his tunic and toga seemed to weigh him down.

Octavianus surveyed the scene with gravity that was far beyond his twenty years. There was no doubt that he had grown in political and military experience since the day he first visited me at Antium. He had been a nineteen-year-old student then, on his way to Roma to claim his inheritance. Now, having fought his and the Republic's foes, he was ready to dictate.

"Conscript Fathers," the young Caesar began, "it is good that you yet wear the military garb, for there is still a state of war. The Republic lacks consuls, and your first obligation is to correct this. So, you will sanction my own and Quintus Pedius' election to the consulate for the remainder of the year."

There it was! The young whelp's thunderbolt shocked the senators, except for his step-father, Philippus, and his brother-in-law, Marcellus. Over much grumbling and murmuring, Octavianus proceeded to outline his agenda.

"All legions of the Republic are to be placed under my command. The forces presently at Ostia will be placed under the command of Quintus Pedius." He looked about the cella and noticed the Tribunes positioned near the doors. Perhaps he anticipated a veto from one or all of them. But none was forthcoming. He called out to them, "Where is Tribune Publius Casca? Where is the murderer of my father?"

Tribune Appuleius stepped forward and responded, "He has fled the City!"

Octavianus was pleased with the news. He turned toward Marcus Agrippa and announced, "I nominate Marcus Agrippa to the vacated tribunate of Publius Casca. The Plebeian Concilium will vote for him accordingly. Once installed in office, Agrippa will prosecute in absentia the assassins of Gaius Julius Caesar. Their properties will be forfeited to the Republic."

The murmuring of dissent among the senators became more agitated. Octavianus held up his hand to quiet them, as Salvidienus made for the door. "Conscript Fathers, the condemnation of the assassins of the Divine Julius is long overdue. Also, my official adoption will be delayed no longer. Accordingly, the Centuriate Assembly will validate the adoption with all expediency."

Salvidienus now re-entered the cella with a unit of armed soldiers who positioned themselves within the cella's perimeter. Stunned into silence by this show of force, the senators had no alternative but to listen quietly to the young Caesar's final dictate. "The Senate will rescind its decrees of outlawry against all adherents of Gaius Julius Caesar.' He paused again. Not a cough or murmur was heard. "This, Conscript Fathers, is my agenda for the settlement of the Republic's woes. The Senate will act and the Citizens' Assemblies will legislate accordingly because this is all for the ultimate welfare of the Republic."

So slyly, he was opening the doors to a truce with Antonius and with the Proconsuls who had been condemned as public enemies.

When Octavianus and his men departed, I looked up at the colossal image of Jupiter. Cold, marmoreal silence stared down at a Senate in the throes of fear and confusion. Suddenly, I noticed that my statuette of Minerva was missing. But upon closer inspection, I recognized its shattered pieces strewn upon the marble floor. Minerva had either been the victim of vandalism or of the previous night's violent storm. Either way, the sight of the destroyed statuette alarmed me, filling me with a sickening sense of foreboding. Even Quintus shared my fear. Publius Figulus, so taken up with signs and portents, also noticed the broken fragments. Though he regarded me anxiously, he offered no comment.

The rest of that day, that fateful nineteenth day of Sextilis, the weather had cleared sufficiently to allow the Centuriate Assembly to convene without the likelihood of any augural invalidation. Octavianus put it through his dictated paces. At long last, his adoption was formally ratified. Now, he was officially Gaius Julius Caesar Octavianus. He bore the name, he inherited the property, and he was well on his way to becoming the Great Man's successor. The very same convention of the Centuriata elected young Caesar and his cousin, Pedius, to the vacant consulates.

With but a few hours of daylight remaining, Octavianus had Tribune Appuleius convene the Plebeian Concilium so that Marcus Agrippa could be elected to the tribunate abandoned by Publius Casca. The next morning, the new Tribune reconvened the Concilium. As his first official act as the People's Tribune, Agrippa secured the condemnation in absentia of Caesar's assassins. We could no longer speak of them as tyrannicides or Liberators. That would have been not only politically inappropriate, but also illegal and even treasonable.

On the Capitoline summit, before the Jovian Temple, the new Consuls were inaugurated. While performing the customary inaugural sacrifices, Octavianus indicated six vultures flying overhead. At the same time, another group of six was flying over the Forum in the vicinity of the Temple of Concord.

The timely appearance of these predatory scavengers may have been contrived, probably by the wily Etruscan Maecenas, as propaganda for Octavianus; or they may have been among the parasites that had flown over the corpses in Mars Field the day before. Nonetheless, their significance was not lost upon many of the senators, particularly Varro, Figulus, and Philippus. Even the more enlightened of the City rabble could not have failed to grasp the auspiciousness of the vultures' flight. Roma's legendary founder, Romulus, had had his first sacrifice attended by twelve vultures. So, it was evident that Octavianus and his agents wanted the senators and the citizenry to infer the gods' favor upon him as a new founder, or at least as the creator of a new order for Roma. But far more ominously, as Romulus had also been Roma's first king, was Octavianus posing as a new master of the Republic?

When the senators queued up to congratulate the new Consuls, I took a position at the end of the line, even though I was senior to all of my colleagues, with the exception of Aurelius Cotta who was first to salute his kinsman, Octavianus. At last, when I approached Octavianus, he facetiously said to me, "Marcus Cicero, the last of my friends to greet me!" I was taken aback by this, but he relieved my discomfiture by thanking me for my efforts on his behalf. Then he said to me, "You would do well to retire from Roma, but only as you desire."

His words were like a command couched as an invitation, or so I thought at the time. I looked askance at him and his sickly colleague and cousin, Pedius, and wondered what was next in store for us.

Omniscient Narrative

THE NEW CONSULS ARE THE guests of honor at the Carinae home of Marcius Philippus and Atia. The peristyle of the house is adorned for the festivity. Lamps have been lit to illumine the dusk; couches have been set out, and tables have been packed with bounteous food and beakers of wine and water.

The family of Gaius Octavius Caepias has gathered to celebrate the elevation of Caesar Octavianus and Quintus Pedius to the consulate. Atia and Philippus are thoroughly proud of them, but they have misgivings about Octavianus' age and Pedius' health.

Seated at a table, Octavianus' brother-in-law, Gaius Marcellus, stuffs a Sicilian olive into his mouth, and while chewing on it he manages to ask him, "Aren't you uncomfortable being twenty-two years *too* young to be Consul?"

The new, young Caesar smiles tolerantly. "I know all of you are surprised and confused by what I've done, though no one before you, Marcellus, has directly questioned me about my actions, or my plans."

Philippus raises his bald head, his pudgy face catching the oil lamplight. His stocky frame seems to overpower the couch upon which he reclines. "Are you trying to imitate your illustrious, adoptive father by twisting the constitution?" His question is laced with a tinge of irony.

Octavianus answers earnestly. "Had I not taken the consulate, then the Senate, having finished with me, would have pushed me aside, relegating me to political oblivion. You think Cicero would have continued to sponsor me once Decimus Brutus was liberated and after Antonius was defeated? You heard his words, did you not Marcellus? You heard him also, Father." Octavianus turns from his brother-in-law and his step-father to face Tribune Publius Appuleius and Senator Sextus Appuleius. "Did you not hear him as well? Did not Cicero announce that I should be exulted all the way to the heavens?"

The men whom Octavianus has addressed answer him affirmatively. The young Consul trusts them all. Philippus, his step-father, has been constant in his love and in his honor for Atia, and in his fatherly solicitude for Octavianus. Similarly, Gaius Marcellus, once Caesar's foe, has been a lovingly faithful husband to Octavia. The young Caesar's other sibling is his half-sister, also named Octavia. She was born of Gaius Octavius' first marriage, and she is married to Sextus Appuleius, a senator of aedilician rank, and a cousin of the like-named Tribune.

These men have consistently supported Octavianus' interests during the entire Mutina war and even earlier, when he had petitioned for his adoption and inheritance. Yet, he senses their continued misgivings.

"Very well then," Philippus asserts, "Cicero is duplicitous. "But why did you change tack only after Antonius retreated?"

"The Consuls had questioned whether we were fighting the real enemy. Before Pansa died, he told me that we might be reconciled with Antonius. He said that the real foes were those men who, after being advanced and promoted by Caesar, conspired against him, killed him, and in so doing, condemned us to new discord. He asked me how we, Caesar's relatives, friends, and supporters, could fight each other when we should have been fighting the Brutuses and Cassius and the other traitors." Octavianus' fervent words almost bring the image of the deceased Consul to every person present. "Tomorrow, I leave for the north," the young Consul announces. "I'm gambling on a truce with Antonius."

"*Truce with Antonius?*" His half-sister interjects. She is dark of complexion and of hair, as her mother, Ancharia had been. Yet, she also resembles her father, the late Gaius Octavius. She is slender in figure, square shouldered, and long-limbed. Her face also is long and her mouth protrudes because of crooked teeth.

"My son, do you truly believe you can trust him?" Atia is incredulous.

"Well, Mother, that remains to be seen. We both have ties to Caesar, ties of blood kinship and ties of service." Octavianus nods reassuringly. "Besides, I have the consulate."

Turning to his cousin and colleague, Octavianus says, "Quintus, I'm relying on you to manage the Senate in my absence."

The sickly, gout-ridden man replies, "Of course, Gaius—I mean, *Caesar.*"

Atia asks herself as she shakes her head disapprovingly: *My son, why him? Was there no one else you could have chosen?*

"Brother, do you so urgently need Antonius?" The younger Octavia's question betrays a political naivete. She resembles her mother in her fair hair and complexion and chiseled features, and she is taller than her slight, younger brother.

"When I learned of my inheritance, I asked an astrologer, Theogenes of Appolonia, to cast my horoscope. After he had done so, he prostrated himself at my feet and told me that my destiny was to rule over all of Roma's imperium." *If* I'm to fulfill my destiny—*yes*—for now, perhaps for some time hereafter, I'll need Marcus Antonius." He turns now to Atia. "Mother, do you remember the story you told me of Father's visit to the Dionysian Shrine in Apollona, when he was Proconsul?"

Atia sighs, "Yes, my son. Your father wrote me about his sacrifice to the god; he described how a flame had shot up from the altar. The priests said it portended that his son would have dominion over the world."

Atia notices her son-in-law, Marcellus, grimacing at Octavianus' tale of the Apollonian soothsayer. He has heard the tale before, and with each telling his skepticism becomes more apparent upon his ruddy, hawk-like features. Impatiently, he shifts his sturdy frame in his chair as Atia speaks on.

"They also explained that once before had a similar phenomenon occurred—when Alexander of Macedon had sacrificed at the same altar." Atia turns to her son, lowering her voice to a religious intonation. "Before we conceived you, Gaius, I dreamt that a snake had entered me and...."

"Oh Mother, please!" Octavia exclaims.

"Don't scoff, child!" Atia upbraids her. "Snakes carry the spirits of the gods!"

Octavianus reverts to his father's experience at Apollonia. "The night of Father's sacrifice, he dreamt of me. Though I was only a child, he saw me in super-human majesty, armed with thunderbolt, scepter, and all the regal trappings of Jupiter. I wore a solar diadem and I was riding in a chariot bedecked with laurel and drawn by twelve magnificent white horses."

More amazing than the revelation is the completely unperturbed, unembarrassed demeanor with which Octavianus tells it. "If I'm to fulfill my destiny, the destiny indicated by these portents and by Father's dream, I must engineer a truce with Antonius. Toward this end, I allowed his friends and their legions to pass freely through my lines so that they could join him. Before that, I released a prisoner and told him to go find Antonius."

Agrippa interjects. "A bold gamble *that* was! Those friends—Bassus, Calenus, and Censorinus—have very likely linked up with Antonius, along with Lepidus and Plancus, and perhaps even Pollio." Like the speaker, his words are direct, simple, and logical.

"My gestures were meant to signal Antonius. I'm gambling that he won't ignore these peace overtures, especially as I've also sent emissaries to the Transalpina to seek out his whereabouts and arrange a meeting with him." Octavianus pauses and looks about the peristyle as though anticipating some objections or questions.

Octavia the Younger asks, "What about Marcus Brutus and Gaius Cassius? Marcellus says that they've built up a great power in Macedonia and Greece and the entire East."

For emphasis, Marcellus adds, "And they must surely have their secret supporters here and all over Italia."

"And there's nothing secretive about the Cicero brothers' support," Philippus puts in.

Octavianus acknowledges their accuracy. "All true; and all the more reason that *all* of Caesar's men unite to destroy his enemies."

Now, the effete, wily Etruscan, Maecenas contributes to the discussion. "Just as surely, Antonius needs *you* because you now officially bear the name of *Caesar*. It would only weaken him in the eyes of the veterans if he were to continue making war upon you."

"What about Sextus Pompeius?" Marcellus is determined to bring out every conceivable obstacle to his brother-in-law.

Octavianus is quick to answer. "For the time being, if he stays planted at Massilia, he'll not concern us."

"But he's more likely to join Brutus and Cassius," the rustic, tough, soldierly Salvidienus points out.

"And if he does," Octavianus allows, "then he too will have to be eliminated."

"*Marcus Antonius*—he's the crux!" says Marcellus. "It all comes back to him. Gaius, you might ally with him, and then again you might *not*. But even if you do, can you really hope for a lengthy alliance with him?"

Unequivocally, Octavianus answers, "Yes, especially if we have a buffer, someone to balance us."

"Another *triumvirate*?" Philippus asks. "I suppose the third member would be one of the Western Proconsuls."

Smiling and nodding his head appreciatively, Octavianus admits, "I was thinking of the Pontifex Maximus."

"*Lepidus?*" Marcellus' hawk-face is grimacing yet again.

"Why not? Both he and Antonius were Caesar's Master of Horse and co-Consuls." Octavianus sees that his family is fully nonplussed at the extent of his calculations. "Yes, there's so much to be worked out. That's why I must leave tomorrow and go back up to the Cisalpina." He looks intently at the entire family gathering. "Father, Marcellus, Sextus, Publius, and Quintus—please continue to look after my interests in the Senate. In particular, watch over Cicero. See that he doesn't get himself into any trouble."

Then to the women, he says, "Mother and sisters, please remember me in your devotions to our family's ancestral spirits. In particular, remember me in your offerings to the Divine Julius—my beloved granduncle and honored adoptive Father."

Octavianus is thinking of Julius Caesar's words on the Rubicon's bank: *The die is cast.*

Cicero's Elysian Voice

Leaving Pedius in Roma, Octavianus set out for the north, ostensibly to encounter Marcus Antonius and his allies. Brilliant sunshine attended his departure. The sun's rays shone through a huge cloud shaped like a sheaf of grain surmounted by a corona. Figulus said it was an auspicious sign betokening the gods' favor for the young, new Consul.

But others read the omen differently. Among them were the praetors. Having stood opposed to Octavianus' consulate, now they knew they were marked men. Marcus Cornutus, the Urban Praetor, gave them a different sign to ponder. Rather than attend Octavianus' inauguration, he had stayed at home and opened his veins in a warm bathtub. It was said that he did not take long to bleed to death.

Roma was now an armed camp. The senators yet wore the military garb betokening a state of war. Consul Pedius had the African cohorts—more of whom arrived each day—patrol the City and keep order. The very soldiers who had been counted on to shield Roma against Antonius and Octavianus were now under the orders of Young Caesar's consular colleague. The war to liberate the Republic from tyranny, from despotism, from dictatorship, had ground to a halt. We were suspended between a young upstart adventurer, who marched his way to supremacy, and a fugitive enemy who was far from beaten. The Republic was adrift in a twilight realm between liberty and tyranny.

There was no purpose in remaining in Roma. So, near the end of Sextilis, I closed up the Palatine house with a queer sense of finality. Then, with Tiro, Metrodorus, and Alexio and about a dozen household servants, I set out for Tusculum.

Caput XX

THERE IS NOTHING MORE ACCEPTABLE to the chief of the gods who rules over the Cosmos, of all things that happen on the Earth, than the councils and gatherings of men who associate together in respect for law and justice; that is, the organizations called states. Their rulers and preservers have come from Heaven and will return there.

From *The Dream of Scipio*

Cicero's Elysian Voice

THE FORCE OR SPIRIT THAT drove me to Tusculum instead of to any of the other rural villas was unknown to me. I had not been there since my *Tulliola* died. Once, I loved to retreat to Tusculum, where woods shut out the world and afforded me an idyllic sanctuary to read and write and reflect.

But now, the house and grounds were permeated with a sense of death. My soul was afflicted with painful memories of Tullia. Yet, I could not bear to leave the morose place. The same force or spirit that had brought me here impelled me to stay.

Before leaving Roma, I had stopped off at the Vestal Residence to bid farewell to Fabia. Receiving me in the atrium, she could not conceal her concern for me. She was so nervous and preoccupied. "Mother Vesta's flame yet burns bright, but disaster is soon to befall us," Fabia warned me. "Marcus, don't tarry at Tusculum, but leave Italia as soon as possible. Go to Greece and put yourself under Brutus' protection, as your son has already done; or go further East to Gaius Cassius. You've been betrayed by this young Caesar. Antonius and his allies are clearly your enemies."

Fabia took my hands in hers and held them tenderly to her bosom. "May Mother Vesta bless you and light your way." I kissed her on both cheeks and embraced her. She said to me, "Farewell, Marcus Cicero; farewell, and gods' speed."

"Good-bye, Fabia," I murmured to her. "Keep us always in your prayers as you safeguard Vesta's fire. Hail and farewell, most holy one."

I PASSED THE AUTUMN IN relative isolation, although I was routinely visited by Atticus, Quintus, Varro, and Figulus. The news they brought from Roma was of an uneasy tranquility. The Eastern provinces remained firmly controlled by Marcus Brutus and Gaius Cassius. Whenever Consul Pedius convened the Senate, it was only for mundane trivia, and he gave no news of his colleague's activities up North.

OCTAVIANUS HAD INDEED BETRAYED THE Republic and me with it. He was the latest in a long line of *imperatori* who had used the legions to force their will on the Senate. By now, the Senate was weak, exhausted, its members depleted by war, banishment, and cynicism. The remnants went with the tide, and Octavianus was riding the crest. But Antonius and his allies could change that.

A hundred years before, the Greek historian, Polybios—himself a captive of Roma – had described the Republic's prime malady in his *Histories*:

When a commonwealth, after warding off many great dangers, has arrived at a high pitch of prosperity and undisputed power, it is evident that, by the lengthened continuance of great wealth within it, the manner of life of its citizens will become more extravagant; and that the rivalry for office, and in other spheres of activity, will become fiercer than it ought to be.

How clearly Polybios foresaw the process of the Republic's decline through generations of foreign conquest, internal strife, and civil war, a process that had brought us to our present state. Was it an inevitable process? Perhaps; yet, I had refused to acknowledge it. My whole life and career was a testament to that.

In my service to the Republic, I had endured banishment several times and in various forms. When the Fates brought me once again to the steerage of the Republic, I led the Senate against Antonius' tyranny. Though defeated and put to flight, he was still not vanquished. And then the young man whom I had sponsored for the Republic's defense betrayed us in order to achieve his own selfish ends.

THERE WAS A STILLNESS AS of death hovering over me as I waited for further news of the upstart Consul and the fugitive Proconsul. I could feel Tullia's presence in this house. My *Tulliola,* my soul, my life, my light—I could smell your freshness and feel your aura and your warmth. I drew strength from you.

As a youth living at the family homestead at Arpinum, I had spent hours reading beneath the great oak on the island watered by the Liris River. Locals called it the "oak of Marius." I derived so much strength and security sitting beneath its broad, expansive branches and leaning against its stout, firm trunk. To stare up into its mass of green summer leaves with the sunlight streaming through was like beholding Eternity. If I could have seen those leaves now, they would be russet and golden and preparing to drop to the earth. As the seasons change, so too, it seems, do men's fortunes. Mine have been no exception.

THE TUSCULANUM HAD A WELL-STOCKED library. One day, near the end of November, I surveyed the collection, running my fingers by each scroll and examining the title tags. I saw copies of my own philosophical works, the products of years of enforced retirement from politics. Now, I turned to these volumes for solace, to dispel my fears of the unknown, and to find meaning for my life.

Here was *On Ends,* which I had written as a speculation on the chief aim or end of all human action. The Epicureans, Atticus' heroes, maintain that the ultimate aim of human endeavors is the pursuit of pleasure and the avoidance of pain. Among the Stoics, the chief aim is the cultivation of virtue. I have generally followed the *New Academy,* a synthesis of these schools, in endeavoring to inculcate a sound, moral attitude.

In all truth, much of my thinking has been eclectic in that I have always drawn inspiration from the Stoical prescription of enduring all adversity with patience and forbearance. Also, though I remained an agnostic where the gods of the state are concerned, I had always been receptive to the Stoical idea of a Divine Intelligence governing the Cosmos. I anticipated that I would soon come to realize the truth or folly of the Stoics' beliefs.

Turning to the treatise, *On Duties*, which I had written as a code of conduct for Marcus, I reviewed the four cardinal virtues. I reflected on the extent to which my own life had exemplified or contradicted them.

We esteem wisdom. Yet, true knowledge is unattainable. Only probabilities are reliable, especially in politics. So, true wisdom enables us to differentiate among probabilities. I have been a temperate man insofar as I've refrained from pleasure as an end in itself, though I've known temptation. However, I've not always refrained from serving my own purposes at the public's expense. In the Republic's service and in the strength of my own convictions, I was courageous, but all too often I compromised and accommodated for the sake of concord and stability. As an advocate in the courts, I always sought to achieve justice for my clients. As a magistrate, I was always motivated to secure justice for the Republic's welfare, for the citizens' liberty, and for the provincials' rights.

Wisdom, temperance, courage, and justice—the cardinal virtues by which I've tried to live. I hoped they would become my son's intimate companions. But my other companions through life have been distress, pain, spiritual disorder, and death. Here in this house, in the months following Tullia's death, I had written the treatise, *The Tusculan Disputations*. In it, I described these conditions from the standpoint of the major philosophical schools.

Though we fear and grieve over it, death is not an evil, but a departure, a deliverance for the soul imprisoned within the corruptible body. That the soul is immortal is confirmed by the practices of our forbears, by the Greeks, and by so many ancient peoples.

While death liberates the body from pain, before it comes, the evil of pain must be despised and overcome. Yielding to pain is inconsistent with wisdom, temperance, courage, and justice. Virtue renders pain insignificant and death is a steady refuge.

Philosophy nurtures and medicates the soul and helps to alleviate distress. The causes of distress and all spiritual disorders are mistaken opinion and judgment, and the longing for or aversion of present or future things. These are abetted by contempt for reason, and as virtue cultivates reason, disorder is the child of vice. However, philosophy can root out error and inculcate virtue. Without it, happiness is unattainable, for just as vice brings misery, so does virtue bring contentment. As nature makes everything perfect in its kind, so the perfection of man is virtue.

While I could call myself a virtuous man, the vicissitudes of my political career would appear to consign me to the ignominy of failure. To endeavor with all good intentions and with one's spirit is not enough. My statecraft could not save the Republic from the military despotism of Caesar or Antonius or Octavianus.

I glossed through my treatise, *On the Republic* and came upon "The Dream of Scipio" in its last book. In his day, two generations before my birth, Scipio Aemilianus had been the Republic's *rector*, the guiding, stabilizing leader who led the legions against implacable foreign enemies and warded off internal unrest. I had always cast Pompeius Magnus in this role for our generation.

In the book, I described the great Roman general and conqueror of Carthage, Scipio Africanus, appearing in a dream to his adoptive grandson, Scipio Aemilianus. The elder Scipio shows the younger man the infinity of the cosmos against which our own imperium is contemptuously dwarfed. The words that I had Scipio speak in this section encouraged me to the belief that my life's endeavors had not been totally in vain.

There is a sure place in Heaven for all who have cared for their fatherland, preserved it, and labored for its growth: a place where they may enjoy life in everlasting bliss. There is nothing more acceptable to the chief of the gods who rules over the cosmos, of all things that happen on the earth, than the councils and gatherings of men who associate together in respect for law and justice; that is, the organizations called states. Their rulers and preservers have come from Heaven and will return there.

I set down the book, closed my eyes, and tried to suppress the tears that were welling up. The whole span of my life flowed through my consciousness. I remembered my early court cases culminating with the prosecution of Gaius Verres by which I earned a virtually unchallenged supremacy among Roman advocates. I remembered my advancement through the course of offices and the distinction of being the first Cicero ever to attain the consulate.

Images of both friends and enemies came to my mind's eye—Atticus, Pompeius, Catilina, Caesar, Cato, Caelius, Publius Clodius, Milo, and Servius Sulpicius. I remembered my first love—at last I acknowledged her—Clodia Pulchra. Over the years, I had never really stopped loving her, or at least my obsession for her never waned, though I came to loathe the wanton sensualist that she had become.

Plato had described the spiritual union of lovers in his *Symposium*. Though we both had gone our separate ways domestically and politically, Clodia remained an indelible presence in my heart, my mind, and my soul. No measure of sarcasm or vitriolic denunciation could expel her. Over the years, I often wondered, as I did now at Tusculum, about what might have been.

Memories of my family brought forth the tears that I could no longer contain—tears for my parents, for Terentia, and most painfully for Tullia. I longed to see my son. *I'll send word to Quintus,* I thought. *We should consider crossing over to Macedonia. There was hardly any reason for us to remain in Italia. In fact, it might soon have become dangerous for us to do so.*

There could be no semblance of neutrality now. I had repeatedly denounced Antonius in the Senate and before the People. And now Octavianus clearly regarded as his enemies all the men who had killed Caesar as well as those who supported the deed. To cross into territory controlled by Marcus Brutus and the Republican forces was to make myself an enemy of the young Caesar.

When he had granted me leave to withdraw from Roma, I thought I had the benefit of his protection. But now, I realized that he had been warning me to attend to my own security. Therefore, it was very much to our purpose to quit Italia and withdraw to the safety of Brutus' army in Macedonia. And yet, I wanted to see how Octavianus would fare against Antonius and his allies.

I was willing to accept death because it was my fate, but how I wished to see my Marcus once more before it came. The scrolls on the shelves of my library were cold and silent. Was my life more than the ideas they contained? It was late.

Omniscient Narrative

A MILITARY JUNTA MEETS ON an island in the middle of the Lavinius River near Bononia in the Cisalpina's Po Valley. It is a cloudless day. Sunshine from the hard, blue sky does little to diminish the November chill. On either side of the river, the might of Roma's Western legions is clearly evident. The Proconsuls Lepidus, Plancus, and Pollio command nine legions and sizeable auxiliary forces. Three legions of veterans recruited by Antonius' chief supporters, Calenus, Bassus, and Censorinus, stand at arms with Antonius' legions. All told, some fifteen legions and auxiliaries and cavalry are aligned with Marcus Antonius.

Opposite them are the Fourth and Martian Legions, the legions that had been recruited by Hirtius and Pansa, and the cohorts that had deserted Decimus Brutus. These soldiers, comprising nearly twelve legions, are firmly committed to Caesar Octavianus.

A leather and canvass tent has been erected on the island so that the young Consul and the renegade Proconsul may confer in relative privacy. Propitiously, the two commanders request the same man to sit at their deliberations. Caesar's former Master of Horse and the current Chief Pontiff, Marcus Lepidus is utterly flattered to be their chosen man. He cannot know, so limited is his political statecraft, that his participation will compromise him for the rest of his life.

As Lepidus enters the conference tent, Antonius and Octavianus salute him most cordially. Antonius adds almost facetiously, "It's always wise to placate the *gods!*"

The three commanders sit on camp stools at a round campaign table. They are unarmed, but they wear the armor and military cloaks commensurate with their rank. As their conference will last for several days, their legionaries will encamp about them. Food and wine and water will be brought in to sustain them, and at times of their own choosing they will recess either to relieve themselves or to defuse their aroused tempers.

"We should form a triumvirate," Octavianus insists and then qualifies, "but unlike the informal partnership of Caesar, Pompeius, and Crassus, ours is to be officially established in order to reorganize the Republic."

Antonius and Lepidus both consent. However, Antonius raises his own qualification. "It's imperative, Octavius—uh, Octavianus, uh, *Caesar* Octavianus"—Antonius purposely and facetiously equivocates—"that you give up the consulate. How can our intentions to reorganize the Republic be taken seriously if one of us is a *boy-consul*?"

"Don't call me *boy*!" Octavianus hisses through clenched teeth.

Lepidus intervenes. "Legally, you're far too young to be consul, just as you were too young to be accorded propraetorian status."

"Give up the consulate, Octavius," Antonius says straight-forwardly, "and Bassus will relinquish his praetorate and then he'll finish out the year as Consul. Agreed?"

Octavianus purses his lips, frowns, and then sighs in resignation. "Very well then, I'll relinquish the consulate."

"Good, good; now we must merge our legions and vanquish Brutus and Cassius and their allies in the East." Antonius nods, expecting no dissent from his fellow triumvirs.

"Yes, as soon as possible," says Octavianus, "or they will invade Italia."

"The campaign will be expensive, and even without it, the legions must be paid," wily Antonius points out. "And there are enemies close to home who need to be eliminated."

"*Enemies?*" Lepidus wonders aloud.

"Yes; there are in the Senate about three hundred; and two thousand among the equites; your enemies, Lepidus, or my enemies, or *your* enemies, Octavianus."

"*Proscriptions?*" Lepidus asks again. "As in the days of Sulla?"

"It's the most efficient way to dispose of our enemies, and their properties and wealth will pay the legions and finance the campaign in the East against Brutus and Cassius."

THE TRIUMVIRS SPEND DAYS REVIEWING the list of the condemned. Lepidus acquiesces in the proscription of his brother, Lepidus Paullus, in return for Antonius' consent to the inclusion of his uncle, Lucius Caesar. These two had been among the first to vote for the decree of outlawry against both Antonius and Lepidus. Now, they are surrendered to the triumvirs' mutual vindication.

One of the proscribed enemies will be difficult to apprehend. The Triumvirs' latest intelligence is that Sextus Pompeius is still at Massilia with his fleet and army of Greek slaves and freedmen. They cannot afford to leave an enemy, however inactive, in their rear once they go to the East. So, their consensus is that, if they cannot remove him immediately, then they will negotiate with him, throw him some scrap or other to satisfy him, however provisionally. They realize, of course, that if they cannot win him over, then they will eventually eliminate him. Had Caesar disposed of him in Spain, then they would not presently have to take into account the surviving son of the Magnus.

Octavianus attempts to quibble over a particular name, but Antonius is adamant in his insistence that this aged consular, and his son, his brother, and his nephew, be included among the condemned. Ultimately, Octavianus consents, but only with a severe twinge of conscience. But in his pursuit of power, this will prove to be short-lived. He also agrees to marry Antonius' step-daughter, Claudia, the daughter of Fulvia and her first husband, Publius Clodius. In doing so, Octavianus replicates Pompeius Magnus, who had married Caesar's daughter in order to solidify their political alliance with a personal bond. So it is again with Roma's new, albeit official Triumvirate.

The Triumvirs arrange for one of their amenable tribunes to propose the formal establishment of their rule, with military iron to implement it. The allocation of the Western provinces will have Gallia Cisalpina and Comata going to Antonius; Gallia Transalpina and Hither Spain remaining under Lepidus; Sicilia, Sardinia, and Africa assigned to Octavianus. Their imperium over the provinces will extend for five years, while in Roma they will share the power of appointment over all magistrates. They anticipate another round of provincial assignments once the East has been regained from Brutus and Cassius.

They agree that the posting of the proscription lists and the commencement of their enemies' elimination will begin under the new Consul, Bassus, and Octavianus' cousin, Consul Pedius. Their sanguinary counsels anticipate the use of the military to implement their decreed liquidation. Military Tribune Popillius Laenas will convey the Triumvirs' orders to the, by now, thoroughly demoralized Senate.

As they conclude their business, each man privately considers his own individual gains. For Lepidus, the Chief Pontiff, the Proconsul, and now Triumvir of the Republic, the prospects of further advancement appear to be almost guaranteed, even though his brothers-in-law, Brutus and Cassius, will be marked among his enemies. Octavianus reckons on future consulates to compensate for what he must now relinquish. Of his two partners, clearly Antonius is the stronger, the more dangerous, and the one requiring the most careful circumspection.

Antonius thinks that the alliance is the best deal he could have cut. He will be satisfied if it lasts at least until after they have disposed of Caesar's murderers. Should Lepidus not die early, then he will endeavor to retire him to some miniscule province befitting his innocuous character. But Octavianus is a different matter. Adopted and bequeathed the Caesar name, he truly takes himself seriously as the *new* Caesar. For the sake of unity among the legions, so crucial to all of their ambitions, Antonius has had to cooperate with him and tolerate his presumptuous airs. Perhaps, a providential accident might befall him or he might be among the fatalities when they finally fight Caesar's killers.

Antonius does not believe that their Triumvirate will last indefinitely. *Did Caesar's?*

THEIR CONFERENCE CONCLUDED, THE TRIUMVIRS emerge from the tent and clasp hands in full view of their cheering legions. Antonius adds a piece of stagecraft and statecraft. There are three aquilifers—eagle standard bearers—representing the three commanders. Antonius goes to his own standard and places his right hand upon the gilded silver eagle's wooden pole. With his left hand, he beckons the troops to silence. "This was Caesar's personal eagle," Antonius announces. "It was with him through all the Gallic campaigns, and it was carried across the Rubicon; it was with him at Pharsalus and at all the other battles. It brought him glorious victories. Let's seal our triumvirate with it!"

Octavianus and Lepidus look from Antonius and then at each other. Cautiously, they walk to the standard. They join their hands to Antonius' on the wooden pole and pledge their loyalty to each other. Once the eagle of Marius, and then of Catilina, and then of Caesar, it now becomes the talisman of Roma's new Triumvirate. The legions cheer and acclaim the Triumvirs.

Later, Gaius Asinius Pollio tells Antonius that he had seen an eagle perch atop Octavianus' tent. It killed two ravens contending with it for the same position. "If this is an omen, Antonius, what do you make of it?" the Proconsul asks.

Antonius laughs contemptuously. "You know I don't even *piss* over omens!"

Octavianus hears about the eagle from Centurion Gaius Herennius, and he wonders: *If it is an omen, what might it portend? The Triumvirate's victory over Brutus and Cassius? Or his own eventual supremacy over his two partners?*

ANTONIUS WRITES A SHORT NOTE to his loving wife and the steadfast partner of his labors. Fulvia will be happy to learn that he will be returning to Roma with a force of twenty-seven legions. The leading cohorts should be in the environs of Roma by month's end.

He sends his salutations to his mother and to the children. Fulvia is invited to share the note with them should they need proof of his imminent return. Also, he wants Fulvia to assure Titus Atticus of his gratitude for the hospitality and protection extended to all of the Antonius family. Antonius is sure that Atticus knows that he will remember the equite's generosity.

Antonius longs to see his tender Fulvia. He advises her to be in readiness for him because he will return with a Herculean, erotic appetite that paltry camp followers have never been fully able to satisfy.

Tribune Popillius Laenas is sent with two cohorts to deliver the Triumvirate's tidings to the Senate and Antonius' note to Fulvia.

Marcus Antonius, the Taurus of Fulvia's desires, believes he is well placed to conquer all before him.

"PORCIA! PORCIA! OPEN THE DOOR!" Servilia cries out against the locked door as she pounds her hands against it. "Porcia! *Open the door!*"

Behind her, Junia is anguished with apprehension. "But Mother, how could she have locked the door? Porcia was too ill to stir from her bed."

Exasperated, Servilia stops pounding on the door, and she chides her daughter, "That's what I fear! What might have happened if she *had!*" She resumes her pounding on the door. "Porcia! For god's sake—open the accursed door—now!"

Tertia arrives with two brawny household slaves. Servilia turns to them. "Well, don't just stand there! Break it down!"

The two slaves assault the door with their broad shoulders. After several tries, they succeed in breaking it off its interior lock. Almost stumbling into the room, they recover themselves and move out of the way.

Servilia and her daughters rush into the room. Immediately, they are assailed by the stench of burned out charcoal and wood. "Open those shutters!" Servilia orders the slaves. "Get some air into the room!"

As soon as the sunlight from the street floods into the dark room, the women emit a collective gasp. On the floor, next to a brazier whose embers have turned white-gray, is the lifeless body of Porcia. She lies on her right side, the hem of her palla pulled upon her head. Her flesh is ashen, and her body is rigid and warped in death's grasp.

"Oh gods!" Tertia shrieks. "But why?"

Servilia slumps into a chair near her daughter-in-law's body. She looks down at it mournfully. Junia and Tertia are too stunned to do or say anything. The slaves who have broken down the door stand nearby, awaiting further orders.

Running through Servilia's mind are thoughts of the previous night's conversation. Brutus and Cassius had written, as had Porcia's brother, urging them to quit Italia and to come to the East. Brutus had been aware that Porcia was ill, but since he had written and sent his letter, his wife's condition had worsened. Porcia became bed-ridden; aches and pains and fever assailed her body, and her lungs became repositories for infectious mucous and phlegm.

"How could I possibly travel to Macedonia in my condition?" she had struggled to say to her in-laws. Yet, she had urged them to go without her, while she would remain, trusting in Marcus Lepidus' kinship and magnanimity.

But Servilia would not hear of it. Even though Junia, Lepidus' wife, offered to care for Porcia, more than likely with Junilla's assistance,

Servilia had said that she and Tertia would not leave them behind. "Either we all go or we all stay," she had insisted. "I've come to believe that Lepidus and Antonius can't be trusted as long as Octavianus wants revenge on the men who killed Caesar."

Weakened and wracked by illness, Porcia had tried in vain to oppose her mother-in-law. "Don't stay on my account, Servilia. Go to my husband. Tertia, Junia—take your mother to Macedonia. All of you—get out of harm's way. Marcus and Cassius and all the others have already been condemned! What's to stop Octavianus from inflicting his spite on us as well?"

Porcia had neither the strength nor the will to offer further argument. But she had resolved to take matters into her own hands, insofar as she was physically able to do so.

Now, Servilia can only surmise through tear-swollen eyes how her son's wife had taken her own life. Porcia must have struggled with her last strength to drag herself out of bed, to close the window shutters facing out onto the street, and then to lock the bedroom door. There were no implements or weapons with which she could have done herself in. So, she had had recourse to the charcoal and wood burning brazier, the room's only source of heat to ward off the autumn night's chill.

How long might Porcia have knelt by the brazier, her head placed over it, the hem of her palla like a tent encompassing herself and the brazier? How long had she breathed in the smoke and fumes as the fire burned her nostrils and mouth and throat, poisoning her ailing lungs? How long might this inhaling and swallowing of fire have taken to kill her? Or had she actually swallowed any of the live, burning coals to wreak havoc upon her internal organs, bringing death and oblivion quickly? Porcia's mouth and lips and fingertips attest to this as they appear to be burned.

Like her father, the tough, uncompromising Cato, Servilia's irrepressibly obnoxious half-brother, Porcia has chosen death rather than capitulation, and self-extinction over accommodation.

Suddenly, Servilia mind's eye beholds her two sons, Marcus Brutus and Marcus Silanus, and her son-in-law, Gaius Cassius, and her nephews, Marcus Cato and Marcus Lucullus. They and Cato's nephew, Gnaeus Domitius Ahenobarbus, the son of Lucius Domitius, are among the few remnants of the once powerful optimate faction. With the exception of Silanus, who has clung to Antonius, they have assembled a mighty host in Greece and Macedonia, a last, desperate attempt to restore the free Republic of old. What have the Fates prepared for them? Will they ultimately triumph? Or will they taste of defeat? And once vanquished, will they emulate Marcus Cato and his daughter, Porcia? Will they too extinguish their own lives?

Servilia breaks down, covering her face with her hands as she sobs pathetically.

CALPURNIA PISO, AS THE DICTATOR'S wife, was once the most powerful woman in Roma, albeit barren and infertile, and therefore unable to give him children. Yet, out of political necessity, their marriage had been sustained. However, Caesar's assassination had changed everything for her, in particular, necessitating her vacating the Regia. Now, she is alone, except for her father.

Lucius Calpurnius Piso has been conspicuously among the Senate's neutrals. He has endeavored to steer the Senate along the elusive path of conciliation among all parties. But Cicero's animosity to Antonius has precluded that possibility. Now, he does not anticipate having a voice in Roma's new political order; there is nothing left for him but oblivion.

For Calpurnia, it is most unlikely that there will be new political marriages. She has served her purpose. Her legacy: she will be remembered as the wife and widow of Gaius Julius Caesar, once the greatest titan to bestride the Roman Republic. She will be the template for the wives of other powerful men who will hold sway over Roma in the years to come.

CICERO'S ELYSIAN VOICE
"YOUR LIFE IS OVER. FAREWELL."

That is what she said to me. Clodia Pulchra, attired in black as though she were in mourning, her black hair undone, seemed like a raven presaging disaster. She came here late in November and told me things that cannot and should not matter. She reached out to me and, though I cannot explain why, I reached for her too. We were together, here in this house laden with death and morbid reminders. Time could not be measured for it seemed not to exist. Tusculum did not exist. Roma, Arpinum, Italia did not exist. We were nowhere except enraptured within our own passions. She brought me back to life. But then, sated and spent, she looked into my eyes and without emotion she whispered, *"Your life is over. Farewell."*

Clodia Pulchra slept in my arms as I held her, excited and afraid. I don't know how long it was before I awoke. I dreamt of a veiled woman who seemed to resemble Fabia. The hem of her palla covered her head and the rest of it swirled around her torso. Her stola was a long-sleeved, close fitting garment that delineated her bosom. In her large hands she held aloft an infant boy who so reminded me of Marcus as a new-born. I awoke as soon as the vision disappeared and saw Clodia Pulchra leave like a black form disappearing into the autumnal mist.

The next day, Quintus and his son called on me. Their mood was as dark as Clodia's raiment. "The ring is getting tighter," Quintus warned. "Every day, more and more soldiers patrol the streets. They've even set up command posts in each district. The whole City is cordoned off. We almost had to bribe our way out. I'm not sure we can get back in." He looked at young Quintus apprehensively. "That's not all. There've been rumors—about Octavianus and Antonius. They may have made some sort of peace, a compact. The Senate has given up asking Pedius because his answer's always the same: *'I've had no word. There's no foundation to the rumors.'* But at the same time Tribune Agrippa and Tribune Titius are said to be preparing a bill for the establishment of an official triumvirate. *Whose?* Well, it's as certain as Juno's teats that Octavianus and Antonius are two-thirds of it! Marcus, we need to plan."

"Leave Italia?" I needlessly asked.

Quintus nodded, "No use putting it off any longer."

He was right, of course, and Atticus brought even more convincing news shortly after Quintus and his son had arrived. "What I tell you now, I learned from a third-hand source, but I would not doubt its authenticity." He was winded, agitated, and distraught. "One of Pilia's maids heard from one of Julia's maids that there's going to be a proscription of senators and equites. It's been put together by Antonius, but with names contributed by Octavianus and Lepidus." He paused and looked away from us as if he were ashamed. Swallowing hard, he looked back at us and said, "All of you—you're all on the list. You're all marked for death."

At that instant, Clodia Pulchra's words resonated in my mind: *"Your life is over. Farewell."*

"You've got to get out of here!" Atticus demanded. *"Now!* And get out of Italia as soon as possible. Cross over to Athens, or better still, go to Apollonia, and put yourselves under Marcus Brutus' protection."

Though alarmed I tried to temporize. "If I went to Marcius Phillipus and asked him to intercede with Octavianus...."

"Listen to me, Marcus," Atticus insisted. "Antonius is his partner now, and he's too hot for your blood to be placated by entreaties. Look—once you're out of the country, I'll speak with Fulvia. She owes me, and perhaps in consideration of my protection over all of them, she might be open to negotiation. But get out now—while you still can!"

There was no point in delaying, except to write a brief letter to Terentia.

I've learned only today of precarious circumstances that render it impossible for me and for Quintus and young Quintus to remain anywhere in Italia. So we're leaving almost immediately for Apollonia via my preferred indirect route so as to avoid the garrison at Brundisium. The reports I've had from Brutus leave no doubt in my mind that our Marcus, our son, is a true patriot of the Republic. I'm immensely proud of him, and I cannot wait to see him again. But the times are more uncertain than ever. I know not when or if I shall see... Italia or Roma again. I commend you, and Fabia and Pomponia, to Atticus' care. Stay well and strong, no matter what may happen. Farewell

Marcus Tullius Cicero

Atticus assured me he would deliver the letter. I gave him my own copy of the treatise, *On Friendship* which I had written the year before. Handing it to him, I quoted from it: *"Friendship makes prosperity brighter, while it lightens adversity by sharing its sorrows and anxieties."*

Atticus held the scroll tightly in his hand and then pressed it against his chest, all the while looking ashamedly at the floor. Then, I embraced him and bade him farewell.

WE SET OUT FOR ASTURA. Quintus and his son travelled by horseback along with Alexio and several household slaves, while Tiro, Metrodorus, and I rode in a coach drawn by a pair of mules. Our journey along the Appian road was uneventful and unhampered, and we made good time.

But once arrived at Astura, my brother insisted on going back to Roma because he needed more money for the journey.

All my entreaties could not prevail upon him to forego such a perilous change in direction. So, pledging to reunite at Rhegium, we embraced and bade each other a sad farewell. The younger Quintus set out with his father for Roma, and we continued on our way from Astura. Rather than proceed by land and risk detection by search parties, I decided that we should hire a small vessel at the shore and sail down to Caieta, the harbor of Formiae.

Tiro negotiated for the rental of the skiff. Its owner and pilot was an old, haggard Greek, inauspiciously named Charon, and he looked as though he might have been the very same creature who ferries the shades of the dead to Hades. Despite my unease and misgivings, I agreed to hire him.

We had planned to stop at my villa at Formiae for a brief rest before continuing on down to Rhegium where we hoped to take ship, skirt the coast, and then cross to Epirus. A dark depression came over me. All during our progress down the coast, I sat motionless, brooding and without speaking. Tiro tried to encourage me and to allay my fears about my brother and nephew, but to no avail. My forlorn mood had me in a trance.

As we rounded the promontory of Circaeium, where there is a shrine to Apollo, the god of prophecy, an extraordinary happening shook me from my stupor. A great flight of crows and ravens wildly emerged from its top and from behind it. Cawing and cackling, they surrounded our vessel and filled us all with an eerie terror. They continued their ominous flight over us until we put in at Caieta. Here, anxious and exhausted, I went ashore to rest at the seaside loggia, a short remove from the Formian villa. I spoke to Tiro briefly, telling him that I wanted to return to Roma and kill myself before the altar of Caesar Octavianus' household gods so that divine retribution would be visited upon him. However, Tiro and Alexio and Metrodorus persuaded me to dispense with such thoughts and to rest before continuing our journey. So, we proceeded to the villa.

As I lay on my bed, the mysterious crows and ravens again came to me. By twos and threes they gathered by the open window and then alighted upon the bed, pecking at my blanket as though trying to remove it from me. My servants beheld this prodigy with much fear and alarm. It must have seemed to them that these weak creatures were attempting to save me while the men stood by helplessly.

By earnest entreaty and gentle force, they at last persuaded me to rise up and again make for the sea. But by this time, there was a commotion outside the front end of the house. We saw a troop of soldiers, swords drawn. I recognized two of them, Military Tribune Popillius Laenas and Centurion Gaius Herennius. Between them was my brother's freedman, Philologus. He was gesticulating wildly.

Everything then happened so quickly. Alexio seized me and almost threw me into a litter. Four slaves carried me out the rear exit and through a wooded path toward the shore and the waiting skiff. As we neared the point where the wooded path opened upon the shore, we saw Popillius and twelve soldiers arrayed before us, and Herennius with Philologus and other soldiers were coming upon our rear. Alexio drew his sword and confronted Popillius' soldiers. He slew one and wounded two others before he was overtaken and killed. The house slaves and Tiro and Metrodorus, though unarmed, tried to fight off the legionaries, but they were easily overcome, knocked down and restrained. Drawn swords ringed the litter. There was a long moment of silence broken only by the muffled, anguished struggles of the men to break free of their captors' restraints.

The Tribune and the Centurion stood at each end of the litter, and Philologus was between them. They seemed to be waiting for him to identify me. He had been with my brother and nephew. I feared they had been taken and killed. I could not be sure whether Philologus had been coerced to lead them to me or if he had volunteered to do so.

I broke the silence. "Well, Philologus, do you not recognize your teacher of the liberal arts?" I pulled back the tunic and the toga and cloak from the back of my neck. "Yes, it is I, Marcus Tullius Cicero." Defiantly, I extended my neck. And with a single, swift stroke, Herennius severed my head. The iron sword was cold and sharp against my flesh, and the gushing blood effused upon my torso and onto the litter's cushions. My severed head plopped onto the blood-dampened ground.

From above the gory scene, I heard Tiro and Metrodorus scream in utter anguish before the soldiers struck them into unconsciousness. My headless torso collapsed onto the ground. Tribune Popillius severed my hands. I felt no pain now.

It was sometime before Tiro, Metrodorus, and the others regained their senses. The soldiers had already left with their grisly trophies. Lest they should return to do further dishonor to my remains, Tiro supervised the burial of my butchered, mutilated corpse.

I met my death on the seventh of December. By the twelfth, Tiro and the others had returned to Roma, a city beset with fire and destruction, bloodshed and death. In all quarters of the City, the proscribed were being hunted down and murdered. Even ailing Consul Pedius had died from undue exhaustion after implementing the earliest murders. An Antonian partisan, Gaius Carrinas, became Consul in his stead and continued the bloody business.

Just outside the Capena Gate, I oversaw Tiro and the others come upon the tortured, mutilated bodies of Quintus, my beloved brother, and his son. I had begged them not to return to Roma. They had been captured on the City's outskirts, probably by the same soldiers who had overtaken us at Formiae. They had been betrayed by Philologus, and then bound to trees and methodically tortured to death. Their gruesome remains were scattered like refuse on either side of the road. Tiro and his companions painstakingly gathered them up and buried them, lest the vultures should feed upon them.

I SAW AND HEARD MY enemies and my loved ones in ways that I could never have experienced had I been alive in a corporeal body.

Fulvia has moved back into her old house in the Aventine district. Sitting in a cathedra chair at a marble table, she reaches into a leather sack, the kind used by soldiers to carry dispatches. She feels the blood-matted hair of my scalp and her body begins to tingle. Placing her hands on either side of my skull, she extracts my head from the sack. A husky, spiteful laugh bursts forth from her throat and she throws her head back. "Greetings, Marcus Tullius Cicero," she says before laughing yet again. "But there might be more of you, I think. Let's see!"

Fulvia reaches into the sack again and feels my severed hands. "Oh! Yes! Here we are!" She pulls my hands out and places them on the table on either side of my head. Passing her fingers through the thick crop of white hair, she fondles my ears as my eyes, brown, dead eyes, stare up at her. She pushes my lips apart and gropes for my tongue. Removing her hairpin, she lets her hair fall in flame-red cascades upon my face. She laughs at me and spits into my dead eyes.

Piercing my tongue with her hairpin, she sneers, "This should hold your putrid tongue in place." The sight of it excites her and fills her with an intense sensual craving. She gratifies herself, moaning, "Can you speak now, *Chick-Pea?* Your pin-pierced tongue hangs down like a spent penis." Then, after licking the fingers of my severed hands, she holds them against her exposed breasts, gratifying herself yet again.

Upon finishing, Fulvia sets them aside. Taking pen and parchment, she writes two short notes.

To Terentia:

Have you been to the Forum lately? If you go, you won't hear speeches and you won't see the likes of your ex-husband haranguing from the Rostra. No, but you will see the relics of that spiteful, hateful man: those sinewy hands with which he wrote the venomous words attacking me and Antonius; that tongue which poured out calumny and vilification upon us will not waggle now with my pin holding it in place. By the way, you needn't rush to go there, for my husband has ordered that they remain on view until they rot....

To Clodia Pulchra:

... I'd have kept these trophies for you to see but Antonius has had them moved to the Rostra. He wants them to serve as an example to any and all others who might criticize his...that is, our *endeavors. So, if you want to see them, you'll have to go down to the Forum. Should you see Terentia there, let me know what she thinks of* Chick-Pea's *adornment of the Rostra.*

Hugs and kisses,
Your Fulvia

ATTICUS IS ASSAILED BY THREE hysterical women. His wife, Pilia, upbraids him for failing to intervene on our behalf. In her passionate zeal, she even threatens to take their daughter and leave him. Pomponia grieves for her murdered ex-husband. "Even in death, he had to follow his brother; but why my son as well, my precious boy, my Quintus? Was his life such an affront to the new masters? I'd have plunged the dagger into my own breast, had you not restrained me!" Atticus looks askance at his sister, for his household servants have strict orders to be attendant upon her so that she will not harm herself.

Pomponia turns to Terentia and sobs, "Terentia, though you may mourn the terrible death of the man who was once your husband, yet be grateful that you still have your son! Mine is lost, gone forever. There's nothing left for me now."

But Terentia is oblivious to the sobbing woman, consumed as she is with her own sorrow and rage. "Atticus, could you have done nothing… to spare us this disgrace, this dishonor? You sheltered Antonius' wife and children; could you not have persuaded him to impose exile instead of death? Was it not enough that they butchered Marcus? Did they have to display him like a hunted animal? What shame! You sheltered that *Lupa*, but you could not shelter your dearest friend, or your brother-in-law or your nephew! Do sesterces and talents weigh more than friendship or family or love? What a fine example you set for your Caecilia Attica!"

Atticus blushes with shame. He would speak, but he knows not what he could possibly say; nor will Terentia allow him an opportunity to answer. "You've made your compact of cash and credit with today's rulers, haven't you? But I've no doubt that should Brutus and Cassius return triumphantly to Italia, you'll negotiate an equally advantageous bargain with *them*!"

Atticus can only look at her as humiliation and sorrow for the Ciceroes swallows up his pride. He makes no attempt to offer any apology or any justification. He has made a life and a career of being *in* with everyone and *out* with no one. He is most unlikely to change now.

I watch Terentia write to our son.

… *Cherish the memory of your father. Though he was often miscalculating and myopic in his judgments, he was consistent in his devotion to the Republic and in his concern for your welfare. I know he was proud of the choice you've made. Remain steadfast in it. Cling to Marcus Brutus, for when the butchery here is ended, the butchers will go to Greece and to Macedonia to expand their blood-letting. Only Brutus and Cassius can defend what is left of the Republic for which your father expended his labors and offered up his life.*

In your father's name, my son, I wish for you peace, health, and life, though you will soon be in the midst of war.

Your loving Mother,
Terentia

I SEE TERENTIA RECEIVE A grieving visitor. It is Clodia Pulchra.

"What do you want here?" Terentia demands so imperiously. "How dare you to come to me! Do you imagine I'd want *your* commiseration?" Terentia is distraught with grief, her eyes red and swollen from weeping, and she wears a stola and palla of the deepest black.

"I cannot commiserate with your grief," Clodia replies sorrowfully, "for I bear my own. You've always resented and suspected me of having designs on Marcus Cicero because of our youthful attachment." She wears the same raiment that she had worn when she came to me at Tusculum. "Know this, Terentia, I've always loved him with my thoughts and in my heart. But I loved him with my entire being only days before he fled for his life."

Terentia's aggrieved face darkens with anger. Her eyes flash with malice. But Clodia speaks on. "Yes, it was at Tusculum that we had each other and loved each other. At first, he was reluctant, but I was so persuasive. I've no shame in this, for I loved him and yet love him. I loved him in every man that I've ever had. His death is as great a wound for me as... more so for me than it could ever be for you, despite your thirty years with him and your children by him...."

"Your shadow fell between me and my husband during our life together," Terentia interrupts, "but you will *not* come between us in death."

"Are you so sure of that, Terentia?"

Terentia hisses back, "If you've nothing else to say, then leave my house!"

OVER HER SHOULDER, I READ the words that Clodia writes.

...and then I said to him, 'Your life is over. Farewell.'

Must you have details, Fulvia? How boorish you can be sometimes! I'll leave those to your own fanciful imagination. Can you not understand that I loved him? You can think what you will of my visits to him at Antium last year. At Tusculum, when we were finished, I wished he could have died in my arms and have been spared the horrible death he subsequently suffered. I'd have hidden his body to spare it mutilation from both the soldiers and you. Are you satisfied with your revenge? Is there anything further you want from him? Is there anything further you want from me?

If not, then I'll take leave of this pointless existence. Only moments ago, I took a draught to end all my grief and pain and longing. I'm told it brings peace quickly and painlessly. Fulvia, I hope you too will soon find peace somehow, somewhere.

It grows late. The darkness covers me. The words on the tablet are blurred. My maid, Renna, will deliver this to you. Please be patient with her as she will probably be distraught.

It is time to close, Fulvia, time to make an end. Farewell.

The stylus drops from Clodia's hand. Her head tilts lifelessly against the back of the chair, and the pulse in her long, lovely neck ceases. Though her luminous dark eyes are closed forever, even in death an enigmatic smile remains upon her mouth.

From Clodia Pulchra to the Rostra is but the merest instant of time. There on the Rostra wall, from which I'd so often addressed the Roman People, my severed head and hands are nailed and exposed. The tongue, from which such eloquence had come forth, protrudes from the open mouth, pierced with Fulvia's hairpin. Above these grisly relics of my mortal existence, there is an inscription on the wall, seemingly carved with blood:

By Order of the Triumvirate for the Re-Constitution of the Republic

Two women look at these bloody trophies. Before they turn away in revulsion, I recognize them as the wife and step-daughter of Lucius Sergius Catilina. When I had saved the Republic from Catilina's subversive conspiracy, Orestilla had warned me that the struggle would not end until either her husband's head or mine graced the Rostra wall. How wrong you were, Orestilla! I see many more years of strife and civil war before the establishment of a new Respublica, a new political order for Roma and her imperium under a young, laurel-crowned rector. But those events belong to another story and to other personages, and they will be chronicled by other hands and voices. Soon, my voice will be stilled as my soul rests in the eternal bliss of Elysium amid amber fields and verdant meadows and tranquil waters.

The light, so long absent, has returned to my soul. I rejoice in its recovery.

Epilogus (Epilogue)

Marcus Tullius Cicero, Consul, to Marcus Tullius Tiro at Arpinum. Written from Roma, eleven days before the Kalends of December, DCCXXIV AB URBE CONDITA

Greetings, Tiro.

I hope you're well and I trust you've found everything in order at the Arpinum farmstead. Before you move on to Antium, Cumae, Formiae, and the others, please write me about any special attention the grounds or the buildings may require. I've no way of knowing if the tenants have taken any pains to maintain Father's villas. Since the Senate, upon Octavianus' motion, has restored all of Father's confiscated properties, I'm most anxious to repair whatever ravages time and neglect may have wrought.

The latest news here is that Octavianus may soon be on his way back to Roma, although he may have to leave his most trustworthy legates in Egypt to complete the task of converting the former client-kingdom into a province of the Republic.

The path I've traveled since Father's murder thirteen years ago has been a bold gamble, steeped with danger. Many of my generation have either sacrificed their lives or have had to compromise their honor in order to survive. I'd thrown in my lot with the Republican Liberators, Brutus and Cassius, the last of Father's heroes. At Philippi, I fought in their legions against Antonius and Octavianus.

In two decisive battles, young men like Marcus Cato, Quintus Hortensius, and Marcus Lucullus, the sons of the Republic's old guardians, were killed. Others, like Lucius Bibulus and Gnaeus

Ahenobarbus eventually defected to the Triumvirs. Brutus and Cassius took their own lives after their forces were vanquished, and I surrendered to the victors.

Antonius would have been content to inflict upon me the same outrages he had inflicted on Father, especially since Brutus had had Antonius' brother, Gaius, executed in retaliation for Father's murder. But Octavianus pardoned me and then allowed me to return to Roma on the condition that I moved in his approved political circles.

Ironically at the same time, Marcus Silanus had a falling out with the Triumvirs, and he joined Sextus Pompeius and his piratical insurgents. Eventually, after Pompeius' death, he returned to Antonius' faction, only to defect to Octavianus shortly before Actium. Octavianus has been grooming him for an inevitable consulate.

During the Triumviral years, I became a follower, an acquaintance, and then an intimate friend of Octavianus. Yet, he kept me in the background as he maneuvered and manipulated his way to power. Gradually, he demoted Lepidus, who was expendable from the start, to a virtual nonentity. Poor Lepidus was ultimately forced into retirement, retaining only his Chief Pontificate.

Octavianus had made a pact with Sextus Pompeius, and it held off the inevitable war until Marcus Agrippa's fleet was battle-ready. After Pompeius' defeat off the Sicilian coast, his fate, like his father's before him, was to be executed as a fugitive.

The years of suspicion and distrust between Octavianus and Antonius finally erupted into open rivalry, especially after Antonius' rough-shod repudiation of Octavianus' sister and his return to his Egyptian consort. As Octavianus needed ammunition to hurl against the Roman People's beloved Antonius, he had recourse to Father's letters and speeches, particularly the *Philippics*. With your editorial supervision, with Atticus' scribes, and with my advice, many of these documents were published. In this way, the Senate and large segments of the Roman and Italian public were turned against Antonius and Queen Cleopatra.

Such widespread support for Octavianus, together with Agrippa's superior naval strategy, contributed decisively to Antonius' defeat at Actium, despite his having had Egypt's bountiful resources at his disposal. That Father's letters and speeches should have been used to help destroy Antonius is very much a vindication for all that Father and our family had suffered. In fact, I felt even more vindicated than I had when Fulvia died after inciting the rebellion at Perusia. Her death and Lucius Antonius' death happened because of their own treachery and unbridled ambition.

But I could not have expected fuller vindication than to have been named Octavianus' consular colleague for this year, the year in which Father's murderer went down to defeat and death by his own hand together with his Egyptian lover and ally.

I could wish that just as the Senate has decreed the restoration of Father's properties to me, there could be some way to restore to life all the victims of the Triumvirate's proscriptions. How I wish I could have been here to prevent Publilia's death. That she should die so young by her own hand and with her mother, the pair of them terrified and impoverished after Publilius had been killed and their properties confiscated... how tragic, how pathetic!

Tiro, you've been good and loyal in keeping in confidence my love for her after all these years. It would have caused Father needless pain to know that I had loved his young, neglected wife. You were so wise in realizing this.

Over the years, I thought of telling Mother about it, but it would only have served to exacerbate her chronic pains in the joints. Besides, why should I distract her from her rents, revenues, and all of the other business concerns that occupy her.? Philotimus continues to look after her accounts. Truly, I could wish for her to appoint someone to look after *him* because his fingers have grown stickier with the years. You know as well as I, however, that with age, Mother has become even more remiss about her freedman than she was when Father complained about him.

Whenever I visit Mother, I find Aunt Fabia with her. Their conversation is quite animated, especially concerning the late Sallustius Crispus. How shamelessly he had insinuated himself into her life! On the pretext of seeking information about Father's politics and private counsels for inclusion in the monograph he was writing on the Catilinian conspiracy, Sallustius charmed Mother into marriage. I knew from the start that he was merely fortune-hunting. Why else would he have been interested in a wealthy widow many years his senior? I warned Mother against him, but I could not persuade her. Fortunately, in the end, the gods or the Fates had their way. He's been dead these last five years.

Aunt Fabia has grown lovelier and more graceful with age. I would never have thought it possible for her to surpass her own youthful beauty and grace. Elevated to the rank of Chief Vestal, she'll undoubtedly serve Vesta for the remainder of her years, instructing the novices, supervising the college, and guarding the Holy Fire.

I've wanted to ask Mother if she's forgiven Atticus for not protecting Father against Antonius' and Fulvia's vengeance. It's nearly two years since his death. Aunt Pomponia told me such horrible details of his suffering, his sores and his bleeding. It's no wonder that he chose to hasten his own death by refusing to eat, for his suffering would have been prolonged by even the most meager amounts of soft food. He certainly lived to a ripe old age, nearly eighty, I believe, since he was Father's senior by about three years. He even outlived his wife, Pilia, who was somewhat younger.

I'm glad that their only child, Caecilia Pomponia, has contracted a good marriage with Marcus Agrippa. At least, she will not be alone, unlike Aunt Pomponia. Though her bombastic temperament may have mellowed somewhat, she's still unpleasant to be with. Her household slaves are dreadfully afraid of her ever since she had Philologus put to death. Then again, the devious bastard deserved it for betraying my uncle, my cousin, and Father.

There's been much discussion, both private and public, concerning Octavianus' political plans. After all, he's now the sole leader of the Republic. There are no triumviral colleagues with whom he must consult or to whom he must defer. Some have said that he should resign all his titles and powers and then retire into private life. Imagine it! Retiring at age thirty-three! Remember he's only two years my junior. Others have said that he should accept the innovative title of First Citizen of the Republic and retain an authority similar to that envisioned by Father's *On the Republic*.

You remember, Tiro, how often Father had written and spoken about a leading citizen whom he had designated "rector" and "gubernator." Though not elected to a specific office, this leading citizen would moderate the Senate's authority, the People's power, and the magistrates' prerogatives. He would be a stabilizing force, a steersman for the ship of state. Father might have fashioned such a figure after Pompeius Magnus, or he might have anticipated such a role for Caesar Octavianus.

It's certain that Octavianus will have to come to some understanding with the Senate. This should not be a difficult endeavor, though he will have to proceed with enormous tact and delicacy. The men of Father's generation are all gone, having died in proscription or in war or of the infirmities of old age. While the Senate will not accept a dictatorship of the Julian mold, I believe that, given peace and security over the Republic and the whole imperium, they will be amenable to sharing the administration of the state with Octavianus as an exalted, albeit *Republican* Princeps.

As to what Octavianus will accept or demand, I remain uncertain. Hopefully, all such speculations will be addressed and resolved upon his return to Roma.

In the meantime, Maecenas, his unofficial prefect of culture, or propaganda, has retained Servius Sulpicius Rufus and his sister to compose panegyrics honoring the conquest of Egypt and extolling the new order that we are most likely to see established. Servius and Sulpicia, the offspring of Father's late, beloved friend, have thus been afforded an opportunity to apply the fruits of their intellectual labors in literature and philosophy to the propagation of a new political regime. They are the latest additions to a collegium that already includes the poets, Quintus Horatius Flaccus and Publius Virgilius Maro.

Both Servius and Sulpicia have confided in me that they see a warped irony in their employment. Unlike his father, Servius never entered the political arena, and yet here he is commissioned to write pieces for the sake of political statecraft. Sulpicia, having always rejected marriage and family domesticity, is now engaged to produce tracts brokering the marriage of Octavianus to the Republic.

I have personal reasons for hoping that a sound constitutional settlement will be in the offing, and literature is at the forefront of my intentions. I've kept Father's history, *Respublica*, and I've read it over and over until the parchment's edges have become frayed. Before Octavianus departed for the war against Antonius and Cleopatra, I showed him the manuscript with a view to getting his approval for its publication. He did not directly reply to my request. Instead, as he had done before, he expressed his remorse at having had to assent to Father's proscription.

Then, he said to me, "Your father was a learned man, and a lover of his country." I remain convinced that after Octavianus has settled the affairs of state, he will sanction *Respublica*'s publication. *Respublica* will help to convince future generations of Father's patriotism, despite his all too human flaws and failings.

Dear friend, it is now time for me to close, as I must be off to preside over the Senate. I bid you peace, health, and life.

Marcus Tullius Cicero

Author's Afterword

HISTORICAL FICTION REQUIRES THE AUTHOR to be knowledgeable about the facts and events of a given era and its major figures, while attempting to tell an engaging story. Often times it is necessary to conflate and telescope personages and their deeds. *Respublica* is no exception to this general rule.

Historically, there were four years between Cicero's and Caesar's consulates. For dramatic purposes, however, Caesar's year of office has been made to follow immediately after Cicero's. Likewise, the Bona Dea scandal, so shrouded in mystery, has been moved to December of Cicero's consulate (63 B.C.) when historically it occurred in 62 B.C.; and Clodius' controversial sacrilege trial was actually held in 61 B.C. and not, as in *Respublica*, at the beginning of Caesar's consulate. Also, Pompeius—better known to English readers as Pompey—was still in the East in 63 B.C. However, it was deemed dramatically useful to have him command the troops in Italy that defeated Catilina in that year. Additionally, Fulvia is a conflation of two women of the same name: The first was the mistress of one Curius, a conspirator who has been jettisoned from the novel and replaced by Clodius; the second was the successive wife of Clodius, Curio, and Marcus Antonius, better known to English readers as Mark Antony. Fulvia's gross abuse of Cicero is historically valid, albeit dramatically interpreted. Clodia Pulchra was most certainly an emancipated woman for her time, or any time. *Respublica* presents her as such, and her sexually charged relationships with Caelius, Fulvia, Dolabella, and Cicero—to name but a few of her lovers—render her a rebel against the Roman Republic's male-dominated society.

License taken with the historical chronology necessitated certain revisions in the ages of some of the characters. It is sincerely hoped that classical and historical purists will not be overly irritated by these and other liberties.

There is a bounteous trove of documentation for Cicero and his era. His speeches, correspondence, and treatises are available in English translation in the Loeb Classical Library. Cicero's life and motivations are rendered particularly accessible by these primary sources. Additionally, Plutarch's biographies of Cicero, Caesar, Marcus Antonius, Pompeius, and Crassus, and Sallust's monograph on Catilina's conspiracy are available in the same collection. These and numerous secondary works from the twentieth and twenty-first centuries have been referenced.

Roman names, particularly of aristocratic males, usually came in groups of three. The *praenomen*, or first name, was a personal name as in Gaius, Gnaeus, Lucius, Marcus, Publius and Quintus. The middle name or *nomen*, identified a Roman's *gens* or clan, as in Tullius or Julius or Claudius or Licinius. The *cognomen*, or last name, indicated a Roman's family name as in Cicero or Caesar or Pulcher or Crassus. Females were usually given the feminine form of the nomen as in Tullia, Julia, Fulvia, and Claudia or Clodia. The system became monotonous for multiple female births resulting in numerous Julias or Licinias or Junias, and it became expedient to differentiate among Major and Minor or Tertia within the same family. Frequently the use of suffixes indicated a daughter's younger status as in Junilla, the diminutive of Junia.

If one were to select an emblematic figure of the Roman Republic it would be the *lictor*, the equivalent of today's security guard or Secret Service agent. Twelve of them accompanied consuls when they went about in public. They carried on their left shoulders the *fasces*, the bound bundles of hickory or birch rods with an axe protruding from their midst. The rods symbolized the magistrates' authority to scourge malefactors, and the axe was indicative of their power to inflict capital punishment when legally justified. Generally, the axe was not borne within the sacred precincts of Rome. While the fasces are suggestive of Fascism as a totalitarian system, it is worth bearing in mind that they also represent strength and unity even in democratic societies. Observant television viewers of Presidential State of the Union Addresses will have surely noticed that a pair of sculpted fasces adorns the wall behind the Capitol podium and are plainly visible over the seated Speaker of the House and the Vice-President.

Most of the references to Roman money are in *sesterces*, silver or bronze coins roughly equivalent to the American nickel. The *denarius*, whether of gold or silver, was worth four times the *sesterce*. The Greek *talentum*, or talent, was the most expensive coin in circulation, roughly equivalent to a thousand dollars. Paper money and credit cards were unknown, but banking deposits were well established, usually in temples to the gods and/or goddesses. Financiers could implement deposits and draughts on their accounts all over the Mediterranean Basin wherever banking sanctuaries were established.

Now, a word about Roman time measurement is in order. The Romans calculated their months in terms of the *Kalends*—the first day of the month; the *Nones*—the fifth or seventh day; and the *Ides*—the thirteenth or fifteenth day. Most of the time, *Respublica* references the Latin names of the months; please note that the Roman months of Quinctilis and Sextilis correspond to our months of July and August. Also, today's paradigm of **Before Christ/Anno Domini** or **Before Common Era/Common Era** was unknown to them. The Romans designated the years as **Ab Urbe Condita**=From the Founding of the City. Hence, the year of Cicero's consulate, by our reckoning 63 **B.C.** or **B.C.E.**, was for the Romans the Year DCXCI (691) **A.U.C.** (Ab Urbe Condita).

The Romans calculated an eight-day interval or *nundinum,* with every eighth day being a market day. For modern readers, the common term *week* has been used instead, along with the conventional *hours* and *minutes. The Oxford Classical Dictionary* Second Edition (1992) was referenced for these and other such details in *Respublica*.

Finally, a few words are offered about *Respublica*'s narrative structure. Essentially, Cicero tells the story via his written testament, compiled for his son, and later in his Elysian voice. Complementing Cicero's narrative is an omniscient voice giving the reader an alternate perspective on characters and events.

It is hoped that reading *Respublica* has been as edifying an experience for you as its writing has been for me.

Pax, Salus, et Vita,
(Peace, Health, and Life)
Richard Braccia, 2009

Acknowledgements

Heartfelt thanks are given to my beautiful wife, Catherine, and to our beautiful daughter, Marian, for their unceasing support and assistance in this project, especially in typing and re-typing the manuscript and in their technical guidance. I love you both infinitely.

Additionally, salutations are extended to Lauren Riles Smith for her painstaking efforts in copy-editing *Respublica*; to Allison Lang for the beautiful cover painting, and to Javier Maldonado for the handsome maps and charts; and Patricia DeLacy for her unstinting technical support.

To the staff of AuthorHouse, particularly to Veronica Zan, a very special word of thanks is extended.

Respublica would not have come to fruition without the contributions of all of the above.